The Collected Supernatural and Weird Fiction of J. Sheridan le Fanu Volume 6

Including One Novel 'Checkmate',
and Six Short Stories
of the Ghostly and Gothic

J. Sheridan le Fanu

The Collected
Supernatural and Weird
Fiction of J. Sheridan le Fanu
Volume 6
Including One Novel 'Checkmate',
and Six Short Stories
of the Ghostly and Gothic
by J. Sheridan le Fanu

FIRST EDITION

Leonaur is an imprint
of Oakpast Ltd

ISBN: 978-0-85706-155-3 (hardcover)
ISBN: 978-0-85706-156-0 (softcover)

http://www.leonaur.com

Publisher's Notes

In the interests of authenticity, the spellings, grammar and place names used have been retained from the original editions.

The opinions of the authors represent a view of events in which he was a participant related from his own perspective, as such the text is relevant as an historical document.

The views expressed in this book are not necessarily those of the publisher.

The Collected Supernatural and Weird Fiction of J. Sheridan le Fanu Volume 6

Contents

Checkmate

Mortlake Hall

There stands about a mile and a half beyond Islington, unless it has come down within the last two years, a singular and grand old house. It belonged to the family of Arden, once distinguished in the Northumbrian counties. About fifty acres of ground, rich with noble clumps and masses of old timber, surround it; old-world fish-ponds, with swans sailing upon them, tall yew hedges, quincunxes, leaden fauns and goddesses, and other obsolete splendours surround it. It rises, tall, florid, built of Caen stone, with a palatial flight of steps, and something of the grace and dignity of the genius of Inigo Jones, to whom it is ascribed, with the shadows of ancestral trees and the stains of two centuries upon it, and a vague character of gloom and melancholy, not improved by some indications not actually of decay, but of something too like neglect.

It is now evening, and a dusky glow envelopes the scene. The setting sun throws its level beams, through tall drawing-room windows, ruddily upon the Dutch tapestry on the opposite walls, and not unbecomingly lights up the little party assembled there.

Good-natured, fat Lady May Penrose, in her bonnet, sips her tea and chats agreeably. Her carriage waits outside. You will ask who is that extremely beautiful girl who sits opposite, her large soft grey eyes gazing towards the western sky with a look of abstraction, too forgetful for a time of her company, leaning upon the slender hand she has placed under her cheek. How silken and golden-tinted the dark brown hair that grows so near her brows, making her forehead low, and marking with its broad line the beautiful oval of her face! Is there carmine anywhere to match her brilliant lips? And when, recollecting something to tell Lady May, she turns on a sudden, smiling, how soft and pretty the dimples, and how even the little row of pearls she discloses!

This is Alice Arden, whose singularly handsome brother Richard, with some of her tints and outlines translated into masculine beauty, stands leaning on the back of a *prie-dieu* chair, and chatting gaily.

But who is the thin, tall man—the only sinister figure in the group—with one hand in his breast, the other on a cabinet, as he leans against the wall? Who is that pale, thin-lipped man, 'with cadaverous aspect and broken beak,' whose eyes never seem to light up, but maintain their dismal darkness while his pale lips smile? Those eyes are fixed on the pretty face of Alice Arden, as she talks to Lady May, with a strangely intense gaze. His eyebrows rise a little, like those of Mephistopheles, towards his temples, with an expression that is inflexibly sarcastic, and sometimes menacing. His jaw is slightly underhung, a formation which heightens the satirical effect of his smile, and, by contrast, marks the depression of his nose.

There was at this time in London a Mr. Longcluse, an agreeable man, a convenient man, who had got a sort of footing in many houses, nobody exactly knew how. He had a knack of obliging people when they really wanted a trifling kindness, and another of holding fast his advantage, and, without seeming to push, or ever appearing to flatter, of maintaining the acquaintance he had once founded. He looked about eight-and-thirty: he was really older. He was gentlemanlike, clever, and rich; but not a soul of all the men who knew him had ever heard of him at school or college. About his birth, parentage, and education, about his 'life and adventures,' he was dark.

How were his smart acquaintance made? Oddly, as we shall learn when we know him a little better. It was a great pity that there were some odd things said about this very agreeable, obliging, and gentlemanlike person. It was a pity that more was not known about him. The man had enemies, no doubt, and from the sort of reserve that enveloped him their opportunity arose. But were there not about town hundreds of men, well enough accepted, about whose early days no one cared a pin, and everything was just as dark?

Now Mr. Longcluse, with his pallid face, his flat nose, his sarcastic eyebrows, and thin-lipped smile, was overlooking this little company, his shoulder leaning against the frame that separated two pieces of the pretty Dutch tapestry which covered the walls.

'By-the-bye, Mr. Longcluse—you can tell me, for you always know everything,' said Lady May—'is there still any hope of that poor child's recovering—I mean the one in that dreadful murder in Thames Street, where the six poor little children were stabbed?'

Mr. Longcluse smiled.

'I'm so glad, Lady May, I can answer you upon good authority! I stopped today to ask Sir Edwin Dudley that very question through his carriage window, and he said that he had just been to the hospital to see the poor little thing, and that it was likely to do well.'

'I'm so glad! And what do they say can have been the motive of the murder?'

'Jealousy, they say; or else the man is mad.'

'I should not wonder. I'm sure I hope he is. But they should take care to put him under lock and key.'

'So they will, rely on it; that's a matter of course.'

'I don't know how it is,' continued Lady May, who was garrulous, 'that murders interest people so much, who ought to be simply shocked at them.'

'We have a murder in our family, you know,' said Richard Arden.

'That was poor Henry Arden—I know,' she answered, lowering her voice and dropping her eyes, with a side glance at Alice, for she did not know how she might like to hear it talked of.

'Oh, that happened when Alice was only five months old, I think,' said Richard; and slipping into the chair beside Lady May, he laid his hand upon hers with a smile, and whispered, leaning towards her—

'You are always so thoughtful; it is *so* nice of you!'

And this short speech ended, his eyes remained fixed for some seconds, with a glow of tender admiration, on those of fat Lady May, who simpered with effusion, and did not draw her hand away until she thought she saw Mr. Longcluse glance their way.

It was quite true, all he said of Lady May. It would not be easy to find a simpler or more good-natured person. She was very rich also, and, it was said by people who love news and satire, had long been willing to share her gold and other chattels with handsome Richard Arden, who being but five-and-twenty, might very nearly have been her son.

'I remember that horrible affair,' said Mr. Longcluse, with a little shrug and a shake of his head. 'Where was I then—Paris or Vienna? Paris it was. I recollect it all now, for my purse was stolen by the very man who made his escape—Mace was his name; he was a sort of low man on the turf, I believe.'

'I was very young then—somewhere about seventeen, I think.'

'You can't have been more, of course,' said good-natured Lady May.

'I should like very much some time to hear all about it,' continued Mr. Longcluse.

'So you shall,' said Richard, 'whenever you like.'

'Every old family has a murder, and a ghost, and a beauty also, though she does not always live and breathe, except in the canvas of Lely, or Kneller, or Reynolds: and they, you know, had roses and lilies to give away at discretion, in their paint-boxes, and were courtiers,' remarked Mr. Longcluse, 'who dealt sometimes in the old-fashioned business of making compliments. *I* say happy the man who lives in those summers when the loveliness of some beautiful family culminates, and who may, at ever such a distance, gaze and worship.'

This ugly man spoke in a low tone, and his voice was rather sweet. He looked as he spoke at Miss Arden, from whom, indeed, his eyes did not often wander.

'Very prettily said!' applauded Lady May affably.

'I forgot to ask you, Lady May,' inquired Alice, cruelly, at this moment, ' how the pretty little Italian greyhound is that was so ill—better, I hope.'

'Ever so much—quite well almost. I'd have taken him out for a drive today, poor dear little Pepsie! but that I thought the sun just a little overpowering. Didn't you?'

'Perhaps a little.'

Mr. Longcluse lowered his eyes as he leaned against the wall and sighed, with a pained smile, that even upon his plain, pallid face, was pathetic.

Did proud Richard Arden perceive the devotion of the dubious Longcluse—undefined in position, in history, in origin, in character, in all things but in wealth? Of course he did, perfectly. But that wealth was said to be enormous. There were Jews, who ought to know, who said he was worth one million eight hundred thousand pounds, and that his annual income was considerably more than a hundred thousand pounds a year.

Was a man like that to be dismissed without inquiry? Had he not found him good-natured and gentlemanlike? What about those stories circulated among Jews and croupiers? Enemies might affect to believe them, and quote the old saw, 'There is never smoke without fire;' but dare one of them utter a word of the kind aloud? Did they stand the test of five minutes' inquiry, such even as he had given them? Had he found a particle of proof, of evidence, of suspicion? Not a spark. What man had ever escaped stories who was worth forging a lie about?

Here was a man worth more than a million. Why, if *he* let him slip through his fingers, some duchess would pounce on him for her daughter.

It was well that Longcluse was really in love—well, perhaps, that he did not appreciate the social omnipotence of money.

'Where is Sir Reginald at present?' asked Lady May.

'Not here, you may be sure,' answered Richard. 'My father does not admit my visits, you know.'

'Really! And is that miserable quarrel kept up still?'

'Only too true. He is in France at present; at Vichy—ain't it Vichy?' he said to Alice.

But she, not choosing to talk, said simply, 'Yes—Vichy.'

'I'm going to take Alice into town again; she has promised to stay with me a little longer. And I think you neglect her a little, don't you? You ought to come and see her a little oftener,' pleaded Lady May, in an undertone. 'I only feared I was boring you all. Nothing, *you* know, would give me half so much pleasure,' he answered.

'Well, then, she'll expect your visits, mind.'

A little silence followed. Richard was vexed with his sister; she was, he thought, snubbing his friend Longcluse.

Well, when once he had spoken his mind and disclosed his treasures, Richard flattered himself he had some influence; and did not Lady May swear by Mr. Longcluse? And was his father, the most despotic and violent of baronets, and very much dipt, likely to listen to sentimental twaddle pleading against a hundred thousand a year? So, Miss Alice, if you were disposed to talk nonsense, it was not very likely to be listened to, and sharp and short logic might ensue.

How utterly unconscious of all this she sits there, thinking, I daresay, of quite another person!

Mr. Longcluse was also for a moment in profound reverie; so was Richard Arden. The secrecy of thought is a pleasant privilege to the thinker—perhaps hardly less a boon to the person pondered upon.

If each man's forehead could project its shadows and the light of his spirit shine through, and the confluence of figures and phantoms that cross and march behind it become visible, how that magic-lantern might appal good easy people!

And now the ladies fell to talking and comparing notes about their guipure lacework.

'How charming yours looks, my dear, round that little table!' exclaimed Lady May in a rapture. 'I'm sure I hope mine may turn out half as pretty. I wanted to compare; I'm not quite sure whether it is exactly the same pattern.'

And so on, until it was time for them to order their wings for town.

The gentlemen have business of their own to transact, or pleasures to pursue. Mr. Longcluse has his trap there, to carry them into town when their hour comes. They can only put the ladies into their places, and bid them good-bye, and exchange parting reminders and good-natured speeches.

Pale Mr. Longcluse, as he stands on the steps, looks with his dark eyes after the disappearing carriage, and sighs deeply. He has forgotten all for the moment but one dream. Richard Arden wakens him, by laying his hand on his shoulder.

'Come, Longcluse, let us have a cigar in the billiard-room, and a talk. I have a box of Manillas that I think you will say are delicious—that is, if you like them full-flavoured.'

Martha Tansey

'By-the-bye, Longcluse,' said Richard, as they entered together the long tiled passage that leads to the billiard-room, 'you like pictures. There is one here, banished to the housekeeper's room, that they say is a Vandyck; we must have it cleaned and backed, and restored to its old place—but would you care to look at it?'

'Certainly, I should like extremely,' said Mr. Longcluse.

They were now at the door of the housekeeper's room, and Richard Arden knocked.

'Come in,' said the quavering voice of the old woman from within.

Richard Arden opened the door wide. The misty rose-coloured light of the setting sun filled the room. From the wall right opposite, the pale portrait of Sir Thomas Arden, who fought for the king during the great Civil War, looked forth from his deep dingy frame full upon them, stern and melancholy; the misty beams touching the softer lights of his long hair and the gleam of his armour so happily, that the figure came out from its dark background, and seemed ready to step forth to meet them. As it happened, there was no one in the room but old Mrs. Tansey, the housekeeper, who received Richard Arden standing.

From the threshold, Mr. Longcluse, lost in wonder at the noble picture, gazed on it, with the exclamation, almost a cry, 'Good heaven! what a noble work! I had no idea there could be such a thing in existence and so little known.' And he stood for awhile in a rapture, gazing from the threshold on the portrait.

At sound of that voice, with a vague and terrible recognition, the housekeeper turned with a start towards the door, expecting, you'd have fancied from her face, the entrance of a ghost. There was a tremble in the voice with which she cried, 'Lord! what's that?' a tremble in the hand extended towards the door, and a shake also in the pale frowning face, from which shone her glassy eyes.

Mr. Longcluse stepped in, and the old woman's gaze became, as he did so, more shrinking and intense. When he saw her he recoiled, as a man might who had all but trod upon a snake; and these two people gazed at one another with a strange, uncertain scowl.

In Mr. Longcluse's case, this dismal caprice of countenance did not last beyond a second or two. Richard Arden, as he turned his eyes from the picture to say a word to his companion, saw it for a moment, and it faded from his features—saw it, and the darkened countenance of the old housekeeper, with a momentary shock. He glanced from one to the other quickly, with a look of unconscious surprise. That look instantly recalled Mr. Longcluse, who, laying his hand on Richard Arden's arm, said, with a laugh—'I do believe I'm the most nervous man in the world.'

'You don't find the room too hot?' said Richard, inwardly ruminating upon the strange looks he had just seen exchanged. 'Mrs. Tansey keeps a fire all the year round—don't you, Martha?'

Martha did not answer, nor seem to hear; she pressed her lean hand, instead, to her heart, and drew back to a sofa and sat down, muttering, 'My God, lighten our darkness, we beseech thee!' and she looked as if she were on the point of fainting.

'That is a true Vandyck,' said Mr. Longcluse, who was now again looking *steadfastly* at the picture. 'It deserves to rank among his finest portraits. I have never seen anything of his more forcible. You really ought not to leave it here, and in this state.' He walked over and raised the lower end of the frame gently from the wall. 'Yes, just as you said, it wants to be backed. That portrait would not stand a shake, I can tell you. The canvas is perfectly rotten, and the paint—if you stand here you'll see—is ready to flake off. It is an awful pity. You shouldn't leave it in such danger.'

'No,' said Richard, who was looking at the old woman. 'I don't think Martha's well—will you excuse me for a moment?' And he was at the housekeeper's side. 'What's the matter, Martha?' he said kindly. 'Are you ill?'

'Very bad, Sir. I beg your pardon for sitting, but I could not help; and the gentleman will excuse me.'

'Of course—but what's the matter?' said Richard.

'A sudden fright like, Sir. I'm all over on a tremble,' she quavered.

'See how exquisitely that hand is painted,' continued Mr. Longcluse, pursuing his criticism, 'and the art with which the lights are managed. It is a wonderful picture. It makes one positively angry to see it in that state, and anywhere but in the most conspicuous and honourable place. If I owned that picture, I should never be tired showing it. I should have it where everyone who came into my house should see it; and I should watch every crack and blur on its surface, as I should the symptoms of a dying child, or the looks of the mistress of my heart. Now just look at this. Where is he? Oh!'

'I beg your pardon, a thousand times, but I find my old friend Martha feels a little faint and ill,' said Richard.

'Dear me! I hope she's better,' said Mr. Longcluse, approaching with solicitude. 'Can I be of any use? Shall I touch the bell?'

'I'm better, Sir, I thank you; I'm much better,' said the old woman. 'It won't signify nothing, only—' She was looking hard again at Mr. Longcluse, who now seemed perfectly at his ease, and showed in his countenance nothing but the commiseration befitting the occasion. 'A sort of a weakness—a fright like—and I can't think, quite, what came over me.'

'Don't you think a glass of wine might do her good?' asked Mr. Longcluse.

'Thanks, Sir, I don't drink it. Oh, lighten our darkness, we beseech thee! Good Lord, a' mercy on us! I take them drops, hartshorn and valerian, on a little water, when I feel nervous like. I don't know when I was took wi' t' creepins before.'

'You look better,' said Richard.

'I'm quite right again, Sir,' she said, with a sigh. She had taken her 'drops,' and seemed restored.

'Hadn't you better have one of the maids with you? I'm going now; I'll send someone,' he said. 'You must get all right, Martha. It pains me to see you ill. You're a very old friend, remember. You must be all right again; and, if you like, we'll have the doctor out, from town.'

He said this, holding her thin old hand very kindly, for he was by no means without good-nature. So sending the promised attendant, he and Longcluse proceeded to the billiard-room, where, having got the lamps lighted, they began to enjoy their smoke. Each, I fancy, was thinking of the little incident in the housekeeper's room. There was a long silence.

'Poor old Tansey! She looked awfully ill,' said Richard Arden at last.

'By Jove! she did. Is that her name? She rather frightened me,' said Mr. Longcluse. 'I thought we had stumbled on a mad woman—she stared so. Has she ever had any kind of fit, poor thing?'

'No. She grumbles a good deal, but I really think she's a healthy old woman enough. She says she was frightened.'

'We came in too suddenly, perhaps?'

'No, that wasn't it, for I knocked first,' said Arden.

'Ah, yes, so you did. I only know she frightened me. I really thought she was out of her mind, and that she was going to stick me with a knife, perhaps,' said Mr. Longcluse, with a little laugh and a shrug.

Arden laughed, and puffed away at his cigar till he had it in a glow again. Was this explanation of what he had seen in Longcluse's countenance—a picture presented but for a fraction of a second, but thenceforward ineffaceable—quite satisfactory?

In a short time Mr. Longcluse asked whether he could have a little brandy and water, which accordingly was furnished. In his first glass there was a great deal of brandy, and very little water indeed; and his second, sipped more at his leisure, was but little more diluted. A very faint flush tinged his pallid cheeks.

Richard Arden was, by this time, thinking of his own debts and ill-luck, and at last he said, 'I wonder what the art of getting on in the world is. Is it communicable? or is it no art at but a simple run of luck?'

Mr. Longcluse smiled scornfully. 'There are men who have immense faith in themselves,' said he, 'who have indomitable will, and who are provided with craft and pliancy for any situation. Those men are giants from the first to the last hour of action, unless, as happened to Napoleon, success enervates them. In the cradle, they strangle serpents; blind, they pull down palaces; old as Dandolo, they burn fleets and capture cities. It is only when they have taken to bragging that the *lues Napoleonica* has set in. Now I have been, in a sense, a successful man—I am worth some money. If I were the sort of man I describe, I should be worth, if I cared for it, ten times what I have in as many years. But I don't care to confess I made my money by flukes. If, having no tenderness, you have two attributes—profound cunning and perfect audacity—nothing can keep you back. I'm a common-place man, I say; but I know what constitutes power. Life is a battle, and the general's qualities win.'

'I have not got the general's qualities, I think; and I know I haven't luck,' said Arden; 'so for my part I may as well drift, with as little trouble as may be, wherever the current drives. Happiness is not for all men.'

'Happiness is for *no* man,' said Mr. Longcluse. And a little silence followed. 'Now suppose a fellow has got more money than ever he dreamed of,' he resumed, 'and finds money, after all, not quite what he fancied, and that he has come to long for a prize quite distinct and infinitely more precious; so that he finds, at last, that he never can be happy for an hour without it, and yet, for all his longing and his pains, sees it is unattainable as that star.' (He pointed to a planet that shone down through the skylight.) 'Is that man happy? He carries with him, go where he may, an aching heart, the pangs of jealousy and despair, and the longing of the damned for Paradise. That is *my* miserable case.'

Richard Arden laughed, as he lighted his second cigar.

'Well, if that's your case, you can't be one of those giants you described just now. Women are not the obdurate and cruel creatures you fancy. They are proud, and vain, and unforgiving; but the misery and the perseverance of a lover constitute a worship that first flatters and then wins them. Remember this, a woman finds it very hard to give up a worshipper, except for another. Now why should you despair? You are a gentleman, you are a clever fellow, an agreeable fellow; you are what is accounted a young man still, and you can make your wife rich. They all like that. It is not avarice, but pride. I don't know the young lady, but I see no good reason why you should fail.'

'I wish, Arden, I dare tell you all; but someday I'll tell you more.'

'The only thing is——You'll not mind my telling you, as you have been so frank with me?'

'Pray say whatever you think. I shall be ever so much obliged. I forget so many things about English manners and ways of thinking—I have lived so very much abroad. Should I be put up for a club?'

'Well, I should not mind a club just yet, till you know more people—quite time enough. But you must manage better. Why should those Jew fellows, and other people, who don't hold, and never can, a position the least like yours, be among your acquaintance? You must make it a rule to drop all objectionable persons, and know none but good people. Of course, when you are strong enough it doesn't so much matter, provided you keep them at arm's length. But you passed your younger days abroad, as you say, and not being yet so well known here, you will have to be particular—don't you see? A man is so much judged by his acquaintance; and, in fact, it is essential.'

'A thousand thanks for any hints that strike you,' said Longcluse good humouredly.

'They sound frivolous; but these trifles have immense weight with women,' said Arden. 'By Jove!' he added, glancing at his watch, 'we shall be late. Your trap is at the door—suppose we go?'

Mr. Longcluse Opens His Heart

The old housekeeper had drawn near her window, and stood close to the pane, through which she looked out upon the starlit night. The stars shine down over the foliage of huge old trees. Dim as shadows stand the horse and tax-cart that await Mr. Longcluse and Richard Arden, who now at length appear. The groom fixes the lamps, one of which shines full on Mr. Longcluse's peculiar face.

'Ay—the voice; I could a' sworn to that,' she muttered. 'It went through me like a scythe. But that's a strange face; and yet there's summat in it, just a hint like, to call my thoughts out a-seeking up and down, and to and fro; and 'twill not let me rest until I come to find the truth. Mace? No, no. Langly? Not he. Yet 'twas summat *that night*, I think—summat awful. And who *was* there? No one. Lighten our darkness, we beseech thee, O Lord! for my heart is sore troubled.'

Up jumped the groom. Mr. Longcluse had the reins in his hand, and he and his companion passed swiftly by the window, and the flash of the lamps crossed the panelled walls of the housekeeper's room. The light danced wildly from corner to corner of the wainscot, accompanied by the shadows of two geraniums in bow-pots on the window-stool. The lamps flew by, and she still stood there, with the palsied shake of her head and hand, looking out into the darkness, in rumination.

Arden and Longcluse glided through the night air in silence, under the mighty old trees that had witnessed generations of Ardens, down the darker, narrow road, and by the faded old inn, once famous in those regions as the *Guy of Warwick*, representing still on its board, in tarnished gold and colours, that redoubted champion, with a boar's head on the point of his sword, and a grotesque lion winding itself fawningly about his horse's legs.

As they passed swiftly along this smooth and deserted road, Longcluse spoke. *Aperit praecordia vinum*. In his brandy and water he had not spared alcohol, and the quantity was considerable.

'I have lots of money, Arden, and I can talk to people, as you say,' he suddenly said, as if Richard Arden had spoken but a moment before; 'but, on the whole, is there on earth a more miserable dog than I? There are things that trouble me that would make you laugh; there are others that would, if I dare tell them, make you sigh. Soon I shall be able; soon you shall know all. I'm not a bad fellow. I know how to give away money, and, what is harder to bestow on others, my time and labour. But who to look at me would believe it? I'm not a worse fellow than Penruddock.

'I can cry for pity and do a kind act like him; but I look in my glass, and I also feel like him, 'the mark of Cain' is on me—cruelty in my face. Why should Nature write on some men's faces such libels on their characters? Then here's another thing to make you laugh—you, a handsome fellow, to whom beauty belongs, I say, by right of birth—it would make me laugh also if I were not, as I am, forced every hour I live to count up, in agonies of hope and terror, my chances in that enterprise in which all my happiness for life is staked so wildly. Common ugliness does not matter, it is got over. But such a face as mine! Come, come! you are too good-natured to say. I'm not asking for consolation; I am only summing up my curses.'

'You make too much of these. Lady May thinks your face, she says, very interesting—upon my honour, she does.'

'Oh, heaven!' exclaimed Mr. Longcluse, with a shrug and a laugh.

'And what is more to the purpose (will you forgive my reporting all this—you won't mind?), some young lady friends of hers who were by said, I assure you, that you had so much expression, and that your features were extremely refined.'

'It won't do, Arden; you are too good-natured,' said he, laughing more bitterly.

'I should much rather be as I am, if I were you, than be gifted with vulgar beauty—plump, pink and white, with black beady eyes, and all that,' said Arden.

'But the heaviest curse upon me is that which, perhaps, you do not suspect—the curse of—secrecy.'

'Oh, really!' said Arden, laughing, as if he had thought up to then that Mr. Longcluse's history was as well known as that of the ex-Emperor Napoleon.

'I don't say that I shall come out like the enchanted hero in a fairy tale, and change in a moment from a beast into a prince; but I am something better than I seem. In a short time, if you cared to be bored with it, I shall have a great deal to tell you.'

There followed here a silence of two or three minutes, and then, on a sudden, pathetically, Mr. Longcluse broke forth—

'What has a fellow like me to do with love? and less than beloved, can I ever be happy? I know something of the world—not of this London world, where I live less than I seem to do, and into which I came too late ever to understand it thoroughly—I know something of a greater world, and human nature is the same everywhere. You talk of a girl's pride inducing her to marry a man for the sake of his riches. Could I possess my beloved on those terms? I would rather place a pistol in my mouth, and blow my skull off. Arden, I'm unhappy; I'm the most miserable dog alive.'

'Come, Longcluse, that's all nonsense. Beauty is no advantage to a man. The being agreeable is an immense one. But success is what women worship, and if, in addition to that, you possess wealth—not, as I said, that they are sordid, but only vain-glorious—you become very nearly irresistible. Now *you* are agreeable, successful and wealthy—you must see what follows.'

'I'm out of spirits,' said Longcluse, and relapsed into silence, with a great sigh.

By this time they had got within the lamps, and were threading streets, and rapidly approaching their destination. Five minutes more, and these gentlemen had entered a vast room, in the centre of which stood a billiard-table, with benches rising tier above tier to the walls, and a gallery running round the building above them, brilliantly lighted, as such places are, and already crowded with all kinds of people. There is going to be a great match of a 'thousand up' played between Bill Hood and Bob Markham. The betting has been unusually high; it is still going on. The play won't begin for nearly half an hour. The 'admirers of the game' have mustered in great force and variety. There are young peers, with sixty thousand a year, and there are gentlemen who live by their billiards. There are, for once in a way, grave persons, bankers, and counsel learned in the law; there are Jews and a sprinkling of foreigners; and there are members of Parliament and members of the swell mob.

Mr. Longcluse has a good deal to think about this night. He *is* out of spirits. Richard Arden is no longer with him, having picked up a friend or two in the room. Longcluse, with folded arms, and his shoulders against the wall, is in a profound reverie, his dark eyes for the time lowered to the floor, beside the point of his French boot. *There* unfold themselves beneath him picture after picture, the scenes of many a year ago. Looking down, there creeps over him an old horror, a supernatural disgust, and he sees in the dark a pair of wide, white eyes, staring up at him in an agony of terror, and a shrill yell, piercing a distance of many years, makes him shake his ears with a sudden chill. Is this the witches' Sabbath of our pale Mephistopheles—his night of goblins? He raised his eyes, and they met those of a person whom he had not seen for a very long time—a third part of his whole life. The two pairs of eyes, at nearly half across the room, have met, and for a moment fixed. The stranger smiles and nods. Mr. Longcluse does neither. He affects now to be looking over the stranger's shoulder at some more distant object. There is a strange chill and commotion at his heart.

Monsieur Lebas

Mr. Longcluse leaned still with folded arms, and his shoulder to the wall. The stranger, smiling and fussy, was making his way to him. There is nothing in this man's appearance to associate him with tragic incident or emotion of any kind. He is plainly a foreigner. He is short, fat, middle-aged, with a round fat face, radiant with good humour and good-natured enjoyment. His dress is cut in the somewhat grotesque style of a low French tailor. It is not very new, and has some spots of grease upon it. Mr. Longcluse perceives that he is now making his way towards him. Longcluse for a moment thought of making his escape by the door, which was close to him; but he reflected, 'He is about the most innocent and good-natured soul on earth, and why should I seem to avoid him? Better, if he's looking for me, to let him find me, and say his say.' So Longcluse looked another way, his arms still folded, and his shoulders against the wall as before.

'Ah, ha! *Monsieur* is thinking profoundly,' said a gay voice in French. 'Ah, ha, ha, ha! you are surprised, Sir, to see me here. So am I, my faith! I saw you. I never forget a face.'

'Nor a friend, Lebas. Who could have imagined anything to bring you to London?' answered Longcluse, in the same language, shaking him warmly by the hand, and smiling down on the little man. 'I shall never forget your kindness. I think I should have died in that *illness* but for you. How can I ever thank you half enough?'

'And the grand secret—the political difficulty—*Monsieur* found it well evaded,' he said, mysteriously touching his upper lip with two fingers.

'Not all quiet yet. I suppose you thought I was in Vienna?'

'Eh? well, yes—so I did,' answered Lebas, with a shrug. 'But perhaps you think this place safer.'

'Hush! You'll come to me tomorrow. I'll tell you where to

find me before we part, and you'll bring your portmanteau and stay with me while you remain in London, and the longer the better.'

'*Monsieur* is too kind, a great deal; but I am staying for my visit to London with my brother-in-law, Gabriel Laroque, the watchmaker. He lives on the Hill of Ludgate, and he would be offended if I were to reside anywhere but in his house while I stay. But if *Monsieur* would be so good as to permit me to call ——' 'You must come and dine with me tomorrow; I have a box for the opera. You love music, or you are not the Pierre Lebas whom I remember sitting with his violin at an open window. So come early, come before six; I have ever so much to ask you. And what has brought you to London?'

'A very little business and a great deal of pleasure; but all in a week,' said the little man, with a shrug and a hearty laugh. 'I have come over here about some little things like that.' He smiled archly as he produced from his waistcoat pocket a little flat box with a glass top, and shook something in it. 'Commerce, you see. I have to see two or three more of the London people, and then my business will have terminated, and nothing remain for the rest of the week but pleasure—ha, ha!'

'You left all at home well, I hope—children?' He was going to say '*Madame*,' but a good many years had passed.

'I have seven children. *Monsieur* will remember two. Three are by my first marriage, four by my second, and all enjoy the very best health. Three are very young—three, two, one year old; and they say a fourth is not impossible very soon,' he added archly.

Longcluse laughed kindly, and laid his hand upon his shoulder.

'You must take charge of a little present for each from me, and one for *Madame*. And the old business still flourishes?'

'A thousand thanks! yes, the business is the same—the file, the chisel, and knife.' And he made a corresponding movement of his hand as he mentioned each instrument.

'*Hush!*' said Longcluse, smiling, so that no one who did not hear him would have supposed there was so much cautious emphasis in the word. 'My good friend, remember there are details we talk of, you and I together, that are not to be mentioned so suitably in a place like this,' and he pressed his hand on his wrist, and shook it gently.

'A thousand pardons! I am, I know, too careless, and let my tongue too often run before my caution. My wife, she says, 'You can't wash your shirt but you must tell the world.' It is my weakness truly. She is a woman of extraordinary penetration.'

Mr. Longcluse glanced from the corners of his eyes about the room. Perhaps he wished to ascertain whether his talk with this man, whom you would have taken to be little above the level of a French mechanic, had excited anyone's attention. But there was nothing to make him think so.

'Now, Pierre, my friend, you must win some money upon this match—do you see? And you won't deny me the pleasure of putting down your stake for you; and, if you win, you shall buy something pretty for *Madame*—and, win or lose, I shall think it friendly of you after so many years, and like you the better.'

'*Monsieur* is too good,' he said with effusion.

'Now look. Do you see that fat Jew over there on the front bench—you can't mistake him—with the velvet waistcoat all in wrinkles, and the enormous lips, who talks to every second person who passes?'

'I see perfectly, *Monsieur*.'

'He is betting three to one upon Markham. You must take his offer, and back Hood. I'm told *he'll* win. Here are ten pounds, you may as well make them thirty. Don't say a word. Our English custom is to *tip,* as we say, our friend's sons at school, and to make presents to everybody, as often as we like. Now there—not a word.' He quietly slipped into his hand a little *rouleau* of ten pounds in gold. 'If you say one word you wound me,' he continued. 'But, good Heaven! my dear friend, haven't you a breast-pocket?'

'No, *Monsieur*; but this is quite safe. I was paid, only five minutes before I came here, fifteen pounds in gold, a cheque of forty-four pounds, and——'

'Be silent. You may be overheard. Speak here in a very low tone, as I do. And do you mean to tell me that you carry all that money in your coat pocket?'

'But in a pocket-book, *Monsieur*.'

'All the more convenient for the *chevalier d'industrie*' said Longcluse. 'Stop. Pray don't produce it; your fate is, perhaps, sealed if you do. There are gentlemen in this room who would hustle and rob you in the crowd as you get out; or, failing that, who, seeing that you are a stranger, would follow and murder you in the streets, for the sake of a twentieth part of that sum.'

'Gabriel thought there would be none here but men distinguished,' said Lebas, in some consternation.'

'Distinguished by the special attention of the police, some of them,' said Longcluse.

'*Hé*! that is very true,' said Monsieur Lebas— 'very true, I am sure of it. See you that man there, *Monsieur*? Regard him for a moment. The tall man, who leans with his shoulder to the metal pillar of the gallery. My faith! he has observed my steps and followed me. I thought he was a spy. But my friend he says 'No, that is a man of bad character, dismissed for bad practices from the police.' Aha! he has watched me sideways, with the corner of his eye. I will watch him with the corner of mine—ha, ha!'

'It proves, at all events, Lebas, that there are people here other than gentlemen and men of honest lives,' said Longcluse.

'But,' said Lebas, brightening a little, 'I have this weapon,' producing a dagger from the same pocket.

'Put it back this instant. Worse and worse, my good friend. Don't you know that just now there is a police activity respecting foreigners, and that two have been arrested only yesterday on no charge but that of having weapons about their persons? I don't know what the devil you had best do.'

'I can return to the Hill of Ludgate—eh?'

'Pity to lose the game; they won't let you back again,' said Longcluse.

'What shall I do?' said Lebas, keeping his hand now in his pocket on his treasure.

Longcluse rubbed the tip of his finger a little over his eyebrow, thinking.

'Listen to me,' said Longcluse, suddenly. 'Is your brother-in-law here?'

'No, *Monsieur*.'

'Well, you have some London friend in the room, haven't you?'

'One—yes.'

'Only be sure he is one whom you can trust, and who has a safe pocket.'

'Oh, yes, *Monsieur*, entirely! and I saw him place his purse so,' he said, touching his coat, over his heart, with his fingers.

'Well, now, you can't manage it here, under the gaze of the people; but *where* is best? Yes—you see those two doors at opposite sides in the wall, at the far end of the room? They open into two parallel corridors leading to the hall, and a little way down there is a cross passage, in the middle of which is a door opening into a smoking-room. That room will be deserted now, and there, unseen, you can place your money and dagger in his charge.'

'Ah, thank you a hundred thousand times, *Monsieur*!' answered Lebas. 'I shall be writing to the Baron van Boeren tomorrow, and I will tell him I have met *Monsieur*.'

'Don't mind; how is the baron?' asked Longcluse.

'Very well. Beginning to be not so young, you know, and thinking of retiring. I will tell him his work has succeeded. If he demolishes, he also secures. If he sometimes sheds blood——'

'*Hush!*' whispered Longcluse, sternly.

'There is no one,' murmured little Lebas, looking round, but dropping his voice to a whisper. 'He also saves a neck sometimes from the blade of the guillotine.'

Longcluse frowned, a little embarrassed. Lebas smiled archly. In a moment Longcluse's impatient frown broke into a mysterious smile that responded.

'May I say one word more, and make one request of *Monsieur*, which I hope he will not think very impertinent?' asked Monsieur Lebas, who had just been on the point of taking his leave.

'It mayn't be in my power to grant it; but you can't be what you say—I am too much obliged to you—so speak quite freely,' said Longcluse.

So they talked a little more and parted, and Monsieur Lebas went on his way.

A Catastrophe

The play has commenced. Longcluse, who likes and understands the game, sitting beside Richard Arden, is all eye. He is intensely eager and delighted. He joins modestly in the clapping that now and then follows a stroke of extraordinary brilliancy. Now and then he whispers a criticism in Arden's ear. There are many vicissitudes in the game. The players have entered on the third hundred, and still 'doubtful it stood.' The excitement is extraordinary. The assembly is as hushed as if it were listening to a sermon, and, I am afraid, more attentive. Now, on a sudden, Hood scores a hundred and sixty-eight points in a single break. A burst of prolonged applause follows, and, during the clapping, in which he had at first joined, Longcluse says to Arden,—

'I can't tell you how that run of Hood's delights me. I saw a poor little friend of mine here before the play began—I had not seen him since I was little more than a boy—a Frenchman, a good-natured little soul, and I advised him to back Hood, and I have been trembling up to this moment. But I think he's safe now to win. Markham can't score this time. If he's in 'Queer Street,' as they whisper round the room, you'll find he'll either give a simple miss, or put himself into the pocket.'

'Well, I'm sure I hope your friend will win, because it will put three hundred and eighty pounds into my pocket,' said Richard Arden.

And now silence was called, and the building became, in a moment, hushed as a cathedral before the anthem; and Markham knocked his own ball into the pocket as Longcluse had predicted.

On sped the game, and at last Hood scored a thousand, and

won the match, greeted by an uproar of applause that, now being no longer restrained, lasted for nearly five minutes. The assemblage had, by this time, descended from the benches, and crowded the floor in clusters, discussing the play or settling bets. The people in the gallery were pouring down by the four staircases, and adding to the crowd and buzz.

Suddenly there is a sort of excitement perceptible of a new kind—a gathering and pressure of men about one of the doors at the far corner of the room. Men are looking back and beckoning to their companions; others are shouldering forward as strenuously as they can. What is it—any dispute about the score?—a pair of men boxing in the passage?

'No suspicion of fire?' the men at this near end exclaim, and sniff over their shoulders, and look about them, and move toward the point where the crowd is thickening, not knowing what to make of the matter. But soon there runs a rumour about the room— 'a man has just been found murdered in a room outside,' and the crowd now press forward more energetically to the point of attraction.

In the cross-passage which connects the two corridors, as Mr. Longcluse described, there is an awful crush, and next to no light. A single jet of gas burns in the smoking room, where the pressure of the crowd is not quite so much felt. There are two policemen in that chamber, in the ordinary uniform of the force, and three detectives in plain clothes, one supporting a corpse already stiffening, in a sitting posture, as it was found, in a far angle of the room, on the bench to your left as you look in. All the people are looking up the room. You can see nothing but hats, and backs of heads, and shoulders. There is a ceaseless buzz and clack of talk and conjecture.

Even the policemen are looking, as the rest do, at the body. The man who has mounted on the chair near the door, with the other beside him, who has one foot on the rung and another on the seat, and an arm round the first gentleman's neck, although he has not the honour of his acquaintance, to support himself, can see, over the others' heads, the one silent face which looks back towards the door, upon so many gaping, and staring, and gabbling ones. The light is faint. It has occurred to no one to light the gas lamps in the centre. But that forlorn face is distinct enough. Fixed and leaden it is, with the chin a little raised. The eyes are wide open, with a deep and awful gaze; the mouth slightly distorted with what the doctors call 'a convulsive smile,' which shows the teeth a little, and has an odd, wincing look.

As I live, it is the little Frenchman, Pierre Lebas, who was talking so gaily tonight with Mr. Longcluse!

The ebony haft of a dagger, sticking straight out, shows where the hand of the assassin planted the last stab of four, through his black satin waistcoat, embroidered with green leaves, red strawberries, and yellow flowers, which, I suppose, was one of the finest articles in the little wardrobe that Madame Lebas packed up for his holiday. It is not worth much now. It has four distinct cuts, as I have said, on the left side, right through it, and is soaked in blood.

His pockets have been rifled. The police have found nothing in them but a red pocket-handkerchief and a *papier-maché* snuff-box. If that dumb mouth could speak but fifty words, what a world of conjecture it would end, and poor Lebas's story would be listened to as never was story of his before!

A policeman now takes his place at the door to prevent further pressure. No newcomers will be admitted, except as others go out. Those outside are asking questions of those within, and transmitting, over their shoulders, particulars, eagerly repeated. On a sudden there is a subsidence of the buzz and gabble within, and one voice, speaking almost at the pitch of a shriek, is heard declaiming. White as a sheet, Mr. Longcluse, in high excitement, is haranguing in the smoking-room, mounted on a table.

'I say,' he cried, 'gentlemen, excuse me. There are so many together here, so many known to be wealthy, it is an opportunity for a word. Things are coming to a pretty pass—garotters in our streets and assassins in our houses of entertainment! Here is a poor little fellow—look at him—here tonight to see the game, perfectly well and happy, murdered by some miscreant for the sake of the money he had about him. It might have been the fate of anyone of us. I spoke to him tonight. I had not seen him since I was a boy almost. Seven children and a wife, he told me, dependent on him. I say there are two things wanted—first, a reward of such magnitude as will induce exertion. I promise, for my own share, to put down double the amount promised by the highest subscriber. Secondly, something should be done for the family he has left, in proportion to the loss they have sustained.

'Upon this point I shall make inquiry myself. But this is plain, the danger and scandal have attained a pitch at which none of us who cares to walk the streets at night, or at any time to look in upon amusements like that we attended this evening, can permit them longer to stand. There is a fatal defect somewhere. Are our police awake and active? Very possibly; but if so the force is not adequate, I say this frightful scandal must be abated if, as citizens of London, we desire to maintain our reputation for common sense and energy.'

There was a tall thin fellow, shabbily dressed, standing nearly behind the door, with a long neck, and a flat mean face, slightly pitted with smallpox, rather pallid, who was smiling lazily, with half-closed eyes, as Mr. Longcluse declaimed; and when he alluded pointedly to the inadequacy of the police, this man's amusement improved, and he winked pleasantly at the clock which he was consulting at the moment with the corner of his eye.

And now a doctor arrived, and Gabriel Laroque the watchmaker, and more police, with an inspector. Laroque faints when he sees his murdered friend. Recovered after a time, he identifies the body, identifies the dagger also as the property of poor Lebas.

The police take the matter now quite into their hands, and clear the room.

To Bed

Mr. Longcluse jumped into a cab, and told the man to drive to his house in Bolton Street, Piccadilly. He rolled his coat about him with a kind of violence, and threw himself into a corner. Then, as it were, *in furore,* and with a stamp on the floor, he pitched himself into the other corner.

'I've seen tonight what I never thought I should see. What devil possessed me to tell him to go into that black little smoking-room?' he muttered. 'What a room it is! It has seized my brain somehow. Am I in a fever, or going mad, or what? That cursed smoking-room! I can't get out of it. It is in the centre of the earth. I'm built round and round in it. The moment I begin to think, I'm in it. The moment I close my eyes, its four stifling walls are round me. There is no way out. It is like hell.'

The wind had come round to the south, and a soft rain was pattering on the windows. He stopped the cab somewhere near St. James's Street, and got out. It was late—it was just past two o'clock, and the streets were quiet. Wonderfully still was the great city at this hour, and the descent of the rain went on with a sound like a prolonged 'hush' all round. He paid the man, and stood for a while on the kerbstone, looking up and down the street, under the downpour of the rain. You might have taken this millionaire for a man who knew not where to lay his head that night. He took off his hat, and let the refreshing rain saturate his hair, and stream down his forehead and temples.

'Your cab's stuffy and hot, ain't it? Standing half the day with the glass in the sun, I daresay,' said he to the man, who was fumbling in his pockets, and pretending a difficulty about finding change.

'See, never mind, if you haven't got change; I'll go on. Heavier rain than I fancied; very pleasant though. When did the rain begin?' asked Mr. Longcluse, who seemed in no hurry to get back again.

'A trifle past ten, Sir.'

'I say, your horse's knees are a bit broken, ain't they? Never mind, I don't care. He can pull you and me to Bolton Street, I daresay.'

'Will you please to get in, Sir?' inquired the cabman.

Mr. Longcluse nodded, frowning and thinking of something

else; the rain still descending on his bare head, his hat in his hand.

The cabman thought this 'cove' had been drinking and must be a trifle 'tight.' He would not mind if he stood so for a couple of hours; it would run his fare up to something pretty. So cabby had thoughts of clapping a nosebag to his horse's jaws, and was making up his mind to a bivouac. But Mr. Longcluse on a sudden got in, repeating his direction to the driver in a gay and brisk tone, that did not represent his real sensations.

'Why should I be so disturbed at that little French fellow? Have I been ill, that my nerve is gone and I such a fool? One would think I had never seen a dead fellow till now. Better for him to be quiet than at his wit's ends, devising ways and means to keep his seven cubs in bread and butter. I should have gone away when the game was over. What earthly reason led me into that d—d room, when I heard the fuss there? I've a mind to go and play hazard, or see a doctor. Arden said he'd look in, in the morning. I should like that; I'll talk to Arden. I sha'n't sleep, I know; I can't, all night; I've got imprisoned in that suffocating room. Shall I ever close my eyes again?'

They had now reached the door of the small, unpretending house of this wealthy man. The servant who opened the door, though he knew his business, stared a little, for he had never seen his master return in such a plight before, and looking so haggard.

'Where's Franklin?'

'Arranging things in your room, Sir.'

'Give me a candle. The cab is paid. Mr. Arden, mind, may call in the morning; if I should not be down, show him to my room. You are not to let him go without seeing me.'

Upstairs went the pale master of the house. 'Franklin!' he called, as he mounted the last flight of stairs, next his bedroom.

'Yes, Sir.'

'I sha'n't want you tonight, I think—that is, I shall manage what I want for myself; but I mean to ring for you by-and-by.' He was in his dressing-room by this time, and looked round to see that his comforts were provided for as usual—his foot-bath and hot water.

'Shall I fetch your tea, Sir?'

'I'll drink no tea tonight; I've been disgusted. I've seen a dead man, quite unexpectedly; and I sha'n't get over it for some hours, I daresay. I feel ill. And what you must do is this: when I ring my bell, you come back, and you must sit up here till eight in the morning. I shall leave the door between this and the next room open; and should you hear me sleeping uneasily, moaning, or anything like nightmare, you must come in and waken me. And you are not to go to sleep, mind; the moment I call, I expect you in my room. Keep yourself awake how you can; you may sleep all tomorrow, if you like.'

With this charge Franklin departed.

But Mr. Longcluse's preparations for bed occupied a longer time than he had anticipated. When nearly an hour had passed, Mr. Franklin ventured upstairs, and quietly approached the dressing-room door; but there he heard his master still busy with his preparations, and withdrew. It was not until nearly half-an-hour more had passed that his bell gave the promised signal, and Mr. Franklin established himself for the night, in the easy-chair in the dressing-room, with the connecting door between the two rooms open.

Mr. Longcluse was right. The shock which his nerves have received did not permit him to sleep very soon. Two hours later he called for the *Eau-de-Cologne* that stood on his dressing table; and although he made belief to wet his temples with it and kept it at his bedside with that professed design, it was Mr Franklin's belief that he drank the greater part of what remained in the capacious cut-glass bottle. It was not until people were beginning to 'turn out' for their daily labour that sleep at length visited the wearied eye-balls of the Croesus. Three hours of death-like sleep, and Mr. Longcluse, with a little start, was wide awake.

'Franklin!'

'Yes, Sir.' And Mr. Franklin stood at his bedside.

'What o'clock is it?'

'Just struck ten, Sir.'

'Hand me the *Times*.' This was done.

'Tell them to get breakfast as usual. I'm coming down. Open the shutters, and draw the curtains, quite.'

When Franklin had done this and gone down, Mr. Longcluse read the *Times* with a stern eagerness, still in bed. The great billiard match between Hood and Markham was given in spirited detail; but he was looking for something else. Just under this piece of news, he found it 'Murder and Robbery, in the Saloon Tavern.' He read this twice over, and then searched the paper in vain for any further news respecting it. After this search, he again read the short account he had seen before, very carefully, and more than once. Then he jumped out of bed, and looked at himself in the glass in his dressing-room.

'How awfully seedy I am looking!' he muttered, after a careful inspection. 'Better by-and-by.'

His hand was shaking like that of a man who had made a debauch, or was worn out with ague. He looked ten years older.

'I should hardly know myself,' muttered he. 'What a confounded, sinful old fogey I look, and I so young and innocent!'

The sneer was for himself and at himself. The delivery of such is an odd luxury which, at one time or other, most men indulge in. Perhaps it should teach us to take them more kindly when other people crack such cynical jokes on our heads, or, at least, to perceive that they don't always argue personal antipathy.

The sour smile which had, for a moment, flickered with a wintry light on his face, gave place suddenly to a dark fatigue; his features sank, and he heaved a long, deep, and almost shuddering sigh.

There are moments, happily very rare, when the idea of suicide is distinct enough to be dangerous, and having passed which, a man feels that Death has looked him very nearly in the face. Nothing more trite and true than the omnipresence of suffering. The possession of wealth exempts the unfortunate owner from, say, two-thirds of the curse that lies heavy on the human race. Two thirds is a great deal; but so is the other third, and it may have in it, at times, something as terrible as human nature can support.

Mr. Longcluse, the *millionaire*, had, of course, many poor enviers. Had any one of all these uttered such a sigh that morning? Or did any one among them feel wearier of life?

'When I have had my tub, I shall be quite another man,' said he.

But it did not give him the usual fillip; on the contrary, he felt rather chilled.

'What can the matter be? I'm a changed man,' said he, wondering, as people do at the days growing shorter in autumn, that time had produced some changes. 'I remember when a scene or an excitement produced no more effect upon me, after the moment, than a glass of champagne; and now I feel as if I had swallowed poison, or drunk the cup of madness. Shaking!—hand, heart, every joint. I have grown such a muff!'

Mr. Longcluse had at length completed his very careless toilet, and looking ill, went downstairs in his dressing-gown and slippers.

Fast Friends

In little more than half-an-hour, as Mr. Longcluse was sitting at his breakfast in his dining-room, Richard Arden was shown in.

'Dressing-gown and slippers—what a lazy dog I am compared with you!' said Longcluse gaily as he entered.

'Don't say another word on that subject, I beg. I should have been later myself, had I dared; but my Uncle David had appointed to meet me at ten.'

'Won't you take something?'

'Well, as I have had no breakfast, I don't mind if I do,' said Arden, laughing.

Longcluse rang the bell.

'When did you leave that place last night?' asked Longcluse.

'I fancy about the same time that you went—about five or ten minutes after the match ended. You heard there was a man murdered in a passage there? I tried to get down and see it but the crowd was awful.'

'I was more lucky—I came earlier,' said Longcluse. 'It was perfectly sickening, and I have been seedy ever since. You may guess what a shock it was to me. The murdered man was that poor little Frenchman I told you of, who had been talking to me, in high spirits, just before the play began—and there he was, poor fellow! You'll see it all there; it makes me sick.'

He handed him the *Times*.

'Yes, I see. I daresay the police will make him out,' said Arden, as he glanced hastily over it. 'Did you remark some awfully ill-looking fellows there?'

'I never saw so many together in a place of the kind before,' said Longcluse.

'That's a capital account of the match,' said Arden, whom it interested more than the tragedy of poor little Lebas did. He read snatches of it aloud as he ate his breakfast: and then, laying the paper down, he said, 'By-the-bye, I need not bother you by asking your advice, as I intended. My uncle David has been blowing me up, and I think he'll make everything straight. When he sends for me and gives me an awful lecture, he always makes it up to me afterwards.'

'I wish, Arden, I stood as little in need of your advice as you do, it seems, of mine,' said Longcluse suddenly, after a short silence. His dark eyes were fixed on Richard Arden's. 'I have been fifty times on the point of making a confession to you, and my heart has failed me. The hour is coming. These things won't wait. I must speak, Arden, soon or never—*very* soon, or never. *Never,* perhaps, would be wisest.'

'Speak *now*, on the contrary,' said Arden, laying down his knife and fork, and leaning back. 'Now is the best time always. If it's a bad thing, why, it's over; and if it's a good one, the sooner we have it the better.'

Longcluse rose, looking down in meditation, and in silence walked slowly to the window, where, for a time, without speaking he stood in a reverie. Then, looking up, he said, 'No man likes a crisis. 'No good general ever fights a pitched battle if he can help it.' Wasn't that Napoleon's saying? No man who has not lost his head likes to get together all he has on earth, and make one stake of it. I have been on the point of speaking to you often. I have always recoiled.'

'Here I am, my dear Longcluse,' said Richard Arden, rising and following him to the window, 'ready to hear you. I ought to say, only too happy if I can be of the least use.'

'Immense! everything?' said Longcluse vehemently. 'And yet I don't know how to ask you—how to begin—so much depends. Don't you conjecture the subject?'

'Well, perhaps I do—perhaps I don't. Give me some clue.'

'Have you formed no conjecture?' asked Longcluse.

'Perhaps.'

'Is it anything in any way connected with your sister, Miss Arden?'

'It may be, possibly.'

'Say what you think, Arden, I beseech you.'

'Well, I think, perhaps, you admire her.'

'Do I? Do I? Is that all? Would to God I could say that is all! Admiration, what is it?—Nothing. Love?— Nothing. Mine is adoration and utter madness. I have told my secret. What do you say? Do you hate me for it?'

'Hate you, my dear fellow! Why on earth should I hate you? On the contrary, I ought, I think, to like you better. I'm only a little surprised that your feelings should so much exceed anything I could have supposed.'

'Yesterday, Arden, you spoke as if you liked me. As we drove into that place, I fancied you half understood me; and cheered by what you then said, I have spoken that which might have died with me, but for that.'

'Well, what's the matter? My dear Longcluse, you talk as if I had shown signs of wavering friendship. Have I? Quite the contrary.'

'Quite the contrary, that is true,' said Longcluse eagerly. 'Yes, you *should* like me better for it—that is true also. Yours is no wavering friendship, I'm sure of it. Let us shake hands upon it. A treaty, Arden, a treaty!'

With a fierce smile upon his pale face, and a sudden fire in his eyes, he extended his hand energetically, and took that of Arden, who answered the invitation with a look in which gleamed faintly something of amusement.

'Now, Richard Arden,' he continued excitedly, 'you have more influence with Miss Arden than falls commonly to the lot of a brother. I have observed it. It results from her having had during her earlier years little society but yours, and from your being some years her senior. It results from her strong affection for you, from her admiration of your talents, and from her having neither brother nor sister to divide those feelings. I never yet saw brother possessed of so evident and powerful an influence with a sister. You must use it all for me.'

He continued to hold Arden's hand in his as he spoke. 'You can withdraw your hand if you decline,' said he. 'I sha'n't complain. But your hand remains—you don't. It is a treaty, then. Henceforward we live *foedere icto.* I'm an exacting friend, but a good one.'

'My dear fellow, you do me but justice. I am your friend, altogether. But you must not mistake me for a guardian or a father in the matter. I wish I could make my sister think exactly as I do upon every subject, and *that* above all others. All I can say is, in me you have a fast friend.'

Longcluse pressed his hand, which he had not relinquished, at these words, with a firm grasp and a quick shake.

'Now listen. I must speak on this point, the one that is in my mind, my chief difficulty. Personally, there is not, I think, a living being in England who knows my history. I am glad of it, for reasons which you will approve by-and-by. But this is an enormous disadvantage, though only temporary, and the friends of the young lady must weigh my wealth against it for the present. But when the time comes, which can't now be distant, upon my honour! upon my soul!—by Heaven, I'll show you I'm of as good and old a family as any in England! We have been gentlemen up to the time of the Conqueror, here in England, and as far before him as record can be traced in Normandy. If I fail to show you this when the hour comes, stigmatise me as you will.'

'I have not a doubt, dear Longcluse. But you are urging a point that really has no weight with us people in England. We have taken off our hats to the gentlemen in *casques* and tabards, and feudal glories are at a discount everywhere but in Debrett, where they are taken with allowance. Your ideas upon these matters are more Austrian than ours. We expect, perhaps, a little more from the man, but certainly less from his ancestors than our forefathers did. So till a title turns up, and the heralds want them, make your mind easy on matters of pedigree, and then you can furnish them with effect. All I can tell you is this—there are hardly fifty men in England who dare tell all the truth about their families.'

'We are friends, then; and in that relation, Arden, if there are privileges, there are also liabilities, remember, and both extend into a possibly distant future.'

Longcluse spoke with a gloomy excitement that his companion did not quite understand.

'That is quite true, of course,' said Arden.

Each was looking in the other's face for a moment, and each face grew suddenly dark, darker—and the whole room darkened as the air was overshadowed by a mass of cloud that eclipsed the sun, threatening thunder.

'By Jove! How awfully dark in a moment!' said Arden, looking from the face thus suddenly overcast through the window towards the sky.

'Dark as the future we were speaking of,' said Longcluse, with a sad smile.

'Dark in one sense, I mean unseen, but not darkened in the ill-omened sense,' said Richard Arden. 'I have great confidence in the future. I suppose I am sanguine.'

'I ought to be sanguine, if having been lucky hitherto should make one so, and yet I'm not. *My* happiness depends on that which I cannot, in the least, control. Thought, action, energy, contribute nothing, and so I but drift, and—my heart fails me. Tell me, Arden, for Heaven's sake, truth—spare me nothing, conceal nothing. Let me but know it, however bitter. First tell me, does Miss Arden dislike me—has she an antipathy to me?'

'Dislike you! Nonsense. How could that be? She evidently enjoys your society, when you are in spirits and choose to be amusing. Dislike you? Oh, my dear Longcluse, you can't have fancied such a thing!' said Arden.

'A man placed as I am may fancy anything—things infinitely more unlikely. I sometimes hope she has never perceived my admiration. It seems strange and cruel, but I believe where a man cannot be beloved, nothing is so likely to make him *hated* as his presuming to love. *There* is the secret of half the tragedies we read of. The man cannot cease to love, and the idol of his passion not only disregards but insults it. It is their cruel nature; and thus the pangs of jealousy and the agitations of despair are heightened by a peculiar torture, the hardest of all hell's torture to endure.' 'Well, I have seen you pretty often together, and you must see there is nothing of that kind,' said Arden.

'You speak quite frankly, do you? For Heaven's sake don't spare me!' urged Longcluse.

'I say exactly what I think. There can't be any such feeling,' said Arden.

Longcluse sighed, looked down thoughtfully, and then, raising his eyes again, he said—

'You must answer me another question, dear Arden, and I shall, for the present, task your kindness no more. If you think it a fair question, will you promise to answer me with unsparing frankness? Let me hear the worst.'

'Certainly,' answered his companion.

'Does your sister like anyone in particular—is she attached to anyone—are her affections quite disengaged?'

'So far as I am aware, certainly. She never cared for any one among all the people who admired her, and I am quite certain such a thing could not be without my observing it,' answered Richard Arden.

'I don't know; perhaps not,' said Longcluse. 'But there is a young friend of yours, who I thought was an admirer of Miss Arden's, and possibly a favoured one. You guess, I daresay, who it is I mean?'

'I give you my honour I have not the least idea.'

'I mean an early friend of yours—a man about your own age—who has often been staying in Yorkshire and at Mortlake with you, and who was almost like a brother in your house—very intimate.'

'Surely you can't mean Vivian Darnley?' exclaimed Richard Arden.

'I do. I mean no other.'

'Vivian Darnley? Why, he has hardly enough to live on, much less to marry on. He has not an idea of any such thing. If my father fancied such an absurdity possible, he would take measures to prevent his ever seeing her more. You could not have hit upon a more impossible man,' he resumed, after a moment's examination of a theory which, notwithstanding, made him a little more uneasy than he would have cared to confess. 'Darnley is no fool either, and I think he is a honourable fellow; and altogether, knowing him as I do, the thing is utterly incredible. And as for Alice, the idea of his imagining any such folly, I can undertake to say, positively never entered her mind.'

Here was another pause. Longcluse was again thoughtful.

'May I ask one other question, which I think you will have no difficulty in answering?' said he.

'What you please, dear Longcluse; you may command me.'

'Only this, how do you think Sir Reginald would receive me?'

'A great deal better than he will ever receive me; with his best bow—no, not that, but with open arms and his brightest smile. I tell you, and you'll find it true, my father is a man of the world. Money won't, of course, do everything; but it can do a great deal. It can't make a vulgar man a gentleman, but it may make a gentleman anything. I really think you would find him a very fast friend. And now I must leave you, dear Longcluse. I have just time, and no more, to keep my appointment with old Mr. Blount, to whom my uncle commands me to go at twelve.'

'Heaven keep us both, dear Arden, in this cheating world! Heaven keep us true in this false London world! And God punish the first who breaks faith with the other!'

So spoke Longcluse, taking his hand again, and holding it hard for a moment, with his unfathomable dark eyes on Arden. Was there a faint and unconscious menace in his pale face, as he uttered these words, which a little stirred Arden's pride?

'That's a comfortable litany to part with—a form of blessing elevated so neatly, at the close, into a malediction. However, I don't object. Amen, by all means,' laughed Arden.

Longcluse smiled.

'A malediction? I really believe it was. Something very like it, and one that includes myself, doesn't it? But we are not likely to earn it. An arrow shot into the sea, it can hurt no one. But oh, dear Arden, what does such language mean but suffering? What is all bitterness but pain? Is any mind that deserves the name ever cruel, except from misery? We are good friends, Arden: and if ever I seem to you for a moment other than friendly, just say, 'It is his heart-ache and not he that speaks. Goodbye! God bless you!'

At the door there was another parting.

'There's a long dull day before me—say, rather, *night;* weary eyes, sleepless brain,' murmured Longcluse, in a rather dismal soliloquy, standing in his slippers and dressing-gown again at the window. 'Suspense! What a hell is in that word! Chain a man across a rail, in a tunnel—pleasant situation! let him listen for the faint fifing and drumming of the engine, miles away, not knowing whether deliverance or death may come first. Bad enough, that suspense. What is it to mine! I shall see her tonight. I shall see her, and how will it all be? Richard Arden wishes it—yes, he does. 'Away, slight man!' It is Brutus who says that, I think. Good Heaven! Think of my life—the giddy steps I go by.

'That dizzy walk by moonlight, when I lost my way in Switzerland—beautiful nightmare!—the two mile ledge of rock before me, narrow as a plank; up from my left, the sheer wall of rock; at my right so close that my glove might have dropped over it, the precipice; and curling vapour on the cliffs above, that seem about to break, and envelope all below in blinding mist. There is my life translated into landscape. It has been one long adventure—danger—fatigue. Nature is full of beauty—many a quiet nook in life, where peace resides; many a man whose path is broad and smooth. Woe to the man who loses his way on Alpine tracks, and is benighted!'

Now Mr. Longcluse recollected himself. He had letters to read and note. He did this rapidly. He had business in town. He had fifty things on his hands; and, the day over, he would see Alice Arden again.

Concerning a Boot

Several pairs of boots were placed in Mr. Longcluse's dressing-room.

'Where are the boots that I wore yesterday?' asked he.

'If you please, Sir,' said Mr. Franklin, 'the man called this morning for the right boot of that pair.'

'What man?' asked Mr. Longcluse, rather grimly.

'Mr. Armagnac's man, Sir.'

'Did you desire him to call for it?' asked Mr. Longcluse. 'No, Sir. I thought you must have told someone else to order him to send for it,' said Franklin.

'*I?* You ought to know I leave those things to *you,*' said Mr. Longcluse, staring at him more aghast and fierce than the possible mislaying of a boot would seem to warrant. 'Did you see Armagnac's man?'

'No, Sir. It was Charles who came up, at eight o'clock, when you were still asleep, and said the shoemaker had called for the right boot of the pair you wore yesterday. I had placed them outside the door, and I gave it him, Sir, supposing it all right.'

'Perhaps it *was* all right; but you know Charles has not been a week here. Call him up. I'll come to the bottom of this.'

Franklin disappeared, and Mr. Longcluse, with a stern frown, was staring vaguely at the varnished boot, as if it could tell something about its missing companion. His brain was already at work. What the plague was the meaning of this manoeuvre about his boot? And why on earth, think I, should he make such a fuss and a tragedy about it? Charles followed Mr. Franklin up the stairs.

'What's all this about my boot?' demanded Mr. Longcluse, peremptorily. '*Who* has got it?'

'A man called for it this morning, Sir.'

'What man?'

'I think he said he came from Mr. Armagnac's, Sir.'

'You *think*. Say what you *know*, Sir. What *did* he say?' said Mr. Longcluse, looking dangerous.

'Well, Sir,' said the man, mending his case, 'he did say, Sir, he came from Mr. Armagnac's, and wanted the right boot.'

'What right boot?—*any* right boot?'

'No, Sir, please; the right boot of the pair you wore last night,' answered the servant.

'And *you* gave it to him?'

'Yes, Sir, 'twas me,' answered Charles.

'Well, you mayn't be quite such a fool as you look. I'll sift all this to the bottom. You go, if you please, this moment, to Monsieur Armagnac, and say I should be obliged to him for a line to say whether he this morning sent for my boot, and got it—and I must have it back, mind; *you* shall bring it back, you understand? And you had better make haste.'

'I made bold, Sir,' said Mr. Franklin, 'to send for it myself, when you sent me down for Charles; and the boy will be back, Sir, in two or three minutes.'

'Well, come you and Charles here again when the boy comes back, and bring him here also. I'll make out who has been playing tricks.'

Mr. Longcluse shut his dressing-room door sharply; he walked to the window, and looked out with a vicious scowl; he turned about, and lifted up his clenched hand, and stamped on the floor. A sudden thought now struck him.

'The right foot? By Jove! it may not be the one.'

The boot that was left was already in his hand. He was examining it curiously.

'Ay, by heaven! The right *was* the boot! What's the meaning of this? Conspiracy? I should not wonder.'

He examined it carefully again, and flung it into its corner with violence.

'If it's an accident, it is a very odd one. It is a suspicious accident. It may be, of course, all right. I daresay it *is* all right. The odds are ten, twenty, a thousand to one that Armagnac has got it. I should have had a warm bath last night, and taken a ten miles' ride into the country this morning. It must be all right, and I am plaguing myself without a cause.'

Yet he took up the boot, and examined it once more; then, dropping it, went to the window and looked into the street—came back, opened his door, and listened for the messenger's return.

It was not long deferred. As he heard them approach, Mr. Longcluse flung open his door and confronted them, in white waistcoat and shirt-sleeves, and with a very white and stern face—face and figure all white.

'Well, what about it? Where's the boot?' he demanded, sharply.

'The boy inquired, Sir,' said Mr. Franklin, indicating the messenger with his open hand, and undertaking the office of spokesman; ' and Mr. Armagnac did not send for the boot, Sir, and has not got it.'

'Oh oh! very good. And now, Sir,' he said, in rising fury, turning upon Charles, 'what have *you* got to say for yourself?'

'The man said he came from Mr. Armagnac, please, Sir,' said Charles, 'and wanted the boot, which Mr. Franklin should have back as early as he could return it.'

'Then you gave it to a common thief with that cock-and-a-bull story, and you wish me to believe that you took it all for gospel. There are men who would pitch you over the banisters for a less thing. If I could be certain of it, I'd put you beside him in the dock. But, by heavens! I'll come to the bottom of the whole thing yet.'

He shut the door with a crash, in the faces of the three men, who stood on the lobby.

Mr. Franklin was a little puzzled at these transports, all about a boot. The servants looked at one another without a word. But just as they were going down, the dressing-room door opened, and the following dialogue ensued: 'See, Charles, it was you who saw and spoke with that man?' said Longcluse.

'Yes, Sir.'

'Should you know him again?'

'Yes, Sir, I think I should.'

'What kind of man was he?'

'A very common person, Sir.'

'Was he tall or short? What sort of figure?'

'Tall, Sir.'

'Go on; what more? Describe him.'

'Tall, Sir, with a long neck, and held himself straight; very flat feet, I noticed; a thin man, broad in the shoulders—pretty well that.'

'Describe his face,' said Longcluse.

'Nothing very particular, Sir; a shabby sort of face—a bad colour.'

'How?'

'A bad white, Sir, and pock-marked something; a broad face and flat, and a very little bit of a nose; his eyes almost shut, and a sort of smile about his mouth, and stingy bits of red whiskers, in a curl, down each cheek.' 'How old?'

'He might be nigh fifty, Sir.'

'Ha, ha! very good. How was he dressed?'

'Black frock coat, Sir, a good deal worn; an old flowered satin waistcoat, worn and dirty, Sir; and a pair of raither dirty tweed trousers. Nothing fitted him, and his hat was brown and greasy, begging your parding, Sir; and he had a stick in his hand, and cotton gloves—a-trying to look genteel.'

'And he asked for the right boot?' asked Mr. Longcluse.

'Yes, Sir.'

'You are quite sure of that? Did he take the boot without looking at it, or did he examine it before he took it away?'

'He looked at it sharp enough, Sir, and turned up the sole, and he said 'It's all right,' and he went away, taking it along with him.'

'He asked for the boot I wore yesterday, or last night—which did he say?' asked Mr. Longcluse.

'I think it was last night he said, Sir,' answered Charles.

'Try to recollect yourself. Can't you be certain? Which was it?'

'I think it was *last night*, Sir, he said.'

'It doesn't signify,' said Mr. Longcluse; 'I wanted to see that your memory was pretty clear on the subject. You seem to remember all that passed pretty accurately.'

'I recollect it perfectly well, Sir.'

'H'm! That will do. Franklin, you'll remember that description—let every one of you remember it. It is the description of a thief; and when you see that fellow again, hold him fast till you put him in the hands of a policeman. And, Charles, you must be prepared, d'ye see, to swear to that description; for I am going to the detective office, and I shall give it to the police.'

'Yes, Sir,' answered Charles.

'I sha'n't want you, Franklin; let someone call a cab.'

So he returned to his dressing-room, and shut the door, and thought—'That's the fellow whom that miserable little fool, Lebas, pointed out to me at the saloon last night. He watched him, he said, wherever he went. *I* saw him. There may be other circumstances. That is the fellow—that is the very man. Here's matter to think over! By heaven! that fellow must be denounced, and discovered, and brought to justice. It is a strong case a pretty hanging case against him. We shall see.'

Full of surmises about his lost boot, Atra Cura walking unheard behind him, with her cold hand on his shoulder, and with the image of the ex-detective always gliding before or beside him, and peering with an odious familiarity over his shoulder into his face, Mr. Longcluse marched eastward with a firm tread and a cheerful countenance. Friends who nodded to him, as he walked along Piccadilly, down Saint James's Street, and by Pall Mall, citywards, thought he had just been listening to an amusing story. Others, who, more deferentially, saluted the great man as he walked lightly by Temple Bar, towards Ludgate Hill, for a moment perplexed themselves with the thought, 'What stock is up, and what down, on a sudden, today, that Longcluse looks so radiant?'

The Man Without a Name

Mr. Longcluse had made up his mind to a certain course—a sharp and bold one. At the police office he made inquiry. 'He understood a man had been lately dismissed from the force, answering to a certain description, which he gave them; and he wished to know whether he was rightly informed, because a theft had been that morning committed at his house by a man whose appearance corresponded, and against whom he hoped to have sufficient evidence.'

'Yes, a man like that had been dismissed from the detective department within the last fortnight.'

'What was his name?' Mr. Longcluse asked.

'Paul Davies, Sir.'

'If it should turn out to be the same, I may have a more serious charge to bring against him,' said Mr. Longcluse.

'Do you wish to go before his worship, and give an information, Sir?' urged the officer, invitingly.

'Not quite ripe for that yet,' said Mr. Longcluse, 'but it is likely very soon.'

'And what might be the nature of the more serious charge, Sir?' inquired the officer, insinuatingly.

'I mean to give my evidence at the coroner's inquest that will be held today, on the Frenchman who was murdered last night at the Saloon Tavern. It is not conclusive—it does not fix anything upon him; it is merely inferential.'

'Connecting him with the murder?' whispered the man,

something like reverence mingling with his curiosity, as he discovered the interesting character of his interrogator.

'I can only say possibly connecting him in some way with it. Where does the man live?'

'He did live in Rosemary Court, but he left that, I think. I'll ask, if you please, Sir. Tompkins—hi! You know where Paul Davies puts up. Left Rosemary Court?'

'Yes, five weeks. He went to Gold Ring Alley, but he's left that a week ago, and I don't know where he is now, but will easy find him. Will it answer at eight this evening, Sir?'

'Quite. I want a servant of mine to have a sight of him,' said Longcluse.

'If you like, Sir, to leave your address and a stamp, we'll send you the information by post, and save you calling here.'

'Thanks, yes, I'll do that.'

So Mr. Longcluse took his leave, and proceeded to the place where the coroner was sitting. Mr. Longcluse was received in that place with distinction. The moneyed man was honoured—eyes were gravely fixed on him, and respectful whispers went about. A seat was procured for him; and his evidence, when he came to give it, was heard with marked attention, and a general hush of expectation.

The reader, with his permission, must now pass away, seaward, from this smoky London, for a few minutes, into a clear air, among the rustling foliage of ancient trees, and the fragrance of hay-fields, and the song of small birds.

On the London and Dover road stands, as you know, the 'Royal Oak,' still displaying its ancient signboard, where you behold King Charles II sitting with laudable composure, and a crown of Dutch gold on his head, and displaying his finery through an embrasure in the foliage, with an ostentation somewhat inconsiderate, considering the proximity of the halberts of the military emissaries in search of him to the royal features. As you drive towards London, it shows at the left side of the road, a good old substantial inn and posting-house. Its business has dwindled to something very small indeed, for the traffic prefers the rail, and the once bustling line of road is now quiet. The sun had set, but a reflected glow from the sky was still over everything; and by this somewhat lurid light Mr. Truelock, the innkeeper, was observing from the steps the progress of a chaise, with four horses and two postilions, which was driving at a furious pace down the gentle declivity about a quarter of a mile away, from the Dover direction towards the 'Royal Oak' and London.

'It's a runaway. Them horses has took head. What do you think, Thomas?' he asked of the old waiter who stood beside him.

'No. See, the post-boys is whipping the hosses. No, Sir, it's a gallop, but no runaway.'

'There's luggage a' top?' said the innkeeper.

'Yes, Sir, there's something,' answered Tom.

'I don't see nothing a-followin' them,' said Mr. Truelock, shading his eyes with his hand as he gazed.

'No—there *is* nothing,' said Tom.

'They're in fear o' summat, or they'd never go at that lick,' observed Mr. Truelock, who was inwardly conjecturing the likelihood of their pulling up at his door.

'Lawk! *there* was a jerk. They *was* nigh over at the fingerpost turn,' said Tom, with a grin. And now the vehicle and the reeking horses were near. The post-boys held up their whips by way of signal to the 'Royal Oak' people on the steps, and pulled up the horses with all their force before the door. Trembling, snorting, rolling up wreaths of steam, the exhausted horses stood.

'See to the gentleman, will ye?' cried one of the postilions.

Mr. Truelock, with the old-fashioned politeness of the English innkeeper, had run down in person to the carriage door, which Tom had opened. Master and man were a little shocked to behold inside an old gentleman, with a very brown, or rather a very bilious visage, thin, and with a high nose, who looked, as he lay stiffly back in the corner of the carriage, enveloped in shawls, with a velvet cap on, as if he were either dead or in a fit. His eyes were half open, and nothing but the white balls partly visible. There was a little froth at his lips. His mouth and delicately-formed hands were clenched, and all the furrows and lines of a selfish face fixed, as it seemed, in the lock of death. John Truelock said not a word, but peered at this visitor with a horrible curiosity.

'If he's dead,' whispered Tom in his ear, 'we don't take in no dead men here. Ye'll have the coroner and his jury in the house, and the place knocked up-side down; and if ye make five pounds one way ye'll lose ten the tother.'

'Ye'll have to take him on, I'm thinkin',' said Mr. Truelock, rousing himself, stepping back a little, and addressing the post-boys sturdily. 'You've no business bringin' a deceased party to my house. You must go somewhere else, if so be he *is* deceased.'

'He's not gone dead so quick as that,' said the postilion, dismounting from the near leader, and throwing the bridle to a boy who stood by, as he strutted round bandily to have a peep into the chaise. The postilion on the 'wheeler' had turned himself about in the saddle in order to have a peep through the front window of the carriage. The innkeeper returned to the door.

If the old London and Dover road had been what it once was, there would have been a crowd about the carriage by this time. Except, however, two or three servants of the 'Royal Oak,' who had come out to see, no one had yet joined the little group but the boy who was detained, bridle in hand, at the horse's head.

'He'll not be dead yet,' repeated the postilion dogmatically.

'What happened him?' asked Mr. Truelock.

'I don't know,' answered the post-boy.

'Then how can you say whether he be dead or no?' demanded the innkeeper.

'Fetch me a pint of half-and-half,' said the dismounted post-boy, aside, to one of the 'Royal Oak' people at his elbow.

'We was just at this side of High Hixton,' said his brother in the saddle, 'when he knocked at the window with his stick, and I got a cove to hold the bridle, and I came round to the window to him. He had scarce any voice in him, and looked awful bad, and he said he thought he was a-dying. 'And how far on is the next inn?' he asked; and I told him the 'Royal Oak' was two miles; and he said, 'Drive like lightning, and I'll give you half a guinea a-piece'—I hope he's not gone dead— 'if you get there in time."

By this time their heads were in the carriage again.

'Do you notice a sort of a little jerk in his foot, just the least thing in the world?' inquired the landlord, who had sent for the doctor. 'It will be a fit, after all. If he's living, we'll fetch him into the 'ouse.'

The doctor's house was just round the corner of the road, where the clump of elms stands, little more than a hundred yards from the sign of the 'Royal Oak'.

'Who is he?' inquired Mr. Truelock.

'I don't know,' answered the postilion.

'What's his name?'

'Don't know that, neither.'

'Why, it'll be on that box, won't it?' urged the innkeeper, pointing to the roof, where a portmanteau with a glazed cover was secured.

'Nothing on that but 'R. A."', answered the man, who had examined it half an hour before, with the same object.

'Royal Artillery, eh?'

While they were thus conjecturing, the doctor arrived. He stepped into the chaise, felt the old man's hand, tried his pulse, and finally applied the stethoscope.

'It is a nervous seizure. He is in a very exhausted state,' said the doctor, stepping out again, and addressing Truelock. 'You must get him into bed, and don't let his head down; take off his handkerchief, and open his shirt-collar—do you mind? I had best arrange him myself.'

So the forlorn old man, without a servant, without a name, is carried from the chaise, possibly to die in an inn.

The Rev. Peter Sprott, the rector, passing that way a few minutes later, and hearing what had befallen, went up to the bed-room, where the old gentleman lay in a four-poster, still unconscious.

'Here's a case,' said the doctor to his clerical friend. 'A nervous attack. He'd be all right in no time, but he's so low. I daresay he crossed the herring-pond today, and was ill; he's in such an exhausted state. I should not wonder if he sank; and here we are, without a clue to his name or people. No servant, no name on his trunk; and, certainly, it would be awkward if he died unrecognised, and without a word to apprise his relations.'

'Is there no letter in his pockets?'

'Not one,' Truelock says.

The rector happened to take up the great-coat of the old gentleman, in which he found a small breast pocket, that had been undiscovered till now, and in this a letter. The envelope was gone, but the letter, in a lady's hand began: 'My dearest papa.'

'We are all right, by Jove, we're in luck!'

'How does she sign herself?' said the doctor.

'Alice Arden, and she dates from 8, Chester Terrace,' answered the clergyman.

'We'll telegraph forthwith,' said the doctor. 'It had best be in your name—the clergyman, you know—to a young lady.'

So together they composed the telegram.

'Shall it be *ill* simply, or *dangerously* ill?' inquired the clergyman.

'Dangerously,' said the doctor.

'But *dangerously* may terrify her.'

'And if we say only *ill,* she mayn't come at all,' said the doctor.

So the telegram was placed in Truelock's hands, who went himself with it to the office; and we shall follow it to its destination.

The Royal Oak

Three people were sitting in Lady May Penrose's drawing-room, in Chester Terrace, the windows of which, as all her ladyship's friends are aware, command one of the parks. They were looking westward, where the sky was all a-glow with the fantastic gold and crimson of sunset. It is quite a mistake to fancy that sunset, even in the heart of London—which this hardly could be termed—has no rural melancholy and poetic fascination in it. Should that hour by any accident overtake you, in the very centre of the city, looking, say, from an upper window, or any other elevation toward the western sky beyond stacks of chimneys, roofs, and steeples, even through the smoke of London, you will feel the melancholy and poetry of sunset, in spite of your surroundings.

A little silence had stolen over the party; and young Vivian Darnley, who stole a glance now and then at beautiful Alice Arden, whose large, dark, grey eyes were gazing listlessly towards the splendid mists, that were piled in the west, broke the silence by a remark that, without being very wise, or very new, was yet, he hoped, quite in accord with the looks of the girl, who seemed for a moment saddened.

'I wonder why it is that sunset, which is so beautiful, makes you all sad!'

'It never made me sad,' said good Lady May Penrose, comfortably. 'There is, I think, something very pleasant in a good sunset; there *must* be, for all the little birds begin to sing in it—it must be cheerful. Don't you think so, Alice?'

Alice was, perhaps, thinking of something quite different, for rather listlessly, and without a change of features, she said, 'Oh, yes, very.'

'So, Mr. Darnley, you may sing, 'Oh, leave me to my sorrow!' for we won't mope with you about the sky. It is a very odd taste, that for being dolorous and miserable. I don't understand it—I never could.'

Thus rebuked by Lady Penrose, and deserted by Alice, Darnley laughed and said—

'Well, I do seem rather to have put my foot in it—but I did not mean miserable, you know; I meant only that kind of thing that one feels when reading a bit of really good poetry—and most people do not think it a rather pleasant feeling.'

'Don't mind that moping creature, Alice; let us talk about something we can all understand. I heard a bit of news today—

perhaps, Mr. Darnley, you can throw a light upon it. You are a distant relation, I think, of Mr. David Arden.'

'Some very remote cousinship, of which I am very proud,' answered the young man gaily, with a glance at Alice.

'And what is that—what about uncle David?' inquired the young lady, with animation.

'I heard it from my banker today. Your uncle, you know, dear, despises us and our doings, and lives, I understand, very quietly; I mean, he has chosen to live quite out of the world, so we have no chance of hearing anything! except by accident, from people we are likely to know. Do you see much of your uncle, my dear?'

'Not a great deal; but I am very fond of him—he is such a good man, or at least, what is better,' she laughed, 'he has always been so very kind to me.'

'You know him, Mr Darnley?' inquired Lady May.

'By Jove, I do!'

'And like him?'

'No one on earth has better reason to like him,' answered the young man warmly— 'he has been my best friend on earth.'

'It is pleasant to know two people who are not ashamed to be grateful,' said fat Lady May, with a smile.

The young lady returned her smile very kindly. I don't think you ever beheld a prettier creature than Alice Arden. Vivian Darnley had wasted many a secret hour in sketching that oval face. Those large, soft, grey eyes, and long dark lashes, how difficult they are to express! And the brilliant lips! Could art itself paint anything quite like her? Who could paint those beautiful dimples that made her smiles so soft, or express the little circlet of pearly teeth whose tips were just disclosed? Stealthily he was now, for the thousandth time, studying that bewitching smile again.

'And what is the story about Uncle David?' asked Alice again.

'Well, what will you say—and you, Mr. Darnley, if it should be a story about a young lady?'

'Do you mean that Uncle David is going to marry? I think it would be an awful pity!' exclaimed Alice.

'Well, dear, to put you out of pain, I'll tell you at once; I only know this—that he is going to provide for her somehow, but whether by adopting her as a child, or taking her for a wife, I can't tell. Only I never saw any one looking archer than Mr. Brounker did today when he told me; and I fancied from that it could not be so dull a business as merely making her his daughter.'

'And who is the young lady?' asked Alice.

'Did you ever happen to meet anywhere a Miss Grace Maubray?'

'Oh, yes,' answered Alice quickly. 'She was staying, and her father, Colonel Maubray, at the Wymerings' last autumn. She's quite lovely, I think, and very clever—but I don't know—I think she's a little ill-natured, but very amusing. She seems to have a talent for cutting people up—and a little of that kind of thing, you know, is very well, but one does not care for it *always.* And is she really the young lady?'

'Yes, and —— Dear me! Mr. Darnley, I'm afraid my story has alarmed you.

'Why should it?' laughed Vivian Darnley, partly to cover perhaps, a little confusion.

'I can't tell, I'm sure, but you blushed as much as a man can; and you know you did. I wonder, Alice, what this underplot can be, where all is so romantic. Perhaps, after all, Mr. David Arden is to adopt the young lady, and someone else, to whom he is also kind, is to marry her. Don't you think that would be a very natural arrangement?'

Alice laughed, and Darnley laughed; but he was embarrassed.

'And Colonel Maubray, is he still living?' asked Alice.

'Oh, no, dear; he died ten or eleven months ago. A very foolish man, you know; he wasted a very good property. He was some distant relation, also; Mr. Brounker said your uncle, Mr. David Arden, was very much attached to him—they were schoolfellows, and great friends all their lives.'

'I should not wonder,' said Alice smiling and then became silent.

'Do you know the young lady, this fortunate Miss Maubray?' said Lady May, turning to Vivian Darnley again.

'I? Yes—that is, I can't say more than a mere acquaintance—and not an old one. I made her acquaintance at Mr. Arden's house. He is her guardian. I don't know about any other arrangements. I daresay there may be.'

'Well, I know her a little, also,' said Lady May. 'I thought her pretty—and she sings a little, and she's clever.'

'She's all that,' said Alice. 'Oh, here comes Dick! What do you say, Richard—is not Miss Maubray very pretty? We are making a plot to marry her to Vivian Darnley, and get Uncle David to contribute her *dot.*'

'What benevolent people! *You* don't object, I dare say, Vivian.'

'I have not been consulted,' said he; 'and, of course, Uncle David need not be consulted, as he has simply to transfer the proper quantity of stock.'

Richard Arden had drawn near Lady May, and said a few words in a low tone, which seemed not unwelcome to her.

'I saw Longcluse this morning. He has not been here, has he?' he added, as a little silence threatened the conversation.

'No, he has not turned up. And what a charming person he is!' exclaimed Lady May.

'I quite agree with you, Lady May,' said Arden. 'He is, take him on every subject, I think, about the cleverest fellow I ever met art, literature, games, *chess*, which I take to be a subject by itself. He is very great at chess—for an amateur, I mean—and when I was chess-mad, nearly a year ago and beginning to grow conceited, he opened my eyes, I can tell you; and Airly says he is the best musical critic in England, and can tell you at any hour who is who in the opera, all over Europe; and he really understands, what so few of us here know anything about, foreign politics, and all the people and their stories and scandals he has at his fingers' ends. And he is such good company, when he chooses, and such a gentleman always!'

'He is very agreeable and amusing when he takes the trouble; I always like to listen when Mr. Longcluse talks,' said Alice Arden, to the secret satisfaction of her brother, whose enthusiasm was, I think, directed a good deal to her—and to, perhaps, the vexation of other people, whom she did not care at that moment to please.

'An admirable Crichton!' murmured Vivian Darnley, with a rather hackneyed sneer. 'Do you like his style of—*beauty,* I suppose I should call it? It has the merit of being very uncommon, at least, don't you think?'

'Beauty, I think, matters very little. He has no beauty, but his face has what, in a man, I think a great deal better—I mean refinement, and cleverness, and a kind of satire that rather interests one,' said Miss Arden, with animation.

'Sir Walter Scott, in his *Rob Roy* thinking, no doubt, of the Diana Vernon of his early days, the then beautiful lady, long afterwards celebrated by Basil Hall as the old Countess Purgstorf (if I rightly remember the title), and recurring to some cherished incident, and the thrill of a pride that had ceased to agitate, but was at once pleasant and melancholy to remember wrote these words: 'She proceeded to read the first *stanza*, which was nearly to the following purpose.' [Then follow the verses.] "There is a great deal of it,' said she, glancing along the paper, and interrupting the sweetest sounds that mortal ears can drink in—those of a youthful poet's verses, namely, read by the lips which are dearest to them.' So writes Walter Scott. On the other hand, in certain states, is there a pain intenser than that of listening to the praises of another man from the lips we love?'

'Well,' said Darnley, 'as you say so, I suppose there is all that, though I can't see it. Of course, if he tries to make himself agreeable (which he never does to me), it makes a difference, it affects everything—it affects even his looks. But I should not have thought him good-looking. On the contrary, he appears to me about as ugly a fellow as one could see in a day.'

'He's not that,' said Alice. 'No one could be ugly with so much animation and so much expression.'

'You take up the cudgels very prettily, my dear, for Mr. Longcluse,' said Lady May. 'I'm sure he ought to be extremely obliged to you.'

'So he would be,' said Richard Arden. 'It would upset him for a week, I have no doubt.'

There are few things harder to interpret than a blush. At these words the beautiful face of Alice Arden flushed, first with a faint, and then, as will happen, with a brighter crimson. If Lady Mary had seen it, she would have laughed, probably, and told her how much it became her. But she was, at that moment, going to her chair in the window, and Richard Arden would, of course, accompany her. He did see it, as distinctly as he saw the glow in the sky over the park trees. But, knowing what a slight matter will sometimes make a recoil, and even found an antipathy, he wisely chose to see it not—and chatting gaily, followed Lady May to the window.

But Vivian Darnley, though he said nothing, saw that blush, of which Alice, with a sort of haughty defiance, was conscious. It did not make him like or admire Mr. Longcluse more.

'Well, I suppose he is very charming—I don't know him well enough myself to give an opinion. But he makes his acquaintances rather oddly, doesn't he? I don't think anyone will dispute that.'

'I don't know really. Lady May introduced him to me, and she seems to like him very much. So far as I can see, people are very well pleased at knowing him, and don't trouble their heads as to how it came about,' said Miss Arden.

'No, of course; but people not fortunate enough to come within the influence of his fascination, can't help observing. How did he come to know your brother, for instance? Did anyone introduce him? Nothing of the kind. Richard's horse was hurt or lame at one of the hunts in Warwickshire, and he lent him a horse, and introduced himself, and they dined together that evening on the way back, and so the thing was done.'

'Can there be a better introduction than a kindness?' asked Alice.

'Yes, where it *is* a kindness, I agree; but no one has a right to push his services upon a stranger who does not ask for them.'

'I really can't see. Richard need not have taken his horse if he had not liked,' she answered.

'And Lady May, who thinks him such a paragon, knows no more about him than anyone else. She had her footman behind her—didn't she tell you all about it?'

'I really don't recollect; but does it very much matter?'

'I think it does—that is, it has been a sort of system. He just gave her his arm over a crossing, where she had taken fright, and then pretended to think her great deal more frightened than she really can have been, and made her sit down to recover in a confectioner's shop, and so saw her home, and *that* affair was concluded. I don't say, of course, that he is never introduced in the regular way; but a year or two ago, when he was beginning, he always made his approaches by means of that kind of stratagem; and the fact is, no one knows anything on earth about him; he has emerged, like a figure in a phantasmagoria, from total darkness, and may lose himself in darkness again at any moment.'

'I am interested in that man, whoever he is; his entrance, and his probable exit, so nearly resemble mine,' said a clear, deep-toned voice close to them; and looking up, Miss Arden saw the pale face and peculiar smile of Mr. Longcluse in the fading twilight.

Mr. Longcluse was greeted by Lady May and by Richard Arden, and then again he drew near Alice, and said, 'Do you recollect, Miss Arden, about ten days ago I told you a story that seemed to interest you—the story of a young and eloquent friar, who died of love in his cell in an abbey in the Tyrol, and whose ghost used to be seen pensively leaning on the pulpit from which he used to preach, too much thinking of the one beautiful face among his audience, which had enthralled him. I had left the enamel portrait I told you of at an artist's in Paris, and I wrote for it, thinking you might wish to see it—hoping you might care to see it,' he added, in a lower tone, observing that Vivian Darnley, who was not in a happy temper, had, with a sudden impulse of disdain, removed himself to another window, there to contemplate the muster of the stars in the darkening sky, at his leisure.

'That was so kind of you, Mr. Longcluse! You have had a great deal of trouble. It *is* such an interesting story!' said Alice.

In his reception, Mr. Longcluse found something that pleased, almost elated him. Had Richard Arden been speaking to her on the subject of their morning's conversation? He thought not, Lady May had mentioned that he had not been with them till just twenty minutes ago, and Arden had told him that he had dined with his uncle David and Mr. Blount, upon the same business on which he had been occupied with both nearly all day. No, he could not have spoken to her. The slight change which made him so tumultuously proud and happy, was entirely spontaneous.

'So it seemed to me—an eccentric and interesting story—but pray do not wound me by speaking of trouble. I only wish you knew half the pleasure it has been to me to get it to show you. May I hold the lamp near for a moment while you look at it?' he said, indicating a tiny lamp which stood on a pier-table, showing a solitary gleam, like a lighthouse, through the gloom; 'you could not possibly see it in this faint twilight.'

The lady assented. Had Mr. Longcluse ever felt happier?

The Telegram Arrives

Mr. Longcluse placed the little oval enamel, set in gold, in Miss Arden's fingers, and held the lamp beside her while she looked.

'How beautiful!—how very interesting!' she exclaimed. 'What suffering in those thin, handsome features! What a strange enthusiasm in those large hazel eyes! I could fancy that monk the maddest of lovers, the most chivalric of saints. And did he really suffer that incredible fate? Did he really die of love?'

'So they say. But why incredible? I can quite imagine that

wild shipwreck, seeing what a raging sea love is, and how frail even the strongest life.'

'Well, I can't say, I am sure. But your own novelists laugh at the idea of any but women—whose business it is, of course, to pay that tribute to their superiors—dying of love. But if any man could die such a death, he must be such as this picture represents. What a wild, agonised picture of passion and asceticism! What suicidal devotion and melancholy rapture! I confess I could almost fall in love with that picture myself.'

'And I think, were I he, I could altogether die to earn one such sentence, so spoken,' said Mr. Longcluse.

'Could you lend it to me for a very few days?' asked the young lady.

'As many—as long as you please. I am only too happy.'

'I should so like to make a large drawing of this in chalks!' said Alice, still gazing on the miniature.

'You draw so beautifully in chalks! Your style is not often found here—your colouring is so fine.'

'Do you really think so?'

'You must know it, Miss Arden. You are too good an artist not to suspect what everyone else must see, the real excellence of your drawings. Your colouring is better understood in France. Your master, I fancy, was a Frenchman?' said Mr. Longcluse.

'Yes, he was, and we got on very well together. Some of his young lady pupils were very much afraid of him.'

'Your poetry is fired by that picture, Miss Arden. Your copy will be a finer thing than the original,' said he.

'I shall aim only at making it a faithful copy; and if I can accomplish anything like that, I shall be only too glad.'

'I hope you will allow me to see it?' pleaded Longcluse.

'Oh, certainly,' she laughed. 'Only I'm a little afraid of you, Mr. Longcluse.'

'What can you mean, Miss Arden?'

'I mean, you are so good a critic in art, everyone says, that I really *am* afraid of you,' answered the young lady, laughing.

'I should be very glad to forfeit any little knowledge I have, if it were attended with such a misfortune,' said Longcluse. 'But I don't flatter; I tell you truly, a critic has only to admire, when he looks at your drawings; they are quite above the level of an amateur's work.'

'Well, whether you mean it or not, I *am* very much flattered,' she laughed. 'And though wise people say that flattery spoils one, I can't help thinking it very agreeable to be flattered.'

At this point of the dialogue Mr. Vivian Darnley—who wished that it should be plain to all, and to one in particular, that he did not care the least what was going on in other parts of the room—began to stumble through the treble of a tune at the piano with his right hand. And whatever other people may have thought of his performance, to Miss Alice Arden it seemed very good music indeed, and inspired her with fresh animation. Such as it was, Mr. Darnley's solo also turned the course of Miss Arden's thoughts from drawing to another art, and she said—

'You, Mr. Longcluse, who know everything about the opera, can you tell me—of course you can—anything about the great *basso* who is coming?'

'Stentoroni?'

'Yes; the newspapers and critics promise wonders.'

'It is nearly two years since I heard him. He was very great, and deserves all they say in '*Robert le Diable*'. But there his greatness began and ended. The voice, of course, you had, but everything else was defective. It is plain, however, that the man who could make so fine a study of one opera, could with equal labour make as great a success in others. He has not sung in any opera for more than a year and a half, and has been working diligently; and so everyone is in the dark very much, and I am curious to hear the result—and nobody knows more than I have told you. You are sure of a good '*Robert le Diable,*' but all the rest is speculation.'

'And now, Mr. Longcluse, I shall try your good-nature.'

'How?'

'I am going to make Lady May ask you to sing a song.'

'Pray don't.'

'Why not?'

'I should so much rather you asked me yourself.'

'That's very good of you; then I certainly shall. I *do* ask you.'

'And I instantly obey. And what shall the song be?' asked he, approaching the piano, to which she also walked.

'Oh, that ghostly one that I liked so much when you sang it here about a week ago,' she answered.

'I know it—yes, with pleasure.' And he sat down at the piano, and in a clear, rich baritone, sang the following odd song:—

The autumn leaf was falling
At midnight from the tree,
When at her casement calling,
'I'm here, my love,' says he.
'Come down and mount behind me,
And rest your little head,
And in your white arms wind me,
Before that I be dead.

You've stolen my heart by magic,
I've kissed your lips in dreams:
Our wooing wild and tragic
Has been in ghostly scenes.
The wondrous love I bear you
Has made one life of twain,
And it will bless or scare you,
In deathless peace or pain.

Our dreamland shall be glowing,
If you my bride will be;
To darkness both are going,
Unless you come with me.
Come now, and mount behind me,
And rest your little head,
And in your white arms wind me,
Before that I be dead.

'Why, dear Alice, will you choose that dismal song, when you know that Mr. Longcluse has so many others that are not only charming, but cheery and natural?'

'It is because it is *un*natural that I like that song so much; the air is so ominous and spectral, and yet so passionate. I think the idea is Icelandic—those ghostly lovers that came in the dark to win their beloved maidens, who as yet knew nothing of their having died, to ride with them over the snowy fields and frozen rivers, to join their friends at a merry-making which they were never to see; but there is something more mysterious even in this lover, for his passion has unearthly beginnings that lose themselves in utter darkness. Thank you very much, Mr. Longcluse. It is so very kind of you! And now, Lady May, isn't it your turn to choose? May she choose, Mr. Longcluse?'

'Any one, if you desire it, may choose anything I possess, and have it,' said he, in a low impassioned murmur.

How the young lady would have taken this, I know not, but all were suddenly interrupted. For at this moment a servant entered with a note, which he presented, upon a salver, to Mr. Longcluse.

'Your servant is waiting, Sir, please, for orders in the awl,' murmured the man.

'Oh, yes—thanks,' said Mr. Longcluse, who saw a shabby letter, with the words 'Private' and 'Immediate' written in a round, vulgar hand over the address.

'Pray read your note, Mr. Longcluse, and don't mind us,' said Lady May.

'Thank you very much. I think I know what this is. I gave some evidence today at an inquest,' began Mr. Longcluse.

'That wretched Frenchman,' interposed Lady May, 'Monsieur Lebrun or—'

'Lebas,' said Vivian Darnley.

'Yes, so it was, Lebas; what a frightful thing that was!' continued Lady May, who was always well up in the day's horrors.

'Very melancholy, and very alarming also. It is a selfish way of looking at it, but one can't help thinking it might just as well have happened to anyone else who was there. It brings it home to one a little uncomfortably,' said Mr. Longcluse, with an uneasy smile and a shrug.

'And you actually gave evidence, Mr. Longcluse?' said Lady May.

'Yes, a little,' he answered. 'It may lead to something. I hope so. As yet it only indicates a line of inquiry. It will be in the papers, I suppose, in the morning. There will be, I daresay, a pretty full report of that inquest.'

'Then you saw something occur that excited your suspicions?' said Lady May.

Mr. Longcluse recounted all he had to tell, and mentioned having made inquiries as to the present abode of the man, Paul Davies, at the police office.

'And this note, I daresay, is the one they promised to send me, telling the result of their inquiries,' he added.

'Pray open it and see,' said Lady May.

He did so. He read it in silence. From his foot to the crown of his head there crept a cold influence as he read. Stream after stream, this *aura* of fear spread upwards to his brain. Pale Mr. Longcluse shrugged and smiled, and smiled and shrugged, as his dark eye ran down the lines, and with a careless finger he turned the page over. He smiled, as prizefighters smile for the spectators, while every nerve quivered with pain. He looked up, smiling still, and thrust the note into his breast-pocket.

'Well, Mr. Longcluse, a long note it seems to have been,' said Lady May, curiously.

'Not very long, but what is as bad, very illegible,' said Mr. Longcluse gaily.

'And what about the man—the person the police were to have inquired after?' she persisted.

'I find it is no police information, nothing of the kind,' answered Longcluse with the same smile. 'It comes by no means from one of that long-headed race of men; on the contrary, poor fellow, I believe he is literally a little mad. I make him a trifling present every Christmas, and that is a very good excuse for his plaguing me all the year round. I was in hopes this letter might turn out an amusing one, but it is not; it is a failure. It is rather sensible, and disgusting.'

'Well, then, I must have my song, Mr. Longcluse,' said Lady May, who, under cover of music, sometimes talked a little, in gentle murmurs, to that person with whom talk was particularly interesting.

But that song was not to be heard in Lady May's drawing-room that night, for a kindred interruption, though much more serious in its effects upon Mr. Longcluse's companions, occurred. A footman entered, and presented on a salver a large brown envelope to Miss Alice Arden.

'Oh, dear! It is a telegram,' exclaimed Miss Arden, who had taken it to the window. Lady May Penrose was beside her by this time. Alice looked on the point of fainting.

'I'm afraid papa is very ill,' she whispered, handing the paper, which trembled very much in her hand, to Lady May.

'H'm! Yes—but you may be sure it's exaggerated. Bring some sherry and water, please. You look a little frightened, my dear. Sit down, darling. There now! These messages are always written in a panic. What do you mean to do?'

'I'll go, of course,' said Alice.

'Well, yes—I think you must go. What is the place? Twyford, the 'Royal Oak?' Look out Twyford, please Mr. Darnley—there's a book there. It must be a post-town. It was thoughtful saying it is on the Dover coach road.'

Vivian Darnley was gazing in deep concern at Alice. Instantly he began turning over the book, and announced in a few moments more—'It is a post-town—only thirty-six miles from London,' said Mr. Darnley.

'Thanks,' said Lady May. 'Oh, here's the wine—I'm so glad! You must have a little, dear; and you'll take Louisa Diaper with you, of course; and you shall have one of my carriages, and I'll send a servant with you, and he'll arrange everything; and how soon do you wish to go?'

'Immediately, instantly—thanks, darling. I'm *so* much obliged!'

'Will your brother go with you?'

'No, dear. Papa, you know, has not forgiven him, and it is, I think, two years since they met. It would only agitate him.'

And with these words she hurried to her room, and in another moment, with the aid of her maid, was completing her hasty preparations.

In wonderfully little time the carriage was at the door. Mr. Longcluse had taken his leave. So had Richard Arden, with the one direction to the servant, 'If anything should go *very* wrong, be sure to telegraph for me. Here is my address.'

'Put this in your purse, dear,' said Lady May. 'Your father is so thoughtless, he may not have brought money enough with him; and you will find it is as I say—he'll be a great deal better by the time you get there; and God bless you, my dear.'

And she kissed her as heartily as she dared, without communicating the rouge and white powder which aided her complexion.

As Alice ran down, Vivian Darnley awaited her outside the drawing-room door, and ran down with her, and put her into the carriage. He leaned for a moment on the window, and said—

'I hope you didn't mind that nonsense Lady May was talking just now about Miss Grace Maubray. I assure you it is utter folly. I was awfully vexed; but you didn't believe it?'

'I didn't hear her say anything, at least seriously. Wasn't she laughing? I'm in such trouble about that message! I am so longing to be at my journey's end!'

He took her hand and pressed it, and the carriage drove away. And standing on the steps, and quite forgetting the footman close behind him, he watched it as it drove rapidly southward, until it was quite out of sight, and then with a great sigh and 'God for ever bless you!' —uttered not above his breath—he turned about, and saw those powdered and liveried effigies, and walked up with his head rather high to the drawing-room, where he found Lady May.

'I sha'n't go to the opera tonight; it is out of the question,' said she. 'But *you* shall. You go to my box, you know; Jephson will put you in there.'

It was plain that the good-natured soul was unhappy about Alice, and, Richard Arden having departed, wished to be alone. So Vivian took his leave, and went away—but not to the opera—and sauntered for an hour, instead, in a melancholy romance up and down the terrace, till the moon rose and silvered the trees in the park.

Sir Reginald Arden

The human mind being, in this respect, of the nature of a kaleidoscope, that the slightest hitch, or jolt, or tremor is enough to change the entire picture that occupies it, it is not to be supposed that the illness of her father, alarming as it was, could occupy Alice Arden's thoughts to the exclusion of every other subject, during every moment of her journey. One picture, a very pretty one, frequently presented itself, and always her heart felt a strange little pain as this pretty phantom appeared. It was the portrait of a young girl, with fair golden hair, a brilliant complexion, and large blue eyes, with something *riant*, triumphant, and arch to the verge of mischief, in her animated and handsome face.

The careless words of good Lady May, this evening, and the very obvious confusion of Vivian Darnley at mention of the name of Grace Maubray, troubled her. What was more likely than that Uncle David, interested in both, should have seriously projected the union which Lady May had gaily suggested? If she—Alice Arden—liked Vivian Darnley, it was not very much, her pride insisted. In her childhood they had been thrown together. He had seemed to like her; but had he ever spoken? Why was he silent? Was she fool enough to like him?—that cautious, selfish young man, who was thinking, she was quite certain now, of a marriage of prudence or ambition with Grace Maubray? It was a cold, cruel, sordid world!

But, after all, why should he have spoken? or why should he have hoped to be heard with favour? She had been to him, thank Heaven, just as any other pleasant, early friend. There was nothing to regret—nothing fairly to blame. It was just that a person whom she had come to regard as a property was about to go, and belong quite, to another. It was the foolish little jealousy that everyone feels, and that means nothing. So she told herself; but constantly recurred the same pretty image, and with it the same sudden little pain at her heart.

But now came the other care. As time and space shorten, and the moment of decision draws near, the pain of suspense increases. They were within six miles of Twyford. Her heart was in a wild flutter—now throbbing madly, now it seemed standing still. The carriage window was down. She was looking out on the scenery—strange to her—all bright and serene under a brilliant moon. What message awaited her at the inn to which they were travelling at this swift pace? How frightful it might be!

'Oh, Louisa!' she every now and then imploringly cried to her maid, 'how do you think it will be? Oh! how will it be? Do you think he'll be better? Oh! do you think he'll be better? Tell me again about his other illness, and how he recovered? Don't you think he will this time? Oh, Louisa, darling! don't you think so? Tell me—*tell* me you do!'

Thus, in her panic, the poor girl wildly called for help and comfort, until at last the carriage turned a curve in the road at which stood a shadowy clump of elms, and in another moment the driver pulled up under the sign of the 'Royal Oak'.

'Oh, Louisa! Here it is,' cried the young lady, holding her maid's wrist with a trembling grasp.

The inn-door was shut, but there was light in the hall, and light in an upper room.

'Don't knock—only ring the bell. He may be asleep, God grant!' said the young lady.

The door was quickly opened, and a waiter ran down to the carriage window, where he saw a pair of large wild eyes, and a very pale face, and heard the question— 'An old *gentleman* has been ill here, and a telegram was sent; is he—how is he?'

'He's better, Ma'am,' said the man.

With a low, long 'O—Oh!' and clasped hands and upturned eyes, she leaned back in the carriage, and a sudden flood of tears relieved her. Yes; he was a great deal better. The attack was quite over; but he had not spoken. He seemed much exhausted; and having swallowed some claret, which the doctor prescribed, he had sunk into a sound and healthy sleep, in which he still lay. A message by telegraph had been sent to announce the good news, but Alice was some way on her journey before it had reached.

Now the young lady got down, and entered the homely old inn, followed by her maid. She could have dropped on her knees in gratitude to her Maker; but true religion, like true affection, is shy of demonstrating its fervours where sympathy is doubtful.

Gently, hardly breathing, guided by the 'chambermaid', she entered her father's room, and stood at his bedside. There he lay, yellow, lean, the lines of his face in repose still forbidding, the thin lips and thin nose looking almost transparent, and breathing deeply and regularly, as a child in his slumbers. In that face Alice could not discover what any stranger would have seen. She only saw the face of her father. Selfish and capricious as he was, and violent too—a wicked old man, if one could see him justly—he was yet proud of her, and had many schemes and projects afloat in his jaded old brain, of which her beauty was the talisman, of which she suspected nothing, and with which his head was never more busy than at the very moment when he was surprised by the *aura* of his coming fit.

The doctor's conjecture was right. He had crossed the Channel that morning. In his French *coupée*, he had for companion the very man he had most wished and contrived to travel homeward with. This was Lord Wynderbroke.

Lord Wynderbroke was fifty years old and upwards. He was very much taken with Alice, whom he had met pretty often. He was a man who was thought likely to marry. His estate was in the nattiest order. He had always been prudent, and cultivated a character. He had, moreover, mortgages over Sir Reginald Arden's estate, the interest of which the baronet was beginning to find it next to impossible to pay. They had been making a little gouty visit to Vichy, and Sir Reginald had taken good care to make the journey homeward with Lord Wynderbroke, who knew that when he pleased he could be an amusing companion, and who also felt that kind of interest in him which everyone experiences in the kindred of the young lady of whom he is enamoured.

The baronet, who tore up or burnt his letters for the most part, had kept this particular one by which his daughter had been traced and summoned to the 'Royal Oak'. It was, he thought, clever. It was amusing, and had some London gossip. He had read bits of it to Lord Wynderbroke in the *coupeé*. Lord Wynderbroke was delighted. When they parted, he had asked leave to pay him a visit at Mortlake.

'Only too happy, if you are not afraid of the old house falling in upon us. Everything *there*, you know, is very much as my grandfather left it. I only use it as a caravanserai, and alight there for a little, on a journey. Everything there is tumbling to pieces. But you won't mind—no more than I do.'

So the little visit was settled. The passage was rough. Peer and baronet were ill. They did not care to reunite their fortunes after they touched English ground. As the baronet drew near London, for certain reasons he grew timid. He got out with a portmanteau and dressing-case, and an umbrella, at Drowark station, sent his servant on with the rest of the luggage by rail, and himself took a chaise; and, after one change of horses, had reached the 'Royal Oak' in the state in which we first saw him.

The doctor had told the people at that inn that he would look in, in the course of the night, sometime after one o'clock, being a little uneasy about a possible return of the old man's malady. There was that in the aristocratic looks and belongings of his patient, and in the very fashionable address to which the message to his daughter was transmitted, which induced in the mind of the learned man a suspicion that a 'swell' might have accidentally fallen into his hands.

By this time, thanks to the diligence of Louisa Diaper, everyone in the house had been made acquainted with the fact that the sick man was no other than Sir Reginald Arden, Bart., and with many other circumstances of splendour, which would not, perhaps, have so well stood the test of inquiry. The doctor and his crony, the rector—simplest of parsons—who had agreed to accompany him in this nocturnal call, being a curious man, as gentlemen inhabiting quiet villages will be—these two gentlemen now heard all this lore in the hall at a quarter past one, and entered the patient's chamber (where they found Miss Arden and her maid) accordingly. In whispers, the doctor made to Miss Arden a most satisfactory report. He made his cautious inspection of the patient, and again had nothing but what was cheery to say.

If the rector had not prided himself upon his manners, and had been content with one bow on withdrawing from the lady's presence, they would not that night have heard the patient's voice—and perhaps, all things considered, so much the better.

'I trust, Madam, in the morning Sir Reginald may be quite himself again. It is pleasant, Madam, to witness slumber so quiet,' murmured the clergyman kindly, and in perfect good faith. 'It is the slumber of a tranquil mind—a spirit at peace with itself.'

Smiling kindly in making the last stiff bow which accompanied these happy words, the good man tilted over a little table behind him, on which stood a decanter of claret, a water *caraffe*, and two glasses, all of which came to the ground with a crash that wakened the baronet. He sat up straight in his bed and stared round, while the clergyman, in consternation, exclaimed—'Good gracious!'

'Hollo! what is it?' cried the fierce, thin voice of the baronet. 'What the devil's all this? Where's Crozier? Where's my servant? Will you, will you, some of you, say where the devil I am?' He was screaming all this, and groping and clutching at either side of the bed's head for a bell-rope, intending to rouse the house. 'Where's Crozier, I say? Where the devil's my servant? eh? He's gone by rail, ain't he? No one came with me. And where's this? What is it? Are you all tongue-tied?—haven't you a word among you?'

The clergyman had lifted his hands in terror at the harangue of the old man of the 'tranquil mind.' Alice had taken his thin hand, standing beside him, and was speaking softly in his ear. But his prominent brown eyes were fiercely scanning the strangers, and the hand which clutched hers was trembling with eager fury. 'Will some of you say what you mean, or what you are doing, or where I am?' and he screeched another sentence or two, that made the old clergyman very uncomfortable.

'You arrived here, Sir Reginald, about six hours ago—extremely ill, Sir,' said the doctor, who had placed himself close to his patient, and spoke with official authority; 'but we have got you all right again, we hope; and this is the 'Royal Oak,' the principal hotel of Twyford, on the Dover and London road; and my name is Proby.'

'And what's all this?' cried the baronet, snatching up one of the medicine-bottles from the little table by his bed, and plucking out the cork and smelling at the fluid. 'By heaven?' he screamed, 'this is the very thing. I could not tell what d——d taste was in my mouth, and here it is. Why, my doctor tells me—and he knows his business—it is as much as my life's worth to give me anything like—like that, pah! *assafoetida*! If my stomach is upset with this filthy stuff, I give myself up! I'm gone. I shall sink, Sir. Was there no one here, in the name of Heaven, with a grain of sense or a particle of pity, to prevent that beast from literally poisoning me? Egad! I'll make my son punish him! I'll make my family hang him if I die!' There was a quaver of misery in his shriek of fury, as if he was on the point of bursting into tears. 'Doctor, indeed! who sent for him? I didn't. Who gave him leave to drug me? Upon my soul, I've been poisoned. To think of a creature in my state, dependent on nourishment every hour, having his digestion destroyed! Doctor, indeed! Pay him? Not I, begad,' and he clenched his sentence with an ugly expletive.

But all this concluding eloquence was lost upon the doctor, who had mentioned, in a lofty 'aside' to Miss Arden, that 'unless sent for he should not call again;' and with a marked politeness to her, and no recognition whatever of the baronet, he had taken his departure.

'I'm not the doctor, Sir Reginald; I'm the clergyman,' said

the Reverend Peter Sprott, gravely and timidly, for the prominent brown eyes were threatening him.

'Oh, the clergyman! Oh, I see. Will you be so good as to ring the bell, please, and excuse a sick man giving you that trouble. And is there a post-office near this?'

'Yes, Sir—close by.'

'This is you, Alice? I'm glad you're here. You must write a letter this moment—a note to your brother. Don't be afraid—I'm better, a good deal—and tell the people, when they come, to get me some strong soup this moment, and—good evening, Sir, or goodnight, or morning, or whatever it is,' he added, to the clergyman, who was taking his leave. 'What o'clock is it?' he asked Alice. 'Well, you'll write to your brother to meet me at Mortlake. I have not seen him, now, for how many years? I forget. He's in town, is he? Very good. And tell him it is perhaps the last time, and I expect him. I suppose he'll come. Say at a quarter past nine in the evening. The sooner it's over the better. I expect no good of it; it is only just to try. And I shall leave this early—immediately after breakfast—as quickly as we can. I hate it!'

On the Road

Next morning the baronet was in high good-humour. He has written a little reminder to Lord Wynderbroke. He will expect him at Mortlake the day he named, to dinner. He remembers he promised to stay the night. He can offer him, still, as good a game of piquet as he is likely to find in his club; and he almost feels that he has no excuse but a selfish one, for exacting the performance of a promise which gave him a great deal of pleasure. His daughter, who takes care of her old father, will make their tea and—*voilà, tout*!

Sir Reginald was in particularly good spirits as he sent the waiter to the post-office with this little note. He thinks within himself that he never saw Alice in such good looks. His selfish elation waxes quite affectionate, and Alice never remembered him so good-natured. She don't know what to make of it exactly; but it pleases her, and she looks all the more brilliant.

And now these foreign birds, whom a chance storm has thrown upon the hospitality of the 'Royal Oak', are up and away again. The old baronet and his pretty daughter, Louisa Diaper sitting behind, in cloaks and rugs, and the footman in front, to watch the old man's signals, are whirling dustily along with a team of four horses; for Sir Reginald's arrangements are never economical, and a pair would have brought them over these short stages and home very nearly as fast. Lady May's carriage pleases the old man, and helps his transitory good-humour: it is so much more luxurious than the jolty hired vehicle in which he had arrived.

Alice is permitted her thoughts to herself. The baronet has taken his into companionship, and is leaning back in his corner, with his eyes closed; and his pursed mouth, with its wonderful involution of wrinkles round it, is working unconsciously; and his still dark eyebrows, now elevating, now knitting themselves, indicate the same activity of brain.

With a silent look now and then at his face—for she need not ask whether Sir Reginald wants anything, or would like anything changed, for the baronet needs no inquiries of this kind, and makes people speedily acquainted with his wants and fancies—she occupies her place beside him, for the most part looking out listlessly from the window, and thinks of many things. The baronet opens his eyes at last, and says abruptly,—

'Charming prospect! Charming day! You'll be glad to hear, Alice, I'm not tired; I'm making my journey wonderfully! It is so pretty, and the sun so cheery. You are looking so well, it is quite a pleasure to look at you—charming! You'll come to me at Mortlake for a few days, to take care of me, you know. I shall go on to Buxton in a week or so, and you can return to Lady May tonight, and come to Mortlake shortly; and your brother, graceless creature! I suppose, will come tonight. I expect nothing from his visit, absolutely. He has been nothing to me but a curse all his life. I suppose, if there's justice anywhere, he'll have his deserts some day. But for the present I put him aside—I sha'n't speak of him. He disturbs me.'

They drove through London over Westminster Bridge, the servant thinking that they were to go to Lady May Penrose's in Chester Terrace. It was the first time that day, since he had talked of his son, that a black shadow crossed Sir Reginald's face. He shrunk back. He drew up his Chinese silk muffler over his chin. He was fearful lest some prowling beak or eagle-eyed Jew should see his face, for Sir Reginald was just then in danger. Glancing askance under the peak of his travelling cap, he saw Talkington, with Wynderbroke on his arm, walking to their club. How free and fearless those happy mortals looked! How the old man yearned for his chat and his glass of wine at B——'s, and his afternoon whist at W——'s! How he chafed and blasphemed inwardly at the invisible obstacle that insurmountably interposed, and with what a fiery sting of malice he connected the idea of his son with the fetters that bound him!

'You know that man?' said Sir Reginald sharply, as he saw Mr. Longcluse raise his hat to her as they passed.

'Yes, I've met him pretty often at Lady May's.'

'H'm! I had not an idea that anyone knew him. He's a man who might be of use to one.'

Here followed a silence.

'I thought, papa, you wished to go direct to Mortlake, and I don't think this is the way,' suggested Alice.

'Eh? heigho! You're right, child; upon my life, I was not thinking,' said Sir Reginald, at the same time signalling vehemently to the servant, who, having brought the carriage to a stand-still, came round to the window.

'We don't stop anywhere in town, we go straight to Mortlake Hall. It is beyond Islington. Have you ever been there? Well, you can tell them how to reach it.'

And Sir Reginald placed himself again in his corner. They had not started early, and he had frequently interrupted their journey on various whimsical pretexts. He remembered one house, for instance, where there was a stock of the very best port he had ever tasted, and then he stopped and went in, and after a personal interview with the proprietor, had a bottle opened, and took two glasses, and so paid at the rate of half a guinea each for them. It had been an interrupted journey, late begun, and the sun was near its setting by the time they had got a mile beyond the outskirts of Islington, and were drawing near the singular old house where their journey was to end.

Always with a melancholy presentiment, Alice approached Mortlake Hall. But never had she felt it more painfully than now. If there be in such misgivings a prophetic force, was it to be justified by the coming events of Miss Arden's life, which were awfully connected with that scene?

They passed a quaint little village of tall stone houses, among great old trees, with a rural and old-world air, and an ancient inn, with the sign of 'Guy of Warwick'—an inn of which we shall see more by-and-by—faded, and like the rest of this little town, standing under the shadow of old trees. They entered the road, dark with double hedge-rows, and with a moss-grown park-wall on the right, in which, in a little time, they reached a great iron gate with fluted pillars. They drove up a broad avenue, flanked with files of gigantic trees, and showing grand old timber also upon the park-like grounds beyond. The dusky light of evening fell upon these objects, and the many windows, the cornices, and the smokeless chimneys of a great old house. You might have fancied yourself two hundred miles away from London.

'You don't stay here tonight, Alice. I wish you to return to Lady May, and give her the note I am going to write. You and she come out to dine here on Friday. If she makes a difficulty, I rely on you to persuade her. I must have someone to meet Mr. Longcluse. I have reasons. Also, I shall ask my brother David, and his ward Miss Maubray. I knew her father: he was a fool, with his head full of romance, and he married a very pretty woman who was a devil, without a shilling on earth. The girl is an orphan, and David is her guardian, and he would like any little attention we can show her. And we shall ask Vivian Darnley also. And that will make a very suitable party.'

Sir Reginald wrote his note, talking at intervals.

'You see, I want Lady May to come here again in a day or

two, to stay only for two or three days. She can go into town and remain there all day, if she likes it. But Wynderbroke will be coming, and I should not like him to find us quite deserted; and she said she'd come, and she may as well do it now as another time. David lives so quietly, we are sure of him; and I commit May Penrose to you. You must persuade her to come. It will be cruel to disappoint. Here is her note—I will send the others myself. And now, God bless you, dear Alice!'

'I am so uncomfortable at the idea of leaving you, papa.' Her hand was on his arm, and she was looking anxiously into his face.

'So of course you should be; only that I am so perfectly recovered, that I must have a quiet evening with Richard; and I prefer your being in town tonight, and you and May Penrose can come out tomorrow. Goodbye, child, God bless you!'

Mr. Longcluse's Boot Finds a Temporary Asylum

In the papers of that morning had appeared a voluminous report of the proceedings of the coroner's inquest which sat upon the body of the deceased Pierre Lebas. I shall notice but one passage referring to the evidence which, it seems, Mr. Longcluse volunteered. It was given in these terms:—

> At this point of the proceedings, Mr. R. D. Longcluse, who had arrived about half an hour before, expressed a wish to be examined. Mr. Longcluse was accordingly sworn, and deposed that he had known the deceased, Pierre Lebas, when he (Mr. Longcluse) was little more than a boy, in Paris. Lebas at that time let lodgings, which were neat and comfortable, in the Rue Victoire. He was a respectable and obliging man. He had some other occupation besides that of letting lodgings, but he (Mr. Longcluse) could not say what it might be.'

Then followed particulars with which we are already acquainted; and the report went on to say:

> He seemed surprised when witness told him that there

might be in the room persons of the worst character; and he then, in considerable alarm, pointed out to him (witness) a man who was and had been following him from place to place, he fancied with a purpose. Witness observed the man and saw him watch deceased, turning his eyes repeatedly upon him. The man had no companions, so far as he could see, and affected to be looking in a different direction. It was sideways and stealthily that he was watching deceased, who had incautiously taken out and counted some of his money in the room.

Deceased did not conceal from the witness his apprehensions from this man, and witness advised him again to place his money in the hands of some friend who had a secure pocket, and recommended, in case his friend should object to take so much money into his care—Lebas having said he had a large sum about him—under the gaze of the public, that he should make the transfer in the smoking-room, the situation of which he described to him. Mr. Longcluse then proceeded to give an exact description of the man who had been dogging the *deceased*; the particulars were as follows:—

Here I arrest my quotation, for I need not recapitulate the details of the tall man's features, dress, and figure, which are already familiar to the reader.

In a court off High Holborn there was, and perhaps is, a sort of coffee-shop, in the small drawing-rooms of which, thrown into one room, are many small and homely tables, with penny and halfpenny papers, and literature with startling woodcuts. Here working mechanics and others snatch a very early breakfast, and take their dinners, and such as can afford time loiter their half-hour or so over this agreeable literature. One penny morning paper visited that place of refection, for three hours daily, and then flitted away to keep an appointment elsewhere. It was this dull time in that peculiar establishment—namely, about nine o'clock in the morning—and there was but one listless guest in the room.

It was the identical tall man in question. His flat feet were planted on the bare floor, and he leaned a shoulder against the window-case, with a plug of tobacco in his jaw, as, at his leisure, he was getting through the coroner's inquest on Pierre Lebas. He was smiling with half-closed eyes and considerable enjoyment, up to the point where Mr. Longcluse's evidence was suddenly directed upon him. There was a twitching scowl, as if from a sudden pain; but his smile continued from habit, although his face grew paler. This man, whose name was Paul Davies, winked hard with his left eye, as he got on, and read fiercely with his right. His face was whiter now, and his smile less easy. It was a queerish situation, he thought, and might lead to consequences.

There was a little bit of a looking-glass, picked up at some rubbishy auction, as old as the hills, with some tarnished gilding about it, in the narrow bit of wall between the windows. Paul Davies could look at nothing quite straight. He looked now at himself in this glass, but it was from the corners of his eyes, askance, and with his sly, sleepy depression of the eye-lids, as if he had not overmuch confidence even in his own shadow. He folded the morning paper, and laid it, with formal precision, on the table, as if no one had disturbed it; and taking up the *Halfpenny Illustrated Broadsheet of Fiction*, and with it flourishing in his hand by the corner, he called the waiter over the bannister, and paid his reckoning, and went off swiftly to his garret in another court, a quarter of a mile nearer to Saint Paul's—taking an obscure and devious course through back-lanes and sequestered courts.

When he got up to his garret. Mr. Davies locked his door and sat down on the side of his creaking settle-bed, and, in his playful phrase, 'put on his considering cap.'

'That's a dangerous cove, that Mr. Longcluse. He's done a bold stroke. And now it's him or me, I do suppose—him or me; me or him. Come, Paul, shake up your knowledge-box; I'll not lose this cast simple. He's gave a description of me. The force will know it. And them feet o' mine, they *are* a bit flat: but any chap can make a pair of insteps with a penn'orth o' rags. I wouldn't care tuppence if it wasn't for them pockmarks. There's no managing them. A scar or a wart you may touch over with paint and sollible gutta-percha, or pink wafers and gelatine, but pock-marks is too many for any man.'

He was looking with some anxiety in the triangular fragment of looking-glass—balanced on a nail in the window-case—at his features.

'I can take off them whiskers; and the long neck he makes so much of, if it was as long as an oystrich, with fourpenn'orth of cotton waste and a cabbage-net, I'd make a bull of it, and run my shoulders up to my ears. I'll take the whiskers off, anyhow. That's no treason; and he mayn't identify me. If I'm not had up for a fortnight my hair would be grew a bit, and that would be a lift. But a fellow must think twice before he begins disguisin'. Juries smells a rat. Howsomever, a cove may shave, and no harm done; or his hair may grow a bit, and how can he help it? Longcluse knows what he's about. He's a sharp lad, but for all that Paul Davies 'ill sweat him yet.'

Mr. Davies turned the button of his old-fashioned window, and let it down. He shut out his two scarlet geraniums, which accompanied him in all his changes from one lodging to another.

'Suppose he tries the larceny—that's another thing he may do, seeing what my lay is. It wouldn't do to lose that thing; no more would it answer to let them find it.'

This last idea seemed to cause Paul Davies a good deal of serious uneasiness. He began looking about at the walls, low down near the skirting, and up near the ceiling, tapping now and then with his knuckles, and sounding the plaster as a doctor would the chest of a wheezy patient. He was not satisfied. He scratched his head, and fiddled with his ear, and plucked his short nose dubiously, and winked hard at his geraniums through the window.

Paul Davies knew that the front garret was not let. He opened his door and listened. Then he entered that room. I think he had a notion of changing his lodgings, if only he could find what he wanted. That was such a hiding-place as professional seekers were not likely to discover. But he could not satisfy himself.

A thought struck him, however, and he went into the lobby again; he got on a chair and pushed open the skylight, and out went Mr. Davies on the roof. He looked and poked about here. He looked to the neighbouring roofs, lest any eye should be upon him; but there was no one. A maid hanging clothes upon a line, on a sort of balcony, midway down the next house, was singing, 'The Ratcatcher's Daughter', he thought rather sweetly—so well, indeed, that he listened for two whole verses—but that did not signify.

Paul Davies kneeled down, and loosed and removed, one after the other, several slates near the lead gutter, between the gables; and, having made a sufficient opening in the roof for his purpose, he returned, let himself down lightly through the skylight, entered his room, and locked himself up. He then unlocked his trunk and took from under his clothes, where it lay, a French boot—the veritable boot of Mr. Longcluse—which, for greater security, he popped under the coarse coverlet of his bed. He next took from his trunk a large piece of paper which, being unfolded at the window, disclosed a rude drawing with a sentence or two underneath, and three signatures, with a date preceding.

Having read this document over twice or thrice, with a rather menacing smile, he rolled it up in brown paper and thrust it into the foot of the boot, which he popped under the coverlet and bolster. He then opened his door wide. Too long a silence might possibly have seemed mysterious, and called up prying eyes, so, while he filled his pipe with tobacco, he whistled, 'Villikins and his Dinah' lustily. He was very cautious about this boot and paper. He got on his great-coat and felt hat, and took his pipe and some matches—the enjoying a quiet smoke without troubling others with the perfume was a natural way of accounting for his visit to the roof. He listened. He slipped his boot and its contents into his capacious great-coat pocket, with a rag of old carpet tied round it; and then, whistling still cheerily, he mounted the roof again, and placed the precious parcel within the roof, which he, having some skill as a slater, proceeded carefully and quickly to restore.

Down came Mr. Davies now, and shaved off his whiskers. Then he walked out, with a bundle consisting of the coat, waistcoat, and blue necktie he had worn on the evening of Lebas's murder. He was going to pay a visit to his mother, a venerable greengrocer, who lived near the Tower of London; and on his way he pledged these articles at two distinct and very remote pawnbrokers', intending on his return to release, with the proceeds, certain corresponding articles of his wardrobe, now in ward in another establishment. These measures of obliteration he was taking quietly. His visit to his mother, a very honest old woman, who believed him to be the most virtuous, agreeable, and beautiful young man extant, was made with a very particular purpose.

'Well, Ma'am,' he said, in reply to the old lady's hospitable greeting, 'I won't refuse a pot of half-and-half and a couple of eggs, and I'll go so far as a cut or two of bacon, bein' 'ungry; and I'm a-goin' to write a paper of some consequence, if you'll obleege me with a sheet of foolscap and a pen and ink; and I may as well write it while the things is a-gettin' ready, accordin' to your kind intentions.'

And accordingly Mr. Paul Davies sat in silence, looking very important—as he always did when stationery was before him—at a small table, in a dark back room, and slowly penned a couple of pages of foolscap.

'And now,' said he, producing the document after his repast, 'will you be so good, Ma'am, as to ask Mr. Sildyke and Mrs. Rumble to come down and witness my signing of this, which I mean to leave it in your hands and safe keepin', under lock and key, until I take it away, or otherwise tells you what you must do with it. It is a police paper, Ma'am, and may be wanted any time. But you keep it dark till I tells you.'

This settled, Mr. Sildyke and Mrs. Rumble arrived obligingly; and Paul Davies, with an adroit wink at his mother—who was a little shocked and much embarrassed by the ruse, being a truth-loving woman—told them that here was his last will and testament, and he wanted only that they should witness his signature; which, with the date, was duly accomplished. Paul Davies was, indeed, a man of that genius which requires to proceed by stratagem, cherishing an abhorrence of straight lines, and a picturesque love of the curved and angular. So, if Mr. Longcluse was doing his duty at one end of the town, Mr. Davies, at the other, was by no means wanting in activity, or, according to the level of his intellect and experience, in wisdom.

We have recurred to these scenes in which Mr. Paul Davies figures, because it was indispensable to the reader's right understanding of some events that follow. Be so good, then, as to find Sir Reginald exactly where I left him, standing on the steps of Mortlake Hall. His daughter would have stayed, but he would not hear of it. He stood on the steps, and smirked a yellow and hollow farewell, waving his hand as the carriage drove away. Then he turned and entered the lofty hall, in which the light was already failing.

Sir Reginald did not like the trouble of mounting the stairs, His bedroom and sitting-room were on a level with the hall. As soon as he came in, the gloom of his old prison-house began to overshadow him, and his momentary cheer and good-humour disappeared.

'Where is Tansey? I suppose she's in her bed, or grumbling in toothache,' he snarled to the footman. 'And where the devil's Crozier? I have the fewest and the worst servants, I believe, of any man in England.'

He poked open the door of his sitting-room with the point of his walking-stick.

'Nothing ready, I dare swear,' he quavered, and shot a peevish and fiery glance round it.

Things were not looking quite so badly as he expected. There was just the little bit of expiring fire in the grate which he liked, even in summer. His sealskin slippers were on the hearth-rug, and his easy-chair was pushed into its proper place.

'Ha! Crozier, at last! Here, get off this coat, and these mufflers, and —— I was d——d near dying in that vile chaise. I don't remember how they got me into the inn. There, don't mind condoling. You're privileged, but don't do that. As near dying as possible—rather an awkward business for useless old servants here, if I had. I'll dress in the next room. My son's coming this evening. Admit him, mind. I'll see him. How long is it since we met last? Two years, egad! And Lord Wynderbroke has his dinner here—I don't know what day, but some day very soon—Friday, I think; and don't let the people here go to sleep. Remember!'

And so on, with his old servant, he talked, and sneered, and snarled, and established himself in his sitting-room, with his reviews, and his wine, and his newspapers.

Night fell over dark Mortlake Hall, and over the blazing city of London. Sir Reginald listened, every now and then, for the approach of his son. Talk as he might, he did expect something—and a great deal—from the coming interview. Two years without a home, without an allowance, with no provision except a hundred and fifty pounds a year, might well have tamed that wilful beast!

With the tremor of acute suspense, the old man watched and listened. Was it a good or an ill sign, his being so late?

The city of London, with its still roaring traffic and blaze of gas-lamps, did not contrast more powerfully with the silent shadows of the forest-grounds of Mortlake, than did the drawing-room of Lady May Penrose, brilliant with a profusion of light, and resonant with the gay conversation of inmates, all disposed to enjoy themselves, with the dim and vast room in which Sir Reginald sat silently communing with his own dismal thoughts.

Nothing so contagious as gaiety. Alice Arden, laughingly, was 'making her book' rather prematurely in dozens of pairs of gloves, for the Derby. Lord Wynderbroke was deep in it So was Vivian Darnley.

'Your brother and I are to take the reins, turn about, Lady May says. He's a crack whip. He's better than I, I think,' said Vivian to Alice Arden.

'You mustn't upset us, though. I am so afraid of you crack whips!' said Alice. 'Nor let your horses run away with us; I've been twice run away with already.'

'I don't the least wonder at Miss Arden's being run away with very often,' said Lord Wynderbroke, with all the archness of a polite man of fifty.

'Very prettily said, Wynderbroke,' smiled Lady May. 'And where is your brother? I thought he'd have turned up to night,' asked she of Alice.

'I quite forgot. He was to see papa this evening. They wanted to talk over something together.'

'Oh, I see!' said Lady May, and she became thoughtful.

What was the exact nature of the interest which good Lady May undoubtedly took in Richard Arden? Was it quite so motherly as years might warrant? At that time people laughed over it, and were curious to see the progress of the comedy. Here was light and gaiety—light within, lamps without; spirited talk in young anticipation of coming days of pleasure; and outside the roll of carriage-wheels making a humming bass to this merry treble.

Over the melancholy precincts of Mortlake the voiceless darkness of night descends with unmitigated gloom. The centre—the brain of this dark place—is the house: and in a large dim room, near the smouldering fire, sits the image that haunts rather than inhabits it.

Father and Son

Sir Reginald Arden Had fallen into a doze, as he sat by the fire with his *Revue des Deux Mondes*, slipping between his finger and thumb, on his knees. He was recalled by Crozier's voice, and looking up, he saw, standing near the door, as if in some slight hesitation, a figure not seen for two years before.

For a moment Sir Reginald doubted his only half-awakened senses. Was that handsome oval face, with large, soft eyes, with such brilliant lips, and the dark-brown moustache, so fine, and silken, that had never known a razor, an unsubstantial portrait hung in the dim air, or his living son? There were perplexity and surprise in the old man's stare.

'I should have been here before, Sir, but your letter did not reach me until an hour ago,' said Richard Arden.

'By heaven! Dick? And so you came! I believe I was asleep. Give me your hand. I hope, Dick, we may yet end this miserable quarrel happily. Father and son can have no real interests apart.'

Sir Reginald Arden extended his thin hand, and smiled invitingly but rather darkly on his son. Graceful and easy this young man was, and yet embarrassed, as he placed his hand within his father's.

'You will take something, Dick, won't you?'

'Nothing, Sir, thanks.'

Sir Reginald was stealthily reading his face. At last he began circuitously—

'I've a little bit of news to tell you about Alice. How long shall I allow you to guess what it is?'

'I'm the worst guesser in the world—pray don't wait for me, Sir.'

'Well, I have in my desk there—would you mind putting it on the table here?—a letter from Wynderbroke. You know him?'

'Yes, a little.'

'Well, Wynderbroke writes—the letter arrived only an hour ago—to ask my leave to marry your sister, if she will consent; and he says all he will do, which is very handsome—very generous indeed. Wait a moment. Yes, here it is. Read that'

Richard Arden did read the letter, with open eyes and breathless interest. The old man's eyes were upon him as he did so.

'Well, Richard, what do you think?'

'There can be but one opinion about it. Nothing can be more handsome. Everything suitable. I only hope that Alice will not be foolish.'

'She sha'n't be that, I'll take care,' said the old man, locking down his desk again upon the letter.

'It might possibly be as well, Sir, to prepare her a little at first. I may possibly be of some little use, and so may Lady May. I only mean that it might hardly be expedient to make it from the first a matter of authority, because she has romantic ideas, and she is spirited.'

'I'll sleep upon it. I sha'n't see her again till tomorrow evening. She does not care about anyone in particular, I suppose?'

'Not that I know of,' said Richard.

'You'll find it will all be right—it *will*—all right. It *shall* be right,' said Sir Reginald. And then there was a silence. He was meditating the other business he had in hand, and again circuitously he proceeded.

'What's going on at the opera? Who is your great *danseuse* at present?' inquired the baronet, with a glimmer of a leer. 'I haven't seen a ballet for more than six years. And why? I needn't tell you. You know the miserable life I lead. Egad! there are fellows placed everywhere to watch me. There would be an execution in this house this night, if the miserable table and chairs were not my brother David's property. Upon my life, Craven, my attorney, had to serve two notices on the sheriff in one term, to caution him not to sell your uncle's furniture for my debts. I shouldn't have had a joint-stool to sit down on, if it hadn't been for that.

'And I had to get out of the railway-carriage, by heaven! for fear of arrest, and come home—if home I can call this ruin—by posting all the way, except a few miles. I did not dare to tell Craven I was coming back. I wrote from Twyford, where I—I—took a fancy to sleep last night, to no human being but yourself. My comfort is that they and all the world believe that I'm still in France. It is a pleasant state of things!'

'I am grieved, Sir, to think you suffer so much.'

'I know it. I knew it. I know you are, Dick,' said the old man eagerly. 'And my life is a perfect hell. I can nowhere in England find rest for the sole of my foot. I am suffering perpetually the most miserable mortifications, and the tortures of the damned. I know you are sorry. It can't be pleasant to you to see your father the miserable outcast, and fugitive, and victim he so often is. And I'll say distinctly—I'll say at once—for it was with this one purpose I sent for you—that no son with a particle of human feeling, with a grain of conscience, or an atom of principle, could endure to see it, when he knew that by a stroke of his pen he could undo it all, and restore a miserable parent to life and liberty! Now, Richard, you have my mind. I have concealed nothing, and I'm sure, Dick, I know, I *know* you won't see your father perish by inches, rather than sign the warrant for his liberation. For God's sake, Dick, my boy speak out! Have you the heart to reject your miserable father's petition? Do you wish me to kneel to you? I love you, Dick, although you don't admit it. I'll kneel to you, Dick—I'll kneel to you. I'll go on my knees to you.'

His hands were clasped; he made a movement. His great prominent eyes were fixed on Richard Arden's face, which he was reading with a great deal of eagerness, it is true, but also with a dark and narrow shrewdness.

'Good heaven, Sir, don't stir, I implore! If you do, I must leave the room,' said Richard, embarrassed to a degree that amounted to agitation. 'And I must tell you, Sir—it is very painful, but, I could not help it, necessity drove me to it—if I were ever so desirous, it is out of my power now. I have dealt with my reversion. I have executed a deed.'

'You have been with the Jews!' cried the old man, jumping to his feet. 'You have been dealing, by way of post obit with my estate!'

Richard Arden looked down. Sir Reginald was as nearly white as his yellow tint would allow; his large eyes were gleaming fire—he looked as if he would have snatched the poker, and brained his son.

'But what could I do, Sir? I had no other resource. I was forbidden your house; I had no money.'

'You lie, Sir!' yelled the old man, with a sudden flash, and a hammer of his thin trembling fist on the table. 'You had a hundred and fifty pounds a year of your mother's.'

'But that, Sir, could not possibly support any one. I was compelled to act as I did. You really, Sir, left me no choice.'

'Now, now, now, now, now! you're not to run away with the thing, you're not to run away with it; you sha'n't run away with it, Sir. You could have made a submission, you know you could. I was open to be reconciled at any time—always too ready. You had only to do as you ought to have done, and I'd have received you with open arms; you know I would—I *would*—you had only to unite our interests in the estates, and I'd have done everything to make you happy, and you know it. But you have taken the step—you have done it, and it is irrevocable. You have done it, and you've ruined me; and I pray to God you have ruined yourself!'

With every sinew quivering, the old man was pulling the bell-rope violently with his left hand. Over his shoulder, on his son, he glanced almost maniacally. 'Turn him out!' he screamed to Crozier, stamping; 'put him out by the collar. Shut the door upon him, and lock it; and if he ever dares to call here again, slam it in his face. I have done with him forever!'

Richard Arden had already left the room, and this closing passage was lost on him. But he heard the old man's voice as he walked along the corridor, and it was still in his ears as he passed the hall-door; and, running down the steps, he jumped into his cab. Crozier held the cab-door open, and wished Mr. Richard a kind goodnight. He stood on the steps to see the last of the cab as it drove down the shadowy avenue and was lost in gloom. He sighed heavily. What a broken family it was! He was an old servant, born on their northern—estate loyal, and somewhat rustic—and, certainly, had the baronet been less in want of money, not exactly the servant he would have chosen.

'The old gentleman cannot last long,' he said, as he followed the sound of the retreating wheels with his gaze, 'and then Master Richard will take his turn, and what one began the other will finish. It is all up with the Ardens. Sir Reginald ruined, Master Harry murdered, and Master David turned tradesman! There's a curse on the old house.'

He heard the baronet's tread faintly, pacing the floor in agitation, as he passed his door; and when he reached the housekeeper's room, that old lady, Mrs. Tansey, was alone and all of a tremble, standing at the door. Before her dim staring eyes had risen an oft-remembered scene: the ivy-covered gatehouse at Mortlake Hall; the cold moon glittering down through the leafless branches; the grey horse on its side across the gig-shaft, and the two villains—one rifling and the other murdering poor Henry Arden, the baronet's gay and reckless brother.

'Lord, Mr. Crozier! what's crossed Sir Reginald?' she said huskily, grasping the servant's wrist with her lean hand. 'Master Dick, I do suppose. I thought he was to come no more. They quarrel always. I'm like to faint, Mr. Crozier.'

'Sit ye down, Mrs. Tansey, Ma'am; you should take just a thimbleful of something. What has frightened you!'

'There's a scritch in Sir Reginald's voice—mercy on us!—when he raises it so; it is the very cry of poor Master Harry—his last cry, when the knife pierced him, I'll never forget it!'

The old woman clasped her fingers over her eyes, and shook her head slowly.

'Well, that's over and ended this many a day, and past cure. We need not fret ourselves no more about it—'tis thirty years since.'

'Two-and-twenty the day o' the Longden steeple-chase. I've a right to remember it.' She closed her eyes again. 'Why can't they keep apart?' she resumed. 'If father and son can't look one another in the face without quarrelling, better they should turn their backs on one another for life. Why need they come under one roof? The world's wide enough.'
'So it is—and no good meeting and argufying; for Mr. Dick will never open the estate,' remarked Mr. Crozier.

'And more shame for him!' said Mrs. Tansey. 'He's breaking his father's heart. It troubles him more,' she added in a changed tone, 'I'm thinking, than ever poor Master Harry's death did. There's none living of his kith or kin cares about it now but Master David. He'll never let it rest while he lives.'

'He *may* let it rest, for he'll never make no hand of it,' said Crozier. 'Would you object, Ma'am, to my making a glass of something hot?—you're gone very pale.'

Mrs. Tansey assented, and the conversation grew more comfortable. And so the night closed over the passions and the melancholy of Mortlake Hall.

A Midnight Meeting

A couple of days passed; and now I must ask you to suppose yourself placed, at night, in the centre of a vast heath, undulating here and there like a sea arrested in a ground-swell, lost in a horizon of monotonous darkness all round. Here and there rises a scrubby hillock of furze, black and rough as the head of a monster. The eye aches as it strains to discover objects or measure distances over the blurred and black expanse. Here stand two trees pretty close together—one in thick foliage, a black elm, with a funereal and plume-like stillness, and blotting out many stars with its gigantic canopy; the other, about fifty paces off, a withered and half barkless fir, with one white branch left, stretching forth like the arm of a gibbet.

Nearly under this is a flat rock, with one end slanting downwards, and half buried in the ferns and the grass that grow about that spot. One other fir stands a little way off, smaller than these two trees, which in daylight are conspicuous far away as landmarks on a trackless waste. Overhead the stars are blinking, but the desolate landscape lies beneath in shapeless obscurity, like drifts of black mist melting together into one wide vague sea of darkness that forms the horizon. Over this comes, in fitful moanings, a melancholy wind. The eye stretches vainly to define the objects that fancy sometimes suggests, and the ear is strained to discriminate the sounds, real or unreal, that seem to mingle in the uncertain distance.

If you can conjure up all this, and the superstitious freaks that in such a situation imagination will play in even the hardest and coarsest natures, you have a pretty distinct idea of the feelings and surroundings of a tall man who lay that night his length under the blighted tree I have mentioned, stretched on its roots, with his chin supported on his hands, and looking vaguely into the darkness. He had been smoking, but his pipe was out now, and he had no occupation but that of forming pictures on the dark background, and listening to the moan and rush of the distant wind, and imagining sometimes a voice shouting, sometimes the drumming of a horse's hoofs approaching over the plain. There was a chill in the air that made this man now and then shiver a little, and get up and take a turn back and forward, and stamp sharply as he did so, to keep the blood stirring in his legs and feet. Then down he would lay again, with his elbows on the ground, and his hands propping his chin. Perhaps he brought his head near the ground, thinking that thus he could hear distant sounds more sharply. He was growing impatient, and well he might.

The moon now began to break through the mist in fierce red over the far horizon. A streak of crimson, that glowed without illuminating anything, showed through the distant cloud close along the level of the heath. Even this was a cheer, like a red ember or two in a pitch-dark room. Very far away he thought now he heard the tread of a horse. One can hear miles away over that level expanse of death-like silence. He pricked his ears, he raised himself on his hands, and listened with open mouth. He lost the sound, but on leaning his head again to the ground, that vast sounding-board carried its vibration once more to his ear. It was the canter of a horse upon the heath. He was doubtful whether it was approaching, for the sound subsided sometimes; but afterwards it was renewed, and gradually he became certain that it was coming nearer.

And now, like a huge, red-hot dome of copper, the moon rose above the level strips of cloud that lay upon the horizon of the heath, and objects began to reveal themselves. The stunted fir, that had looked to the fancy of the solitary watcher like a ghostly policeman, with arm and truncheon raised, just starting in pursuit, now showed some lesser branches, and was more satisfactorily a tree; distances became measurable, though not yet accurately, by the eye; and ridges and hillocks caught faintly the dusky light, and threw blurred but deep shadows backward.

The tread of the horse approaching had become a gallop as the light improved, and horse and horseman were soon visible.

Paul Davies stood erect, and took up a position a few steps in advance of the blighted tree at whose foot he had been stretched. The figure, seen against the dusky glare of the moon, would have answered well enough for one of those highwaymen who in old times made the heath famous. His low-crowned felt hat, his short coat with a cape to it, and the leather casings, which looked like jack-boots, gave this horseman, seen in dark outline against the glow, a character not unpicturesque. With a sudden strain of the bridle, the gaunt rider pulled up before the man who awaited him.

'What are you doing there?' said the horseman roughly.

'Counting the stars,' answered he.

Thus the signs and countersigns were exchanged, and the stranger said—

'You're alone, Paul Davies, I take it.'

'No company but ourselves, mate,' answered Davies.

'You're up to half a dozen dodges, Paul, and knows how to lime a twig; that's your little game, you know. This here tree is clean enough, but that 'ere has a hatful o' leaves on it.'

'I didn't put them there,' said Paul, a little sulkily.

'Well, no. I do suppose a sight o' you wouldn't exactly put a tree in leaf, or a rose-bush in blossom; nor even make wegitables grow. More like to blast 'em, like that rum un over your head.'

'What's up?' asked the ex-detective. '

'Jest this—there's leaves enough for a bird to roost there, so this won't do. Now, then, move on you with me.'

As the gaunt rider thus spoke, his long red beard was blowing this way and that in the breeze; and he turned his horse, and walked him towards that lonely tree in which, as he lay gazing on its black outline, Paul had fancied the shape of a phantom policeman.

'I don't care a cuss,' said Davies. 'I'm half sorry I came a leg to meet yer.'

'Growlin', eh?' said the horseman.

'I wish you was as cold as me, and you'd growl a bit, maybe, yourself,' said Paul. 'I'm jolly cold.'

'Cold, are ye?'

'Cold as a lock-up.'

'Why didn't ye fetch a line o' the old author with you?' asked the rider—meaning brandy.

'I had a pipe or two.'

'Who'd a-guessed we was to have a night like this in summertime?'

'I do believe it freezes all the year round in this queer place.'

'Would ye like a drop of the South-Sea mountain (gin)?' said the stranger, producing a flask from his pocket, which Paul Davies took with a great deal of good-will, much to the donor's content, for he wished to find that gentleman in good-humour in the conversation that was to follow.

'Drink what's there, mate. D'ye like it?'

'It ain't to be by no means sneezed at,' said Paul Davies.

The horseman looked back over his shoulder. Paul Davies remarked that his shoulders were round enough to amount almost to a deformity. He and his companion were now a long way from the tree whose foliage he feared might afford cover to some eavesdropper.

'This tree will answer. I suppose you like a post to clap your back to while we are palaverin',' said the rider. 'Make a finish of it, Mr. Davies,' he continued, as that person presented the half-emptied flask to his hand. 'I'm as hot as steam, myself, and I'd rather have a smoke by-and-by.'

He touched the bridle here, and the horse stood still, and the rider patted his reeking neck, as he stooped with a shake of his ears and a snort, and began to sniff the scant herbage at his feet.

'I don't mind if I have another pull,' said Paul, replenishing the goblet that fitted over the bottom of the flask.

'Fill it again, and no heel-taps,' said his companion.

Mr. Davies sat down, with his mug in his hand, on the ground, and his back against the tree. Had there been a donkey near, to personate the immortal Dapple, you might have fancied, in that uncertain gloom, the Knight and Squire of La Mancha overtaken by darkness, and making one of their adventurous bivouacs under the boughs of the tree.

'What you saw in the papers three days ago did give you a twist, I take it?' observed the gentleman on horseback, with a grin that made the red bristles on his upper lip curl upwards and twist like worms.

'I can't tumble to a right guess what you means,' said Mr. Davies.

'Come, Paul, that won't never do. You read every line of that there inquest on the French cove at the Saloon, and you have by rote every word Mr. Longcluse said. It must be a queer turning of the tables, for a clever chap like you to have to look slippy, for fear other dogs should lag you.'

''Tain't me that'll be looking slippy, as you and me well knows; and it's jest because you knows it well you're here. I suppose it ain't for love of *me* quite?' sneered Paul Davies.

'I don't care a rush for Mr. Longcluse, no more nor I care for you; and I see he's goin' where he pleases. He made a speech in yesterday's paper, at the meetin' at the Surrey Gardens. He was canvassin' for Parliament down in Derbyshire a week ago; and he printed a letter to the electors only yesterday. He don't care two pins for you.'

'A good many rows o' pins, I'm thinkin',' sneered Mr. Davies.

'Thinkin' won't make a loaf, Mr. Davies. Many a man has bin too clever, and *thought* himself into the block-house. You're making too fine a game, Mr. Davies; a playin' a bit too much with edged tools, and fiddlin' a bit too freely with fire. You'll burn your fingers, and cut 'em too, do ye mind? unless you be advised, and close the game where you stand to win, as I rather think you do now.'

'So do I, mate,' said Paul Davies, who could play at brag as well as his neighbour.

'I'm on another lay, a safer one by a long sight. My maxim is the same as yours, 'Grab all you can;' but *I* do it safe, d'ye see? You are in a fair way to end your days on the twister.'

'Not if I knows it,' said Paul Davies. 'I'm afeared o' no man livin'. Who can say black's the white o' my eye? Do ye take me for a child? What do ye take me for?'

'I take you for the man that robbed and done for the French cove in the Saloon. That's the child I take ye for,' answered the horseman cynically.

'You lie! You don't! You know I han't a pig of his money, and never hurt a hair of his head. You say that to rile me, jest.'

'Why should I care a cuss whether you're riled or no? Do you think I want to get anything out o' yer? I knows everything as well as you do yourself. You take me for a queer gill, I'm thinking; that's not my lay. I wouldn't wait here while you'd walk round my hoss to have every secret you ever know'd.'

'A queer gill, mayhap. I think I know you,' said Mr. Davies, archly.

'You do, do ye? Well, come, who do you take me for?' said the stranger, turning towards him, and sitting erect in the saddle, with his hand on his thigh, to afford him the amplest view of his face and figure.

'Then I take you for Mr. Longcluse,' said Paul Davies, with a wag of his head.

'For Mr. Longcluse!' echoed the horseman, with a boisterous laugh. 'Well, *there's* a guess to tumble to! The worst guess I ever heer'd made. Did you ever see him? Why, there's not two bones in our two bodies the same length, and not two inches of our two faces alike. There's a guess for a detective! Be my soul, it's well for you it ain't him, for I think he'd a shot ye!'

The rider lifted his hand from his coat-pocket as he said this, but there was no weapon in it. Mistaking his intention, however, Paul Davies skipped behind the tree, and levelled a revolver at him.

'Down with that, you fool!' cried the horseman. 'There's nothing here.' And he gave his horse the spur, and made him plunge to a little distance, as he held up his right hand. 'But I'm not such a fool as to meet a cove like you without the lead towels, too, in case you should try that dodge.' And dipping his hand swiftly into his pocket again, he also showed in the air the glimmering barrels of a pistol. 'If you must be pullin' out your barkers every minute, and can't talk like a man, where's the good of coming all this way to palaver with a cove. It ain't not tuppence to me. Crack away if you likes it, and see who shoots best; or, if you likes it better, I don't mind if I get down and try who can hit hardest t'other way, and you'll find my fist tastes very strong of the hammer.'

'I thought you were up for mischief,' said Davies, 'and I won't be polished off simple, that's all. It's best to keep as we are, and no nearer; we can hear one another well enough where we stand.'

'It's a bargain,' said the stranger, 'and I don't care a cuss who you take me for. I'm not Mr. Longcluse; but you're welcome, if it pleases you, to give me his name, and I wish I could have the old bloke's tin as easy. Now here's my little game, and I don't find it a bad one. When two gentlemen—we'll say, for instance, you and Mr. Longcluse—differs in opinion (you says he did a certain thing, and he says he didn't, or goes the whole hog and says *you* did it, and not him), it's plain, if the matter is to be settled amigable, it's best to have a man as knows what he's about, and can find out the cove as threatens the rich fellow, and deal with him handsome, according to circumstances. My terms is moderate. I takes five shillins in the pound, and not a pig under; and that puts you and I in the same boat, d'ye see?

'Well, I gets all I can out of him, and no harm can happen me, for I'm but a cove a-carryin' of messages betwixt you, and the more I gets for you the better for me. I settled many a business amigable the last five years that would never have bin settled without me. I'm well knowing to some of the swellest lawyers in town, and whenever they has a dilikite case, like a gentleman threatened with informations or the like, they sends for me, and I arranges it amigable, to the satisfacshing of both parties. It's the only way to settle sich affairs with good profit and no risk. I have spoke to Mr. Longcluse. He was all for having your four bones in the block-house, and yourself on the twister; and he's not a cove to be bilked out of his tin. But he would not like the bother of your cross-charge, either, and I think I could make all square between ye. What do you say?'

'How can I tell that you ever set eyes on Mr. Longcluse?' said Davies, more satisfied as the conference proceeded that he had misdirected his first guess at the identity of the horseman. 'How can I tell you're not just a-gettin' all you can out o' me, to make what you can of it on your own account in that market?'

'That's true, you can't tell, mate.'

'And what do I know about you? What's your name?' pursued Paul Davies.

'I forgot my name, I left it at home in the cupboard; and you know nothing about me, that's true, excepting what I told you, and you'll hear no more.'

'I'm too old a bird for that; you're a born genius, only spoilt in the baking. I'm thinking, mate, I may as well paddle my own canoe, and sell my own secret on my own account. What can you do for me that I can't do as well for myself?'

'You don't think that, Paul. You dare not show to Mr. Longcluse, and you know he's in a wax; and who can you send to him? You'll make nothing o' that brag. Where's the good of talking like a blast to a chap like me? Don't you suppose I take all that at its vally? I tell you what, if it ain't settled now, you'll see me no more, for I'll not undertake it.' He pulled up his horse's head, preparatory to starting.

'Well, what's up now?—what's the hurry?' demanded Mr. Davies.

'Why, if this here meetin' won't lead to business, the sooner we two parts and gets home again, the less time wasted,' answered the cavalier, with his hand on the crupper of the saddle, as he turned to speak.

Each seemed to wait for the other to add something.

Mr. Longcluse at Mortlake Hall

'If you let me go this time, Mr. Wheeler, you'll not catch me a-walking out. here again,' said Mr Davies sourly. 'If there's business to be done, now's the time.'

'Well, I can't make it no plainer—'tis as clear as mud in a

wine-glass,' said the mounted man gaily, and again he shook the bridle and hitched himself in the saddle, and the horse stirred uneasily, as he added, 'Have you any more to say?'

'Well, supposin' I say ay, how soon will it be settled?' said Paul Davies, beginning to think better of it.

'These things doesn't take long with a rich cove like Mr. Longcluse. It's where they has to scrape it up, by beggin' here and borrowin' there, and sellin' this and spoutin' that—there's a wait always. But a chap with no end o' tin—that has only to wish and have—that's your sort. He swears a bit, and threatens, and stamps, and loses his temper summat, ye see; and if I was the prencipal, like you are in this 'ere case, and the police convenient, or a poker in his fist, he might make a row. But seein' I'm only a messenger like, it don't come to nothin'. He claps his hand in his pocket, and outs with the rino, and there's all; and jest a bit of paper to sign. But I won't stay here no longer. I'm getting a bit cold myself; so it's on or off *now.* Go yourself to Longcluse, if you like, and see if you don't catch it. The least you get will be seven-penn'orth, for extortin' money by threatenin' a prosecution, if he don't hang you for the murder of the Saloon cove. How would you like that?'

'It ain't the physic that suits my complaint, guvnor. But I have him there. I have the statement wrote, in sure hands, and other hevidence, as he may suppose, and dated, and signed by respectable people; and I know his dodge. He thinks he came out first with his charge against me, but he's out there; and if he *will* have it, and I split, he'd best look slippy.'

'And how much do you want? Mind, I'll funk him all I can, though he's a wide-awake chap; for it's my game to get every pig I can out of him.'

'I'll take two thousand pounds, and go to Canada or to New York, my passage and expenses being paid, and sign anything in reason he wants; and that's the shortest chalk I'll offer.'

'Don't you wish you may get it? *I* do, I know, but I'm thinking you might jest as well look for the naytional debt.'

'What's your name?' again asked Davies, a little abruptly.

'My name fell out o' window and was broke, last Tuesday mornin'. But call me Tom Wheeler, if you can't talk without calling me something.'

'Well, Tom, that's the figure,' said Davies.

'If you want to deal, speak now,' said Wheeler. 'If I'm to stand between you, I must have a power to close on the best offer I'm like to get. I won't do nothing in the matter elseways.'

With this fresh exhortation, the conference on details proceeded; and when at last it closed, with something like a definite understanding, Tom Wheeler said,—'Mind, Paul Davies, I comes from no one, and I goes to no one; and I never seed you in all my days.'

'And where are you going?' 'A bit nearer the moon,' said the mysterious Mr. Wheeler, lifting his hand and pointing towards the red disk, with one of his bearded grins. And wheeling his horse suddenly, away he rode at a canter, right toward the red moon, against which for a few moments the figure of the retreating horse and man showed black and sharp, as if cut out of cardboard.

Paul Davies looked after him with his left eye screwed close, as was his custom, in shrewd rumination. Before the horseman had got very far, the moon passed under the edge of a thick cloud, and the waste was once more enveloped in total darkness. In this absolute obscurity the retreating figure was instantaneously swallowed, so that the shrewd ex-detective, who had learned by rote every article of his dress, and every button on it, and could have sworn to every mark on his horse at York Fair, had no chance of discovering in the ultimate line of his retreat, any clue to his destination. He had simply emerged from darkness, and darkness had swallowed him again.

We must now see how Sir Reginald's little dinner-party, not a score of miles away, went off only two days later. He was fortunate, seeing he had bidden his guests upon very short notice, not one disappointed.

I daresay that Lady May—whose toilet, considering how quiet everything was, had been made elaborately—missed a face that would have brightened all the rooms for her. But the interview between Richard Arden and his father had not, as we know, ended in reconciliation, and Lady May's hopes were disappointed, and her toilet labour in vain.

When Lady May entered the room with Alice, she saw standing on the hearthrug, at the far end of the handsome room, a tall and very good-looking man of sixty or upwards, chatting with Sir Reginald, one of whose feet was in a slipper, and who was sitting in an easy-chair. A little bit of fire burned in the grate, for the day had been chill and showery. This tall man, with white silken hair, and a countenance kind, frank, and thoughtful, with a little sadness in it, was, she had no doubt, David Arden, whom she had last seen with silken brown locks, and the cheerful aspect of early manhood.

Sir Reginald stood up, with an uncomfortable effort, and, smiling, pointed to his slippers in excuse for his limping gait, as he shuffled forth across the carpet to meet her, with a good-humoured shrug.

'Wasn't it good of her to come?' said Alice.

'She's better than good,' said Sir Reginald, with his thin, yellow smile, extending his hand, and leading her to a chair; 'it is visiting the sick and the halt, and doing real good, for it is a pleasure to see her—a pleasure bestowed on a miserable soul who has very few pleasures left;' and with his other thin hand he patted gently the fingers of her fat hand. 'Here is my brother David,' continued the baronet. 'He says you will hardly know him.'

'She'll hardly believe it. She was very young when she last saw me, and the last ten years have made some changes,' said Uncle David, laughing gently.

At the baronet's allusion to that most difficult subject, the lapse of time, Lady May winced and simpered uneasily; but she expanded gratefully as David Arden disposed of it so adroitly.

'We'll not speak of years of change. I knew you instantly,' said Lady May happily. 'And you have been to Vichy, Reginald. What stay do you make here?'

'None, almost; my crippled foot keeps me always on a journey. It seems a paradox, but so it is. I'm ordered to visit Buxton for a week or so, and then I go, for change of air, to Yorkshire.'

As Alice entered, she saw the pretty face, the original of the brilliant portrait which had haunted her on her night journey to Twyford, and she heard a very silvery voice chatting gaily. Mr. Longcluse was leaning on the end of the sofa on which Grace Maubray sat: and Vivian Darnley, it seemed in high spirits, was standing and laughing nearly before her. Alice Arden walked quickly over to welcome her handsome guest. With a misgiving and a strange pain at her heart, she saw how much more beautiful this young lady had grown. Smiling radiantly, with her hand extended, she greeted and kissed her fair kinswoman; and, after a few words, sat down for a little beside her; and asked Mr. Longcluse how he did; and finally spoke to Vivian Darnley, and then returned to her conventional dialogue of welcome and politeness with her cousin—*how* cousin, she could not easily have explained.

The young ladies seemed so completely taken up with one another that, after a little waiting, the gentlemen fell into a desultory talk, and grew gradually nearer to the window. They were talking now of dogs and horses, and Mr. Longcluse was stealing rapidly into the good graces of the young man.

'When we come up after dinner, you must tell me who these people are,' said Grace Maubray, who did not care very much what she said. 'That young man is a Mr. Vivian, ain't he?'

'No—Darnley,' whispered Alice; 'Vivian is his Christian name.'

'Very romantic names; and, if he really means half he says, he is a very romantic person.' She laughed.

'What has he been saying?' Alice wondered. But, after all, it was possible to be romantic on almost any subject.

'And the other?'

'He's a Mr. Longcluse,' answered Alice.

'He's rather clever,' said the young lady, with a grave decision that amused Alice.

'Do you think so? Well, so do I; that is, I know he can interest one. He has been almost everywhere, and he tells things rather pleasantly.'

Before they could go any further, Vivian Darnley, turning from the window toward the two young ladies, said— 'I've just been saying that we must try to persuade Lady May to get up that party to the Derby,'

'I can place a drag at her disposal,' said Mr. Longcluse.

'And a splendid team—I saw them,' threw in Darnley.

'There's nothing I should like so much,' said Alice. 'I' ve never been to the Derby. What do you say, Grace? Can you manage Uncle David?'

'I'll try,' said the young lady gaily.

'We must all set upon Lady May,' said Alice. 'She is good-natured, she can't resist us.'

'Suppose we begin now?' suggested Darnley.

'Hadn't we better wait till we have her quite to ourselves? Who knows what your papa and your uncle might say?' said Grace Maubray, turning to Alice. 'I vote for saying nothing to them until Lady May has settled, and then they must only submit.'

'I agree with you quite,' said Alice laughing.

'Sage advice!' said Mr. Longcluse, with a smile; 'and there's time enough to choose a favourable moment. It comes off exactly ten days from this.'

'Oh, anything might be done in ten days,' said Grace. 'I'm sorry it is so far away.'

'Yes, a great deal might be done in ten days; and a great deal might happen in ten days,' said Longcluse, listlessly looking down at the floor— 'a great deal might happen.'

He thought he saw Miss Arden's eye turned upon him, curiously and quickly, as he uttered this common-place speech, which was yet a little odd.

'In this busy world, Miss Arden, there is no such thing as quiet, and no one acts without imposing on other people the necessity for action,' said Mr. Longcluse; 'and I believe that often the greatest changes in life are the least anticipated by those who seem to bring them about spontaneously.'

At this moment, dinner being announced, the little party transferred itself to the dining-room, and Miss Arden found herself between Mr. Longcluse and Uncle David.

The Party in the Dining-Room

And now, all being seated, began the talk and business of dinner.

'I believe,' said Mr. Longcluse, with a laugh. 'I am growing metaphysical.'

'Well, shall I confess, Mr. Longcluse, you do sometimes say things that are, I fear, a little too wise for my poor comprehension?'

'I don't express them; it is my fault,' he answered, in a very low tone. 'You have *mind*, Miss Arden, for anything. There is no one it is so delightful to converse with, owing in part to that very faculty—I mean quick apprehension. But I know my own defects. I know how imperfectly I often express myself. By-the-way, you seemed to wish to have that curious little wild Bohemian air I sang the other night. 'The Wanderer's Bride'—the song about the white lily, you know. I ventured to get a friend, who really is a very good musician, to make a setting of it, which I so very much hope you will like. I brought it with me. You will think me very presumptuous, but I hoped so much you might be tempted to try it.'

When Mr. Longcluse spoke to Alice, it was always in a tone so very deferential, that it was next to impossible that a very young girl should not be flattered by it—considering, especially, that the man was reputed clever, had seen the world, and had met with a certain success, and that by no means of a kind often obtained, or ever quite despised. There was also a directness in his eulogy which was unusual, and which spoken with a different manner would have been embarrassing, if not offensive. But in Mr. Longcluse's manner, when he spoke such phrases, there appeared a real humility, and even sadness, that the boldness of the sentiment was lost in the sincerity and dejection of the speaker, which seemed to place him on a sudden at the immeasurable distance of a melancholy worship.

'I am so much obliged!' said Alice. 'I did wish so much to have it when you sang it. It may not do for my voice at all, but I longed to try it. When a song is sung so as to move one, it is sure to be looked out and learned, without any thought wasted on voice, or skill, or natural fitness. It is, I suppose, like the vanity that makes one person dress after another. Still, I do wish to sing that song, and I am so much obliged!'

From the other side her uncle said very softly—'What do you think of my ward, Grace Maubray?'

'Oughtn't I to ask, rather, what you think of her?' she laughed archly.

'Oh! I see,' he answered, with a pleasant and honest smile; 'you have the gift of seeing as far as other clever people into a millstone. But, no—though perhaps I ought to thank you for giving me credit for so much romance and good taste—I don't think I shall ever introduce you to an aunt. You must guess again, if you will have a matrimonial explanation; though I don't say there is any such design. And perhaps, if there were, the best way to promote it would be to leave the intended hero and heroine very much to themselves. They are both very good-looking.'

'Who?' asked Alice, although she knew very well whom he meant.

'I mean that pretty creature over there, Grace Maubray, and Vivian Darnley,' said he quietly.

She smiled, looking very much pleased and very arch.

With how Spartan a completeness women can hide the shootings and quiverings of mental pain, and of bodily pain too, when the motive is sufficient! Under this latter they are often clamorous, to be sure; but the demonstration expresses not want of patience, but the feminine yearning for compassion.

'I fancy nothing would please the young rogue Vivian better. I wish I were half so sure of her. You girls are so unaccountable, so fanciful, and—don't be angry—so uncertain.'

'Well, I suppose, as you say, we must only have patience, and leave the matter in the hands of Time, who settles most things pretty well.'

She raised her eyes, and fancied she saw Grace Maubray at the same moment withdraw hers from her face. Lady May was talking from the end of the table with Mr. Longcluse.

'Your neighbour who is talking to Lady May is a Mr. Longcluse?'

'Yes.'

'He is a City notability; but oddly, I never happened to see him till this evening. Do you think there is something curious in his appearance?'

'Yes, a little, perhaps. Don't you.'

'So odd that he makes my blood run cold,' said Uncle David, with a shrug and a little laugh. 'Seriously, I mean unpleasantly odd. What is Lady May talking about? Yes—I thought so—that horrid murder at the 'Saloon Tavern'. For so good-natured a person, she has the most bloodthirsty tastes I know of; she's always deep in some horror.'

'My brother Dick told me that Mr. Longcluse made a speech there.'

'Yes, so I heard; and I think he said what is true enough. London is growing more and more insecure; and that certainly was a most audacious murder. People make money a little faster, that is true; but what is the good of money, if their lives are not their own? It is quite true that there are streets in London, which I remember as safe as this room, through which no one suspected of having five pounds in his pocket could now walk without a likelihood of being garotted.'

'How dreadful!' said Alice, and Uncle David laughed a little at her horror.

'It is too true, my dear. But, to pass to pleasanter subjects, when do you mean to choose among the young fellows, and present me to a new nephew?' said Uncle David.

'Do you fancy I would tell anyone if I knew?' she answered, laughing. 'How is it that you men, who are always accusing us weak women of thinking of nothing else, can never get the subject of matrimony out of your heads? Now, uncle, as you and I may talk confidentially, and at our ease, I'll tell you two things. I like my present spinster life very well—I should like it better, I think, if it were in the country; but town or country, I don't think I should ever like a married life. I don't think I'm fit for command.'

'Command! I thought the prayer-book said something about obeying, on the contrary,' said Uncle David.

'You know what I mean. I'm not fit to rule a household; and I am afraid I am a little idle, and I should not like to have it to do—and so I could never do it well.'

'Nevertheless, when the right man comes, he need but beckon with his finger, and away you go, Miss Alice, and undertake it all.'

'So we are whistled away, like poodles for a walk, and that kind of thing! Well, I suppose, uncle, you are right, though I can't see that I'm quite so docile a creature. But if my poor sex is so willing to be won, I don't know how you are to excuse your solitary state, considering how very little trouble it would have taken to make some poor creature happy.'

'A very fair retort!' laughed Uncle David. And he added, in a changed tone, for a sudden recollection of his own early fortunes crossed him— 'But even when the right man does come, it does not always follow, Miss Alice, that he dares make the sign; fate often interposes years, and in them death may come, and so the whole card-castle falls.'

'I've had a long talk,' he resumed, 'with Richard; he has made me promises, and I hope he will be a better boy for the future. He has been getting himself into money troubles, and acquiring—I'm afraid I should say cultivating—a taste for play. I know you have heard something of this before; I told you myself. But he has made me promises, and I hope, for your sake, he'll keep them; because, you know, I and your father can't last forever, and he ought to take care of you; and how can he do that, if he's not fit to take care of himself? But I believe there is no use in thinking too much about what is to come. One has enough to do in the present. I think poor Lady May has been disappointed,' he said, with a very cautious smile, his eye having glanced for a moment on her; ' she looks a little forlorn, I think.'

'Does she? And why?'

'Well, they say she would not object to be a little more nearly related to you than she is.'

'You can't mean papa—or *yourself!*'

'Oh, dear, no!' he answered, laughing. 'I mean that she misses Dick a good deal.'

'Oh, dear! uncle, you can't be serious!'

'It might be a very serious affair for her; but I don't know that he could do a wiser thing. The old quarrel is still raging, he tells me, and that he can't appear in this house.'

'It is a great pity,' said she.

'Pity! Not at all. They never could agree; and it is much better for Dick they should not—on the terms Reginald proposes, at least. I see Lady May trying to induce you to make her the sign at which ladies rise, and leave us poor fellows to shift for ourselves.'

'Ungallant old man! I really believe she is.'

And in a moment more the ladies were floating from the room, Vivian Darnley standing at the door. Somehow he could not catch Alice's eye as they passed; she was smiling an answer to some gabble of Lady May's. Grace gave him a very kind look with her fine eyes as she went by; and so the young man, who had followed them up the massive stairs with his gaze, closed the door and sat down again, before his claret glass, and his little broken cluster of grapes, and half-dozen distracted bits of candied fruit, and sighed deeply.

'That murder in the City that you were speaking of just now to Lady May is a serious business for men who walk the streets, as I do sometimes, with money in their pockets," said David Arden, addressing Mr. Longcluse.

'So it struck me—one feels that instinctively. When I saw that poor little good-natured fellow dead, and thought how easily I might have walked in there myself, with the assassin behind me, it seemed to me simply the turn of a die that the lot had not fallen upon me,' said Longcluse.

'He was robbed, too, wasn't he?' croaked Sir Reginald, who was growing tired; and with his fatigue came evidences of his temper.

'Oh, yes,' said David; 'nothing left in his pockets.'

'And Laroque, a watchmaker, a relation of his, said he had cheques about him, and foreign money,' said Longcluse; 'but, of course, the cheques were not presented, and foreign money is not easily traced in a big town like London. I made him a present of ten pounds to stake on the game; I could not learn that he did stake it, and I suppose the poor fellow intended applying it in some more prudent way. But my present was in gold, and that, of course, the robber applied without apprehension.

'Now, you fellows who have a stake in the City, it is a scandal your permitting such a state of things to continue,' said Sir Reginald; 'because, though your philanthropy may not be very diffuse, each of you cares most tenderly for one individual at least in the human race—I mean *self*—and whatever you may think of personal morality, and even life—for you don't seem to me to think a great deal of grinding operatives in the cranks of your mills, or blowing them up by bursting steamboilers, to say nothing of all the people you poison with adulterated food, or with strychnine in beer, or with arsenic in candles, or pretty green papers for bed-rooms—or smash or burn alive on railways—yet you should, on selfish grounds, set your faces against a system of assassination for pocket-books and purses, the sort of things precisely you have always about you.

'Don't you see? And it's inconsistent besides, because, as I said, although you care little for life—other people's, I mean—in the abstract, yet you care a great deal for property. I think it's your idol, by Jove! and worshipping money—positively *worshipping* it, as you do, it seems a scandalous inconsistency that you should—of course, I don't mean you two individually,' he said, perhaps recollecting that he might be going a little too fast; 'you never, of course, fancied *that.* I mean, of course, the class of men we have all heard of, or seen—but I do say, with that sort of adoration for money and property, I can't understand their allowing their pockets to be profaned and their purses made away with.'

Sir Reginald, having thus delivered himself with considerable asperity, poured some claret into his glass, and pushed the jugs on to his brother, and then, closing his eyes, composed himself either to listen or to sleep.

'City or country, East End or West End, I fancy we are all equally anxious to keep other people's hands out of our pockets,' said David Arden; ' and I quite agree with Mr. Longcluse in all he is reported to have said with respect to our police system.'

'But is it so certain that the man was robbed?' said Vivian Darnley.

'Everything he had about him was taken,' said Mr. Longcluse.

'But they pretend to rob men sometimes, when they murder them, only to conceal the real motive,' persisted Vivian Darnley.

'Yes, that's quite true; but then there must be *some* motive,' said Mr. Longcluse, with something a little supercilious in his smile: 'and it isn't easy to conceive a motive for murdering a poor little good-natured letter of lodgings, a person past the time of life when jealousy could have anything to do with it, and a most inoffensive and civil creature. I confess, if I were obliged to seek a motive other than the obvious one, for the crime, I should be utterly puzzled.'

'When I was travelling in Prussia,' said Vivian Darnley, 'I saw two people in different prisons—one a woman, the other a middle-aged man—both for murder. They had been found guilty, and had been kept there only to get a confession from them before execution. They won't put culprits to death there, you know, unless they have first admitted their guilt; and one of these had actually confessed. Well, each had borne an unexceptionable character up to the time when suspicion was accidentally aroused, and then it turned out that they had been poisoning and otherwise making away with people, at the rate of two or three a year, for half their lives.

'Now, don't you see, these masked assassins, having, as it appeared, absolutely no intelligible motive, either of passion or of interest, to commit these murders, could have had no inducement, as the woman had actually confessed, except a sort of lust of murder. I suppose it is a sort of madness, but these people were not otherwise mad; and it is quite possible that the same sort of thing may be going on in other places. People say that the police would have got a clue to the mystery by means of the foreign coin and the bank-notes, if they had not been destroyed.'

'But there are traces of organisation,' said Mr. Longcluse. 'In a crowded place like that, such things could hardly be managed without it, and insanity such as you describe is very rare; and you'll hardly get people to believe in a swell-mob of madmen, committing murder in concert simply for the pleasure of homicide. They will all lean to a belief in the coarse but intelligible motive of the highwayman.'

'I saw in the newspapers,' said David Arden, 'some evidence of yours, Mr. Longcluse, which seemed rather to indicate a particular man as the murderer.'

'I have my eye upon him,' said Longcluse. 'There are suspicious circumstances. The case in a little time may begin to clear; at present the police are only groping.'

'That's satisfactory; and those fellows are paid so handsomely for groping,' said Sir Reginald, opening his eyes suddenly. 'I believe that we are the worst-governed and the worst-managed people on earth, and that our merchants and tradespeople are rich simply by flukes—simply by a concurrence of lucky circumstances, with which they have no more to do than Prester John or the Man in the Moon. Take a little claret, Mr. Longcluse, and send it on.'

'No more, thanks.'

And all the guests being of the same mind, they marched up the broad stairs to the ladies.

In Mrs. Tansey's Room

There were sounds of music and laughter faintly audible through the drawing-room door. The music ceased as the door opened, and the gentlemen entered an atmosphere of brilliant light, and fragrant with the pleasant aroma of tea.

'Pray, Miss Arden, don't let us interrupt you,' said Mr. Longcluse. 'I thought I heard singing as we came up the stairs.' He had come to the piano, and was now at her side.

She did not sing or play, but Vivian Darnley thought that her conversation with Longcluse, as, with one knee on his chair, he leaned over the back of it and talked, seemed more interesting than usual.

'I say, Reginald,' said David Arden softly to his brother, 'I must run down and pay Martha Tansey my usual visit. She's in her room, I suppose. I'll steal away and return quietly.'

And so he was gone. He closed the door softly behind him, and slowly descended the wide staircase, with many vague conjectures and images revolving in his mind. He paused at the great window on the landing, and looked out upon the solemn and familiar landscape. A brilliant moon was high in the sky, and the stars glimmered brightly. His hand was on the window as he looked out, thinking.

Uncle David was a man impulsive, prompt, sanguine—a temperament, in short, which, directed by an able intellect, would have made a good general. When an idea had got into his head, he could not rest until he had worked it out. On the whole, throughout his life these fits of sudden and feverish concentration had been effective, and aided his fortunes. It is, perhaps, an unbusiness-like temperament; but commercial habits and example had failed to control that natural ardour, and when once inflamed, it governed his actions implicitly.

An idea, very vague, very little the product of reason, had now taken possession of his brain, and he relied upon it as an intuition. He had been thinking over it. It first warmed, then simmered, then, as it were, boiled. The process had been one of an hour and more, as he sat at his brother's table and took his share in the conversation. When the steam got up and the pressure rose to the point of action, forth went Uncle David to have his talk with his early friend Tansey. He stopped, as I have said, at the great window on the staircase, and looked out and up. The moon was splendid; the stars were glimmering brightly; they looked down like a thousand eyes set upon him, to watch the prowess and perseverance of the man on whom fate had imposed a mission.

Some idea like this seized him, for, like many men of a similar temperament, he had an odd and unconfessed vein of poetry in his nature. He had looked out and up in a listless abstraction, and the dark heaven above him, brilliant with its eternal lights, had for a moment withdrawn and elevated his thoughts as if he had entered a cathedral.

'What specks and shadows we are, and how eternal is duty! And if we are in another place to last like those unfailing lights—to become happy or wretched, and, in either state, indestructible for ever—what signify the labour and troubles of life, compared with that by which our everlasting fate is fixed? God help us! Am I consulting revenge or conscience in pursuing this barren inquiry? Do I mistake for the sublime impulse of conscience a vulgar thirst for blood? I think not. I never harboured malice; I hate punishing people. But murder is a crime against God himself, respecting which he imposes duties upon man, and seconds them by all the instincts of affection. Dare I neglect them, then, in the case of poor loving Harry, my brother?'

The drawing-room door had been opened a little, the night being sultry, and through it now came the clear tones of a well-taught baritone. It was singing a slow and impassioned air, and its tones, though sweet, chilled him with a strange pain. It seemed like instinct that told him it was the stranger's voice. One moment's thought would have proved it equally. There was no one else present to suspect but Vivian Darnley, and he was no musician; but to David Arden it seemed that if a hundred people were there he should have felt it all the same, and intuitively recognised it as Longcluse's voice.

'What is it in that voice which is so hateful? What is it in that passion which sounds insincere? What gives to those sweet tones a latent discord, that creeps so coldly through my nerves?'

So thought David Arden, as, with one hand still upon the window-sash, he listened and turned toward the open door, with a frown akin to one of pain.

Spell-bound, he listened till the song was over, and sighed and shook his ears with a sort of shudder when the music ceased.

'I don't know why I stayed to listen. Face—voice—what is the agency about that fellow? I daresay I'm a fool, but I can't help it, and I must bring the idea to the test.'

He descended the stairs slowly, crossed the hall, and walked thoughtfully down the passage leading to the housekeeper's room. At this hour the old woman had it usually to herself. He knocked at the housekeeper's door, and recognised the familiar voice that answered.

'How do you do, Martha?' said he, striding cheerily into the room.

'Ah! Master David? So it is, sure!'

'Ay, sure and sure, Martha,' said he, taking the old woman's hand, with his kind smile. 'And how are you, Martha? Tell me how you are.'

'I won't say much. I'm not so canty as you'll mind me. I'm an old wife now, Master David, and not much for this world, I'm thinking,' she answered dolorously.

'You may outlive much younger people, Martha; we are all in the hands of God,' said David, smiling. 'It seems to me but yesterday that I and poor Harry used to run in here to you from our play in the grounds, and you had always a bit of something for us hungry fellows to eat, come when we might.'

'Ah, ha! Yes, ye were hungry fellows then—spirin' up, fine tall lads. Reginald was never like ye; he was seven years older than you. And hungry? Yes! The cold turkey and ham, ye mind—by Jen! I *have* seen ye eat hearty; and pancakes—ye liked them best of all. And it went a' into a good skin. I will say—you and Master Harry (God be wi' him!) a fine, handsome pair o' lads ye were.

And you're a handsome fellow still, Master David, and might have married well, no doubt; but *man proposes and God disposes*, and *time and tide'll wait for no man*, and *what's one man's meat's another man's poison.* Who knows and all may be for the best? And that Mr. Longcluse is dining here today?' she added, not very coherently, and with a sudden gloom.

'Yes, Martha, that Mr. Longcluse is dining here today; and Master Dick tells me you did not fall in love with him at first sight, when they paid you a visit here. Is that true?'

'I don't know. I don't know what. The sight of him—or the sound of his voice, I don't know which—gave me a turn,' said the old woman.

'Well, Martha, I don't like his face, either. He gave me, also, what you call a turn. He's very pale, and I felt as if I had been frightened by him when I was a child; and yet he must be some five and twenty years younger than I am, and I'm almost certain I never saw him before. So I say it must be something that's no' canny as you used to say. What do you think, Martha?'

'Ye may be funnin', Master David. Ye were always a canty lad. But it's o'er true. I can't bring to mind what it is—I can't tell—but something in that man's face gev me a sten. I conceited I was just goin' to swound; and he looked sa straight at me, like a ghost.'

'Master Richard says you looked very hard at Mr. Longcluse; you had both a good stare at each other,' said Uncle David. 'He thought there was going to be a recognition.'

'Did I?' Well, no: I don't know him, I *think.* 'Tis all a jummlement, like. I couldn't bring nout to mind.'

'I know, Martha, you liked poor Harry well,' said David Arden, not with a smile, but with a very sad countenance.

'That I did,' said Mrs. Tansey.

'And I think you like me, Martha?'

'Ye're not far wrong there, Master David.'

'And for both our sakes—for mine and his, for the dead no less than the living—I am sure you won't allow any thought of trouble, or nervousness, or fear of lawyers' browbeating, or that sort of thing, to deter you from saying, wherever and whenever justice may require it, everything you know or suspect respecting that dreadful occurrence.'

'The death o' Master Harry, ye mean!' exclaimed Mrs. Tansey sternly, drawing herself up on a sudden, with a pale frown, and looking full at him. '*Me* to hide or hold back aught that could bring the truth to light! Oh! Master David, do you know what ye're sayin'?'

'Perfectly,' said he, with a melancholy smile; ' and I am glad it vexes you, Martha, because I need no answer on that point more than your honest voice and face.'

'Keep back aught, man!' she repeated, striking her hand on the table. 'Why, lad, I'd lose that old hand under the chopper for one gliff o' the truth into that damned story. Why, lawk! where's yer head, boy? Wasn't I maist killed myself, for sake o' him that night?'

'Ay, Martha, brave girl, I'm satisfied; and I ask your pardon for the question. But years bring alteration, you know; and I'm changed in mind myself in many ways I never could have believed. And everyone doesn't see with me that it is our duty to explore a crime like that, to track the villain, if we can, and bring him to justice. *You* do, Martha; but there are many in whose veins poor Harry's blood is running who don't feel like you. Master Richard said that the gentleman looked as if he did not know what to make of you; 'and, by Jove!' said he, '*I* didn't either—Martha stared so."

'I couldn't help. 'Twas scarce civil; but truly I couldn't, Sir,' said Martha Tansey, who had by this time recovered her equanimity. 'He did remind me of summat.'

'We will talk of that by-and-by, Martha; we will try to recall it. What I want you first to tell me is exactly your recollection of the lamentable occurrence of that night. I have a full note of it at home; but I have not looked at it for years, and I want my recollection confirmed tonight, that you and I may talk over some possibilities which I should like to examine with your help.'

'I can talk of it now,' said the old woman; 'but for many a year after it happened I dare not. I could not sleep for many a night after I told it to anyone. But now I can bear it. So, Master David, you may ask what you please.'

'First let me hear your recollection of what happened,' said David Arden.

'Ay, Master David, that I will. Sit ye down, for my old bones won't carry me standing no time now, and sit I must. Right well ye're lookin', and right glad am I to see it, Master David; and ye were always a handsome laddie. God bless ye, and God be wi' the old times! And poor Master Harry—poor laddie!—I liked him well. You two looked beautiful, walkin' up to t' house together—two conny, handsome boys ye were.'

Mrs. Tansey's Story

'The sun don't touch these windows till nigh nightfall. In the short days o' winter, the last sunbeam at the settin' just glints along the wall, and touches a sprig or two o' them scarlet geraniums on the windastone. 'Tis a cold room, Master David. In summer evenins, like this, ye have just a chilly flush o' the sun' settin', and, before it's well on the windas, the bats and beetles is abroad, and the moth is flittin', and the gloamin' fa's,' said the old woman. 'The windas looks to the west, but also a bit to the north, ye'll mind, and that's the cause o't.

'I don't complain. I ha' suffered it these thirty years and more, and 'tain't worth while, for the few years that's left, makin' a blub and a blither about it. I'm an old wife now, Master David, and there can't be many more years for me left aboon the grass, sa I e'en let be and taks the world easy, ye see; and that's the reason I aye keep a bit o' wood burnin' on the hearth—it keeps the life in my old bones—and I hope it ain't too warm for you, Master David?'

'Not a bit, Martha. This side of the house is cool. I remember that our room, when we were boys, looked out from it, high up, you recollect, and it never was hot.'

'That's it, ye were in the top o' the house; and poor Harry, wi' his picturs o' horses and dogs hangin' up on the wa's. Lawk!

it seems but last week. How the years flits! I often thinks of him. See what a moon there is tonight. 'Twas just such a moon that night, only frostier, ye see—the same clear sky and bright moon; 'twould make ye wink to look at. Ye're not too hot wi' that bit o' wood lightin' in the grate?'

'I like the fire, Martha, and I like the moon, and I like your company best of all.'

The truth was, he did like the flicker of the wood fire. The flame was cheery, and took off something of the dismal shadow that stole over everything whenever he applied his affectionate mind to the horrors of the dreadful night on which he was now ruminating. One of the window-shutters was open, and the chill brilliancy of the moon, and the deep blue sky, were serenely visible over the black foreground of trees. The wavering of the redder light of the fire, as its reflection spread and faded upon the wainscot, was warm and pleasant; and, had their talk been of less ghastly things, would have brightened their thoughts with a sense of comfort.

'I have not very long to stay, Martha,' said David Arden, looking at his watch, 'so tell me your recollection as accurately as you can. Let me hear *that* first; and then I want to ask you for some particular information, which I am sure you can give me.'

'Why not? Who should I give it sooner to? Will ye take a cup o' coffee? No. Well, a glass o' *curaçoa*? No. And what will ye take?'

'You forget that I have taken everything, and come to you with all my wants supplied. So now, dear Martha, let me hear it all.'

'I'll tell ye all about it. I was younger and stronger, mind, than I am now, by twenty years and more. 'Tis a short time to look back on, but a good while passing, and leaves many a gap and change, and many a scar and wrinkle.'

There was a palpable tremble always in Mrs. Tansey's voice, in the thin hand she extended towards him, and in the head from which her old eyes glittered glassily on him.

'The road is very lonely by night—the loneliest road in all

England. When it passes ten o'clock, you might listen till cock-crow for a footfall. Well, I, and Thomas Ridley, and Anne Haslett, was all the people at Mortlake just then, the family being in the North, except Master Harry. He went to a race across country, that was run that day; and he told me, laughing, he would not ask me to throw an old shoe after him, as he stood sure to win two thousand pounds. And away he went, little thinking, him and me, how our next meetin' would be. At that time old Tom Clinton—ye'll mind Clinton?'

'To be sure I do,' acquiesced David Arden.

'Well, Tom was in the gatehouse then; after he died, his daughter's husband got it, ye know. And when he had outstayed his time by two hours—for he was going northwards in the morning, and told me he'd be surely back before ten—I began to grow frightened, and I put on my bonnet and cloak, and down I runs to the gatehouse, and knocks up Tom Clinton. It was nigh twelve o'clock then. When Tom came to the door, having dressed in haste, I said, "Tom, which way will Master Harry return? he's not been since." And says Tom, "If he's comin' straight from the course, he'll come down from the country; but if he's dinin' instead in London, he'll come up the Islington way." "Well," said I, "go you, Tom, to the turn o' the road, and look and listen for sight or sound, and bring me word."

'I don't know what was frightenin' me. He was often later, and I never minded; but something that night was on my mind, like a warning, for I couldn't get the fear out o' my heart. Well, who comes ridin' back but Dick Wallock, the groom, that had drove away with him in the gig in the mornin'; and glad I was to see his face at the gate. It was bright moonlight, and says I, "Dick, how is Master Harry? Is all well with him?" So he tells me, ay, all was well, and he goin' to drive the gig out himself from town. He was at a place—*you'll* mind the name of it—where it turned out they played cards and dice, and won and lost like—like fools, or worse, as some o' them no doubt was. "Well," says I, "go you up, as he told you, with the horse, and I'll stay here till he comes back, if it wasn't till daybreak." For all the time, ye see, my heart misgave me that there was summat bad to happen; and when Tom Clinton came back, says I, "Tom, you go in, and get to your room, and let me sit down in your kitchen; and I'll let him in when he comes, for I can't go up to the house, nor close an eye, till he comes." Well, it was a full hour after, and I was sittin' in the kitchen window that looks out on the road, starin' wide awake, and lookin', now one way and now another, up and down, when I hears the clink of a footfall on the stones, and a tall, ill-favoured man walks slowly by, and turns his face toward the window as he passed.'

'You saw him distinctly, then?' said David.

'As plain as ever I saw you. An ill-favoured fellow in a light drab great coat wi' a cape to it. He looked white wi' fear, and wild big eyes, and a high hooked nose—a tall chap wi' his hands in his pockets, and a low-crowned hat on. He went on slow, till a whistle sounded, and then he ran down the road a bit toward the signal.'

'That was toward the Islington side?'

'Ay, Sir, and I grew more uneasy. I was scared wi' the sight o' such a man at that time o' night, in that lonesome place, and the whistlin' and runnin'.'

'Did you see the same man again that night?' asked David.

'Yes, 'twas the same I saw afterwards—Lord ha' mercy on us! I saw him again, at his murderin' work. Oh, Master David! it makes my brain wild, and my skin creep, to think o' that sight.'

'I did wrong to interrupt you—tell it your own way, Martha, and I can afterwards ask you the questions that lie near my heart,' said Mr. Arden.

''Tis easy told, Sir; the candle was burnt down almost in the socket, and I went to look out another—but before I could find one, it went out. 'Twas but a stump I found and lighted, after I saw that fellow in the light drab *surtout* go by. I wished to let them know, if they had any ill design, there was folks awake in the lodge. But he was gone by before I found the matches, and now that he was comin' again, the candle went out—things goes so cross. It was to be, ye see. Well, while I was rummagin' about, looking for a candle, I heard the sound of a horse trotting hard, and wheels rollin' along; so says I, 'Thank God!' for then I was sure it must be Harry, poor lad. So I claps on my bonnet, and out wi' me, wi' t' key. I thought I heard voices, as the hoofs and wheels came clinkin' up to the gate; but I could not be quite sure. I was huffed wi' Master Harry for the long wait he gev me, and the fright, and I took my time comin' round the corner of the gatehouse.

'And thinks I to myself, he'll be offerin' me a seat in the gig up to the house, but I won't take it. God forgi'e me for them angry thoughts to the poor laddie that I was never to have a word wi' more! When I came to the gate there was never a call, and nothing but voices talking and gaspin' like, under their breath a'most, and a queer scufflin' sound, that I could not make head nor tail on. So I unlocked the wicket, and out wi' me, and, Lord ha' mercy on us, what a sight for me! The gig was there, with its shafts on the ground, and its back cocked up, and the iron-grey flat on his side, lashin' and scramblin', poor brute, and two villains in the gig, both pullin' at poor Master Harry, one robbin', and t'other murderin' him. I took one o' them—a short, thick fellow—by the skirt o' his coat, to drag him out, and I screamed for Tom Clinton to come out.

'The short fellow turned, and struck at me wi' somethin'; but, lucky for me, 'appen, the lashin' horse that minute took me on the foot, and brought me down. But up I scrambles wi' a stone in my hand, and I shied it, the best I could, at the head o' the villain that was killin' Master Harry. But what can a woman do? It did not go nigh him, I'm thinkin'. I was, all the time, calling on Tom to come, and cryin' "Murder!" that you'd think my throat'd split. That bloody wretch in the gig had got poor Master Harry's head back over the edge of it, and his knee to his chest, a-strivin' to break his neck across the back-rails; and poor dear lad, Master Harry, he just scritched, "Yelland Mace! for God's sake!"

They were the last words I ever heard from him, and I'll never forget that horrid scritch, nor the face of the villain that was over him, like a beast over its prey. He was tuggin' at his throat, like you'd be tryin' to tear up a tree by the roots—you never see such a face. His teeth was set, and the froth comin' through, and his black eyebrows screwed together, you'd think they'd crack the thin hooked nose of him between them, and he pantin' like a wild beast. He looked like a madman, I tell you; 'twas bright moonlight, and the trees bare, and the shadows of the branches was switchin' across his face.'

'You saw that face distinctly?' asked David Arden.

'As clear as yours this minute.'

'Now tell me—and think first—was he a bit like that Mr. Longcluse whose appearance startled you the other evening?' asked Mr. Arden, in a very low tone, with his eyes fixed on her intensely.

'No, no, no! not a bit. He had a small mouth and white teeth, and a great beak of a nose. No, no, no! not he. I saw him strike somethin' that shone—a knife or a dagger—into the poor lad's throat, and he struck it down at my head, as you know, and I mind nothin' after that. I'll carry the scar o' that murderer's blow to my grave. There's the whole story, and God forgi'e ye for asking me, for it gi'es me t' creepins for a week after; and I didn't conceit 'twould 'a' made me sa excited, Sir, or I would not 'a' bargained to tell it tonight—not that I blame ye, Master David, for I thought, myself, that I could bear it better—and I do believe, as I have gone so far in it, 'tis better to make one job of it, and a finish. So ye'll ask me any question ye like, and I'll make the best answer I can; only, Master David, ye'll not be o'er long about it?'

'You are a good creature, Martha. I am sorry to pain you, but I pain myself, and you know why I ask these questions.'

'Ay, Sir, and I'd rather hear ye ask them than see you sit as easy under all that as some does, that owed the poor fellow as much love as ever you did, and were as near akin.'

'I am puzzled, Martha, and hitherto I have been baffled, but I won't give it up yet. You say that the wretch who struck you was a singular-looking man, at least as you describe him. I know, Martha, I can rely upon your caution—you will not repeat to anyone what passes in our interview.' He lowered his voice. 'You do not think that this Mr. Longcluse—a rich gentleman, you know and a person who thinks he's of some consequence, a person whom we must not look at, you know, as if he had two heads—you really don't think that this Mr. Longcluse has any resemblance to the villain whom you saw stab my brother, and who struck you?'

'Not he—no more than I have. No, no, Mr. Longcluse is quite another sort of face; but for all that, when he came in here, and I saw him before me, his face and his speech reminded me of that night.'

'How was that, Martha? Did he resemble the other man—the man who was aiding?'

'That fellow was hanged, ye'll mind, Master David.'

'Yes, but a likeness might have struck and startled you.'

'No, Sir—no, Master David, not him; surely not him. I can't bring it to mind, but it frightens me. It *is* queer, Sir. All I can say for certain is this, Master David. The minute I heard his voice, and got sight of his face, like that,' and she dropped her hand on the table, 'the thought of that awful night came back, bright and cold, Sir, and them black shadows—'twas all about me, I can't tell how, and I hope I may never see him again.'

'Do you think there was another man by, besides the two villains in the gig?' suggested David Arden.

'Not a living soul except them and myself. Poor Master Harry said to Tom Clinton, ye'll mind, for he lived half-an-hour after, and spoke a little, though faint and with great labour, and says he, 'There were two: Yelland Mace killed me, and Tom Todry took the money.' Tom Clinton heard him say that, and swore to it before the justice o' peace, and after, on the trial. No, no, there wasn't a soul there but they two villains, and the poor dear lad they murdered, and me and Tom Clinton, that might as well 'a' bin in York for any good we did. Oh, no, Heaven forbid I should be so unmannerly as to compare a gentleman like Mr. Longcluse to such folk as that! Oh, lawk, no, Sir! But there's something, there's a look—or a sound in his voice—I can't get round it quite—but it reminds me of something about that night, with a start like, I can't tell how—something unlucky and awful—and I would not see him again for a deal.'

'Well, Martha, a thousand thanks. I'm puzzled, as I said. Perhaps it is only something strange in his face that caused that odd misgiving. For *I* who saw but one of the wretches engaged in the crime, the man who was convicted, who certainly did not in the slightest degree resemble Mr. Longcluse, experienced the same unpleasant sensation on first seeing him. I don't know how it is, Martha, but the idea clings to me, as it does to you. Some light may come. Something may turn up. I can't get it out of my mind that somehow—it may be circuitously—he has, at least, got the thread in his fingers that may lead us right. Goodnight, Martha. I have got the Bible with large print you wished for; I hope you will like the binding. And now, God bless you! It is time I should bid them goodnight upstairs. Farewell, my good old friend.' And, so saying, he shook her hard and shrivelled hand.

His steps echoed along the long tiled passage, with its one dim light, and his mind was still haunted by its one obscure idea.

'It is strange,' he thought, 'that Martha and I—the only two living persons, I believe, who care still for poor Harry, and feel alike respecting the expiation that is due to his memory—should both have been struck with the same odd feeling on seeing Longcluse. From that white sinister face, it seems to me, I know not why, will shine the light that will yet clear all up.'

A Walk by Moonlight

While Martha Tansey was telling her grisly story in the housekeeper's room, and David Arden listening to the oft-told tale, for the sake of the possible new lights which the narration might throw upon his present theory, the little party in the drawing-room had their music and their talk. Mr. Longcluse sang the song which, standing beside Uncle David on the landing, near the great window on the staircase, we have faintly heard; and then he sang that other song, of the goblin wooer, at

Alice's desire.

'Was the poor girl fool enough to accept his invitation?' inquired Miss Maubray.

'That I really can't say,' laughed Mr. Longcluse.

'Yes, indeed, poor thing! I so hope she didn't,' said Lady May.

'It's very likely she did,' interposed Sir Reginald, opening his eyes—everyone thought he was dozing— 'nothing more foolish, and therefore, nothing more likely. Besides, if she didn't, she probably did worse. Better to go straight to the——'

'Oh, dear Reginald!' exclaimed Lady May.

'Than by a tedious circumbendibus. I suppose her parents highly disapproved of the goblin; wasn't that alone an excellent reason for going away with him?'

And Sir Reginald closed his eyes again.

'Perhaps,' said Miss Maubray aside to Vivian Darnley, 'that romantic young lady may have had a cross papa, and thought that she could not change very much for the worse.'

'Shall I tell that to Sir Reginald?—it would amuse him,' inquired Darnley.

'Not as my remark; but I make you a present of it.'

'Thanks; but that, even with your permission, would be a plagiarism, and robbing you of his applause.'

Vivian Darnley was very inattentive to his own nonsense. He was talking very much at random, for his mind, and occasionally his eyes, were otherwise occupied.

Alice Arden was sitting near the piano, and talking to Mr. Longcluse.

'Is that meant to be a ghost, I wonder, in our sense, like the ghost of Wilhelm in the ballad of Leonora? or is the lover a demon?'

'A demon, surely,' answered Longcluse, 'a spirit appointed to her destruction. In an old ghostly writer there is a Latin sentence, *Unicuique nascenti, adest daemon vitae mystagogus*, which I will translate, 'There is present at the birth of every human being a demon, who is the conductor of his life.' Be it fortunate, or be it direful, to this supernatural influence he owes it all. So they thought; and to families such a demon is allotted also, and they prosper or wane as his function is ordained. I wonder whether such demons ever enter into human beings, and, in the shape of living men, haunt, plague, and ruin their predestinated victims.'

This sort of mysticism for a time they talked, and then wandered away to other themes, and the talk grew general; and Mr. Longcluse, with a pang, discovered that it was late. He had something on his mind that night. He had an undivulged use, also, to which to apply David Arden. As the hour drew near it weighed more and more heavily at his heart. That hour must be observed; he wished to be away before it arrived. There was still ample time; but Lady May was now talking of going, and he made up his mind to say farewell.

Lingeringly Mr. Longcluse took his leave. But go he must; and so, a last touch of the hand, a last look, and the parting is over. Down-stairs he runs; his groom and his brougham are at the door. What a glorious moon! The white light upon all things around is absolutely dazzling. How sharp and black the shadows! How light and filmy rises the old house! How black the nooks of the thick ivy! Every drop of dew that hangs upon its leaves, or on the drooping stalks of the neglected grass, is transmuted into a diamond. As he stands for an instant upon the broad platform of the steps, he looks round him with a deep sigh, and with a strange smile of rapture. The man standing with the open door of the brougham in his hand caught his eye.

'Go you down as far as the little church, before you reach the 'Guy of Warwick', in the village, quite close to this—you know it—and wait there for me. I shall walk.'

The man touched his hat shut the door, and mounted the box beside the driver, and away went the brougham. Mr. Longcluse lit a cigarette, and slowly walked down the broad avenue after the vehicle. By the time he had got about half-way, he heard the iron gates swing together, the sound of the wheels was lost in distance, and the feeling of seclusion returned. In the same vague intoxication of poetry and romance, he paused and looked round again, and sighed. The trunk of a great tree overthrown in the last year's autumnal gales, with some of its boughs lopped off, lay on the grass at the edge of the avenue. There remained a little of his cigarette to smoke, and the temptation of this natural seat was irresistible; so he took it, and smoked, and gazed, and dreamed, and sometimes, as he took the cigarette from his lips, he sighed—never was man in a more romantic vein.

He looked back on the noble front of the picturesque old house. The cold moonlight gleamed on most of the window-panes; but from a few tall windows glowed faintly the warmer light of candles. If anyone had ever felt the piercing storms of life, the treachery of his species, and the mendacity of the illusions that surround us, Longcluse was that man. He had accepted the conditions of life, and was a man of the world; but no boy of eighteen was ever more in love than he at this moment.

Gazing back at the dim glow that flushed through the tall window-blinds of the distant drawing-room, his fancy weaving all those airy dreams that passion lives in, this pale, solitary man—whom no one quite knew, who trusted no one, who had his peculiar passions, his sorrows, his fears, and strange remembrances; everything connected with his origin, vicissitudes, and character, except this one wild hope, locked up, as it were, in an iron casket, and buried in a grave fathoms deep—was now floated back, he knew not how, to that time of sweet perturbation and agonising hope at which the youth of Shakespeare's time were wont to sigh like a furnace, and indite woeful ballads to their mistress's eyebrows.

Now he saw lights in an upper room. Imagination and conjecture were in a moment at work. No servant's apartment, its dimensions were too handsome; and had not Sir Reginald mentioned that his room was upon a level with the hall? Just at this moment Lady May's carriage drove down the avenue and past him. Yes, she had run up direct to her room on bidding Lady May good ight. How he drank in these rosy lights through his dark eyes! and how their tremble seemed to quicken the pulsations of his heart! Gradually his thoughts saddened, and his face grew dark.

'Two doors in life—only in this life, if all bishops and curates speak truth—one or other shut for ever in the next. The gate to heaven, the gate to hell. Heaven! *Facilis decensus.* Life is such a sophism. Yet even those canting dogs in the pulpit can't bark away the truth. God sees not with our eyes! Revealed religion—Mahomet, Moses, Mormon, Borgia! What is the first lesson inscribed by his Maker on every man's heart, instinct, intellect? I read the mandate thus: 'Take the best care you can of number one.' Bah! 'It is he that hath made us, and not we ourselves."

Uncle David's carriage now drove by.

'There goes that sharp girl—pretty, vain—and they're all vain; they ought to be vain; they could not please if they were not. Vain she is—devoured, mind, soul, passion, by vanity. Yes, and power—the lust of power, conquest, acquisition. She's greedy and crafty, I daresay. Oh! Alice, who was ever quite like you? The most beautiful, the best, my darling! Oh! enchantress, work the miracle, and make this forlorn man what he might be!'

It passed like a magic-lantern picture, and was gone. The distant clang of the iron gate was heard again, the avenue was deserted and silent, and Longcluse once more alone in his dream. He was looking towards the house, sometimes breaking into a few murmured words, sometimes smoking, and just as his cigarette was out he saw a figure approaching. It was Uncle David, who was walking down the avenue. It so happened that his mind was at that moment busy with Mr. Longcluse, and it was with an odd little shock, therefore, that he saw the very man—whom he fancied by that time to be at least two miles away—rise up in his path, and stand before him, smiling, in the moonlight.

'Oh!—Mr. Longcluse?' exclaimed David Arden, coming suddenly to a halt.

'So it is,' said Longcluse, with a little laugh. 'You are surprised to find me here, and I fancied I had seen you carriage go on.'

'So you did; it is waiting near the gate for me. Can I give you a seat into town?'

'Thanks,' said Longcluse, smiling; 'mine is waiting for me a little further on.'

Longcluse walked slowly on toward the gate, with David Arden at his side.

'My ward, Miss Maubray, has gone on with Lady May, and Darnley went with them. So I'm not such a brute as I should be if I were making a young lady wait while I was enjoying the moonlight.'

'It was this wonderful moon that led me, also, into this night-ramble on foot,' said Mr. Longcluse; 'I found the temptation absolutely irresistible.'

As they thus talked, Mr. Longcluse had formed the resolution of choosing that moment for a confidence which, considering how slender was his acquaintance with Mr. David Arden, was, to say the least, a little bold and odd. They had not very far to walk before reaching the gate, so, a little abruptly turning the course of their talk, Mr. Longcluse said, with a chilly little laugh, and a smile more pallid than ever in the moonlight—

'By-the-bye, we were talking of that shocking occurrence in the Saloon Tavern; and connected with it, I have had two threatening letters.'

'Indeed!' said David Arden.

'Fact, I assure you,' said Mr. Longcluse, with a shrug and another cold little laugh.

Mr. Longcluse Makes an Odd Confidence

David Arden looked at Mr. Longcluse with a sudden glance, that was, for a moment, shrinking and sharp. This confidence connected with such a scene chimed in, with a harmony that was full of pain, with the utterly vague suspicions that had somehow got into his imagination.

'Yes, and I have been a little puzzled,' continued Longcluse. 'They say the man who is his own lawyer has a fool for his client; but there are other things besides law to which the spirit of the canon more strongly still applies. I think you could give me just the kind of advice I need, if you were not to think my asking it too great a liberty. I should not dream of doing so if the matter were simply a private one, and began and ended in myself; but you will see in a moment that public interests of some value are involved, and I am a little doubtful whether the course I am taking is in all respects the right one. I have had two threatening letters; would you mind glancing at them? The moon is so brilliant, one has no difficulty in reading. This is the first. And may I ask you, kindly, until I shall have determined, I hope, with your aid, upon a course, to treat the matter as quite between ourselves? I have mentioned it to but one other person.'

'Certainly,' said David, 'you have a right to your own terms.'

He took the letter and stopped short where he was, unfolding it. The light was quite sufficient, and he read the odd and menacing letter which Mr. Longcluse had received a few evenings before, as we know, at Lady May's. It was to the following effect:

> Sir,—
>
> The unfortunate situation in which you stand, the proof being so, as you must suppose, makes it necessary for you to act considerately, and no nonsense can be permitted by your well wishers. The poor man has his conscience all one as 'as the rich, and must be cautious as well as him. I cannot put myself in no dainger for you, Sir, nor won't hold back the truth, so welp me. I have heerd tell of your boote bin took away. I would be happy to lend an and, Sir, to recover that property. How all will end otherwise I regrett. Knowing well who it will be that takes so mutch consern for your safety, you cannot doubt who I am, and if you wishes to meat me quiet to consult, you need only to name the place and time in the times newspaper, which I sees it every day. It must be put part in one days times, for the daite, saying a friend will show on sich a night, and in next days times for the place, saying the dogs will meet at sich and sich a place, and it shall hev the attenshen of your
>
> *Fast Frend.*

'That's a cool letter, upon my word,' said David Arden. 'Have you an idea who wrote it?'

'Yes, a very good guess. I'll tell you all that if you allow me, just now. I should say, indeed, an absolute certainty, for I have had another this afternoon with the name of the writer signed, and he turns out to be the very man whom I suspected. Here it is.'

David Arden's curiosity was piqued. He took the last note and read as follows:—

> Sir,—
>
> My last Letter must have came to Hand, and you been in resect of it since the 11th instant, has took no Notice thereoff, I have No wish for justice, as you may Suppose, and has no Fealing against you Mr. Longcluse Persanelly and to shew you plainly that Such is the case, I will meet you for an intervue if such is your Wishes in your Own house, if you should Raython than name another place. I do not objeck To one frend been Present providing such Be not a lawyer. The subjek been Dellicat, I will Attend any hour and Place you appoint. If you should faile I must put my Proofs in the hands of the police, for I will take it for a sure sine of guilt if you fail after this to appoint for a meating.
>
> I remain, Sir, Your obedient servent,
>
> PAUL DAVIES.
>
> No. 2 Rosemary Court.

'Well, that's pretty frank,' said Longcluse, observing that he had read to the end.

'Extremely. What do you suppose his object to be—to extort money?'

'Possibly; but he may have another object. In any case, he wants to make money by this move.'

'Very audacious, then. He must know, if he is fit for his trade, how much risk there is in it; and his signing his name and address to his letter, and seeking an interview with a witness by seems to me utterly infatuated,' said David Arden, with his eye upon Mr. Longcluse.

'So it does, except upon one supposition; I mean that the man believes his story,' said Mr. Longcluse, walking beside him, for they had resumed their march towards the gate.

'Really! believes that you committed the murder?' said Uncle David, again coming to a halt and looking full at him.

'I can't quite account for it otherwise,' said Longcluse; 'and I think the right course is for me to meet him. But I have no intimacies in London, and that is my difficulty.'

'How? Why don't you arrest him?' said David Arden.

David Arden had seldom felt so oddly. A quarter-of-an-hour since, he expected to have been seated in his carriage with his ward and Vivian Darnley, driving into town in quiet humdrum fashion, by this time. How like a dream was the actual scene! Here he was, standing on the grass among the noble timber, under the moonlight, with the pale face beside him which had begun to haunt him so oddly. The strange smile of his mysterious companion, the cold tone that jarred sweetly, somehow, on his ear, lending a sinister eccentricity to the extraordinary confession he was making.

In this situation, which had come about almost unaccountably, there was a strange feeling of unreality. Was this man, from whom he had felt an indescribable repulsion, now by his side, and drawing him, in this solitude, into a mysterious confidence? and had not this confidence an *unaccountable* though distant relation to the vague suspicions that had touched his mind? With a little effort he resumed,—

'I beg pardon, but if the case were mine I should put the letters at once into the hands of the police and prosecute him.'

'Precisely my own first impulse. But the letters are more cautiously framed than you might at first sight suppose. I should be placed in an awkward position were my prosecution to fail. *I* am obliged to think of this because, although I am nothing to the public, I am a good deal to myself. But I've resolved to take a course not less bold, though less public. I am determined to meet him face to face with an unexceptionable witness present, and to discover distinctly whether he acts from fraud or delusion, and then to proceed accordingly. I have communicated with him.'

'Oh, really!'

'Yes, I was clear I ought to meet him, but I would consent to nothing with an air of concealment.'

'I think you were right, Sir.'

'He wanted our meeting by night on board a Thames boat; then in a dilapidated house in Southwark; then in a deserted house that is to be let in Thames Street; but I named my own house, in Bolton Street, at half-past twelve tonight.'

'Then you really wish to see him. I suppose you have thought it well over; but I am always for taking such miscreants promptly by the throat. However, as you say, cases differ, and I daresay you are well advised.'

'And now may I venture a request, which, were it not for two facts within my knowledge, I should not presume to make? But I venture it to you, who take so special an interest in this case, because you have already taken trouble and, like myself, contributed money to aid the chances of discovery; and because only this evening you said you would bestow more labour, more time, and more money with pleasure to procure the least chance of an additional light upon it: now it strikes me as just possible that the writer of those letters may be, to some extent, honest. Though utterly mistaken about me, still he may have evidence to give, be it worth much or little; and so, Mr. Arden, having the pleasure of being known to some members of your family, although till tonight by name only to you, I beg as a great kindness to a man in a difficulty, and possibly in the interests of the public, that you will be so good as to accompany me, and be present at the interview, that cannot be so well conducted before any other witness whom I can take with me.'

David Arden paused for a moment, but independently quite of his interest in this case: he felt a strange curiosity about this pale man, whose eyes from under their oblique brows gleamed back the cold moonlight; while a smile, the character of which a little puzzled him, curled his nostril and his thin lip, and showed the glittering edge of his teeth. Did it look like treachery? or was it defiance, or derision? It was a face, thus seen, so cadaverous and Mephistophelian, that an artist would have given something for a minute to fix a note of it in white and black.

David Arden was not to be disturbed in a practical matter by a pictorial effect, however, and in another moment he said—

'Yes, Mr. Longcluse, as you desire it I will accompany you, and see this fellow, and hear what he has to say. *Certainly.*'

'That's very kind—only what I should have expected, also, from your public spirit. I'm extremely obliged.'

They resumed their walk towards the gate.

'I shall get into my brougham and call at home, to tell them not to expect me for an hour or so. And what is the number of your house?'

He told him; and David Arden having offered to take him, in his carriage, to the place where his own awaited him, which however he declined, they parted for a little time, and Mr. Arden's brougham quickly disappeared under the shadow of the tall trees that lined the curving road.

The Meeting

As David Arden drove towards town, his confusion rather increased. Why should Mr. Longcluse select him for this confidence? There were men in the City whom he must know, if not intimately, at least much better than he knew him. It was a very strange occurrence; and was not Mr. Longcluse's manner, also, strange? Was he not, somehow, very oddly cool under a charge of murder? There was something, it seemed, indefinably incongruous in the nature of his story, his request, and his manner.

It was five or ten minutes before the appointed time when David Arden and Longcluse met in the latter gentleman's 'study' in Bolton Street. There was a slight, odd flutter at Longcluse's heart, although his pale face betrayed no sign of agitation, as the shuffling tread of a heavy foot was heard on the doorsteps, followed by a faint knock, like that of a tremulous postman. It was the preconcerted summons of Mr. Paul Davies.

Longcluse smiled at David Arden and raised his finger, as he lightly drew near the room door, with an air of warning. He wished to remind his companion that he was to receive their visitor alone. Mr. Arden nodded, and Mr. Longcluse withdrew. In a minute more the servant opened the study-door, and said—

'Mr. Davies, Sir.'

And the tall ex-detective entered, and looked with a silky simper stealthily to the right and to the left from the corners of his eyes, and glided in, shutting the door behind him.

Uncle David received this man without even a nod. He eyed him sternly, from his chair at the end of the table.

'Sit in that chair, please,' said he, pointing to a seat at the other end.

The ex-policeman made his best bow, and turning out his toes very much, he shuffled with his habitual sly smirk on, to the chair, in which he seated himself, and with his big red hands on the table began turning, and twisting, and twiddling a short pencil, which was a good deal bitten at the uncut end, between his fingers and thumbs.

'You came here to see Mr. Longcluse?' asked David Arden.

'A few words of business at his desire. Sir, I ask your parding, I came, Sir, by his wishes, not mine, which has brought me here at his request.'

'And who am I, do you suppose?'

The man, still smiling, looked at him shrewdly. 'Well, I don't know, I'm sure; I may 'a' seen you.'

'Did you ever see that gentleman?' said David Arden, as Mr. Longcluse entered the room.

The ex-detective looked also shrewdly at Longcluse, but without any light of recognition. 'I may have seen him, Sir. Yes, I saw him in Saint George's, Hanover Square, the day Lord Charles Dillingsworth married Miss Wygram, the *hairess.* I saw him at Sydenham the second week in February last when the Freemasons' dinner was there; and I saw him on the night of the match between Hood and Markham, at the Saloon Tavern.'

'Do you know my name?' said David Arden.

'Well, no, I don't at present remember.'

'Do you know that gentleman's name!'

'His name?'

'Ay, his name.'

'Well, no; I may have heard it, and I may bring it to mind, by-and-by.'

Longcluse smiled and shrugged, looking at Mr. Arden, and he said to the man—

'So you don't know *that* gentleman's name, nor mine?'

The man looked at each, hard and a little anxiously, like a person who feels that he may be making a very serious mistake; but after a pause he said decisively—'No, I don't at present. I say I don't know your names, either of you gentlemen, and I *don't*.'

The two gentlemen exchanged glances.

'Is either of us as tall as Mr. Longcluse?' asked David Arden, standing up.

The man stood up also, to make his inspection.

'You're both' he said, after a pause, 'much about his height.'

'Is either of us like him?'

'No,' answered Davies, after a pause.

'Did you write these letters?' asked Mr. Longcluse laughing.

'Well, I did, or I didn't, and what's that to you?'

'Something, as you shall know presently.'

'I think you're trying it on. I reckon this is a bit of a plant. I don't care a scratch o' that pencil if it be. I wrote them letters, and I said nothin' but what's true, and I'll go with you now to the station if you like, and tell all I knows.'

The fellow seemed nettled, and laughed viciously a little, and swaggered at the close of his speech. The faintest flush imaginable tinged Longcluse's forehead, as he shot a searching glance at him.

'No, we don't want that,' said he; 'but you may be of more use in another way, although just now you are in the wrong box, and have mistaken your man, for *I* am Mr. Longcluse. You have been misinformed, you see, as to the *identity* of the person you suspect; but some person you have, no doubt, in your mind, and possibly a case worth sifting, although you have been deceived as to his name. Describe the appearance of the man you supposed to be Mr. Longcluse. You may be frank with me; I mean you no harm.'

'I defy any man to harm me, Sir, if you please, so long as I do my dooty,' said Paul Davies. 'Mr. Longcluse, if that be his name, the man I mean, he's about your height, with round shoulders and red hair, and talks with a north-country twang on his tongue; he's a bit rougher, and a swaggering cove, and a yard o' red beard over his waistcoat, and bigger hands a deal than you, and broader feet.'

'And have you a case against him?'

'Partly, but it ain't, Sir, if you please, by no means so complete as would answer as yet. If I was sure you were really Mr. Longcluse, I could say more, for I partly guess who this other gent—is a most respectable party. I think I do know you, Sir, by appearance; if you had your 'at on, Sir, I could say to a certainty. But I think, Sir, if you please, I'm not very far wrong when I say that I would identify you for Mr. David Arden.'

'So I am; that is quite true.'

'Thank you, Sir, I am obleeged; that's very quietin' to my mind, Sir, having full confidence in your character; and if you, Sir, please to tell me *that* gentleman is undoubtingly Mr. Longcluse, the propperieter of this house, I must 'a' been let into a mistake; I don't think they was agreenin' of me, but it was a mistake, if you please, Sir, if you say so.'

'This is Mr. Longcluse—I know of no other—and he resides in this house,' said David Arden. 'But if you have information to give respecting that red-bearded fellow, there is no reason why you should not give it forthwith to the police.'

'Parding me, Sir, if you please, Mr. Arden. There is, I would say, strong reasons for a poor man in rayther anxious circumstances, like myself, Sir, 'aving an affectionate mother to, in a measure, support, and been himself unfortunately rayther hard up, he can't answer it nohow to his conscience if he lets a hoppertunity like the present pass him and his aged mother by unimproved. There been a reward offered, Sir, I naturally wish, Sir, if you please, to earn it myself by valuable evidence leading to the conviction of the guilty cove; and if I was to tell all I knows and 'av' made out by my own hindustry to the force, Sir, other persons would, don't you conceive, Sir, draw the reward, and me and my mother should go without. If I could get a hinterview with the man I 'av' bin a-gettin' things together for, I'd lead him, I 'av' no doubt, to make such hadmissions as would clench the prosecution, and vendicate justice.'

'I see what you mean,' said David Arden.

'And fair enough, I think,' added Longcluse.

Mr. Longcluse Follows a Shadow

The ex-detective cleared his voice, shook his head, and smirked.

'A hinterview, gentlemen,' said he, 'is worth much in the hands of a persuasive party. I have hanged several obnoxious characters, and let others in for penal for life, by means of a hinterview. You remember Spikes, gentlemen, as got into difficulties for breaking Mr. Winterbotham's desk? Spikes would have frusterated justice, if it wasn't for me. It was done in one hinterview. Says I, 'Mr. Spikes, you have a wife and five children."

The recollection of Mr. Paul Davies' diplomacy was so gratifying to that smiling gentleman, that he could not forbear winking at his auditors as he proceeded.

"And my belief is, Mr. Spikes, Sir," he continued, "that it was all the hinfluence of Tom Sprowles. It was Sprowles persuaded yer—it was him as got the whole thing up. That's my belief; and you did not want to do it, no-wise, and only consented to force the henges in the belief that Sprowles wanted to read the papers, and no more. I have a bad opinion of Sprowles,' says I, 'for deceiving you, I may say innocently;' and talking this way, you conceive, I got it all out of him, and he's under penal for life. Whenever you want to get round a man, and to turn him inside out, your way is to sympath*ise* with him. If I had but an hinterview with that man, I know enough to draw it out of him, every bit. It's all done by sympath*ising*'

'But do you think you can discover the man?' asked Mr. Arden.

'I'm sure to make him out, if you please, Sir; I'll find out all about him. I'd a found out the facks long ago, but for the mistake, which it occurred most unlucky. I saw him twice sence, and I know well where to look for him; and I'll have it all right before long, I'm thinkin'.'

'That will do, then, for the present,' said Mr. Longcluse. 'You have said all you have to say, and you see into what a serious mistake you have blundered; but I sha'n't give you any trouble about it—it is too ridiculous. Goodnight, Mr. Davies.'

'No mistake of mine, Sir, please. Misinformed, Sir, you will kindly remark—misinformed, if you please—misinformed, as may occur to the sharpest party going. Goodnight, gentlemen; I takes my leave without no unpleasant feelin', and good wishes for your 'ealth and 'appiness, both, gentlemen.' And blandly, and with a sly sleepy smile, this insinuating person withdrew.

'It is the reward he is thinking of,' said Longcluse.

'Yes, he won't spare himself; you mentioned that your own suspicions respecting him were but vague,' said David Arden.

'I merely stated what I saw to the coroner, and it was answered that he was watching the Frenchman Lebas, because the detective police, before Paul Davies' dismissal, had received orders to keep an eye on all foreigners; and he hoped to conciliate the authorities, and get a pension, by collecting and furnishing information. The police did not seem to think his dogging and watching the unfortunate little fellow really meant more than this.'

'Very likely. It is a very odd affair. I wonder who that fellow is whom he described. He did not give a hint as to the circumstances which excited his suspicions.'

'It *is* strange. But that man, Paul Davies, kept his eye upon Lebas from the motive I mentioned, and this circumstance may have led to his seeing more of the matter than, with the reward in his mind, he cares to make known at present. I think I did right in meeting him face to face.'

'Quite right, Sir.'

'It has been always a rule with me to go straight at everything. I think the best diplomacy is directness, and that the truest caution lies in courage.'

'Precisely my opinion, Mr. Longcluse,' said Uncle David, looking on him with eyes of approbation. He was near adding something hearty in the spirit of our ancestors' saying, 'I hope you and I, Sir, may be better acquainted;' but something in the look and peculiar face of this unknown Mr. Longcluse chilled him and he only said—

'As you say, Mr. Longcluse, courage is safety, and honesty the best policy. Goodnight, Sir.'

'A thousand thanks, Mr. Arden. Might I ask one more favour, that you will endorse on each of these threatening letters a memorandum of the facts of this strange interview?—

I mean a sentence or two, which may at any time confound this fellow, should he turn out to be a villain.'

'Certainly,' said Mr. Arden thoughtfully, and he sat down again, and wrote a few lines on the back of each, which, having signed, he handed them to Mr. Longcluse, with the question, 'Will that answer?'

'Perfectly, thank you very much; it is indeed impossible for me to thank you as I ought and wish to,' said Mr. Longcluse with effusion, extending his hand at the same time; but Mr. Arden took it without much warmth, and said, in comparison a little drily—

'No need to thank me, Mr. Longcluse; as you said at first, there are motives quite sufficient, of a kind for which you can owe me, personally, no thanks whatever, to induce the very slight trouble of coming here.'

'Well, Mr. Arden, I *am* very *much* obliged to you, notwithstanding;' and so he gratefully saw him to the door, and smiled and bowed him off, and stood for a moment as his carriage whirled down the short street.

'He does not like me—nor I, perhaps, him. Ha! ha! ha!' he laughed, very softly and reservedly, looking down on the flags. 'What an odd thing it is! Those instincts and antipathies, they are very odd.' All this, except the faint laughter, was in thought.

Mr. Longcluse stepped back. He was negatively happy—he was rid of an anxiety. He was positively happy—he had been better received by Miss Arden, this evening, than he had ever been before. So he went to his bed with a light heart, and a head full of dreams.

All the next day, one beautiful image haunted Longcluse's imagination. He was delayed in town; he had to consult about operations in foreign stocks; he had many words to say, directions to modify, and calls to make on this man and that. He had hoped to be at Mortlake Hall at three o'clock. But it was past six before he could disentangle himself from the tenacious meshes of his business. Never had he thought it so irksome. Was he not rich enough—too rich? Why should he longer submit to a servitude so wearisome? It was high time he should begin to enjoy his days in the sunshine of his gold and the companionship of his beautiful idol. But *man proposes*, says the ancient saw, *and God disposes*.

It was just seven o'clock when Mr. Longcluse descended at the steps of old Mortlake Hall.

Sir Reginald, who is writhing under a letter from the attorney of the millionaire mortgagee of his Yorkshire estate, making an alternative offer, either to call in the principal sum or to allow it to stand out on larger interest, had begged of Mr. Longcluse, last night, to give him a few words of counsel some day. He had, in a quiet talk the evening before, taken the man of huge investments rather into his confidence.

'I don't know, Mr.—a—Mr. Longcluse, whether you are aware how cruelly my property is tied up,' he said, as he talked in a low tone with him, in a corner of the drawing-room. 'A life estate, and my son, who declines bearing any part of the burden of his own extravagance, will do nothing to facilitate my efforts to pay his debts for him; and I declare solemnly, if they raise the interest on this very oppressive mortgage, I don't know how on earth I can pay my insurances. I don't see how I am to do it. I should be so extremely obliged to you, Mr. Longcluse, if you would, with your vast experience and knowledge in all—all financial matters, give me any advice that strikes you—if you could, with perfect convenience, afford so much time. I don't really know what rate of interest is usual. I only know this, that interest, as a rule, has been steadily declining ever since I can remember—perpetually declining; I mean, of course, upon perfect security like this; and now this confounded harpy wants, after ten years, to *raise* it! I believe they want to drive me out of the world, among them! and they well know the cruelty of it, for I have never been able to pay them a single half-year punctually. Will you take some tea?'

So Longcluse had promised his advice very gladly next day; and now he asked for Sir Reginald. Sir Reginald was very particularly engaged at this moment on business; Mr. Arden was with him at present; but if Mr. Longcluse would wait for a few minutes, Sir Reginald would be most happy to see him. So there was to be a little wait. How could he better pass the interval than in Miss Arden's company?

A Tête-à-tête

Up to the drawing-room went Mr. Longcluse, and there he found Miss Arden finishing a drawing. He fancied a very slight flush on her cheek as he entered. Was there really a heightening of that beautiful tint as she smiled? How lovely her long lashes, and her even little teeth, and the lustrous darkness of her eyes, in that subdued light!

'I so wanted advice, Mr. Longcluse, and you have come in so fortunately! I am not satisfied with my sky and mountains, and the foreground where the light touches that withered branch is a horrible failure. In nature, it looked quite beautiful. I remember it so well. It looked on fire, almost. This is Saxteen Castle, near Golden Friars, and that is a bit of the lake and those are the fells. I sketched it in pencil, and trusted to memory for colouring. It was just at the most picturesque moment, when the sun was going down between the two mountains that overhang the little town on the west.'

'Sunset is very well expressed. You indicated all those long shadows, Miss Arden, in pencil, and I envy your perspective, and I think your colouring so extremely good! The distances are admirably marked. Try a little cadmium, burnt sienna, and lake for the intense touches of light in the foreground, on that barkless branch. Your own eye will best regulate the proportions. I am one of those vandals who prefer colour a little too bold and overdone to any timidity in that respect. Exuberance in a beginner is always, in my mind, an augury of excellence. It is so easy to moderate afterwards.'

'Yes, I daresay; I'm very glad you advise that, because I always thought so myself; but I was half afraid to act on it. I think that is about the tint—a little more yellow, perhaps. Yes; how does it look now?—what do you think?'

'Now judge yourself, Miss Arden. Do not those three sharp little touches of reflected fire light up the whole drawing? I say it is admirable. It is really quite a beautiful little drawing.'

'I'm growing so vain! you will quite spoil me, Mr. Longcluse.'

'Truth will never spoil any one. Praise is very delightful. I have not had much of it in my day, but I think it makes one better as well as happier; and to speak simple truth of you, Miss Arden, is inevitably to praise you.'

'Those are compliments, Mr. Longcluse, and they bewilder me—anything one does not know how to answer; so I would rather you pointed me out four or five faults in my drawing, and I should be very well content if you said no more. I believe you know the scenery of Golden Friars.'

'I do. Beautiful, and so romantic, and full of legends! the whole place with its belongings is a poem.'

'So I think. And the hotel—the inn I prefer calling it—the 'George and Dragon', is so picturesque and delightfully old, and so comfortable! Our headquarters were there for two or three weeks. And did you see Childe Waylin's Leap?'

'Yes, an awful scene; what a terrible precipice! I saw it to great advantage from a boat, while a thunderstorm was glaring and pealing over its summit. You know the legend, of course?'

'No, I did not hear it.'

'Oh, it is a very striking one, and won't take many words to tell. Shall I tell it?'

'Pray do,' said Alice, with her bright look of expectation.

He smiled sadly. Perhaps the story returned with an allegoric melancholy to his mind. With a sigh and a smile he continued—

'Childe Waylin fell in love with a phantom lady, and walked day and night along the fells—people thought in solitude—really lured on by the beautiful apparition, which, as his love increased, grew less frequent, more distant and fainter, until last, in the despair of his wild pursuit, he throw himself over that terrible precipice, and so perished. I have faith in instinct—faith in passion, which is but a form of instinct, am sure he did wisely.'

'I sha'n't dispute it; it is not a case likely to happen ofter. These phantom ladies seem to have given up practice of late years, or else people have become proof against their wiles, neither follow, nor adore, nor lament them.'

'I don't think these phantom ladies are at all out of date,' said Mr. Longcluse.

'Well, men have grown wiser, at all events.'

'No wiser, no happier; in such a case there is no room for what the world calls wisdom. Passion is absolute, and as for happiness, that or despair hangs on the turn of a die.'

'I have made that shadow a little more purple—do you think it an improvement?'

'Yes, certainly. How well it throws out that bit of the ruin that catches the sunlight! You have made a very poetical sketch; you have given not merely the outlines, but the character of that singular place—the *genus loci* is there.'

Just as Mr. Longcluse had finished this complimentary criticism, the door opened, and rather unexpectedly Richard Arden entered the room. Very decidedly *de trop* at that moment, his friend thought Mr. Arden. Longcluse meant again to have turned the current of their talk into the channel he liked best, and here was interruption. But was not Richard Arden his sworn brother, and was he not sure to make an excuse of some sort, and take his leave, and thus restore him to his *tête-à-tête.*

But was there—or was it fancy—a change scarcely perceptible, but unpleasant, in the manner of this sworn brother? Was it not very provoking, and a little odd, that he did not go away, but stayed on and on, till at length a servant came in with a message from Sir Reginald to Mr. Longcluse, to say that he would be very happy to see him whenever he chose to come to his room? Mr. Longcluse was profoundly vexed. Richard Arden, however, had resumed his old manner pretty nearly. Was the interruption he had persisted in designed, or only accidental? Could he suppose Richard Arden so stupid? He took his leave smiling, but with an uncomfortable misgiving at his heart.

Richard Arden now proceeded in his own way, with some colouring and enormous suppression at discretion, to give his sister such an account as he thought would best answer of the interview he had just had with his father. Honestly related, what occurred between them was as follows:—

Richard Arden had come on summons from his father. Without a special call, he never appeared at Mortlake while his father was there, and never in his absence but with an understanding that Sir Reginald was to hear nothing of it. He sat for a considerable time in the apartment that opened from his father's dressing-room. He heard the baronet's peevish voice ordering Crozier about. Something was dropped and broken, and the same voice was heard in angrier alto. Richard Arden looked out of the window and waited uncomfortably. He hated his father's pleadings with him, and he did not know for what purpose he had appointed this interview.

The door opened, and Sir Reginald entered, limping a little, for his gout had returned slightly. He was leaning on a stick. His thin, dark face and prominent eyes looked angry, and he turned about and poked his dressing-room door shut with the point of his stick, before taking any notice of his son.

'Sit down, if you please, in that chair,' he said, pointing to the particular seat he meant him to occupy with two vicious little pokes, as if he were running a small-sword through it. 'I wrote to ask you to come, Sir, merely to say a word respecting your sister, for whom, if not for other members of your family, you still retain, I suppose, some consideration and natural affection.'

Here was a pause which Richard Arden did not very well know what to do with. However, as his father's fierce eyes were interrogating him, he murmured—

'Certainly, Sir.'

'Yes, and under that impression I showed you Lord Wynderbroke's letter. He is to dine here tomorrow at a quarter to eight—please to recollect—precisely. Do you hear?'

'I do, Sir, everything.'

'You must meet him. Let us not appear more divided than we are. You know Wynderbroke—he's peculiar. Why the devil shouldn't we appear united? I don't say *be* united, for you won't. But there is something owed to decency. I suppose you admit that? And before people, confound you, Sir, can't we appear affectionate? He's a quiet man, Wynderbroke, and makes a great deal of these domestic sentiments. So you'll please to show some respect and affection while he's present—and I mean to show some affection for you; and after that, Sir, you may go to the devil for me! I hope you understand?'

'Perfectly, Sir.'

'As to Wynderbroke, the thing is settled—it is *there*.' He pointed to his desk. 'What I told you before, I tell you now—you must see that your sister doesn't make a fool of herself. I have nothing more to say to you at present—unless you have something to say to me?'

This latter part of the sentence had something sharp and interrogative in it. There was just a chance, it seemed to imply, that his son might have something to say upon the one point that lay near the old man's heart.

'Nothing, Sir,' said Richard, rising.

'No, no; so I supposed. You may go, Sir—nothing.'

Of this interview, one word of the real purport of which he could not tell to his sister, he gave her an account very slight indeed, but rather pleasant.

The Garden at Mortlake

Alice leaned back in her chair, smiling, and very much pleased.

'So my father seems disposed to relent ever so little—and ever so little, you know, is better than nothing,' said Richard Arden.

'I'm so glad, Dick, that he wishes you to take your dinner with us tomorrow; it is a very good sign. It would be so delightful if you could be at home with us, as you used to be.'

'You are a good little soul, Alice—a dear little thing! This is very pretty,' he said, looking at her drawing. 'What is it?'

'The ruined castle near the northern end of the lake at Golden Friars. Mr. Longcluse says it is pretty good. Is he to dine here, do you know?'

'No—I don't know—I hope not,' said Richard shortly.

'Hope not! why?' said she. 'I thought you liked him extremely.'

'I thought he was very well for a sort of outdoor acquaintance for *men;* but I don't even know *that,* now. There's no use in speaking to Lady May, but I warn you—you had better drop him. There is very little known about him, but there is a great deal that is not pleasant *said.*'

'Really?'

'Yes, really.'

'But you used to speak so highly of him. I'm so surprised!'

'I did not know half what people said of him. I've heard a great deal since.'

'But is it true?' asked Alice.

'It is nothing to me whether it is true or not. It is enough if a man is talked about uncomfortably, to make it unpleasant to know him. We owe nothing to Mr. Longcluse; there is no reason why you should have an acquaintance that is not desirable. *I* mean to drop him quietly, and you *can't* know him, really you *mustn't,* Alice.'

'I don't know. It seems to me very hard,' said Miss Alice spiritedly. 'It is not many days since you spoke of him so highly; and I was quite pained when you came in just now. I don't know whether he perceived it, but I think he must. I only know that I thought you were so cold and strange to him, your manner so unlike what it always was before. I thought you had been quarrelling. I fancied he was vexed, and I felt quite sorry; and I don't think what you say, Richard, is manly, or like yourself. You used to praise him so, and fight his battles; and he is, though very distinguished in some ways, rather a stranger in London; and people, you told me, envy him, and try in a cowardly way to injure him; and what more easy than to hint discreditable things of people? and you did not believe a word of those reports when last you spoke of him; and considering that he had no people to stand by him in London, or to take his part, and that he may never even hear the things that are said by low people about him, don't you think it would be cowardly of us, and positively base to treat him so?'

'Upon my word, Miss Alice, that is very good oratory indeed! I don't think I ever heard you so eloquent before, at least upon the wrongs of one of my sex.'

'Now, Dick, that sneer won't do. There may possibly be reasons why it would have been wiser never to have made Mr. Longcluse's acquaintance; I can't say. Those reasons, however, you treated very lightly indeed a little time ago—you know you did—and now, upon no better, you say you are going to cut him. *I* can't bring myself to do any such thing. He is always looking in at Lady May's, and I can't help meeting him unless I am to cut her also. Now don't you see how odious I should appear, and how impossible it is?'

'I won't argue it now, dear Alice; there is quite time enough. I shall come an hour before dinner, tomorrow, and we can have a quiet talk; and I am quite sure I shall convince you. Mind, I don't say we should insult him,' he laughed. 'I only say this, and I'll maintain it—and I'll show you why—that he is not a desirable acquaintance. We have taken him up very foolishly, and we *must* drop him And now, darling, goodbye.'

He kissed her—she kissed him. She looked grave for a moment after, after he had run down the stairs. He has quarrelled with Mr. Longcluse about something, she thought, as she stood at the window with the tip of her finger to her lip, looking at her brother as he mounted the showy horse which had cantered with him up and down Rotten Row for two hours or more, before he had ridden out to Mortlake. She saw him now ride away.

It was near eight o'clock, and all this time Mr. Longcluse had been in confidence with Sir Reginald about his miserable mortgage. Mr. Longcluse was cautious; but there floated in his mind certain possible contingencies, under which he might perhaps make the financial adjustment, which Sir Reginald desired, very easy indeed to the worthy baronet.

It was the tempting hour of evening when the birds begin to sing, and the level beams from the west glorify all objects. Alice put on her hat and ran out to the old gardens of Mortlake. They are enclosed in a grey wall, and lie one above the other in three terraces, with tall standard fruit trees, so old that their fruit was now dwarfed in size to half its earlier bearings, standing high with a dark and sylvan luxuriance, and at this moment, sheltering among their sunlit leaves, nestle and flutter the small birds whose whistlings cheer and sadden the evening air. Every tree and bush that bore fruit, in this old garden, had grown quite beyond the common stature of its kind, and a good gardener would have cut them all down fifty years ago. But there was a kind of sylvan and stately beauty in those wonderful lofty pear-trees, with their dense dark foliage, and in the standard cherries so tall and prim, and something homely and comfortable in the great straggling apples and plums, dappled with grey lichens and tufted with moss. There were flowers as well as fruits, of all sorts, in this garden. All its arrangements were out of date. There was an air, not actually of neglect—for it was weeded, and the walks were trim and gravelled—but of carelessness and rusticity, not unpleasant, in the place. Trees were allowed to straggle and spread, and rise aloft in the air, just as they pleased. Tall roses climbed the walls about the door, and clustered in nodding masses overhead; and no end of pretty annuals and other flowers, quite out of fashion, crowded the dishevelled currant bushes, and the forest of raspberries. Here and there were very tall myrtles, and the quince, and obsolete medlars, were discoverable among the other fruit-trees. The summits of the walls were in some places crowned, to the scandal of all decent gardening, with ivy, and a carved shaft in the centre of each garden supported a sun-dial as old as the Hall itself.

There are fancies, as well as likings and lovings. Where there is a real worship, however cautiously masked—and Mr. Longcluse was by no means so—it is never a mystery to a clever girl. And such adoration, although it be not at all reciprocated, is sometimes hard to part with. There is something of the nature of compassion, with a little gratitude, perhaps, mingling in the pang which a gentle lady feels at having to discharge for ever an honest love and a true servant, and send him away to solitary suffering for her sake. Some little pang of reproach of this sensitive kind had, perhaps, armed her against her brother's sudden sentence of exclusion pronounced against Mr. Longcluse.

The evening sunlight travelled over the ivy on the discoloured wall, and glittered on the leaves of the tall fruit-trees, in whose thick foliage the birds were still singing their vespers. Walking down the broad walk towards the garden-door, she felt the saddening influence of the hour returning; and as she reached the door, overclustered with roses, it opened, and Mr. Longcluse stood in the shadow before her.

Miss Arden, thus surprised in the midst of thoughts which at that moment happened to be employed about him, showed for a second, as she suddenly stopped, something in her beautiful face almost amounting to embarrassment.

'I was called away so suddenly to see Sir Reginald, that I went without saying goodbye; so I ran up to the drawing-room, and the servant told me I should probably find you here; and, really without reflecting—I act, I'm afraid, so much from impulse that I might appear very impertinent—I ventured to follow. What a beautiful evening! How charming the light! You, who are such an artist, and understand the poetry of colour so, must admire this cloister-like garden, so beautifully illuminated.'

Was Mr. Longcluse also a very little embarrassed as he descanted thus on light and colour?

'a It is a very old garden and does very little credit, I'm afraid, to our care; but I greatly prefer it to our formal gardens and their finery, in Yorkshire.'

She moved her hand as if she expected Mr. Longcluse to take it and his leave, for it was high time her visitor should 'order his wings and be off the west,' in which quarter, as we know lay Mr. Longcluse's habitation. He had stepped in, however and the door closed softly before the light evening breeze that swung it gently. She was standing under the wild canopy of roses, and he under the sterner arch of grooved and fluted stone that overhung the doorway.

Winged Words

'I was afraid I had vexed your brother somehow,' said Mr Longcluse—'I thought he seemed to meet me a little formally. I should be so sorry if I had annoyed him by any accident!'

He paused, and Miss Arden said, half laughing—'Oh, don't you know, Mr. Longcluse, that people are out of spirits sometimes, and now and then a little offended with all the world? It is nothing, of course.'

'What a fib!' whispered conscience in the young lady's pretty ear, while she smiled and blushed.

Again she raised her hand a little, expecting Mr. Longcluse's farewell. But she looked a great deal too beautiful for a farewell. Mr. Longcluse could not deny himself a minute more, and he said, 'It is a year, Miss Arden, since I first saw you.'

'Is it really? I daresay.'

'Yes, at Lady May Penrose's. Yes, I remember it distinctly—so distinctly that I shall never forget any circumstance connected with it. It is exactly a year and four days. You smile, Miss Arden, because for you the event can have had no interest; for me it is different—how different I will not say.'

Miss Arden coloured and then grew pale. She was very much embarrassed. She was about to say a word to end the interview, and go. Perhaps Mr. Longcluse was, as he said, impulsive—too precipitate and impetuous. He raised his hand entreatingly,—

'Oh, Miss Arden, pray, only a word!—I must speak it. Ever since then—ever since that hour—I have been the slave of a single thought; I have worshipped before one beautiful image, with an impious adoration, for there is nothing—no sacrifice, no crime—I would shrink from for your sake. You can make of me what you will; all I possess, all my future, every thought and feeling and dream—all are yours. No, no; don't interrupt the few half desperate words I have to speak, they may move you to pity. Never before, in a life of terrible vicissitude, of much suffering, of many dangers, have I seen the human being who could move me as you have done. I did not believe my seared heart capable of passion. And I stand now aghast at what I have spoken. I stand at the brink of a worse death, by the word that trembles on your lips, than the cannon's mouth could give me. I see I have spoken rashly—I see it in your face—oh, Heaven! I see what you would say.'

His hands were clasped in desperate supplication, as he continued; and the fitful breeze shook the roses above them, and the fading leaves fell softly in a shower about his feet.

'No, don't speak—your silence is sacred. I sha'n't misinterpret—I conjure you, don't answer! Forget that I have spoken. Oh! let it, in mercy, be all forgotten, and let us meet again as if there never had been this moment of madness, and in pity—as you look for mercy—forget it and forgive it!'

He waited for no answer: he was gone: the door closed as it was before. Another breath of wind ruffled the roses, and a few more sere leaves fell where he had just been standing. She drew a long breath, like one awaking from a vision. She was trembling slightly. Never before had she seen such agony in a human face! All had happened so suddenly. It was an effort to believe it real. It seemed as if she could see nothing while he spoke, but that intense, pale face. She heard nothing but his deep and thrilling words. Now it seemed as if flowers, and trees, and wall, and roses, all emerged suddenly again from mist and as if all the birds had resumed their singing after a silence.

'Forget—it forgive it! Let it, as you look for mercy, be all forgotten. Let us meet again as if it never was.' This strange petition still rang in the ears of the astonished girl.

She was still too much flurried by the shock of this wild and sudden outbreak of passion, and appeal to mercy, quite to see her true course in the odd combination that had arisen. She was a little angry, and a little flattered. There was a confusion of resentment and compassion. What business had this Mr. Longcluse to treat her to those heroics! What right had he to presume that he would be listened to? How dared he ask her to treat all that had happened as if it had never been? How dared he seek to found on this unwarrantable liberty relations of mystery between them? How dared he fancy that she would consent to play at this game of deception with him?

Mingled with these angry thoughts, however, were the recollections of his homage, his tone of melancholy deference ever since she had know him, and his admiration.

Underlying all his trifling talk, there had always been toward her a respect which flattered her, which could not have been exceeded had she been an empress in her own right. No, if he had said more than he had any right to suppose would be listened to, the extravagance was due to no want of respect for her, but to the vehemence of passion.

He was driving now into town, at a great pace. His cogitations were still more perturbed. Had he, by one frantic precipitation, murdered his best hopes?

One consolation at least he had. Being a man, not without

reason, prone to suspicion, he had a deep conviction that, for some reason, Richard Arden was opposed to his suit, and had already begun to work upon Miss Arden's mind to his prejudice. His best chance, then, he still thought, was to anticipate that danger by a declaration. If that declaration could only be forgiven, and the little scene at old Mortlake garden door sponged out, might not his chances stand better far than before? Would not the past, though never spoken of, give meaning, fire, and melancholy to things else insignificant, and keep him always before her, and her alone, be his demeanour and language ever so reserved and cold, as an impassioned lover? Did not his knowledge of human nature assure him that these relations of mystery would, more than any other, favour his fortunes?

'That she should consign what has passed, in a few impetuous moments, to oblivion and silence, is no unreasonable prayer, and one as easy to grant as to will it. She will think it over, and, for my part, I will meet her as if nothing had ever happened to change our trifling but friendly relations. I wish I knew what Richard Arden was about. I soon shall. Yes, I shall—I soon shall.'

An opportunity seemed to offer sooner even than he had hoped; for as he drove towards St. James's Street, passing one of Richard Arden's clubs, he saw that young gentleman ascending the steps with Lord Wynderbroke.

Longcluse stopped his brougham, jumped out, and overtook Richard Arden in the hall, where he stood, taking his letters from the hall-porter.

'How d'ye do, again? I sha'n't detain you a minute. I have had a long talk with your father about business,' said Longcluse, seizing the topic most likely to secure a few minutes, and speaking very low. 'You can bring me into a room here, and I'll tell you all that is necessary in two minutes.'

'Certainly,' said Richard, yielding to his curiosity. 'I have only two or three minutes. I dine here with a friend, who is at this moment ordering dinner; so, you see, I am rather hurried.'

He opened a door, and looking in said—

'Yes, we shall be quite to ourselves here.'

Longcluse shut the door. There was no one to overhear them.

Richard Arden sat down on a sofa, and Mr. Longcluse threw himself into a chair.

'And what did he say?' asked Richard.

'They want to raise his interest on the Yorkshire estate; and he says you won't help him; but that of course is your affair, and I declined, point-blank, to intervene in it. And before I go further, it strikes me, as it did today at Mortlake, that your manner to me has undergone a slight change.'

'Has it? I did not mean it, I assure you,' said Richard Arden, with a little laugh.

'Oh! yes, Arden, it *has,* and you must know it, and—pardon me—you must *intend* it also; and now I want to know what I have done, or how I have hurt you, or who has been telling lies of me?'

'Nothing of all these, that I know of,' said Richard, with a cold little laugh.

'Well, of course, if you prefer it, you may decline an explanation. I must however, remind you, because it concerns my happiness, and possibly other interests dearer to me than my life, too nearly to be trifled with, that you heard all I said respecting your sister with the friendliest approbation and encouragement. You knew as much and as little about me then as you do now. I am not conscious of having said or done anything to warrant the slightest change in your feelings or opinion; and in your manner there *is* a change, and a very decided change, and I tell you frankly I can't understand it.'

Thus directly challenged, Richard Arden looked at him hard for a moment. He was balancing in his mind whether he should evade or accept the crisis. He preferred the latter.

'Well, I can only say I did not intend to convey anything by my manner; but, as you know, when there is anything in one's mind it is not always easy to prevent its affecting, as you say, one's manner. I am not sorry you have asked me, because I spoke without reflection the other day. No one should answer, I really think, for anyone else, in ever so small a matter, in this world.'

'But you didn't—you spoke only for yourself. You simply promised me your friendship, your kind offices—you said, in fact, all I could have hoped for.'

'Yes, perhaps—yes, I may, I suppose I did. But don't you see, dear Longcluse, things may come to mind, on thinking over.'

'*What* things?' demanded Longcluse quickly, with a sudden energy that called a flush to his temples; and fire gleamed for a moment from his deep-set, gloomy eyes.

'What things? Why, young ladies are not always the most intelligible problems on earth. I think you ought to know that; and really I do think, in such matters, it is far better that they should be left to themselves as much as possible; and I think, besides, that there are some difficulties that did not strike us. I mean, that I now see that there really are great difficulties—insuperable difficulties.'

'Can you define them?' said Longcluse coldly.

'I don't want to vex you, Longcluse, and I don't want to quarrel.'

'That's extremely kind of you.'

'I don't know whether you are serious, but it is quite true. I don't wish any unpleasantness between us. I don't think I need say more than that; having thought it over, I don't see how it could ever be.'

'Will you give me your reasons?'

'I really don't see that I can add anything in particular to what I have said.'

'I think, Mr. Arden, considering all that has passed between us on this subject, that you are *bound* to let me know your reasons for so marked a change of opinion.'

'I can't agree with you, Mr. Longcluse. I don't see in the least why I need tell you my particular reasons for the opinion I have expressed. My sister can act for herself, and I certainly shall not account to you for my reasons or opinions in the matter.'

Mr. Longcluse's pale face grew whiter, and his brows knit, as he fixed a momentary stare on the young man; but he mastered his anger, and said in a cold tone—

'We disagree totally upon that point, and I rather think the time will come when you *must* explain.' 'I have no more to say upon the subject, Sir, except this,' said Arden, very tartly, 'that it is certain your hopes can never lead to anything, and that I object to your continuing your visits at Mortlake.'

'Why, the house does not belong to you it—belongs to Sir Reginald Arden, who objects to your visits and receives mine. Your ideas seem a little confused,' and he laughed gently and coldly.

'Very much the reverse, Sir. I object to my sister being exposed to the least chance of annoyance from your visits. I protest against it, and you will be so good as to understand that I distinctly forbid them.'

'The young lady's father, I presume, will hardly ask your advice in the matter, and *I* certainly shall not ask your leave. I shall call when I please, so long as I am received at Mortlake, and shall direct my own conduct, without troubling you for counsel in my affairs.' Mr. Longcluse laughed again icily.

'And so shall I, mine,' said Arden sharply.

'You have no right to treat anyone so,' said Longcluse angrily—'as if one had broken his honour, or committed a crime.'

'A crime!' repeated Richard Arden. 'Oh! *That,* indeed, would pretty well end all relations.'

'Yes, as, perhaps, you shall find,' answered Longcluse, with sudden and oracular ferocity.

Each gentleman had gone a little farther than he had at first intended. Richard Arden had a proud and fierce temper when it was roused. He was near saying what would have amounted to insult. It was a chance opening of the door that prevented it. Both gentlemen had stood up.

'Please, Sir, have you done with the room, Sir?' asked the man.

'Yes,' said Longcluse, and laughed again as he turned on his heel.

'Because three gentlemen want the room, if it's not engaged,

Sir. And Lord Wynderbroke is waiting for you, please, Mr. Arden.'

So with a little toss of his head, which he held unusually high, and a flushed and 'glooming' countenance, Richard Arden marched a little swaggeringly forth, to his dinner *tête-à-tête* with Lord Wynderbroke.

Stories About Mr. Longcluse

The irritation of this unpleasant interview soon subsided, but Mr. Longcluse's anxiety rather increased.

Next day early in the afternoon he drove to Lady May's and she received him just as usual. He learned from her, without appearing to seek the information, that Alice Arden was still at Mortlake. His visit was one of but two or three minutes. He jumped into a hansom and drove out to Mortlake. He knocked. Man of the world as he was, his heart beat faster.

'Is Miss Arden at home?'

'No, Sir.'

'Not at home?'

'Miss Arden is gone out, Sir.'

'Oh! perhaps in the garden?'

'No, Sir; she has gone out, and won't be back for some time.'

The man spoke with the promptitude and decision of a servant instructed to deny his mistress to the visitor. He had not a card; he would call again another day.

He heard the piano faintly, and, he thought, Alice's voice also; and certainly he saw Vivian Darnley in the drawing-room window, as his cab turned away from the door. With a swelling heart he drove into town. The portcullis, then, had fallen; access was denied him; and he should see her no more!

Good Heaven! what had he done? He walked distractedly, for a while, up and down his study. Should he employ Lady May's intervention, and tell her the whole story? Good-natured Lady May! Perhaps she would undertake his cause, and plead for his re-admission. But was even that so certain? How could he tell what view she might take of the matter? And were she to intercede for him ever so vehemently, how could he tell that she had any chance of prevailing?

No; on the whole it was better to be his own advocate. He would sit down then and there, and write to the offended or alarmed lady, and lay his piteous case before her in his own words and rely on her compassion, without an intervenient.

How many letters he began, how many he even finished, and rejected, I need not tire you by telling. Some were composed in the first, others in the third person. Not one satisfied him. Here was the man of a million and more, who would dash off a note to his stock-broker, to buy or sell a hundred thousand pounds' worth of stock—who would draft a resolution of the bank of which he was the chairman, directing an operation which would make men open their eyes, without the tremor of a nerve or the hesitation of a moment—unmanned, helpless, distracted in the endeavour to write a note to a young and inexperienced girl!

O beautiful sex! what a triumph is here! O Love! what fools will you not make of us poor masculine wiseacres! The letter he dispatched was in these terms. I daresay he had torn better ones to pieces:—

> Dear Miss Arden,—
>
> I had hoped that my profound contrition might have atoned for a momentary indiscretion—the declaration, though in terms the most respectful, of feelings which I had not self command sufficient to suppress, and which had for nearly a year remained concealed in my own breast. I am sure, Miss Arden, that you are incapable of a gratuitous cruelty. Have I not sworn that one word to recall the remembrance of that, to me, all but fatal madness shall never escape my lips, in your presence? May I not entreat that you will forget it, that you will forbear to pass upon me the agonising sentence of exclusion? You shall never again have to complain of my uttering one word that the merest acquaintance, who is permitted the happiness of conversing with you, might not employ. You shall

never regret your forbearance.

I shall never cease to bless you for it; and whatever decision you arrive at, it shall be respected by me as sacred law. I shall never cease to reverence and bless the hand that spares or—afflicts me. May I be permitted this one melancholy hope, may I be allowed to interpret your omitting to answer this miserable letter as a concession of its prayer? Unless forbidden, I will endeavour to construe your silence as oblivion.

I have the honour to remain, dear Miss Arden, with deep compunction and respect, but not altogether without hope in your mercy,

Yours the most unhappy and distracted man in England,

Walter Longcluse.

Mr. Longcluse sealed this letter in its envelope, and addressed it. He would have liked to send it that moment, by his servant, but an odd shyness prevented. He did not wish his servants to conjure and put their heads together over it; he could not endure the idea; so with his own hand he dropped it in the post. Somewhat in the style of the old novel was this composition of Mr. Longcluse's—a little theatrical, and, one would have fancied, even affected; yet never was man more desperately sincere.

Night came, and brought no reply. Was no news good news, or would the morning bring, perhaps from Richard Arden, a withering answer? Morning came, and no answer: what was he to conjecture?

That day, in Grosvenor Square, he passed Richard Arden, who looked steadily and sternly a little to his right, and *cut* him.

It was a marked and decided cut. His ears tingled as if he had received a slap in the face. So things had assumed a very decided attitude indeed! Longcluse felt very oddly enraged, at first; then anxious. It was insulting that Richard Arden should have taken the initiative in dissolving relations. But had he not been himself studiously impertinent to Arden, in that brief colloquy of yesterday? He ought to have been prepared for this. Without explanation, and the shaking of hands, it was impossible that relations of amity should have been resumed between them. But Longcluse had been entirely absorbed by a threatened alienation that affected him much more nearly. There was a thesis for conjecture in the situation, which made him still more anxious. A very little time would probably clear all up.

He was walking homeward, saying to himself as he went, 'No, I shall find no answer; I should be a fool to fancy anything else;' and yet walking all the more quickly, as he approached his house, in the hope of the very letter which he affected, to himself, to have quite rejected as an impossibility. Some letters had come, but none from Mortlake. His letter to Alice was still unanswered. He was now in the agony of suspense and distraction.

The same evening Richard Arden was talking about him, as he leaned with his elbow on the mantelpiece at Mortlake. He and Alice were alone in the drawing-room, awaiting the arrival of the little dinner-party. This, as you know, was to include Lord Wynderbroke, before whose advances, in Richard Arden's vision, Mr. Longcluse had waned, and even become an embarrassment and a nuisance.

'It is easier to cut him than to explain,' thought Richard Arden. 'It bores one so inexpressibly, giving reasons for what one does, and I'm so glad he has saved me the trouble by his vulgar impertinence.'

They had talked for some time, Alice chiefly a listener. How was she affected toward Mr. Longcluse? He was agreeable; he flattered her; he was passionately in love with her. All but this latter condition she liked very well; but this was embarrassing, and quite impracticable. Who knows what that tiny spark we term a fancy, a whim, a *penchant* might have grown to, had it not been blown away by this untimely gust? But, for my part, I don't think it ever would have grown to a matter of the heart. There was something in the way. A fancy is one thing, and passion quite another. Pique is a common state of mind, and comes and goes, and comes again, in many a courtship. But a liking that has once entered the heart cannot be torn out in a hasty moment, and takes a long time, and many a struggle, to kill.

She was a little sorry, just then, to lose him so inevitably. Perhaps his letter, to which he had trusted to move her, had rendered the return of old relations impossible. In this letter she felt herself the owner of a secret—a secret which she could not keep without a sort of understanding growing up between them—which therefore she had no idea of keeping.

She was resolved to tell it. The letter she had locked, in marked isolation, as if no property of hers, but simply a document that was in her keeping, in the pretty ormolu casket that stood on the drawing-room chimney-piece. She had intended showing it, and telling the story of the scene in the garden, to Richard. But he was speaking with a mysterious asperity of Mr. Longcluse, which made her hesitate. A very little thing, it seemed to her, might suffice to make a very violent quarrel out of a coldness. Instinctively, therefore, she refrained, and listened to Richard while, with his arm touching the casket on the chimney-piece, he descanted on the writer of the unknown letter.

She experienced an odd feeling of insecurity as, in the course of his talk, his fingers began to trifle with the pretty fingers that stood out in relief upon the casket; for she knew that the ordeal of the pistol, discountenanced in England, was still in force on the Continent, and Mr. Longcluse's ideas were all Continental; and how near were those fingers to the letter which might suffice to explode the dangerous element that had already accumulated!

'He has talked of us to his low companions; he chooses to associate with usurers and worse people; and he has been speaking of us in the most insolent terms.'

'Really!' said Alice. Her large eyes looked larger as they fixed on him.

'Yes, and I'll tell you how I heard it. You must know, dear Alice, that I happened to want a little money; and when one does, the usual course is to borrow it. So I paid a visit to my harpy—and a harpy in need is a harpy indeed. Being hard up, he fleeced me; and the gentleman, I suppose, thinking he might be familiar, told me he was on confidential terms with Mr. Longcluse and wished me a good deal of joy. 'Of what?' I ventured to ask, for he had just hit me rather hard. 'Of your chance,' or, as he called it *chanshe*, he said, with a delightfully arch leer. I thought he meant I had backed the right horse for the Derby, but it turned out he meant our chance of inducing Mr. Longcluse to make up his mind to marry you. I was very near knocking him down; but a man who has one's bill for three hundred pounds must be respected. So I merely ventured to ask on whose authority he congratulated me, when it appeared it was on Mr. Longcluse's own, who, it seems, had said a great deal more, equally intolerable. In plain, coarse terms, he says that, being poor, we have conspired with you to secure him, Mr. Longcluse, for your husband. As to the fact of his having actually conveyed that, and to more people than one, there is and can be no doubt whatever. I can imagine, considering all things, nothing more vulgar, audacious, and cowardly.'

A blush of anger glowed in Alice's face. Richard Arden liked the proud fire that gleamed from her dark grey eyes. It satisfied him that his words were not lost.

'I lighted on a man who knew more about him than I had learned before,' resumed Richard Arden. 'He was suspected at Berlin of having been engaged in a conspiracy to pigeon Dacre and Wilmot, who were travelling. He did not appear, but he is said to have supplied the money, and had a lion's share of the spoil. There is no good in repeating these things generally, you know, because they are so hard to prove; and a fellow like that is dangerous. They say he is very litigious.'

'Upon my word, if your information is at all to be relied on, it is plain we *have* made a great mistake. It is a disappointing world, but I could not have fancied him doing anything so low; and I must say for him that he was gentlemanlike and quiet, and very unlike the person he appears to be. I think I never heard of anything so outrageous! Vivian Darnley told me that he was a great duellist, and thought to be a very quarrelsome, dangerous companion abroad. But he had only heard this, and what you tell me is so much worse, so mean, so utterly intolerable!'

'Oh! There's worse than that,' said Richard, with a faint sinister smile.

'What?' said she, returning it with an almost frightened gaze.

'There was a very beautiful girl at the opera in Vienna; her name was Piccardi, a daughter of a good old Roman family. You can't imagine how admired she was! And she was thought to be on the point of marrying Count Baddenoff; Mr. Longcluse, it seems, chose to be in love with her; he was not then anything like so rich as he became afterwards—and this poor girl was killed.'

'Good heavens! Richard—what can you mean?'

'I mean that she was assassinated, and that from that day Mr. Longcluse was never received in society in Vienna, and had to leave it.'

'You ought to tell May Penrose,' said she, after a silence of dismay.

'Not for the world,' said Richard; 'she talks enough for six—and where's the good? She'll only take up the cudgels for him, and we shall be in the centre of a pretty row.'

'Well, if you think it best——' she began.

'Certainly,' said he. And a silence followed.

'Here is a carriage at the door,' said Richard Arden. 'Let us dismiss Longcluse, and look a little more like ourselves.'

That evening there came letters as usual to Mr. Longcluse, and among others a note from Lady Mary Penrose, reminding him of her little garden-party at Richmond next day.

'By Jove!' he exclaimed, starting up and reading the cards on his chimney, 'I thought it was the day after. It was very good-natured, poor old thing, her reminding me. I shall see Alice Arden there. Not one line does she vouchsafe. But is not she right? I think the more highly of her for not writing. I don't think she ought to write. Oh, Heaven grant she may meet me as usual? Does she mean it? If she did not, would she not have got her brother to write, or have written herself a cold line, to end our acquaintance?'

So he tried to comfort himself, and to keep alive his dying

hope by these artificial stimulants.

The Garden Party

Next morning Mr. Longcluse rose with a sense of something before him.

'So I shall see her today! If she's the girl I've thought her, she will meet me as usual. That frantic scene, in which I risked all on the turn of a die, will be forgotten. Hasty words, or precipitate letters, are passed over every day; the man who commits such follies, under a transitory insanity, is allowed the privilege of recalling them. There were no witnesses present to make forgiveness difficult. It all lies with her own good sense, and a heart proud but gentle. Let but those mad words be sponged out, and I am happy. Alice, if you forgive me, I forgive your brother, and take his name from where it is, and write it in my heart. Oh, beautiful Alice! will you belie your looks? Oh, clear bright mind! will you be clouded and perverted? Oh, gentle heart! can you be merciless?'

Mr. Longcluse made his simple morning toilet very carefully. A very plain man, extremely ugly some pronounce him; yet his figure is good, his get-up unexceptionable, and altogether he is a most gentlemanlike man to look upon, and in his movements and attitudes, quite unstudied, there is an undefinable grace. His accent is a little foreign—he slightest thing in the world, and Lady May Penrose declares it is so very pretty. Then he is so agreeable, when he pleases; and he is so very rich!

Some people wonder why he does not withdraw from all speculations, retire upon his enormous wealth, and with his elegant tastes, and the art of being magnificent without glare, even gorgeous without vulgarity—for has he not shown this refined talent in the service of others, who have taken him into council?—he could eclipse all the world in splendid elegance, and make his way, *force d'argent,* to the pinnacle of half the world's ambition. Were those stories true that Richard Arden told his sister on the night before?

I don't think that Richard Arden stuck at trifles, where he

had an object to gain, and I don't believe a word of his story of Mr. Longcluse's insulting talk. It was not his way to boast and vapour; and he had a secret contempt for many of the Jewish and other agents whom he chose to employ. But undoubtedly Mr. Longcluse had the reputation among his discounting admirers of being a dangerous man to quarrel with; and also it was true that he had fought three or four savage duels in the course of his Continental life. There were other stories, unauthenticated, unpleasant. There were whispered with sneers by Mr. Longcluse's enemies. But there's a divinity doth hedge a King Croesus, and his character bore a charmed life, among the missiles that would have laid that of many a punier man in the dust.

With an agitated heart, Mr. Longcluse approached the pretty little place known as Raleigh Court, to which he had been invited. Through the quaint, old-fashioned gateway, under the embowering branches of tall trees, he drove up a short, broad avenue, clumped at each side with old timber, to the open hall-door of the pretty Elizabethan house. Carriages of all sorts were discernible under the branches, assembled at the further side to the right of the hall-door, over the wide steps of which was spread a scarlet cloth. Croquet parties were already visible on the shorn grass, under boughs that spread high in the air, and cast a pleasant shadow on the sward. Groups were strolling among the flower-beds—some walking in, some emerging from the open door—and the scene presented the usual variety of dress, and somewhat listless to-ing and fro-ing.

Did anyone, of all the guests of Lady May, mask so profound an agitation, under the conventional smile, as that which beat at Walter Longcluse's heart? Two or three people whom he knew, he met and talked to—some for a minute, others for a longer time—as he drew near the steps. His eye all the time was busy in the search after one pretty figure, the least glimpse of which he would have recognised with the thrill of a sure intuition, far or near. He would have liked to ask the friends he met whether the Ardens were here. But what would have been easy to him a week before, was now an effort for which he could not find courage.

He entered the hall, quaint and lofty, rising to the entire height of the house, with two galleries, one above the other, surrounding it on three sides. Ancestors of the late Mr. Penrose, who had left all this and a great deal more to his sorrowing relict, stood on the panelled walls at full length—some in ruffs and trunk-hose, others in *perukes* and cut-velvet, one with a *bâton* in his hand, and three with falcon on fist—all stately and gentlemanlike, according to their several periods; with corresponding ladies, some stiff and pallid, who figured in the days of the virgin queen, and others in the graceful *déshabille* of Sir Peter Lely. This quaint oak hall was now resonant with the buzz and clack of modern gossip, prose, and flirtation, and a great deal crowded, notwithstanding its commodious proportions. Lady May was still receiving her company near the doorway of the first drawing-room, and her kindly voice was audible from within as the visitor approached. Mr. Longcluse was very graciously received.

'I want you so particularly, to introduce you to Lady Hummington. She is such a charming person. She is so thoroughly up in German literature. She's a great deal too learned for me, but you and she will understand one another so perfectly, and you will be quite charmed with her. Mr. Addlings, did you happen to see Lady Hummington, or have you any idea where she's gone?'

'I shall go and look for her, with pleasure. Is not she the tall lady with grey hair? Shall I tell her you want to say a word to her?'

'You're very kind, but I'll not mind, thank you very much. It is so provoking, Mr. Longcluse! you would have been perfectly charmed with her.'

'I shall be more fortunate, by-and-by, perhaps,' said Mr. Longcluse. 'Are any of our friends from Mortlake here?' he added, looking a little fixedly in her eyes, for he was thinking whether Alice had betrayed his secret, and was trying to read an answer there.

Lady May answered quite promptly—

'Oh, yes, Alice is here, and her brother. He went out that way with some friends,' she said, indicating with a little nod a door which, from a second hall, opened on a terrace. 'I asked him to show them the three fountains. You must see them also; they are in the Dutch garden; they were put up in the reign of George the First.—How d'ye do, Mrs. Frumply? How dye do, Miss Frumply?'

'What a charming house!' exclaims Mrs. Frumply, 'and what a day! We were saying, Arabella and I, as we drove out, that you must really have an influence with the clerk of the weather, ha, ha, ha! didn't we, Arabella? So charming!'

Lady May laughed affably, and said— 'Won't you and your daughter go in and take some tea? Mr. (she was going to call on Longcluse, but he had glided away)—Oh, Mr. Darnley!'

And the introduction was made, and Vivian Darnley, with Mrs. Frumply on his arm, attended by her daughter Arabella, did as he was commanded and got tea for that simpering lady, and fruit and Naples biscuits, and plum-cake, and was rewarded with the original joke about the clerk of the weather.

Mr. Longcluse, in the meantime, had passed the door indicated by Lady May, and stood upon the short terrace that overlooked the pretty flower-garden cut out in grotesque patterns, so that looking down upon its masses of crimson, blue, and yellow, as he leaned on the balustrade, it showed beneath his eye like a wide deep-piled carpet, on the green ground of which were walking groups of people, the brilliant hues of the ladies' dresses rivalling the splendour of the verbenas, and making altogether a very gay picture.

The usual paucity of male attendance made Mr. Longcluse's task of observation easy. He was looking for Richard Arden's well-known figure among the groups, thinking that probably Alice was not far off. But he was not there, nor was Alice; and Walter Longcluse, gloomy and lonely in this gay crowd, descended the steps at the end of this terrace, and sauntered round again to the front of the house, now and then passing someone he knew, with an exchange of a smile or a bow, and then lost again in the Vanity Fair of strange faces and voices.

Now he is at the hall door—he mounts the steps. Suddenly, as he stands upon the level platform at top, he finds himself within four feet of Richard Arden. He looks on him as he might on the carved pilaster, at the side of the hall door; no one could have guessed, by his inflexible but unaffected glance, that he and Mr. Arden had ever been acquainted. The younger man showed something in his countenance, a sudden hauteur, a little elevation of the chin, a certain sternness, more melodramatic, though less effective, than the simple blank of Mr. Longcluse's glance.

That gentleman looked about coolly. He was in search of Miss Arden, but he did not see her. He entered the hall again, and Richard Arden a little awkwardly resumed his conversation, which had suddenly subsided into silence on Longcluse's appearance.

By this time Lady May was more at ease, having received all her company that were reasonably punctual, and in the hall Longcluse now encountered her.

'Have you seen Mr. Arden?' she inquired of him.

'Yes, he's at the door, at the steps.'

'Would you mind telling him kindly that I want to say a word to him?'

'Certainly, most happy,' said Longcluse, without any distinct plan as to how he was to execute her awkward commission.

'Thank you very much. But, oh! dear, here is Lady Hummington, and she wishes so much to know you; I'll send someone else. I must introduce you, come with me—Lady Hummington, I want to introduce my friend, Mr. Longcluse.'

So Mr. Longcluse was presented to Lady Hummington, who was very lean, and a 'blue,' and most fatiguingly well up in archaeology, and all new books on dry and difficult subjects. So that Mr. Longcluse felt that he was, in *Joe Willett's* phrase, 'tackled' by a giant, and was driven to hideous exertions of attention and memory to hold his own. When Lady Hummington, to whom it was plain kind Lady May, with an unconscious cruelty, had been describing Mr. Longcluse's accomplishments and acquirements, had taken some tea and other refection, and when Mr. Longcluse's kindness 'had her wants supplied,' and she, like Scott's 'old man' in the *Lay of the Last Minstrel*, 'was gratified,' she proposed visiting the music-room, where she had heard a clever organist play, on a harmonium, three distinct tunes at the same time, which being composed on certain principles, that she explained with much animation and precision, harmonised very prettily.

So this clever woman directed, and Mr. Longcluse led, the way to the music-room.

He Sees Her

Mr. Longcluse's attention was beginning to wander a little, and his eyes were now busy in search of someone whom he had not found; and knowing that the duration of people's stay at a garden-party is always uncertain, and that some of those gaily-plumed birds who make the nutter, and chirping, and brilliancy of the scene, hardly alight before they take wing again, he began to fear that Alice Arden had gone.

'Just like my luck!' he thought bitterly; 'and if she is gone, when shall I have an opportunity of seeing her again?'

Lady Hummington's well-informed conversation had been, unheeded, accompanying the ruminations and distractions of this 'passionate pilgrim;' and as they approached the door of the music-room, the little crush there brought the learned lady's lips so near to his ear, that with a little start he heard the words—'All strictly arithmetical, you know, and adjusted by the relative frequency of vibrations. That theory, I am sure, you approve, Mr. Longcluse.'

To which the distracted lover made answer, 'I quite agree with you, Lady Hummington.'

The music-room at Raleigh Court is an apartment of great size, and therefore when, with Lady Hummington on his arm, he entered, it was at no great distance that he saw Miss Arden standing near the window, and talking with an elderly gentleman, whose appearance he did not know, but who seemed to be extremely interested in her conversation. She saw him, he had not a doubt, for she turned a little quickly and looked ever so little more directly out at the window, and a very slight tinge flushed her cheek. It was quite plain, he thought, and a dreadful pang stole through his breast, that she did not choose to see him—quite plain that she did see him—and he thought, from a subtle scrutiny of her beautiful features, quite plain also that it gave her pain to meet without acknowledging him.

Lady Hummington was conversing with volubility; but the air felt icy, and there was a strange trembling at his heart, and this, in many respects, hard man of the world, felt that the tears were on the point of welling from his eyes. The struggle was but for a few moments, and he seemed quite himself again. Lady Hummington wished to go to the end of the room where the piano was, and the harmonium on which the organist had performed his feat of the three tunes. That artist was taking his departure, having a musical assignation of some kind to keep. But to oblige Lady Hummington, who had heard of Thalberg's doing something of the kind, he sat down and played an elaborate piece of music on the piano with his thumbs only. This charming effort over, and applauded, the performer took his departure. And Lady Hummington said—

'I am told, Mr. Longcluse, that you are a very good musician.'

'A very indifferent performer, Lady Hummington.'

'Lady May Penrose tells a very different tale.'

'Lady May Penrose is too kind to be critical,' said Longcluse; and as he maintained this dialogue, his eye was observing every movement of Alice Arden. She seemed, however, to have quite made up her mind to stand her ground. There was a strange interest, to him, even in being in the same room with her. Perhaps Miss Arden saw that Mr. Longcluse's movements were dependent upon those of the lady whom he accompanied, and might have thought that, the musician having departed, their stay in that room would not be very long.

'I should be so glad to hear you sing, Mr. Longcluse,' pursued

Lady Hummington. 'You have been in the East, I think; have you any of the Hindostanee songs? There are some, I have read, that embody the theories of the Brahmin philosophy.'

'Long-winded songs, I fancy,' said Mr. Longcluse, laughing; 'it is a very voluminous philosophy, but the truth is, I've got a little cold, and I should not like to make a bad impression so early.'

'But surely there are some simple little things, without very much compass, that would not distress you. How pretty those old English songs are that they are collecting and publishing now! I mean songs of Shakespeare's time—Ben Jonson's, Beaumont and Fletcher's, and Massinger's, you know. Some of them are so extremely pretty!'

'Oh! yes, I'll sing you one of those with pleasure,' said he with a strange alacrity, quite forgetting his cold, sitting down at the instrument, and striking two or three fierce chords.

I am sure that most of my readers are acquainted with that pretty old English song, of the time of James the First, entitled, *Once I Loved a Maiden Fair.* That was the song he chose.

Never, perhaps, did he sing so well before, with a fluctuation of pathos and scorn, tenderness and hatred, expressed with real dramatic fire, and with more power of voice than at moments of less excitement he possessed. He sang it with real passion, and produced, exactly where he wished, a strange but unavowed sensation. He omitted one verse, and the song as he delivered it was thus:—

Once I loved a maiden fair,
But she did deceive me:
She with Venus could compare,
In my mind, believe me.
She was young, and among
All our maids the sweetest:
Now I say, Ah, well-a-day,
Brightest hopes are fleetest.

Maidens wavering and untrue
Many a heart have broken;

Sweetest lips the world e'er knew
Falsest words have spoken.
Fare thee well, faithless girl,
I'll not sorrow for thee:
Once I held thee dear as pearl,
Now I do abhor thee.

When he had finished the song, he said coldly, but very distinctly, as he rose—

'I like that song, there is a melancholy psychology in it. It is a song worthy of Shakespeare himself.'

Lady Hummington urged him with an encore, but he was proof against her entreaties. And so, after a little, she took Mr. Longcluse's arm; and Alice felt relieved when the room was rid of them.

About the Grounds

Lady Hummington, well pleased at having found in Mr. Longcluse what she termed a kindred mind, was warned by the hour that she must depart. She took her leave of Mr. Longcluse with regret, and made him promise to come to luncheon with her on the Thursday following. Mr. Longcluse called her carriage for her, and put in, besides herself, her maiden sister and two daughters, who all exhibited the family leanness, with noses more or less red and aquiline, and small black eyes, set rather close together.

As he ascended the steps he was accosted by a damsel in distress.

'Mr. Longcluse, I'm so glad to see you! You must do a very good-natured thing,' said handsome Miss Maubray, smiling on him. 'I came here with old Sir Arthur and Lady Tramway, and I've lost them; and I've been bored to death by a Mr. Bagshot, and I've sent him to look for my pocket-handkerchief in the tea-room; and I want you, as you hope for mercy, to show it now, and rescue me from my troubles.'

'I'm too much honoured. I'm only too happy, Miss Maubray. I shall put Mr. Bagshot to death, if you with it, and Sir Arthur and Lady Tramway shall appear the moment you command.'

Mr. Longcluse was talking his nonsense with the high spirits which sometimes attend a painful excitement.

'I told them I should get to that tree if I were lost in the crowd, and that they would be sure to find me under it after six o'clock. Do take me there; I am so afraid of Mr. Bagshot's returning!'

So over the short grass that handsome girl walked, with Mr Longcluse at her side.

'I'll sit at this side, thank you; I don't want to be seen by Mr. Bagshot.'

So she sat down, placing herself at the further side of the great trunk of the old chestnut-tree. Mr. Longcluse stood nearly opposite, but so placed as to command a view of the hall-door steps. He was still watching the groups that emerged, with as much interest as if his life depended on the order of their to-ing and fro-ing. But, in spite of this, very soon Miss Maubray's talk began to interest him.

'Whom did Alice Arden come with?' asked Miss Maubray. 'I should like to know; because, if I should lose my people, I must find someone to take me home.'

'With her brother, I fancy.'

'Oh! yes, to be sure—I saw him here. I forgot. But Alice's very independent, just now, of his protection,' and she laughed.

'How do you mean?'

'Oh! Lord Wynderbroke, of course, takes care of her while she's here. I saw them walking about together, so happy! I suppose it is all settled.'

'About Lord Wynderbroke?' suggested Longcluse, with a gentle carelessness, as if he did not care a farthing—as if a dreadful pain had not at that moment pierced his heart.

'Yes, Lord Wynderbroke. Why, haven't you heard of that?'

'Yes, I believe—I think so. I am sure I have heard something of it; but one hears so many things, one forgets, and I don't know him. What kind of man is he?'

'He's hard to describe; he's not disagreeable, and he's not dull;

he has a great deal to say for himself about pictures, and the East, and the Crimea, and the opera, and all the people at all the courts in Europe, and he ought to be amusing; but I think he is the driest person I ever talked to. And he is really good-natured; but I think him much more teasing than the most ill-natured man alive, he's so insufferably punctual and precise.'

'You know him very well, then?' said Longcluse, with an effort to contribute his share to the talk.

'Pretty well,' said the young lady, with just a slight tinge flushing her haughty cheek 'But no one, who has been a week in the same house with him, could fail to see all that.'

Miss Maubray herself, I am told, had hopes of Lord Wynderbroke about a year before, and was not amiably disposed towards him now, and looked on the triumph of Alice a little sourly; although something like the beginning of a real love had since stolen into her heart—not, perhaps, destined to be much more happy.

'Lord Wynderbroke—I don't know him. Is that gentleman he whom I saw talking to Miss Arden in the music-room, I wonder? He's not actually thin, and he is not at all stout; he's a little above the middle height, and he stoops just a little. He appears past fifty, and his hair looks like an old-fashioned brown wig, brushed up into a sort of cone over his forehead. He seems a little formal, and very polite and smiling, with a flower in his button-hole; a blue coat; and he has a pair of those little gold Paris glasses, and was looking out through the window with them.'

'Had he a high nose?'

'Yes, rather a thin, high nose, and his face is very brown.'

'Well, if he was all that, and had a brown face and a high nose, and was pretty near fifty-three, and very near Alice Arden, he was positively Lord Wynderbroke.'

'And has this been going on for some time, or is it a sudden thing?'

'Both, I believe. It has been going on a long time, I believe, in old Sir Reginald's head; but it has come about, after all, rather suddenly; and my guardian says—Mr. David Arden, you know—that he has written a proposal in a letter to Sir Reginald, and you see how happy the young lady looks. So I think we may assume that the course of true love, for once, runs smooth—don't you?'

'And I suppose there is no objection anywhere?' said Longcluse, smiling. 'It is a pity he is not a little younger, perhaps.'

'I don't hear any complaints; let us rather rejoice he is not ten or twenty years older. I am sure it would not prevent his happiness, but it would heighten the ridicule. Are you one of Lady May Penrose's party to the Derby tomorrow?' inquired the young lady.

'No; I haven't been asked.'

'Lord Wynderbroke is going.'

'Oh! of course he is.'

'I don't think Mr. David Arden likes it; but, of course, it is no business of his if other people are pleased. I wonder you did not hear all this from Richard Arden, you and he are so intimate.'

So said the young lady, looking very innocent. But I think she suspected more than she said.

'No, I did not hear it,' he said carelessly; 'or, if I did, I forgot it. But do you blame the young lady?'

'Blame her! not at all. Besides, I am not so sure that she knows.'

'How can you think so?'

'Because I think she likes quite another person.'

'Really! And who is he?'

'Can't you guess?'

'Upon my honour, I can't.'

There was something so earnest, and even vehement, in this sudden asseveration, that Miss Maubray looked for a moment in his face; and seeing her curious expression, he said more quietly, 'I assure you I don't think I ever heard; I'm rather curious to know.'

'I mean Mr. Vivian Darnley.'

'Oh! Well, I've suspected that a long time. I told Richard Arden, one day—I forget how it came about but he said no.'

'Well, I say yes,' laughed the young lady, 'and we shall see who's right.'

'Oh! Recollect I'm only giving you his opinion. I rather lean to yours, but he said there was positively nothing in it, and that Mr. Darnley is too poor to marry.'

'If Alice Arden resembles me,' said the young lady, 'she thinks there are just two things to marry for—either love or ambition.'

'You place love first, I'm glad to hear,' said Mr. Longcluse, with a smile.

'So I do, because it is most likely to prevail with a pig-headed girl; but what I mean is this: that social pre-eminence—I mean rank, and not trumpery rank; but such as, being accompanied with wealth and precedence, is also attended with power—is worth an immense sacrifice of all other objects; my reason tells me, worth the sacrifice of love. But that is a sacrifice which impatient, impetuous people can't always so easily make—which I daresay I could not make if I were tried; but I don't think shall ever be fool enough to become so insane, for the state of a person in love is a state of simple idiotism. It is pitiable, allow, but also contemptible; but, judging by what I see, it appears to me a more irresistible delusion than ambition. But I don't understand Alice well. I think, if I knew a little more of her brother—certain qualities so run in families—I should able to make a better guess. What do you think of him?'

'He's very agreeable, isn't he? and, for the rest, really, until men are tried as events only can try them, it is neither wise nor safe to pronounce.'

'Is he affectionate?'

'His sister seems to worship him,' he answered; 'but young ladies are so angelic, that where they like they resent nothing, and respect selfishness itself as a manly virtue.'

'But you know him intimately; surely you must know something of him.'

Under different circumstances, this audacious young lady's

cross-examination would have amused Mr. Longcluse; but in his present relations, and spirits, it was otherwise.

'I should but mislead you if I were to answer more distinctly. I answer for no man, hardly for myself. Besides, I question your theory. I don't think, except by accident, that a brother's character throws any light upon a sister's; and I hope—I think, I mean—that Miss Arden has qualities illimitably superior to those of her brother. Are these your friends, Miss Maubray?' he continued.

'So they are,' she answered. 'I'm so much obliged to you, Mr. Longcluse! I think they are leaving.'

Mr. Longcluse, having delivered her into the hands of her chaperon, took his leave, and walked into the broad alleys among the trees , and in solitude under their shade, sat himself down by a pond, on which two swans were sailing majestically. Looking down upon the water with a pallid frown, he struck the bank beneath him viciously with his heel, peeling off little bits of the sward, which dropped into the water.

'It is all plain enough now. Richard Arden has been playing me false. It ought not to surprise me, perhaps. The girl, I still believe, has neither act nor part in the conspiracy. She has been duped by her brother. I have thrown myself upon her mercy; I will now appeal to her *justice.* As for him—what vermin mankind are! He must return to his allegiance; he will. After all, he may not like to lose me. He will act in the way that most interests his selfishness. Come, come! it is no impracticable problem. I'm not cruel? Not I! No, I'm not cruel; but I am utterly just. I would not hang a mouse up by the tail to die, as they do in France, head downwards, of hunger, for eating my cheese; but should the vermin nibble at my heart, in that case, what says justice?

'Alice, beautiful Alice, you shall have every chance before I tear you from my heart—oh, forever! Ambition! That coarse girl, Miss Maubray, can't understand you. Ambition, in her sense, you have none; there is nothing venal in your nature. Vivian Darnley, is there anything in that either? I think nothing. I observed them closely, that night, at Mortlake. No, there was nothing. My conversation and music interested her, and when I was by, he was nothing.'

'They are going to the Derby tomorrow. I think Lady May has treated me rather oddly, considering that she had all but borrowed my drag. She might have put me off civilly; but I don't blame her. She is good-natured, and if she has any idea that I and the Ardens are not quite on pleasant terms, it quite excuses it. Her asking me here, and her little note to remind, were meant to show that she did not take up the quarrel against me. Never mind; I shall know all about it, time enough. They are going to the Derby tomorrow. Very well, I shall go also. It will all be right yet. When did I fail? When did I renounce an object? By Heaven, one way or other, I'll accomplish this!'

Tall Mr. Longcluse rose, and looked round him, and in deep thought, marched with a resolute step towards the house.

Under the Lime-Trees

At this garden-party, marvellous as it may appear, Lord Wynderbroke has an aunt. How old she is I know not, nor yet with what conscience her respectable relations can permit her to haunt such places, and run a risk of being suffocated in doorways, or knocked down the steps by an enamoured couple hurrying off to more romantic quarters, or of having her maundering old head knocked with a croquet mallet, as she totters drearily among the hoops.

This old lady is worth conciliating, for she has plate and jewels, and three thousand a-year to leave; and Lord Wynderbroke is a prudent man. He can bear a great deal of money, and has no objection to jewels, and thinks that the plate of his bachelor and old-maid kindred should gravitate to the centre and head of the house. Lord Wynderbroke was indulgent, and did not object to her living a little longer, for this aunt conduced to his air of juvenility more than the flower in his button-hole. However, she was occasionally troublesome, and on this occasion made an unwise mixture of fruit and other things; and a servant glided into the music-room, and with a proper inclination of his person, in a very soft tone said,—

'My lord, Lady Witherspoons is in her carriage at the door, my lord, and says her ladyship is indisposed, and begs, my lord, that your lordship will be so good as to hacompany her 'ome in her carriage, my lord.'

'Oh! tell her ladyship I am so *very* sorry, and will be with her in a moment.' And he turned with a very serious countenance to Alice. 'How extremely unfortunate! When I saw those miserable cherries, I knew how it would be; and now I am torn away from this charming place; and I'm sure I hope she may be better soon, it *is* so (disgusting, he thought, but he said) melancholy! With whom shall I leave you, Miss Arden?'

'Thanks, I came with my brother, and here is my cousin, Mr. Darnley, who can tell me where he is.'

'With a croquet party, near the little bridge. I'll be your guide, if you'll allow me,' said Vivian Darnley eagerly.

'Pray, Lord Wynderbroke, don't let me delay you longer. I shall find my brother quite easily now. I so hope Lady Witherspoons may soon be better!'

'Oh, yes, she always *is* better soon; but in the meantime one is carried away, you see, and everything upset; and all because, poor woman, she won't exercise the smallest restraint. And she has, of course, a right to command me, being my aunt, you know, and—and—the whole thing is ineffably provoking.'

And thus he took his reluctant departure, not without a brief but grave scrutiny of Mr. Vivian Darnley. When he was gone, Vivian Darnley proffered his arm, and that little hand was placed on it, the touch of which made his heart beat faster. Though people were beginning to go, there was still a crush about the steps. This little resistance and mimic difficulty were pleasant to him for her sake. Down the steps they went together, and now he had her all to himself; and silently for a while he led her over the closely-shorn grass, and into the green walk between the lime-trees, that leads down to the little bridge.

'Alice,' at last he said— 'Miss Arden, what have I done that you are so changed?'

'Changed! I don't think I am changed. What is there to change me?' she said carelessly, but in a low tone, as she looked along towards the flowers.

'It won't do, Alice, repeating my question, for that is all you have done. I like you too well to be put off with mere words. You are changed, and without a cause—no, I could not say that—not without a cause. Circumstances are altered; you are in the great world now, and admired; you have wealth and titles at your feet—Mr. Longcluse with his millions, Lord Wynderbroke with his coronet.'

'And who told you that these gentlemen were at my feet?' she exclaimed, with a flash from her fine eyes, that reminded him of moments of pretty childish anger, long ago. 'If I am changed—and perhaps I am—such speeches as that would quite account for it. You accuse me of caprice—has anyone ever accused you of impertinence?'

'It is quite true, I deserve your rebuke. I have been speaking as freely as if we were back again at Arden Court, or Ryndelmere, and ten years of our lives were *as a mist that rolls away*.'

'That's a quotation from a song of Tennyson's.'

'I don't know what it is from. Being melancholy myself, I say the words because they are melancholy.'

'Surely you can find some friend to console you in your affliction.'

'It is not easy to find a friend at any time, much less when things go wrong with us.'

'It is very hard if there is really no one to comfort you. Certainly *I* sha'n't try anything so hopeless as comforting a person who is resolved to be miserable. *There's such a charm in melancholy, I would not if I could, be gay*. There's a quotation for you, as you like verses—particularly what I call moping verses.'

'Come, Alice! this is not like you; you are not so unkind as your words would seem; you are not cruel, Alice—you are cruel to no one else, only to me, your old friend.'

'I have said nothing cruel,' said Miss Alice, looking on the grass before her; 'cruelty is too sublime a phrase. I don't think I have ever experienced cruelty in my life; and I don't think it likely that you have; I certainly have never been cruel to anyone. I'm a very good-natured person, as my birds and squirrel would testify if they could.'

She laughed.

'I suppose people call that cruel which makes them suffer very much; it may be but a light look, or a cold word, but still it may be more than years of suffering to another. But I don't think, Alice, you ought to be so with me. I think you might remember old times a little more kindly.'

'I remember them very kindly—as kindly as you do. We were always very good friends, and always, I daresay, shall be. *I* sha'n't quarrel. But I don't like heroics, I think they are so unmeaning. There may be people who like them very well and —— There is Richard, I think, and he has thrown away his mallet. If his game is over, he will come now, and Lady May doesn't want the people to stay late; she is going into town, and I stay with her tonight. We are going to the Derby tomorrow.'

'I am going also—it was so kind of her!—she asked me to be of her party,' said Vivian Darnley.

'Richard is coming also; I have never been to the Derby, and I daresay we shall be a very pleasant party; I know I like it of all things. Here comes Richard—he sees me. Was my uncle David here?'

'No.'

'I hardly thought he was, but I saw Grace Maubray, and I fancied he might have come with her,' she said carelessly.

'Yes, she was here; she came with Lady Tramways. They went away about half-an-hour ago.' So Richard joined her, and they walked to the house together, Vivian Darnley accompanying them.

'I think I saw you a little spooney today, Vivian, didn't I?' said Richard Arden, laughing. He remembered what Longcluse once said to him, about Vivian's *tendre* for his sister, and did not choose that Alice should suspect it. 'Grace Maubray is a very pretty girl.'

'She may be that, though it doesn't strike me,' began Darnley.

'Oh! come, I'm too old for that sort of disclaimer; and I don't see why you should be so modest about it. She is clever and pretty.'

'Yes, she is very pretty,' said Alice.

'I suppose she is, but you're quite mistaken if you really fancy I admire Miss Maubray. I *don't,* I give you my *honour,* I don't,' said Vivian vehemently.

Richard Arden laughed again, but prudently urged the point no more, intending to tell the story that evening as he and Alice drove together into town, in the way that best answered his purpose.

The Derby

The morning of the Derby day dawned auspiciously. The weather-cocks, the sky, and every other prognostic portended a fine cloudless day, and many an eye peeped early from bed-room window to read these signs, rejoicing.

'Ascot would have been more in *our* way,' said Lady May, glancing at Alice, when the time arrived for taking their places in the carriage. 'But the time answered, and we shall see a great many people we know there. So you must not think I have led you into a very fast expedition.'

Richard Arden took the reins. The footmen were behind, in charge of hampers from Fortnum and Mason's, and inside, opposite to Alice, sat Lord Wynderbroke; and Lady May's *vis-à-vis* was Vivian Darnley. Soon they had got into the double stream of carriages of all sorts. There are closed carriages with pairs or fours, gigs, hansom cabs fitted with gauze curtains, dog-carts, open carriages with hampers lashed to the foot-boards, dandy drags, bright and polished, with crests; vans, cabs, and indescribable contrivances. There are horses worth a hundred and fifty guineas a-piece, and there are others that look as if the knacker should have them. There are all sorts of raws, and sand-cracks, and broken knees. There are kickers and roarers, and bolters and jibbers, such a crush and medley in that densely packed double line, that jogs and crushes along you can hardly tell how.

Sometimes one line passes the other, and then sustains a momentary check, while the other darts forward; and now and then a panel is smashed, with the usual altercation, and dust unspeakable eddying and floating everywhere in the sun; all sorts of chaff exchanged, mail-coach horns blowing, and general impudence and hilarity; gentlemen with veils on, and ladies with light hoods over their bonnets, and all sorts of gauzy defences against the dust. The utter novelty of all these sights and sounds highly amuses Alice, to whom they are absolutely strange.

'I am so amused,' she said, 'at the gravity you all seem to take these wonderful doings with. I could not have fancied anything like it. Isn't that Borrowdale?' 'So it is,' said Lady May. 'I thought he was in France. He doesn't see us, I think.'

He did see them, but it was just as he was cracking a personal joke with a busman, in which the latter had decidedly the best of it, and he did not care to recognise his lady acquaintances at disadvantage.

'What a fright that man is!' said Lord Wynderbroke.

'But his team is the prettiest in England, except Longcluse's,' said Darnley; 'and, by Jove, there's Longcluse's drag!'

'Those are very nice horses,' said Lord Wynderbroke looking at Longcluse's team, as if he had not heard Darnley's observation. 'They are worth looking at, Miss Arden.'

Longcluse was seated on the box, with a veil on, through which his white smile was indistinctly visible.

'And what a fright *he* is, also! He looks like a picture of Death I once saw, with a cloth half over his face; or the Veiled Prophet. By Jove, a curious thing that the two most hideous men in England should have between them the two prettiest teams on earth!'

Lord Wynderbroke looks at Darnley with raised brows, vaguely. He has been talking more than his lordship perhaps thinks he has any business to talk, especially to Alice.

'You will be more diverted still when we have got upon the

course,' interposes Lord Wynderbroke. 'The variety of strange people there—gipsies, you know, and all that—mountebanks, and thimble-riggers, and beggars, and musicians—you'll wonder how such hordes could be collected in all England, or where they come from.'

'And although they make something of a day like this, how on earth they contrive to exist all the other days of the year when people are sober, and minding their own business,' added Darnley.

'To me the pleasantest thing about the drive is our finding ourselves in the open country. Look out of the window there—trees and farmsteads—it is so rural, and such an odd change!' said Lady May.

'And the young corn, I'm glad to see, is looking very well' said Lord Wynderbroke, who claimed to be something of an agriculturist.

'And the oddest thing about it is our being surrounded, in the midst of all this rural simplicity, with the population of London,' threw in Vivian Darnley.

'Remember, Miss Arden, our wager,' said Lord Wynderbroke; 'you have backed May Queen.'

'May! she should be a cousin of mine,' said good Lady May, firing off her little pun, which was received very kindly by her audience.

'Ha, ha! I did not think of that; she should certainly be the most popular name on the card,' said Lord Wynderbroke. 'I hope I have not made a great mistake, Miss Arden, in betting against so—so auspicious a name.'

'I sha'n't let you off, though. I'm told I'm very likely to win—isn't it so?' she asked Vivian.

'Yes, the odds are in favour of May Queen now; you might make a capital hedge.'

'You don't know what a hedge is, I daresay. Miss Arden; ladies don't always quite understand our turf language,' said Lord Wynderbroke, with a consideration which he hoped that very forward young man, on whom he fancied Miss Arden looked good-naturedly, felt as he ought. 'It is called a hedge, by betting men, when——' and he expounded the meaning of the term.

The road had now become more free, as they approached the course, and Dick Arden took advantage of the circumstance to pass the omnibuses, and other lumbering vehicles, which he soon left far behind. The grand stand now rose in view—and now they were on the course. The first race had not yet come off, and young Arden found a good place among the triple line of carriages. Off go the horses! Miss Arden is assisted to a cushion on the roof; Lord Wynderbroke and Vivian take places beside her. The sun is growing rather hot, and the parasol is up.

Good-natured Lady May is a little too stout for climbing, but won't hear of anyone's staying to keep her company. Perhaps when Richard Arden, who is taking a walk by the ropes, and wants to see the horses which are showing, returns, she may have a little talk with him at the window. In the meantime, all the curious groups of figures, and a hundred more, which Lord Wynderbroke promised—the monotonous challenges of the fellows with games of all sorts, the whine of the beggar for a little penny, the guitarring, singing, barrel-organing, and the gipsy inviting Miss Arden to try her lucky sixpence—all make a curious and merry Babel about her.

A Sharp Colloquy

In foot, near the weighing stand, is a tall, powerful, and clumsy fellow, got up gaudily—a fellow with a lowering red face, in loud good-humour, very ill-looking. He is now grinning and chuckling with his hands in his pockets, and talking with a little Hebrew, young, sable-haired, with the sallow tint, great black eyes, and fleshy nose that characterise his race. A singularly sullen mouth aids the effect of his vivid eyes, in making this young Jew's face ominous.

'Young Dick Harden's 'ere,' said Mr. Levi.

'Eh? is he?' said the big man with the red face and pimples, the green cut-away coat, gilt buttons, purple neck-tie, yellow waistcoat, white cord tights, and top boots.

'Walking down there,' said Levi, pointing with his thumb

over his shoulder. 'I shaw him shpeak to a fellow in chocolate and gold livery.'

'And an eagle on the button, I know. That's Lady May Penrose's livery,' said his companion. 'He came down with her, I lay you fifty. And he has a nice sister as ever you set eyes on—pretty gal, Mr. Levi—a reg'lar little angel,' and he giggled after his wont. 'If there's a dragful of hangels anyvere, she's one of them. I saw her yesterday in one of Lady May Penrose's carriages in St. James' Street. Mr. Longcluse is engaged to get married to her; you may see them linked arm-in-arm, any day you please, walkin' hup and down Hoxford Street. And her brother, Richard Harden, is to marry Lady May Penrose. That will be a warm family yet, them Hardens, arter all.'

'A family with a title, Mr. Ballard, be it never so humble, Sir, like 'ome shweet 'ome, hash nine livesh in it; they'll be down to the last pig, and not the thickness of an old tizzy between them and the glue-pot; and while you'd write your name across the back of a cheque, all's right again. The title doesh it. You never shaw a title in the workus yet, Mr. Ballard, and you'll wait awhile before you 'av a hoppertunity of shayin', 'My lord Dooke, I hope your grashe's water-gruel is salted to your noble tasht thish morning,' or, 'My noble marquishe, I humbly hope you are pleashed with the fit of them pepper-and-salts;' and, 'My lord earl, I'm glad to see by the register you took a right honourable twisht at the crank thish morning.' No, Mishter Ballard, you nor me won't shee that, Shir.'

While these gentlemen enjoyed their agreeable banter, and settled the fortunes of Richard Arden and Mr. Longcluse, the latter person was walking down the course in the direction in which Mr. Levi had seen Arden go, in the hope of discovering Lady May's carriage. Longcluse was in an odd state of excitement. He had entered into the spirit of the carnival. Voices all around were shouting, 'Twenty to five on Dotheboys;' or, 'A hundred to five against Parachute.'

'In what?' called Mr. Longcluse to the latter challenge.

'In assassins!' cried a voice from the crowd.

Mr. Longcluse hustled his way into the thick of it.

'Who said that?' he thundered.

No one could say. No one else had heard it. Who cared? He recovered his coolness quickly, and made no further fuss about it. People were too busy with other things to bother themselves about his questions, or his temper. He hurried forward after young Arden, whom he saw at the turn of the course a little way on.

'The first race no one cares much about; compared with the great event of the day, it is as the farce before the pantomime, or the oyster before the feast.'

The bells had not yet rung out their warning, and Alice said to Vivian,—

'How beautifully that girl with the tambourine danced and sang! I do so hope she'll come again; and she is, I think, so perfectly lovely. She is so like the picture of La Esmeralda; didn't you think so?'

'Do you really wish to see her again?' said Vivian. 'Then if she's to be found on earth you shall see her.'

He was smiling, but he spoke in the low tone that love is said to employ and understand, and his eyes looked softly on her. He was pleased that she enjoyed everything so. In a moment he had jumped to the ground, and with one smile back at the eager girl he disappeared.

And now the bells were ringing, and the police clearing the course. And now the cry, 'They're off, they're off!' came rolling down the crowd like a hedge-fire. Lord Wynderbroke offered Alice his race-glass, but ladies are not good at optical aids, and she prefers her eyes; and the Earl constitutes himself her sentinel, and will report all he sees, and stands on the roof beside her place, with the glasses to his eyes. And now the excitement grows. Beggar-boys, butcher-boys, stable-helps, jump up on carriage-wheels unnoticed, and cling to the roof with filthy fingers. And now they are in sight, and a wild clamour arises. 'Red's first!' 'No, Blue!' 'White leads!' 'Pink's first!'

And here they are! White, crimson, pink, black, yellow—the

silk jackets quivering like pennons in a storm—the jockeys tossing their arms madly about, the horses seeming actually to fly; swaying, reeling, whirring, the whole thing passes in a beautiful drift of a moment, and is gone!

Lord Wynderbroke is standing on tiptoe, trying to catch a glimpse of the caps as they show at the opening nearer the winning-post. Vivian Darnley is away in search of La Esmeralda. Miss Arden has seen the first race of the day, the first she has ever seen, and is amazed and delighted. The intruders who had been clinging to the carriage now jump down, and join the crowd that crush on towards the winning-post, or break in on the course. But there rises at the point next her a figure she little expected to see so near that day. Mr. Longcluse has swung himself up, and stands upon the wheel. He is bare-headed, his hat is in the hand he clings by. In the other hand he holds up a small glove—a lady's glove. His face is very pale. He is not smiling; he looks with an expression of pain, on the contrary, and very great respect.

'Miss Arden, will you forgive my venturing to restore this glove, which I happened to see you drop as the horses passed?'

'She looked at him with something of surprise and fear, and drew back a little instead of taking the proffered glove.

'I find I have been too presumptuous,' he said gently. 'I place it there. I see, Miss Arden, I have been maligned. Someone has wronged me cruelly. I plead only for a fair chance—for God's sake, give me a chance. I don't say hear me now, only say you won't condemn me utterly unheard.'

He spoke vehemently, but so low that, amid the hubbub of other voices, no one but Miss Arden, on whom his eyes were fixed, could hear him.

'I take my leave, Miss Arden, and may God bless you. But I rest in the hope that your noble nature will refuse to treat any creature as my enemies would have you treat me.'

His looks were so sad and even reverential, and his voice though low, so full of agony, that no one could suppose the speaker had the least idea of forcing his presence upon the lady a moment longer than sufficed to ascertain that it was not welcome. He was about to step to the ground, when he saw Richard Arden striding rapidly up with a very angry countenance. Then and there seemed likely to occur what the newspapers term an ungentlemanlike fracas. Richard Arden caught him, and pulled him roughly to the ground. Mr. Longcluse staggered back a step or two, and recovered himself. His pale face glared wickedly, for a moment or two, on the flushed and haughty young man; his arm was a little raised, and his fist clenched. I daresay it was just the turn of a die, at that moment, whether he struck him or not.

These two bosom friends, and sworn brothers, of a week or two ago, were confronted now with strange looks, and in threatening attitude. How frail a thing is the worldly man's friendship, hanging on flatteries and community of interest! A word or two of truth, and a conflict or even a divergence of interest, and where is the liking, the friendship, the intimacy?

A sudden change marked the face of Mr. Longcluse. The vivid fires that gleamed for a moment from his eyes sunk in their dark sockets, the intense look changed to one of sullen gloom. He beckoned, and said coldly, 'Please follow me;' and then turned and walked, at a leisurely pace, a little way inward from the course.

Richard Arden, perhaps, felt that had he hesitated it would have reflected on his courage. He therefore disregarded the pride that would have scorned even a seeming compliance with that rather haughty summons, and he followed him with something of the odd dreamy feeling which men experience when they are stepping, consciously, into a risk of life. He thought that Mr. Longcluse was inviting the interview for the purpose of arranging the preliminaries of who were to act as their 'friends,' and where each gentleman was to be heard of that evening. He followed, with oddly conflicting feelings, to a place in the rear of some tents. Here was a sort of booth. Two doors admitted to it—one to the longer room, where was whirling that roulette round which men who, like Richard Arden, could not deny themselves, even on the meanest scale, the excitement of chance gain and loss, were betting and bawling. Into the smaller room of plank, which was now empty, they stepped.

'Now, Sir, you'll be so good as to observe that you have taken upon you a rather serious responsibility in laying your hand on me,' said Longcluse, in a very low tone, coldly and gently. 'In France, such a profanation would be followed by an exchange of shots, and here, under other circumstances, I should exact the same chance of retaliation. I mean to deal differently—quite differently. I have fought too many duels, as you know, to be the least apprehensive of being misunderstood or my courage questioned. For your sister's sake, not yours, I take a peculiar course with you. I offer you an alternative; you may have reconciliation—here is my hand' (he extended it)— 'or you may abide the other consequence, at which I sha'n't hint, in pretty near futurity. You don't accept my hand?'

'No, Sir,' said Arden haughtily—more than haughtily, insolently. 'I can have no desire to renew an acquaintance with you. I sha'n't do that. I'll fight you, if you like it. I'll go to Boulogne, or wherever you like, and we can have our shot, Sir, whenever you please.'

'No, if you please—not so fast. You decline my friendship—that offer is over,' said Longcluse, lowering his hand resolutely. 'I am not going to shoot you—I have not the least notion of that. I shall take, let me see, a different course with you, and I shall obtain on reflection your entire concurrence with the hopes I have no idea of relinquishing. You will probably understand me pretty clearly by-and-by.'

Richard Arden was angry; he was puzzled; he wished to speak, but could not light quickly on a suitable answer. Longcluse stood for some seconds, smiling his pale sinister smile upon him, and then turned on his heel, and walked quietly out upon the grass, and disappeared in the crowd.

Richard Arden was irresolute. He threw open the door, and entered the roulette-room—looked round on all the strange faces, that did not mind him, or seem to see that he was there—

then, with a sudden change of mind, he retraced his steps more quickly, and followed Longcluse through the other door. But there he could not trace him. He had quite vanished. Perhaps, next morning, he was glad that he had missed him, and had been compelled to 'sleep upon it.'

Now and then, with a sense of disagreeable uncertainty, recurred to his mind the mysterious intimation, or rather menace, with which he had taken his departure. It was not, however, his business to look up Longcluse. He had himself seemed to intimate that the balance of insult was the other way. If 'satisfaction,' in the slang of the duellist, was to be looked for the initiative devolved undoubtedly upon Longcluse.

Alice was so placed on the carriage, that she did not see what passed immediately beside it, between Longcluse and her brother. Still, the appearance of this man, and his having accosted her, had agitated her a good deal, and for some hour the unpleasant effect of the little scene spoiled her enjoyment of this day of wonders.

Very gaily, notwithstanding, the party returned—except, perhaps, one person who had reason to remember that day.

Dinner at Mortlake

Lady May's party from the Derby dined together late, that evening, at Mortlake. Lord Wynderbroke, of course, was included. He was very happy, and extremely agreeable. When Alice, and Lady May, who was to stay that night at Mortlake, and Miss Maubray, who had come with Uncle David, took their departure for the drawing-room, the four gentlemen who remained over their claret drew more together, and chatted at their ease.

Lord Wynderbroke was in high spirits. He admired Alice more than ever. He admired everything. A faint rumour had got about that something was not very unlikely to be. It did not displease him. He had been looking at diamonds the day before; he was not vexed when that amusing wag, Pokely, who had surprised him in the act, asked him that day, on the Downs, some sly questions on the subject, with an arch glance at beautiful

Miss Arden. Lord Wynderbroke pooh-pooh'd this impertinence very radiantly. And now this happy peer, pleased with himself, pleased with everybody, with the flush of a complacent elation on his thin cheeks, was simpering and chatting most agreeably, and commending everything to which his attention was drawn.

In very marked contrast with this happy man was Richard Arden, who talked but little, was absent, utterly out of spirits, and smiled with a palpable effort when he did smile. His conversation with Lady May showed the same uncomfortable peculiarities. It was intermittent and bewildered. It saddened the good lady. Was he ill? or in some difficulty?

Now that she had withdrawn, Richard Arden seemed less attentive to Lord Wynderbroke than to his uncle. In so far as a wight in his melancholy mood could do so, he seemed to have laid himself out to please his uncle in those small ways where, in such situations, an anxiety to please can show itself. Once his father's voice had roused him with the intimation, 'Richard, Lord Wynderbroke is speaking to you;' and he saw a very urbane smile on his thin lips, and encountered a very formidable glare from his dark eyes. The only subject on which Richard Arden at all brightened up was the defeat of the favourite. Lord Wynderbroke remarked,—

'It seems to have caused a good deal of observation. I saw Hounsley and Crackham, and they shake their heads at it a good deal, and——'

He paused, thinking that Richard Arden was going to interpose something, but nothing followed, and he continued,—

'And Lord Shillingsworth, he's very well up in all these things, and he seems to think it is a very suspicious affair; and old Sir Thomas Fetlock, who should have known better, has been hit very hard, and says he'll have it before the Jockey Club.'

'I don't mind Sir Thomas, he blusters and makes a noise about everything,' said Richard Arden; 'but it was quite palpable, when the horse showed, he wasn't fit to run. I don't suppose Sir Thomas will do it, but it certainly will be done. I know a dozen men who will sell their horses, if it isn't done. I don't see how any man can take payment of the odds on Dotheboys—I don't, I assure you—till the affair is cleared up: *gentlemen*, of course, I mean; the other people would like the money all the better if it came to them by a swindle. But it certainly can't rest where it is.'

No one disputing this, and none of the other gentlemen being authorities of any value upon turf matters, the subject dropped, and others came on, and Richard Arden was silent again. Lord Wynderbroke, who was to pass two or three days at Mortlake, and who had made up his mind that he was to leave that interesting place a *promesso sposo*, was restless, and longed to escape to the drawing-room. So the sitting over the wine was not very long.

Richard Arden made an effort, in the drawing-room, to retrieve his character with Lady May and Miss Maubray, who had been rather puzzled by his hang-dog looks and flagging conversation.

'There are times, Lady May,' said he, placing himself on the sofa beside her, 'when one loses all faith in the future—when everything goes wrong, and happiness becomes incredible. Then one's wisest course seems to be, to take off one's hat to the good people in this planet, and go off to another.'

'Only that I know you so well,' said Lady May, 'I should tell Reginald—I mean your father—what you say; and I think your uncle, there, is a magistrate for the county of Middlesex, and could commit you, couldn't he? for any such foolish speech. Did you observe today—you saw him, of course—how miserably ill poor Pindledykes is looking? I don't think, really, he'll be alive in six months.'

'Don't throw away your compassion, dear Lady May. Pindledykes has always looked dying as long as I can remember, and on his last legs; but those last legs carry some fellows a long way, and I'm very sure he'll outlive me.'

'And what pleasure can a person so very ill as he looks take in going to places like that?'

'The pleasure of winning other people's money,' laughed Arden sourly. 'Pindledykes knows very well what he's about. He turns his time to very good account, and wastes very little of it, I assure you, in pitying other people's misfortunes.'

'I'm glad to see that you and Richard are on pleasanter terms,' said David Arden to his brother, as he sipped his tea beside him.

'Egad! we are *not,* though. I hate him worse than ever. Would you oblige me by putting a bit of wood on the fire? I told you how he has treated me. I wonder, David, how the devil you could suppose we were on pleasanter terms!'

Sir Reginald was seated with his crutch-handled stick beside him, and an easy fur slipper on his gouty foot, which rested on a stool, and was a great deal better. He leaned back in a cushioned arm-chair, and his fierce prominent eyes glanced across the room, in the direction of his son, with a flash like a scimitar's.

'There's no good, you know, David, in exposing one's ulcers to strangers—there's no use in plaguing one's guests with family quarrels.'

'Upon my word, you disguised this one admirably, for I mistook you for two people on tolerably friendly terms.'

'I don't want to plague Wynderbroke about the puppy; there is no need to mention that he has made so much unhappiness. *You* won't, neither will I.' David nodded.

'Something has gone wrong with him,' said David Arden, 'and I thought you might possibly know.'

'Not I.'

'I think he has lost money on the races today,' said David.

'I hope to Heaven he has! I'm glad of it. It will do me good; let him settle it out of his blackguard post-obit' snarled Sir Reginald, and ground his teeth.

'If he has been gambling, he has disappointed me. He can, however, disappoint me but once. I had better thoughts of him.'

So said David Arden, with displeasure in his frank and manly face.

'Playing? Of course he plays, and of course he's been making a blundering book for the Derby. He likes the hazard-table and the turf, he likes play, and he likes making books; and what he likes he does. He always did. I'm rather pleased you have been trying to manage him. You'll find him a charming person, and you'll understand what I have had to combat with. He'll never do any good; he is so utterly graceless.'

'I see my father looking at me, and I know what he means,' said Richard Arden, with a smile, to Lady May; 'I'm to go and talk to Miss Maubray. He wishes to please Uncle David, and Miss Maubray must be talked to; and I see that Uncle David envies me my little momentary happiness, and meditates taking that empty chair beside you. You'll see whether I am right. By Jove! here he comes; I sha'n't be turned away so——'

'Oh, but, really, Miss Maubray has been quite alone,' urged poor Lady May, very much pleased; 'and you *must,* to please *me;* I'm sure you will.'

Instantly he arose.

'I don't know whether that speech is most kind or *un*-kind; you banish me, but in language so flattering to my loyalty, that I don't know whether to be pleased or pained. Of course I obey.' He said these parting words in a very low tone, and had hardly ended them, when David Arden took the vacant chair beside the good lady, and began to talk with her.

Once or twice his eyes wandered to Richard Arden, who was by this time talking with returning animation to Grace Maubray, and the look was not cheerful. The young lady, however, was soon interested, and her good-humour was clever and exhilarating. I think that she a little admired this handsome and rather clever young man, and who can tell what such a fancy may grow to?

That night, as Richard Arden bid him goodbye, his uncle said, coldly enough,—

'By-the-bye, Richard, would you mind looking in upon me tomorrow, at five in the afternoon? I shall have a word to say to you.'

So the appointment was made, and Richard entered his cab, and drove into town dismally.

Mr. Longcluse Sees a Lady's Note

Next day Mr. Longcluse paid an early visit at Uncle David's house, and saw Miss Maubray in the drawing-room. The transition from that young lady's former, to her new life, was not less dazzling than that of the heroine of an Arabian tale, who is transported by friendly genii, while she sleeps, from a prison to the palace of a sultan. Uncle David did not care for finery; no man's tastes could be simpler and more camp-like. But these drawing-rooms were so splendid, so elegant and refined, and yet so gorgeous in effect, that you would have fancied that he had thought of nothing else all his life but china, *marqueterie*, buhl, Louis Quatorze clocks, mirrors, pale-green and gold cabriole chairs, bronzes, pictures, and all the textile splendours, the names of which I know not, that make floors and windows magnificent.

The feminine nature, facile and self-adapting, had at once accommodated itself to the dominion over all this, and all that attended it. And Miss Maubray being a lady, a girl who had, in her troubled life, been much among high-bred people—her father a gentle, fashionable, broken-down man, and her mother a very elegant and charming woman—there was no contrast, in look, air, or conversation, to mark that all this was new to her: on the contrary, she became it extremely.

The young lady was sitting at the piano when Longcluse came in, and to the expiring vibration of the chord at which she was interrupted she rose, with that light, floating ascent which is so pretty, and gave him her hand, and welcomed him with a very bright smile. She thought he was a likely person to be able to throw some light upon two rumours which interested her.

'How do you contrive to keep your rooms so deliciously cool? The blinds are down and the windows open, but that alone won't do, for I have just left a drawing-room that is very nearly insupportable; yours must be the work of some of those pretty sylphs that poets place in attendance upon their heroines. How fearfully hot yesterday was! You did not go to the Derby with Lady May's party, I believe.'

He watched her clever face, to discover whether she had heard of the scene between him and Richard Arden—'I don't think she has.'

'No,' she said, 'my guardian, Mr. Arden, took me there instead. On second thoughts, I feared I should very likely be in the way. One is always *de trop* where there is so much love-making; and I am a very bad gooseberry.'

'A very dangerous one, I should fancy. And who are all these lovers?'

'Oh, really, they are so many, it is not easy to reckon them up. Alice Arden, for instance, had *two* lovers—Lord Wynderbroke and Vivian Darnley.'

'What, two lovers charged upon one lady? Is not that false heraldry? And does she really care for that young fellow, Darnley?'

'I'm told she really is deeply attached to him. But that does not prevent her accepting Lord Wynderbroke. He has spoken, and been accepted. Old Sir Reginald told my guardian his brother, last night, and *he* told me in the carriage, as we drove home. I wonder how soon it will be. I should rather like to be one of her bridesmaids. Perhaps she will ask me.'

Mr. Longcluse felt giddy and stunned; but he said, quite gaily—

'If she wishes to be suitably attended, she certainly will. But young ladies generally prefer a foil to a rival, even when so very beautiful as she is.'

'And there was Vivian Darnley at one side I'm told, whispering all kinds of sweet things, and poor old Wynderbroke at the other, with his glasses to his eyes, reporting all he saw. Only think! What a goose the old creature must have looked!' And the young lady laughed merrily. 'But can you tell me about the other affair?' she asked.

'What is it?'

'Oh! you know, of course—Lady May and Richard Arden; is it true that it was all settled the day before yesterday, at that kettle-drum?'

'There again my information is quite behind yours. I did not hear a word of it.'

'But you must have seen how very much in love they both are! Poor young man! I really think it would have broken his heart if she had been cruel, particularly if it is true that he lost so much as they say at the Derby yesterday. I suppose he did. Do you know?'

'I'm sorry to say,' said Mr. Longcluse, 'I'm afraid it's only too true. I don't know exactly how much it is, but I believe it is more than he can, at present, very well bear. A mad thing for him to do. I'm really sorry, although he has chosen to quarrel with me most unreasonably.'

'Oh? I wasn't aware. I fancied you would have heard all from him.'

'No, not a word—no.'

'Lady May was talking to me at Raleigh Court, the day we were there—she can talk of no one else, poor old thing!—and she said something had happened to make him and his sister very angry. She would not say what. She only said, 'You know how very proud they are, and I really think,' she said, 'they ought to have been very much pleased, for everything, I think, was most advantageous.' And from this I conclude there must have been a proposal for Alice; I shall ask her when I see her.'

'Yes, I daresay they are proud. Richard Arden told me so. He said that his family were always considered proud. He was laughing, of course, but he meant it.'

'He's proud of being proud, I daresay. I thought you would be likely to know whether all they say is true. It would be a great pity he should be ruined; but, you know, if all the rest is true, there are resources.'

Longcluse laughed.

'He has always been very particular and a little tender in that quarter; very sweet upon Lady May, I thought,' said he.

'Oh, very much gone, poor thing!' said Grace Maubray. 'I think my guardian will have heard all about it. He was very angry, once or twice, with Richard Arden about his losing so much money at play. I believe he has lost a great deal at different times.'

'A great many people do lose money so. For the sake of excitement, they incur losses, and risk even their utter ruin.'

'How foolish!' exclaimed Miss Maubray. 'Have you heard anything more about that affair of Lady Mary Playfair and Captain Mayfair? He is now, by the death of his cousin, quite sure of the title, they say.'

'Yes it must come to him. His uncle has got something wrong with his leg, a fracture that never united quite; it is an old hurt, and I'm told he is quite breaking up now. He is at Buxton, and going on to Vichy, if he lives, poor man.'

'Oh, then, there can be no difficulty now.'

'No, I heard yesterday it is all settled.'

'And what does Caroline Chambray say to that?'

And so on they chatted, till his call was ended, and Mr, Longcluse walked down the steps with his head pretty busy.

At the corner of a street he took a cab; and as he drove to Lady May's, those fragments of his short talk with Grace Maubray that most interested him were tumbling over and over in his mind. 'So they are angry, very angry; and very proud and haughty people. I had no business dreaming of an alliance with Mr. Richard Arden. Angry, he may be—he may affect to be—but I don't believe she is. And proud, is he? Proud of her he might be, but what else has he to boast of? Proud and angry—ha, ha! Angry and proud. We shall see. Such people sometimes grow suddenly mild and meek. And she has accepted Lord Wynderbroke. I doubt it. Miss Maubray, you are such a good-natured girl that, if you suspected the torture your story inflicted, you would invent it, rather than spare a fellow-mortal that pang.'

In this we know he was a little unjust.

'Well, Miss Arden, I understand your brother; I shall soon understand *you*. At present I hesitate. Alas! must I place you, too, in the schedule of my lost friends? Is it come to this?—'

Once I held thee dear as pearl,
Now I do abhor thee.

Mr. Longcluse's chin rests on his breast as, with a faint smile, he thus ruminates.

The cab stops. The light frown that had contracted his eyebrows disappears, he glances quickly up at the drawing-room windows, mounts the steps, and knocks at the hall door.

'Is Lady May Penrose at home?' he asked.

'I'll inquire, Sir.'

Was it fancy, or was there in his reception something a little unusual, and ominous of exclusion?

He was, notwithstanding, shown upstairs. Mr. Longcluse enters the drawing-room: Lady May will see him in a few minutes. He is alone. At the further end of this room is a smaller one, furnished like the drawing-room, the same curtains, carpet, and style, but much more minute and elaborate in ornamentation—an extremely pretty *boudoir.* He just peeps in. No, no one there. Then slowly he saunters into the other drawing-room, picks up a book, lays it down, and looks round. Quite solitary is this room also. His countenance changes a little. With a swift, noiseless step, he returns to the room he first entered.

There is a little *marqueterie* table, to which he directs his steps, just behind the door from the staircase, under the pretty old buhl clock that ticks so merrily with its old wheels and lever, exciting the reverential curiosity of Monsieur Racine, who keeps it in order, and comments on its antique works with a mysterious smile every time he comes, to anyone who will listen to him. The door is a little bit open. All the better, Mr. Longcluse will hear any step that approaches. On this little table lies an open note, hastily thrown there, and the pretty handwriting he has recognised. He knows it is Alice Arden's. Without the slightest scruple, this odd gentleman takes it up and reads a bit, and looks toward the door; reads a little more, and looks again, and so on to the end.

On the principle that listeners seldom hear good of themselves, Mr. Longcluse's cautious perusal of another person's letter did not tell him a pleasant tale.

What Alice Could say

The letter which Mr. Longcluse held before his eyes was destined to throw a strong light upon the character of Alice Arden's feelings respecting himself. After a few lines, it went on to say:—'And, darling, about going to you this evening, I hardly know what to say, or, I mean, I hardly know how to say it. Mr. Longcluse, you know, may come in at any moment, and I have quite made up my mind that I cannot know him.

I told you all about the incredible scene in the garden at Mortlake, and I showed you the very cool letter with which he saw fit to follow it—and yesterday the scene at the races, by which he contrived to make everything so uncomfortable—so, my dear creature, I mean to be cruel, and cut him. I am quite serious. He has not an idea how to behave himself; and the only way to repair the folly of having made the acquaintance of such an ill-bred person is, as I said, to cut him—you must not be angry—and Richard thinks exactly as I do. So, as I long to see you, and, in fact, can't live away from you very long, we must contrive some way of meeting now and then, without the risk of being disturbed by him. In the meantime, you must come more to Mortlake. It is too bad that an impertinent, conceited man should have caused me all this real vexation.'

There was but little more, and it did not refer to the only subject that interested Longcluse just then. He would have liked to read it through once more, but he thought he heard a step. He let it fall where he had found it, and walked to the window. Perhaps, if he had read it again, it would have lost some of the force which a first impression gives to sentences so terrible; as it was, they glared upon his retina, through the same exaggerating medium through which his excited imagination and feelings had scanned them at first.

Lady May entered, and Mr. Longcluse paid his respects, just as usual. You would not have supposed that anything had occurred to ruffle him. Lady May was just as affable as usual, but very much graver. She seemed to have something on her mind, and not to know how to begin.

At length, after some little conversation, which flagged once or twice—

'I have been thinking, Mr. Longcluse, I must have appeared very stupid,' says Lady May. 'I did not ask you to be one of our party to the Derby: and I think it is always best to be quite frank, and I know you like it best. I'm afraid there has been some little misunderstanding. I hope in a short time it will be all got over, and everything quite pleasant again. But some of our friends—you, no doubt, know more about it than I do, for I must confess, I don't very well understand it—are vexed at something that has occurred, and——'

Poor Lady May was obviously struggling with the difficulties of her explanation, and Mr. Longcluse relieved her.

'Pray, dear Lady May, not a word more; you have always been so kind to me. Miss Arden and her brother choose to visit me with displeasure. I have nothing to reproach myself with, except with having misapprehended the terms on which Miss Arden is pleased to place me. She may however, be very sure that I sha'n't disturb her happy evenings here, or anywhere assume my former friendly privileges.'

'But Mr. Longcluse, I'm not to lose your acquaintance,' said kindly Lady May, who was disposed to take an indulgent and even a romantic view of Mr. Longcluse's extravagances. 'Perhaps it may be better to avoid a risk of meeting, under present circumstances; and, therefore, when I'm quite sure that no such awkwardness can occur, I can easily send you a line, and you will come if you can. You will do just as it happens to answer you best at the time.'

'It is extremely kind of you, Lady May. My evenings here have been so very happy that the idea of losing them altogether would make me more melancholy than I can tell.'

'Oh, no, I could not consent to lose you, Mr. Longcluse, and I'm sure this little quarrel can't last very long. Where people are amiable and friendly, there may be a misunderstanding, but there can't be a real quarrel, I maintain.'

With this little speech the interview closed, and the gentleman took a very friendly leave.

Mr. Longcluse was in trouble. Blows had fallen rapidly upon

him of late. But, as light is polarised by encountering certain incidents of reflection and refraction, grief entering his mind changed its character.

The only articles of expense in which Mr. Longcluse indulged—and even in those his indulgence was very moderate—were horses. He was something of a judge of horses, and had that tendency to form friendships and intimacies with them which is proper to some minds. One of these he mounted, and rode away into the country, unattended. He took a long ride, at first at a tolerably hard pace. He chose the loneliest roads he could find. His exercise brought him no appetite; the interesting hour of dinner passed unimproved. The horse was tired now. Longcluse was slowly returning, and looking listlessly to his right, he thus soliloquised:—

'Alone again. Not a soul in human shape to disclose my wounds to, not a soul. This is the way men go mad. He knows too well the torture he consigns me to. How often has my hand helped him out of the penalties of the dice-box and betting-book! How wildly have I committed myself to him!—how madly have I trusted him! How plausibly has he promised. The confounded miscreant! Has he good-nature, gratitude, justice, honour? Not a particle. He has betrayed me, slandered me fatally, where only on earth I dreaded slander, and he knew it; and he has ruined the only good hope I had on earth. He has launched it: sharp and heavy is the curse. Wait: it shall find him out. And *she!* I did not think Alice Arden could have written that letter. My eyes are opened. Well, she has refused to hear my good angel; the other may speak differently.'

He was riding along a narrow old road, with palings, and quaint old hedgerows, and now and then an old-fashioned brick house, staid and comfortable, with a cluster of lofty timber embowering it, and chimney smoke curling cosily over the foliage; and as he rode along, sometimes a window, with very thick white sashes, and a multitude of very small panes, sometimes the summit of a gable appeared. The lowing of unseen cows was heard over the fields, and the whistle of the birds in the hedges;

and behind spread the cloudy sky of sunset, showing a peaceful old-world scene, in which Izaak Walton's milkmaid might have set down her pail, and sung her pretty song.

Not another footfall was heard but the clink of his own horse's hoofs along the narrow road; and, as he looked westward, the flush of the sky threw an odd sort of fire-light over his death-pale features.

'Time will unroll his book,' said Longcluse, dreamily, as he rode onward, with a loose bridle on his horse's neck, 'and my fingers will trace a name or two on the pages that are passing. That sunset, that sky—how grand, and glorious, and serene—the same always. Charlemagne saw it, and the Caesars saw it, and the Pharoahs saw it, and we see it today. Is it worth while troubling ourselves here? How grand and quiet nature is, and how beautifully imperturbable! Why not we, who last so short a time—why not drift on with it, and take the blows that come, and suffer and enjoy the facts of life, and leave its dreadful dreams untried? Of all the follies we engage in, what more hollow than revenge—vainer than wealth?'

Mr. Longcluse was preaching to himself, with the usual success of preachers. He knew himself what his harangue was driving at, although it borrowed the vagueness of the sky he was looking on. He fancied that he was discussing something with himself, which, nevertheless, was settled—so fixed, indeed, that nothing had power to alter it.

Gentlemen in Trouble

Mr. Longcluse had now reached a turn in the road, at which stands an old house that recedes a little way and has four poplars growing in front of it, two at each side of the door. There are mouldy walls, and gardens, fruit and vegetables, in the rear, and in one wing of the house the proprietor is licenced to sell beer and other refreshing drinks. This quaint greengrocery and pothouse was not flourishing, I conjecture, for a cab was at the door, and Mr Goldshed, the eminent Hebrew, on the steps, apparently on the point of leaving.

He is a short, square man, a little round shouldered. He is very bald, with coarse, black hair, that might not unsuitably stuff a chair. His nose is big and drooping, his lips large and moist. He wears a black satin waistcoat, thrust up into wrinkles by his habit of stuffing his short hands, bedizened with rings, into his trousers pockets. He has on a peculiar low-crowned hat. He is smoking a cigar, and talking over his shoulder, at intervals, in brief sentences that have a harsh, brazen ring, and are charged with scoff and menace. No game is too small for Mr. Goldshed's pursuit. He ought to have made two hundred pounds of this little venture. He has not lost, it is true; but when all is squared, he'll not have made a shilling, and that for a Jew, you know, is very hard to bear.

In the midst of this intermittent snarl, the large, dark eyes of this man lighted on Mr. Longcluse, and he arrested the sentence that was about to fly over his shoulder, in the disconsolate faces of the broken little family in the passage. A smile suddenly beamed all over his dusky features, his airs of lordship quite forsook him, and he lifted his hat to the great man with a cringing salutation. The weaker spirit was overawed by the more potent.

It was the *catape* doing homage to Mephistopheles, in the witch's chamber.

He shuffled out upon the road, with a lazy smile, lifting his hat again, and very deferentially greeted 'Mishter Longclooshe.' He had thrown away his exhausted cigar, and the red sun glittered in sparkles on the chains and jewellery that were looped across his wrinkled black satin waistcoat.

'How d'ye do, Mr. Goldshed? Anything particular to say to me?'

'Nothing, no, Mr. Longclooshe. I sposhe you heard of that dip in the Honduras?'

'They'll get over it, but we sha'n't see them so high again soon. Have you that cab all to yourself, Mr. Goldshed?'

'No, Shir, my partner'sh with me. He'll be out in a minute; he'sh only puttin' a chap on to make out an inventory.'

'Well, I don't want him. Would you mind walking down the

road here, a couple of hundred steps or so? I have a word for you. Your partner can overtake you in the cab.'

'Shertainly, Mr. Longclooshe, shertainly, Shir.'

And he halloed to the cabman to tell the 'zhentleman' who was coming out to overtake him in the cab on the road to town.

This settled, Mr. Longcluse, walking his horse along the road, and his City acquaintance by his side, slowly made their way towards the City, casting long shadows over the low fence into the field at their left; and Mr. Goldshed's stumpy legs were projected across the road in such slender proportions that he felt for a moment rather slight and elegant, and was unusually disgusted, when he glanced down upon the substance of those shadows, at the unnecessarily clumsy style in which Messrs. Shears and Goslin had cut out his brown trousers.

Mr. Longcluse had a good deal to say when they got on a little. Being earnest, he stopped his horse; and Mr. Goldshed, forgetting his reverence in his absorption, placed his broad hand on the horse's shoulder, as he looked up into Mr. Longcluse's face, and now and then nodded, or grunted a 'Surely.' It was not until the shadows had grown perceptibly longer, until Mr. Longcluse's hat had stolen away to the gilded stem of the old ash-tree that was in perspective to their left, and until Mr. Goldshed's legs had grown so taper and elegant as to amount to the spindle, that the talk ended, and Mr. Longcluse, who was a little shy of being seen in such company, bid him good evening, and rode away townward at a brisk trot.

That morning Richard Arden looked as if he had got up after a month's fever. His dinner had been a pretence, and his breakfast was a sham. His luck, as he termed it, had got him at last pretty well into a corner. The placing of the horses was a dreadful record of moral impossibilities accomplished against him. Five minutes before the start he could have sold his book for three thousand pounds; five minutes after it no one would have accepted fifteen thousand to take it off his hands. The shock, at first a confusion, had grown in the night into ghastly order. It was all, in the terms of the good old simile, 'as plain as a pikestaff.' He simply could not pay. He might sell everything he possessed, and pay about ten shillings in the pound, and then work his passage to another country, and become an Australian drayman, or a New Orleans billiard-marker.

But not pays his bets! And how could he? Ten shillings in the pound? Not five. He forgot how far he was already involved. What *was* to become of him. Breakfast he could eat none. He drank a cup of tea, but his tremors grew worse. He tried claret, but that, too, was chilly comfort. He was driven to an experiment he had never ventured before. He had a 'nip,' and another, and with this Dutch courage rallied a little, and was able to talk to his friend and admirer, Vandeleur, who had made a miniature book after the pattern of Dick Arden's and had lost some hundreds, which he did not know how to pay; and who was, in his degree, as miserable as his chief; for is it not established that—

The poor beetle, that we tread upon,
In corporal sufferance feels a pang as great
As when a giant dies?

Young Vandeleur, with light silken hair, and innocent blue eyes, found his paragon the picture of 'grim-visaged, comfortless despair,' drumming a tattoo on the window, in slippers and dressing-gown, without a collar to his shirt.

'You lost, of course,' said Richard savagely; 'you followed my lead. Any fellow that does is sure to lose.'

'Yes,' answered Vandeleur, 'I did, heavily; and, I give you my honour, I believe I'm ruined.'

'How much?'

'Two hundred and forty pounds!'

'*Ruined!* What nonsense! Who are you? or what the devil are you making such a row about? Two hundred and forty! How can you be such an ass? Don't you know it's nothing?'

'Nothing! By Jove! I wish I could see it,' said poor Van; 'everything's something to any one, when there's nothing to pay it with. I'm not like you, you know; I'm awfully poor. I have just a hundred and twenty pounds from my office, and forty my aunt gives me, and ninety I get from home, and, upon my honour, that's all; and I owed just a hundred pounds to some fellows that were growing impertinent. My tailor is sixty-four, and the rest are rifling, but they were the most impertinent, and I was so sure of this unfortunate thing that I told them I—really did—to call next week; and now I suppose it's all up with me, I may as well make a bolt of it. Instead of having any money to pay them, I'm two hundred and forty pounds worse than ever. I don't know what on earth to do. Upon my honour, I haven't an idea.'

'I wish we could exchange our accounts,' said Richard grimly: 'I wish you owed my sixteen thousand. I think you'd sink through the earth. I think you'd call for a pistol, and blow'— (he was going to say, 'your brains out,' but he would not pay him that compliment)—'blow your head off.'

So it was the old case—'*Enter Tilburina, mad, in white satin; enter her maid, mad, in white linen*.'

And Richard Arden continued—

'What's your aunt good for? You *know* she will pay that; don't let me hear a word more about it.'

'And your uncle will pay yours, won't he?' said Van, with an innocent gaze of his azure eyes.

'My uncle has paid some trifles before, but this is too big a thing. He's tired of me and my cursed misfortunes, and he's not likely to apply any of his overgrown wealth in relieving a poor tortured beggar like me. I'm simply ruined.'

Between Friends

Van was looking ruefully out of the window, down upon the deserted pavement opposite. At length he said,—

'And why don't you give your luck a chance?'

'Whenever I give it a chance it hits me so devilish hard,' replied Richard Arden.

'But I mean at play to retrieve,' said Van.

'So do I. So I did, last night, and lost another thousand. It is utterly monstrous.'

'By Jove! that is really very extraordinary,' exclaimed little Van. 'I tried it, too, last night. Tom Franklyn had some fellows to sup with him, and I went in, and they were playing too; and I lost thirty-seven pounds more!'

'Thirty-seven confounded flea-bites! Why, don't you see how you torture me with your nonsense? If you can't talk like a man of sense, for Heaven's sake, shut up, and don't distract me in my misery.'

He emphasised the word with a Lilliputian thump with the side of his fist—that which presents the edge of the doubled-up little finger and palm—a sort of buffer, which I suppose he thought he might safely apply to the pane of glass on which he had been drumming. But he hit a little too hard, or there was a flaw in the glass, for the pane flew out, touching the window-sill, and alighted in the area with a musical jingle.

'There! see what you made me do. My luck! Now we can't talk without those brutes at that open window, over the way, hearing every word we say. By Jove, it is later than I thought! I did not sleep last night.'

'Nor I, a moment,' said Van.

'It seems like a week since that accursed race, and I don't know whether it is morning or evening, or day or night. It is past four, and I must dress and go to my uncle—he said five. Don't leave me, Van, old fellow! I think I should cut my throat if I were alone.'

'Oh, no, I'll stay with pleasure, although I don't see what comfort there is in me, for I am about the most miserable dog in London.'

'Now don't make a fool of yourself anymore,' said Richard Arden. 'You have only to tell your aunt, and say that you are a prodigal son, and that sort of thing, and it will be paid in a week. I look as if I was going to be hanged—or is it the colour of that glass? I hate it. I'll leave these cursed lodgings. Did you ever see such a ghost?'

'Well, you do look a trifle seedy: you'll look better when you're dressed. It's an awful world to live in,' said poor Van.

'I'll not be five minutes; you must walk with me a bit of the way. I wish I had some fellow at my other side who had lost a hundred thousand. I daresay he'd think me a fool. They say Chiffington lost a hundred and forty thousand. Perhaps he'd think me as great an ass as I think you—who knows? I may be making too much of it—and my uncle is so very rich, and neither wife nor child; and, I give you my honour, I am sick of the whole thing. I'd never take a card or a dice-box in my hand, or back a horse, while I live, if I was once fairly out of it.

'He *might* try me, don't you think? I'm the only near relation he has on earth—I don't count my father, for he's—it's a different thing, you know—I and my sister, just. And, really, it would be nothing to him. And I think he suspected something about it last night; perhaps he heard a little of it. And he's rather hot, but he's a good-natured fellow, and he has commercial ideas about a man's going into the insolvent court; and, by Jove, you know, I'm ruined, and I don't think he'd like to see our name disgraced—eh, do you?'

'No, I'm quite sure,' said Van. 'I thought so all along.'

'Peers and peeresses are very fine in their way, and people, whenever the peers do anything foolish, and throw out a bill, exclaim 'Thank Heaven we have still a House of Lords!' but you and I, Van, may thank Heaven for a better estate, the order of aunts and uncles. Do you remember the man you and I saw in the vaudeville, who exclaims every now and then, '*Vive mon oncle! Vive ma tante!*?"

So, in better spirits, Arden prepared to visit his uncle.

'Let us get into a cab; people are staring at you,' said Richard Arden, when they had walked a little way towards his uncle's house. 'You look so utterly ruined, one would think you had swallowed poison, and were dying by inches, and expected to be in the other world before you reached your doctor's door. Here's a cab.'

They got in, and sitting side by side, said Vandeleur to him, after a minute's silence,—

'I've been thinking of a thing—why did not you take Mr.

Longcluse into council? He gave you a lift before, don't you remember? and he lost nothing by it, and made everything smooth. Why don't you look him up?'

'I've been an awful fool, Van.'

'How so?'

'I've had a sort of row with Longcluse, and there are reasons—I could not, at all events, have asked him. It would have been next to impossible, and now it is *quite* impossible.'

'Why should it be? He seemed to like you; and I venture to say he'd be very glad to shake hands.'

'So he might, but *I* shouldn't,' said Richard imperiously. 'No, no, there's nothing in that. It would take too long to tell; but I should rather go over the precipice than hold by that stay. I don't know how long my uncle may keep me. Would you mind waiting for me at my lodgings? Thompson will give you cigars and brandy and water; and I'll come back and tell you what my uncle intends.'

This appointment made, they parted, and he knocked at his uncle's door. The sound seemed to echo threateningly at his heart, which sank with a sudden misgiving.

An Interview in the Study

'Is my uncle at home?'

'No, Sir; I expect him at five. It wants about five minutes; but he desired me to show you, Sir, into the study.'

He was now alone in that large square room. The books, each in its place, in a vellum uniform, with a military precision and nattiness—seldom disturbed, I fancy, for Uncle David was not much of a book-worm—chilled him with an aspect of inflexible formality; and the busts, in cold white marble, standing at intervals on their pedestals, seemed to have called up looks, like Mrs. Pentweezle, for the occasion. Demosthenes, with his wrenched neck and square brow, had evidently heard of his dealings with Lord Pindledykes, and made up his mind, when the proper time came, to denounce him with a tempest of appropriate eloquence. There was in Cicero's face, he *thought*, something satirical and conceited which was new and odious; and under Plato's external solemnity he detected a pleasurable and roguish anticipation of the coming scene.

His uncle was very punctual. A few minutes would see him in the room, and then two or three sentences would disclose the purpose he meditated. In the midst of the trepidation which had thus returned, he heard his uncle's knock at the hall-door, and in another moment he entered the study.

'How d'ye do, Richard? You're punctual. I wish our meeting was a pleasanter one. Sit down. You haven't kept faith with me. It is scarcely a year since, with a large sum of money, such as at your age I should have thought a fortune, I rescued you from bad hands and a great danger. Now, Sir, do you remember a promise you then made me? and have you kept your word?'

'I confess, uncle, I know I can't excuse myself; but I was tempted, and I am weak—I am a fool, worse than a fool—whatever you please to call me, and I'm sorry. Can I say more?' pleaded the young man.

'That is saying nothing. It simply means that you do the thing that pleases you, and break your word where your inclination prompts; and you are sorry because it has turned out unluckily. I have heard that you are again in danger. *I* am not going to help you.' His blue eyes looked cold and hard, and the oblique light showed severe lines at his brows and mouth. It was a face which, generally kindly, could yet look, on occasion, stern enough. 'Now, observe, I'm not going to help you; I'm not even going to reason with you—you can do that for yourself, if you please—I will simply help you with *light*. Thus forewarned, you need not, of course, answer any one of the questions I am about to put, and to ask which, I have no other claim than that which rests upon having put you on your feet, and paid five thousand pounds for you, only a year ago.'

'But I entreat that you do put them. I'm ashamed of myself, dear Uncle David; I implore of you to ask me whatever you please: I'll answer everything.'

'Well, I think I know everything; Lord Pindledykes makes no

secret of it. He's the man, isn't he?'

'Yes, Sir.'

'That's the sallow, dissipated-looking fellow, with the eye that squints outward. I know his appearance very well; I knew his good-for-nothing father. No one likes to have transactions with that fellow—he's shunned—and you chose him, of all people; and he has pigeoned you. I've heard all about it. Everybody knows by this time. And you have really lost fifteen thousand pounds to him?'

'I am afraid, uncle, it is very near that.'

'This, you know,' resumed Uncle David, 'is not debt: it is ruin. You chose to mortgage your reversion to some Jews, for fifteen hundred a year, during your father's lifetime. Three hundred would have been ample, with the hundred a year you had before—ample; but you chose to do it, and the estates, whenever you succeed to them, will come to you with a very heavy debt charged, for those Jews, upon them. I don't suppose the estates are destined to continue long in our family; but this is a vexation which don't touch you, nephew. *I* am, I confess, sorry. They were in our family, some of them, before the Conquest.

'No matter. What you have to consider is your present position. They will come to you, if ever, saddled with a heavy debt; and, in the meantime, you have fifteen hundred a year for your father's life; and I don't think it will sell for anything like the fifteen thousand pounds you have just lost. You are therefore insolvent; there is the story told. I see nothing for it but your becoming formally an insolvent.

'It is the *bourgeoisie* who shrink from that sort of thing; titled men, and men of pleasure and fashion, don't seem to mind it. There are Lord Harry Newgate, and the Honourable Alfred Pentonville, and Sir Aymerick Pigeon, one of the oldest baronets in England, have been in the *Gazette* within the last twelve months. The money I paid, on the faith of your promise, is worse than wasted. I'll pay no more into the pockets of rooks and scoundrels; I'll divide no more of my money among blackguard jockeys and *villainous* peers, simply to defer for a few months the consequences of a fool's incorrigible folly.'

'But, you know, uncle, I was not quite so mad. The thing was a swindle; it can't stand. The horse was not fairly treated.'

'I daresay: I suppose it was doctored. I don't care; I only think that unless you meant to go in for drugging horses and bribing jockeys, you had no business among such people, and at that sort of game. All I want is that you clearly understand that in this matter—though I would gladly see you safely out of it—I'll waste no more money in paying gambling debts.'

'This might have happened to anyone, Sir; it might indeed, uncle. Every second man you meet is more or less on the turf, and they never come to grief by it. No one, of course, can stand against a barefaced swindle, like this thing.'

'I don't care a farthing about other people; I've seen how it tells upon you. I don't affect to value your promises, Dick; I don't think that they are worth a shilling. How many have you made me, and broken? To me it seems the vice is incurable, like drunkenness. Tattersall's, or whatever is your place of business, is no better than the gin-palace; and when once a fellow is fairly on the turf, the sooner he is under it, the better for himself and all who like him. And you have lost money at play besides. I heard that quite accidentally; and I daresay that is a ruinous item in what I may call your schedule.'

'I know what people are saying; but it isn't so immense a sum, by any means.'

'I'm sorry to hear it. I wish it was enormous; I wish it was a million. I wish your failure could ruin every blackguard in England: the more heavily you have hit them all round, the better I am pleased. They hit you and me, Dick, pretty hard last time; it is our turn now. It is not my fault now, Dick, if you don't understand me perfectly. If at any future time I should do anything for you—by my *will*, mind—I shall take care so to tie it up that you can't make away with a guinea. My advice is not worth much to you, but I venture to give it, and I think the best thing you can do is to submit to your misfortune, and file your schedule; and when you are your own master again, I shall see if I can manage some small thing for you.

'You will have to work for your bread, you know, and you can't expect very much at first; but there are things—of course, I mean in commercial establishments, and railways, and that kind of thing—where I have an influence, of from a hundred and twenty to two hundred pounds a year, and for some of them you would answer pretty well, and you can tide over the time till you succeed to the title: and after a little while I may be able to get you raised a step; and when once you get accustomed to work, you can't think how you will come to like it. So that, on the whole, the knock you have got may do you some good, and make you prize your position more when you come to it. Will you go upstairs, and take a cup of tea with Miss Maubray?'

He used to call her Grace, when speaking to Richard. Perhaps, in the concussion of this earthquake, the fabric of a matrimonial scheme may have fallen to the ground.

Richard Arden was too dejected and too agitated to accept this invitation, I need hardly tell you. He took his leave, chapfallen.

Van Appoints Himself to a Diplomatic Post

Mr. Vandeleur had availed himself very freely of Richard Arden's invitation, to amuse himself during his absence with his cheroots and manillas, as the clouded state of the atmosphere of his drawing-room testified to that luckless gentleman—if indeed he was in a condition to observe anything, on returning from his dreadful interview with his uncle.

Richard's countenance was full of thunder and disaster. Vandeleur looked in his face, with his cigar in his fingers, and said in a faint and hollow tone—

'Well?'

To which inappropriate form of inquiry, Richard Arden deigned no reply; but in silence stalked to the box of cigars on the table, threw himself into a chair, and smoked violently for awhile.

Some minutes passed. Vandeleur's eyes were fixed, through

the smoke, on Richard's, who had fixed his on the chimney-piece. Van respected his ruminations. With a delicate and noiseless attention, indeed, he ventured to slide gently to his side the water carafe, and the brandy, and a tumbler.

Still silence prevailed. After a time, Richard Arden poured brandy and water suddenly into his glass.

'Think of that fellow, that uncle of mine—pretty uncle! Kind relation—rolling in money! He sends for me simply to tell me that he won't give me a guinea. He might have waited till he was asked. If he had nothing better to say, he need not have given me the trouble of going to his odious, bleak study, to hear all his vulgar advice and arithmetic, ending in—what do you think? He says that I'm to be had up in the bankrupt court, and when all that is over he'll get me appointed a ticket-taker on a railway, or a clerk in a pawn-office, or something. By Heaven! when I think of it, I wonder how I kept my temper. I'm not quite driven to those curious expedients, that he seems to think so natural. I've some cards still left in my hand, and I'll play them first, if it is the same to him; and, hang it! my luck can't always run the same way. I'll give it another chance before I give up, and tomorrow morning things may be very different with me.'

'It's an awful pity you quarrelled with Longcluse!' exclaimed Vandeleur.

'That's done, and can't be undone,' said Richard Arden, resuming his cigar.

'I wonder why you quarrelled with him. Why, good heavens! that man is made of money, and he got you safe out of that fellow's clutches—I forget his name—about that bet with Mr. Slanter, don't you remember—and he was so very kind about it; and I'm sure he'd shake hands if you'd only ask him, and one way or another he'd pull you through.'

'I can't ask him, and I won't; he may ask *me* if he likes. I'm very sure there is nothing he would like better, for fifty reasons, than to be on good terms with me again, and I have no wish to quarrel any more than he has. But if there is to be a reconciliation, I can't begin it. He must make the overtures, and that's all.'

'He seemed such an awfully jolly fellow that time. And it is such a frightful state we are both in. I never came such mucker before in my life. I know him pretty well. I met him at Lady May Penrose's, and at the Playfairs', and one night I walked home with him from the opera. It is an awful pity you are not on terms with him, and—by Jove! I must go and have something to eat; it is near eight o'clock.'

Away went Van, and out of the wreck of his fortune contrived a modest dinner at Verey's; and pondering, after dinner, upon the awful plight of himself and his comrade, he came at last to the heroic resolution of braving the dangers of a visit to Mr. Longcluse, on behalf of his friend; and as it was now past nine, he hastily paid the waiter, took his hat, and set out upon his adventure. It was a mere chance, he knew, and a very unlikely one, his finding Mr. Longcluse at home at that hour. He knew that he was doing a very odd thing in calling at past nine o'clock; but the occasion was anomalous, and Mr. Longcluse would understand. He knocked at the door, and learned from the servant that his master was engaged with a gentleman in the study, on business. From this room he heard a voice faintly discoursing in a deep metallic drawl.

'Who shall I say, Sir?' asked the servant.

If his mission had been less monotonous, and he less excited and sanguine as to his diplomatic success, he would have, as he said, 'funked it altogether,' and gone away. He hesitated for a moment, and determined upon the form most likely to procure an interview.

'Say Mr. Vandeleur—a friend of Mr. Richard Arden's; you'll remember, please—a friend of Mr. Richard Arden's.'

In a moment the man returned.

'Will you please to walk upstairs?' and he showed him into the drawing-room.

In little more than a minute, Mr. Longcluse himself entered. His eyes were fixed on the visitor with a rather stern curiosity. Perhaps he had interpreted the term ' friend' a little too technically. He made him a ceremonious bow, in French fashion, and placed a chair for him.

'I had the pleasure of being introduced to you, Mr. Longcluse, at Lady May Penrose's. My name is Vandeleur.' 'I have had that honour, Mr. Vandeleur, I remember perfectly. The servant mentioned that you announced yourself as Mr. Arden's friend, if I don't mistake.'

DIPLOMACY

Mr. Vandeleur and Mr. Longcluse were now seated, and the former gentleman said—

'Yes, I am a friend of Mr. Arden's—so much so, that I have ventured what I hope you won't think a very impertinent liberty. I was so very sorry to hear that a misunderstanding had occurred—I did not ask him about what—and he has been so unlucky about the Derby, you know—I ought to say that I am, upon my honour, a mere volunteer, so perhaps you will think I have no right to ask you to listen to me.'

'I shall be happy to continue this conversation, Mr. Vandeleur, upon one condition.'

'Pray name it.'

'That you report it fully to the gentleman for whom you are so kind as to interest yourself.' 'Yes, I'll certainly do that.'

Mr. Longcluse looked by no means so jolly as Van remembered him, and he thought he detected, at mention of Richard Arden's name, for a moment, a look of positive malevolence—I can't say absolutely, it may have been fancy—as he turned quickly, and the light played suddenly on his face.

Mr. Longcluse could, perhaps, dissemble as well as other men; but there were cases in which he would not be at the trouble to dissemble. And here his expression was so unpleasant, upon features so strangely marked and so white, that Van thought the effect ugly, and even ghastly.

'I shall be happy, then, to hear anything you have to say' said Longcluse gently.

'You are very kind. I was just going to say that he has been too unlucky—he has lost so much money——'

'I had better say, I think, at once, Mr. Vandeleur, that nothing shall tempt me to take any part in Mr. Arden's affairs.'

Van's mild blue eyes looked on him wonderingly.

'You could be of so much use, Mr. Longcluse!'

'I don't desire to be of any.'

'But—but that may be, I think it must, in consequence of the unhappy estrangement.'

He had been conning over phrases on his way, and thought that a pretty one.

'A very happy estrangement, on the contrary, for the man who is straight and true, and who is by it relieved of a great—mistake.'

'I should be so extremely happy,' said Van lingeringly, 'if I were instrumental in inducing both parties to shake hands.'

'I don't desire it.'

'But, surely, if Richard Arden were the first to offer——'

'I should decline.'

Van rose; he fiddled with his hat a little; he hesitated. He had staked too much on this—for had he not promised to report the whole thing to Richard Arden, who was not likely to be pleased?—to give up without one last effort.

'I hope I am not very impertinent,' he said, 'but I can hardly think, Mr. Longcluse, that you are quite indifferent to a reconciliation.'

'I'm not indifferent—I'm averse to it.'

'I don't understand.'

'Will you take some tea?'

'No, thanks; I do so hope that I don't quite understand.'

'That's hardly my fault; I have spoken very distinctly.'

'Then what you wish to convey is——' said Van, with his hand now at the door.

'Is this,' said Longcluse, 'that I decline Mr. Arden's acquaintance, that I won't consider his affairs, and that I peremptorily refuse to be of the slightest use to him in his difficulties. I hope I am now sufficiently distinct.'

'Oh, perfectly!'

'Pray take some tea.'

'And my visit is a failure. I'm awfully sorry I can't be of any use!'

'None here, Sir, to Mr. Arden—none, no more than I.'

'Then I have only to beg of you to accept my apologies for having given you a great deal of trouble, and to beg pardon for having disturbed you, and to say goodnight.'

'No trouble—none. I am glad everything is clear now. Goodnight.'

And Mr. Longcluse saw him politely to the door, and said again, in a clear, stern tone, but with a smile and another bow, 'Goodnight,' as he parted at the door.

About an hour later a servant arrived with a letter for Mr. Longcluse. That gentleman recognised the hand, and suspended his business to read it. He did so with a smile. It was thus expressed:—

SIR,

I beg to inform you, in the distinctest terms, that neither Mr. Vandeleur, nor any other gentleman, had any authority from me to enter into any discussion with you, or to make the slightest allusion to subjects upon which Mr. Vandeleur, at your desire, tells me he, this evening, thought fit to converse with you. And I beg, in the most pointed manner, to disavow all connection with, or previous knowledge of, that gentleman's visit and conversation. And I do so lest Mr. Vandeleur's assertion to the same effect should appear imperfect without mine.—

I remain, Sir, your obedient servant,

Richard Arden.

To Walter Longcluse, Esq.

'Does anyone wait for an answer?' he asked, still smiling.

'Yes, Sir: Mr. Thompson, please, Sir.'

'Very well; ask him to wait a moment,' said he, and he wrote as follows:—

'Mr. Longcluse takes the liberty of returning Mr. Arden's letter, and begs to decline any correspondence with him.'

And this note, with Richard Arden's letter, he enclosed in an envelope, and addressed to that gentleman.

While this correspondence, by no means friendly, was proceeding, other letters were interesting, very profoundly, other persons in this drama.

Old David Arden had returned early from a ponderous dinner of the magnates of that world which interested him more than the world of fashion, or even of politics, and he was sitting in his study at half-past ten, about a quarter of a mile westward of Mr. Longcluse's house in Bolton Street.

Not many letters had come for him by the late post. There were two which he chose to read forthwith. The rest would, in Swift's phrase, keep cool, and he could read them before breakfast in the morning. The first was a note posted at Islington. He knew his niece's pretty hand. This was an 'advice' from Mortlake. The second which he picked up from the little pack was a foreign letter, of more than usual bulk.

A Letter and a Summons

Paris? Yes, he knew the hand well. His face darkened a little with a peculiar anxiety. This he will read first. He draws the candles all together, near the corner of the table at which he sits. He can't have too much light on these formal lines, legible and tall as the letters are. He opens the thin envelope, and reads what follows:—

Dear and honoured Sir,

I am in receipt of yours of the 13th instant. You judge me rightly in supposing that I have entered on my mission with a willing mind, and no thought of sparing myself. On the 11th instant I presented the letter you were so good as to provide me with to M. de la Perriere. He received me with much consideration in consequence. You have not been misinformed with regard to his position. His influence is, and so long as the present Cabinet remain in power will continue to be, more than sufficient to procure for me the information and opportunities you so much desire. He explained to me very fully the limits of that assistance which official people here have it in their power to afford. Their prerogative is more extensive than with us, but at the same time it has its points of circumscription. Every private citizen has his well-defined rights, which they can in no case invade.

He says that had I come armed with affidavits criminating any individual, or even justifying a strong and distinct suspicion, their powers would be much larger. As it is, he cautions me against taking any steps that might alarm Vanboeren. The baron is a suspicious man, it seems, and has, moreover, once or twice been under official surveillance, which has made him crafty. He is not likely to be caught napping. He ostensibly practises the professions of a surgeon and dentist. In the latter capacity he has a very considerable business. But his principal income is derived, I am informed, from sources of a different kind.

'H'm! what can he mean? I suppose he explains a little further on,' mused Mr. Arden.

He is, in short, a practitioner about whom suspicions of an infamous kind have prevailed. One branch of his business, a rather strange one, has connected him with persons, more considerable in number than you would readily believe, who were, or are, political refugees.

'Can this noble baron be a distiller of poisons?' David Arden ruminated.

In all his other equivocal doings, he found, on the few occasions that seemed to threaten danger, mysterious protectors, sufficiently powerful to bring him off scot-free. His relations of a political character were those which chiefly brought him under the secret notice of the police. It is believed that he has amassed a fortune, and it is certain that he is about to retire from business. I can much better explain to you, when I see you, the remarkable circumstances to which I have but alluded, I hope to be in town again, and to have the honour of waiting upon you, on Thursday, the 29th instant.

'Ay, that's the day he named at parting. What a punctual fellow that is!'

They appear to me to have a very distinct bearing upon some possible views of the case in which you are so justly interested. The Baron Vanboeren is reputed very wealthy, but he is by no means liberal in his dealings, and is said to be insatiably avaricious. This last quality may make him practicable——

'Yes, so it may,' acquiesced Uncle David.

. . so that disclosures of importance may be obtained, if he be approached in the proper manner. Lebas was connected, as a mechanic, with the dentistry department of his business. Mr. L—— has been extremely kind to Lebas' widow and children, and has settled a small annuity upon her, and fifteen hundred *francs* each upon his children.

'Eh? Upon my life, that is very handsome—extremely handsome. It gives me rather new ideas of this man—that is, if there's nothing odd in it,' said Mr. Arden.

The deed by which he has done all this is, in its reciting part, an eccentric one. I waited, as I advised you in mine of the 12th, upon M. Arnaud, who is the legal man employed by Madame Lebas, for the purpose of handing him the ten *napoleons* which you were so good as to transmit for the use of his family; which sum he has, with many thanks on the part of Madame Lebas, declined, and which, therefore, I hold still to your credit. When explaining to me that lady's reasons for declining your remittance, he requested me to read a deed of gift from Mr. Longcluse, making the provisions I have before referred to, and reciting, as nearly in these words as I can remember:—

'Whereas I entertained for the deceased Pierre Lebas, in whose house in Paris I lodged when very young, for more than a year and a half, a very great respect and regard: and whereas I hold myself to have been the innocent cause of his having gone to the room, as appears from my evidence, in which, unhappily, he lost his life: and whereas I look upon it as a disgrace to our City of London that such a crime could have been committed in a place of public resort, frequented as that was at the time, without either interruption or detection; and whereas, so regarding it, I think that such citizens as could well afford to subscribe money, adequately to compensate the family of the deceased for the pecuniary loss which both his widow and children have sustained by reason of his death, were bound to do so; his visit to London having been strictly a commercial one; and all persons connected with the trade of London being more or less interested in the safety of the commercial intercourse between the two countries: and whereas the citizens of London have failed, although applied to for the purpose, to make any such compensation; now this deed witnesseth, etc.'

'Well, in all that, I certainly go with him. We Londoners ought to be ashamed of ourselves.'

The widow has taken her children to Avranches, her native place, where she means to live. Please direct me whether I shall proceed thither, and also upon what particular points you would wish me to interrogate her. I have learned, this moment, that the Baron Vanboeren retires in October next. It is thought that he will fix his residence after that at Berlin. My informant undertakes to advise me of his address, whenever it is absolutely settled. In approaching this baron, it is thought you will have to exercise caution and dexterity, as he has the reputation of being cunning and unscrupulous.

'I'm not good at dealing with such people—I never was. I

must engage some long-headed fellow who understands them,' said he.

I debit myself with two thousand five hundred *francs*, the amount of your remittance on the 15th inst., for which I will account at sight.—

I remain, dear and honoured Sir, your attached and most obedient servant,

Christopher Blount.

'I shall learn all he knows in a few days. What is it that deprives me of quiet till a clue be found to the discovery of Yelland Mace? And why is it that the fancy has seized me that Mr. Longcluse knows where that villain may be found? He admitted, in talking to Alice, she says, that he had seen him in his young days. I will pick up all the facts, and then consider well all that they may point to. Let us but get the letters together, and in time we may find out what they spell. Here am I, a rich but sad old bachelor, having missed forever the best hope of my life. Poor Harry long dead, and but one branch the old tree with fruit upon it—Reginald, with his two children: Richard, my nephew—Richard Arden, in a few years the sole representative of the whole family of Arden, and he such a scamp and fool! If a childless old fellow could care for such things, it would be enough to break my heart. And poor little Alice! So affectionate and so beautiful, left, as she will be, alone, with such a protector as that fellow! I pity her.'

At that moment her unopened note caught his eye, as it lay on the table. He opened it, and read these words:—

My Dearest Uncle David,

I am so miserable and perplexed, and so utterly without any one to befriend or advise me in my present unexpected trouble, that I must implore of you to come to Mortlake, if you can, the moment this note reaches you. I know how unreasonable and selfish this urgent request will appear. But when I shall have told you all that has happened, you will say, I know, that I could not have avoided imploring your aid. Therefore, I entreat, distracted creature as I am, that you, my beloved uncle, will come to aid and counsel me; and believe me when I assure you that I am in extreme distress, and without, at this moment, any other friend to help me.—Your very unhappy niece,

Alice.

He read this short note over again.

'No; it is not a sick lap-dog, or a saucy maid: there is some real trouble. Alice has, I think, more sense—I'll go at once. Reginald is always late, and I shall find them' (he looked at his watch)—'yes, I shall find them still up at Mortlake.'

So instantly he sent for a cab, and pulled on again a pair boots, instead of the slippers he had donned, and before five minutes was driving at a rapid pace towards Mortlake.

The Reason of Alice's Note

The long drive to Mortlake was expedited by promises to the cabman; for, in this acquisitive world, nothing for nothing is the ruling law of reciprocity. It was about half-past eleven o'clock when they reached the gate of the avenue; it was a still night, and a segment of the moon was high in the sky, faintly silvering the old fluted piers and urns, and the edges of the gigantic trees that overhung them. They were now driving up the avenue. How odd was the transition from the glare and hurly-burly of the town to the shadowy and silent woodlands on which this imperfect light fell so picturesquely.

There were associations enough to induce melancholy as he drove through those neglected scenes, his playground in boyish days, where he, and Harry whom he loved, had passed so many of the happy days that precede school. He could hear his laugh floating still among the boughs of the familiar trees, he could see his handsome face smiling down through the leaves of the lordly chestnut that stood, at that moment, by the point of the avenue they were passing, like a forsaken old friend overlooking the way without a stir.

'I'll follow this clue to the end,' said David Arden. 'I sha'n't make much of it, I fear; but if it ends, as others in the same inquiry have, in smoke, I shall, at least, have done my utmost, and may abandon the task with a good grace, and conclude that Heaven declines to favour the pursuit. Taken for all-in-all, he was the best of his generation, and the fittest to head the house. Something, I thought, was due, in mere respect to his memory. The coldness of Reginald insulted me. If a favourite dog had been poisoned, he would have made more exertion to commit the culprit. And once in pursuit of this dark shadow, how intense and direful grew the interest of the chase, and——'Here we are at the hall-door. 'Don't mind knocking, ring the bell,' he said to the driver.

He was himself at the threshold before the door was opened.

'Can I see my brother?' he asked.

'Sir Reginald is in the drawing-room—a small dinner-party today, Sir—Lady May Penrose, and Lady Mary Maypol, they returned to town in Lady May Penrose's carriage, Lord Wynderbroke remains, Sir, and two gentlemen, they are at present with Sir Reginald in the smoking-room.'

He learned that Miss Arden was alone in the small sitting-room, called the card-room. David Arden had walked through the vestibule, and into the capacious hall. The lights were all out, but one.

'Well, I sha'n't disturb him. Is Miss Alice——'

'Yes, Alice is here. It is so kind of you to come!' said a voice he well knew. 'Here I am! Won't you come up to the drawing-room, Uncle David?'

'So you want to consult Uncle David,' he said, entering the room, and looking round. 'In my father's time the other drawing-rooms used to be open; it is a handsome suite—very pretty rooms. But I think you have been crying, my poor little Alice. What on earth is all this about, my dear! Here I am, and it is past eleven; so we must come to the point, if I am to hear it tonight. What is the matter?'

'My dear uncle, I have been so miserable!'

'Well, what is it?' he said, taking a chair; 'you have refused some fellow you like, or accepted some fellow you don't like. I am sure you are at the bottom of your own misery, foolish little creature! Girls generally are, I think, the architects of their own penitentiaries. Sit there, my dear, and if it is anything I can be of the least use in, you may count of my doing my utmost. Only you must tell me the whole case, and you mustn't colour it a bit.'

So they sat down on a sofa, and Miss Alice told him in her own way that, to her amazement, that day Lord Wynderbroke had made something very like a confession of his passion, and an offer of his hand, which this unsophisticated young lady was on the point of repelling, when Lady May entered the room, accompanied by her friend, Lady Mary Maypol; and, of course, the interesting situation, for that time, dissolved. About an hour after, Alice, who was shocked at the sudden distinction of which she had become the object, and extremely vexed at the interruption which had compelled her to suspend her reply, and very anxious for an opportunity to answer with decision, found that opportunity in a little saunter which she and the two ladies took in the grounds, accompanied by Lord Wynderbroke and Sir Reginald.

When the opportunity came, with a common inconsistency, she rather shrank from the crisis; and a slight uncertainty as to the actual meaning of the noble lord, rendered her perplexity still more disagreeable. It occurred thus: the party had walked some little distance, and when Alice was addressed by her father—

'Here is Wynderbroke, who says he has never seen my Roman inscription! You, Alice, must do the honours, for I daren't yet venture on the grass,' —he shrugged and shook his head over his foot— 'and I will take charge of Lady Mary and Lady May, who want to see the Derbyshire thistles—they have grown so enormous under my gardener's care. You said, May, the other evening, that you would like to see them.'

Lady May acquiesced with true feminine sympathy with the baronet's stratagem, notwithstanding an imploring glance from Alice! and Lady Mary Maypol, exchanging a glance with Lady

May, expressed equal interest in the Derbyshire thistles.

'You will find the inscription at the door of the grotto, only twenty steps from this; it was dug up when my grandfather made the round pond, with the fountain in it. You'll find us in the garden.'

Lord Wynderbroke beamed an insufferable smile on Alice, and said something pretty that she did not hear. She knew perfectly what was coming, and although resolved, she was yet in a state of extreme confusion.

Lord Wynderbroke was talking all the way as they approached the grotto; but not one word of his harmonious periods did she clearly hear. By the time they reached the little rocky arch under the evergreens, through the leaves of which the marble tablet and Roman inscription were visible, they had each totally forgotten the antiquarian object with which they had set out.

Lord Wynderbroke came to a standstill, and then with a smiling precision and distinctness, and in accents that seemed, somehow to ring through her head, he made a very explicit declaration and proposal; and during the entire delivery of this performance, which was neat and lucid rather than impassioned, she remained tongue-tied, listening as if to a tale told in a dream.

She withdrew her hand hastily from Lord Wynderbroke's tender pressure, and the young lady with a sudden effort, replied collectedly enough, in a way greatly to amaze Lord Wynderbroke.

When she had done, that nobleman was silent for some time, and stood in the same attitude of attention with which he had heard her. With a heightened colour he cleared his voice, and his answer, when it came, was dry and pettish. He thought with great deference, that he was, perhaps entitled to a little consideration, and it appeared to him that he had quite unaccountably misunderstood what had seemed the very distinct language of Sir Reginald. For the present he had no more to say. He hoped to explain more satisfactorily to Miss Arden, after he had himself had a few words of explanation, to which he thought he had a claim, from Sir Reginald; and he must confess that, after the lengths to which he had been induced to proceed, he was quite taken by surprise, and inexpressibly wounded by the tone which Miss Arden had adopted.

Side by side, at a somewhat quick pace, Miss Arden with a heightened colour, and Lord Wynderbroke with his ears tingling, rejoined their friends.

'Well, my dear child,' said Uncle David, with a laugh, 'if you have nothing worse to complain of, though I am very glad to see you, I think we might have put off our meeting till daylight.'

'Oh! but you have not heard half what has happened. He has behaved in the most cowardly, treacherous, ungentlemanlike way,' she continued vehemently. 'Papa sent for me, and I never saw him so angry in my life. Lord Wynderbroke has been making his unmanly complaints to him, and papa spoke so violently. And *he,* instead of going away, having had from me the answer which nothing on earth shall ever induce me to change, *he* remains here; and actually had the audacity to tell me, very nearly in so many words, that my decision went for nothing. I spoke to him quite frankly, but said nothing that was at all rude—nothing that could have made him the least angry. I implored of him to believe me that I never could change my mind; and I could not help crying, I was so agitated and wretched.

'But he seemed very much vexed, and simply said that he placed himself entirely in papa's hands. In fact, I've been utterly miserable and terrified, and I do not know how I can endure those terrible scenes with papa. The whole thing has come upon me so suddenly. Could you have imagined any gentleman capable of acting like Lord Wynderbroke—so selfish, cruel, and dastardly?' and with these words she burst into tears.

'Do you mean to say that he won't take your refusal?' said her uncle, looking very angry.

'That is what he says,' she sobbed. 'He had an opportunity only for a few words, and that was the purport of them; and I was so astounded, I could not reply; and, instead of going away, he remains here. Papa and he have arranged to prolong his visit; so I shall be teased and frightened, and I am so nervous and agitated; and it is such an outrage!'

'Now, we must not lose our heads, my dear child; we must consult calmly. It seems you don't think it possible that you may come to like Lord Wynderbroke sufficiently to marry him.'

'I would rather *die!* If this goes on, I sha'n't stay here. I'd go and be a governess rather.'

'I think you might give my house a trial first,' said Uncle David merrily; 'but it is time to talk about that by-and-by. What does May Penrose think of it? She sometimes, I believe, on an emergency, lights on a sensible suggestion.'

'She had to return to town with Lady Mary, who dined here also; I did not know she was going until a few minutes before they left. I've been so *miserably* unlucky! and I could not make an opportunity without its seeming so rude to Lady Mary, and I don't know her well enough to tell her; and, you have no idea, papa is so incensed, and so peremptory; and what *am* I to do? Oh! dear uncle, think of something. I know you'll help me.'

'That I will,' said the old gentleman. 'But allowances are to be made for a poor old devil so much in love as Lord Wynderbroke.'

'I don't think he likes me now—he can't like me,' said Alice. 'But he is angry. It is simply pride and vanity. From something papa said, I am sure of it, Lord Wynderbroke has been telling his friends, and speaking, I fancy, as if everything was arranged, and he never anticipated that I could have any mind of my own; and I suppose he thinks he would be laughed at, and so I am to undergo a persecution, and he won't hear of anything but what he pleases; and papa is determined to accomplish it. And, oh! what *am* I to do?'

'I'll tell you, but you must do exactly as I bid you. Who's there?' he said suddenly, as Alice's maid opened the door.

'Oh! I beg pardon—Miss Alice, please,' she said, dropping a curtsey and drawing back.

'Don't go,' said Uncle David, 'we shall want you. What's the matter?'

'Sir Reginald has been took bad with his foot again, please,

Miss.'

'Nothing serious?' said Uncle David.

'Only pain, please, Sir, in the same place.'

'All the better it should fix itself well in his foot. You need not be uneasy about it, Alice. You and your maid must be in my cab, which is at the hall door, in five minutes. Take leave of no one, and don't waste time over finery; just put a few things up, and take your dressing-case; and you and your maid are coming to town with me. Is my brother in the drawing-room?'

'No, Sir, please; he is in his own room.'

'Are the gentlemen who dined still here?'

'Two left, Sir, when Sir Reginald took ill; but Lord Wynderbroke remains.'

'Oh! and where is he?'

'Sir Reginald sent for him, please, Sir—just as I came up—to his room.'

'Very good, then I shall find them both together. Now, Alice, I must find you and your maid in the cab in five minutes. I shall get your leave from Reginald, and you order the fellow to drive down to the little church gate in the village close by, and I'll walk after and join you there in a few minutes. Lose no time.'

With this parting charge, Uncle David ran down the stairs, and met Lord Wynderbroke at the foot of them, returning from his visit of charity to Sir Reginald's room.

Collision

'Lord Wynderbroke!' said Uncle David, and bowed rather ceremoniously.

Lord Wynderbroke, a little surprised, extended two fingers and said, 'How d'ye do, Mr. Arden?' and smiled drily, and then seemed disposed to pass on.

'I beg your pardon, Lord Wynderbroke,' said David Arden, 'but would you mind giving me a few minutes? I have something you may think a little important to say, and if you will allow me, I'll say it in this room'—he indicated the half-open door of the dining-room, in which there was still some light—'I shall not detain you long.'

The urbane and smiling peer looked on him for a moment—rather darkly—with a shrewd eye; and he said, still smiling,—

'Certainly, Mr. Arden; but at this hour, and being about to write a note, you will see that I have very little time indeed—I'm very sorry.'

He was speaking stiffly, and any one might have seen that he suspected nothing very agreeable as the result of Mr. Arden's communication.

When they had got into the dining-room, and the door was closed, Lord Wynderbroke, with his head a little high, invited Mr. Arden to proceed.

'Then, as you are in a hurry, you'll excuse my going direct to the point. I've come here in consequence of a note that reached me about an hour ago, informing me that my niece, Alice Arden, has suffered a great deal of annoyance. You know, of course, to what I refer?'

'I should extremely regret that the young lady, your niece, should suffer the least vexation, from any cause; but I should have fancied that her happiness might be more naturally confided to the keeping of her father, than of a relation residing in a different house, and by no means so nearly interested in consulting it.'

'I see, Lord Wynderbroke, that I must address you very plainly, and even coarsely. My brother Reginald does not consult her happiness in this matter, but merely his own ideas of a desirable family connection. She is really quite miserable; she has unalterably made up her mind. You'll not induce her to change it. There is no chance of that. But by permitting my brother to exercise a pressure in favour of your suit—'

'You'll excuse my interrupting for a moment, to say that there is, and can be, nothing but the perfectly legitimate influence of a parent. *Pressure,* there is none—none in the world, Sir; although I am not, like you, Mr. Arden, a relation—and a very near one—of Sir Reginald Arden's, I think I can undertake to say that he is quite incapable of exercising what you call a pressure upon the young lady his daughter; and I have to beg that you will be so good as to spare me the pain of hearing that term employed, as you have just now employed it—or *at all,* Sir, in connection with me. I take the liberty of insisting upon that, *peremptorily.*'

Mr. Arden bowed, and went on:

'And when the young lady distinctly declines the honour you propose, you persist in paying your addresses, as though her answer meant just nothing.'

'I don't quite know, Sir, why I've listened so long to this kind of thing from you; you have no right on earth, Sir, to address that sort of thing to me. How dare you talk to me, Sir, in that—a—a—audacious tone upon my private affairs and conduct?'

Uncle David was a little fiery, and answered, holding his head high,—

'What I have to say is short and clear. I don't care twopence about your affairs, or your conduct, but I do very much care about my niece's happiness; and if you any long' decline to take the answer she has given you, and continue to cause her the slightest trouble, I'll make it a personal matter with you. Good-*night!*' he added, with an inflamed visage, and a stamp on the floor, thundering his valediction. And forth he went to pay his brief visit to his brother—not caring twopence, as he said, what Lord Wynderbroke thought of him.

Sir Reginald had got into his dressing-gown. He was not now in any pain to speak of, and expressed great surprise at the sudden appearance of his brother.

'You'll take something, won't you?'

'Nothing, thanks' answered David, 'I came to beg a favour.'

'Oh! did you? You find me very poorly,' said the baronet, in a tone that seemed to imply, 'You might easily kill me, by imposing the least trouble just now.'

'You'll be all the better, Reginald, for this little attack; it is so comfortably established in your foot.'

'Comfortably! I wish you felt it,' said Sir Reginald, sharply; 'and it's confoundedly late. Why didn't you come to dinner?'

David laughed good-humouredly.

'You forgot, I think, to ask me,' said he.

'Well, well, you know there is always a chair and a glass for you; but won't it do to talk about any cursed thing you wish tomorrow? I—I never, by any chance, hear anything agreeable. I have been tortured out of my wits and senses all day long by a tissue of pig-headed, indescribable frenzy. I vow to Heaven there's a conspiracy to drive me into a mad-house, or into my grave; and I declare to my Maker, I wish the first time I'm asleep, some fellow would come in and blow my brains out on the pillow.'

'I don't know an easier death,' said David; and his brother, who meant it to be terrific, did not pretend to hear him. 'I have only a word to say,' he continued, 'a request you have never refused to other friends, and, in fact, dear Reginald, I ventured to take it for granted you would not refuse me; so I have taken Alice into town, to make me a little visit of a day or two.'

'You haven't taken Alice—you don't mean—she's not gone?' exclaimed the baronet, sitting up with a sudden perpendicularity, and staring at his brother as if his eyes were about to leap from their sockets.

'I'll take the best care of her. Yes, she *is* gone,' said David.

'But my dear, excellent, worthy—why, curse you, David, you can't possibly have done anything so clumsy! Why, you forgot that Wynderbroke is here; how on earth am I to entertain Wynderbroke without her?'

'Why, it is exactly because Lord Wynderbroke is here, that I thought it the best time for her to make me a visit.'

'I protest to Heaven, David, I believe you're deranged! Do you the least know what you are saying?'

'Perfectly. Now, my dear Reginald, let us look at the matter quietly. The girl does not like him; she would not marry him, and never will; she has grown to hate him; his own conduct has made her despise and detest him; and she's not the kind of girl who would marry for a mere title. She has unalterably made up her mind; and these are not times when you can lock a young lady into her room, and starve her into compliance; and Alice is a spirited girl—all the women of our family were. You're no goose like Wynderbroke—you only need to know that the girl has quite made up her mind, or her heart, or her hatred, or whatever it is, and she won't marry him. It is as well he should know it at first, as at last; and I don't think, if he were a gentleman, peer though he be, he would have been in this house to-night. He counted on his title: he was too sure. I am very proud of Alice. And now he can't bear the mortification—having, like a fool, disclosed his suit to others before it had succeeded—of letting the world know he has been refused; and to this petty vanity he would sacrifice Alice, and prevail on you, if he could, to bully her into accepting him, a plan in which, if he perseveres, I have told him he shall, besides failing ridiculously, give me a meeting; for I will make it a personal quarrel with him.'

Sir Reginald sat in his chair, looking very white and wicked, with his eyes gleaming fire on his brother. He opened his mouth once or twice, to speak, but only drew a short breath at each attempt.

David Arden rather wondered that his brother took all this so quietly. If he had observed him a little more closely, he would have seen that his hands were trembling, and perceived also that he had tried repeatedly to speak, and that either voice or articulation failed him. On a sudden he recovered, and regardless of his gout started to his feet, and limped along the floor, exclaiming,—'Help us—help us—God help us! What's this? My—my—oh, my God! It's very bad!' He was stumping round and round the table, near which he had sat, and restlessly shoving the pamphlets and books hither and thither as he went. 'What have I done to earn this curse?—was ever mortal so pursued? The last thing, this was; now all's gone—quite gone—it's over, quite.

'They've done it—they've done it. *Bravo! bravi tutti! brava*! All—all, and everything gone! To think of her—only to think of her! She was my pet.' (And in his bleak, trembling voice, he cried a horrid curse at her.) 'I tell you,' he screamed, dashing his hand on the table, at the other of which he had arrested his monotonous shuffle round it, when his brother caught suddenly his vacant eye, 'you think, because I'm down in the world, and you are prosperous, that you can do as you like. If I was where I should be, you daren't. I'll have her back, Sir. I'll have the police with you. I'll—I'll indict you—it's a police-office affair. They'll take her through the streets. Where's the wretch like her? I charge her—let them take her by the shoulder. And my son, Richard—to think of him!—the cursed puppy!—his post obit! One foot in the grave, have I? No, I'm not so near smoked out as you take me—I've a long time for it—I've a long life. I'll live to see him broken—without a coat to his back—you *villainous*, swindling dandy, and I'll——'

His voice got husky, and he struck his thin fist on the table, and clung to it, and the room was suddenly silent.

David Arden rang the bell violently, and got his arm round his brother, who shook himself feebly, and shrugged, as if he disdained and hated that support.

In came Crozier, who looked aghast, but wheeled his easy-chair close to where he stood, and between them they got him into it, trembling from head to foot.

Martha Tansey came in and lent her aid, and beckoning her to the door, David Arden asked her if she thought him very ill.

'I 'a' seen him just so a dozen times over. He'll be well enough, soon, and if ye knew him as weel in they takins, ye'd ho'd wi' me, there's nothing more than common in't; he's a bit teathy and short-waisted, and always was, and that's how he works himself into them fits.'

So spoke Tansey, into whose talk, in moments of excitement returned something of her old north-country dialect.

'Well, so he was, vexed with me, as with other people, and he has over-excited himself; but as he has this little gout about him, I may as well send out his doctor as I return.'

This little conversation took place outside Sir Reginald's room-door, which David did not care to re-enter, as his brother might have again become furious on seeing him. So he took his leave of Martha Tansey, and their whispered dialogue ended. One or two sighs and groans showed that Sir Reginald's energies were returning. David Arden walked quickly across the vast hall, in which now burned duskily but a single candle, and let himself out into the clear, cold night; and as he walked down the broad avenue he congratulated himself on having cut the Gordian knot, and liberated his niece.

It was a pleasant walk by the narrow road, with its lofty groining of foliage, down to the village outpost of Islington, where, under the shadow of the old church-spire, he found his cab waiting, with Alice and her maid in it.

An Unknown Friend

As they drove into town, Uncle David was thinking how awkward it would be if Sir Reginald should have recovered his activity, and dispatched a messenger to recall Alice, and await their arrival at his door. Well, he did not want a quarrel; he hated a fracas; but he would not send Alice back till next morning, come what might; and then he would return with her, and see Lord Wynderbroke again, and take measures to compel an immediate renunciation of his suit. As for Reginald, he would find arguments to reconcile him to the disappointment. At all events, Alice had thrown herself upon his protection and he would not surrender her except on terms.

Uncle David was silent, having all this matter to ruminate upon. He left a pencilled line for Sir Henry Margate, his brother's physician, and then drove on towards home.

Turning into Saint James's Street, Alice saw her brother standing at the side of a crossing, with a great-coat and a white muffler en, the air being sharp. A couple of carriages drawn up near the pavement, and the passing of two or three others on the outside, for a moment checked their progress, and Alice, had not the window been up, could have spoken to him as they passed. He did not see them, but the light of lamp was on his face, and she was shocked to see how ill he looked.

'There is Dick,' she said, touching her uncle's arm, 'looking so miserable! Shall we speak to him!'

'No, dear, never mind him—he's well enough.' David Arden

peeped at his nephew as they passed. 'He is beginning to take an interest in what really concerns him.'

She looked at her uncle, not understanding his meaning.

'We can talk of it another time, dear,' he added with a cautionary glance at the maid, who sat in the corner at the other side.

Richard Arden was on his way to the place where he meant to recover his losses. He had been playing deep at Colonel Marston's lodgings, but not yet luckily. He thought he had used his credit there as far as he could successfully press it.

The polite young men who had their supper there that night, and played after he left till nearly five o'clock in the morning, knew perfectly what he had lost at the Derby; but they did not know how perilously, on the whole, he was already involved. Was Richard Arden, who had lost nearly seven hundred pounds at Colonel Marston's little gathering, though he had not paid them yet, now quite desperate? By no means. It is true he had, while Vandeleur was out, made an excursion to the City, and, on rather hard terms, secured a loan of three hundred pounds—a trifle which, if luck favoured, might grow to a fortune; but which, if it proved contrary, half an hour would see out.

He had locked this up in his desk, as a reserve for a theatre quite different from Marston's little party; and on his way to that more public and also more secret haunt, he had called at his lodgings for it. It was not that small deposit that cheered him, but a curious and unexpected little note which he found there. It presented by no means a gentlemanlike exterior. The hand was a round clerk's-hand, with flourishing capitals, on an oblong blue envelope, with a vulgar little device. A dun, he took it to be; and he was not immediately relieved when he read at the foot of it, 'Levi.' Then he glanced to the top, and read, 'Dear Sir'.

This easy form of address he read with proper disdain.

> I am instructed by a most respectable party who is desirous to assist you, to the figure of £1,000 or upwards, at nominal discounts, to meet you and ascertain your wishes thereupon, if possible tonight, lest you should suffer in-

convenience.

Yours truly,

ISRAEL LEVI.

P.S.—In furtherance of the above, I shall be at Dignum's Divan, Strand, from 11 p.m. tonight to 1 a.m.

Here then, at last, was a sail in sight!

With this note in his pocket, he walked direct to the place of rendezvous, in the Strand. It was on his way that, unseen by him, his sister and his uncle had observed him, on their drive to David Arden's house.

There were two friends only whom he strongly suspected of this very well-timed interposition—there was Lady May Penrose, and there was Uncle David. Lady May was rich, and quite capable of a generous sacrifice for him. Uncle David, also rich, would like to show an intimidating front, as he had done, but would hardly like to see him go to the wall. There was, I must confess, a trifling bill due to Mr. Longcluse, who had kindly got or given him cash for it. It was something less than a hundred pounds—a mere nothing; but in their altered relations, it would not do to permit any miscarriage of this particular bill. He might have risked it in the frenzy of play.

But to stoop to ask quarter from Longcluse was more than his pride could endure. No; nor would the humiliation avail to arrest the consequences of his neglect. In the general uneasiness and horror of his situation, this little point was itself a centre of torture, and now his unknown friend had come to the rescue, and in the golden sunshine of his promise it, like a hundred minor troubles, was dissolving.

In Pall Mall he jumped into a cab, feeling strangely like himself again. The lights, the clubs, the well-known perspectives, the stars above him, and the gliding vehicles and figures that still peopled the streets, had recovered their old cheery look; he was again in the upper world, and his dream of misery had broken up and melted. Under the great coloured lamp, yellow, crimson, and blue, that overhung the pavement, emblazoned on every side with transparent arabesques, and in gorgeous capitals proclaiming to all whom it might concern 'DIGNUM'S DIVAN', he dismissed his cab, took his counter in the cigar shop, and entered the great rooms beyond. The first of these, as many of my readers remember, was as large as a good-sized Methodist Chapel; and five billiard-tables, under a blaze of gas, kept the many-coloured balls rolling, and the marker busy, calling 'Blue on brown, and pink your player,' and so forth; and gentlemen young and old, Christians and Hebrews, in their shirt-sleeves, picked up shillings when they took 'lives,' or knocked the butts of their cues fiercely on the floor when they unexpectedly lost them.

Among a very motley crowd, Richard Arden slowly sauntering through the room found Mr. Levi, whose appearance he already knew, having once or twice had occasion to consult him financially. His play was over for the night. The slim little Jew, with black curly head, large fierce black eyes and sullen mouth, stood with his hands in his pockets, gaping luridly over the table where he had just, he observed to his friend Isaac Blumer, who did not care if he was hanged, 'losht sheven pound sheventeen, ash I'm a shinner!'

Mr. Levi saw Richard Arden approaching, and smiled on him with his wide show of white fangs. Richard Arden approached Mr. Levi with a grave and haughty face. Here, to be sure, was nothing but what Horace Walpole used to call 'the mob.' Not a human being whom he knew was in the room; still he would have preferred seeing Mr. Levi at his office; and the audacity of his presuming to grin in that familiar fashion! He would have liked to fling one of the billiard-balls in his teeth. In a freezing tone, and with his head high, he said,—

'I think you are Mr. Levi.'

'The shame,' responded Levi, still smiling; 'and 'ow ish Mr. Harden thish evening?'

'I had a note from you,' said Arden, passing by Mr. Levi's polite inquiry, 'and I should like to know if any of that money you spoke of may be made available tonight'

'Every shtiver,' replied the Jew cheerfully.

'I can have it all? Well, this is rather a noisy place,' hesitated

Richard Arden, looking around him.

'I can get into Mishter Dignum's book-offish here, Mr. Harden, and it won't take a moment. I haven't notes, but I'll give you our cheques, and there'sh no place in town they won't go down as slick as gold. I'll fetch you to where there's pen and ink.'

'Do so,' said he.

In a very small room, where burned a single jet of gas, *Mr.* Arden signed a promissory note for £1,012 10s., for which Mr. Levi handed him cheques of his firm for £1,000.

Having exchanged these securities, Richard Arden said—

'I wish to put one or two questions to you, Mr. Levi.' He glanced at a clerk who was making 'tots' from a huge folio before him, on a slip of paper, and transferring them to a small book, with great industry.

Levi understood him and beckoned in silence, and when they both stood in the passage he said—

'If you want a word private with me, Mr. Harden, where there'sh no one can shee us, you'll be as private as the deshert of Harabia if you walk round the corner of the shtreet.'

Arden nodded, and walked out into the Strand, accompanied by Mr. Levi. They turned to the left, and a few steps brought them to the corner of Cecil Street. The street widens a little after you pass its narrow entrance. It was still enough to justify Mr. Levi's sublime comparison.

The moon shone mistily on the river, which was dotted and streaked at its further edge with occasional red lights from windows, relieved by the black reflected outline of the building which made their background. At the foot of the street, at that time, stood a clumsy rail, and Richard Arden leaned his arm on this, as he talked to the Jew, who had pulled his short cloak about him; and in the faint light he could not discern his features, near as he stood, except, now and then, his white eyeballs, faintly, as he turned, or his teeth when he smiled.

By the River

'You mentioned, Mr. Levi, in your note, that you were instructed, by some person who takes an interest in me, to open this business,' said Richard Arden, in a more conciliatory tone. 'Will your instructions permit you to tell me who that person is?'

'No, no,' drawled Mr. Levi, with a slow shake of his head; 'I declare to you sholemnly, Mr. Harden, I couldn't. I'm employed by a third party, and though I may make a tolerable near guess who's firsht fiddle in the bishness, I can't shay nothin''

'Surely you can say this—it is hardly a question, I am so sure of it—is the friend who lends this money a gentleman?'

'I think the pershon as makesh the advanshe is a bit of a shwell. There, now, that'sh enough.'

'But I said a *gentleman*' persisted Arden.

'You mean to ask, hashn't a lady got nothing to do with it?'

'Well, suppose I do?'

Mr. Levi shook his head slowly, and all his white teeth showed dimly, as he answered with an unctuous significance that tempted Arden strongly to pitch him into the river.

'We puts the ladiesh first; ladiesh and shentlemen, that's the way it goes at the theaytre; if a good-looking chap's a bit in a fix, there'sh no one like a lady to pull him through.'

'I really want to know,' said Richard Arden, with difficulty restraining his fury. 'I have some relations who are likely enough to give me a lift of this kind; some *are* ladies, and some gentlemen, and I have a right to know to whom I owe this money.'

'To our firm; who elshe? We have took your paper, and you have our cheques on Childs'.'

'*Your* firm lend money at five per cent!' said Arden with contempt. 'You forget, Mr. Levi, you mentioned in your note distinctly, that you act for another person. Who is that principal for whom you act?'

'I don't know.'

'Come, Mr. Levi! you are no simpleton; you may as well tell me—no one shall be a bit the wiser—for I will know.'

'Azh I'm a shinner—as I hope to be shaved——' began Mr. Levi.

'It won't do—you may just as well tell me—out with it!'

'Well, here now; I *don't* know, but if I did, upon my shoul, I wouldn't tell you.'

'It is pleasant to meet with so much sensitive honour, Mr. Levi,' said Richard Arden very scornfully. 'I have nothing particular to say, only that your firm were mistaken, a little time ago, when they thought that I was without resources; I've friends, you now perceive, who only need to learn that I want money, to volunteer assistance. Have you anything more to say?'

Richard Arden saw the little Jew's fine fangs again displayed in the faint light, as he thus spoke; but it was only prudent to keep his temper with this lucky intervenient.

'I have nothing to shay, Mr. Harden, only there'sh more where that came from, and I may tell you sho, for that'sh no shecret. But don't you go too fasht, young gentleman—not that you won't get it—but don't you go too fasht.'

'If I should ever ask your advice, it will be upon other things. I'm giving the lender as good security as I have given to anyone else. I don't see any great wonder in the matter. Goodnight,' he said haughtily, not taking the trouble to look over his shoulder as he walked away.

'Goodnight,' responded Mr. Levi, taking one of Dignum's cigars from his waistcoat-pocket, and preparing to light it with a lazy grin, as he watched the retreating figure lessening in the perspective of the street, 'and take care of yourshelf for my shake, *do*, and don't you be lettin' all them fine women be throwin' their fortunes like that into your 'at, and bringin' themshelves to the workus, for love of your pretty fashe—poor, dear, love-sick little fools! There you go, right off to Mallet and Turner's, I dareshay, and good luck attend you, for a reglar lady-killin', 'ansome, sweet-spoken, broken-down jackass!'

At this period of his valediction the vesuvian was applied to his cigar, and Richard Arden, turning the far corner of the street, escaped the remainder of his irony, as the Jew, with his hands in his pockets, sauntered up its quiet pavement, in the direction in which Richard Arden had just disappeared. It seemed to that young gentleman that his supplies, no less than thirteen hundred pounds, would all but command the luck of which, as his spirits rose, he began to feel confident. 'Fellows,' he thought, 'who have gone in with less than fifty, have come out, to my knowledge, with thousands; and if less than fifty could do that, what might not be expected from thirteen hundred?'

He picked up a cab. Never did lover fly more impatiently to the feet of his mistress than Richard Arden did, that night, to the shrine of the goddess whom he worshipped.

The muttered scoffs, the dark fiery gaze, the glimmering teeth of this mocking, malicious little Jew, represented an influence that followed Richard Arden that night.

Sudden News

What is luck? Is there such an influence? What type of mind rejects altogether, and consistently, this law or power? Call it by what name you will, fate or fortune, did not Napoleon, the man of death and of action, and did not Swedenborg, the man of quietude and visions, acknowledge it? Where is the successful gamester who does not 'back his luck,' when once it has declared itself, and bow before the storms of fortune when they in turn have set in? I take Napoleon and Swedenborg—the man of this visible world, and the man of the invisible world—as the representatives of extreme types of mind. People who have looked into Swedenborg's works will remember curious passages on the subject, and find more dogmatical, and less metaphysical admissions in Napoleon's conversations everywhere.

In corroboration of this theory, that luck is an element, with its floods and ebbs, against which it is fatuity to contend, the result of Richard Arden's play.

Before half-past two, he had lost every guinea of his treasure. He had been drinking champagne. He was flushed, dismal, profoundly angry. Hot and headachy, he was ready to choke with gall. There was a big, red-headed, vulgar fellow beside him, with a broad-brimmed white hat, who was stuffing his pockets and piling the table before him, as though he had found the secret of an 'open sesame,' and was helping himself from the sacks of the Forty Thieves.

When Richard had lost his last pound, he would have liked to smash the gas-lamps and windows, and the white hat and the red head in it, and roar the blasphemy that rose to his lips. But men can't afford to make themselves ridiculous, and as he turned about to make his unnoticed exit, he saw the little Jew, munching a sandwich, with a glass of champagne beside him.

'I say,' said Richard Arden, walking up to the little man, whose big mouth was full of sandwich, and whose fierce black eyes encountered his instantaneously, 'you don't happen to have a little more, on the same terms, about you?'

Mr. Levi waited to bolt his sandwich, and then swallow down his champagne.

'Shave me!' exclaimed he, when this was done. 'The thoushand gone! every rag! and' (glancing at his watch) 'only two twenty-five! Won't it be rayther young, though, backin' such a run o' bad luck, and throwin' good money after bad, Mr. Harden?'

'That's my affair, I fancy; what I want to know is whether you have got a few hundreds more, on the same terms—I mean, from the same lender. Hang it, say yes or no—can't you?'

'Well, Mr. Harden, there's five hundred more—but 'twasn't expected you'd a' drew it so soon. How much do you say, Mr. Harden?'

'I'll take it all,' said Richard Arden. 'I wish I could have it without these blackguards seeing.'

'They don't care, blesh ye! if you got it from the old boy himself. That *is* a rum un!' There were pen and ink on a small table beside the wall, at which Mr. Levi began rapidly to fill in the blanks of a bill of exchange. 'Why, there's not one o' them, almost, but takes a hundred now and then from me, when they runs out a bit too fast. You'd better shay one month.'

'Say two, like the other, and don't keep me waiting.' 'You'd better shay one—your friend will think you're going a bit too quick to the devil. Remember, as your proverb shays, 'taint the thing to kill the gooshe that laysh the golden eggs—shay one month.'

Levi's large black eye was fixed on him, and he added, 'If you want it pushed on a bit when it comes due, there won't be no great trouble about it, I calculate.'

Richard Arden looked at the large fierce eyes that were silently fixed on him: one of those eyes winked solemnly and significantly.

'Well, what way you like, only be quick,' said Richard Arden.

His new sheaf of cheques were quickly turned into counters; and, after various fluctuations, these counters followed the rest, and in the grey morning he left that haunt jaded and savage, with just fifteen pounds in his pocket, the wreck of the large sum which he had borrowed to restore his fortunes.

It needs some little time to enable a man, who has sustained such a shock as Richard Arden had, to collect his thoughts and define the magnitude of his calamity. He let himself in by a latch-key: the grey light was streaming through the shutters, and turning the chintz pattern of his window-curtains here and there, in streaks, into transparencies. He went into his room and swallowed nearly a tumbler of brandy, then threw off his clothes, drank some more, and fell into a flushed stupor, rather than a sleep, and lay for hours as still as any dead man on the field of battle.

Some four hours of this lethargy, and he became conscious, at intervals, of a sound of footsteps in his room. The shutters were still closed. He thought he heard a voice say, 'Master Richard!' but he was too drowsy, still, to rouse himself.

At length a hand was laid upon him, and a voice that was familiar to his ear repeated twice over, more urgently, 'Master Richard! Master Richard!' He was now awake: very dimly, by his bedside, he saw a figure standing. Again he heard the same words, and wondered, for a few seconds, where he was.

'That's Crozier talking,' said Richard.

'Yes, Sir,' said Crozier, in a low tone; 'I'm here half-an-hour, Sir, waiting till you should wake.'

'Let in some light; I can't see you.'

Crozier opened half the window-shutter, and drew the curtain.

'Are ye ailin', Master Richard—are ye bad, Sir?'

'Ailing—yes, I'm bad enough, as you say—I'm miserable. I don't know where to turn or what to do. Hold my coat while count what's in the pocket. If my father, the old scoundrel——'

'Master Richard, don't ye say the like o' that no more; all's over, this morning, wi' the old master—Sir Reginald's dead, Sir,' said the old follower, sternly.

'Good God!' cried Richard, starting up in his bed and staring at old Crozier with a frightened look.

'Ay, Sir,' said the old servant, in a low stern tone, 'he's gone at last: he was took just a quarter past five this mornin', by the clock at Mortlake, about four minutes before St. Paul's chimed the quarter. The wind being southerly, we heard the chimes. We thought he was all right, and I did not leave him until half-past twelve o'clock, having given him his drops, and waited till he went asleep. It was about three he rang his bell, and in I goes that minute, and finds him sitting up in his bed, talking quite silly-like about old Wainbridge, the groom, that's dead and buried, away in Skarkwynd Churchyard, these thirty year.'

Crozier paused here. He had been crying hours ago, and his eyes and nose still showed evidences of that unbecoming weakness. Perhaps he expected Richard, now Sir Richard Arden, to say something, but nothing came.

''Tis a change, Sir, and I feel a bit queer; and as I was sayin', when I went in, 'twas in his head he saw Tom Wainbridge leadin' a horse saddled and all into the room, and standin' by the side of his bed, with the bridle in his hand, and holdin' the stirrup for him to mount. And what the devil brings Wainbridge here, when he has his business to mind in Yorkshire? and where could he find a horse like that beast? He's waiting for me; I can hear the roarin' brute, and I see Tom's parchment face at the door—*there*,' he'd say, 'and *there*—where are your eyes, Crozier, can't you see, man? Don't be afraid—can't you look—and don't you hear him? Wainbridge's old nonsense.' And he'd laugh a bit to himself every now and again, and then he'd whimper to me, looking a bit frightened, 'Get him away, Crozier, will you? He's annoying me, he'll have me out,' and this sort o' talk he went on wi' for full twenty minutes. I rang the bell to Mrs. Tansey's room, and when she was come we agreed to send in the brougham for the doctor. I think he was a bit wrong i' the garrets, and we were both afraid to let it be no longer.'

Crozier paused for a moment, and shook his head.

'We thought he was goin' asleep, but he wasn't. His eyes was half shut, and his shoulders against the pillows, and Mrs. Tansey was drawin' the eider-down coverlet over his feet, softly, when all on a sudden—I thought he was laughin'—a noise like a little flyrin' laugh, and then a long, frightful yellock, that would make your heart tremble, and awa' wi' him into one o' them fits, and so from one into another, until when the doctor came he said he was in an apoplexy; and so, at just a quarter past five the auld master departed. And I came in to tell you, Sir; and have you any orders to give me, Master Richard? and I'm going on, I take it you'd wish me, to your uncle, Mr. David, and little Miss Alice, that han't heard nout o' the matter yet.'

'Yes, Crozier—go,' said Richard Arden, staring on him as if his soul was in his eyes; and, after a pause, with an effort, he added—'I'll call there as I go on to Mortlake; tell them I'll see them on my way.'

When Crozier was gone, Richard Arden got up, threw his dressing-gown about him, and sat on the side of his bed, feeling very faint. A sudden gush of tears relieved the strange paroxysm. Then come other emotions less unselfish. He dressed hastily. He was too much excited to make a breakfast. He drank a cup of coffee, and drove to Uncle David's house.

Vows For the Future

As he drove to his uncle's house, he was tumbling over facts and figures, in the endeavour to arrive at some conclusion as to how he stood in the balance-sheet that must now be worked out. What a thing that post-obit had turned out! Those cursed Jews who had dealt with him must have known ever so much more about his poor father's health than he did. They are such fellows to worm out the secrets of a family—all through one's own servants, and doctors, and apothecaries. The spies! They stick at nothing—such liars! How they pretended to wish to be off! What torture they kept him in! How they talked of the old man's nervous fibre, and pretended to think he would live for twenty years to come!

'And the deed was not six weeks signed when I found out he had those epileptic fits, and they knew it, the wretches!—and so I've been hit for that huge sum of money. And there is interest, two years' nearly, on that other charge, and that swindle that half ruined me on the Derby. And there are those bills that Levi has got, but that is only fifteen hundred, and I can manage that any time, and a few other trifles.'

And he thought what yeoman's service Longcluse might and *would* have rendered him in this situation. How translucent the whole opaque complexity would have become in a hour or two, and at what easy interest he would have procured him funds to adjust these complications! But here, too, fortune had dealt maliciously. What a piece of cross-grained luck that Longcluse should have chosen to fall in love with Alice! And now they two had exchanged, not shots, but insults, harder to forgive. And that officious fool, Vandeleur, had laid him open to a more direct and humiliating affront than had before befallen him. Henceforward, between him and Longcluse no reconciliation was possible. Fiery and proud by nature was this Richard Arden, and resentful. In Yorkshire the family had been accounted a vindictive race. I don't know. I have only to do with those inheritors of the name who figure in this story.

There remained an able accountant and influential man on 'Change, on whose services he might implicitly reckon—his uncle, David Arden. But he was separated from him by the undefinable chasm of years—the want of sympathy, the sense of authority. He would take not only the management of this financial adjustment, but the carriage of the future of this young, handsome, full-blooded fellow, who had certainly no wish to take unto himself a Mentor.

Here have been projected on this page, as in the disk of an oxy-hydrogen microscope, some of the small and active thoughts that swarmed almost unsuspected in Richard Arden's mind. But it would be injustice to Sir Richard Arden (we may as well let him enjoy at once the title which stately Death has just presented him with—it seems to me a mocking obeisance) to pretend that higher and kinder feelings had no place in his heart.

Suddenly redeemed from ruin, suddenly shocked by an awful spectacle, a disturbance of old associations where there had once been kindness, where estrangements and enmity had succeeded: there was in all this something moving and agitating, that stirred his affections strangely when he saw his sister.

David Arden had left his house an hour before the news reached its inmates. Sir Richard was shown to the drawing-room, where there was no one to receive him; and in a minute Alice, looking very pale and miserable, entered, and running up to him, without saying a word threw her arms about his neck, and sobbed piteously.

Her brother was moved. He folded her to his heart. Broken and hurried words of tenderness and affection he spoke, as he kissed her again and again. Henceforward he would live a better and wiser life. He had tasted the dangers and miseries that attend on play. He swore he would give it up. He had done with the follies of his youth. But for years he had not had a home. He was thrown into the thick of temptation. A fellow who had no home was so likely to amuse himself with play; and he had suffered enough to make him hate it, and she should see what a brother he would be, henceforward, to her.

Alice's heart was bursting with self-reproach; she told Richard the whole story of her trouble of the day before, and the circumstances of her departure from Mortlake, all in an agony of tears; and declared, as young ladies often have done before, that she never could be happy again.

He was disappointed, but generous and gentle feelings had been stirred within him.

'Don't reproach yourself, darling; that is mere lolly. The entire responsibility of your leaving Mortlake belongs to my uncle; and about Wynderbroke, you must not torment yourself; you had a right to a voice in the matter, surely, and I daresay you would not be happier now if you had been less decided, and found yourself at this moment committed to marry him. I have more reason to upbraid myself, but I'm sure I was right, though I sometimes lost my temper; I know my Uncle David thinks I was right; but there is no use now in thinking more about it; right or wrong, it is all over, and I won't distract myself uselessly. I'll try to be a better brother to you than I ever *have* been; and I'll make Mortlake our head-quarters: or we'll live, if you like it better, at Arden Manor, or I'll go abroad with you. I'll lay myself out to make you happy. One thing I'm resolved on, and that is to give up play, and find some manly and useful pursuit; and you'll see I'll do you some credit yet, or at least, as a country squire, do some little good, and be not quite useless in my generation; and I'll do my best, dear Alice, to make you a happy home, and to be all that I ought to be to you, my darling.'

Very affectionately he both spoke and felt, and left Alice with some of her anxieties lightened, and already more interest in the future than she had thought possible an hour before.

Richard Arden had a good deal upon his hands that morning. He had money liabilities that were urgent. He had to catch his friend Mardykes at his lodgings, and get him to see the people in whose betting-books he stood for large figures, to represent to them what had happened, and assure them that a few days should see all settled. Then he had to go to the office of his father's attorney, and learn whether a will was forthcoming; then to consult with his own attorney, and finally to follow his uncle, David Arden, from place to place, and find him at last at home, and talk over details, and advise with him generally about many things, but particularly about the further dispositions respecting the funeral; for a little note from his Uncle David had offered to relieve him of the direction of those hateful details transacted with the undertaker, which everyone is glad to depute.

Uncle David's Suspicions

Mr. David Arden, therefore, had made a call at the office of Paller, Crapely, Plumes, and Co., eminent undertakers in the most gentleman-like, and, indeed, aristocratic line of business, with immense resources at command, and who would undertake to bury a duke, with all the necessary draperies, properties, and *dramatis personae*, if required, before his grace was cold in his bed.

A little dialogue occurred here, which highly interested Uncle David. A stout gentleman, with a muddy and melancholy countenance, and a sad suavity of manner, and in the perennial mourning that belongs to a *gentleman* of his doleful profession, presents himself to David Arden, to receive his instructions respecting the deceased baronet's obsequies. The top of his head is bald, his face is furrowed and baggy; he looks fully sixty-five, and he announces himself as the junior partner, Plumes by name.

Having made his suggestions and his notes, and taken his order for a strictly private funeral in the neighbourhood of London, Mr. Plumes thoughtfully observes that he remembers the name well, having been similarly employed for another member of the same family.

'Ah! How was that? How long ago?' asked Mr. Arden.

'About twenty years, Sir.'

'And where was that funeral?'

'The same place, Sir, Mortlake.'

'Yes, I know that was——?'

'It was Mr. 'Enry, or raything 'Arry Harden. We 'ad to take back the plate, Sir, and change 'Enry to 'Arry—'Arry being the name he was baptised by. There was a hinquest connected with that horder.'

'So there was, Mr. Plumes,' said Uncle David with awakened interest, for that gentleman spoke as if he had something more to say on the subject.

'There was, Sir,—and it affected me very sensibly. My niece, Sir, had a wery narrow escape.'

'Your niece! Really? How could that be?'

'There was a Mister Yelland Mace, Sir, who paid his haddresses to her, and I do believe, Sir, she rayther liked him. I don't know, I'm sure, whether he was serious in 'is haddresses, but it looked very like as if he meant to speak; though I do suppose he was looking 'igher for a wife. Well, he was believed to 'ave 'ad an 'and in that 'orrible business.'

'I know—so he undoubtably had—and the poor young lady, I suppose, was greatly shocked and distressed.'

'Yes, Sir, and she died about a year after.'

David Arden expressed his regret, and then he asked—

'You have often seen that man, Yelland Mace?'

'Not often, Sir.'

'You remember his face pretty well, I daresay?'

'Well, no, Sir, not very well. It is a long time.'

'Do you recollect whether there was anything noticeable in his features?—had he, for instance, a remarkably prominent nose?'

'I don't remember that he 'ad, Sir. I rather think not, but I can't by no means say for certain. It is a long time, and I 'aven't much of a memory for faces. There is a likeness of him among my poor niece's letters.'

'Really? I should be so much obliged if you would allow me to see it.'

'It is at 'ome, Sir, but I shall be 'ome to dinner before I go out to Mortlake; and, if you please, I shall borrow it of my sister, and take it with me.'

This offer David Arden gladly accepted.

When the events were recent, he could have no difficulty in identifying Yelland Mace, by the evidence of fifty witnesses, if necessary. But it was another thing now. The lapse of time had made matters very different. It was recent impressions of a vague kind about Mr. Longcluse that had revived the idea, and prompted a renewal of the search. Martha Tansey was aged now, and he had misgivings about the accuracy of her recollection. Was it possible, after all, that he was about to see that which would corroborate his first vague suspicions?

Sir Richard had a busy and rather harassing day, the first of his succession to an old title and a new authority, and he was not sorry when it closed. He had stolen about from place to place in a hired cab, and leaned back to avoid a chance recognition, like an absconding debtor; and had talked with the people whom he was obliged to call on and see, in low and hurried colloquy, through the window of the cab. And now night had fallen, the lamps were glaring, and tired enough he returned to his lodgings, sent for his tailor, and arranged promptly about the

——inky cloak, good mother,
And customary suits of solemn black;

and that done, he wrote two or three notes to kindred in Yorkshire, with whom it behoved him to stand on good terms; and then he determined to drive out to Mortlake Hall. An unpleasant mixture of feelings was in his mind as he thought of that visit, and the cold tenant of the ancestral house, whom in the grim dignity of death, it would not have been seemly to leave for a whole day and night unvisited. It was to him a repulsive visit, but how could he postpone it?

Behold him, then, leaning back in his cab, and driving through glaring lamps, and dingy shops, and narrow ill-thriven streets, eastward and northward; and now, through the little antique village, with trembling lights, and by the faded splendours of the 'Guy of Warwick.' And he sat up and looked out of the windows, as they entered the narrow road that is darkened by the tall overhanging timber of Mortlake grounds.

Now they are driving up the broad avenue, with its noble old trees clumped at either side; and with a shudder Sir Richard Arden leans back and moves no more until the cab pulls up at the door-steps, and the knock sounds through hall and passages, which he dared not so have disturbed, uninvited, a day or two before. Crozier ran down the steps to greet Master Richard.

'How are you, old Crozier?' he said, shaking hands from the cab-window, for somehow he liked to postpone entering the house as long as he could. 'I could not come earlier. I have been detained in town all day by business, of various kinds, connected with this.' And he moved his hand toward the open hall-door, with a gloomy nod or two. 'How is Martha?'

'Tolerable, Sir, thankye, considerin'. It's a great upset to her.'

'Yes, poor thing, of course. And has Mr. Paller been here—the person who is to—to——'

'The undertaker? Yes, Sir, he was here at two o'clock, and some of the people has been busy in the room, and his men has come out again with the coffin, Sir. I think they'll soon be leaving; they've been here a quarter of an hour, and—if I may make bold to ask, Sir,—what day will the funeral be?'

'I don't know myself, Crozier; I must settle that with my uncle. He said he thought he would come here himself this evening, at about nine, and it must be very near that now. Where is Martha?'

'In her room, Sir, I think.'

'I won't see her there. Ask her to come to the oak-room.'

Richard got out and entered the house of which he was now the master, with an oppressive misgiving.

The oak-parlour was a fine old room, and into the panels were let four full-length portraits. Two of these were a lady and gentleman, in the costume of the beginning of Charles the Second's reign. The lady held an Italian greyhound by a blue ribbon, and the *gentleman* stood booted for the field, and falcon on fist. It struck Richard, for the first time, how wonderfully like Alice that portrait of the beautiful lady was. He raised the candle to examine it. There was a story about this lady. She had been compelled to marry the companion portrait, with the hawk on his hand, and those beautiful lips had dropped a curse, in her despair, when she was dying, childless, and wild with grief. She prayed that no daughter of the house of Arden might ever wed the man of her love, and it was said that a fatality had pursued the ladies of that family, which looked like the accomplishment of the malediction; and a great deal of curious family lore was connected with this legend and portrait.

As he held the candle up to this picture, still scanning its features, the door slowly opened, and Martha Tansey, arrayed in a black silk dress of a fashion some twenty years out of date, came in. He set down the candle, and took the old woman's hand, and greeted her very kindly.

'How's a' wi' you, Master Richard? A dowly house ye've come too. Ye didna look to see this sa soon?'

'Very sudden, Martha—awfully sudden. I could not let the day pass without coming out to see you.'

'Not me, Master Richard, but to ha'e a last look at the face of the father that begot ye. He'll be shrouded and coffined by this time—the light'll not be lang on that face. The lid will be aboon it and screwed down tomorrow, I dar' say. Ay, there goes the undertaker's men; and there's a man from Mr. Paller—Mr. Plumes is his name—that says he'll stay still your Uncle David comes, for he told him he had something very particular to say to him; and I desired him to wait in my room after his business about the poor master was over; and the a'ad things is passin' awa' and it's time auld Martha was fittin' herself.'

'Don't say that, Martha, unless you would have me think you expect to find me less kind than my father was.'

'There's good and there's bad in every one, Master Richard.

Ye can't take it in meal and take it in malt. A bit short-waisted he was, there's no denyin', and a sharp word now and again; but none so hard to live wi' as many a one that was cooler-tempered, and more mealy-mouthed; and I think ye were o'er hard wi' him, Master Richard. Ye should have opened the estate. It was that killed him,' she continued considerately. 'Ye broke his heart, Master Richard; he was never the same man after he fell out wi' you.'

'Some day, Martha, you'll learn all about it,' said he gently. 'It was no fault of mine—ask my Uncle David. I'm not the person to persuade you; and, beside, I have not courage to talk over that cruel quarrel now.'

'Come and see him,' said the old woman grimly, taking up the candle.

'No, Martha, no; set it down again—I'll not go.'

'And when will you see him?'

'Another time—not now—I can't.'

'He's laid in his coffin now; they'll be out again in the mornin'. If you don't see him now, ye'll never see him; and what will the folk down in Yorkshire say, when it's told at Arden Court that Master Richard never looked on his dead father's face, nor saw more of him after his flittin' than the plate on his coffin. By Jen! 'twill stir the blood o' the old tenants and gar them clench their fists and swear, I warrant, at the very sound o' yer name; for there never was an Arden died yet, at Arden Court, but he was waked, and treated wi' every respect, and visited by every living soul of his kindred, for ten mile round.'

'If you think so, Martha, say no more. I'll—go as well now as another time—and, as you say, sooner or later it must be done.'

'He's lookin' very nice and like himself,' mumbled the old woman, as she led the way.

At the open door of Sir Reginald's room stood Mr. Plumes, in professional black with a pensive and solemn countenance, intending politely to do the honours.

'Thank you, Sir,' said the old woman graciously, taking the lead in the proceedings. 'This is the young master, and he won't mind troublin' you, Mr. Plumes. If you please to go to my room, Sir, the third door on the right, you'll find tea made, Sir; and Mr. Crozier, I think, will be there.'

And having thus disposed of the stranger, they entered the room, in which candles were burning.

Sir Reginald had, as it were, already made dispositions for his final journey. He had left his bed, and lay instead, in the handsomely upholstered coffin which stood on trestles beside it. Thin and fixed were the cold, earthly features that looked upward from their white trimmings. Sir Richard Arden checked his step and held his breath as he came in sight of these stern lineaments. The pale light that surrounds the dead face of the martyr was wanting here: in its stead, upon selfish lines and contracted features, a shadow stood.

Mrs. Tansey, with a feather-brush placed near, drove away a fly that was trying to alight on the still face.

'I mind him when he was a boy,' she said, with a groan and shake of the head. 'There was but six years between us, and the life that's ended is but a dream, all like yesterday—nothing to look back on; and, I'm sure, if there's rest for them that has been troubled on earth, he's happy now: a blessed change 'twill be.'

'Yes, Martha, we all have our troubles.'

'Ay, it's well to know that in time: the young seldom dees,' she answered sardonically.

'I'll go, Martha. I'll return to the oak-room. I wish my uncle were come.'

'Well, you have took your last look, and that's but decent, and——Dear me, Master Richard, you do look bad!'

'I feel a little faint, Martha. I'll go there; and will you give me a glass of sherry?'

He waited at the room door, while Martha nimbly ran to her room, and returned with some sherry and a wine-glass. He had hardly taken a glass, and begun to feel himself better, when David Arden's step was heard approaching from the hall. He greeted his nephew and Martha in a hushed undertone, as he might in church; and then, as people will enter such rooms, he passed in and crossed with a very soft tread, and said a word or two in whispers. You would have thought that Sir Reginald was tasting the sweet slumber of precarious convalescence, so tremendously does death simulate sleep.

When Uncle David followed his nephew to the oak-room, where the servants had now placed candles, he appeared a little paler, as a man might who had just witnessed an operation. He looked through the unclosed shutters on the dark scene; then he turned, and placed his hand kindly on his nephew's arm, and said he, with a sigh—

'Well, Dick, you're the head of the house now; don't run the old ship on the rocks. Remember, it is an old name, and, above all, remember, that Alice is thrown upon your protection. Be a good brother, Dick. She is a true-hearted, affectionate creature: be you the same to her. You can't do your duty by her unless you do it also by yourself. For the first time in your life, a momentous responsibility devolves upon you. In God's name, Dick, give up play and do your duty!'

'I have learned a lesson, uncle; I have not suffered in vain. I'll never take a dice-box in my hand again; I'd as soon take a burning coal. I shall never back a horse again while I live. I am quite cured, thank God, of that madness. I sha'n't talk about it; let time declare how I am changed.'

'I am glad to hear you speak so. You are right, that is the true test. Spoken like a man!' said Uncle David, and he took his hand very kindly.

The entrance of Martha Tansey at this moment gave the talk a new turn.

'By-the-bye, Martha,' said he, 'has Mr. Plumes come? He said he would be here at eight o'clock.'

'He's waitin', Sir; and 'twas to tell you so I came in. Shall I tell him to come here?'

'I asked him to come, Dick; I knew you would allow me.

He has some information to give me respecting the wretch who murdered your poor Uncle Harry.'

'May I remain?' asked Richard.

'Do; certainly.'

'Then, Martha, will you tell him to come here?' said Richard, and in another minute the sable garments and melancholy visage of Mr. Plumes entered the room slowly.

When Mr. Plumes was seated, he said, with much deliberation, in reply to Uncle David's question—

'Yes, Sir, I have brought it with me. You said, I think, you wished me to fetch it, and as my sister was at home, she hobleeged me with a loan of it. It belonged, you may remember, to her deceased daughter—my niece. I have got it in my breast-pocket;

perhaps you would wish me now to take it hout?'

'I'm most anxious to look at it,' said Uncle David, approaching with extended hand. 'You said you had seen him; was this a good likeness?'

These questions and the answers to them occupied the time during which Mr. Plumes, whose proceedings were slow as a funeral, disengaged the square parcel in question from his pocket, and then went on to loosen the knots in the tape which tied it up, and afterwards to unfold the wrappings of paper which enveloped it.

'I don't remember him well enough, only that he was good-looking. And this was took by machinery, and it *must* be like. The ball and socket they called it. It must be hexact, Sir.'

So saying, he produced a square black leather case, which being opened displayed a black profile, the hair and whiskers being indicated by a sort of gilding which, laid upon sable, reminded one of the decorations of a coffin, and harmonised cheerfully with Mr. Plumes' profession.

'Oh!' exclaimed Uncle David with considerable disappointment, 'I thought it was a miniature; this is only a silhouette; but you are sure it *is* the profile of Yelland Mace?'

'That is certain, Sir. His name is on the back of it, and she kept it, poor young woman! with a lock of his 'air and some hother relics in her work-box.'

By this time Uncle David was examining it with deep interest The outline demolished all his fancies about Mr. Longcluse. The nose, though delicately formed, was decidedly the ruling feature of the face. It was rather a parrot face, but with a good forehead. David Arden was disappointed. He handed it to his nephew.

'That is a kind of face one would easily remember,' he observed to Richard as he looked. 'It is not like any one that I know, or *ever* knew.'

'No,' said Richard; 'I don't recollect any one the least like it.' And he replaced it in his uncle's hand.

'We are very much obliged to you, Mr. Plumes; it was your

mention of it this morning, and my great anxiety to discover all I can respecting that man, Yelland Mace, that induced me to make the request. Thank you very much,' said old Mr. Arden, placing the profile in the fat fingers of Mr. Plumes. 'You must take a glass of sherry before you leave. And have you got a cab to return in?'

'The men are waiting for me, I thank you, and I have just 'ad my tea, Sir, much obleeged, and I think I had best return to town, gentlemen, as I have some few words to say tonight to our Mr. Trimmer; so, with your leave, gentlemen, I'll wish you goodnight.'

And with a solemn bow, first to Mr. Arden, then to the young scion of the house, and lastly a general bow to both, that grave gentleman withdrew.

'I could see no likeness in that thing to any one,' repeated old Mr. Arden. 'Mr. Longcluse is a friend of yours?' he added a little abruptly.

'I can't say he was a friend; he was an acquaintance, but even that is quite ended.'

'What! you don't know him any longer?'

'No.'

'You're quite sure!'

'Perfectly.'

'Then I may say I'm very glad. I don't like him, and I can't say why; but I can't help connecting him with your poor uncle's death. I must have dreamed about him and forgot the dream, while the impression continues; for I cannot discover in any fact within my knowledge the slightest justification for the unpleasant persuasion that constantly returns to my mind. I could not trace a likeness to him in that silhouette.'

He looked at his nephew, who returned his steady look with one of utter surprise.

'Oh, dear! no. There is not a vestige of a resemblance,' said Richard. 'I know his features very well.'

'No,' said Uncle David, lowering his eyes to the table, on which he was tapping gently with his fingers; 'no, there certainly is not—not any. But I can't dismiss the suspicion. I can't get it out of my head, Richard, and yet I can't account for it,' he said, raising his eyes to his nephew's. 'There is something in it; I could not else be so haunted.'

Mr. Longcluse Employed

The funeral was not to be for some days, and then to be conducted in the quietest manner possible. Sir Reginald was to be buried in a small vault under the little *church*, whose steeple cast its shadow every sunny evening across the garden-hedges of the 'Guy of Warwick', and could be seen to the left from the door of Mortlake Hall, among distant trees. Further it was settled by Richard Arden and his uncle, on putting their heads together, that the funeral was to take place after dark in the evening; and even the undertaker's people were kept in ignorance of the exact day and hour.

In the meantime, Mr. Longcluse did not trouble any member of the family with his condolences or inquiries. As a raven perched on a solitary bough surveys the country round, and observes many things—very little noticed himself-so Mr. Longcluse made his observations from his own perch and in his own way. Perhaps he was a little surprised on receiving from Lady May Penrose a note, in the *following* terms:—

Dear Mr. Longcluse,

I have just heard something that troubles me; and as know of no one who would more readily do me a kindness, I hope you won't think me very troublesome if I beg of you to make me a call tomorrow morning, at any time before twelve.

Ever yours sincerely,

May Penrose.

Mr. Longcluse smiled darkly, as he read this note again. 'It is better to be sought after than to offer one's self.'

Accordingly, next morning, Mr. Longcluse presented himself in Lady May's drawing-room; and after a little waiting, that good-natured lady entered the room. She liked to make herself miserable about the troubles of her friends, and on this occasion, on entering the door, she lifted her hands and eyes, and quickened her step towards Mr. Longcluse, who advanced a step or two to meet her.

'Oh! Mr. Longcluse, it is so kind of you to come,' she exclaimed; 'I am in such a sea of troubles! and you are such a friend, I know I may tell you. You have heard, of course, of poor Reginald's death. How horribly sudden!—shocking! and dear Alice is so broken by it! He had been, the day before, so cross—poor Reginald, everybody knows he had a temper, poor old soul!—and had made himself so disagreeable to her, and now she is quite miserable, as if it had been her fault. But no matter; it's not about that. Only do you happen to know of people—bankers or something—called Childers and Ballard?'

'Oh! dear, yes; Childers and Ballard; they are City people, on 'Change—stockbrokers. They are people you can quite rely on, so far as their solvency is concerned.'

'Oh! it isn't that. They have not been doing any business for me. It is a very unpleasant thing to speak about, even to a kind friend like you; but I want you to advise what is best to be done; and to ask you, if it is not very unreasonable, to use any influence you can—without trouble, of course, I mean—to prevent anything so distressing as may possibly happen.'

'You have only to say, dear Lady May, what I can do. I am too happy to place my poor services at your disposal.'

'I knew you would say so,' said Lady May, again shaking hands in a very friendly way; 'and I know what I say won't go any further. I mean, of course, that you will receive it entirely as a confidence.'

Mr. Longcluse was earnest in his assurances of *secrecy* and good faith.

'Well,' said Lady May, lowering her voice, 'poor Reginald, he was my cousin, you know, so it pains me to say it; but he was a good deal embarrassed; his estates were very much in debt. He owed money to a great many people, I believe.'

'Oh! Really?' Mr. Longcluse expressed his well-bred surprise very creditably.

'Yes, indeed; and these people, Childers and Ballard, have something they call a judgment, I think. It is a kind of debt, for about twelve hundred pounds, which they say must be paid at once; and they vow that if it is not they will seize the coffin, and—and—all that, at the funeral. And David Arden is so angry, you can't think! and he says that the money is not owed to them, and that they have no right by law to do any such thing; and that from beginning to end it is a mere piece of extortion. And he won't hear of Richard's paying a farthing of it; and he says that Richard must bring a law-suit against them, for ever so much money, if they attempt anything of the kind, and that he's sure to win. But that is not what I am thinking of—it is about poor Alice, she is so miserable about the mere chance of its happening. The profanation—the *fracas*—all so shocking and so public—the funeral, you know.'

'You are quite sure of that, Lady May?' said Longcluse.

'I heard it all as I tell you. My man of business told me; and I saw David Arden,' she answered.

'Oh! yes; but I mean, with respect to Miss Arden. Does *she,* in particular, so very earnestly desire intervention in this awkward business?'

'Certainly; *only* she—only Miss Arden—only Alice.'

He looked down in thought, and then again in her face, paler than usual. He had made up his mind.

'I shall take measures,' he said quietly. 'I shall do everything—anything in my power. I shall even expose myself to the risk of insult, for her sake; only let it soften her. After I have done it, ask her, not before, to think mercifully of me.'

He was going.

'Stay, Mr. Longcluse, just a moment. I don't know what I am to say to you; I am so much obliged. And yet how can I undertake that anything you do may affect other people as you wish?'

'Yes, of course you are right; I am willing to take my chance of that. Only, dear Lady May, will you *write* to her? All I plead for—and it is the *last* time I shall sue to her for anything—is that my folly may be forgotten, and I restored to the humble privileges of an acquaintance.'

'But do you really wish me to write? I'll take an opportunity of speaking to her. Would not that be less formal?'

'Perhaps so; but, forgive me, it would not answer. I beg of you to write.'

'But why do you prefer my writing?'

'Because I shall then read her answer.'

'Then I must tell her that you are to read her reply.'

'Certainly, dear Lady May; I meant nothing else.'

'Well, Mr. Longcluse, there is no great difficulty.'

'I only make it a request, not a condition. I shall do my utmost in any case. Pray tell her that.'

'Yes, I'll write to her, as you wish it; or, at least, I'll ask her to put on paper what she desires me to say, and I'll read it to you.'

'That will answer as well. How can I thank you?'

'There is no need of thanks. It is I who should thank you for taking, I am afraid, a great deal of trouble so promptly and kindly.'

'I know those people; they are cunning and violent, difficult to deal with, harder to trust,' said Longcluse, looking down in thought. 'I should be most happy to settle with them, and afterwards the executor might settle with me at his convenience; but, from what you say, Mr. David Arden and his nephew won't admit their claim. I don't believe such a seizure would be legal; but they are people who frequently venture illegal measures, upon the calculation that it would embarrass those against whom they adopt them more than themselves to bring them into court. It is not an easy card to play, you see, and they are people I hate; but I'll try.'

In another minute Mr. Longcluse had taken his leave, and was gone.

The Night of the Funeral

Mr. Longcluse smiled as he sat in his cab, driving city-ward to the office of Messrs. Childers and Ballard.

'How easily, now, one might get up a scene! Let Ballard, the monster—he would look the part well—with his bailiffs, seize the coffin and its precious burden in the church; and I, like Sir Edward Maulay, step forth from behind a pillar to stay the catastrophe. We could make a very fine situation, and I the hero; but the girl is too clever for that, and Richard as sharp—that is, as base—as I; knowing my objects, he would at once see a *plant,* and all would be spoiled. I shall do it in the least picturesque and most probable way. I should like to know the old housekeeper, Mrs. Tansey, better; I should like to be on good terms with her. An awkward meeting with Arden. What the devil do I care? besides, it is but one chance in a hundred. Yes, that is the best way. Can I see Mr. Ballard in his private room for a minute?' he added aloud, to the clerk, Mr. Blotter, behind the mahogany counter, who turned from his desk deferentially, let himself down from his stool, and stood attentive before the great man, with his pen behind his ear.

'Certainly, Mr. Longcluse—certainly, Sir. Will you allow me, Sir, to conduct you?'

Most men would have been peremptorily denied; the more fortunate would have had to await the result of an application to Mr. Ballard; but to Mr. Longcluse all doors flew open, and wherever he went, like Mephistopheles, the witches received him gaily, and the cat-apes did him homage.

Without waiting for the assistance of Mr. Blotter, he ran up the back-stairs familiarly to see Mr. Ballard; and when Mr. Longcluse came down, looking very grave, Mr. Ballard, with the red face and lowering countenance which he could not put off, accompanied him downstairs deferentially, and held open the office-door for him; and could not suppress his grins for some time in the consciousness of the honour he had received. Mr. Ballard hoped that the people over the way had seen Mr. Longcluse step from his door; and mentioned to everyone he talked to for a week, that he had Mr. Longcluse in his private office in consultation—first it was 'for a quarter of an hour by the clock over the chimney,' speedily it grew to 'half-an-hour,' and finally to 'upwards of an hour, by——,' with a stare in the face of the wondering, or curious, listener.

And when clients looked in, in the course of the day, to consult him, he would say, with a wag of his head and a little looseness about minutes, 'There was a man sitting here a minute ago, Mr. Longcluse—you may have met him as you came up the stairs—that could have given us a wrinkle about that;' or, 'Longcluse, who was here consulting with me this morning, is clearly of opinion that Italian bonds will be down a quarter by settling day;' or, 'Take my advice, and don't burn your fingers with those things, for it is possible something queer may happen any day after Wednesday. I had Longcluse—I daresay you may have heard of him,' he parenthesised jocularly—'sitting in that chair today for very nearly an hour and a half, and that's a fellow one doesn't sit long with without hearing something worth remembering.'

From the attorney of Sir Richard Arden was served upon Messrs. Childers and Ballard, that day, a cautionary notice in very stern terms respecting their threatened attack upon Sir Reginald's funeral appointments and body; to which they replied in terms as sharp, and fixed three o'clock for payment of the bond.

It was a very short mile from Mortlake to that small old church near the 'Guy of Warwick,' the bit of whose grey spire and the pinnacle of whose weather-cock you could see between the two great clumps of elms to the left. Sir Reginald, feet foremost, was to make this little journey that evening under a grove of black plumes, to the small, quiet room, which he was henceforward to share with his ancestor Sir Hugh Arden, of Mortlake Hall, Baronet, whose pillard monument decorated the little church.

He lies now, soldered up and screwed down, in his strait bed, triply secured in lead, mahogany, and oak, and as safe as 'the old woman of Berkeley' hoped to be from the grip of marauders. Once there, and the stone door replaced and mortared in, the irritable old gentleman might sleep the quietest sleep his body had ever enjoyed, to the crack of doom. The space was short, too, which separated that from the bed-room he was leaving; but the interval was 'Jew's ground,' trespassing on which, it was thought, he ran a great risk of being clutched by frantic creditors. A whisper of the danger had got into the housekeeper's room; and Crozier, whose north-country blood was hot, and temper warlike, had loaded the horse-pistols, and swore that he would shoot the first man who laid a hand unfriendly on the old master's coffin.

There was an agitation simmering under the grim formalities and tip-toe treadings of the house of death. Martha Tansey grew frightened, angry as she was, and told Richard Arden that Crozier was 'neither to hold nor to bind, and meant to walk by the hearse, and stand by the coffin till it was shut into the vault, with loaded pistols in his coat-pockets, and would make food for worms so sure as they villains dar'd to interrupt the funeral.'

Whereupon Richard saw Crozier, took the pistols from him, shook him very hard by the hand, for he liked him all the more, and told him that he would desire nothing better than their attempting to accomplish their threats, as he was well advised the law would make examples of them. Then he went upstairs, and saw Alice, and he could not help thinking how her black crapes became her. He kissed her, and, sitting down beside her, said,—'Martha Tansey says, darling, that you are unhappy about something she has been telling you concerning this miserable funeral. She ought not to have alarmed you about it. If I had known that you were frightened, or, in fact, knew anything about it, I should have made a point of coming out here yesterday, although I had fifty things to do.'

'I had a very good-natured note today, Dick, from Lady May,' she said— 'only a word, but very kindly intended.' And she placed the open note in his fingers. When he had read it, Richard dropped the note on the table with a sneer.

'That man, I suspect, is himself the secret promoter of this outrage—a very inexpensive way, this, of making character with

Lady May, and placing you under an obligation—the scoundrel!'

Looks and language of hatred are not very pretty at any time, but in the atmosphere of death they acquire a character of horror. Some momentary disturbance of this kind Richard may have seen in his sisters pale face, for he said,—

'Don't mind what I say about that fellow, for I have no patience with myself for having ever known him.'

'I am so glad, Dick, you have dropped *that* acquaintance!' said the young lady.

'You have come at last to think as I do,' said Richard, 'It is not so much thinking as something different; the uncertainty about him—the appalling stories you have heard—and, oh! Richard, I had such a dream last night! I dreamt that Mr. Longcluse murdered you. You smile, but I could not have imagined anything that was not real, so vivid, and it was in this room, and—I don't know how, for I forget the beginning of it—the candles went out, and you were standing near the door talking to me, and bright moonlight was at the window, and showed you quite distinctly, and the open door; and Mr. Longcluse came from behind it with a pistol, and I tried to scream, but I couldn't. But you turned about and stabbed at him with a knife or something; it shone in the moonlight, and instantly there was a line of blood across his face; he fired, and I saw you fall back on the floor; I knew you were dead, and I awoke in terror. I thought I still saw his wicked face in the dark, quite white as it was in my dream. I screamed, and thought I was going mad.'

'It is only, darling, that all that has happened has made you nervous, and no wonder. Don't mind your dreams. Longcluse and I will never exchange a word more. We have turned our backs on one another, and our paths lie in very different directions.'

This was a melancholy and grizzly evening at Mortlake Hall. The undertakers were making some final and mysterious arrangements about the coffin, and stole in and out of the dead baronet's room, of which they had taken possession.

Martha Tansey was alone in her room. It was a lurid sunset. Immense masses of black cloud were piled in the west, and from a long opening in that sombre screen, near the horizon, the expiring light glared like the red fire at night, through the clink of a smithy. Mrs. Tansey, dressed in deepest mourning, awaited the hour when she was to accompany the funeral of her old master.

Without succumbing to the threat of Messrs. Childers and Ballard, David Arden and his nephew would have been glad to evade the risk of the *fracas*, which would no doubt have been a dismal scandal. Martha Tansey herself was not quite sure at what hour the funeral was to leave Mortlake. Opposite the window from which she looked, stand groups of gigantic elms that darken that side of the house, and underwood forms a thick screen among their trunks. Upon the edges of this foliage glinted that fierce farewell gleam, and among the glimmering leaves behind she thought she saw the sinister face of Mr. Longcluse looking toward her.

Her fear and horror of Longcluse had increased, and if the very remembrance of him visited her with a sudden qualm, you may be sure that the sight of him, on this melancholy evening, was a shock. Alice's wild dream, which she had recounted to her, did not serve to dissociate him from the vague misgivings that his image called up. She stared aghast at the apparition—itself uncertain—while in the deep shadow, with a foreground of fiercely flashing leaves, had on a sudden looked at her, and before she could utter an exclamation it was gone.

'I think it is my old eyes that plays me tricks, and my weary head that's 'wildered wi' all this dowly jummlement! What sud bring him there? It was never him I sid, only a fancy, and it's past and gone; and so, in the name of God, be it now, and ever, amen! For an evil sight it is, and bodes us no good. Who's there?'

'It's me, Mrs. Tansey,' said Crozier, who had just come in. 'Master Richard desired me to tell you it is to be at ten o'clock tonight. He and Mr. David thinks that best, and you're to please not to mention it to no one.'

'Ten o'clock! That's very late, ain't it? No, surely, I'll not blab to no one; let him tell them when he sees fit. Martha Tansey's na that sort; she has had mony a secret to keep, and always the confidence o' the family, and 'twould be queer if she did not know to ho'd her tongue by this time. Sit ye down, Mr. Crozier—ye're wore off yer feet, man, like myself, ever since this happened and rest a bit; the kettle's boilin', and ye'll tak' a cup o' tea. It's hours yet to ten o'clock.'

So Mr. Crozier, who was in truth a tired man, complied, and took his seat by the fire, and talked over Sir Reginald's money matters, his fits, and his death; and, finally, he fell asleep in his chair, having taken three cups of tea.

The twilight had melted into darkness by this time, and the clear, cold moonlight was frosting all the landscape, and falling white and bright on the carriage-way outside, and casting on the floor the sharp shadows of the window-sashes, and giving the brilliant representations of the windows and the very veining of the panes of glass upon the white boards.

As Martha sat by the table, with her eyes fixed, in a reverie, on one of these reflections upon the floor, the shadow of a man was suddenly presented upon it, and raising her eyes she saw a figure, black against the moonlight, beckoning gently to her to approach.

Martha Tansey was an old lass of the Northumbrian counties, and had in her veins the fiery blood of the Border. The man wore a great-coat, and she could not discern his features; but he was tall and slight, and she was sure he was Mr. Longcluse. But 'what dar' Longcluse say or do that she need fear?' And was not Crozier dozing there in the chair, 'ready at call?'

Up she got, and stalked boldly to the window, and, drawing near, she plainly saw, as the stranger drew himself up from the window-pane through which he had been looking, and the moonlight glanced on his features, that the face was indeed that of Mr. Longcluse. He looked very pale, and was smiling. He nodded to her in a friendly way once or twice as she approached. She stood stock-still about two yards away, and though she knew him well, she deigned no sign of recognition, for she had learned vaguely something of the feud that had sprung up between him and the young head of the family, and no daughter of the marches was ever a fiercer partisan than lean old Martha. He tapped at the window, still smiling, and beckoned her nearer. She did come a step nearer, and asked sternly—

'What's your will wi' me?'

'I'm Mr. Longcluse,' he said, in a low tone, but with sharp and measured articulation. 'I have something important to say. Open the window a little; I must not raise my voice, and I have this to give you.' He held a note by the corner, and tapped it on the glass.

Martha Tansey thought for a moment. It could not be a law-writ he had to serve; a rich man like him would never do that. Why should she not take his note, and hear what he had to say? She removed the bolt from the sash, and raised the window. There was not a breath stirring.

Among the Trees

Then the old woman had raised the window, 'Thanks,' said Mr. Longcluse, almost in a whisper. 'There are people, Lady May Penrose told me this morning, threatening to interrupt the funeral tonight. Of course you know—you must know.'

'I have heard o' some such matter, but 'tis nout to no one here. We don't care a snap for them, and if they try any sich lids, by my sang, we'll fit them. And I think, Sir, if ye've any thing o' consequence to tell to the family, ye'll not mind my saying 'twould be better ye sud go, like ither folk, to the hall-door, and leave your message there.'

'Your reproof would be better deserved, Mrs. Tansey,' he answers good-humouredly, 'if there had not been a difficulty. Mr. Richard Arden is not on pleasant terms with me, and my business will not afford to wait. I understand that Miss Arden has suffered much anxiety. It is entirely on her account that I have interested myself so much in it; and I don't see, Mrs. Tansey, why you and I should not be better friends,' he adds, extending his long slender hand gently towards her.

She does not take it, but makes a stiff little curtsey instead, and draws back about six inches.

Perhaps Mr. Longcluse had meditated making her a present, but her severe looks daunted him, and he thought that he might as well be a little better acquainted before he made that venture. He went on—

'You have spoken very wisely, Mrs. Tansey; I am sure if these people do as they threaten, it will be contrary to law, and so, as you say, you may snap your fingers at them at last. But in the meantime they may enter the house and seize the coffin, or possibly cause some disgraceful interruption on the way. Lady May tells me that Miss Alice has suffered a great deal in consequence. Will you tell her to set her mind at ease? Pray assure her that I have seen the people, that I have threatened them into submission, that I am confident no such attempt will be made, and that should the slightest annoyance be attempted, Crozier has only to present the notice enclosed in this to the person offering it, and it will instantly be discontinued. I have done all this *entirely* on her account, and pray lose no time in quieting her alarms. I am sure, Mrs. Tansey, you and I shall be better friends some day.'

Mrs. Tansey curtseyed again.

'Pray take this note.'

She took it.

'Give it to Crozier; and pray tell Miss Alice Arden, immediately, that she need have no fears. Goodnight.'

And pale Mr. Longcluse, with his smile and his dismally dark gaze, and the strange suggestion of something undefined in look or tone, or air, that gradually overcome her more and more till she almost felt faint, as he smiled and murmured at the open window, in the moonlight, was gone. Then she stood with the note in her thin fingers, without moving, and called to Crozier with a shrill and earnest summons as one who has just had a frightful dream will call up a sleeper in the same room.

Mr. Longcluse walks boldly and listlessly through this forbidden ground. He does not care who may meet him. Near the house, indeed, he would not like an encounter with Sir Richard Arden, because he knows that his being involved in a quarrel at such a moment, so near, especially with her brother, would not subserve his interests with Alice Arden.

For hours he strode or loitered alone through the solitary woodlands. The moonlight was beautiful; the old trees stand mournful and black against the luminous sky; there is for him a fascination in the solitude, as his noiseless steps lead him alternately into the black shadow cast on the sward by the towering foliage, and into the clear moonlight, on dewy grass that shows grey in that cold brightness. He was in the excitement of hope and suspense. Things had looked very black, but a door had opened and light came out. Was it a dream?

He leans with folded arms against the trunk of one of the trees that stand there, and from the slight elevation of the ground he can see the avenue under the boughs of the trees that flank it, and the chimneys of Mortlake Hall through the summits of the opening clumps. How melancholy and still the whole scene looks under that light!

'When I succeed to all this, who will be mistress of it?' he says, with his strange smile, looking toward the summits of the chimneys, that indicate the site of the Hall. 'No one knows who I am; who can tell my history? What about that opera-girl? What about my money?—money is alway exaggerated. How many humbugs! how many collapses! stealing into society by evasions, on false pretences, in disguise! The man in the mask, ha! ha! Really perhaps *two* masks; not a bad fluke, that. The villain! You would not take a thousand pounds and know me—that is speaking boldly.

'A thousand pounds is still something in your book. You would not take it. The time will come, perhaps, when you'd *give* a thousand—ten thousand, if you had them—that I were your friend. Slanderous villain! To think of his talking so of me! The man in the mask trying to excite suspicion. My two masks are broken, and I all the better. By —! you shall meet me yet without a mask. Alice! will you be my idol? There is no neutrality with one like me in such a case. If I don't worship, I must *break* the image. What a speck we stand on between the illimitable—the eternal past and the eternal future—always looking for a present that shall be something tangible; always finding it a mathematical point, *cujus nulla est pars*—the mere stand-point of a retrospect and a conjecture. Ha! There are the wheels: there goes the funeral!'

He holds his breath, and watches. How interesting is everything connected with Alice? Slowly it passes along. Through one opening made by the havoc of a storm in the line of trees that form the avenue, he sees it plainly enough. A very scanty procession—the plumed hearse and three carriages, and a few persons walking beside. It passes. The great iron gate shrieks its long and dolorous note as it opened, and Longcluse heard it clang after the last carriage had passed, and with this farewell the old gate sent forth the dead master of Mortlake.

'Farewell to Mortlake,' murmured Longcluse, as he heard these sounds, with a shrug and his peculiar smile; 'farewell, the lights, the claret-jug, the whist, and all the rest. You 'fear neither justices nor bailiffs,' as the song says, any longer. Very easy about your interest and your premiums; very careless who arrests you in your leaden vesture; and having paid, if nothing else, at least your beloved son's post obit. Courage, Sir Reginald! your earthly troubles are over. Here am I, erect as this tree, and as like to live my term out, with all that money, and no will made, and yet as tired as ever you were, and very willing, if the transaction were feasible, to die, and be bothered no more, instead of you.'

He sighs, and looks toward the house, and sighs again.

'Does she relent? Was it not she who told Lady May to ask this service of me? If I could only be sure of that, I should stand here, this moment, the proudest man in England. I think I know myself—a very simple character; just two principles—love and malice; for the rest, unscrupulous. Mere cruelty gives me no pleasure: well for some people it don't. Revenge does make me happy: well for some people if it didn't. Except for those I love or those I hate, I live for none. The rest live for me. I owe them no more than I do this rotten stick. Let them rot and fatten my land; let them burn and bake my bread.'

With these words he kicked the fragments of a decayed branch that lay at his foot, and glided over the short grass, like a ghost, toward the gate.

Mr. Longcluse Sees a Friend

Sir Reginald Arden, then, is actually dead and buried, and is quite done with the pomps and vanities, the business and the miseries of life—dead as King Duncan, and cannot come out of his grave to trouble any one with protest or interference; and his son, Sir Richard, is in possession of the title, and seized of the acres, and uses them, without caring to trouble himself with conjectures as to what his father would have liked or abhorred.

A week has passed since the funeral. Lady May has spent two days at Mortlake, and then gone down to Brighton. Alice does not leave Mortlake; her spirits do not rise. Kind Lady May has done her best to persuade her to come down with her to Brighton, but the perversity or the indolence of grief has prevailed, and Alice has grown more melancholy and self-up-braiding about her quarrel with her father, and will not be persuaded to leave Mortlake, the very worst place she could have chosen, as Lady May protests, for a residence during her mourning. Perhaps in a little while she may feel equal to the effort, but now she can't. She has quite lost her energy, and the idea of a place like Brighton, or even the chance of meeting people, is odious to her.

'So, my dear, do what I may, there she will remain, in that *triste* place,' says Lady May Penrose; 'and her brother, Sir Richard, has so much business just now on his hands, that he is often away two or three days at a time, and then she stays moping there quite alone; and only that she likes gardening and flowers, and that kind of thing, I really think she would go melancholy mad. But you know that kind of folly can't go on always, and I am determined to take her away in a month or so. People at first are so morbid, and make recluses of themselves.'

Lady May stayed away at Brighton for about a week. On her return, Mr. Longcluse called to see her.

'It was so kind of you, Mr. Longcluse, to take all the trouble you did about that terrible business! and it was perfectly successful. There was not the slightest unpleasantness.'

'Yes, I knew I had made anything of that kind all but impossible, but you are not to thank me. It made me only too happy to have an opportunity of being of any use—of relieving any anxiety.'

Longcluse sighed.

'You have placed me, I know, under a great obligation, and if everyone felt it as I do, you would have been thanked as you deserved before now.'

A little silence followed.

'How is Miss Arden?' asked he in a low tone, and hardly raising his eyes.

'Pretty well,' she answered, a little dryly. 'She's not very wise, I think, in planning to shut herself up so entirely in that melancholy place, Mortlake. You have seen it?'

'Yes, more than once,' he answered.

Lady May appeared more embarrassed as Mr. Longcluse grew less so. They became silent again. Mr. Longcluse was the first to speak, which he did a little hesitatingly.

'I was going to say that I hoped Miss Arden was not vexed at my having ventured to interfere as I did.'

'Oh! about that, of course there ought to be, as I said, but one opinion; but you know she is not herself just now, and I shall have, perhaps, something to tell by-and-by; and, to say truth—you won't be vexed, but I'm sorry I undertook to speak to her, for on that point I really don't quite understand her; and I am a little vexed—and—I'll talk to you more another time. I'm obliged to keep an appointment just now, and the carriage,' she added, glancing at the *pendule* on the bracket close by, 'will be at the door in two or three minutes; so I must do a very ungracious thing, and say goodbye; and you must come again very soon—come to luncheon tomorrow—you must, really; I won't let you off, I assure you; there are two or three people coming to see me, whom I think you would like to meet.'

And, looking very good-natured, and a little flushed, and rather avoiding Mr. Longcluse's dark eyes, she departed.

He had been thinking of paying Miss Maubray a visit, but he had not avowed, even to himself, how high his hopes had mounted; and here was, in Lady May's ominous manner and determined evasion, matter to disturb and even shock him. Instead, therefore, of pursuing the route he had originally designed, he strolled into the park, and under the shade of green boughs he walked, amid the twitter of birds and the prattle of children and nursery-maids, with despair at his heart, and a brain in chaos.

As he sauntered, with downcast looks, under the trees, he came upon a humble Hebrew friend, Mr. Goldshed, a magnate in his own circle, but dwarfed into nothing beside the paragon of Mammon who walked on the grass, so unpretentiously, and with a face as anxious as that of the greengrocer who had just been supplicating the Jew for a renewal of his twenty-five pound bill.

Mr. Goldshed came to a full stop a little way in advance of Mr. Longcluse, anxious to attract his attention. Mr. Longcluse did see him, as he sauntered on; and the fat old Jew, with the seedy velvet waistcoat, crossed with gold chains, and with an old-fashioned gold eye-glass dangling at his breast, first smiled engagingly, then looked reverential and solemn, and then smiled again with his great moist lips, and raised his hat. Longcluse gave him a sharp, short nod, and intended to pass him.

'Will you shpare me one word, Mr. Lonclushe?'

'Not today, Sir.'

'But I've been to your chambers, Sir, and to your houshe, Mr. Lonclushe.'

'You've wasted time—waste no more.'

'I do assure you, Shir, it'sh very urgent.'

'I don't care.'

'It'sh about that East Indian thing,' and he lowered his voice as he concluded the sentence.

'I don't care a pin, Sir.'

The amiable Mr. Goldshed hesitated; Mr. Longcluse passed him as if he had been a post. He turned, however, and walked a few steps by Mr. Longcluse's side.

'And everything elshe is going sho vell; and it would look fishy, don't you think, to let thish thing go that way?'

'Let them go—and go you with them. I wish the earth would swallow you all—scrip, bonds, children, and *beldames*.' And if a stamp could have made the earth open at his bidding, it would have yawned wide enough at that instant 'If you follow me another step, by Heaven, I'll make it unpleasant to you.'

Mr. Longcluse looked so angry, that the Jew made him a unctuous bow, and remained fixed for a while to the earth, gazing after his patron with his hands in his pockets; and, with a gloomy countenance, he took forth a big cigar from his case, lighted a vesuvian, and began to smoke, still looking after Mr. Longcluse.

That gentleman sauntered on, striking his stick now and then to the ground, or waving it over the grass in as many odd flourishes as a magician in a pantomime traces with his wand.

If men are prone to tease themselves with imaginations, they are equally disposed to comfort themselves with the same shadowy influences.

'I'm so nervous about this thing, and so anxious, that I exaggerate everything that seems to tell against me. How did I ever come to love her so? And yet, would I kill that love if I could? Should I not kill myself first? I'll go and see Miss Maubray—I may hear something from her. Lady May *was* embarrassed: what then? Were I a simple observer of such a scene in the case of another, I should say there was nothing in it more than this—that she had quite forgotten all about her promise. She never mentioned my name, and when the moment came, and I had come to ask for an account, she did not know what to say. It was well done, to see old Mrs. Tansey as I did. Lady May is so good-natured, and would feel her little neglect so much, and she will be sure to make it up. Fifty things may have prevented her. Yes, I'll go and hear what Miss Maubray has to say, and I'll lunch with Lady May tomorrow. I suspect that her visit today was to Mortlake.'

With these reflections, Mr. Longcluse's pace became brisker, and his countenance brightened.

A Hope Expires

Mr. Longcluse knocked at Mr. David Arden's door. Yes, Miss Maubray was at home. He mounted the stairs, and was duly announced at the drawing-room door, and saw the brilliant young lady, who received him very graciously. She was alone.

Mr. Longcluse began by saying that the weather was cooler, and the sun much less intolerable.

'I wish we could say as much for the people, though, indeed, they are cool enough. There are some people called Tramways: he's a baronet—a very new one. Do you know anything of them? Are they people one can know?'

'I only know that Lady Tramway chaperoned a very charming young lady, whom everybody is very glad to know, to Lady May's garden-party the other day, at Richmond.'

'Yes, very true; I'm that young lady, and that is the very reason I want to know. My uncle placed me in their hands.'

'Oh, he knows everybody.'

'Yes, and every one, which is quite another thing; and the woman has never given me an hour's quiet since. She presents me with bouquets, and fruit, and every imaginable thing I don't want, herself included, at least once a day; and I assure you I live in hourly terror of her getting into the drawing-room. You don't know anything about them?'

'I only know that her husband made a great deal of money by a contract.'

'That sounds very badly, and she is such a vulgar woman.'

'I know no more of them; but Lady May had her to Raleigh Hall, and surely she can satisfy your scruples.'

'No, it was my guardian who asked for their card, so that goes for nothing. It is really too bad.'

'My heart bleeds for you.'

'By-the-bye, talking of Lady May, I had a visit from her not a quarter-of-an-hour ago. What a fuss our friends at Mortlake do make about the death of that disagreeable old man!—Alice, I mean. Richard Arden bears it wonderfully. When did you see either?' she asked, innocently.

'You forget he has not been dead three weeks, and Alice Arden is not likely to see anyone but very intimate friends for a long time; and—and I daresay you have heard that Sir Richard Arden and I are not on very pleasant terms.'

'*Oh! Pity such difference should be* ——.'

'Thanks, and Tweedledum and Tweedledee are not likely to make it up. I'm afraid people aren't always reasonable, you know, and expect, often, things that are not quite fair.'

'He ought to marry someone with money, and give up play.'

'What! give up play, and commence husband? I'm afraid he'd think that a rather dull life.'

'Well, I'm sure I'm no judge of that, although I give an opinion. Whatever he may be, you have a very staunch friend in Lady May.'

'I'm glad of that; she's always so kind.' And he looked rather oddly at the young lady.

Perhaps she seemed conscious of a knowledge more than she had yet divulged.

This young lady was, I need not tell you, a little coarse. She had, when she liked, the frankness that can come pretty boldly to the point; but I think she could be sly enough when she pleased; and was she just a little mischievous?

'Lady May has been talking to me a great deal about Alice Arden. She has been to see her very often since that poor old man died, and she says—she says, Mr. Longcluse—will you be upon honour not to repeat this?'

'Certainly, upon my honour.'

'Well, she says——'

Miss Maubray gets up quickly, and settles some flowers over the chimney-piece.

'She says that there is a coolness in that quarter also.'

'I don't quite see,' says Mr. Longcluse.

'Well, I must tell you she has taken me into council, and told me a great deal; and she spoke to Alice, and wrote to her. Did she say she would show you the answer? I have got it; she left it with me, and asked me—she's so good-natured—to use my influence—she said *my* influence! She ought to know I've *no* influence.'

Longcluse felt very oddly indeed during this speech; he had still presence of mind not to add anything to the knowledge the young lady might actually possess.

'You have not said a great deal, you know; but Lady May certainly did promise to show me an answer which she expected to a note she wrote about three weeks ago, or less, to Miss Arden.'

'I really don't know of what use I can be in the matter. I have no excuse for speaking to Alice on the subject of her note—none in the world. I think I may as well let you see it; but you will promise—you *have* promised not to tell anyone?'

'I have—I do—I promise. Lady May herself said she would show me that letter.'

'Well, I can't, I suppose, be very wrong. It is only a note: it does not say much, but quite enough, I'm afraid, to make it useless, and almost impertinent, for me, or anyone else, to say a word more on the subject to Alice Arden.'

All this time she is opening a very pretty *marqueterie* writing-desk, on spiral legs, which Longcluse has been listlessly admiring, little thinking what it contains. She now produced a little note, which, disengaging from its envelope, she places in the hand that Mr. Longcluse extended to receive it.

'I do so hope,' she said, as she gave it to him, 'that I am doing what Lady May would wish. I think she shrank a little from showing it to you herself, but I am certain she wished you to know what is in it.'

He opened it quickly. It ran thus ('Merry,' I must remark, was a pet name, originating, perhaps, in Shakespeare's song that speaks of '*the merry month of May*'):—

Dearest Merry,

I hope you will come to see me tomorrow. I cannot yet bear the idea of going into town. I feel as if I never should, and I think I grow more and more miserable every day. You are one of the very few friends whom I can see. You can't think what a pleasure a call from you is—if, indeed, in my miserable state, I can call anything a pleasure. I have read your letter about Mr. Longcluse, and parts of it a little puzzle me. I can't say that I have anything to forgive, and am sure he has acted just as kindly as you say. But our acquaintance has ended, and nothing shall ever induce me to renew it. I can give you fifty reasons, when I see you, for my not choosing to know him.

Darling Merry, I have quite made up my mind upon this point. I *don't* know Mr. Longcluse, and I *won't* know Mr. Longcluse; and I'll tell you *all* my reasons, if you wish to hear them, when we meet. Some of them, which seem to me *more* than sufficient, you do know. The only condition I make is that you don't discuss them with me. I have grown so stupid that *I* really cannot. I only know that I am right, and that *nothing* can change me. Come, darling, and see me very soon. You have no idea how very wretched I am. But I do not complain: it has drawn me, I hope, to higher and better thoughts. The world is not what it was to me, and I pray it never may be. Come and see me soon, darling; you cannot think how I long to see you.—

Your affectionate,

Alice Arden.

'What mountains of molehills!' said Mr. Longcluse, very gently, smiling with a little shrug, as he placed the letter again in Miss Maubray's hand.

'Making such a fuss about that poor old man's death! It certainly does look a little like a pretty affectation. Isn't that what you mean? He *was* so *insupportable!*'

'No, I know nothing about that. I mean such a ridiculous fuss about nothing. Why, people cease to be acquainted every day for much less reason. Sir Reginald chose to talk over his money matters with me, and I think he expected me to do things which no stranger could be reasonably invited to do. And I suppose, now that he is gone, Miss Arden resents my insensibility to his hints; and I daresay Sir Richard, who, I may say, on precisely similar grounds, chooses to quarrel with me, does not spare invective, and has, of course, a friendly listener in his sister. But how absurdly provoking that Lady May should have made such a diplomacy, and given herself so much trouble! And—I'm afraid I appear so foolish—I merely assented to Lady May's kind proposal to mediate, and I could not, of course, appear to think it a less important mission than she did; and—where are you going—Scotland? Italy?'

'My guardian, Mr. Arden, has not yet settled anything,' she answered; and upon this, Mr. Longcluse begins to recommend, and with much animation to describe, several Continental routes, and then he tells her all his gossip, and takes his leave, apparently in very happy spirits.

I doubt very much whether the face can ever be taught to lie as impudently as the tongue. Its muscles, of course, can be trained; but the young lady thought that Mr. Longcluse's pallor, as he smiled and returned the note, was more intense, and his dark eyes strangely fierce.

'He was more vexed than he cared to say,' thought the young lady. 'Lady May has not told me the whole story yet. There has been a great deal of fibbing, but I shall know it all.'

Mr. Longcluse had to dine out. He drove home to dress. On arriving, he first sat down and wrote a note to Lady May.

Dear Lady May,

I am so grateful. Miss Maubray told me today all the trouble you have been taking for me. Pray think no more of that little vexation. I never took so serious a view of so commonplace an unpleasantness, as to dream of tasking your kindness so severely. I am quite ashamed of having given you so much trouble.—

Yours, dear Lady May, sincerely,

Walter Longcluse.

P.S.—I don't forget your kind invitation to lunch tomorrow.

Longcluse dispatched this note, and then wrote a few words of apology to the giver of the City dinner, to which he had intended to go. He could not go. He was very much agitated: he knew that he could not endure the long constraint of that banquet. He was unfit, for the present, to bear the company of any one. Gloomy and melancholy was the pale face of this man, as if he were going to the funeral of his beloved, when he stepped from his door in the dark. Was he going to walk out to Mortlake, and shoot himself on the steps?

As Mr. Longcluse walked into town, he caught a passing sight of a handsome young face that jarred upon him. It was that of Richard Arden, who was walking, also alone, not under any wild impulse, but to keep an appointment. This handsome face appeared for a moment gliding by, and was lost. Melancholy and thoughtful he looked, and quite unconscious of the near vicinity of his pale adversary. We shall follow him to his place of rendezvous.

He walked quickly by Pall Mall, and down Parliament Street, into the ancient quarter of Westminster, turned into a street near the Abbey, and from it into another that ran toward the river. Here were tall and dingy mansions, some of which were let out as chambers. In one of these, in a room over the front drawing-room, Mr. Levi received his Westend clients; and here, by appointment, he awaited Sir Richard Arden.

The young baronet, a little paler, and with the tired look of a man who was made acquainted with care, enters this room, hot with the dry atmosphere of gaslight. With his back towards the door, and his feet on the fender, smoking, sits Mr. Levi. Sir Richard does not remove his hat, and he stands by the table, which he slaps once or twice sharply with his stick.

Mr. Levi turns about, looking, in his own phrase, unusually 'down in the mouth,' and his big black eyes are glowing angrily.

'Ho! Shir Richard Harden,' he says, rising, 'I did not think we was sho near the time. Izh it a bit too soon?'

'A little later than the time I named.'

'Crikey! sho it izh.'

Levi's Apologue

The room had once been a stately one. Three tall windows looked toward the street. Its cornices and door-cases were ponderous, and its furniture was heterogeneous, and presented the contrasts that might be expected in a broker's store. A second-hand Turkey carpet, in a very dusty state, covered part of the floor; and a dirty canvas sack lay by the door for people coming in to rub their feet on. The table was a round one, that turned on a pivot; it was oak, massive and carved, with drawers; there were two huge gilt arm-chairs covered with Utrecht velvet, a battered office-stool, and two or three bed-room chairs that did not match. There were two great iron safes on trestles.

On the top of one was some valuable old china, and on the other an electrifying machine; a French harp with only half-a-dozen strings stood in the corner near the fire-place, and several dusty pictures of various sizes leaned with their faces against the wall. A jet of gas burned right over the table, and had blackened the ceiling by long use, and a dip candle, from which Mr. Levi lighted his cigars, burned in a brass candlestick on the hob of the empty grate. Over everything lay a dark grey drift of dust. And the two figures, the elegant young man in deep mourning, and the fierce vulgar little Jew, shimmering all over with chains, rings, pins, and trinkets, stood in a narrow circle of light, in strong relief against the dim walls of the large room.

'So you *will* want that bit o' money in hand?' said Mr. Levi.

'I told you so.'

'Don't you think they'll ever get tired helpin' you, if you keep pulling alwaysh the wrong way?'

'You said, this morning, I might reckon upon the help of that friend to any extent within reason,' said Sir Richard, a little sourly.

'Ye're goin' fashter than yer friendsh li-likesh; ye're goin' al-ash—ye're goin' a terrible lick, you are!' said Mr. Levi, solemnly.

His usually pale face was a little flushed; he was speaking rather thickly, and there came at intervals a small hiccough, which indicated that he had been making merry.

'That's my own affair, I fancy,' replied Sir Richard, as haughtily as prudence would permit. 'You are simply an agent.'

'Wish shome muff would take it off my hands; 'shan agenshy tha'll bring whoever takesh it more tr-tr-ouble than tin. By my shoul I'll not keepsh long! I'm blowsh if I'll be fool any longer!'

'I'm to suppose, then, that you have made up your mind to act no longer for my friend, whoever that friend may be?' said Sir Richard, who boded no good to himself from that step.

Mr. Levi nodded surlily.

'Have you drawn those bills?'

Mr. Levi gave the table a spin, unlocked a drawer, and threw two bills across to Sir Richard, who glancing at them said,—

'The date is ridiculously short!'

'How can I 'elp 't? and the interesht shlesh than nothin': sh-shunder the bank termsh f-for the besht paper going—I'm blesht if it ain't—it ain't f-fair interesh—the timesh short becaushe the partiesh, theysh—they shay they're 'ard hup, Shir, 'eavy sharge to pay hoff, and a big purchashe in Austriansh!'

'My uncle, David Arden, I happen to know, is buying Austrian stock this week; and Lady May Penrose is to pay off a charge on her property next month.'

The Jew smiled mysteriously.

'You may as well be frank with me,' added Sir Richard, pleased at having detected the coincidence, which was strengthened by his having, the day before, surprised his uncle in conference with Lady May.

'If you don't like the time, why don't you try shomwhere else? why don't you try Lonclushe? There'sh a shwell! Two millionsh, if he's worth a pig! A year, or a month, 'twouldn't matter a tizhy to him, and you and him'sh ash thick ash two pickpockets!'

'You're mistaken; I don't choose to have any transactions with Mr. Longcluse.'

There was a little pause.

'By-the-bye, I saw in some morning paper—I forget which—a day or two ago, a letter attacking Mr. Longcluse for an alleged share in the bank-breaking combination; and there was a short reply from him.'

'I know, in the *Timesh*', interposed Levi.

'Yes,' said Arden, who, in spite of himself, was always drawn into talk with this fellow more than he intended; such was the force of the ambiguously confidential relations in which he found himself. 'What is thought of that in the City?'

'There'sh lotsh of opinionsh about it; not a shafe chap to quar'l with. If you rub Lonclushe this year, he'll tear you for itsh the next. He'sh a bish—a bish—a bit—bit of a bully, is Lonclushe, and don't alwaysh treat 'ish people fair. If you've quar'led with him, look oush—I shay, look oush!'

'Give me the cheque,' said Sir Richard, extending his fingers.

'Pleashe, Shir Richard, accept them billsh,' replied Levi, pushing an ink-stand toward him, 'and I'll get our cheque for you.'

So Mr. Levi took the dip candle and opened one of the safes, displaying for a moment cases of old-fashioned jewellery, and a number of watches. I daresay Mr. Levi and his partner made advances on deposits.

'Why don't you cut them confounded rasesh, Shir Richard? I'm bleshed if I didn't lose five pounds on the Derby myself! There'sh lotsh of field sportsh,' he continued, approaching the table with his cheque-book. 'Didn't you never shee a ferret kill a rabbit? It'sh a beautiful thing; it takesh it shomeway down the back, and bit by bit it mendsh itsh grip, moving up to-*wards* the head. It *is* really beautiful, and not a shound from either, only you'll see the rabbitsh big eyes lookin' sho wonderful! and the ferret hangsh on, swinging this way and that like a shna-ake—'tish wery pretty!—till he worksh hish grip up to where the backbone joinish in with the brain; and then in with itsh teeth, through the shkull! and the rabbit givesh a screetch like a child in a fit. Ha, ha, ha! I'm blesht if it ain't done ash clever ash a doctor could do it. 'Twould make you laugh. That will do.'

And he took the bills from Sir Richard, and handed him two cheques, and as he placed the bills in the safe, and locked them up, he continued,—

'It *ish* uncommon pretty! I'd rayther shee it than a terrier on fifty rats. The rabbit's sho shimple—there'sh the fun of it—and looksh sho foolish; and every rabbit had besht look sharp,' he continued, turning about as he put the keys in his pocket, and looking with his burning black eyes full on Sir Richard, 'and not let a ferret get a grip anywhere; for if he getsh a good purchase, he'll never let go till he hash his teeth in his brain, and then he'sh off with a shqueak, and there's an end of him.'

'I can get notes for one of these cheques tonight?' said Sir Richard.

'The shmall one, yesh, eashy,' answered Mr. Levi. 'I'm a bachelor,' he added jollily, in something like a soliloquy, 'and whenever I marry I'll be the better of it; and I'm no muff, and no cove can shay that I ever shplit on no one. And what do I care for Lonclushe? Not the snuff of this can'le!' And he snuffed the dip scornfully with his fingers, and flung the sparkling wick over the bannister, as he stood at the door, to light Sir Richard down the stairs.

The Baron Comes to Town

Weeks flew by. The season was in its last throes: the session was within a day or two of its death. Lady May drove out to Mortlake with a project in her head.

Alice Arden was glad to see her.

'I've travelled all this way,' she said, 'to make you come with me on Friday to the Abbey.'

'On Friday? Why Friday, dear?' answered Alice.

'Because there is to be a grand *oratorio* of Handel's. It is for the benefit of the clergy's sons' school, and it is one that has not been performed in England for I forget how many years. It is *Saul*. You have heard the Dead March in Saul, of course; everyone has; but no one has ever heard the *oratorio*, and come you must. There shall be no one but ourselves—you and I, and your uncle and your brother to take care of us. They have promised to come; and Stentoroni is to take *Saul*, and they have the finest voices in Europe; and they say that Herr Von Waasen, the conductor, is the greatest musician in the world.

'There have been eight performances in that great room—oh! what do you call it?—while I was away; and now there is only to be this one, and I'm longing to hear it; but I won't go unless you come with me—and you need not dress. It begins at three o'clock, and ends at six, and you can come just as you are now; and an *oratorio* is really exactly the same as going to church, so you have no earthly excuse; and I'll send out my carriage at one for you; and you'll see, it will do you all the good in the world.'

Alice had her difficulties, but Lady May's vigorous onset overpowered them, and at length she consented.

'Does your uncle come out here to see you?' asks Lady May.

'Often; he's very kind,' she replies.

'And Grace Maubray?'

'Oh, yes; I see her pretty often—that is, she has been here twice, I think—quite often enough.'

'Well, do you know, I never could admire Grace Maubray as I have heard other people do,' says Lady May. 'There is something harsh and bold, don't you think?—something a little cruel. She is a girl that I don't think could ever be in love.'

'I don't know that,' says Alice.

'Oh! really?' says Lady May, 'and who is it?'

'It is merely a suspicion,' says Alice.

'Yes—but you think she likes some one—do, like a darling, tell me who it is,' urges Lady May, a little uneasily.

'You must not tell anyone, because they would say it was sisterly vanity, but I think she likes Dick.'

'Sir Richard?' says Lady May, with as much indifference as she could.

'Yes, I think she likes my brother.'

Lady May smiles painfully.

'I always thought so,' she says; 'and he admires her, of course?'

'No, I don't think he admires her at all—I'm certain he doesn't,' said Alice.

'Well, certainly he always does speak of her as if she belonged to Vivian Darnley,' remarks Lady May, more happily.

'So she does, and he to her, I hope,' said Alice.

'Hope?' repeated Lady May, interrogatively.

'Yes—I think nothing could be more suitable.'

'Perhaps so; you know them better than I do.'

'Yes, and I still think Uncle David intends them for one another.'

'I would have asked Mr. Longcluse,' Lady May begins, after a little interval, 'to use his influence to get us good hearing-places, but he is in such disgrace—is he still, or is there any chance of his being forgiven?'

'I told you, darling, I have really nothing to forgive—but I have a kind of fear of Mr. Longcluse—a fear I can't account for. It began, I think, with that affair that seemed to me like a piece of insanity, and made me angry and bewildered; and then there was a dream, in which I saw such a horrible scene, and fancied he had murdered Richard, and I could not get it out of my head. I suppose I am in a nervous state—and there were other things; and, altogether, I think of him with a kind of horror—and I find that Martha Tansey has an unaccountable dread of him exactly as I have; and even Uncle David says that he has a misgiving about him that he can't get rid of, or explain.'

'I can't think, however, that he is a ghost or even a malefactor,' said Lady May, 'or anything worse than a very agreeable, good-natured person. I never knew anything more zealous than his good-nature on the occasion I told you of; and he has always approached you with so much devotion and respect—he seemed to me so sensitive, and to watch your very looks; I really think that a frown from you would have almost killed him.'

Alice sighs, and looked wearily through the window, as if the subject bored her; and she said listlessly,—

'Oh, yes, he was kind, and gentlemanlike, and sang nicely, I grant you everything; but—there is something ominous about him, and I hate to hear him mentioned, and with my consent I'll never meet him more.'

Connected with the musical venture which the ladies were discussing, a remarkable person visited London. He had a considerable stake in its success. He was a penurious German, reputed wealthy, who ran over from Paris to complete arrangements about ticket-takers and treasurer, so as to ensure a system of check, such as would made it next to impossible for the gentlemen his partners to rob him. This person was the Baron Vanboeren.

Mr. Blount had an intimation of this visit from Paris, and Mr. David Arden invited him to dine, of which invitation he took absolutely no notice; and then Mr. Arden called upon him in his lodging in St. Martin's Lane. There he saw him, this man, possibly the keeper of the secret which he had for twenty years of his life been seeking for. If he had a feudal ideal of this baron, he was disappointed. He beheld a short, thick man, with an enormous head and grizzled hair, coarse pug features, very grimy skin, and a pair of fierce black eyes, that never rested for a moment, and swept the room from corner to corner with a rapid and unsettled glance that was full of fierce energy.

'The Baron Vanboeren?' inquires Uncle David courteously.

The baron, who is smoking, nods gruffly.

'My name is Arden—David Arden. I left my card two days ago, and having heard that your stay was but for a few days, I ventured to send you a very hurried invitation.'

The baron grunts and nods again.

'I wrote a note to beg the pleasure of a very short interview, and you have been so good as to admit me.'

The baron smokes on.

'I am told that you possibly are possessed of information which I have long been seeking in vain.'

Another nod.

'Monsieur Lebas, the unfortunate little Frenchman who was murdered here in London, was, I believe in your employment?'

The baron here had a little fit of coughing.

Uncle David accepted this as an admission.

'He was acquainted with Mr. Longcluse?'

'Was he?' says the baron, removing and replacing his pipe quickly.

'Will you, Baron Vanboeren, be so good as to give me any information you possess respecting Mr. Longcluse? It is not, I assure you, from mere curiosity I ask these questions, and I hope you will excuse the trouble I give you.'

The baron took his pipe from his mouth, and blew out a thin stream of smoke.

'I have heard,' said he, in short, harsh tones, 'since I came to London, nosing but good of Mr. Longcluse. I have ze greadest respect for zat excellent gendleman. I will say nosing bud zat—ze greadest respect.'

'You knew him in Paris, I believe?' urges Uncle David.

'Nosing but zat—ze greadest respect,' repeats the baron. 'I sink him a very worzy gendleman.'

'No doubt, but I venture to ask whether you were acquainted with Mr. Longcluse in Paris?'

'Zere are a gread many beoble in Paris. I have nosing to say of Mr. Longcluse, nosing ad all, only he is a man of high rebudation.'

And on completing this sentence the baron replaced his pipe, and delivered several rapid puffs.

'I took the liberty of enclosing a letter from a friend explaining who I am, and that the questions I should entreat you to answer are not prompted by any idle or impertinent curiosity; perhaps, then, you would be so good as to say whether you know anything of a person named Yelland Mace, who visited Paris some twenty years since?'

'I am in London, Sir, ubon my business, and no one else's. *I* am sinking of myself, and not about Mace or Longcluse, and I will not speak about eizer of zem. I am well baid for my dime. I will nod waste my dime on dalking—I will nod,' he continues, warming as he proceeds; 'nosing shall induce me do say one word aboud zoze gendlemen. I dake my oas I'll not, mein Gott! What do you mean by asking me aboud zem?'

He looks positively ferocious as he delivers this expostulation. 'My request must be more unreasonable than it appeared to me.'

'Nosing can be more unreasonable!'

'And I am to understand that you positively object to giving me any information respecting the persons I have named?'

The baron appeared extremely uneasy. He trotted to the door on his short legs, and looked out. Returning, he shut the door carefully. His grimy countenance, under the action of fear, assumes an expression peculiarly forbidding; and he said, with angry volubility—

'Zis visit must end, Sir, zis moment. Donnerwesser! I will nod be combromised by you. But if you bromise as a Christian, ubon your honour, never to mention what I say——'

'Never, upon my honour.'

'Nor to say you have talked with me here in London——'

'Never.'

'I will tell you that I have no objection to sbeak wis you, *privately* in Paris, whenever you are zere—now, now! zat is all. I will not have one ozer word—you shall not stay one ozer minude.'

He opens the door and wags his head peremptorily, and points with his pipe to the lobby.

'You'll not forget your promise, Baron, when I call? for visit you I will.'

'I never forget nosing. Monsieur Arden, will you go or *nod?*'

'Farewell, Sir,' says his visitor, too much excited by the promise opened to him, for the moment to apprehend what was ridiculous in the scene or in the brutality of the baron.

When he was gone the Baron Vanboeren sat down and panted; his pipe had gone out, and he clutched it in his hand like a weapon and continued for some minutes, in the good old phrase, very much disordered. 'That old fool,' he mutters, in his native German, 'won't come near me again while I remain in London.'

This assurance was, I suppose, consolatory, for the baron repeated it several times; and then bounced to his feet, and made a few hurried preparations for an appearance in the streets. He put on a short cloak which had served him for the last thirty years, and a preposterous hat; and with a thick stick in his hand, and a cigar lighted, sallied forth, square and short, to make Mr. Longcluse a visit by appointment.

By this time the lamps were lighted. There had been a performance of *Saul*, a very brilliant success, although it pleased the baron to grumble over it that day. He had not returned from the great room where it had taken place more than an hour, when David Arden had paid his brief visit. He was now hastening to an interview which he thought much more momentous. Few persons who looked at that vulgar seedy figure, strutting through the mud, would have thought that the thread-bare black cloak, over which a brown autumnal tint had spread, and the monstrous battered felt hat, in which *a* coster-monger would scarcely have gone abroad, covered a man worth a hundred and fifty thousand pounds.

Man is mysteriously so constructed that he cannot abandon himself to selfishness, which is the very reverse of heavenly love, without in the end contracting *some* incurable insanity; and that insanity of the higher man constitutes, to a great extent, his mental death. The Baron Vanboeren's insanity was avarice; and his solitary expenses caused him all the sordid anxieties which haunt the unfortunate gentleman who must make both ends meet on five-and-thirty pounds a year.

Though not *sui profusus*, he was *alieni appetens* in a very high degree; and his visit to Mr. Longcluse was not one of mere affection.

Mr. Longcluse was at home in his study. The baron was instantly shown in. Mr. Longcluse, smiling, with both hands extended to grasp his, advances to meet him.

'My dear Baron, what an unexpected pleasure! I could scarcely believe my eyes when I read your note. So you have a stake in this musical speculation, and though it is very late, and, of course, everything at a disadvantage, I have to congratulate you on an immense success.'

The baron shrugs, shakes his head, and rolls his eyes dismally. 'Ah, my friend, ze exbenses are enormous.'

'And the receipts still more so,' says Longcluse cheerfully; 'you must be making, among you, a mint of money.'

'Ah! Monsieur Longcluse, id is nod what it should be! zay are all such sieves and robbers! I will never escape under a loss of a sousand bounds.'

'You must be cheerful, my dear Baron. You shall dine with me today. I'll take you with me to half a dozen places of amusement worth seeing after dinner. Tomorrow morning you shall run down with me to Brighton—my yacht is there—and when you have had enough of that, we shall run up again and have a whitebait dinner at Greenwich; and come into town and see those fellows, Markham and the other, that poor little Lebas saw play, the night he was murdered. You must see them play the return match, so long postponed. Next day we shall——'

'Bardon, *Monsieur*, bardon! I am doo old. I have no spirits.'

'What, not enough to see a game of billiards between Markham and Hood! Why, Lebas was charmed so far as he saw it, poor fellow, with their play.'

'No, no, no, no, *Monsieur*; a sousand sanks, no, bardon, cannod,' says the baron. 'I do not like billiards, and your friends have not found it a lucky game.'

'Well, if you don't care for billiards, we'll find something else,' replies hospitable Mr. Longcluse.

'Nosing else, nosing else,' answers the baron hastily, 'I hade all zese sings, ze seatres, ze bubbedshows, and all ze ozer amusements, I give you my oas. Did you read my liddle node?'

'I did indeed, and it amused me beyond measure,' says Longcluse joyously.

'Amuse!' repeats the baron, 'how so?'

'Because it is so diverting; one might almost fancy it was meant to ask me for fifteen hundred pounds.'

'I have lost, by zis sing, a vast deal more zan zat.'

'And, my dear Baron, what on earth have I to do with that?'

'I am an old friend, a good friend, a true friend,' says the baron, while his fierce little eyes sweep the walls, from corner to corner, with quivering rapidity. 'You would not like to see me quide in a corner. You're the richest man in England, almost; what's one sousand five hundred to you? I have not wridden to you, or come to England, dill now. You have done nosing for your old friend yet: what are you going to give him?'

'Not as much as I gave Lebas,' said Longcluse, eyeing him askance, with a smile.

'I don't know what you mean.'

'Not a *napoleon*, not a *franc*, not a *sou*.'

'You are jesding; sink, sink, sink, *Monsieur*, what a friend I have been and *am* to you.'

'So I do, my dear Baron, and consider how I show my gratitude. Have I ever given a hint to the French police about the identity of the clever gentleman who managed the little tunnel through which a river of champagne flowed into Paris, under the barrier, duty free? Have I ever said a word about the confiscated jewels of the Marchioness de la Sarnierre? Have I ever asked how the Comte de Loubourg's little boy is, or directed an unfriendly eye upon the conscientious physician who extricates ladies and gentlemen from the consequences of late hours, nervous depression, and fifty other things that war against good digestion and sound sleep? Come, come, my good Baron, whenever we come to square accounts, the balance will stand very heavily in my favour. I don't want to press for a settlement, but if you urge it, by Heaven, I'll make you pay the uttermost farthing!'

Longcluse laughs cynically. The baron looks very angry. His face darkens to a leaden hue. The fingers which he plunged into his snuff-box are trembling. He takes two or three great pinches of snuff before speaking.

Mr. Longcluse watches all these symptoms of his state of mind with a sardonic enjoyment, beneath which, perhaps, is the sort of suspense with which a beast-tamer watches the eye of the animal whose fury he excites only to exhibit the coercion which he exercises through its fears, and who is for a moment doubtful *whether* its terrors or its fury may prevail.

The baron's restless eyes roll wickedly. He puts his hand into his pocket irresolutely, and crumbles some papers there. There was no knowing, for some seconds, what turn things might take. But if he had for a moment meditated a crisis, he thought better of it. He breaks into a fierce laugh, and extends his hand to Mr. Longcluse, who as frankly places his own in it, and the baron shakes it vehemently. And Mr. Longcluse and he laugh boisterously and oddly together. The baron takes another great pinch of snuff, and then he says, sponging out as it were, as an ignored parenthesis, the critical part of their conversation—

'No, no, I sink not; no, no, surely not I am not fit for all zose amusements. I cannot knog aboud as I used; an old fellow, you know: beace and tranquilidy. No, I cannot dine with you. I dine with Stentoroni tomorrow; today I have dined with our *tenore*. How well you look! What nose, what tees, what chin! I am proud of you. We bart good friends, *bon soir*, Monsieur Longcluse, farewell. I am already a liddle lade.'

'Farewell, dear Baron. How can I thank you enough for this kind meeting? Try one of my cigars as you go home.'

The baron, not being a proud man, took half-a-dozen, and with a final shaking of hands these merry gentlemen parted, and Longcluse' s door closed for ever on the Baron Vanboeren.

'That bloated spider?' mused Mr. Longcluse. 'How many flies has he sucked! It is another matter when spiders take to catching wasps.'

Every man of energetic passions has within him a principle

of self-destruction. Longcluse had his. It had expressed itself in his passion for Alice Arden. That passion had undergone a wondrous change, but it was imperishable in its new as in its pristine state.

This gentleman was in the dumps so soon as he was left alone. Always uncertainty; always the sword of Damocles; always the little reminders of perdition, each one contemptible, but each one in succession touching the same set of nerves, and like the fall of the drop of water in the inquisition, *non vi, sed saepe cadendo*, gradually heightening monotony into excitement, and excitement into frenzy. Living always with a sense of the unreality of life and the vicinity of death, with a certain stern tremor of the heart, like that of a man going into action, no wonder if he sometimes sickened of his bargain with Fate, and thought life purchased too dear on the terms of such a lease.

Longcluse bolted his door, unlocked his desk, and there what do we see? Six or seven miniatures—two enamels, the rest on ivory—all by different hands; some English, some Parisian; very exquisite, some of them. Everyone was Alice Arden. Little did she dream that such a gallery *existed*. How were they taken? Photographs are the colourless phantoms from which these glowing life-like beauties start.

Tender-hearted Lady May has in confidence given him, from time to time, several of these from her album; he has induced foreign artists to visit London, and managed opportunities by which, at parties, in theatres, and I am sorry to say even in church, these clever persons succeeded in studying from the life, and learning all the tints which now glow before him. If I had mentioned what this little collection cost him, you would have opened your eyes. The Baron Vanboeren would have laughed and cursed him with hilarious derision, and a money-getting Christian would have been quite horror-struck, on reading the scandalous row of figures.

Each miniature he takes in turn, and looks at for a long time, holding it in both hands, his hands resting on the desk, his face inclined and sad, as if looking down into the coffin of his darling.

One after the other he puts them by, and returns to his favourite one; and at last he shuts it up also, with a snap, and places it with the rest in the dark, under lock and key.

He leaned back and laid his thin hand across his eyes. Was he looking at an image that came out in the dark on the retina of memory? Or was he shedding tears?

Saul

The day arrived on which Alice Arden had agreed to go with Lady May to Westminster Abbey, to hear the masterly performance of *Saul*. When it came to the point, she would have preferred staying at home; but that was out of the question. Everyone has experienced that ominous foreboding which overcomes us sometimes with a shapeless forecasting of evil. It was with that vague misgiving that she had all the morning looked forward to her drive to town, and the long-promised *oratorio*. It was a dark day, and there was a thunderous weight in the air, and the melancholy atmosphere deepened her gloom.

Her Uncle David arrived in Lady May's carriage, to take care of her. They were to call at Lady May's house, where its mistress and Sir Richard Arden awaited them.

A few kind words followed Uncle David's affectionate greeting, as they drove into town. He did not observe that Alice was unusually low. He seemed to have something not very pleasant himself to think upon, and he became silent for some time.

'I want,' said he at last, looking up suddenly, 'to give you a little advice, and now mind what I say. Don't sign any legal paper without consulting me, and don't make any promise to Richard. It is just possible—I hope he may not, but it is just possible—that he may ask you to deal in his favour with your charge on the Yorkshire estate. Do you tell him if he should that you have promised me faithfully not to do anything in the matter, except as I shall advise. He may, as I said, never say a word on the subject, but in any case my advice will do you no harm. I have had bitter experience, my dear, of which I begin to grow rather ashamed, of the futility of trying to assist Richard. I have thrown away a great deal of money upon him, utterly thrown it away. *I* can afford it, but *you* cannot, and you shall not lose your little provision.' And here he changed the subject of his talk, I suppose to avoid the possibility of discussion. 'How very early the autumn has set in this year! It is the extraordinary heat of the summer. The elms in Mortlake are quite yellow already.'

And so they talked on, and returned no more to the subject at which he had glanced. But the few words her uncle had spoken gave Alice ample matter to think on, and she concluded that Richard was in trouble again.

Lady May did not delay them a moment, and Sir Richard got into the carriage after her, with the tickets in his charge. Very devoted, Alice thought him, to Lady May, who appeared more than usually excited and happy.

We follow our party without comment into the choir, where they take possession of their seats. The chorus glide into their places like shadows, and the vast array of instrumental musicians as noiselessly occupy the seats before their desks. The great assembly is marshalled in a silence almost oppressive, but which is perhaps the finest preparation for the wondrous harmonies to come.

And now the grand and unearthly oratorio has commenced. Each person in our little group hears it with different ears. I wonder whether any two persons in that vast assembly heard it precisely alike. Sir Richard Arden, having many things to think about, hears it intermittently as he would have listened to a bore, and with a secret impatience. Lady May hears it not much better, but felt as if she could have sat there forever. Old David Arden enjoyed music, and is profoundly delighted with this. But his thoughts also begin to wander, for as the mighty *basso* singing the part of Saul delivers the words,

I would that, by thy art, thou bring me up
The man whom I shall name,

David Arden's eye lighted, with a little shock, upon the enormous head and repulsive features of the Baron Vanboeren. What a mask for a witch! The travesty lost its touch of the ludicrous, in Uncle David's eye, by virtue of the awful interest he felt in the possible revelations of that ugly magician, who could, he fancied, by a word, call up the image of Yelland Mace. The baron is sitting about the steps in front of him, face to face. He wonders he has not seen him till now. His head is a little thrown back, displaying his short bull neck. His restless eyes are fixed now in a sullen reverie. His calculation as to the exact money value of the audience is over; he is polling them no longer, and his unresting brain is projecting pictures into the darkness of the future.

His face in a state of apathy was ill-favoured and wicked, and now lighted with a cadaverous effect, by the dull purplish halo which marks the blending of the feeble daylight, with the glow of the lamp that is above him.

The baron had seen and recognised David Arden, and a train of thoughts horribly incongruous with the sacred place was moving through his brain. As he looks on, impassive, the great *basso* rings out:—

If heaven denies thee aid, seek it from hell.

And the *soprano* sends forth the answering incantation, wild and piercing—

Infernal spirits, by whose power
Departed ghosts in living forms appear,
Add horror to the midnight hour,
And chill the boldest hearts with fear;
To this stranger's wondering eyes
Let the man he calls for rise.

If Mr. Longcluse had been near, he might have made his own sad application of the air so powerfully sung by the alto to whom was committed the part of David—

Such haughty beauties rather move
Aversion, than engage our love.

He might with an undivulged anguish have heard the adoring strain—

O lovely maid! thy form beheld
Above all beauty charms our eyes,
Yet still within that form concealed,
Thy mind a greater beauty lies.

In a rapture Alice listened on. The famous *Dead March* followed, interposing its melancholy instrumentation, and arresting the vocal action of the drama by the pomp of that magnificent dirge.

To her the whole thing seemed stupendous, unearthly, glorious beyond expression. She almost trembled with excitement. She was glad she had come. Tears of ecstasy were in her eyes.

And now, at length, the three parts are over, and the crowd begin to move outward. The organ peals as they shuffle slowly along, checked every minute, and then again resuming their slow progress, pushing on in those little shuffling steps of two or three inches by which well-packed crowds get along, every one wondering why they can't all step out together, and what the people in front can be about.

In two several channels, through two distinct doors, this great human reservoir floods out. Sir Richard has undertaken the task of finding Lady May's carriage, and bringing it to a point where they might escape the tedious waiting at the door; and David Arden, with Lady May on one arm and Alice on the other, is getting on slowly in the thick of this well-dressed and aristocratic mob.

'I think, Alice,' said Uncle David, 'you would be more out of the crush, and less likely to lose me, if you were to get quite close behind us—do you see? between Lady May and me, and hold me fast.'

The pressure of the stream was so unequal, and a front of three so wide, that Alice gladly adopted the new arrangement, and with her hand on her uncle's arm, felt safer and more comfortable than before.

This slow march, inch by inch, is strangely interrupted. A well-known voice, close to her ear, says—

'Miss Arden, a word with you.'

A pale face, with flat nose and Mephistophelian eyebrows, was stooping near her. Mr. Longcluse's thin lips were close to her ear. She started a little aside, and tried to stop. Recovering, she stretched her hand to reach her uncle, and found that there were strangers between them.

A Waking Dream

There is something in that pale face and spectral smile that fascinates the terrified girl; she cannot take her eyes off him. His dark eyes are near hers; his lips are still close to her; his arm is touching her dress; he leans his face to her, and talks on, in an icy tone little above a whisper, and an articulation so sharply distinct that it seems to pain her ear.

'The *oratorio*!' he continued: 'the music! The words, here and there are queer—a little sinister—eh? There are better words and wilder music—you shall hear them some day! Saul had his evil spirit, and a bad family have theirs—ay, they have a demon who is always near, and shapes their lives for them; they don't know it, but, sooner or later justice catches them. Suppose *I* am the demon of your family—it is very funny, isn't it? I tried to serve you both, but it wouldn't do. I'll set about the other thing now: the evil genius of a bad family; I'm appointed to that.

'It almost makes me laugh—such cross-purposes! You're frightened? That's a pity; you should have thought of that before. It requires some nerve to fight a man like me. I don't threaten you, mind, but you are frightened. There is such a thing as getting a dangerous fellow bound over to keep the peace. Try that. I should like to have a talk with you before his worship in the police-court, across the table, with a corps of clever newspaper reporters sitting there. What fun in the *Times* and all the rest next morning.'

It is plain to Miss Arden that Mr. Longcluse is speaking all this time with suppressed fury, and his countenance expresses a sort of smiling hatred that horrifies her.

'I'm not bad at speaking my mind,' he continues. 'It is unfortunate that I am so well thought of and listened to in London.

Yes, people mind what I say a good deal. I rather think they'll choose to believe *my* story. But there's another way, if you don't like that. Your brother's not afraid—*he*'ll protect you. Tell your brother what a miscreant I am, and send him to me—do, pray! Nothing on earth I should like better than to have a talk with that young gentleman. Do pray, send him. I entreat. He'd like satisfaction—ha! ha!—and, by Heaven, I'll give it him! Tell him to get his pistols ready; he shall have his shop! Let him come to Boulogne, or where he likes—I'll stand it— and I don't think he'll need to pay his way back again. He'll stay in France; he'll not walk in at your hall-door, and call for luncheon, I promise you. Ha! ha! ha!'

This pale man enjoys her terror cruelly.

'I'm not worthy to speak to you, I believe—eh? That's odd, for the time isn't far off when you'll pray to God I may have mercy on you. You had no business to encourage me. I'm afraid the crowd is getting on very slowly, but I'll try to entertain you: you *are* such a good listener!'

Miss Arden often wondered afterwards at her own passiveness through all this. There were, no doubt, close by, many worthy citizens, fathers of families, who would have taken her for a few minutes under their protection with honest alacrity. But it was a fascination; her state was cataleptic: and she could no more escape than the bird that is throbbing in the gaze of a snake. The cold murmur went distinctly on and on: 'Your brother will probably think I should treat you more ceremoniously. Don't you agree with him? Pray, do complain to him. Pray, send him to me, and I'll thank him for his share in this matter. He wanted to make it a match between us—I'm speaking coarsely, for the sake of distinctness—till a title turned up. What has become of the title, by-the-bye?—I don't see him here. The peer wasn't in the running, after all: didn't even start! Ha! ha! ha! Remember me to your brother, pray, and tell him the day will come when he'll not need to be reminded of me: I'll take care of that.

'And so Sir Richard is doomed to disappointment! It is a

world of disappointment. The earl is nowhere! And the proudest family on earth—what is left of it—looks a little foolish. And well it may: it has many follies to expiate. You had no business encouraging me, and you are foolish enough to be terribly afraid now—ha! ha! ha! Too late, eh? I daresay you think I'll punish you! Not I! Nothing of the sort! I'll never punish anyone. Why should I take that trouble about you. Not I: not even your brother. Fate does that. Fate has always been kind to me, and hit my enemies pretty hard. You had no business encouraging me. Remember this: the day is not far off when you will *both* rue the hour you threw me over!'

She is gazing helplessly into that dreadful face. There is a cruel elation in it. He looks on her, I think, with admiration. Mixed with his hatred, did there remain a fraction of love?

On a sudden the voice, which was the only sound she heard, was in her ear no longer. The face which had transfixed her gaze was gone. Longcluse had apparently pushed a way for her to her friends, for she found herself again next her Uncle David. Holding his arm fast, she looked round quickly for a moment: she saw Mr. Longcluse nowhere. She felt on the point of fainting. The scene must have lasted a shorter time than she supposed, for her uncle had not missed her.

'My dear, how pale you look! Are you tired?' exclaims Lady May, when they have come to a halt at the door.

'Yes, indeed, so she does. Are you ill, dear?' added her uncle.

'No, nothing, thanks, only the crowd. I shall be better immediately.' And so waiting in the air, near the door, they were soon joined by Sir Richard, and in his carriage he and she drove home to Mortlake. Lady May, taking hers, went to a tea at old Lady Elverstone's; and David Arden, bidding them goodbye, walked homeward across the park.

Richard had promised to spend the evening at Mortlake with her, and side by side they were driving out to that sad and sombre scene. As they entered the shaded road upon which the great gate of Mortlake opens, the setting sun streamed through the huge trunks of the trees, and tinted the landscape with a subdued splendour.

'I can't imagine, dear Alice, why you *will* stay here. It is enough to kill you,' says Sir Richard, looking out peevishly on the picturesque woodlands of Mortlake, and interrupting a long silence. 'You never can recover your spirits while you stay here. There is Lady May going all over the world—I forget where, but she will be at Naples—and she absolutely longs to take you with her; and you won't go! I really sometimes think you want to make yourself melancholy mad.'

'I don't know,' said she, waking herself from a reverie in which, against the dark background of the empty arches she had left, she still saw the white, wicked face that had leaned over her, and heard the low murmured stream of insult and menace. 'I'm not sure that I shall not be worse anywhere else. I don't feel energy to make a change. I can't bear the idea of meeting people. By-and-by, in a little time, it will be different. For the present, quiet is what I like best.

'But you, Dick, are not looking well, you seem so overworked and anxious. You really do want a little holiday. Why don't you go to Scotland to shoot, or take a few weeks' yachting? All your business must be pretty well settled now.'

'It will never be settled,' he said, a little sourly. 'I assure you there never was property in such a mess—I mean leases and everything. Such drudgery, you have no idea; and I owe a good deal. It has not done me any good. I'd rather be as I was before that miserable Derby. I'd gladly exchange it all for a clear annuity of a thousand a year.'

'Oh! my dear Dick, you can't mean that! All the northern property, and this, and Morley?'

'I hate to talk about it. I'm tired of it already. I have been so unlucky, so foolish, and if I had not found a very good friend, I should have been utterly ruined by that cursed race; and he has been aiding me very generously, on rather easy terms, in some difficulties that have followed; and you know I had to raise money on the estate before all this happened, and have had to make a very heavy mortgage, and I am getting into such a mess—a confusion, I mean—and really I should have sold the estates, if it had not been for my unknown friend, for I don't know his name.'

'What friend?'

'The friend who has aided me through my troubles—the best friend I ever met, unless it be as I half suspect. Has anyone spoken to you lately, in a way to lead you to suppose that he, or anyone else among our friends, has been lending me a helping hand?'

'Yes, as were driving into town today, Uncle David told me so distinctly; but I am not sure that I ought to have mentioned it. I fancy, indeed,' she added, as she remembered the reflection with which it was accompanied, 'that he meant it as a secret, so you must not get me into disgrace with him by appearing to know more than he has told you himself.'

'No, certainly,' said Richard; 'and he said it was he who lent it?'

'Yes, distinctly.'

'Well, I all but knew it before. Of course it is very kind of him. But then, you know he is very wealthy; he does not feel it; and he would not for the world that our house should lose its position. I think he would rather sell the coat off his back, than that our name should be slurred.'

Sir Richard was pleased that he had received this light in corroboration of his suspicions. He was glad to have ascertained that the powerful motives which he had conjectured were actually governing the conduct of David Arden, although for obvious reasons he did not choose that his nephew should be aware of his weakness.

The carriage drew up at the hall-door. The old house in the evening beams, looked warm and cheery, and from every window in its broad front flamed the reflection which showed like so many hospitable winter fires.

Love and Play

'Here we are, Alice,' says Sir Richard, as they entered the hall.

'We'll have a good talk this evening. We'll make the best of everything; and I don't see if Uncle David chooses to prevent it, why the old ship should founder after all.'

They are now in the house. It is hard to get rid of the sense of constraint that, in his father's time, he always experienced within those walls; to feel that the old influence is exorcised and utterly gone, and that he is himself absolute master where so lately he hardly ventured to move on tip-toe.

They did not talk so much as Sir Richard had anticipated. There were upon his mind some things that weighed heavily. He had got from Levi a list of the advances made by his luckily found friend, and the total was much heavier than he had expected. He began to fear that he might possibly exceed the limits which his uncle must certainly have placed somewhere. He might not, indeed, allow him to suffer the indignity of a bankruptcy; but he would take a very short and unpleasant course with him. He would seize his rents, and, with a friendly roughness, put his estates to nurse, and send the prodigal on a Childe Harold's pilgrimage of five or six years, with an allowance, perhaps, of some three hundred a year, which in his frugal estimate of a young man's expenditure, would be handsome.

While he was occupied in these ruminations, Alice cared not to break the silence. It was a very unsociable *tête-à-tête*. Alice had a secret of her own to brood over. If anything could have made Longcluse now more terrible to her imagination, it would have been a risk of her brother's knowing anything of the language he had dared to hold to her. She knew from her brother's own lips, that he was a duellist; and she was also persuaded that Mr. Longcluse was, in his own playful and sinister phrase, very literally a 'miscreant.' His face, ever since that interview, was always at her right side, with its cruel pallor, and the vindictive sarcasm of lip and tone. How she wished that she had never met that mysterious man! What she would have given to be exempted from his hatred, and blotted from his remembrance!

One object only was in her mind, distinctly, with respect to that person. She was, thank God, quite beyond his power. But men, she knew, live necessarily a life so public, and have so many points of contact, that better opportunities present themselves for the indulgence of a masculine grudge; and she trembled at the thought of a collision. Why, then, should not Dick seek a reconciliation with him, and, by any honourable means, abate that terrible enmity.

'I have been thinking, Dick, that, as Uncle David makes the interest he takes in your affairs a secret, and you can't consult him, it would be very well indeed if you could find someone else able to advise, who would consult with you when you wished.'

'Of course, I should be only too glad,' says Sir Richard, yawning and smiling as well as he could at the same time; 'but an adviser one can depend on in such matters, my dear child, is not to be picked up every day.'

'Poor papa, I think, was very wise in choosing people of that kind. Uncle David, I know, said that he made wonderfully good bargains about his mortgages, or whatever they are called.'

'I daresay—I don't know—he was always complaining, and always changing them,' says Sir Richard. 'But if you can introduce me to a person who can disentangle all my complications, and take half my cares off my shoulders, I'll say you are a very wise little woman indeed.'

'I only know this—that poor papa had the highest opinion of Mr. Longcluse, and thought he was the cleverest person, and the most able to assist, of any one he knew.'

Sir Richard Arden hears this with a stare of surprise.

'My dear Alice, you seem to forget everything. Why, Longcluse and I are at deadly feud. He hates me implacably. There never could be anything but enmity between us. Not that I care enough about *him* to hate him, but I have the worst opinion of him. I have heard the most shocking stories about him lately. They insinuate that he committed a murder! I told you of that jealousy and disappointment, about a girl he was in love with and wanted to marry, and it ended in *murder!* I'm told he had the reputation of being a most unscrupulous villain. They say he was engaged in several conspiracies to pigeon young fellows. He was the utter ruin, they say, of young Thornley, the poor muff who shot himself some years ago; and he was thought to be a principal proprietor of that gaming-house in Vienna, where they found all the apparatus for cheating so cleverly contrived.'

'But are any of these things proved?' urges Miss Arden.

'I don't suppose he would be at large if they were,' says Sir Richard, with a smile. 'I only know that I believe them.'

'Well, Dick, you know I reminded you before—you used not to believe those stories till you quarrelled with him.'

'Why, what do you want, Alice?' he exclaims, looking hard at her. 'What on earth can you mean? And what can possibly make you take an interest in the character of such a ruffian?'

Alice's face grew pale under his gaze. She cleared her voice and looked down; and then she looked full at him, with burning eyes, and said—

'It is because I am afraid of him, and think he may do you some dreadful injury, unless you are again on terms with him. I can't get it out of my head; and I daresay I am wrong, but I am sure I am miserable.'

She burst into tears.

'Why, you darling little fool, what harm can he do me?' said Richard fondly, throwing his arms about her neck and kissing her, as he laughed tenderly. 'He exhausted his utmost malice when he angrily refused to lend me a shilling in my extremity, or to be of the smallest use to me, at a moment when he might have saved me, without risk to himself, by simply willing it. *I* didn't ask him, you may be sure. An officious, foolish little friend, doing all, of course, for the best, *did,* without once consulting me, or giving me a voice in the matter, until he had effectually put his foot in it, as I told you. I would not for anything on earth have applied to him, I need not tell you; but it was done, and it only shows with what delight he would have seen me ruined, as, in fact, I should have been, had not my own relations taken the matter up. I do believe, Alice, the best thing I could do for myself and for you would be to marry,' he says, a little suddenly, after a considerable silence.

Alice looks at him, doubtful whether he is serious.

'I really mean it. It is the only honest way of making or mending a fortune now-a-days.'

'Well, Dick, it is time enough to think of that by-and-by, don't you think?'

'Perhaps so; I hope so. At present it seems to me that, as far as I am concerned, it is just a race between the bishop and the bailiff which shall have me first. If any lady is good enough to hold out a hand to a poor drowning fellow, she had better——'

'Take care, Dick, that the poor drowning fellow does not pull her in. Don't you think it would be well to consider first what you have got to live on?'

'I have plenty to live on; I know that exactly,' said Dick.

'What is it?'

'My wife's fortune.'

'You are never serious for a minute, Dick! Don't you think it would be better first to get matters a little into order, so as to know distinctly what you are worth?'

'Quite the contrary; she'd rather not know. She'd rather exercise her imagination than learn distinctly what I am worth. Any woman of sense would prefer marrying me so.'

'I don't understand you.'

'Why, if I succeed in making matters quite lucid, I don't think she would marry me at all. Isn't it better to say, "My Angelina," or whatever else it may be, "you see before you Sir Richard Arden, who has estates in Yorkshire, in Middlesex, and in Devonshire, thus spanning all England from north to south. We had these estates at the Conquest. There is nothing modern about them but the mortgages. I have never been able to ascertain exactly what they bring in by way of rents, or pay out by way of interest. That I stand here, with flesh upon my bones, and pretty well-made clothes, I hope, upon both, is evidence in a confused way that an English gentleman—a baronet—can subsist upon them; and this magnificent muddle I lay at your feet with the devotion of a passionate admirer of your personal—property!" That, I say, is better than appearing with a balance-sheet in your hand, and saying,

"Madam, I propose marrying you, and I beg to present you with a balance-sheet of the incomings and outgoings of my estates, the intense clearness of which will, I hope, compensate for the nature of its disclosures. I am there shown in the most satisfactory detail to be worth exactly fifteen shillings *per annum*, and how unlimited is my credit will appear from the immense amount and variety of my debts. In pressing my suit I rely entirely upon your love of perspicuity and your passion for arithmetic which will find in the ledgers of my steward an almost inexhaustible gratification and indulgence." However, as you say, Alice, I have time to look about me, and I see you are tired. We'll talk it over tomorrow morning at breakfast. Don't think I have made up my mind; I'll do exactly whatever you like best. But get to your bed, you poor little soul; you do look so tired!'

With great affection they parted for the night. But Sir Richard did not meet her at breakfast.

After she had left the room some time, he changed his mind and left a message for his sister with old Crozier, ordered his servant and trap to the door, and drove into town. It was not his good angel who prompted him. He drove to a place where he was sure to find high play going on, and there luck did not favour him.

What had become of Sir Richard Arden's resolutions? The fascinations of his old vice were irresistible. The ring of the dice, the whirl of the roulette, the plodding pillage of whist—any rite acknowledged by Fortune, the goddess of his soul, was welcome to that keen worshipper. Luck was not always adverse; once or twice he might have retreated in comparative safety; but the temptation to 'back his luck' and go on prevailed, and left him where he was.

About a week after the evening passed at Mortlake, a black and awful night of disaster befell him.

Every other extravagance and vice draws its victim on at a regulated pace, but this of gaming is an hourly trifling with life, and one infatuated moment may end him. How short had been the reign of the new baronet, and where were prince and princedom now?

Before five o'clock in the morning, he had twice spent a quarter of an hour tugging at Mr. Levi's office-bell, in the dismal old street in Westminster. Then he drove off toward his lodgings. The roulette was whirling under his eyes whenever for a moment he closed them. He thought he was going mad.

The cabman knew a place where, even at that unseasonable hour, he might have a warm bath; and thither Sir Richard ordered him to drive. After this, he again essayed the Jew's office. The cool early morning was over still quiet London—hardly a soul was stirring. On the steps he waited, pulling the office-bell at intervals. In the stillness of the morning, he could hear it distinctly in the remote room, ringing unheeded in that capacious house.

Plans

It was, of course, in vain looking for Mr. Levi there at such an hour. Sir Richard Arden fancied that he had, perhaps, a sleeping-room in the house, and on that chance tried what his protracted alarm might do.

Then he drove to his own house. He had a latch-key, and let himself in. Just as he is, he throws himself into a chair in his dressing-room. He knows there is no use in getting into his bed. In his fatigued state, sleep was quite out of the question. That proud young man was longing to open his heart to the mean, cruel little Jew.

Oh, madness! why had he broken with his masterly and powerful friend, Longcluse? Quite unavailing now, his repentance. They had spoken and passed like ships at sea, in this wide life, and now who could count the miles and billows between them! Never to cross or come in sight again!

Uncle David! Yes, he might go to him; he might spread out the broad evidences of his ruin before him, and adjure him, by the God of mercy, to save him from the great public disgrace that was now imminent; implore of him to give him any pittance he pleased, to subsist on in exile, and to deal with the estates as he himself thought best. But Uncle David was away, quite out of reach. After his whimsical and inflexible custom, lest business should track him in his holiday, he had left no address with his man of business, who only knew that his first destination was Scotland; none with Grace Maubray, who only knew that, attended by Vivian Darnley, she and Lady May were to meet him in about a fortnight on the Continent, where they were to plan together a little excursion in Switzerland or Italy.

Sir Richard quite forgot there was such a meal as breakfast. He ordered his horse to the door, took a furious two hours' ride beyond Brompton, and returned and saw Levi at his office, at his usual hour, eleven o'clock. The Jew was alone. His large lowering eyes were cast on Sir Richard as he entered and approached.

'Look, now; listen,' says Sir Richard, who looks woefully wild and pale, and as he seats himself never takes his eyes off Mr. Levi. 'I don't care very much who knows it—I think I'm totally *ruined*.'

The Jew knows pretty well all about it, but he stares and gapes hypocritically in the face of his visitor as if he were thunderstruck, and he speaks never a word. I suppose he thought it as well, for the sake of brevity and clearness, to allow his client 'to let off the shteam' first, a process which Sir Richard forthwith commenced, with both hands on the table—sometimes clenched, sometimes expanded, sometimes with a thump, by blowing off a cloud of oaths and curses, and incoherent expositions of the wrongs and perversities of fortune. 'I don't think I can tell you how much it is. I don't know,' says Sir Richard bleakly, in reply to a pertinent question of the Jew's. 'There was that rich fellow, what's his name, that makes candles—he's always winning. By Jove, what a thing luck is! He won—I know it is more than two thousand.

'I gave him I O U's for it. He'd be very glad, of course, to know me, curse him! I don't care, now, who does. And he'd let me owe him twice as much, for as long as I like. I daresay, only too glad—as smooth as one of his own filthy candles. And there were three fellows lending money there. I don't know how much I got—I was stupid. I signed whatever they put before me. Those things can't stand, by heavens; the Chancellor will set them all aside. The confounded villains! What's the Government doing? What's the Government about, I say? Why don't Parliament interfere, to smash those cursed nests of robbers and swindlers? Here I am, utterly robbed—I know I'm *robbed*—and all by that cursed temptation; and—and—and I don't know what cash I got, nor what I have put my name to!'

'I'll make out that in an hour's time. They'll tell me at the houshe who the shentleman wazh.'

'And—upon my soul that's true—I owe the people there something too; it can't be much—it isn't much. And, Levi, like a good fellow—by Heaven, I'll *never* forget it to you, if you'll think of something. You've pulled me through so often; I am sure there's good-nature in you; you wouldn't see a fellow you've known so long driven to the wall and made a beggar of, without—without thinking of something.'

Levi looked down, with his hands in his pockets, and whistled to himself, and Sir Richard gazed on his vulgar features as if his life or death depended upon every variation of their expression.

'You know,' says Levi, looking up and swaying his shoulders a little, 'the old chap can't do no more. He's taken a share in that Austrian contract, and he'll want his capital, every pig. I told you lasht time. Wouldn't Lonclushe give you a lift?'

'Not he. He'd rather give me a shove under.'

'Well, they tell me you and him wazh very thick; and your uncle'sh man, Blount, knowshe him, and can just aslik him, from himself, mind, not from you.'

'For money?' exclaimed Richard.

'Not at a—all,' drawled the Jew impatiently. 'Lishen—mind. The old fellow, your friend——'

'He's out of town,' interrupted Richard.

'No, he'sh not. I shaw him lasht night. You're a—all wrong. He'sh not Mr. David Harden, if that'sh what you mean. He'sh a better friend, and he'll leave you a lot of tin when he diesh—an old friend of the family—and if all goeshe shmooth he'll come and have a talk with you fashe to fashe, and tell you all his plansh about you, before a week'sh over. But he'll be at hish lasht pound for five or six weeksh to come, till the firsht half-million of the new shtock is in the market; and he shaid, 'I can't draw out a pound of my balanshe,' but if he can get Lonclushe's na—name, I'll get him any shum he wantsh, and bear Lonclushe harmlesh.'

'I don't think I can,' said Sir Richard; 'I can't be quite sure, though. It is just possible he might.'

'Well, let Blount try,' said he.

There was another idea also in Mr. Levi's head. He had been thinking whether the situation might not be turned to some more profitable account, for him, than the barren agency for the 'friend of the family,' who 'lent out money gratis,' like Antonio; and if he did not 'bring down the rate of usance,' at all events, deprived the Shylocks of London, in one instance at least, of their fair game.

'If he won't do that, there'sh but one chansh left.'

'What is that?' asked Sir Richard, with a secret flutter at his heart. It was awful to think of himself reduced to his last chance, with his recent experience of what a chance is.

'Well,' says Mr. Levi, scrawling florid capitals on the table with his office pen, and speaking with much deliberation, 'I heard you were going to make a very rich match; and if the shettlementsh was agreed on, I don't know but we might shee our way to advancing all you want.'

Sir Richard gets up, and walks slowly two or three times up and down the room.

'I'll see about Blount,' said he;' I'll talk to him. I think those things are payable in six or eight days; and that tallow-chandler won't bother me tomorrow, I daresay. I'll go today and talk to Blount, and suppose you come to me tomorrow evening at Mortlake. Will nine o'clock do for you? I sha'n't keep you half-an-hour.'

'A—all right, Shir—nine, at Mortlake. If you want any diamondsh, I have a beoo—ootiful collar and pendantsh, in that shaafe—brilliantsh. I can give you the lot three thoushand under cosht prishe. You'll wa—ant a preshent for the young la—ady.'

'Yes, I suppose so,' said Sir Richard, abstractedly. 'Tomorrow night—tomorrow evening at nine o'clock.'

He stopped at the door, looking silently down the stairs, and then without leave-taking or looking behind him, he ran down, and drove to Mr. Blount's house, close by, in Manchester Buildings.

For more than a year the young gentleman whom we are following this morning had cherished vague aspirations, of which good Lady May had been the object. There was nothing to prevent their union, for the lady was very well disposed to listen. But Richard Arden did not like ridicule, and there was no need to hurry; and besides, within the last half-year had arisen another flame, less mercenary; also, perhaps, reciprocated.

Grace Maubray was handsome, animated; she had that combination of air, tact, cleverness, which enter into the idea of *chic*. With him it had been a financial, but notwithstanding rather agreeable, speculation. Hitherto there seemed ample time before him, and there was no need to define or decide.

Now, you will understand, the crisis had arrived, which admitted of neither hesitation nor delay. He was now at Blount's hall-door. He was certain that he could trust Blount with anything, and he meant to learn from him what *dot* his Uncle David intended bestowing on the young lady.

Mr. Blount was at home. He smiled kindly, and took the young gentleman's hand, and placed a chair for him.

From Flower to Flower

Mr. Blount was intelligent: he was an effective though not an artful diplomatist. He promptly undertook to sound Mr. Longcluse without betraying Sir Richard.

Richard Arden did not allude to his losses. He took good care to appear pretty nearly as usual. When he confessed his *tendresse* for Miss Maubray, the grave gentleman smiled brightly, and took him by the hand.

'If *you* should marry the young lady, mark you, she will have sixty thousand pounds down, and sixty thousand more after Mr. David Arden's death. That is splendid, Sir, and I think it will please him *very* much.'

'I have suffered a great deal, Mr. Blount, by neglecting his advice hitherto. It shall be my chief object, henceforward, to reform, and to live as he wishes. I believe people can't learn wisdom without suffering.'

'Will you take a biscuit and a glass of sherry, Sir Richard?' asked Mr. Blount.

'Nothing, thanks,' said Sir Richard. 'You know, I'm not as rich as I might have been, and marriage is a very serious step; and you are one of the oldest and most sensible friends I have, and you'll understand that it is only right I should very sure before taking such a step, involving not myself only, but another who ought to be dearer still, that there should no mistake about the means on which we may reckon. Are you quite sure that my uncle's intentions are still exactly what you mentioned?'

'Perfectly; he authorised me to say so two months ago, and on the eve of his departure on Friday last he repeated his instructions,'

Sir Richard, in silence, shook the old man very cordially by the hand, and was gone.

As he drove to his house in May Fair, Sir Richard's thoughts, among other things, turned again upon the question, 'Who could bis mysterious benefactor be?'

Once or twice had dimly visited his mind a theory which, ever since his recent conversation with Mr. Levi, had been growing more solid and vivid. An illegitimate brother of his father's, Edwin Raikes, had gone out to Australia early in life, with a purse to which three brothers, the late Sir Reginald, Harry, and David, had contributed. He had not maintained any correspondence with English friends and kindred; but rumours from time to time reached home that he had amassed a fortune. His feelings to the family of Arden had always been kindly. He was older than Uncle David, and had well earned a retirement from the life of exertion and exile which had consumed all the vigorous years of his manhood. Was this the 'old party' for whom Mr. Levi was acting?

With this thought opened a new and splendid hope upon the mind of Sir Richard. Here was a fortune, if rumour spoke truly, which, combined with David Arden's, would be amply sufficient to establish the old baronetage upon a basis of solid magnificence such as it had never rested on before.

It would not do, however, to wait for this. The urgency of the situation demanded immediate action. Sir Richard made an elaborate toilet, after which, in a hansom, he drove to Lady May Penrose's.

If our hero had had fewer things to think about he would have gone first, I fancy, to Miss Grace Maubray. It could do no great harm, however, to feel his way a little with Lady May, he thought, as he chatted with that plump alternative of his tender dilemma. But in this wooing there was a difficulty of a whimsical kind. Poor Lady May was so easily won, and made so many openings for his advances, that he was at his wits' end to find evasions by which to postpone the happy crisis which she palpably expected. He did succeed, however; and with a promise of calling again, with the lady's permission, that evening, he took his leave.

Before making his call at his uncle's house, in the hope of seeing Grace Maubray, he had to return to Mr. Blount, in Manchester Buildings, where he hoped to receive from that gentleman a report of his interview with Mr. Longcluse.

I shall tell you here what that report related. Mr. Longcluse was fortunately still at his house when Mr. Blount called, and immediately admitted him. Mr. Longcluse's horse and groom were at the door; he was on the point of taking his ride. His gloves and whip were beside him on the table as Mr. Blount entered.

Mr. Blount made his apologies, and was graciously received.

His visit was, in truth, by no means unwelcome.

'Mr. David Arden very well, I hope?'

'Quite well, thanks. He has left town.'

'Indeed! And where has he gone—the moors?'

'To Scotland, but not to shoot, I think. And he's going abroad then—going to travel.'

'On the Continent? How nice that is! What part?'

'Switzerland and Italy, I think,' said Mr. Blount, omitting all mention of Paris, where Mr. Arden was going first to make a visit to the Baron Vanboeren.

'He's going over ground that I know very well,' said Mr. Longcluse. 'Happy man! He can't quite break away from his business, though, I daresay.'

'He never tells us where a letter will find him, and the consequence is his holidays are never spoiled.'

'Not a bad plan, Mr. Blount. Won't he visit the Paris Exhibition?'

'I rather think not.'

'Can I do anything for you, Mr. Blount?'

'Well, Mr. Longcluse, I just called to ask you a question. I have been invited to take part in arranging a little matter which I take an interest in, because it affects the Arden estates.'

'Is Sir Richard Arden interested in it?' inquired Mr. Longcluse, gently and coldly.

'Yes, I rather fancy he would be benefited.'

'I have had a good deal of unpleasantness, and, I might add, a great deal of ingratitude from that quarter, and I have made up my mind never again to have anything to do with him or his affairs. I have no unpleasant *feeling,* you understand; no resentment; there is nothing, of course, he could say or do that could in the least affect me. It is simply that, having coolly reviewed his conduct, I have quite made up my mind to aid in nothing in which he has act, part, or interest.'

'It was not *directly,* but simply as a surety——'

'All the same, so far as I'm concerned,' said Mr. Longcluse sharply.

'And only, I fancied, it might be, as Mr. David Arden is absent, and you should be protected by satisfactory joint security——'

'I won't do it,' said Mr. Longcluse, a little brusquely; and he took out his watch and glanced at it impatiently.

'Sir Richard, I think, will be in funds immediately,' said Mr. Blount.

'How so?' asked Mr. Longcluse. 'You'll excuse me, as you press the subject, for saying *that* will be something new.'

'Well,' said Mr. Blount, who saw that his last words had made an impression, 'Sir Richard is likely to be married, very advantageously, immediately.'

'Are settlements agreed on?' inquired Mr. Longcluse, with real interest.

'No, not yet; but I know all about them.'

'He is accepted then?'

'He has not proposed yet; but there can be, I fancy, no doubt that the lady likes him, and all will go right.'

'Oh! and who is the lady?'

'I'm not at liberty to tell.'

'Quite right; I ought not to have asked,' says Mr. Longcluse. and looks down, slapping at intervals the side of his trousers lightly with his whip. He raises his eyes to Mr. Blount's face, and looks on the point of asking another question, but he does not.

'It is my opinion,' said Mr. Blount, 'the kindness would involve absolutely no risk whatever.'

There was a little pause. Mr. Longcluse looks rather dark and anxious; perhaps his mind has wandered quite from the business before them. But it returns, and he says,—

'Risk or no risk, Mr. Blount, I don't mean to do him that kindness; and for how long will Mr. David Arden be absent?'

'Unless he should take a sudden thought to return, he'll be away at least two months.'

'Where is he?—in Scotland?'

'I *really* don't know.'

'Couldn't one see him for a few minutes before he starts? Where does he take the steamer?'

'Southampton.'

'And on what day?'

'You really want a word with him?' asked Blount, whose hopes revived.

'I may.'

'Well, the only person who will know that is Mr. Humphries, of Pendle Castle, near that town; for he has to transact some trust-business with that gentleman as he passes through.'

'Humphries, of Pendle Castle. Very good; thanks.'

Mr. Longcluse looks again at his watch.

'And perhaps you will reconsider the matter I spoke of?'

'No use, Mr. Blount—not the least. I have quite made up my mind. Anything more? I am afraid I must be off.'

'Nothing, thanks,' said Mr. Blount.

And so the interview ended.

When he was gone, Mr. Longcluse thought darkly for a minute.

'That's a straightforward fellow, they say. I suppose the facts are so. It can't be, though, that Miss Maubray, that handsome creature with so much money, is thinking of marrying that insolent coxcomb. It may be Lady May, but the other is more likely. We must not allow *that,* Sir Richard. That would never do.'

There was a fixed frown on his face, and he was smiling in his dream. Out he went. His pale face looked as if he meditated a wicked joke, and, frowning still in utter abstraction, he took the bridle from his groom, mounted, looked about him as if just wakened, and set off at a canter, followed by his servant, for David Arden's house.

Smiling, gay, as if no care had ever crossed him, Longcluse enters the drawing-room, where he finds the handsome young lady writing a note at that moment.

'Mr. Longcluse, I'm so glad you've come!' she says, with a brilliant smile. 'I was writing to poor Lady Ethel, who is mourning, you know, in the country. The death of her father in the house was so awfully sudden, and I'm telling her all the news I can think of to amuse her. And is it really true that old Sir Thomas Giggles has grown so cross with his pretty young wife, and objects to her allowing Lord Knocknea to make love to her?'

'Quite true. It is a very bad quarrel, and I'm afraid it can't be made up,' said Mr. Longcluse.

'It must be very bad, indeed, if Sir Thomas can't make it up; for he allowed his first wife, I am told, to do anything she pleased. Is it to be a separation?'

'At *least.* And you heard, I suppose, of poor old Lady Glare?'

'No!'

'She has been rolling ever so long, you know, in a sea of troubles, and now, at last, she has fairly foundered.'

'How do you mean?'

'They have sold her diamonds,' said Mr. Longcluse. 'Didn't you hear?'

'No! Really? Sold her diamonds? Good Heaven! Then there's nothing left of her but her teeth. I hope they won't sell them.'

'It is an awful misfortune,' said Mr. Longcluse.

'Misfortune! She's utterly ruined. It was her diamonds that people asked. I am really sorry. She was such fun; she was so fat, and such a fool, and said such delicious things, and dressed herself so like a macaw. Alas! I shall never see her more; and people thought her only use on earth was to carry about her diamonds. No one seemed to perceive what a delightful creature she was. What about Lady May Penrose? I have not seen her since I came back from Cowes, the day before yesterday, and we leave London together on Tuesday.'

'Lady May! Oh! she is to receive a very interesting communication, I believe. She is one name on a pretty long and very distinguished list, which Sir Richard Arden, I am told, has made out, and carries about with him in his pocket-book.'

'You're talking riddles; pray speak plainly.'

'Well, Lady May is one of several ladies who are to be honoured with a proposal.'

'And would you have me believe that Sir Richard Arden has really made such a fool of himself as to make out a list of eligible ladies whom he is about to ask to marry him, and that he has had the excellent good sense and taste to read this list to his acquaintance?'

'I mean to say this—I'll tell the whole story—Sir Richard has ruined himself at play; take that as a fact to start with. He is literally ruined. His uncle is away; but I don't think any man in his senses would think of paying his losses for him. He turns, therefore, naturally, to the more amiable and less arithmetical sex, and means to invite, in turn, a series of fair and affluent admirers to undertake, by means of suitable settlements, that interesting office for him.'

'I don't think you like him, Mr. Longcluse; is not that a story a little too like *The Merry Wives of Windsor?*'

'It is quite certain I don't like him, and it is quite certain,' added Mr. Longcluse, with one of his cold little laughs, 'that if I did like him, I should not tell the story; but it is also certain that the story is, in all its parts, strictly fact. If you permit me the pleasure of a call in two or three days, you will tell me you no longer doubt it.'

Mr. Longcluse was looking down as he said that with a gentle and smiling significance. The young lady blushed a little, and then more intensely, as he spoke, and looking through the window, asked with a laugh,—

'But how shall we know whether he really speaks to Lady May?'

'Possibly by his marrying her,' laughed Mr. Longcluse. 'He certainly will if he can, unless he is caught and married on the way to her house.'

'He was a little unfortunate in showing you his list, wasn't he?' said Grace Maubray.

'I did not say that. If there had been any, the least, confidence, nothing on earth could have induced me to divulge it. We are not even, at present, on speaking terms. He had the coolness to send a Mr. Blount, who transacts all Mr. David Arden's affairs, to ask me to become his security, Mr. Arden being away; and by way of inducing me to do so, he disclosed, with the coarseness which is the essence of business, the matrimonial schemes which are to recoup, within a few days, the losses of the roulette, the whist-table, or the dice-box.'

'Oh! Mr. Blount, I'm told, is a very honest man.'

'Quite so; particularly accurate, and I don't think anything on earth would induce him to tell an untruth,' testifies Mr. Longcluse.

After a little pause, Miss Maubray laughs.

'One certainly does learn,' she said, 'something new every day. Could any one have fancied a *gentleman* descending to so gross a meanness?'

'Everybody is a gentleman now-a-days,' remarked Mr. Longcluse with a smile; 'but every one is not a hero—they give way, more or less, under temptation. Those who stand the test of the crucible and the furnace are seldom met with.'

At this moment the door opened, and Lord Wynderbroke was announced. A little start, a lighting of the eyes, as Grace rose, and a fluttered advance, with a very pretty little hand extended, to meet him, testified, perhaps, rather more surprise than one would have quite expected. For Mr. Longcluse, who did not know him so well as Miss Maubray, recognised his voice, which was peculiar, and resembling the caw of a jay, as he put a question to the servant on his way up.

Mr. Longcluse took his leave. He was not sorry that Lord Wynderbroke had called. He wished no success to Sir Richard's wooing. He thought he had pretty well settled the question in Miss Maubray's mind, and smiling, he rode at pleasant canter to Lady May's. It was as well, perhaps, that she should hear the same story. Lady May, however, unfortunately, had just gone out for a drive.

Behind the Arras

It was quite true that Lady May was not at home. She was actually, with a little charming palpitation, driving to pay a very interesting visit to Grace Maubray. In affairs of the kind that now occupied her mind, she had no confidants but very young people.

Miss Maubray was at home—and instantly Lady May's plump instep was seen on the carriage step. She disdained assistance, and descended with a heavy skip upon the flags, where she executed an involuntary frisk that carried her a little out of the line of advance.

As she ascended the stairs, she met her friend Lord Wynderbroke coming down. They stopped for a moment on the landing, under a picture of Cupid and Venus; Lady May, smiling, remarked, a little out of breath, what a charming day it was, and expressed her amazement at seeing him in town—a surprise which he agreeably reciprocated. He had been at Glenkiltie in the Highlands, where he had accidentally met Mr. David Arden. 'Miss Maubray is in the drawing-room,' he said, observing that the eyes of the good lady glanced unconsciously upward at the door of that room. And then they parted affectionately, and turned their backs on each other with a sense of relief.

'Well, my dear,' she said to Grace Maubray as soon as they had kissed, 'longing to have a few minutes with you, with ever so much to say. You have no idea what it is to be stopped on the stairs by that tiresome man—I'll never quarrel with you again for calling him a bore. No matter, here I am; and really, my dear, it *is* such an odd affair—not quite that; such an odd scene, I don't know where or how to begin.'

'I wish I could help you,' said Miss Maubray laughing.

'Oh, my dear, you'd never guess in a hundred years.'

'How do you know? Hasn't a certain baronet something to do with it?'

'Well, well—dear me! That is *very* extraordinary. Did he tell you he was going to—to—Good gracious! My dear, it *is* the most extraordinary thing. I believe you hear everything; but—a—but *listen.* Not an hour ago he came—Richard Arden, of course, we mean—and, my dear Grace, he spoke so very nicely of his troubles, poor fellow, you know—debts I mean, of course—not the least his fault, and all that kind of thing, and—he went on—I really don't know how to tell you. But he said—he said—he said he liked me, and no one else on earth; and he was on the very point of saying *everything,* when, just at that moment, who should come in but that gossiping old woman, Lady Botherton—and he whispered, as he was going, that he would return, after I had had my drive. The carriage was at the door, so, when I got rid of the old woman, I got into it, and came straight here to have a talk with you; and what do you think I ought to say? Do tell me, like a darling, do!'

'I wish you would tell *me* what one ought to say to that question,' said Grace Maubray with a slight disdain (that young lady was in the most unreasonable way piqued), 'for I'm told he's going to ask me precisely the same question.'

'*You,* my dear?' said Lady May after a pause, during which she was staring at the smiling face of the young lady; 'you can't be serious!'

'*He* can't be serious, you mean,' answered the young lady, 'and—who's this?' she broke off, as she saw a cab drive up to the hall-door. 'Dear me! is it? No. Yes, indeed, it is Sir Richard Arden. We must not be seen together. He'll know you have been talking to me. Just go in here.'

She opened the door of the *boudoir* adjoining the room.

'I'll send him away in a moment. You may hear every word I have to say. I should like it—I shall give him a lecture.'

As she thus spoke she heard his step on the stair, and motioned Lady May into the inner room, into which she hurried and closed the door, leaving it only a little way open.

These arrangements are hardly completed when Sir Richard is announced. Grace is positively angry. But never had she looked so beautiful; her eyes so tenderly lustrous under their long lashes; her colour so brilliant—an expression so maidenly and sad. If it was acting, it was very well done. You would have sworn that the melancholy and agitation of her looks, and the slightly quickened movement of her breathing, were those of a person who felt that the hour of her fate had come.

With what elation Richard Arden saw these beautiful signs!

After a few words had been exchanged, Grace said in reply to a question of Sir Richard's,—

'Lady May and I are going together, you know: in a day or two we shall be at Brighton. I mean to bid Alice goodbye today. There—I mean at Brighton—we are to meet Vivian Darnley, and possibly another friend; and we go to meet your uncle at that pretty little town in Switzerland, where Lady May —— I wonder, by-the-bye, you did not arrange to come with us; Lady May travels with us the entire time. She says there are some very interesting ruins there.'

'Why, dear old soul!' said Sir Richard, who felt called upon to say something to set himself right with respect to Lady May, 'she's thinking of quite another place. She will be herself the only interesting ruin there.'

'I think you wish to vex me,' said pretty Grace, turning away with a smile, which showed, nevertheless, that this kind of joke was not an unmixed vexation to her. 'I don't care for ruins myself.'

'Nor do I,' he said, archly.

'But you don't think so of Lady May. I know you don't. You are franker with her than with me, and you tell her a very different tale.'

'I must be very frank, then, if I tell her more than I know myself. I never said a civil thing of Lady May, except once or twice, to the poor old thing herself, when I wanted her to do one or two little things, to please *you*.'

'Oh! come, you can't deceive me; I've seen you place your hand to your heart, like a theatrical hero, when you little fancied any one but she saw it.'

'Now, really, that is too bad. I may have put my hand to my side, when it ached from laughing.'

'How can you talk so? You know very well I have heard you tell her how you admire her music and her landscapes.'

'No, no—not landscapes—she paints faces. But her colouring is, as artists say, too chalky—and nothing but red and white, like—what is it like?—like a clown. Why did not she get the late Mr. Etty—she's always talking of him—to teach her something of his tints?'

'You are not to speak so of Lady May. You forget she is my particular friend,' says the young lady; but her pretty face does not express so much severity as her words. 'I do think you like her. You merely talk so to throw dust in people's eyes. Why should not you be frank with me?'

'I wish I dare be frank with you,' said Sir Richard.

'And why not?'

'How can I tell how my disclosures might be punished? My frankness might extinguish the best hope I live for; a few rash words might make me a very unhappy man for life.'

'Really? Then I can quite understand that reflection alarming you in the midst of a *tête-à-tête.* with Lady May; and even interrupting an interesting conversation.'

Sir Richard looked at her quickly, but her looks were perfectly artless.

'I really do wish you would spare me all further allusion to that good woman. I can bear that kind of fun from any one but you. Why will you? she is old enough to be my mother. She is fat, and painted, and ridiculous. You think me totally without romance? I wish to heaven I were. There is a reason that makes your saying all that particularly cruel. I am not the sordid creature you take me for. I'm not insensible. I'm not a mere stock of stone. Never was human being more capable of the wildest passion. Oh, if I dare tell you all!'

Was all this acting? Certainly not. Never was shallow man, for the moment, more in earnest. Cool enough he was, although he had always admired this young lady, when he entered the room. He had made that entrance, nevertheless, in a spirit quite dramatic. But Miss Maubray never looked so brilliant, never half so tender. He took fire—the situation aiding quite unexpectedly—and the flame was real. It might have been over as quickly as a balloon on fire; but for the moment the conflagration was intense.

How was Miss Maubray affected? An immensely abler performer than the young gentleman who had entered the room with his part at his fingers' ends, and all his looks and emphasis arranged—only to break through all this, and begin extemporising wildly—she, on the contrary, maintained her *rôle* with admirable coolness. It was not, perhaps, so easy; for notwithstanding appearances, her histrionic powers were severely tasked; for never was she more angry. Her self-esteem was wounded; the fancy (it was no more), she had cherished for him was gone, and a great disgust was there instead.

'You shall ask me no questions till I have done asking mine,' said the young lady, with decision; 'and I will speak as much as I please of Lady May!'

This jealousy flattered Sir Richard.

'And I will say this,' continued Grace Maubray, 'you never address her except as a lover, in what you romantic people would call the language of love.'

'Now, now, now! How can you say that? Is that fair?'

'You do.'

'No, really, I swear—that's *too* bad!'

'Yes, the other day, when you spoke to her at the carriage window—you did not think I heard—you accused her so tenderly of having failed to go to Lady Harbroke's garden-party, and you couldn't say what you meant in plain terms, but you said, 'Why were you false?"

'I didn't, I swear.'

'Oh! you did; I heard every syllable; 'false' was the word.'

'Well, if I said 'false', I must have been thinking of her hair; for she is really a very honest old woman.'

At this moment a female voice in distress is heard, and poor Lady May comes pushing out of the pretty little room, in which Grace Maubray had placed her, sobbing and shedding floods of tears.

'I can't stay there any longer, for I hear everything; I can't help hearing every word—honest old woman, and all—opprobrious. Oh! how *can* people be so? how *can* they? Oh! I'm very angry—I'm very angry—I'm very angry!'

If Miss Maubray were easily moved to pity she might have been at sight of the big innocent eyes turned up at her, from which rolled great tears, making visible channels through the paint down her cheeks. She sobbed and wept like a fat, good-natured child, and pitifully she continued sobbing, 'Oh, I'm a-a-ho—very angry; wha-at shall I do-o-o, my dear? I-I'm very angry—oh, oh—I'm very a-a-angry!'

'So am I,' said Grace Maubray, with a fiery glance at the young baronet, who stood fixed where he was, like an image of death; 'and I had intended, dear Lady May, telling you a thing which Sir Richard Arden may as well hear, as I mean to write to tell Alice today; it is that I am to be married—I have accepted Lord Wynderbroke—and—and that's all.'

Sir Richard, I believe, said 'Goodbye.' Nobody heard him. I don't think he remembers how he got on his horse. I don't think the ladies saw him leave the room—only, he was gone.

Poor Lady May takes her incoherent leave. She has got her veil over her face, to baffle curiosity. Miss Maubray stands at the window, the tip of her finger to her brilliant lip, contemplating Lady May as she gets in with a great jerk and swing of the carriage, and she hears the footman say 'Home,' and sees a fat hand, in a lilac glove, pull up the window hurriedly. Then she sits down on a sofa, and laughs till she quivers again, and tears overflow her eyes; and she says in the intervals, almost breathlessly,—

'Oh, poor old thing! I really am sorry. Who could have thought she cared so much? Poor old soul! what a ridiculous old thing!'

Such broken sentences of a rather contemptuous pity rolled and floated along the even current of her laughter.

Bond and Deed

The summer span of days was gone; it was quite dark, and long troops of withered leaves drifted in rustling trains over the avenue, as Mr. Levi, observant of his appointment, drove up to the grand old front of Mortlake, which in the dark spread before him like a house of white mist.

'I shay,' exclaimed Mr. Levi, softly, arresting the progress of the cabman, who was about running up the steps, ' I'll knock myshelf—wait you there.'

Mr. Levi was smoking. Standing at the base of the steps, he looked up, and right and left with some curiosity. It was too dark; he could hardly see the cold glimmer of the windows that reflected the gray horizon. Vaguely, however, he could see that it was a grander place than he had supposed. He looked down the avenue, and between the great trees over the gate he saw the distant lights, and heard through the the dim air the chimes, far off, from London steeples, succeeding one another, or mingling faintly, and telling all whom it might concern the solemn lesson of the flight of time.

Mr. Levi thought it might be worth while coming down in the daytime, and looking over the house and place to see what could be made of them; the thing was sure to go a dead bargain. At present he could see nothing but the wide, vague, grey front, and the faint glow through the hall windows, which showed their black outlines sharply enough.

'Well, *he*'sh come a mucker, anyhow,' murmured Mr. Levi, with one of his smiles that showed so wide his white sharp teeth.

He knocked at the door and rang the bell. It was not a footman, but Crozier who opened it. The old servant of the family did not like the greasy black curls, the fierce jet eyes, the sallow face and the large, moist, sullen mouth, that presented themselves under the brim of Mr. Levi's hat, nor the tawdry glimmer of chains on his waistcoat, nor the cigar still burning in his fingers. Sir Richard had told Crozier, however, that a Mr. Levi, whom he described, was to call at a certain hour, on very particular business, and was to be instantly admitted.

Mr. Levi looks round him, and extinguishes his cigar before following Crozier, whose countenance betrays no small contempt and dislike, as he eyes the little man askance, as if he would like well to be uncivil to him.

Crozier leads him to the right, through a small apartment, to a vast square room, long disused, still called the library, though but few books remain on the shelves, and those in disorder. It is a chilly night, and a little fire burns in the grate, over which Sir Richard is cowering. Very haggard, the baronet starts up as the name of his visitor is announced.

'Come in,' cries Sir Richard, walking to meet him. 'Here—here I am, Levi, utterly ruined. There isn't a soul I dare tell how I am beset, or anything to, but you. Do, for God's sake take pity on me, and think of something! my brain's quite gone—you're such a clever fellow' (he is dragging Levi by the arm all this time towards the candles: 'do now, you're sure to see some way out. It is a matter of *honour;* I only want time. If I could only find my Uncle David: think of his selfishness—good heaven! was there ever man so treated? and there's the bank letter—there—on the table; you see it—dunning me, the ungrateful harpies, for the trifle—what is it? three hundred and something, I overdrew; and that blackguard tallow-chandler has been three times to my house in town, for payment today, and it's more than I thought—near four thousand, he says—the scoundrel! It's just the same to him two months hence; he's full of money, the beast—a fellow like that—it's delight to him to get hold of a gentleman, and he won't take a bill—the lying rascal!

'He is pressed for cash just now—a pug-faced villain with three hundred thousand pounds! Those scoundrels! I mean the people, whatever they are, that lent me the money; it turns out it was all but at sight, and they were with my attorney today, and they won't wait. I wish I was shot; I envy the dead dogs rolling in the Thames! By heaven; Levi, I'll say you're the best friend man ever had on earth, I will, if you manage something! I'll never forget it to you; I'll have it in my power, yet! no one ever said I was ungrateful; I swear I'll be the making of you! *Do,* Levi, think; you're accustomed to—to emergency, and unless you will, I'm utterly ruined—ruined, by heaven, before I have time to think?'

The Jew listened to all this with his hands in his pockets,

leaning back in his chair, with his big eyes staring on the wild face of the baronet, and his heavy mouth hanging. He was trying to reduce his countenance to vacancy.

'What about them shettlements, Sir Richard—a nishe young lady with a ha-a-tful o' money?' insinuated Levi.

'I've been thinking over that, but it wouldn't do, with my affairs in this state, it would not be honourable or straight. Put that quite aside.'

Mr. Levi gaped at him for a moment solemnly, and turned suddenly, and, brute as he was, spit on the Turkey carpet. He was not, as you perceive, ceremonious; but he could not allow the baronet to see the laughter that without notice caught him for a moment, and could think of no better way to account for his turning away his head.

'That'sh wery honourable indeed,' said the Jew, more solemn than ever; 'and if you can't play in that direction, I'm afraid you're in queer shtreet.'

The baronet was standing before Levi, and at these words from that dirty little oracle, a terrible chill stole up from his feet to the crown of his head. Like a frozen man he stood there, and the Jew saw that his very lips were white. Sir Richard feels, for the first time, actually, that he is ruined.

The young man tries to speak, twice. The big eyes of the Jew are staring up at the contortion. Sir Richard can see nothing but those two big fiery eyes; he turns quickly away and walks to the end of the room.

'There's just one fiddle-string left to play on,' muses the Jew.

'For God's sake!' exclaims Sir Richard, turning about, in a voice you would not have known, and for fully a minute the room was so silent you could scarcely have believed that two men were breathing in it.

'Shir Richard, will you be so good as to come nearer a bit? There, that'sh the cheeshe. I brought thish 'ere thing.'

It is a square parchment with a good deal of printed matter, and blanks, written in, and a law stamp fixed with an awful regularity, at the corner.

'Casht your eye over it,' says Levi, coaxingly, as he pushes it over the table to the young gentleman, who is sitting now at the other side.

The young man looks at it, reads it, but just then, if it had been a page of *Robinson Crusoe*, he could not have understood it.

'I'm not quite myself, I can't follow it; too much to think of. What is it?'

'A bond and warrant to confess judgment.'

'What is it for?'

'Ten thoushand poundsh.'

'Sign it, shall I? Can you do anything with it?'

'Don't raishe your voishe, but lishten. Your friend'— and at the phrase Mr. Levi winked mysteriously— 'has enough to do it twishe over; and upon my shoul, I'll shwear on the book, azh I hope to be shaved, it will never shee the light; he'll never raishe a pig on it, sho' 'elp me, nor let it out of hish 'ands, till he givesh it back to you. He can't ma-ake no ushe of it; I knowshe him well, and he'll pay you the ten thoushand tomorrow morning, and he wantsh to shake handsh with you, and make himself known to you, and talk a bit.'

'But—but my signature wouldn't satisfy him,' began Sir Richard bewildered.

'Oh! *no*—no, no?' murmured Mr. Levi, fiddling with the corner of the bank's reminder which lay on the table. 'Mr. Longcluse won't sign it,' said Sir Richard. Mr. Levi threw himself back in his chair, and looked with a roguish expression still upon the table, and gave the corner of the note a little fillip.

'Well,' said Levi, after both had been some time silent, 'it ain't much, only to write his name on the penshil line, *there,* you see, and *there*—he shouldn't make no bonesh about it. Why, it's done every day. Do you think I'd help in a thing of the short if there was any danger? The Sheneral's come to town, is he? What are you afraid of? Don't you be a shild—ba-ah!'

All this Mr. Levi said so low that it was as if he were whispering to the table, and he kept looking down as he put the parchment over to Sir Richard, who took it in his hand, and the bond trembled so much that he set it down again.

'Leave it with me,' he said faintly.

Levi got up with an unusual hectic in each cheek, and his eyes very brilliant.

'I'll meet you what time you shay tonight; you had besht take a little time. It'sh ten now. Three hoursh will do it. I'll go on to my offish by one o'clock, and you come any time from one to two.'

Sir Richard was trembling.

'Between one and two, mind. Hang it! Shir Richard, don't you be a fool about nothing,' whispers the Jew, as black as thunder.

He is fumbling in his breast-pocket, and pulling out a sheaf of letters; he selects one, which he throws upon the parchment that lies open on the table.

'That'sh the note you forgot in my offish yeshterday, *with hish* name shined to it. There, now you have everything.'

Without any form of valediction, the Jew had left the room. Sir Richard sits with his teeth set, and a strange frown upon his face, scarcely breathing. He hears the cab drive away. Before him on the table lie the papers.

Sir Richard's Resolution

Two hours had passed, and more, of solitude. With a candle in his hand, and his hat and great-coat on, Sir Richard Arden came out into the hall. His trap awaited him at the door.

In the interval of his solitude, something incredible has happened to him. It is over. A spectral secret accompanies him henceforward. A devil sits in his pocket, in that parchment. He dares not think of himself. Something sufficient to shake the world of London, and set all English Christian tongues throughout the earth wagging on one theme, has happened.

Does he repent? One thing is certain: he dares not falter. Something within him once or twice commanded him to throw his crime into the fire, while yet it is obliterable. But what then?

what of tomorrow? Into that sheer black sea of ruin, that reels and yawns as deep as eye can fathom beneath him, he must dive and see the light no more. Better his chance.

He won't think of what he has done, of what he is going to do. He suspects his courage: he dares not tempt his cowardice. Braver, perhaps, it would have been to meet the worst at once. But surely, according to the theory of chances, we have played the true game. Is not a little time gained, everything? Are we not in friendly hands? Has not that little scoundrel committed himself, by an all but actual participation in the affair? It can never come to *that*. 'I have only to confess, and throw myself at Uncle David's feet, and the one dangerous debt would instantly be brought up and cancelled.'

These thoughts came vaguely, and on his heart lay an all but insupportable load. The sight of the staircase reminded him that Alice must long since have gone to her room. He yearned to see her and say goodnight. It was the last farewell that the brother she had known from her childhood till now should ever speak or look. That brother was to die tonight, and a spirit of guilt to come in his stead.

He taps lightly at her door. She is asleep. He opens it, and dimly sees her innocent head upon the pillow. If his shadow were cast upon her dream, what an image would she have seen looking in at the door! A sudden horror seizes him—he draws back and closes the door; on the lobby he pauses. It was a last moment of grace. He stole down the stairs, mounted his tax-cart, took the reins from his servant in silence, and drove swiftly into town. In Parliament Street, near the corner of the street leading to Levi's office, they passed a policeman, lounging on the flagway. Richard Arden is in a strangely nervous state; he fancies he will stop and question him, and he touches the horse with the whip to get quickly by.

In his breast-pocket he carried his ghastly secret. A pretty business if he happened to be thrown out, and a policeman should make an inventory of his papers, as he lay insensible in an hospital—a pleasant thing if he were robbed in these villanous streets, and the bond advertised, for a reward, by a pretended finder. A nice thing, good heaven! if it should wriggle and slip its way out of his pocket, in the jolting and tremble of the drive, and fall into London hands, either rascally or severe. He pulled up, and gave the reins to the servant, and felt, however gratefully, with his fingers, the crisp crumple of the parchment under the cloth! Did his servant look at him oddly as he gave him the reins? Not he; but Sir Richard began to suspect him and everything. He made him stop near the angle of the street, and there he got down, telling him rather savagely—for his fancied look was still in the baronet's brain—not to move an inch from that spot.

It was half-past one as his steps echoed down the street in which Mr. Levi had his office. There was a figure leaning with its back in the recess of Levi's door, smoking. Sir Richard's temper was growing exasperated.

It was Levi himself. Upstairs they stumble in the dark. Mr. Levi has not said a word. He is not treating his visitor with much ceremony. He lets himself into his office, secured with a heavy iron bar, and a lock that makes a great clang, and proceeds to light a candle. The flame expands and the light shows well-barred shutters, and the familiar objects.

When Mr. Levi had lighted a second candle, he fixed his great black eyes on the young baronet, who glances over his shoulder at the door, but the Jew has secured it. Their eyes meet for a moment, and Sir Richard places his hand nervously in his breast-pocket and takes out the parchment. Levi nods and extends his hand. Each now holds it by a corner, and as Sir Richard lets it go hesitatingly, he says faintly—

'Levi, you wouldn't—you could not run any risk with that?'

Levi stands by his great iron safe, with the big key in his hand. He nods in reply, and locking up the document, he knocks his knuckles on the iron door, with a long and solemn wink.

'*Sha-afe!*—that'sh the word,' says he, and then he drops the keys into his pocket again.

There was a silence of a minute or more. A spell was stealing over them; an influence was in the room. Each eyed the other, shrinkingly, as a man might eye an assassin. The Jew knew that there was danger in that silence; and yet he could not break it. He could not disturb the influence acting on Richard Arden's mind. It was his good angel's last pleading, before the long farewell.

In a dreadful whisper Richard Arden speaks:—

'Give me that parchment back,' says he.

Satan finds his tongue again.

'Give it back?' repeats Levi, and a pause ensues. 'Of course I'll give it back; and I wash my hands of it and you, and you're throwing away ten thoushand poundsh for *nothing.*'

Levi was taking out his keys as he spoke, and as he fumbled them over one by one, he said—

'You'll want a lawyer in the Insholwent Court, and you'd find Mishter Sholomonsh azh shatisfactory a shengleman azh any in London. He'sh an auctioneer, too; and there'sh no good in your meetin' that friendly cove here tomorrow, for he'sh one o' them honourable chaps, and he'll never look at you after your schedule's lodged, and the shooner that'sh done the better; and them women we was courting, won't they laugh!'

Hereupon, with great alacrity, Mr. Levi began to apply the key to the lock.

'Don't mind. Keep it; and mind, you d——d little swindler, so sure as you stand there, if you play me a trick, I'll blow your brains out, if it were in the police-office!'

Mr. Levi looked hard at him, and nodded. He was accustomed to excited language in certain situations.

'Well,' said he coolly, a second time returning the keys to his pocket, 'your friend will be here at twelve tomorrow, and if you please him as well as he expects, who knows wha-at may be? If he leavesh you half hish money, you'll not 'ave many bill transhactionsh on your handsh.'

'May God Almighty have mercy on me!' groans Sir Richard, hardly above his breath.

'You shall have the cheques then. He'll be here all right.'

'I—I forget; did you say an hour?'

Levi repeats the hour. Sir Richard walks slowly to the stairs, down which Levi lights him. Neither speaks.

In a few minutes more the young gentleman is driving rapidly to his town house, where he means to end that long-remembered night.

When he had got to his room, and dismissed his valet, he sat down. He looked round, and wondered how collected he now was. The situation seemed like a dream, or his sense of danger had grown torpid. He could not account for the strange indifference that had come over him. He got quickly into bed. It was late, and he exhausted, and aided, I know not by what narcotic, he slept a constrained, odd sleep—black as Erebus—the thread of which snaps suddenly, and he is awake with a heart beating fast, as if from a sudden start. A hard bitter voice has said close by the pillow, 'You are the first Arden that ever did that!' and with these words grating in his ears, he awoke, and had a confused remembrance of having been dreaming of his father.

Another dream, later on, startled him still more. He was in Levi's office, and while they were talking over the horrid document, in a moment it blew out of the window; and a lean, ill-looking man, in a black coat, like the famous person who, in old woodcuts picked up the shadow of Peter Schlemel, caught the parchment from the pavement, and with his eyes fixed cornerwise upon him, and a dreadful smile, tapped his long finger on the bond, and with wide paces stepped swiftly away with it in his hand.

Richard Arden started up in his bed; the cold moisture of terror was upon his forehead, and for a moment he did not know where he was, or how much of his vision was real. The grey twilight of early morning was over the town. He welcomed the light; he opened the window-shutters wide. He looked from the window down upon the street. A lean man with tattered black, with a hammer in his hand, just as the man in his dream had held the roll of parchment, was slowly stepping with long strides away from his house, along the street.

As his thoughts cleared, his panic increased. Nothing had happened between the time of his lying down and his up-rising to alter his situation, and the same room sees him now half mad.

The Meeting

Near the appointed hour, he walked across the park, and through the Horse Guards, and in a few minutes more was between the tall old-fashioned houses of the street in which Mr. Levi's office is be found. He passes by a dingy hired coach, with a tarnished crest on the door, and sees two Jewish-looking men inside, both smiling over some sly joke. Whose door are they waiting at? He supposes another Jewish office seeks the shade of that pensive street.

Mr. Levi opened his office door for his handsome client. They were quite to themselves. Mr. Levi did not look well. He received him with a nod. He shut the door when Sir Richard was in the room.

'He'sh not come yet. We'll talk to him inshide.' He indicates the door of the inner room, with a little side jerk of his head. 'That'sh private. He hazh that—*thing* all right.'

Sir Richard says nothing. He follows Levi into a small inner room, which had, perhaps, originally been a lady's *boudoir*, and had afterwards, one might have conjectured, served as the treasury of cash and jewels of a pawn-office; for its door was secured with iron bars, and two great locks, and the windows were well barred with iron. There were two huge iron safes in the room, built into the wall.

'I'll show you a beauty of a dresshing-ca-ashe,' said Levi, rousing himself; 'I'll shell it a dead bargain, and give time for half, if you knowsh any young shwell as wantsh such a harticle. Look here; it was made for the Duchess of Horleans—all in gold, hemerald, and brilliantsh.'

And thus haranguing, he displayed its contents, and turned them over, staring on them with a livid admiration. Sir Richard is not thinking of the duchess's dressing-case, nor is he much more interested when Mr. Levi goes on to tell him, 'There'sh three executions against peersh out thish week—two gone down to the country. Sholomonsh nobbled Lord Bylkington's carriage outshide Shyner's at two o'clock in the morning, and his lordship had to walk home in the rain;' and Levi laughs and wriggles pleasantly over the picture. 'I think he'sh coming,' says Levi suddenly, inclining his ear toward the door. He looked back over his shoulder with an odd look, a little stern, at the young gentleman.

'Who?' asked the young man, a little uncertain, in consequence of the character of that look.

'Your—that—your friend, of course,' said Levi, with his eyes again averted, and his ear near the door.

It was a moment of trepidation and of hope to Richard Arden. He hears the steps of several persons in the next room. Levi opens a little bit of the door, and peeps through, and with a quick glance towards the baronet, he whispers, 'Ay, it's him.'

Oh, blessed hope! here comes, at last, a powerful friend to take him by the hand, and draw him, in his last struggle, from the whirlpool.

Sir Richard glances towards the door through which the Jew is still looking, and signing with his hand as, little by little, he opens it wider and wider; and a voice in the next room, at sound of which Sir Richard starts to his feet, says sharply, 'Is all right?' 'All *right,*' replies Levi, getting aside; and Mr. Longcluse entered the room and shut the door.

His pale face looked paler than usual, his thin cruel lips were closed, his nostrils dilated with a terrible triumph, and his eyes were fixed upon Arden, as he held the fatal parchment in his hand.

Levi saw a scowl so dreadful contract Sir Richard Arden's face—was it pain, or was it fury?—that, drawing back as far as the wall would let him, he almost screamed, 'It ain't me!—it ain't my fault!—I can't help it!—I couldn't!—I can't!' His right hand was in his pocket, and his left, trembling violently, extended toward him, as if to catch his arm.

But Richard Arden was not thinking of him—did not hear

him. He was overpowered. He sat down in his chair. He leaned back with a gasp and a faint laugh, like a man just overtaken by a wave, and lifted half-drowned from the sea. Then, with a sudden cry, he threw his hands and head on the table.

There was no token of relenting in Longcluse's cruel face. There was a contemptuous pleasure in it. He did not remove his eyes from that spectacle of abasement as he replaced the parchment in his pocket. There is a silence of about a minute, and Sir Richard sits up and says vaguely,—

'Thank God, it's over! Take me away; I'm ready to go.' 'You shall go, time enough; I have a word to say first,' said Longcluse, and he signs to the Jew to leave them.

On being left to themselves, the first idea that struck Sir Richard was the wild one of escape. He glanced quickly at the window. It was barred with iron. There were men in the next room—he could not tell how many—and he was without arms. The hope lighted up, and almost at the same moment expired.

Mr. Longcluse Proposes

'Clear your head,' says Mr. Longcluse, sternly, seating himself before Sir Richard, with the table between; 'you must conceive a distinct idea of your situation, Sir, and I shall then tell you something that remains. You have committed a forgery under aggravated circumstances, for which I shall have you convicted and sentenced to penal servitude at the next sessions. I have been a good friend to you on many occasions; you have been a false one to me—who baser?—and while I was anonymously helping you with large sums of money, you forged my name to a legal instrument for ten thousand pounds, to swindle your unknown benefactor, little suspecting who he was.'

Longcluse smiled.

'I have heard how you spoke of me. I'm an adventurer, a leg, an assassin, a person whom you were compelled to drop; rather a low person, I fear, if a felon can't afford to sit beside me! You were always too fine a man for me. Your get up was always peculiar; you were famous for that. It will soon be more singular still, when your hair and your clothes are cut after the fashion of the great world you are about to enter. How your friends will laugh?'

Sir Richard heard all this with a helpless stare.

'I have only to stamp on the ground, to call up the men who will accomplish your transformation. I can change your life by a touch, into convict dress, diet, labour, lodging, for the rest of your days. What plea have you to offer to my mercy?'

Sir Richard would have spoken, but his voice failed him. With a second effort, however, he said—'Would it not be more manly if you let me meet my fate, without this.'

'And you are such an admirable judge of what is manly; or even gentlemanlike!' said Longcluse. 'Now, mind, I shall arrest you in five minutes, on your three over-due bills. The men with the writ are in the next room. I sha'n't immediately arrest you for the forgery. That shall hang over you. I mean to make you, for a while, my instrument. Hear, and understand; I mean to marry your sister. She don't like me, but she suits me; I have chosen her, and I'll not be baulked. When that is accomplished, you are safe. No man likes to see his brother a spectacle of British justice, with cropped hair, and a log to his foot.

'I may hate and despise you, as you deserve, but that would not do. Failing that, however, you shall have justice, I promise you. The course I propose taking is this: you shall be arrested here, for *debt*. You will be good enough to allow the people who take you, to select your present place of confinement. It is arranged. I will then, by a note, appoint a place of meeting for this evening, where I shall instruct you as to the particulars of that course of conduct I prescribe for you. If you mean to attempt an escape, you had better try it *now;* I will give you fourteen hours' start, and undertake to catch and bring you back to London as a forger. If you make up your mind to submit to fate, and do precisely as you are ordered, you may emerge. But on the slightest evasion, prevarication, or default, the blow descends. In the meantime we treat each other civilly before these people. Levi is in my hands, and you, I presume, keep your own secret.'

'That is all?' inquired Sir Richard, faintly, after a minute's silence.

'All for the *present,*' was the reply; 'you will see more clearly, by-and-by, that you are my property, and you will act accordingly.'

The two Jewish-looking gentlemen, whom Richard had passed in a conference in their carriage which stood now at the steps of the house, were the sheriff's officers destined to take charge of the fallen gentleman, and convey him, by Levi's direction, to a 'sponging house,' which, I believe, belonged jointly to him and his partner, Mr. Goldshed.

It was on the principle, perhaps, on which hunters tame wild beasts, by a sojourn at the bottom of a pit-fall, that Mr. Longcluse doomed the young baronet to some ten hours' solitary contemplation of his hopeless immeshment in that castle of Giant Despair, before taking him out and setting him again before him, for the purpose of instructing him in the conditions and duties of the direful life on which he was about to enter.

Mr. Longcluse left the baronet suddenly, and returned to Levi's office no more.

Sir Richard's *rôle* was cast. He was to figure, at least first, as a captive in the drama for which fate had selected him. He had no wish to retard the progress of the piece. Nothing more odious than his present situation was likely to come.

'You have something to say to me?' said the baronet, making tender, as it were, of himself. The offer was, obligingly, accepted, and the sheriffs, by his lieutenants, made prisoner of Sir Richard Arden, who strode down the stairs between them, and entered the seedy coach, and sitting as far back as he could, drove rapidly toward the City.

Stunned and confused, there was but one image vividly present to his recollection, and that was the baleful face of Walter Longcluse.

NIGHT

At about eight o'clock that evening, a hurried note reached

Alice Arden, at Mortlake. It was from her brother, and said,—

My darling Alice,

I can't get away from town tonight, I am overwhelmed with business; but tomorrow, before dinner, I hope to see you, and stay at Mortlake till next morning.—

Your affectionate brother,

Dick

The house was quiet earlier than in former times, when Sir Reginald, of rakish memory, was never in his bed till past three o'clock in the morning. Mortlake was an early house now, and all was still by a quarter past eleven. The last candle burning was usually that in Mrs. Tansey's room. She had not yet gone to bed, and was still in 'the housekeeper's room,' when a tapping came at the window. It reminded her of Mr. Longcluse's visit on the night of the funeral.

She was now the only person up in the house, except Alice, who was at the far side of the building, where, in the next room her maid was in bed asleep. Alice, who sat at her dressing-table, reading, with her long rich hair dishevelled over her shoulders, was, of course, quite out of hearing.

Martha went to the window with a little frown of uncertainty Opening a bit of the shutter, she saw Sir Richard's face close to her. Was ever old housekeeper so pestered by nightly tappings at her window-pane?

'La! who'd a thought o' seeing you, Master Richard! why you told Miss Alice you'd not be here till tomorrow!' she says (hectishly). holding the candle high above her head.

He makes a sign of caution to her, and placing his lips near he pane, says,—

'Open the window the least bit in life.'

With a dark stare in his face, she obeys. An odd approach, surely, for a master to make to his own house!

'No one up in the house but you?' he whispers, as soon as the window is open.'

'Not one!'

'Don't say a word, only listen: come, softly, round to the hall-door, and let me in; and light those candles there, and bring them with you to the hall. Don't let a creature know I have been here, and make no noise for your life!'

The old woman nodded with the same little frown; and he, pointing toward the hall door, walks away silently in that direction.

'What makes you look so white and dowley?' mutters the old woman, as she secures the window, and bars the shutters again.

'Good creature!' whispers Sir Richard, as he enters the hall, and places his hand kindly on her shoulder, and with a very dark look; 'you have always been true to me, Martha, and I depend on your good sense; not a word of my having been here to any one—not to Miss Alice! I have to search for papers. I shall be here but an hour or so. Don't lock or bar the door, mind, and get to your bed! Don't come up this way again—goodnight!'

'Won't you have some supper?'

'No, thanks.'

'A glass of sherry and a bit o' something?'

'Nothing.'

And he places his hand on her shoulder gently, and looks toward the corridor that led to her room; then taking up one of the candles she had left alight on the table in the hall, he says,—

'I'll give you a light,' and he repeats, with a wondrous heavy sigh, 'Goodnight, dear old Martha.'

'God bless ye, Master Dick. Ye must chirp up a bit, mind,' she says very kindly, with an earnest look in her face. 'I'm getting to rest—ye needn't fear me walkin' about to trouble ye. But ye must be careful to shut the hall-door close. I agree, as it is a thing to be done; but ye must also knock at my bed-room window when ye've gane out, for I must get up, and lock the door, and make a' safe; and don't ye forget, Master Richard, what I tell ye.'

He held the candle at the end of the corridor, down which the wiry old woman went quickly; and when he returned to the hall, and set the candle down again, he felt faint. In his ears are ever the terrible words: 'Mind, *I* take command of the house, *I* dispose of and appoint the servants; I don't appear, you do all ostensibly—but from garret to cellar, I'm *master.* I'll look it over, and tell you what is to be done.'

Sir Richard roused himself, and having listened at the staircase, he very softly opened the hall-door. The spire of the old church showed hoar in the moonlight. At the left, from under a deep shadow of elms, comes silently a tall figure, and softly ascends the hall-door steps. The door is closed gently.

Alice sitting at her dressing-table, half an hour later, thought she heard steps—lowered her book, and listened. But no sound followed. Again the same light foot-falls disturbed her—and again, she was growing nervous. Once more she heard them, very stealthily, and now on the same floor on which her room was. She stands up breathless. There is no noise now. She was thinking of waking her maid, but she remembered that she and Louisa Diaper had in a like alarm, discovered old Martha, only two or three nights before, poking about the china-closet, dusting and counting, at one o'clock in the morning, and had then exacted a promise that she would visit that repository no more, except at seasonable hours. But old Martha was so pig-headed, and would take it for granted that she was fast asleep, and would rather fidget through the house and poke up everything at that hour than at any other.

Quite persuaded of this, Alice takes her candle, determined to scold that troublesome old thing, against whom she is fired with the irritation that attends on a causeless fright. She walks along the gallery quickly, in slippers, flowing dressing-gown and hair, with her candle in her hand, to the head of the stairs, through the great window of which the moonlight streams brightly. Through the keyhole of the door at the opposite side, a ray of candlelight is visible, and from this room opens the china-closet, which is no doubt the point of attraction for the troublesome visitant. Holding the candle high in her left hand, Alice opens the door.

What she sees is this—a pair of candles burning on a small table, on which, with a pencil, Mr. Longcluse is drawing, it seems, with care, a diagram; at the same moment he raises his eyes, and Richard Arden, who is standing with one hand placed on the table over which he is leaning a little, looks quickly round, and rising walks straight to the door, interposing between her and Longcluse.

'Oh, Alice? You didn't expect me. I'm very busy, looking for—looking over papers. Don't mind.'

He had placed his hands gently on her shoulders, and she receded as he advanced.

'Oh! it don't matter. I thought—I thought—I did not know.'

She was smiling her best. She was horrified. He looked like a ghost. Alice was gazing piteously in his face, and with a little laugh, she began to cry convulsively.

'What is the matter with the little fool! There, there—don't, don't—nonsense!'

With an effort she recovered herself.

'Only a little startled, Dick; I did not think you were there—goodnight.'

And she hastened back to her chamber, and locked the door; and running into her maid's room, sat down on the side of her bed, and wept hysterically. To the imploring inquiries of her maid, she repeated only the words, 'I am frightened,' and left her in a startled perplexity.

She knew that Longcluse had seen her, and he, that she had seen him. Their eyes had met. He saw with a bleak rage the contracting look of horror, so nearly hatred, that she fixed on him for a breathless moment. There was a tremor of fury at his heart, as if it could have sprung at her, from his breast, at her throat, and murdered her; and—she looked so beautiful! He gazed with an idolatrous admiration. Tears were welling to his eyes, and yet he would have laughed to see her weltering on the floor. A madman for some tremendous seconds!

Measures

About twelve o'clock next day Richard Arden showed himself at Mortlake. It was a beautiful autumnal day, and the mellow sun fell upon a foliage that was fading into russet and yellow. Alice was looking out from the open window, on the noble old timber whose wide-spread boughs and thinning leaves caught the sunbeams pleasantly. She had heard her brother and his companion go down the stairs, and saw them, from the window, walk quickly down the avenue, till the trees hid them from view. She thought that some of the servants were up, and that the door was secured on their departure; and the effect of the shock she had received gradually subsiding, she looked to her next interview with her brother for an explanation of the occurrence which had so startled her.

That interview was approaching; the cab drove up to the steps, and her brother got out. Anxiously she looked, but no one followed him, and the driver shut the cab-door. Sir Richard kissed his hand to her, as she stood in the window.

From the hall the house opens to the right and left, in two suites of rooms. The room in which Alice stood was called the sage-room, from its being hung in sage-green leather, stamped in gold. It is a small room to the left, and would answer very prettily for a card party or a *tête-à-tête.*. Alice had her work, her books, and her music there; she liked it because the room was small and cheery.

The door opened, and her brother comes in.

'Good Dick, to come so early! welcome, darling,' she said, putting her arms about his neck, as he stooped and kissed her, smiling.

He looked very ill, and his smile was painful.

'That was an odd little visit I paid last night,' said he, with his dark eyes fixed on her, inquiringly she thought—'very late—quite unexpected. You are quite well today?—you look flourishing.'

'I wish I could say as much for you, Dick; I'm afraid you are tiring yourself to death.'

'I had some one with me last night,' said Sir Richard, with his eye still upon her; 'I—I don't know whether you perceived that.'

Alice looked away, and then said carelessly, but very gravely—

'I did—I saw Mr. Longcluse. I could not believe my eyes, Dick. You must promise me one thing.'

'What is that?'

'That he sha'n't come into this house any more—while I am here, I mean.

'That is easily promised,' said he.

'And what did he come about, Dick?'

'Oh! he came—he came—I thought I told you; he came about papers. I did not tell you; but he has, after all, turned out very friendly. He is going to do me a very important service.'

She looked very much surprised.

The young man glanced through the window, to which he walked; he seemed embarrassed, and then turning to her, he said peevishly—

'You seem to think, Alice, that one can never make a mistake, or change an opinion.'

'But I did not say so; only, Dick, I must tell you that I have such a horror of that man—a *terror* of him—as nothing can ever get over.'

'I'm to blame for that.'

'No, I can't say you are. I don't mind stories so much as——'

'As what?'

'As looks.'

'Looks! Why, you used to think him a gentlemanly-looking fellow, and so he is.'

'Looks *and language*' said Alice.

'I thought he was a very civil fellow.'

'I sha'n't dispute anything. I suppose you have found him a good friend after all, as you say.'

'As good a friend as most men,' said Sir Richard, growing pale; 'they all act from interest: where interests are the same, men are friends. But he has saved me from a great deal, and he may do more; and I believe I was too hasty about those stories, and I think you were right when you refused to believe them without proof.'

'I daresay—I don't know—I believe my senses—and all I say is this, if Mr. Longcluse is to come here any more, I must go. He is no gentleman, I think—that is, I can't describe how I dislike him—how I hate him! I'm afraid of him! Dick, you look ill and unhappy: what's the matter!'

'I'm well enough—I'm better; we shall be better—all better by-and-by. I wish the next five weeks were over! We must leave this, we must go to Arden Court; I will send some of the servants there first. I am going to tell them now, they must get the house ready. You shall keep your maid here with you; and when all is ready in Yorkshire, we shall be off—Alice, Alice, don't mind me—I'm miserable—mad!' he says suddenly, and covers his face with his hands, and for the first time for years, he is crying bitter tears.

Alice was by his side, alarmed, curious, grieved; and with all these emotions mingling in her dark eyes and beautiful features, as she drew his hand gently away, with a rush of affectionate entreaties and inquiries.

'It is all very fine, Alice,' he exclaims, with a sudden bitterness; 'but I don't believe, to save me from destruction, you would sacrifice one of your least caprices, or reconcile one of your narrowest prejudices.'

'What can you mean, dear Richard? only tell me how I can be of any use. You can't mean, of course——'

She stops with a startled look at him. 'You know, dear Dick, that was always out of the question: and surely you have heard that Lord Wynderbroke is to be married to Grace Maubray? It is all settled.'

Quite another thought had been in Richard's mind, but he was glad to accept Alice's conjecture.

'Yes, so it is—so, at least, it is said to be—but I am so worried and distracted, I half forget things. Girls are such jolly fools; they throw good men away, and lose themselves. What is to become of you, Alice, if things go wrong with me! I think the old times were best, when the old people settled who was to marry whom, and there was no disputing their decision, and marriages were just as happy, and courtships a great deal simpler; and I am very sure there were fewer secret repinings, and broken hearts, and—threadbare old maids. Don't *you* be a fool, Alice; mind what I say.'

He is leaving the room, but pauses at the door, and returns, and places his hand on her arm, looking in her face, and says—

'Yes, mind what I say, for God's sake, and we may all be a great deal happier.'

He kisses her, and is gone. Her eyes follow him, as she thinks with a sigh—

'How strange Dick is growing! I'm afraid he has been playing again, and losing. It must have been something very urgent that induced him to make it up again with that low malignant man; and this break-up, and journey to Arden Court! I think I should prefer being there. There is something ominous about this place, picturesque as it is, and much as I like it. But the journey to Yorkshire is only another of the imaginary excursions Dick has been proposing every fortnight; and next year, and the year after, will find us, I suppose, just where we are.'

But this conjecture, for once, was mistaken. It was, this time, a veritable break-up and migration; for Martha Tansey came in, with the importance of a person who has a matter of moment to talk over.

'Here's something sudden, Miss Alice; I suppose you've heard. Off to Arden Court in the mornin'. Crozier and me: the footman discharged, and you to follow with Master Richard in a week.'

'Oh, then, it *is* settled. Well, Martha, I am not sorry, and I daresay you and Crozier won't be sorry to see old Yorkshire faces again, and the Court, and the rookery, and the orchard.'

'I don't mind; glad enough to see a'ad faces, but I'm a bit o'er a'ad myself for such sudden flittins, and Manx and Darwent, and the rest, is to go by night train tomorrow, and not a housemaid left in Mortlake. But Master Richard says a's provided, and 'twill be but a few days after a's done; and ye'll be down, then, at Arden by the middle o' next week, and I'm no sa sure the change mayn't serve ye; and as your uncle, Master David, and Lady May Penrose, and Miss Maubray—a strackle-brained lass she is, I doubt—and to think o' that a'ad fule, Lord Wynderbroke, takin' sich a young, bonny hizzy to wife! La bless ye, she'll play the hangment wi' that a'ad gowk of a lord, and all his goold guineas won't do.

'His kist o' money won't hod na time, I warrant ye, when once that lassie gets her pretty fingers under the lid. There'll be gaains on in that house, I warrant, not but he's a gude man, and a fine gentleman as need be,' she added, remembering her own strenuous counsel in his favour, when he was supposed to be paying his court to Alice; 'and if he was mated wi' a gude lassie, wi' gude blude in her veins, would doubtless keep as honourable a house, and hod his head as high as any lord o' them a'. But as I was saying, Miss Alice, now that Master David, and Lady May, and Miss Maubray, has left Lunnon, there's no one here to pay ye a visit, and ye'd be fairly buried alive here in Mortlake, and ye'll be better, and sa will we a', down at Arden, for a bit; and there's gentle folk down there as gude as ever rode in Lunnon streets, mayhap, and better; and mony a squire, that ony leddy in the land might be proud to marry, and not one but would be glad to match wi' an Arden.'

'That is a happy thought,' said Alice, laughing.

'And so it is, and no laughing matter,' said Martha, a little offended, as she stalked out of the room, and closed the door, grandly, after her.

'And God bless you, dear old Martha,' said the young lady, looking towards the door through which she had just passed; 'the truest and kindest soul on earth.'

Sir Richard did not come back. She saw him no more that evening.

Next Evening there came, not Richard, but a note saying that he would see Alice the moment he could get away from town. As the old servant departed northward, her solitude for the first time began to grow irksome, and as the night approached, worse even than gloomy.

Her extemporised household made her laugh. It was not even a skeleton establishment. The kitchen department had dwindled to a single person, who ordered her luncheon and dinner, only two or three *plats,* daily, from the 'Guy of Warwick'. The housemaid's department was undertaken by a single servant, a short, strong woman of some sixty years of age.

This person puzzled Alice a good deal. She came to her, like the others, with a note from her brother, stating her name, and that he had engaged her for the few days they meant to remain roughing it at Mortlake, and that he had received a very good account of her.

This woman has not a bad countenance. There is, indeed, no tenderness in it; but there is a sort of hard good-humour. There are quickness and resolution. She talks fluently of herself and her qualifications, and now and then makes a short curtsey. But she takes no notice of any one of Alice's questions.

A silence sometimes follows, during which Alice repeats her interrogatory perhaps twice, with growing indignation, and then the new comer breaks into a totally independent talk, and leaves the young lady wondering at her disciplined impertinence. It was not till her second visit that she enlightened her. 'I did not send for you. You can go!' said Alice.

'I don't like a house that has children in it, they gives a deal o' trouble,' said the woman.

'But I say you may go; you must go, please.'

The woman looked round the room.

'When I was with Mrs. Montgomery, she had five, three girls and two boys; *la*! there never was five such——'

'Go, this moment, please, I insist on your going; do you hear me, pray?'

But so far from answering, or obeying, this cool intruder continues her harangue before Miss Arden gets half way to the end of her little speech.

'That woman was the greatest fool alive—nothing but spoiling and petting—I could not stand it no longer, so I took Master Tommy by the lug, and pulled him out of the kitchen, the limb, along the passage to the stairs, every inch, and I gave him a slap in the face, the fat young rascal; you could hear all over the house! and didn't he rise the roof! So missus and me, we quarrelled upon it.'

'If you don't leave the room, *I* must; and I shall tell my brother, Sir Richard, how you have behaved yourself; and you may rely upon it——'

But here again she is overpowered by the strong voice of her visitor.

'It was in my next place, at Mr. Crump's, I took cold in my head, very bad, Miss, indeed, looking out of window to see two fellows fighting, in the lane—in both ears—and so I lost my hearing, and I've been deaf as a post ever since!'

Alice could not resist a laugh at her own indignant eloquence quite thrown away; and she hastily wrote with a pencil on a slip of paper:—

'Please don't come to me except when I send for you.'

'*La*! Ma'am, I forgot!' exclaims the woman, when she had examined it; 'my orders was not to read any of *your* writing.'

'Not to read any of my writing!' said Alice, amazed; 'then, how am I to tell you what I wish about anything?' she inquires, for the moment forgetting that not one word of her question was heard. The woman makes a curtsey and retires. 'What can Richard have meant by giving her such a direction? I'll ask him when he comes.'

It was likely enough that the woman had misunderstood him, still she began to wish the little interval destined to be passed at Mortlake before her journey to Yorkshire, ended.

She told her maid, Louisa Diaper, to go down to the kitchen and find out all she could as to what people were in the house, and what duties they had undertaken, and when her brother was likely to arrive.

Louisa Diaper, slim, elegant, and demure, descended among these barbarous animals. She found in the kitchen, unexpectedly, a male stranger, a small, slight man, with great black eyes, a big sullen mouth, a sallow complexion, and a profusion of black ringlets. The deaf woman was conning over some writing of his on a torn-off blank leaf of a letter, and he was twiddling about the pencil, with which he had just traced it, in his fingers, and, in a singing drawl, holding forth to the other woman, who, with a long and high canvas apron on, and the handle of an empty saucepan in her right hand, stood gaping at him, with her arms hanging by her sides.

On the appearance of Miss Diaper, Mr. Levi, for he it was, directs his solemn conversation to that young lady.

'I was just telling them about the robberies in the City and Wesht Hend. La! there'sh bin nothin' like it for twenty year. They don't tell them in the papersh, blesh ye! The 'ome Shecretary takesh precious good care o' that; they don't want to frighten every livin' shoul out of London. But there'll be talk of it in Parliament, I promish you. I know three opposition membersh myshelf that will move the 'oushe upon it next session.'

Mr. Levi wagged his head darkly as he made this political revelation.

'Thish day twel'month the number o' burglariesh in London and the West Hend, including Hizzlington, was no more than fifteen and a half a night; and two robberiesh attended with wiolensh. What wazh it lasht night? I have it in confidensh, from the polishe offish thish morning.'

He pulled a pocket-book, rather greasy, from his breast, and from this depositary, it is to be presumed, of statistical secrets, he read the following official memorandum:—

'Number of 'oushes burglarioushly hentered lasht night, including private banksh, charitable hinshtitutions, shops, lodging-'oushes, female hacadamies, and private dwellings, and robbed with more or less wiolench, one thoushand sheven hundred and shixty-sheven. We regret to hadd,' he continued, the official return stealing, as it proceeded, gradually into the style of *The Pictorial Calendar of British Crime*, a half-penny paper which he took in—'this hinundation of crime seems flowing, or rayther rushing northward, and hazh already enweloped Hizhlington, where a bald-headed clock and watch maker, named Halexander Goggles, wazh murdered with his sheven shmall children, with unigshampled ba-arba-arity.'

Mr. Levi eyed the women horribly all round as he ended the sentence, and he added,—

'Hizhlington'sh only down there. It ain't five minutesh walk; only a pleasant shtep; just enough to give a fellow azh has polished off a family there a happetite for another up here. Azh I 'ope to be shaved, I shleep every night with a pair of horshe pishtols, a blunderbush, and a shabre by my bed; and Shir Richard wantsh every door in the 'oushe fasht locked, and the keysh with him, before dark, thish evening, except only such doors as you want open; and he gave me a note to Miss Harden.' And he placed the note in Miss Diaper's hand. 'He wantsh the 'oushe a bit more schecure,' he added, following her towards the hall. 'He wishes to make you and she quite shafe, and out of harm's way, if anything should occur. It will be only a few days, you know, till you're both away.'

The effect of this little alarm, accompanied by Sir Richard's note, was that Mr. Levi carried out a temporary arrangement, which assigned the suite of apartments in which Alice's room was as those to which she would restrict herself during the few days she was to remain there, the rest of the house, except the kitchen and a servant's room or two down-stairs, being locked up.

By the time Mr. Levi had got the keys together, and all safe in Mortlake, the sun had set, and in the red twilight that followed he set off in his cab towards town. At the 'Guy of Warwick'—from the bar of which already was flaring a good broad gaslight—he stopped and got out. There was a full view of the bar from where he stood; and, pretending to rummage his pockets for something, he was looking in to see whether 'the coast was clear.'

'She's just your sort—not too bad and not too good—not too nashty, and not too nishe; a good-humoured lash, rough and ready, and knowsh a thing or two.'

'Ye're there, are ye?' inquired Mr. Levi, playfully, as he crossed the door-stone, and placed his fists on the bar grinning.

'What will you take, Sir, please?' inquired the young woman, at one side of whom was the usual row of taps and pump-handles. 'Now, Miss Phoebe, give me a brandy and shoda, pleashe. When I talked to you in thish 'ere place 'tother night, you wished to engage for a lady's maid. What would you shay to me, if I was to get you a firsht-chop tip-top pla-ashe of the kind? Well, don't you shay a word—that brandy ain't fair measure—and I'll tell you. It'sh a la-ady of ra-ank! where wagesh ish no-o object; and two years' savings, and a good match with a well-to-do 'and-some young fellow, will set you hup in a better place than this 'ere.'

'It comes very timely, Sir, for I'm to leave tomorrow, and I was thinking of going home to my uncle in a day or two, in Chester.'

'Well it's all settled. Come you down to my offishe, you know where it is, tomorrow, at three, and I'll 'av all partickulars for you, and a note to the lady from her brother, the baronet; and if you be a good girl, and do as you're bid, you'll make a little fortune of it.'

She curtsied, with her eyes very round, as he, with a wag of his head drank down what remained of his brandy and soda, and wiping his mouth with his glove, he said, 'Three o'clock sha-arp, mind; goodbye, Phoebe, lass, and don't you forget all I said.'

He stood ungallantly with his back towards her on the threshold lighting a cigar, and so soon as he had it in his own phrase, 'working at high blast,' he got into his cab, and jingled towards his office, with all his keys about him.

While Miss Arden remained all unconscious, and even a little amused at the strange shifts to which her brief stay and extemporised household at Mortlake exposed her, a wily and determined strategist was drawing his toils around her.

The process of isolation was nearly completed, without having once excited her suspicions; and, with the same perfidious skill, the house itself was virtually undergoing those modifications which best suited his designs.

Sir Richard appeared at his club as usual. He was compelled to do so. The all-seeing eye of his pale tyrant pursued him everywhere; he lived under terror. A dreadful agony all this time convulsed the man, within whose heart Longcluse suspected nothing but the serenity of death.

What easier than to tell the story to the police. Meditated duresse. Compulsion. Infernal villain! And then: what then? A pistol to his head, a flash, and—darkness!

A Letter

Mr. Longcluse knocked at Sir Richard's house in May Fair, and sent upstairs for the baronet. It was about the same hour at which Mr. Levi was drinking his thirsty potation of brandy and soda at the 'Guy of Warwick'. The streets were darker than that comparatively open place, and the gas lamp threw its red outline of the sashes upon the dark ceiling, as Mr. Longcluse stood in the drawing-room between the windows, in his great-coat, with his hat on, looking in the dark like an image made of fog.

Sir Richard Arden entered the room.

'You were not at Mortlake today,' said he.

'No.'

'There's a cab at the door that will take you there; your absence for a whole day would excite surmise. Don't stay more than five minutes, and don't mention Louisa Diaper's name, and account for the locking up of all the house, but one suite of rooms, I directed, and come to my house in Bolton Street, direct from Mortlake. That's all.'

Without another word, Mr. Longcluse took his departure.

In this cavalier way, and in a cold tone that conveyed all the menace and insult involved in his ruined position, had this conceited young man been ordered about by his betrayer, on his cruel behests, ever since he had come under his dreadful rod. The iron trap that held him fast, locked him in a prison from which, except through the door of death, there seemed no escape.

Outraged pride, the terrors of suspense, the shame and remorse of his own enormous perfidy against his only sister, peopled it with spectres.

As he drove out to Mortlake, pale, frowning, with folded arms, his handsome face thinned and drawn by the cords of pain, he made up his mind. He knocked furiously at Mortlake Hall door. The woman in the canvas apron let him in. The strange face startled him; he had been thinking so intently of one thing. Going up, through the darkened house, with but one candle, and tapping at the door, on the floor above the drawing-room, within which Alice was sitting, with Louisa Diaper for company, and looking at her unsuspicious smile, he felt what a heinous conspirator he was.

He made an excuse for sending the maid to the next room after they had spoken a few words, and then he said,—

'Suppose, Alice, we were to change our plan, would you like to come abroad? Out of this you must come immediately.' He was speaking low. 'I am in great danger; I must go abroad. For your life, don't seem to suspect anything. Do exactly as I tell you, or else I am utterly ruined, and you, Alice, on your account, very miserable. Don't ask a question, or look a look, that may make Louisa Diaper suspect that you have any doubt as to your going to Arden, or any suspicion of any danger. She is quite true, but not wise, and your left hand must not know what your right hand is doing. Don't be frightened, only be steady and calm. Get together any jewels and money you have, and as little else as you can possibly manage with. Do this yourself; Louisa Diaper must know nothing of it. I will mature our plans, and tomorrow or next day I shall see you again; I can stay but a moment now, and have but time to bid you goodnight.'

Then he kissed her. How horribly agitated he looked! How

cold was the pressure of his hand!

'Hush!' he whispered, and his dark eyes were fixed on the door through which he expected the return of the maid. And as he heard her step, 'Not a word, remember!' he said; then bidding her goodnight aloud, he quitted the room almost as suddenly as he had appeared, leaving her, for the first time, in the horrors of a growing panic.

Sir Richard leaned back in the cab as he drove into town, He had as yet no plan formed. It was a more complicated exploit that he was at the moment equal to. In Mortlake were two fellows, by way of protectors, placed there for security of the house and people.

These men held possession of the keys of the house, and sat and regaled themselves with their hot punch, or cold brandy and water, and pipes; always one awake, and with ears erect, they kept watch and ward in the room to the right of the hall-door, in which Sir Richard and Uncle David had conversed with the sad Mr. Plumes, on the evening after the old baronet's death. To effect Alice's escape, and reserve for himself a chance of accomplishing his own, was a problem demanding skill, cunning and audacity.

While he revolved these things an alarm had been sounded in another quarter, which unexpectedly opened a chance of extrication, sudden and startling.

Mr. Longcluse was destined to a surprise tonight. Mr. Longcluse, at his own house, was awaiting the return of Sir Richard. Overlooked in his usually accurate though rapid selection, a particularly shabby and vulgar-looking letter had been thrown aside among circulars, pamphlets, and begging letters, to await his leisure. It was a letter from Paris, and vulgar and unbusiness-like as it looked, there was yet, in its peculiar scrivenery that which, a little more attentively scanned, thrilled him with a terrible misgiving. The post-mark showed it had been delivered four days before. When he saw from whom it came, and had gathered something of its meaning from a few phrases, his dark eyes gleamed and his face grew stern. Was this wretch's hoof to strike to pieces the plans he had so nearly matured? The letter was as follows:—

Sir,

Mr Longcluse, I have been unfortunate With your money which you have Gave me to remove from England, and Keep me in New York. My boxes, and other things, and Ballens of the money in Gold, except about a Hundred pounds, which has kep me from want ever sense, went Down in the Mary Jane, of London, and my cousin went down in her also, which I might as well av Went down myself in her, only for me Stopping in Paris, where I made a trifle of Money, intending to go Out in August. Now, Sir, don't you Seppose I am not in as good Possition as I was when I Harranged with sum difculty With you.

The boot with The blood Mark on the Soul is not Lost nor Distroyed, but it is Safe in my Custody; so as Likewise in safe Keeping is The traising, in paper, of the foot Mark in blood on the Floar of the Smoaking Room in question, with the signatures of the witnesses attached; and, Moreover, my Staitment made in the Form of a Information, at the Time, and signed In witness of My signature by two Unekseptinible witnesses.

And all Is ready to Produise whenever his worshop shall Apoynt. i have wrote To mister david Arden on this Supget. i wrote to him just a week ago, he seaming To take a Intrast in this Heer case; and, moreover, the two ieyes that sawd a certain Person about the said smoaking Room, and in the saime, is Boath wide open at This presen Time. mister Longcluse i do not Want to have your Life, but gustice must Taike its coarse unless it is settled of hand Slik. i will harrange the Same as last time, And i must have two hundred And fifty pounds More on this Settlement than i Had last time, for Dellay and loss of Time in this town. I will sign any law paper ir. reason you may ask of me. My hadress is under cover to Monseer Letexier, air-dresser, and incloses his card, which you Will please send an Anser by return Of post, or else i Must sepose you chose. The afare shall take Its coarse; and I am as ever,

Your obeediant servant to command,

Paul Davies.

Never did paper look so dazzlingly white, or letters so intensely black, before Mr. Longcluse's eyes, as those of this ominous letter. He crumpled it up, and thrust it in his trousers pocket, and gave to the position a few seconds of intense thought.

His first thought was, what a fool he was for not having driven Davies to the wall, and settled the matter with the high hand of the law at once. His next, what could bring him to Paris? He was there for something. To see possibly the family of Lebas, and collect and dovetail pieces of evidence, after his detective practice, a process which would be sure to conduct him to the Baron Vanboeren! Was this story of the boot and the tracing of the bloodstained footprint true? Had this scoundrel reserved the strongest part of his case for this new extortion? Was his trouble to be never ending? If this accursed ferret were once to get into his warren, what power could unearth him, till the mischief was done?

His eye caught again the words, on which, in the expressive phrase which Mr. Davies would have used, his 'sight spred' as he held the letter before his eyes—'Mister Loncluse, i do not want to have your life.' He ground his teeth, shook his fist in the air, and stamped on the floor with fury, at the thought that a brutal detective, not able to spell two words, and trained for such game as London thieves and burglars, should dare to hold such language to a man of thought and skill, altogether so masterly as he! That he should be outwitted by that clumsy scoundrel!

Well, it was now to begin all over again. It should all go right this time. He thought again for a moment, and then sat down and wrote, commencing with the date and address—

Paul Davies,

I have just received your note, which states that you have succeeded in obtaining some additional information, which you think may lead to the conviction of the murderer of M. Lebas, in the Saloon Tavern. I shall be most happy to pay handsomely any expense of any kind you may be put to in that matter. It is, indeed, no more than I had already undertaken. I am glad to learn that you have also written on the subject to Mr. David Arden, who feels entirely with me. I shall take an early opportunity of seeing him. Persist in your laudable exertions, and I shall not shrink from rewarding you handsomely.

Yours,

Walter Longcluse.

He addressed the letter carefully, and went himself and put it in the post-office.

By this time Sir Richard Arden was awaiting him at home in his drawing-room, and as he walked homeward, under the lamps, in inward pain, one might have moralised with Peter Pindar—

These fleas have other fleas to bite 'em
And so on ad infinitum.

The secret tyrant had in his turn found a secret tyrant, not less cruel perhaps, but more ignoble.

'You made your visit?' asked Mr. Longcluse.

'Yes.'

'Anything to report?'

'Absolutely nothing.'

A silence followed.

'Where is Mr. Arden, your uncle?'

'In Scotland.'

'How soon does he return?

'He will not be in town till spring, I believe; he is going abroad, but he passes through Southampton on his way to the Continent, on Friday next.'

'And makes some little stay there?'

'I think he stays one night'

'Then I'll go down and see him, and you shall come with me.'

Sir Richard stared.

'Yes, and you had better not put your foot in it; and clear your head of all notion of running away,' he said, fixing his fiery eyes on Sir Richard, with a sudden ferocity that made him fancy that his secret thoughts had revealed themselves under that piercing gaze. 'It is not easy to levant now-a-days, unless one has swifter wings than the wires can carry news with; and if you are false, what more do I need than to blast you? and with your name in the *Hue-and-Cry*, and a thousand pounds reward for the apprehension of Sir Richard Arden, Baronet, for forgery, I don't see much more that infamy can do for you.'

A dark flush crossed Arden's face as he rose.

'Not a word now,' cried Longcluse harshly, extending hand quickly towards him; 'I may do that which can't be undone.'

Blight and Change

Danger to herself, Alice suspected none. But she was full of dreadful conjectures about her brother. There was, she was persuaded, no good any longer in remonstrance or entreaty. She could not upbraid him; but she was sure that the terrible fascination of the gaming-table had caused the sudden ruin he vaguely confessed.

'Oh,' she often repeated, 'that Uncle David were in town, or that I knew where to find him!'

'But no doubt,' she thought, 'Richard will hide nothing from him, and perhaps my hinting his disclosures, even to him, would aggravate poor Richard's difficulties and misery.'

It was not until the next evening that, about the same hour, she again saw her brother. His good resolutions in the interval had waxed faint. They were not reversed, but only in the spirit of indecision, and something of the apathy of despair, postponed to a more convenient season.

To her he seemed more tranquil. He said vaguely that the reasons for flight were less urgent and that she had better continue her preparations, as before, for her journey to Yorkshire.

Even under these circumstances the journey to Yorkshire was

pleasant. There was comfort in the certainty that he would there be beyond the reach of that fatal temptation which had too plainly all but ruined him. From the harrassing distractions, also, which in London had of late beset him, almost without intermission, he might find in the seclusion of Arden a temporary calm. There, with Uncle David's help, there would be time, at least, to ascertain the extent of his losses, and what the old family of Arden might still count upon as their own, and a plan of life might be arranged for the future.

Full of these more cheery thoughts, Alice took leave of her brother.

'I am going,' he said, looking at his watch, 'direct to Brighton; I have just time to get to the station nicely; business, of course—a meeting tonight with Bexley, who is staying there, and in the morning a long and, I fear, angry discussion with Charrington, who is also at Brighton.'

He kissed his sister, sighed deeply, and looking in her eyes for a little, fixedly, he said—

'Alice, darling, you must try to think what sacrifice you can make to save your wretched brother.'

Their eyes met as she looked up, her hands about his neck, his on her shoulders; he drew his sister to him quickly, and with another kiss, turned, ran down stairs, got into his cab, and drove down the avenue. She stood looking after him with a heavy heart. How happy they two might have been, if it had not been for the one incorrigible insanity!

About an hour later, as the sun was near its setting, she put on her hat and short grey cloak, and stepped out into its level beams, and looked round smiling. The golden glow and transparent shadows made that beautiful face look more than ever lovely. All around the air was ringing with the farewell songs of the small birds, and, with a heart almost rejoicing in sympathy with that beautiful hour, she walked lightly to the old garden, which in that luminous air, looked, she thought, so sad and pretty.

The well-worn aphorism of the Frenchman, 'History repeats itself,' was about to assert itself. Sometimes it comes in literal sobriety, sometimes in derisive travesti, sometimes in tragic aggravation.

She is in the garden now. The associations of place recall her strange interview with Mr. Longcluse but a few months before. Since then a blight has fallen on the scenery, and what a change upon the persons! The fruit-leaves are yellow now, and drifts of them lie upon the walks. Mantling ivy, as before, canopies the door, interlaced with climbing roses; but they have long shed their honours. This thick mass of dark green foliage and thorny tendrils forms a deep arched porch, in the shadow of which, suddenly, as on her return she reached it, she sees Mr. Longcluse standing within a step or two of her.

He raises his hand, it might be in entreaty, it might be in menace; she could not, in the few alarmed moments in which she gazed at his dark eyes and pale equivocal face, determine anything.

'Miss Arden, you may hate me; you can't despise me. You *must* hear me, because you are in my power. I relent, mind you, thus far, that I give you one chance more of reconciliation; don't, for God's sake, throw it from you!' (he was extending his open hand to receive hers). 'Why should you prefer an unequal war with me? I tell you frankly you are in my power—don't misunderstand me—in *my power* to this degree, that you shall *voluntarily*, as the more tolerable of two alternatives, submit with abject acquiescence to every one of my conditions. Here is my hand; think of the degradation I submit to in asking you to take it. You gave me no chance when I asked forgiveness. I tender you a full forgiveness; here is my hand, beware how you despise it.'

Fearful as he appeared in her sight, her fear gave way before her kindling spirit. She had stood before him pale as death—anger now fired her eye and cheek.

'How dare you, Sir, hold such language to me! Do you suppose, if I had told my brother of your cowardice and insolence as I left the abbey the other day, you would have dared to speak to him, much less to me? Let me pass, and never while you live presume to address me more.'

Mr. Longcluse, with a slow recoil, smiling fixedly, and bowing, drew back and opened the door for her to pass. He did not any longer look like a villain whose heart had failed him.

Her heart fluttered violently with fear as she saw that he stepped out after her, and walked by her side toward the house. She quickened her pace in great alarm.

'If you had liked me ever so little,' said he in that faint and horrible tone she remembered— 'one, the smallest particle, of disinterested liking—the grain of mustard-seed—I would have had you fast, and made you happy, made you *adore* me; *such* adoration that you could have heard from my own lips the confession of my crimes, and loved me still—loved me more desperately. Now that you hate me, and I hate *you,* and have you in my power, and while I hate still admire you—still choose you for my wife—you shall hear the same story, and think me all the more dreadful. You sought to degrade me, and I'll humble you in the dust.

'Suppose I tell you I'm a criminal—the kind of man you have read of in trials, and can't understand, and can scarcely even believe in—the kind of man that seems to you as unaccountable and monstrous as a ghost—your terrors and horror will make my triumph exquisite with an immense delight. I don't want to smooth the way for you; you do nothing for me. I disdain hypocrisy. Terror drives you on; fate coerces you; you can't help yourself, and my delight is to make the plunge terrible. I reveal myself that you may know the sort of person you are yoked to. Your sacrifice shall be the agony of agonies, the death of deaths, and yet you'll find yourself unable to resist.

'I'll make you submissive as ever patient was to a mad doctor. If it took years to do it, you shall never stir out of this house till it is done. Every spark of insolence in your nature shall be trampled out; I'll break you thoroughly. The sound of my step shall make your heart jump; a look from me shall make you dumb for an hour. You shall not be able to take your eyes off me while I'm in sight, or to forget me for a moment when I am gone. The smallest thing you do, the least word you speak, the very thoughts of your heart, shall all be shaped under one necessity and one fear.' (She had reached the hall door). 'Up the steps! Yes; you wish to enter? Certainly.'

With flashing eyes and head erect, the beautiful girl stepped into the hall, without looking to the right or to the left, or uttering one word, and walked quickly to the foot of the great stair.

If she thought that Mr. Longcluse would respect the barrier of the threshold, she was mistaken. He entered but one step behind her, shut the heavy hall door with a crash, dropped the key into his coat pocket, and signing with his finger to the man in the room to the right, that person stood up briskly, and prepared for action. He closed the door again, saying simply, 'I'll call.'

The young lady, hearing his step, turned round and stood on the stair, confronting him fiercely.

'You must leave this house this moment,' she cried, with a stamp, with gleaming eyes and very pale.

'By-and-by,' he replied, standing before her.

Could this be the safe old house in which childish days had passed, in which all around were always friendly and familiar faces? The window stood reflected upon the wall beside her in dim sunset light, and the shadows of the flowers sharp and still that stood there.

'I have friends here who will turn you out, Sir!'

'You have *no* friends here,' he replied, with the same fixed smile.

She hesitated; she stepped down, but stopped in the hall. She remembered instantly that, as she turned, she had seen him take the key from the hall door.

'My brother will protect me.'

'Is he here?'

'He'll call you to account tomorrow, when he comes.'

'Will he say so?'

'Always—brave, true Richard!' she sobbed, with a strange cry in her words.

'He'll do as I bid him: he's a forger, in my power.'

To her wild stare he replied with a low, faint laugh. She

clasped her fingers over her temples.

'Oh! no, no, no, no, no, no!' she screamed, and suddenly she rushed into the great room at her right. Her brother—was it a phantom?—stood before her. With one long, shrill scream, she threw herself into his arms, and cried, 'It's a lie, darling, it's a lie!' and she had fainted.

He laid her in the great chair by the fireplace. With white lips, and with one fist shaking wildly in the air, he said, with a dreadful shiver in his voice,—

'You villain! you villain! you villain!'

'Don't you be a fool,' said Longcluse. 'Ring for the maid. There must have been a crisis some time. I'm giving you a fair chance—trying to save you; they all faint—it's a trick with women.'

Longcluse looked into her lifeless face, with something of pity and horror mingling in the villany of his countenance.

Phoebe Chiffinch

Mr. Longcluse passed into the inner room, as he heard a step approaching from the hall. It was Louisa Diaper, in whose care, with the simple remedy of cold water, the young lady recovered. She was conveyed to her room, and Richard Arden followed, at Longcluse's command, to 'keep things quiet.'

In an agony of remorse, he remained with his sister's hand in his, sitting by the bed on which she lay. Longcluse had spoken with the resolution that a few sharp and short words should accomplish the crisis, and show her plainly that her brother was, in the most literal and terrible sense, in his power, and thus, indirectly, she also. Perhaps, if she must know the fact, it was as well she should know it now.

Longcluse, I suppose, had reckoned upon Richard's throwing himself upon his sister's mercy. He thought he had done so before, and moved her as he would have wished. Longcluse, no doubt, had spoken to her, expecting to find her in a different mood. Had she yielded, what sort of husband would he have made her? Not cruel, I daresay. Proud of her, he would have been. She should have had the best diamonds in England. Jealous, violent when crossed, but with all his malice and severity, easily by Alice to have been won, had she cared to win him, to tenderness.

Was Sir Richard now seconding his scheme?

Sir Richard had no plan—none for escape, none for a catastrophe, none for acting upon Alice's feelings.

'I am so agitated—in such despair, so stunned! If I had but one clear hour! Oh, God! if I had but one clear hour to think in!'

He was now trying to persuade Alice that Longcluse had, in his rage, used exaggerated language—that it was true he was in his power, but it was for a large sum of money, for which he was his debtor.

'Yes, darling,' he whispered, 'only be firm. I shall get away, and take you with me—only be secret, and don't mind one word he says when he is angry—he is literally a madman; there is no limit to the violence and absurdity of what he says.'

'Is he still in the house?' she whispered.

'Not he.'

'Are you certain?'

'Perfectly; with all his rant, he dares not stay: it would be a police-office affair. He's gone long ago.'

'Thank God!' she said, with a shudder.

Their agitated talk continued for some time longer. At last, darkly and suddenly, as usual, he took his leave.

When her brother had gone, she touched the bell for Louisa Diaper. A stranger appeared.

The stranger had a great deal of pink ribbon in her cap, she looked shrewd enough, and with a pair of rather good eyes; she looked curiously and steadily on the young lady.

'Who are you?' said Alice, sitting up. 'I rang for my maid, Louisa Diaper.'

'Please, my lady,' she answers, with a short curtsey, 'she went into town to fetch some things here from Sir Richard's house.'

'How long ago?'

'Just when you was getting better, please, my lady.'

'When she returns send her to me. What is your name?'

'Phoebe Chiffinch, please 'm.'

'And you are here ——'

'In her place, please my lady.'

'Well, when she comes back you can assist. We shall have a great deal to do, and I like your face, Phoebe, and I'm so lonely, I think I'll get you to sit here in the window near me.'

And on a sudden the young lady burst into tears, and sobbed and wept bitterly.

The new maid was at her side, pouring all sorts of consolation into her ear, with odd phrases—quite intelligible, I daresay, over the bar of the 'Guy of Warwick'—dropping h's in all directions, and bowling down grammatic rules like nine-pins.

She was wonderfully taken by the kind looks and tones of the pretty lady whom she saw in this distress, and with the silk curtains drawn back in the fading flush of evening.

Hard work, hard fare, and harder words had been her portion from her orphaned childhood upward, at the old 'Guy of Warwick', with its dubious customers, failing business, and bitter and grumbling old hostess. Shrewd, hard, and not overnice had Miss Phoebe grown up in that godless school.

But she had taken a fancy, as the phrase is, to the looks of the young lady, and still more to her voice and words, that in her ears sounded so new and strange. There was not an unpleasant sense, too, of the superiority of rank and refinement which inspires an admiring awe in her kind; and so, in a voice that was rather sweet and very cheery, she offered, when the young lady was better, to sit by the bed and tell her a story, or sing her a song.

Everyone knows how his view of his own case may vary within an hour. Alice was now of opinion that there was no reason to reject her brother's version of the terrifying situation. A man who could act like Mr. Longcluse, could, of course, say anything. She had begun to grow more cheerful, and in a little while she accepted the offer of her companion, and heard, first a story, and then a song; and, after all, she talked with her for some time.

'Tell me, now, what servants there are in the house,' asked Alice.

'Only two women and myself, please, Miss.'

'Is there anyone else in the house, besides ourselves?'

The girl looked down, and up again, in Alice's eyes, and then away to the floor at the other end of the room.

'I was told, Ma'am, not to talk of nothing here, Miss, except my own business, please, my lady.'

'My God! This girl mayn't speak truth to me,' exclaimed Alice, clasping her hands aghast.

The girl looked up uneasily.

'I should be sent away, Ma'am, if I do.'

'Look—listen: in this strait you must be for or against me; you can't be divided. For God's sake be a friend to me now. I may yet be the best friend you ever had. Come, Phoebe, trust me, and I'll never betray you.'

She took the girl's hand. Phoebe did not speak. She looked in her face earnestly for some moments, and then down, and up again.

'I don't mind. I'll do what I can for you, Ma'am; I'll tell you what I know. But if you tell them, Ma'am, it will be awful bad for me, my lady.'

She looked again, very much frightened, in her face, and was silent.

'No one shall ever know but I. Trust me entirely, and I'll never forget it to you.'

'Well, Ma'am, there is two men.'

'Who are they?'

'Two men, please 'm, I knows one on 'em—he was keeper on the 'Guy o'Warwick', please, my lady, when there was a hexecution in the 'ouse. They're both sheriffs men.'

'And what are they doing here?'

'A hexecution, my lady.'

'That is, to sell the furniture and everything for a debt, isn't that it?' inquired the lady, bewildered.

'Well, that was it below at the 'Guy o' Warwick', Miss; but Mr. Vargers, he was courting me down there at the 'Guy o' Warwick', and offered marriage if I would 'av 'ad him, and he tells me heverything, and he says that there's a paper to take you, please, my lady.'

'Take *me?*'

'Yes, my lady; he read it to me in the room by the hall-door. Halice Harden, spinster, and something about the old guv'nor's will, please; and his horder is to take you, please, Miss, if you should offer to go out of the door; and there's two on 'em, and they watches turn about, so you can't leave the 'ouse, please, my lady; and if you try they'll only lock you up a prisoner in one room a-top o' the 'ouse; and, for your life, my lady, don't tell no one I said a word.'

'Oh! Phoebe. What can they mean? What's to become of me? Somehow or other you must get me out of this house. Help me, for God's sake! I'll throw myself from the window—I'll kill myself rather than remain in their power.'

'Hush! My lady, please, I may think of something yet. But don't you do nothing 'and hover 'ead. You must have patience. They won't be so sharp, maybe, in a day or two. I'll get you out if I can; and, if I can't, then God's will be done. And I'll make out what I can from Mr. Vargers; and don't you let no one think you likes me, and I'll be sly enough, you may count on me, my lady.'

Trembling all over, Alice kissed her.

More News of Paul Davies

Louisa Diaper did not appear that night, nor next morning. She had been spirited away like the rest. Sir Richard had told her that his sister desired that she should go into town, and stay till next day, under the care of the housekeeper in town, and that he would bring her a list of commissions which she was to do for her mistress preparatory to starting for Yorkshire. I daresay this young lady liked her excursion to town well enough. It was not till the night after that she started for the North.

Alice Arden, for a time, lost heart altogether. It was no wonder she should.

That her only brother should be an accomplice against her, in a plot so appalling, was enough to overpower her; her horror of Longcluse, the effectual nature of her imprisonment, and the strange and, as she feared, unscrupulous people by whom she had been so artfully surrounded, heightened her terrors to the pitch of distraction.

At times she was almost wild; at others stupefied in despair; at others, again, soothed by the kindly intrepidity of Phoebe, she became more collected. Sometimes she would throw herself on her bed, and sob for an hour in helpless agony; and then, exhausted and overpowered, she would fall for a time into a deep sleep, from which she would start, for several minutes, without the power of collecting her thoughts, and with only the stifled cry, 'What is it?—Where am I?' and a terrified look round.

One day, in a calmer mood, as she sat in her room after a long talk with Phoebe, the girl came beside her chair with an oddly made key, with a little strap of white leather to the handle, in her hands.

'Here's a latch-key, Miss; maybe you know what it opens?'

'Where did you find it?'

'In the old china vase over the chimney, please 'm.'

'Let me see—oh! dear, yes, this opens the door in the wall of the grounds, in that direction,' and she pointed. 'Poor papa lent it to my drawing-master. He lived somewhere beyond that, and used to let himself in by it when he came to give me my lessons.'

'I remember that door well, Miss,' said Phoebe, looking earnestly on the key— 'Mr. Crozier let me out that way, one day. Mr. Longcluse has put strangers, you know, in the gate-house. That's shut against us. I'll tell you what, Miss—wait—well, I'll *think*. I'll keep this key safe, anyhow; and—the more the merrier,' she added with a sudden alacrity, and lifting her finger, by way of signal, for everything now was done with caution here, she left the room, and passed through the suite to the landing, and quietly took out the door-keys, one by one, and returned with her spoil to Alice's room.

'You thought they might lock us up?' whispered Alice.

The girl nodded. 'No harm to have 'em, Miss—it won't hurt us.' She folded them tightly in a handkerchief, and thrust the parcel as far as her arm could reach between the mattress and the bed. 'I'll rip the ticken a bit just now, and stitch them in,' whispered the girl.

'Didn't I hear another key clink as you put your hand in?' asked Alice.

The girl smiled, and drew out a large key, and nodded, still smiling as she replaced it.

'What does that open?' whispered Alice eagerly.

'*Nothing,* Miss,' said the girl gravely— 'it's the key of the old back-door lock; but there's a new one there now, and this won't open nothing. But I have a use for it. I'll tell you all in time, Miss; and, please, you must keep up your heart, mind.'

Sir Richard Arden was not the cold villain you may suppose. He was resolved to make an effort of some kind for the extrication of his sister. He could not bear to open his dreadful situation to his Uncle David, nor to kill himself, nor to defy the vengeance of Longcluse. He would effect her escape and his own simultaneously. In the meantime he must acquiesce, ostensibly at least, in every step determined on by Longcluse.

It was a bright autumnal day as Sir Richard and Mr. Longcluse took the rail to Southampton. Longcluse had his reasons for taking the young baronet with him.

It was near the hour, by the time they got there, when David Arden would arrive from his northern point of departure. Longcluse looked animated—smiling; but a stupendous load lay on his heart. A single clumsy phrase in the letter of that detective scoundrel might be enough to direct the formidable suspicions of that energetic old gentleman upon him. The next hour might throw him altogether upon the defensive, and paralyse his schemes.

Alice Arden, you little dream of the man and the route by

which, possibly, deliverance is speeding to you.

Near the steps of the large hotel that looks seaward, Longcluse and Sir Richard lounges, expecting the arrival of David Arden almost momentarily. Up drives a fly, piled with portmanteaus, hat-case, dressing-case, and all the other travelling appurtenances of a comfortable wayfarer. Beside the driver sits a servant. The fly draws up at the door near them.

Mr. Longcluse's seasoned heart throbs once or twice oddly. Out gets Uncle David, looking brown and healthy after his northern excursion. On reaching the top of the steps, he halts, and turns round to look about him. Again Mr. Longcluse feels the same odd sensation.

Uncle David recognises Sir Richard, and smiling greets him. He runs down the steps to meet him. After they have shaken hands, and, a little more coldly, he and Mr. Longcluse, he says,—

'You are not looking yourself, Dick; you ought to have run down to the moors, and got up an appetite. How is Alice?'

'Alice? Oh! Alice is very well, thanks.'

'I should like to run up to Mortlake to see her. She has been complaining, eh?'

'No, no—better,' says Sir Richard.

'And you forget to tell your uncle what you told me,' interposes Mr. Longcluse, 'that Miss Arden left Mortlake for Yorkshire, yesterday.'

'Oh!' said Uncle David, turning to Richard again.

'And the servants went before—two or three days ago,' said Sir Richard, looking down for a moment, and hastening, under that clear eye, to speak a little truth.

'Well, I wish she had come with us,' said David Arden; 'but as she could not be persuaded, I'm glad she is making a little change of air and scene, in any direction. By-the-bye, Mr. Longcluse, you had a letter, had not you, from our friend, Paul Davies?'

'Yes; he seemed to think he had found a clue—from Paris it was—and I wrote to tell him to spare no expense in pushing his inquiries and to draw upon me.'

'Well, I have some news to tell you. His exploring voyage will come to nothing; you did not hear?'

'No.'

'Why, the poor fellow's dead. I got a letter—it reached me, forwarded from my house in town, yesterday, from the person who hires the lodgings—to say he had died of scarlatina very suddenly, and sending an inventory of the things he left. It is a pity, for he seemed a smart fellow, and sanguine about getting to the bottom of it'

'An awful pity!' exclaimed Longcluse, who felt as if a mountain were lifted from his heart, and the entire firmament had lighted up; 'an awful pity! Are you quite sure?'

'There can't be a doubt, I'm sorry to say. Then, as Alice has taken wing, I'll pursue my first plan, and cross by the next mail'

'For Paris?' inquired Mr. Longcluse, carelessly.

'Yes, Sir, for Paris,' answered Uncle David deliberately, looking at him; 'yes, for Paris.'

And then followed a little chat on indifferent subjects. Then Uncle David mentioned that he had an appointment, and must dine with the dull but honest fellow who had asked him to meet him here on a matter of business, which would have done just as well next year, but he wished it now. Uncle David nodded, and waved his hand, as on entering the door he gave them a farewell smile over his shoulder.)

The Catacombs

At his disappearance, for Sir Richard the air darkened as when, in the tropics, the sun sets without a twilight, and the silence of an awful night descended.

It seemed that safety had been so near. He had laid his hand upon it, and had let it glide ungrasped between his fingers; and now the sky was black above him, and an unfathomable sea beneath.

Mr. Longcluse was in great spirits. He had grown for a time like the Walter Longcluse of a year before.

They two dined together, and after dinner Mr. Longcluse grew happy, and as he sat with his glass by him, he sang, looking over the waves, a sweet little sentimental song, about ships that pass at sea, and smiles and tears, and 'true, boys, true,' and 'heaven shows a glimpse of its blue.' And he walks with Sir Richard to the station, and he says, low, as he leans and looks into the carriage window, of which young Arden was the only occupant—

'Be true to me now, and we may make it up yet.'

And so saying, he gives his hand a single pressure as he looks hard in his eyes.

The bell had rung. He was remaining there, he said, for another train. The clapping of the doors had ceased. He stood back. The whistle blew its long piercing yell, and as the train began to glide towards London, the young man saw the white face of Walter Longcluse in deep shadow, as he stood with his back to the lamp, still turned towards him.

The train was now thundering on its course; the solitary lamp glimmered in the roof. He threw himself back, with his foot against the opposite seat.

'Good God! what is one to resolve! All men are cruel when they are exasperated. Might not good yet be made of Longcluse? What creatures women are!—what fools! How easy all might have been made, with the least temper and reflection! What d——d selfishness!'

Uncle David was now in Paris. The moon was shining over that beautiful city. In a lonely street, in a quarter which fashion had long forsaken—over whose pavement, as yet unconscious of the Revolution, had passed, in the glare of torchlight, the carved and emblazoned carriages of an aristocracy, as shadowy now as the courts of the Caesars—his footsteps are echoing.

A huge house presents its front. He stops and examines it carefully for a few seconds. It is the house of which he is in search.

At one time the Baron Vanboeren had received patients from the country, to reside in this house. For the last year, during which he had been gathering together his wealth, and detaching himself from business, he had discontinued this, and had gradually got rid of his establishment.

When David Arden rang the bell at the hall-door, which he had to do repeatedly, it was answered at last by an old woman, high-shouldered, skin and bone, with a great nose, and big jawbones, and a high-cauled cap. This lean creature looks at him with a vexed and hollow eye. Her bony arm rests on the lock of the hall-door, and she blocks the narrow aperture between its edge and the massive door-case. She inquires in very nasal French what *Monsieur* desires.

'I wish to see Monsieur the Baron, if he will permit me an interview,' answered Mr. Arden in very fair French.

'*Monsieur* the Baron is not visible; but if *Monsieur* will, notwithstanding, leave any message he pleases for Monsieur the Baron, I will take care he receives it punctually.'

'But *Monsieur* the Baron appointed me to call tonight at ten o'clock.'

'Is *Monsieur* sure of that?'

'Perfectly.'

'Eh, very well; but, if he pleases, I must first learn *Monsieur's* name.'

'My name is Arden.'

'I believe *Monsieur* is right.' She took a bit of notepaper from her capacious pocket, and peering at it, spelled aloud, 'D-a-v-i-d ——'

'A-r-d-e-n,' interrupted and continued the visitor, spelling his name, with a smile.

'A-r-d-e-n,' she followed, reading slowly from her paper; 'yes, *Monsieur* is right. You see, this paper says, 'Admit Monsieur David Arden to an interview.' Enter, if you please *Monsieur*, and follow me.'

It was a decayed house of superb proportions, but of a fashion long passed away. The gaunt old woman, with a bunch of large keys clinking at her side, stalked up the broad stairs and into a gallery, and through several rooms opening *en suite*. The rooms were hung with cobwebs, dusty, empty, and the shutters closed, except here and there where the moonlight gleamed through chinks and seams.

David Arden, before he had seen the Baron Vanboeren in London, had pictured him in imagination a tall old man with classic features, and manners courteous and somewhat stately.

We do not fabricate such images; they rise like exhalations from a few scattered data, and present themselves spontaneously. It is this self-creation that invests them with so much reality in our imaginations, and subjects us to so odd a surprise when the original turns out quite unlike the portrait with which we have been amusing ourselves.

She now pushed open a door, and said, '*Monsieur* the Baron here is arrived Monsieur David d'Ardennes.'

The room in which he now stood was spacious, but very nearly dark. The shutters were closed outside, and the moonlight that entered came through the circular hole cut in each. A large candle on a bracket burned at the further end of the room. There the baron stood. A reflector which interposed between the candle and the door at which David Arden entered directed its light strongly upon something which the baron held, and laid upon the table, in his hand; and now that he turned toward his visitor, it was concentrated upon his large face, revealing, with the force of a Rembrandt, all its furrows and finer wrinkles. He stood out against a background of darkness with remarkable force.

The baron stood before him—a short man in a red waistcoat. He looked more broad-shouldered and short-necked than ever in his shirt-sleeves. He had an instrument in his hand resembling a small bit and brace, and some chips and sawdust on his flannel waistcoat, which he brushed off with two or three sweeps of his short fat fingers. He looked now like a grim old mechanic. There was no vivacity in his putty-coloured features, but there were promptitude and decision in every abrupt gesture. It was his towering, bald forehead, and something of command and savage energy in his lowering face, that redeemed the *tout ensemble* from an almost brutal vulgarity.

The baron was not in the slightest degree 'put out,' as the phrase is, at being detected in his present occupation and *deshabille.*

He bowed twice to David Arden, and said, in English, with a little foreign accent—

'Here is a chair, Monsieur Arden; but you can hardly see it until your eyes have grown a little accustomed to our *crépuscula.*'

This was true enough, for David Arden, though he saw him advance a step or two, could not have known what he held in the hand that was in shadow. The sound, indeed, of the legs of the chair, as he set it down upon the floor, he heard.

'I should make you an apology, Mr. Arden, if I were any longer in my own home, which I am not, although this is still my house; for I have dismissed my servants, sold my furniture, and sent what things I cared to retain over the frontier to my new habitation, whither I shall soon follow; and this house too, I shall sell. I have already two or three gudgeons nibbling, *Monsieur.*'

'This house must have been the hotel of some distinguished family, Baron; it is nobly proportioned,' said David Arden.

As his eye became accustomed to the gloom, David Arden saw traces of gilding on the walls. The shattered frames on which the tapestry was stretched in old times remained in the panels, with crops of small, rusty nails visible. The faint candlelight glimmered on a ponderous gilded cornice, which had also sustained violence. The floor was bare, with a great deal of litter, and some scanty furniture. There was a lathe near the spot where David Arden stood, and shavings and splinters under his feet. There was a great block with a vice attached. In a portion of the fireplace was built a furnace. There were pincers and other instruments lying about the room, which had more the appearance of an untidy workshop than of a, study, and seemed a suitable enough abode for the uncouth figure that confronted him.

'Ha! *Monsieur,*' growls the baron, 'stone walls have ears, you say if only they had tongues; what tales *these* could tell! This house was one of Madame du Barry's, and was sacked in the great Revolution. The mirrors were let into the plaster in the walls. In some of the rooms there are large fragments still stuck in the wall so fast, you would need a hammer and chisel to dislodge and break them up. This room was an ante-room, and admitted to the lady's bedroom by two doors, this and that. The panels of that other, by which you entered from the stair, were of mirror. They were quite smashed.

'The furniture, I suppose, flew out of the window; everything was broken up in small bits, and torn to rags, or carried off to the broker after the first fury, and *sansculotte* families came in and took possession of the wrecked apartments. You will say then, what was left? The bricks, the stones, hardly the plaster on the walls. Yet, Monsieur Arden, I have discovered some of the best treasures the house contained, and they are at present in this room. Are you a collector, Monsieur Arden?'

Uncle David disclaimed the honourable imputation. He was thinking of cutting all this short, and bringing the baron to the point. The old man was at the period when the egotism of age asserts itself, and was garrulous, and being, perhaps, despotic and fierce (he looked both), he might easily take fire and become impracticable. Therefore, on second thoughts, he was cautious.

'You can now see more plainly,' said the baron. 'Will you approach? Concealed by a double covering of strong paper pasted over it, and painted and gilded, each of these two doors on its six panels contains six distinct master-pieces of Watteau's. I have know that for ten years, and have postponed removing them. Twelve Watteaus, as fine as any in the world! I would not trust their removal to any other hand, and so, the panel comes out without a shake. Come here, *Monsieur*, if you please. This candle affords a light sufficient to see, at least, some of the beauties of these incomparable works.'

'Thanks, Baron, a glance will suffice, for I am nothing of an artist.'

He approached. It was true that his sight had grown accustomed to the obscurity, for he could now see the baron's features much more distinctly. His large waxen face was shorn smooth, except on the upper lip, where a short moustache still bristled; short black eyebrows contrasted also with the bald massive forehead, and round the eyes was a complication of mean and cunning wrinkles. Some peculiar lines between these contracted brows gave a character of ferocity to this forbidding and sensual face.

'Now! See there! Those four pictures—I would not sell those four Watteaus for one hundred thousand *francs*. And the other door is worth the same. Ha!'

'You are lucky, Baron.'

'I think so. I do not wish to part with them: I don't think of selling them. See the folds of that brocade! See the ease and grace of the lady in the *sacque*, who sits on the bank there, under the myrtles, with the guitar on her lap! and see the animation and elegance of that dancing boy with the tambourine! This is a *chef-d'oeuvre.* I ought not to part with that, on any terms—no, never! You no doubt know many collectors, wealthy men, in England. Look at that shot silk, green and purple; and whom do you take that to be a portrait of, that lady with the *castanets*?'

He was pointing out each object, on which he descanted, with his stumpy finger, his hands being, I am bound to admit, by no means clean.

'If you do happen to know such people, nevertheless, I should not object to your telling them where this treasure may be seen, I've no objection. I should not like to part with them, that is true. No, no, *no;* but every man may be tempted, it is possible—possible, just possible.'

'I shall certainly mention them to some friends.' 'Wealthy men, of course,' said the baron.

'It is an expensive taste. Baron, and none but wealthy people can indulge it.'

'True, and these would be *very* expensive. They are unique; that lady there is the *Du Barry*—a portrait worth, alone, six thousand *francs*. Ha! he! Yes, when I take zese out and place zem, as I mean before I go, to be seen, they will bring all Europe together. *Mit Speck fängt man Mäuse*—with bacon one catches mice!'

'No doubt they will excite attention, Baron. But I feel I am wasting your time and abusing your courtesy in permitting my visit, the immediate object of which was to earnestly beg from you some information which, I think, no one else can give me.'

'Information? Oh! ah! Pray resume your chair, Sir. Information? yes, it is quite possible I may have information such as you need, Heaven knows! But knowledge, they say, is power, and if I do you a service I expect as much from you. *Eine Hand wäscht die andere* one hand, *Monsieur*, washes ze ozer. No man parts wis zat which is valuable, to strangers, wisout a proper honorarium. I receive no more patients here; but you understand, I may be induced to attend a patient: I may be *tempted,* you understand.'

'But this is not a case of attending a patient, Baron,' said David Arden, a little haughtily.

'And what ze devil *is* it, then?' said the baron, turning on him suddenly. '*Monsieur* will pardon me, but we professional men must turn our time and knowledge to account, do you see? And we don't give eizer wizout being paid, and *well* paid for them, eh?'

'Of course. I meant nothing else,' said David Arden.

'Then, Sir, we understand one another so far, and that saves time. Now, what information can the Baron Vanboeren give to Monsieur David Arden?'

'I think you would prefer my putting my questions quite straight.'

'Straight as a sword-thrust, Sir.'

'Then, Baron, I want to know whether you were acquainted with two persons, Yelland Mace and Walter Longcluse.'

'Yes, I knew zem bos, slightly and yet intimately—intimately and yet but slightly. You wish, perhaps to learn particulars about those gentlemen?'

'I do.'

'Go on: interrogate.'

'Do you perfectly recollect the features of these persons?'

'I ought.'

'Can you give me an accurate description of Yelland Mace?'

'I can bring you face to face with both.'

'By Jove! Sir, are you serious?'

'Mr. Longcluse is in London.'

'But you talk of bringing me face to face with them; how soon?'

'In five minutes.'

'Oh, you mean a photograph, or a picture?'

'No, in the the solid. Here is the key of the catacombs.' And he took a key that hung from a nail on the wall.

'Bah, ha, yah!' exploded the baron, in a ferocious sneer, rather than a laugh, and shrugging his great shoulders to his ears, he shook them in barbarous glee, crying—'What clever fellow you are, Monsieur Arden! you see so well srough ze millstone! *Ich bin klug und weise*— you sing zat song. I am intelligent and wise, eh, he! gra-a, ha, ha!'

He seized the candlestick in one hand, and shaking the key in the other by the side of his huge forehead, he nodded once or twice to David Arden.

'Not much life where we are going; but you shall see zem bose.'

'You speak riddles, Baron; but by all means bring me, as you say, face to face with them.'

'Very good, *Monsieur*; you'll follow me,' said the baron. And he opened a door that admitted to the gallery, and, with the candle and the keys, he led the way, by this corridor, to an iron door that had a singular appearance, being sunk two feet back in a deep wooden frame, that threw it into shadow. This he unlocked, and with an exertion of his weight and strength, swung slowly open.

Resurrections

David Arden entered this door, and found himself under a vaulted roof of brick. These were the chambers, for there was at least two, which the baron termed his catacombs. Along both walls of the narrow apartment were iron doors, in deep recesses, that looked like the huge ovens of an ogre, sunk deep in the wall, and the baron looked himself not an unworthy proprietor. The baron had the General's faculty of remembering faces and names.

'Monsieur Yelland Mace? Yes, I will show you him; he is among ze dead.'

'Dead?'

'Ay, zis right side is *dead*—all zese.'

'Do you mean,' says David Arden, '*literally* that Yelland Mace is no longer living?'

'A, B, C, D, E, F, G,' mutters the baron, slowly pointing his finger along the right wall.

'I beg your pardon, Baron, but I don't think you heard me,' said David Arden.

'*Perfectly,* excuse me: H, I, J, K, L, M—M. I will show you *now,* if you desire it, Yelland Mace; you shall see him now, and never behold him more. Do you wish very much?'

'Intensely—*most* intensely!' said Uncle David earnestly.

The baron turned full upon him, and leaned his shoulders against the iron door of the recess. He had taken from his pocket a bunch of heavy keys, which he dangled from his clenched fingers, and they made a faint jingle in the silence that followed, for a few seconds.

'Permit me to ask,' said the baron, 'are your inquiries directed to a legal object?'

'I have no difficulty in saying yes,' answered he; 'a legal object, strictly.'

'A legal object, by which you gain considerably?' he asked slowly.

'By which I gain the satisfaction of seeing justice done upon a villain.'

'That is fine, *Monsieur.* Eternal justice! I have thought and said that very often: *Vive la justice eternelle!* especially when her sword shears off the head of my enemy, and her scale is laden with *napoleons* for my purse.'

'*Monsieur le Baron* mistakes, in my case; I have absolutely nothing to gain by the procedure I propose; it is strictly criminal,' said

David Arden drily.

'Not an estate? not a slice of an estate? Come, come! *Thorheit!* That is foolish talk.'

'I have told you already, nothing,' repeated David Arden.

'Then you don't care, in truth, a single *napoleon*, whether you win or lose. We have been wasting our time, Sir. I have no time to bestow for nothing; my minutes count by the crown, while I remain in Paris. I shall soon depart, and practise no more; and my time will become my own—still my own, by no means *yours.* I am candid, Sir, and I think you cannot misunderstand me; I must be paid for my time and opportunities.'

'I never meant anything else,' said Mr. Arden sturdily; 'I shall pay you liberally for any service you render me.'

'That, Sir, is equally frank; we understand now the principle on which I assist you. You wish to see Yelland Mace, so you shall.'

He turned about, and struck the key sharply on the iron door.

'There he waits,' said the baron, 'and—did you ever see him?'

'No.'

'Bah! what a wise man. Then I may show you whom I please, and you know nothing. Have you heard him described?'

'Accurately.'

'Well, there is some little sense in it, after all You shall see.'

He unlocked the safe, opened the door, and displayed shelves, laden with rudely-made deal boxes, each of a little more than a foot square. On these were marks and characters in red, some, and some in black, and others in blue.

'*Hé*! you see,' said the baron, pointing with his key, 'my mummies are cased in hieroglyphics. Come! *Here* is the number, the date, and the man.'

And lifting them carefully one off the other, he took out a deal box that had stood in the lowest stratum. The cover was loose, except for a string tied about it. He laid it upon the floor, and took out a plaster mask, and brushing and blowing off the sawdust, held it up.

David Arden saw a face with large eyes closed, a very high and thin nose, a good forehead, a delicately chiselled mouth; the upper lip, though well formed after the Greek model, projected a little, and gave to the chin the effect of receding in proportion. This slight defect showed itself in profile; but the face, looked at full front, was on the whole handsome, and in some degree even interesting.

'You are quite sure of the identity of this?' asked Uncle David earnestly.

There was a square bit of parchment, with two or three short lines, in a character which he did not know, glued to the concave reverse of the mask. The baron took it, and holding the light near, read, 'Yelland Mace, suspect for his politics, May 2nd, 1844.'

'Yes,' said Mr. Arden, having renewed his examination, 'it very exactly tallies with the description; the nose aquiline, but very delicately formed. Is that writing in cypher?'

'Yes, in cypher.'

'And in what language?'

'German.'

David Arden looked at it.

'You will make nothing of it. In these inscriptions, I have employed eight languages—five European, and three Asiatic—I am, you see, something of a linguist—and four distinct cyphers; so having that skill, I gave the benefit of it to my *friends;* this being secret.'

'Secret?—oh!' said Uncle David.

'Yes, secret; and you will please to say nothing of it to any living creature until the twenty-first of October next, when I retire. You understand commerce, Mr. Arden. My practice is confidential, and I should lose perhaps eighty thousand *francs* in the short space that intervenes, if I were thought to have played a patient such a trick. It is but twenty days of reserve, and then I go and laugh at them, every one. Piff, puff, paff! ha! ha!'

'Yes, I promise that also,' said Uncle David dryly, and to himself he thought, 'What a consummate old scoundrel!'

'Very good, Sir; we shall want this of Yelland Mace again, just now; his face and coffin, ha! ha! can rest there for the present.' He had replaced the mask in its box, and that lay on the floor. The door of the iron press he shut and locked. 'Next, I will show you Mr. Longcluse: those are dead.'

He waved his short hand toward the row of iron doors which he had just visited.

'Please, Sir, walk with me into this room. Ay, so. Here are the *resurrections.* Will you be good enough—L, Longcluse, M, one, two, three, four; *three,* yes, to hold this candlestick for a moment?'

The baron unlocked this door, and, after some rummaging, he took forth a box similar to that he had taken out before.

'Yes, right, Walter Longcluse. I tell you how you will see it best: there is brilliant moonlight, stand there.'

Through a circular hole in the wall there streamed a beam of moonlight, that fell upon the plaster-wall opposite with the distinctness of the circle of a magic-lantern.

'You see it—you know it! Ha! ha! His pretty face!'

He held the mask up in the moonlight, and the lineaments, sinister enough, of Mr. Longcluse stood, sharply defined in every line and feature, in intense white and black, against the vacant shadow behind. There was the flat nose, the projecting underjaw, the oblique, sarcastic eyebrow, even the line of the slight but long scar, than ran nearly from his eye to his nostril. The same, but younger.

'There is no doubt about *that.* But when was it taken? Will you read what is written upon it?'

Uncle David had taken out the candle, and he held it beside the mask. The baron turned it round, and read, 'Walter Longcluse, 15th October, 1844.'

'The same year in which Mace's was taken?'

'So it is, 1844.'

'But there is a great deal more than you have read, written upon the parchment in this one.'

'It looks more.'

'And *is* more. Why, count the words, one, two, four six, eight. There must be thirty, or upwards.'

'Well, suppose there are, Sir: I have read, nevertheless, all I mean to read for the present. Suppose we bring these three masks together. We can talk a little then, and I will perhaps tell you more, and disclose to you some secrets of nature and art, of which perhaps you suspect nothing. Come, come. *Monsieur*! kindly take the candle.'

The baron shut the iron door with a clang, and locked it, and, taking up the box, marched into the next room, and placing the boxes one on top of the other, carried them in silence out upon the gallery, accompanied by David Arden.

How desolate seemed the silence of the vast house, in all which, by this time, perhaps, there did not burn another light!

They now re-entered the large and strangely-littered chamber in which he had talked with the baron; they stop among the chips and sawdust with which his work has strewn the floor.

'Set the candle on this table,' says he. 'I'll light another for a time. See all the trouble and time you cost me!'

He placed the two boxes on the table.

'I am extremely sorry——'

'Not on my account, you needn't. You'll pay me well for it.'

'So I will, Baron.'

'Sit you down on that, *Monsieur*.'

He placed a clumsy old chair, with a balloon-back, for his visitor, and, seating himself upon another, he struck his hand on the table, and said, arresting for a moment the restless movement of his eyes, and fixing on him a savage stare—

'You shall see wonders and hear marvels, if only you are willing to pay what they are worth.' The baron laughed when be had said this.

Another

'You shall sit here, Mr. Arden,' said the baron, placing a chair for him. 'You shall be comfortable. I grow in confidence with you. I feel inwardly an intuition when I speak wis a man of honour; my demon, as it were, whispers 'Trust him, honour him, make much of him.' Will you take a pipe, or a mug of beer?'

This abrupt invitation Mr. Arden civilly declined.

'Well, I shall have my pipe and beer. See, there is ze barrel—not far to go.' He raised the candle, and David Arden saw for the first time the outline of a veritable beer-barrel in the corner, on tressels, such as might have regaled a party of boors in the clear shadow of a Teniers.

'There is the comely beer-cask, not often seen in Paris, in the corner of our *boudoir*, resting against the only remaining rags of the sky-blue and gold silk—it is rotten now—with which the room was hung, and a gilded cornice—it is black now—over its head; and now, instead of beautiful women and graceful youths, in gold lace and cut velvets and perfumed powder, there are but one rheumatic and crooked old woman, and one old Prussian doctor, in his shirt-sleeves, ha! ha! mutat terra vices! Come, we shall look at these again, and you shall hear more.'

He placed the two masks upon the chimney-piece, leaning against the wall.

'And we will illuminate them,' says he; and he takes, one after the other, half a dozen pieces of wax candle, and dripping the melting wax on the chimney-piece, he sticks each candle in turn in a little pool of its own wax.

'I spare nothing, you see, to make all plain. Those two faces present a marked contrast. Do you, Mr. Arden, know anything, ever so little, of the fate of Yelland Mace?'

'Nothing. Is he living?'

'Suppose he is dead, what then?'

'In that case, of course, I take my leave of the inquiry, and of you, asking you simply one question, whether there was any correspondence between Yelland Mace and Walter Longcluse?'

'A very intimate correspondence,' said the baron.

'Of what nature?'

'Ha! They have been combined in business, in pleasures, in crimes,' said the baron. 'Look at them. Can you believe it? So dissimilar! They are opposites in form and character, as if fashioned in expression and in feature each to contradict the other; yet so united!'

'And in crime, you say?'

'Ay, in crime—in all things.'

'Is Yelland Mace still living?' urged David Arden.

'Those features, in life, you will never behold, Sir.'

'He is dead. You said that you took that mask from among the dead. *Is* he dead?'

'No, Sir; not actually dead, but under a strange condition. Bah; Don't you see I have a secret? Do you prize very highly learning where he is?'

'Very highly, provided he may be secured and brought to trial; and you, Baron, must arrange to give your testimony to prove his identity.'

'Yes; that would be indispensible,' said the baron, whose eyes were sweeping the room from corner to corner, fiercely and swiftly. 'Without me you can never lift the veil; without me you can never unearth your stiff and pale Yelland Mace, nor without me identify and hang him.'

'I rely upon your aid, Baron,' said Mr. Arden, who was becoming agitated. 'Your trouble shall be recompensed; you may depend upon my honour.'

'I am running a certain risk. I am not a fool, though, like little Lebas. I am not to be made away with like a kitten; and once I move in this matter, I burn my ships behind me, and return to my splendid practice, under no circumstances, ever again.'

The baron's pallid face looked more bloodless, his accent was fiercer, and his countenance more ruffianly as he uttered all this.

'I understood, Baron, that you had quite made up your mind to retire within a very few weeks,' said David Arden.

'Does any man who has lived as long as you or I quite trust his own resolution? No one likes to be nailed to a plan of action an hour before he need be. I find my practice more lucrative every day. I may be tempted to postpone my retirement, and for a while longer to continue to gather the golden harvest that ripens round me. But once I take this step, all is up with that, You see—you understand. Bah! you are no fool; it is plain, all I sacrifice.'

'Of course, Baron, you shall take no trouble, and make no sacrifice, without ample compensation. But are you aware of the nature of the crime committed by that man?'

'I never trouble my head about details; it is enough, the man is a political refugee, and his object concealment.'

'But he was no political refugee; he had nothing to do with politics—he was simply a murderer and a robber.'

'What a little rogue! Will you excuse my smoking a pipe and drinking a little beer? Now, he never hinted that, although I knew him very intimately, for he was my patient for some months; never hinted it, he was so sly.'

'And Mr. Longcluse, was *he* your patient also?

'Ha! to be sure he was. You won't drink some beer? No; well, in a moment.'

He drew a little jugful from the cask, and placed it, and a pewter goblet, on the table, and then filled, lighted, and smoked his pipe as he proceeded.

'I will tell you something concerning those gentlemen, Mr. Longcluse and Mr. Mace, which may amuse you. Listen.'

Broken

'My hands were very full,' said the baron, displaying his stumpy fingers. 'I received patients in this house; I had what you call many irons in ze fire. I was making *napoleons* then, I don't mind telling you, as fast as a man could run bullets. My minutes counted by the crown. It was in the month of May, 1844, late at night, a man called here, wanting to consult me. He called himself Herr von Königsmark. I went down and saw him in my audience room. He knew I was to be depended upon. Such people tell one another who may be trusted. He told me he was an Austrian proscribed: very good. He proposed to place himself in my hands: very well. I looked him in the face—you have *there* exactly what I saw.'

He extended his hand toward the mask ofYelland Mace.

"You are an Austrian' I said, 'a native subject of the empire?"

'Yes.'

'Italian?'

'Hungarian?'

'No.'

'Well, you are not *German*—ha, ha!—I can swear to that.'

He was speaking to me in German.

'Your accent is foreign. Come, confidence. You must be no impostor. I must make no mistake, and blunder into a national type of features, all wrong; if I make your mask, it must do us credit. I know many gentlemen's secrets, and as many ladies' secrets. A man of honour! What are you afraid of?'

'You were not a statuary?' said Uncle David, astonished at his versatility.

'Oh, yes! A statuary, but only in grotesque, you understand. I will show you some of my work by-and-by.'

'And I shall perhaps understand.'

'You *shall, perfectly.* With some reluctance, then, he admitted that what I positively asserted was true; for I told him I knew from his accent he was an Englishman. Then, with some little pressure, I invited him to tell his name. He did—it was Yelland Mace. *That* is Yelland Mace.'

He had now finished his pipe: he went over to the chimney-piece, and having knocked out the ashes, and with his pipe pointing to the tip of the long thin plaster nose, he said, 'Look well at him. Look till you know all his features by rote. Look till you fix them for the rest of your days well in memory, and then say what in the devil's name you could make of them. Look at that high nose, as thin as a fish-knife. Look at the line of the mouth and chin; see the mild gentlemanlike contour. If you find a fellow with a flat nose, and a pair of upper tusks sticking out an inch, and a squint that turns out one eye like the white of an egg, you pull out the tusks, you raise the skin of the nose, slice a bit out of the cheek, and make a false bridge, as high as you please; heal the cheek with a stitch or two, and operate with the lancet for the squint, and your bust is complete. Bravo! you understand?'

'I confess, Baron, I do not.'

'You shall, however. Here is the case—a political refugee, like Monsieur Yelland Mace——'

'But he was no such thing.'

'Well, a criminal—any man in such a situation is, for me, a political refugee zat, for reasons, desires to revisit his country, and yet must be so thoroughly disguised zat by no surprise, and by no process, can he be satisfactorily recognised; he comes to me, tells me his case, and says, 'I desire, Baron, to become your patient,' and so he places himself in my hands, and so—ha, ha! You begin to perceive?'

'Yes, I do! I think I understand you clearly. But, Lord bless me! what a nefarious trade!' exclaimed Uncle David.

The baron was not offended; he laughed.

'Nevertheless,' said he, 'There's no harm in that. Not that I care much about the question of right or wrong in the matter; but there's none. Bah! who's the worse of his going back? or, if he did not, who's the better?'

Uncle David did not care to discuss this point in ethics, but simply said,—

'And Mr. Longcluse was also a patient of yours?'

'Yes, certainly,' said the baron.

'We Londoners know nothing of his history,' said Mr. Arden.

'A political refugee, like Mr. Mace,' said the baron. 'Now, look at Herr Yelland Mace. It was a severe operation, but a beautiful one! I opened the skin with a single straight cut from the lachrymal gland to the nostril, and one underneath meeting it, you see' (he was tracing the line of the scalpel with the stem of his pipe), 'along the base of the nose from the point. Then I drew back the skin over the bridge, and then I operated on the bone and cartilage, cutting them and the muscle at the extremity down to a level with the line of the face, and drew the flap of skin back, cutting it to meet the line of the skin of the cheek; *there,* you see, so much for the nose. Now see the curved eyebrow. Instead of that very well marked arch, I resolved it should slant from the radix of the nose in a straight line obliquely upward; to effect which I removed at the upper edge of each eyebrow, at the corner next the temple, a portion of the skin and muscle, which, being reunited and healed, produced the requisite contraction, and thus drew that end of each brow upward. And now, having disposed of the nose and brows, I come to the mouth. Look at the profile of this mask.'

He was holding that of Yelland Mace toward Mr. Arden, and with the bowl of the pipe in his right hand, pointed out the lines and features on which he descanted, with the amber point of the stem.

'Now, if you observe, the chin in this face, by reason of the marked prominence of the nose, has the effect of receding, but it does not. If you continue the perpendicular line of ze forehead, ze chin, you see, meets it. The upper lip, though short and well-formed, projects a good deal. Ze under lip rather retires, and this adds to the receding effect of the chin, you see. My *coup-d'oeil* assured me that it was practicable to give to this feature the character of a projecting under-jaw. The complete depression of the nose more than half accomplished it. The rest is done by cutting away two upper and four under-teeth, and substituting false ones at the desired angle. By that application of dentistry I obtained zis new line.' (He indicated the altered outline of the features, as before, with his pipe). 'It was a very pretty operation. The effect you could hardly believe.

'He was two months recovering, confined to his bed, ha! ha! We can't have an immovable mask of living flesh, blood, and bone for nothing. He was threatened with erysipelas, and there was a rather critical inflammation of the left eye. When he could sit up, and bear the light, and looked in the glass, instead of thanking me, he screamed like a girl, and cried and cursed for an hour, ha, ha, ha! He was glad of it afterward: it was so complete. Look at it' (he held up the mask of Yelland Mace): 'a face, on the whole, good-looking, but a little of a parrot-face, you know.

I took him into my hands with that face, and' (taking up the mask of Mr. Longcluse, and turning it with a slow oscillation so as to present it in every aspect), he added, 'these are the features of Yelland Mace as I sent him into the world with the name of Herr Longcluse!'

'You mean to say that Yelland Mace and Walter Longcluse are the same person?' cried David Arden, starting to his feet.

'I swear that here is Yelland Mace *before,* and here *after* the operation, call him what you please. When I was in London, two months ago, I saw Monsieur Longcluse. *He* is Yelland Mace; and these two masks are both masks of the same Yelland Mace.'

'Then the evidence is complete,' said David Arden, with awe in his face, as he stood for a moment gazing on the masks which the Baron Vanboeren held up side by side before him.

'Ay, the masks and the witness to explain them,' said the baron, sturdily.

'It is a perfect identification,' murmured Mr. Arden, with his eyes still riveted on the plaster faces. 'Good God! how wonderful that proof, so complete in all its parts, should remain!'

'Well, I don't love Longcluse, since so he is named; he disobliged me when I was in London,' said the baron. 'Let him hang, since so you ordain it. I'm ready to go to London, give my evidence, and produce these plaster casts. But my time and trouble must be considered.'

'Certainly.'

'Yes,' said the baron; 'and to avoid tedious arithmetic, and for the sake of convenience, I will agree to visit London, at what time you appoint, to bring with me these two masks, and to give my evidence against Yelland Mace, otherwise Walter Longcluse, my stay in London not to exceed a fortnight, for ten thousand pounds sterling.'

'I don't think, Baron, you can be serious,' said Mr. Arden, as soon as he had recovered breath.

'*Donner-wetter*! I will show you that I am!' bawled the baron. 'Now or never, Sir. Do as you please. I sha'n't abate a *franc.* Do you like my offer?'

On the event of this bargain are depending issues of which David Arden knows nothing; the dangers, the agonies, the salvation of those who are nearest to him on earth. The villain Longcluse, and the whole fabric of his machinations, may be dashed in pieces by a word.

How, then, did David Arden, who hated a swindle, answer the old extortioner, who asked him, 'Do you like my offer?'

'Certainly not, Sir,' said David Arden, sternly.

'Then *was scheert's mich*! What do I care! No more, no more about it!' yelled the baron in a fury, and dashed the two masks to pieces on the hearthstone at his feet, and stamped the fragments into dust with his clumsy shoes.

With a cry, old Uncle David rushed forward to arrest the demolition, but too late. The baron, who was liable to such accesses of rage, was grinding his teeth, and rolling his eyes, and stamping in fury.

The masks, those priceless records, were gone, past all hope of restoration. Uncle David felt for a moment so transported with anger, that I think he was on the point of striking him. How it would have fared with him, if he had, I can't tell.

'Now!' howled the baron, 'ten times ten thousand pounds would not place you where you were, Sir. You fancied, perhaps, I would stand haggling with you all night, and yield at last to your obstinacy. What is my answer? The floor strewn with the fragments of your calculation. Where will you turn—what will you do now?'

'Suppose I do this,' said Uncle David fiercely—'report to the police what I have seen—your masks and all the rest, and accomplish, besides, all I require, by my own evidence as to what I myself saw?'

'And I will confront you, as a witness,' said the baron, with a cold sneer, 'and deny it all—swear it is a dream, and aid your poor relatives in proving you unfit to manage your own money matters.'

Uncle David paused for a moment. The baron had no idea how near he was, at that moment, to a trial of strength with his

English visitor. Uncle David thinks better of it, and he contents himself with saying, 'I shall have advice, and you shall *most certainly* hear from me again.'

Forth from the room strides David Arden in high wrath. Fearing to lose his way, he bawls over the banister, and through the corridors, 'Is any one there?' and after a time the old woman, who is awaiting him in the hall, replies, and he is once more in the open street.

Doppelganger

It was late, he did not know or care how late. He was by no means familiar with this quarter of the city. He was agitated and angry, and did not wish to return to his hotel till he had a little walked off his excitement. Slowly he sauntered along, from street to street. These were old-fashioned, such as were in vogue in the days of the Regency. Tall houses, with gables facing the street; few of them showing any light from their windows, and their dark outlines discernible on high against the midnight sky. Now he heard the voices of people near, emerging from a low theatre in a street at the right. A number of men come along the *trottoir*, toward Uncle David. They were going to a gaming-house and restaurant at the end of the street, which he had nearly reached. This troop of idlers he accompanies. They turn into an open door, and enter a passage not very brilliantly lighted. At the left was the open door of a restaurant. The greater number of those who enter follow the passage, however, which leads to the roulette-room.

As Uncle David, with a caprice of curiosity, follows slowly in the wake of this accession to the company, a figure passes and goes before him into the room.

With a strange thrill he takes or mistakes this figure for Mr. Longcluse. He pauses, and sees the tall figure enter the roulette-room. He follows it as soon as he recollects himself a little, and goes into the room. The players are, as usual, engrossed by the game. But at the far side beyond these busy people, he sees this person, whom he recognises by a light great-coat, stooping with his lips pretty near the ear of a man who was sitting at the table. He raises himself in a moment more, and stands before Uncle David, and at the first glance he is quite certain that Mr. Longcluse is before him. The tall man stands with folded arms, and looks carelessly round the room, and at Uncle David among the rest.

'Here,' he thought, 'is the man; and the evidence, clear and conclusive, and so near this very spot, now scattered in dust and fragments, and the witness who might have clenched the case impracticable!'

This tall man, however, he begins to perceive, has points, and strong ones, of dissimilarity, notwithstanding his general resemblance to Mr. Longcluse. His beard and hair are red; his shoulders are broader, and very round; much clumsier and more powerful he looks; and there is an air of vulgarity and swagger and boisterous good spirits about him, certainly in marked contrast with Mr. Longcluse's very quiet demeanour.

Uncle David now finds himself in that uncomfortable state of oscillation between two opposite convictions which, in a matter of supreme importance, amounts very nearly to torture.

This man does not appear at all put out by Mr. Arden's observant presence, nor even conscious of it. A place becomes vacant at the table, and he takes it, and stakes some money, and goes on, and wins and loses, and at last yawns and turns away, and walks slowly round to the door near which David Arden is standing. Is not this the very man whom he saw for a moment on board the steamer, as he crossed? As he passes a jet of gas, the light falls upon his face at an angle that brings out lines that seem familiar to the Englishman, and for the moment determines his doubts. David Arden, with his eyes fixed upon him, says, as he was about to pass him,—

'How d'ye do, Mr. Longcluse?'

The gentleman stops, smiles, and shrugs.

'Pardon, *Monsieur*,' he says in French, 'I do not speak English or German.'

The quality of the voice that spoke these words was, he

thought, different from Mr. Longcluse's—less tone, less depth, and more nasal.

The gentleman pauses and smiles with his head inclined, evidently expecting to be addressed in French.

'I believe I have made a mistake, Sir,' hesitates Mr. Arden.

The gentleman inclines his head lower, smiles, and waits patiently for a second or two. Mr. Arden, a little embarrassed, says,—
'I thought, *Monsieur*, I had met you before in England.'
'I have never been in England, *Monsieur*,' says the patient and polite Frenchman, in his own language. 'I cannot have had the honour, therefore, of meeting *Monsieur there*.'

He pauses politely.

'Then I have only to make an apology. I beg your—I beg—but surely—I think—by Jove!' he breaks into English, 'I can't be mistaken—you *are* Mr. Longcluse.'

The tall gentleman looks so unaffectedly puzzled, and so politely good-natured, as he resumes, in the tones which seem perfectly natural, and yet one note in which David Arden fails to recognise, and says,—

'*Monsieur* must not trouble himself of having made a mistake: my name is St. Ange.'

'I believe I *have* made amistake, *Monsieur*—pray excuse me.'

The gentleman bows very ceremoniously, and Monsieur St. Ange walks slowly out, and takes a glass of *curaçoa* in the outer room. As he is paying the *garçon*, Mr. Arden again appears, once more in a state of uncertainty, and again leaning to the belief that this person is indeed the Mr. Longcluse who at present entirely possesses his imagination.

The tall stranger with the round shoulders in truth resembled the person who, in a midnight interview on Hampstead Heath, had discussed some momentous questions with Paul Davies, as we remember; but that person spoke in the peculiar accent of the northern border. *His* beard, too, was exorbitant in length, and flickered wide and red, in the wind. This beard, on the contrary, was short and trim, and hardly so red, I think, as that moss-trooper's. On the whole, the likeness in both cases was somewhat rude and general. Still the resemblance to Longcluse again struck Mr. Arden so powerfully, that he actually followed him into the street and overtook him only a dozen steps away from the door, on the now silent pavement.

Hearing his hurried step behind him, the object of his pursuit turns about and confronts him for the first time with an offended and haughty look.

'*Monsieur*!' says he a little grimly, drawing himself up as he comes to a sudden halt.

'The impression has forced itself upon me again that you *are* no other than Mr. Walter Longcluse,' says Uncle David.

The tall gentleman recovered his good-humour, and smiled as before, with a shrug.

'I have not the honour of that gentleman's acquaintance, *Monsieur*, and cannot tell, therefore, whether he in the least resembles me. But as this kind of thing is unusual, and grows wearisome, and may end in putting me out of temper—which is not easy, although quite possible—and as my assurance that I am really myself seems insufficient to convince *Monsieur*, I shall be happy to offer other evidence of the most unexceptionable kind. My house is only two streets distant. There my wife and daughter await me, and our *curé* partakes of our little supper at twelve. I am a little late,' says he, listening, for the clocks are tolling twelve; 'however, it is a little more than two hundred metres, if you will accept my invitation, and I shall be very happy to introduce you to my wife, to my daughter Clotilde, and to our good *curé*, who is a most agreeable man.

'Pray come, share our little supper, see what sort of people we are, and in this way—more agreeable, I hope, than any other, and certainly less fallacious—you can ascertain whether I am Monsieur St. Ange, or that other gentleman with whom you are so obliging as to confound me. Pray come; it is not much—a *fricasée*, a few cutlets, an omelette, and a glass of wine. Madame St. Ange will be charmed to make your acquaintance, my daughter will sing us a song, and you will say that *Monsieur le Curé* is really a most entertaining companion.'

There was something so simple and thoroughly good-natured in this invitation, under all the circumstances, that Mr. Arden felt a little ashamed of his persistent annoyance of so hospitable a fellow, and for the moment he was convinced that he must have been in error.

'Sir,' says David Arden, 'I am now convinced that I must have been mistaken; but I cannot deny myself the honour of being presented to Madame St. Ange, and I assure you I am quite ashamed of the annoyance I must have caused you, and I offer a thousand apologies.'

'Not one, pray,' replies the Frenchman, with great good-humour and gaiety. 'I felicitate myself on a mistake which promises to result so happily.'

So side by side, at a leisurely pace, they pursued their way through these silent streets, and unaccountably the conviction again gradually stole over Uncle David that he was actually walking by the side of Mr. Longcluse.

A Short Parting

The fluctuations of Mr. Arden's conviction continued. His new acquaintance chatted gaily. They passed a transverse street, and he saw him glance quickly right and left, with a shrewd eye that did not quite accord with his careless demeanour.

Here for a moment the moon fell full upon them, and the effect of this new light was, once more, to impair Mr. Arden's confidence in his last conclusions about this person. Again he was at sea as to his identity.

There were the gabble and vociferation of two women quarrelling in the street to the left, and three tipsy fellows, marching home, were singing a trio some way up the street to the right.

They had encountered but one figure a—seedy scrivener, slip-shod, shuffling his way to his garret, with a baize bag of law-papers to copy in his left hand, and a sheaf of quills in his right, and a pale, careworn face turned up towards the sky. The streets were growing more silent and deserted as they proceeded.

He was sauntering onward by the side of this urbane and

garrulous stranger, when, like a whisper, the thought came, 'Take care!'

David Arden stopped short.

'*Eh, bien*?' said his polite companion, stopping simultaneously, and staring in his face a little grimly.

'On reflection, *Monsieur*, it is so late, that I fear I should hardly reach my hotel in time if I were to accept your agreeable invitation, and letters probably await me, which I should, at least, *read* tonight.'

'Surely *Monsieur* will not disappoint me—surely *Monsieur* is not going to treat me so oddly?' expostulated Monsieur St. Ange.

'Goodnight, Sir. Farewell!' said David Arden, raising his hat as he turned to go.

There intervened not two yards between them, and the polite Monsieur St. Ange makes a stride after him, and extends his hand—whether there is a weapon in it, I know not; but he exclaims fiercely,—

'Ha! robber! my purse!'

Fortunately, perhaps, at that moment, from a lane only a few yards away, emerge two *gendarmes*, and Monsieur St. Ange exclaims, 'Ah, *Monsieur, mille pardons*! Here it is! All safe, *Monsieur*. Pray excuse my mistake as frankly as I have excused yours. *Adieu*!'

Monsieur St. Ange raises his hat, shrugs, smiles, and withdrew.

Uncle David thought, on the whole, he was well rid of his ambiguous acquaintance, and strode along beside the gendarmes, who civilly directed him upon his way, which he had lost.

So, then, upon Mr. Longcluse's fortunes the sun shone; his star, it would seem, was in the ascendant. If the evil genius who ruled his destiny was contending, in a chess game, with the good angel of Alice Arden, her game seemed pretty well lost, and the last move near.

When David Arden reached his hotel a note awaited him, in the hand of the Baron Vanboeren. He read it under the gas in the hall. It said:—

> We must, in this world, forgive and reconsider many things. I therefore pardon you, you me. So soon as you have slept upon our conversation, you will accept an offer which I cannot modify. I always proportion the burden to the back. The rich pay me handsomely; for the poor I have prescribed and operated, sometimes, for nothing! You have the good fortune, like myself, to be childless, wifeless, and rich. When I take a fancy to a thing, nothing stops me; you, no doubt, in like manner. The trouble is something to me; the danger, which you count nothing, to me is *much.* The compensation I name, estimated without the circumstances, is large; compared with my wealth, trifling; compared with your wealth, nothing; as the condition of a transaction between you and me, therefore, not worth mentioning. The accident of last night I can repair. The original matrix of each mask remains safe in my hands: from this I can multiply casts *ad libitum.* Both these matrices I will hammer into powder at twelve o'clock tomorrow night, unless my liberal offer shall have been accepted before that hour. I write to a man of honour. We understand each other.
>
> *Emmanuel Vanboeren.*

The ruin, then, was not irretrievable; and there was time to take advice, and think it over. In the baron's brutal letter there was a coarse logic, not without its weight.

In better spirits David Arden betook himself to bed. It vexed him to think of submitting to the avarice of that wicked old extortioner; but to that submission, reluctant as he is, it seems probable he will come.

And now his thoughts turn upon the hospitable Monsieur St. Ange, and he begins, I must admit not altogether without reason, to reflect what a fool he has been. He wonders whether that hospitable and polite gentleman had intended to murder him, at the moment when the *gendarmes* so luckily appeared. And in the midst of his speculations, overpowered by fatigue, he fell asleep, and ate his breakfast next morning very happily.

Uncle David had none of that small diplomatic genius that helps to make a good attorney. That sort of knowledge of human nature would have prompted a careless reception of the baron's note, and an entire absence of that promptitude which seems to imply an anxiety to seize an offer.

Accordingly, it was at about eleven o'clock in the morning that he presented himself at the house of the Baron Vanboeren.

He was not destined to conclude a reconciliation with that German noble, nor to listen to his abrupt loquacity, nor ever more to discuss or negotiate anything whatsoever with him, for the Baron Vanboeren had been found that morning close to his hall door on the floor, shot with no less than three bullets through his body, and his pipe in both hands clenched to his blood-soaked breast like a crucifix. The baron is not actually dead. He has been hours insensible. He cannot live; and the doctor says that neither speech nor recollection can return before he dies.

By whose hands, for what cause, in what manner the world had lost that excellent man, no one could say. A great variety of theories prevail on the subject. He had sent the old servant for Pierre la Roche, whom he employed as a messenger, and he had given him at about a quarter to eleven a note addressed to David Arden, Esquire, which was no doubt that which Mr. Arden had received.

Had Heaven decreed that this investigation should come to naught? This blow seemed irremediable.

David Arden, however, had, as I mentioned, official friends, and it struck him that he might through them obtain access to the rooms in which his interviews with the baron had taken place; and that an ingenious and patient artist in plaster might be found who would search out the matrices, or, at worst, piece the fragments of the mask together, and so, in part, perhaps, restore the demolished evidence. It turned out, however, that the destruction of these relics was too complete for any such experiments; and all that now remained was, upon the baron's letter of the evening before, to move in official quarters for a search for those 'matrices' from which it was alleged the masks were taken.

This subject so engrossed his mind, that it was not until after his late dinner that he began once more to think of Monsieur St. Ange, and his resemblance to Mr. Longcluse; and a new suspicion began to envelope those gentlemen in his imagination. A thought struck him, and up got Uncle David, leaving his wine unfinished, and a few minutes more saw him in the telegraph office, writing the following message:—

From Monsieur David Arden, etc. to Monsieur Blount, 5 Manchester Buildings, Westminster, London.

'Pray telegraph immediately to say whether Mr. Longcluse is at his house, Bolton Street, Piccadilly.'

No answer reached him that night; but in the morning he found a telegram dated 11.30 of the previous night, which said—

> Mr. Longcluse is ill at his house at Richmond—better today.

To this promptly he replied—

> See him, if possible, immediately at Richmond, and say how he looks. The surrender of the lease in Crown Alley will be an excuse. See him if there. Ascertain with certainty where. Telegraph immediately.

No answer had reached Uncle David at three o'clock P.M.; he had despatched his message at nine. He was impatient, and walked to the telegraph office to make inquiries, and to grumble. He sent another message in querulous and peremptory laconics. But no answer came till near twelve o'clock, when the following was delivered to him:—

> Yours came while out. Received at 6 p.m. Saw Longcluse at Richmond. Looks seedy. Says he is all right now.

He read this twice or thrice, and lowered the hand whose

fingers held it by the corner, and looked up, taking a turn or two about the room; and he thought what a precious fool he must have appeared to Monsieur St. Ange, and then again, with another view of that gentleman's character, what an escape he had possibly had.

So there was no distraction any longer; and he directed his mind now exclusively upon the distinct object of securing possession of the moulds from which the masks were taken; and for many reasons it is not likely that very much will come of his search.

At Mortlake

Events do not stand still at Mortlake. It is now about four o'clock on a fine autumnal afternoon. Since we last saw her, Alice Arden has not once sought to pass the hall-door. It would not have been possible to do so. No one passed that barrier without a scrutiny, and the aid of the key of the man who kept guard at the door, as closely as ever did the office at the hatch of the debtor's prison. The suite of five rooms upstairs, to which Alice is now strictly confined, is not only comfortable, but luxurious. It had been fitted up for his own use by Sir Reginald years before he exchanged it for those rooms downstairs which, as he grew older, he preferred.

Levi every day visited the house, and took a report of all that was said and planned upstairs, in a *tête-à-tête.* with Phoebe Chiffinch, in the great parlour among the portraits. The girl was true to her young and helpless mistress, and was in her confidence, outwitting the rascally Jew, who every time, by Longcluse's order, bribed her handsomely for the information that was misleading him.

From Phoebe the young lady concealed no pang of her agony. Well was it for her that in their craft they had exchanged the comparatively useless Miss Diaper for this poor girl, on whose apprenticeship to strange ways, and a not very fastidious life, they relied for a clever and unscrupulous instrument. Perhaps she had more than the cunning they reckoned upon. 'But I 'av' took a liking to ye, Miss, and they'll not make nothing of Phoebe Chiffinch.'

Alice was alone in her room, and Phoebe Chiffinch came running up the great staircase singing, and through the intervening suite of rooms, entered that in which her young mistress awaited her return. Her song falters, and dies into a strange ejaculation, as she passes the door.

'The Lord be thanked, that's over and done!' she exclaims, with a face pale from excitement—

'Sit down, Phoebe; you are trembling; you must drink a little water. Are you well?'

'La! quite well, Miss,' said Phoebe, more cheerily, and then burst into tears. She gulped down some of the water which the frightened young lady held to her lips, and recovering quickly, she gets on her feet, and says impatiently—'I'm sure, Miss, I don't know what makes me such a fool; but I'm all right now, Ma'am; and you asked me, the other day, about the big key of the old back-door lock that I showed you, and I said, though it could not open no door, I would find a use for it, yet. So I 'av', Miss.'

'Go on; I recollect perfectly.'

'You remember the bit of parchment I asked you to write the words on yesterday evening, Miss? They was these: 'Passage on the left, from main passage to housekeeper's room,' & etc. Well, I was with Mr. Vargers when he locked that passage up, and it leads to a door in the side of the 'ouse, which it opens into the grounds; and in that houter door he left a key, and only took with him the key of the door at the other end, winch it opens from the 'ousekeeper's passage. So all seemed sure—sure it is, so long as you can't get into that side passage, which it is locked.'

'I understand; go on, Phoebe.'

'Well, Miss, the reason I vallied that key I showed you so much, was because it's as like the key of the side passage as one egg is to another, only it won't turn in the lock. So, as that key I must 'av' , I tacked the bit of parchment you wrote to the 'andle of the other, which the two matches exactly, and I didn't tell you, Miss, thinking what a taking you'd be in, but I went down to try if I could not take it for the right one.'

'It was kind of you not to tell me; go on,' said the young lady.

'Well, Miss, I 'ad the key in my pocket, ready to change; and I knew well how 'twould be, if I was found out—I'd get the sack, or be locked up 'ere myself, more likely, and no more chances for you. Mr. Vargers was in the room—the porter's room they calls it now and—in I goes. I did not see no one there, but Vargers and he was lookin' sly, I thought, and him and Mr. Boult has been talking me over, I fancy, and they don't quite trust me. So I began to talk, wheedling him the best I could to let me go into town for an hour; 'twas only for talk, for well I knew I shouldn't get to go; but nothing but chaff did he answer. And then, says I, is Mr. Levice come yet, and he said, he is, but he has a second key of the back door and he may 'av' let himself hout.

'Well, I says, thinking to make Vargers jealous, he's a werry pleasant gentleman, a bit too pleasant for me, and I'm a-going to the kitchen, and I'd rayther he wastnt there, smoking as he often does, and talking nonsense, when I'm in it. There's others that's nicer, to my fancy, than him—so, jest you go and see, and I'll take care of heverything 'ere till you come back—and don't you be a minute. There was the keys, lying along the chimney-piece, at my left, and the big table in front, and nothing to hinder me from changing mine for his, but Vargers' eye over me. Little I thought he'd 'av' bin so ready to do as I said. But he smiled to himself-like, and he said he'd go and see. So away he went; and I listens at the door till I heard his foot go on the tiles of the passage that goes down by the 'ousekeeper's room, and the billiard-room, to the kitchen; and then on tiptoe, as quick as light, I goes to the chimney-piece, and without a sound, I takes the very key I wanted in my fingers, and drops it into my pocket, but putting down the other in its place, I knocked down the big leaden hink-bottle, and didn't it make a bang on the floor—and a terrible hoarse voice roars out from the tother side of the table— "What the devil are you doing there, huzzy?"

'Saving your presence, Miss; and up gets Mr. Boult, only half awake, looking as mad as Bedlam, and I thought I would have fainted away! Who'd 'av' fancied he was in the room? He had his 'ead on the table, and the cloak over it, and I think, when they 'eard me a-coming downstairs, they agreed he should 'ide hisself so, to catch me, while Vargers would leave the room, to try if I would meddle with the keys, or the like—and while Mr. Boult was foxing, he fell asleep in right earnest. Warn't it a joke, Miss? So I brazent it hout, Miss, the best I could, and I threatened to complain to Mr. Levi, and said I'd stay no longer, to be talked to, that way, by sich as he. And Boult could not tell Vargers he was asleep, and so I saw him count over the keys, and up I ran, singing.'

By this time the girl was on her knees, concealing the key between the beds, with the others.

'Thank God, Phoebe, you have got it! But, oh! all that is before us still!'

'Yes, there's work enough, Miss. I'll not be so frightened no more. Tom Chiffinch, that beat the Finchley pet, after ninety good rounds, was my brother, and I won't show nothing but pluck, Miss, from this out—you'll see.'

Alice had proposed writing to summon her friends to her aid. But Phoebe protested against that extremely perilous measure. Her friends were away from London; who could say where? And she believed that the attempt to post the letters would miscarry, and that they were certain to fall into the hands of their jailors. She insisted that Alice should rely on the simple plan of escape from Mortlake.

Martha Tansey, it is true, was anxious. She wondered how it was that she had not once heard from her young mistress since her journey to Yorkshire. And a passage in a letter which had reached her, from the old servant, at David Arden's town house, who had been mystified by Sir Richard, perplexed and alarmed her further, by inquiring how Miss Alice looked, and whether she had been knocked up by the journey to Arden on Wednesday.

So matters stood.

Each evening Mr. Levi was in attendance, and this day, according to rule, she went down to the grand old dining-room.

'How'sh Miss Chiffinch?' said the little Jew, advancing to meet her; 'how'sh her grashe the duchess, in the top o' the houshe? Ish my Lady Mount-garret ash proud ash ever?'

'Well, I do think, Mr. Levice, there's a great change; she's bin growing better the last two days, and she's got a letter last night that's seemed to please her.'

'Wha'at letter?'

'The letter you gave me last night for her.'

'O-oh! Ah! I wonder—eh? Do you happen to know what wa'azh in that ere letter?' he asked, in an insinuating whisper.

'Not I, Mr. Levice. She don't trust me not as far as you'd throw a bull by the tail. You might 'av' managed that better. You must 'a frightened her some way about me. I try to be agreeable all I can, but she won't a-look at me.'

'Well, I don't want to know, *I'm* sure. Did she talk of going out of doors since?'

'No; there's a frost in the hair still, and she says till that's gone she won't stir out.'

'That frost will last a bit, I guess. Any more newshe?'

'Nothing.'

'Wait a minute 'ere,' said Mr. Levi, and he went into the room beyond this, where she knew there were writing materials.

She waited some time, and at length took the liberty of sitting down. She was kept a good while longer. The sun went down; the drowsy crimson that heralds night overspread the sky. She coughed; several fits of coughing she tried at short intervals. Had Mr. Levice, as she called him, forgotten her? He came out at length in the twilight.

'Shtay you 'ere a few minutes more,' said that gentleman, as he walked thoughtfully through the room and paused. 'You wazh asking yesterday where izh Sir Richard Arden. Well, hezh took hishelf off to Harden in Yorkshire, and he'll not be 'ome again for a week.'

Having delivered this piece of intelligence, he nodded, and slowly went to the hall, and closed the door carefully as he left the room. She followed to the door and listened. There was plainly a little fuss going on in the hall. She heard feet in motion, and low talking. She was curious and would have peeped, but the door was secured on the outside. The twilight had deepened, and for the first time she saw that a ray of candle-light came through the key-hole from the inner room. She opened the door softly, and saw a gentleman writing at the table. He was quite alone. He turned, and rose: a tall, slight gentleman, with a singular countenance that startled her.

'You are Phoebe Chiffinch,' said a deep, clear voice, sternly, as the gentleman pointed towards her with the plume end of the pen he held in his fingers. 'I am Mr. Longcluse. It is I who have sent you two pounds each day by Levi. I hear you have got it all right?'

The girl curtseyed, and said 'Yes, Sir,' at the second effort, for she was startled. He had taken out and opened his pocketbook.

'Here are *ten* pounds,' and he handed her a rustling new note by the corner. 'I'll treat you liberally, but you must speak truth, and do exactly as you are ordered by Levi.' She curtseyed again. There was something in that gentleman that frightened her awfully.

'If you do so, I mean to give you a hundred pounds when this business is over. I have paid you as my servant, and if you deceive me I'll punish you; and there are two or three little things they complain of at the 'Guy of Warwick', and' (he swore a hard oath) 'you shall hear of them if you do.'

She curtseyed, and felt, not angry, as she would if any one else had said it, but frightened, for Mr. Longcluse's was a name of power at Mortlake.

'You gave Miss Arden a letter last night. You know what was in it?'

'Yes, Sir.'

'What was it?'

'An offer of marriage from you, Sir.'

'Yes: how do you know that?'

'She told me, please, Sir.'

'How did she take it? Come, don't be afraid.'

'I'd say it pleased her well, Sir.'

He looked at her in much surprise, and was silent for a time.

He repeated his question, and receiving a similar answer, reflected on it.

'Yes; it *is* the best way out of her troubles; she begins to see that,' he said, with a strange smile.

He walked to the chimney-piece, and leaned on it; and forgot the presence of Phoebe. She was too much in awe to make any sign. Turning he saw her, suddenly.

'You will receive some directions from Mr. Levi; take care you understand and execute them.'

He touched the bell, and Levi opened the door; and she and that person walked together to the foot of the stair, where in a low tone they talked.

The Crisis

When Phoebe Chiffinch returned to Alice's room, it was about ten o'clock; a brilliant moon was shining on the old trees, and throwing their shadows on the misty grass. The landscape from these upper windows was sad and beautiful, and above the distant trees that were softened by the haze of night rose the silvery spire of the old church, in whose vault her father sleeps with a cold brain, thinking no more of mortgages and writs.

Alice had been wondering what had detained her so long, and by the time she arrived had become very much alarmed.

Relieved when she entered, she was again struck with fear when Phoebe Chiffinch had come near enough to enable her to see her face. She was pale, and with her eyes fixed on her, raised her finger in warning, and then glanced at the door which she had just closed.

Her young mistress got up and approached her, also growing pale, for she perceived that danger was at the door.

'I wish there was bolts to these doors. They've got other keys.

Never mind; I know it all know,' she whispered, as she walked softly up to the end of the room farthest from the door. 'I said I'd stand by you, my lady; don't you lose heart. They're coming here in about a hour.'

'For God's sake, what is it?' said Alice faintly, her eyes gazing wider and wider, and her very lips growing white.

'There's work before us, my lady, and there must be no fooling,' said the girl, a little sternly. 'Mr. Levi, please, has told me a deal, and all they expect from me, the villains. Are you strong enough to take your part in it, Miss? If not, best be quiet; best for both.'

'Yes; quite strong, Phoebe. Are we to leave this?'

'I hope, Miss. We can but try.'

'There's light, Phoebe,' she said, glancing with a shiver from the window. 'It's a bright night.'

'I wish 'twas darker; but mind you what I say. Longcluse is to be here in a hour. Your brother's coming, God help you! and that little limb o' Satan, that black-eyed, black-nailed, dirty little Jew, Levice! They're not in town, they're out together near this, where a man is to meet them with writings. There's a licence got, Christie Vargers saw Mr. Longcluse showing it to your brother, Sir Richard; and I daren't tell Vargers that I'm for you. He'd never do nothing to vex Mr. Levice, he daren't. There's a parson here, a rum 'un, you may be sure. I think I know something about him; Vargers does. He's in the room now, only one away from this, next the stair head, and Vargers is put to keep the door in the same room. All the doors along, from one room to t'other, is open, from this to the stairs, except the last, which Vargers has the key of it; and all the doors opening from the rooms to the gallery is locked, so you can't get out o' this 'ere without passing through the one where parson is, and Mr. Vargers, please.'

'I'll speak to the clergyman,' whispered Alice, extending her hands towards the far door; 'God be thanked, there's one good man here, and he'll save me!'

'*La*, bless you child! why that parson had his two pen'orth long ago, and spends half his nights in the lock-up.'

'I don't understand, Phoebe.'

'He had two years. He's bin in jail, Miss, Vargers says, as often as he has fingers and toes: and he's at his brandy and water as I came through, with his feet on the fender, and his pipe in his mouth. He's here to marry you, please 'm, to Mr Longcluse, and *there's* all the good *he'll* do you; and your brother will give you away, Miss, and Levice and Vargers for witnesses, and me I dessay. It's every bit harranged, and they don't care the rinsing of a tumbler what you say or do; for through with it, slicks, they'll go, and say 'twas all right, in spite of all you can do; and who is there to make a row about it? Not you, after all's done.'

'We must get away! I'll lose my life, or I'll escape!'

Phoebe looked at her in silence. I think she was measuring her strength, and her nerve, for the undertaking.

'Well, 'm, it's time it was begun. The time is come. Here's your cloak, Miss, I'll tie a handkerchief over my head, if we get out; and here's the three keys, betwixt the bed and the mattress.'

After a moment's search on her knees, she produced them.

'The big one and this I'll keep, and you'll manage this other, please; take it in your right hand—you must use it first. It opens the far door of the room where Vargers is, and if you get through, you'll be at the stair-head then. Don't you come in after me, till you see I have Vargers engaged another way. Go through as light as a bird flies, and take the key out of the door, at the other end, when you unlock it; and close it softly, else he'll see it, and have the house about our ears; and you know the big window at the drawing-room lobby; wait in the hollow of that window till I come. Do you understand, please, Miss?'

Alice did perfectly.

'Hish-sh!' said the maid, with a prolonged caution.

A dead silence followed; for a minute—several minutes neither seemed to breathe.

Phoebe whispered at length—

'*Now,* Miss, are you ready?'

'Yes,' she whispered, and her heart beat for a moment as if it would suffocate her, and then was still; an icy chill stole over her, and as on tiptoe she followed Phoebe, she felt as if she glided without weight or contact, like a spirit.

Through a dark room they passed, very softly, first, a little light under the door showed that there were candles in the next. They halted and listened. Phoebe opened the door and entered.

Standing back in the shadow, Alice saw the room and the people in it, distinctly. The parson was not the sort of contraband clergyman she had fancied, by any means, but a thin hectic man of some four-and-thirty years, only looking a little dazed by brandy and water, and far gone in consumption. Handsome thin features, and a suit of seedy black, and a white choker, indicated that lost gentleman, who was crying silently as he smoked his pipe, I daresay a little bit tipsy, gazing into the fire, with his fatal brandy and water at his elbow.

'Eh! Mr. Vargers, smoking after *all* I said to you!' murmured Miss Phoebe severely, advancing toward her round-shouldered sweetheart, with her finger raised.

Mr. Vargers replied pleasantly; and as this tender 'chaff' flew lightly between the interlocutors, the parson looked still into the fire, hearing nothing of their play and banter, but sunk deep in the hell of his sorrowful memory.

As Phoebe talked on, Vargers grew agreeable and tender, and in about three minutes after her own entrance, she saw with a thrill, imperfectly, just with the 'corner of her eye,' something pass behind them swiftly toward the outer door. The crisis, then, had come. For a moment there seemed a sudden light before her eyes, and then a dark mist; in another she recovered herself.

Vargers stood up suddenly.

'Hullo! what's gone with the door there?' said he, sternly ending their banter.

If he had been looking on her with an eye of suspicion, he might have seen her colour change. But Phoebe was quick-witted and prompt, and saying, in hushed tones—

'Well, dear, ain't I a fool, leaving the lady's door open? Look ye, now, Mr. Vargers, she's lying fast asleep on her bed; and that's the reason I took courage to come here and ask a favour. But

I'd raything you'd lock her door, for if she waked and missed me she'd be out here, and all the fat in the fire.'

'I dessay you're right, Miss,' said he, with a more businesslike gallantry; and as he shut the door and fumbled in his pocket for the key, she stole a look over her shoulder.

The prisoner had got through, and the door at the other end was closed.

With a secret shudder, she thanked God in her heart, while with a laugh she slapped Mr. Vargers' lusty shoulder, and said wheedlingly, 'And now for the favour, Mr. Vargers: you must let me down to the kitchen for five minutes.'

A little more banter and sparring followed, which ended in Vargers kissing her in spite of the usual squall and protest; and on his essaying to let her out, and finding the door unlocked, he swore that it was well she asked, as he'd 'av' got it hot and heavy for forgetting to lock it, when the 'swells' came up. The door closed upon her: so far the enterprise was successful.

She stood at the head of the stairs; she went down a few steps, and listened; then cautiously she descended. The moon shone resplendent through the great window at the landing below the drawing-room. It was that at which Uncle David had paused to listen to the minstrelsy of Mr. Longcluse.

Here in that flood of white light stands Alice Arden, like a statue of horror. The girl, without saying a word, takes her by the cold hand, and leads her quickly down to the arch that opens on the hall.

Just as they reached this point, the door of the room, at the right of the hall door, occupied by Mr. Boult, who did duty as porter, opens, and stepping out with a candle in his hand, he calls in a savage tone—

'What's the row?'

Phoebe pushed Alice's hand in the direction of the passage that leads to the housekeeper's room. For a moment the young lady stands irresolute. Her presence of mind returns. She noiselessly takes the hint, and enters the corridor; Phoebe advances to answer his challenge.

'Well, Mr. Boult, and what *is* the row, pray?' she pertly inquires, walking up to that gentleman, who eyes her sulkily, raising his candle, and displaying as he does so a big patch of red on each cheek-bone, indicative of the brandy, of which he smells potently.

'What's the row?—*you're* the row! What brings you down here, Miss Chivvige?'

'My legs! There's your answer, you cross boy.' She laughed wheedlingly.

'Then walk you up again, and be d——d.'

'On! Mr. Boult.'

'P! Miss Phibbie.'

Mr. Boult was speaking thick, and plainly was in no mood to stand nonsense.

'Now Mr. Boult, where's the good of making yourself disagreeable?'

'Look at this 'ere,' he replied, grimly holding a mighty watch, of some white metal, under her eyes—'you know your clock as well as me, Miss Chavvinge. The gentlemen will be in this 'ere awl in twenty minutes.'

'All the more need to be quick, Mr. Boult, Sir, and why will you keep me 'ere talking?' she replies.

'You'll go up them 'ere stairs, young 'oman; you'll not put a foot in the kitchen tonight,' he says more doggedly.

'Well, we'll see how it will be when they comes and I tells 'em—'Please, gentlemen, the young lady, which you told me most particular to humour her in everything she might call for, wished a cup of tea, which I went down, having locked her door first, which here is the key of it,' and she held it up for the admiration of Mr. Boult, 'which I consider it the most importantest key in the 'ouse; and though the young lady, she lay on her bed a-gasping, poor thing, for her cup of tea, Mr. Boult stopt me in the awl, and swore she shouldn't have a drop, which I could not get it, and went hup again, for he smelt all over of brandy, and spoke so wiolent, I daren't do as you desired.'

'I don't smell of brandy; no, I don't; do I?' he says, appealing to an imaginary audience. 'And I don't want to stop you, if so be the case is so. But you'll come to this door and report yourself in five minute's time, or I'll tell 'em there's no good keepin' me 'ere no longer I don't want no quarrellin' nor disputin', only I'll do my dooty, and I'm not afraid of man, woman, or child!'

With which magnanimous sentiment he turned on his clumsy heel, and entered his apartment again.

In a moment more Phoebe and Alice were at the door which admits to a passage leading literally to the side of the house. This door Phoebe softly unlocks, and when they had entered, locks again on the inside. They stood now on the passage leading to a side door, to which a few paces brought them. She opens it. The cold night air enters, and they step out upon the grass. She locks the door behind them, and throws the key among the nettles that grew in a thick grove at her right.

'Hold my hand, my lady; it's near done now,' she whispers almost fiercely; and having listened for a few seconds, and looked up to see if any light appeared in the windows, she ventures, with a beating heart, from under the deep shadow of the gables, into the bright broad moonlight, and with light steps together they speed across the grass, and reach the cover of a long grove of tall trees and underwood. All is silent here.

Soon a distant shouting brings them to a terrible standstill. Breathlessly Phoebe listens. No; it was not from the house. They resume their flight.

Now under the ivy-laden branches of a tall old tree an owl startles them with its shriek.

As Alice stares around her, when they stop in such momentary alarm, how strange the scene looks! How immense and gloomy the trees about them! How black their limbs stretch across the moon-lit sky! How chill and wild the moonlight spreads over the undulating sward! What a spectral and exaggerated shape all things take in her scared and over-excited gaze!

Now they are approaching the long row of noble beeches that line the boundary of Mortlake. The ivy-bowered wall is near them, and the screen of gigantic hollies that guard the lonely postern through which Phoebe has shrewdly chosen to direct their escape.

Thank God! they are at it. In her hand she holds the key, which shines in the moon-beams.

Hush! what is this? Voices close to the door! Step back behind the holly clump, for your lives, quickly! A key grinds in the lock; the bolt works rustily; the door opens, and tall Mr. Longcluse enters, with every sinister line and shadow of his pale face marked with a death-like sternness, in the moonlight Mr. Levi enters almost beside him; how white his big eyeball gleam, as he steps in under the same cold light! Who next?

Her *brother!* Oh, God! The mad impulse to throw he arms about his neck, and shriek her wild appeal to his manhood, courage, love, and stake all on that momentary frenzy!

As this group halts in silence, while Sir Richard locks the door, the Jew directs his big dark eyes, as she thinks, right upon Phoebe Chiffinch, who stands in the shadow, and is therefore, she saintly hopes, not visible behind the screen of glittering leaves. Her eyes, nevertheless, meet his. He advances his head a little, with more than his usual prying malignity, she thinks. Her heart flutters, and sinks. She is on the point of stepping from her shelter and surrendering. With his cane he strikes at the leaves, aiming, I daresay, at a moth, for nothing is quite below his notice, and he likes smashing even a fly. In this case, having hit or missed it, he turns his fiery eyes, to the infinite relief of the girl, another way.

The three men who have thus stept into the grounds of Mortlake don't utter a word as they stand there. They now recommence their walk toward the house.

Phoebe Chiffinch, breathless, is holding Alice Arden's wrist with a firm grasp. As they brush the holly-leaves, in passing, the very sprays that touch the dresses of the scared girls are stirring. The pale group drifts by in silence. They have each something to meditate on. They are not garrulous. On they walk, like three shadows. The distance widens, the shapes grow fainter.

'They'll soon be at the house, Ma'am, and wild work then.

You'll do something for poor Vargers? Well, time enough! You must not lose heart now, my lady. You're all right, if you keep up for ten minutes longer. You don't feel faint-like! Good lawk, Ma'am! rouse up.'

'I'm better, Phoebe; I'm quite well again. Come on—come on!'

Carefully, to make as little noise as possible she turned the key in the lock, and they found themselves in a narrow lane running by the wall, and under the trees of Mortlake.

'Which way?'

'Not toward the 'Guy of Warwick'. They'll soon be in chase of us, and that is the way they'll take. 'Twould never do. Come away, my lady; it won't be long till we meet a cab or something to fetch us where you please. Lean on me. I wish we were away from this wall. What way do you mean to go?'

'To my Uncle David's house.'

And having exchanged these words, they pursued their way side by side, for a time, in silence.

Pursuit

Arrived at Mortlake, when Mr. Longcluse had discovered with certainty the flight of Alice Arden, his first thought was that Sir Richard had betrayed him. There was a momentary paroxysm of insane violence, in which, if he could only have discovered that he was the accomplice of Alice's escape, I think he would have killed him.

It subsided. How could Alice Arden have possessed such an influence over this man, who seemed to hate her? He sat down, and placed his hand to his broad, pale forehead, his dark eyes glaring on the floor, in what seemed an intensity of thought and passion. He was seized with a violent trembling fit. It lasted only for a few minutes. I sometimes think he loved that girl desperately, and would have made her an idolatrous husband.

He walked twice or thrice up and down the great parlour in which they sat, and then with cold malignity said to Sir Richard—

'But for you she would have married me; but for you I should have secured her now. *Consider,* how shall I settle with you?'

'Settle how you will—do what you will. I swear (and he did swear hard enough, if an oath could do it, to satisfy any man) I've had *nothing* to do it. I've never had a hint that she meditated leaving this place. I can't conceive how it was done, nor who managed it, and I know no more than you do where she is gone.' And he clenched his vehement disclaimer with an imprecation.

Longcluse was silent for a minute.

'She has gone, I assume, to David Arden's house,' he said, looking down. 'There is no other house to receive her in town, and she does not know that he is away still. She knows that Lady May, and other friends, have gone. She's *there.* The will makes you, colourably, her guardian. You shall claim the custody of her person. We'll go there, and remove her.'

Old Sir Reginald's will, I may remark, had been made years before, when Richard was not twenty-two, and Alice little more than a child, and the baronet and his son good friends.

He stalked out. At the steps was his trap, which was there to take Levi into town. That gentleman, I need not say, he did not treat with much ceremony. He mounted, and Sir Richard Arden beside him; and, leaving the Jew to shift for himself, he drove at a furious pace down the avenue. The porter placed there by Longcluse, of course, opened the gate instantaneously at his call. Outside stood a cab, with a trunk on it. An old woman at the lodge-window, knocking and clamouring, sought admission.

'Let no one in,' said Longcluse sternly to the man, who locked the iron gate on their passing out.

'Hallo! What brings *her* here? That's the old housekeeper!' said Longcluse, pulling up suddenly.

It was quite true. Her growing uneasiness about Alice had recalled the old woman from the North. Martha Tansey, who had heard the clang of the gate and the sound of wheels and hoofs, turned about and came to the side of the tax-cart, over which Longcluse was leaning. In the brilliant moonlight, on the white road, the branches cast a network of black shadow. A patch of light fell clear on the side of the trap, and on Longcluse's ungloved hand as he leaned on it.

'Here am I, Martha Tansey, has lived fifty year wi' the family, and what for am I shut out of Mortlake now?' she demanded, with stern audacity.

A sudden change, however, came over her countenance, which contracted in horror, and her old eyes opened wide and white as she gazed on the back of Longcluse's hand, on which was a peculiar star-shaped scar. She drew back with a low sound, like the growl of a wicked old cat; it rose gradually to such a yell and a cry to God as made Richard's blood run cold, and lifting her hand toward her temple, waveringly, the old woman staggered back, and fell in a faint on the road.

Longcluse jumped down and hammered at the window. 'Hallo!' he cried to the man, 'send one of your people with this old woman; she's ill. Let her go in that cab to Sir Richard Arden's house in town; you know it.' And he cried to the cabman, 'Lift her in, will you?'

And having done his devoir thus by the old woman, he springs again into his tax-cart, snatches the reins from Sir Richard, and drives on at a savage pace for town.

Longcluse threw the reins to Sir Richard when they reached David Arden's house, and himself thundered at the door.

They had searched Mortlake House for Alice, and that vain quest had not wasted more than half-an-hour. He rightly conjectured that, if Alice had fled to David Arden's house, some of the servants who received her must be still on the alert. The door is opened promptly by an elderly servant woman.

'Sir Richard Arden is at the door, and he wants to know whether his sister, Miss Arden, has arrived here from Mortlake.'

'Yes, Sir; she's upstairs; but not by no means well, Sir.'

Longcluse stepped in, to secure a footing, and beckoning excitedly to Sir Richard, called, 'Come in; all right. Don't mind the horse; it will take its chance.' He walked impatiently to the foot of the stairs, and turned again toward the street door.

At this moment, and before Sir Richard had time to come

in, there come swarming out of David Arden's study, most unexpectedly, nearly a dozen men, more than half of whom are in the garb of gentlemen, and some three of them police. Uncle David himself, in deep conversation with two gentlemen, one of whom is placing in his breast-pocket a paper which he has just folded, leads the way into the hall.

As they there stand for a minute under the lamp, Mr. Longcluse, gazing at him sternly from the stair, caught his eye. Old David Arden stepped back a little, growing pale, with a sudden frown.

'Oh! Mr. Arden?' says Longcluse, advancing as if he had come in search of him.

'That's enough, Sir,' cries Mr. Arden, extending his hand peremptorily toward him; and he adds, with a glance at the constables, 'There's the man. That is Walter Longcluse.'

Longcluse glances over his shoulder, and then grimly at the group before him, and gathered himself as if for a struggle; next moment he walks forward frankly, and asks, 'What is meaning of all this?'

'A warrant, Sir,' answers the foremost policeman, clutching him by the collar.

'No use, Sir, making a row,' expostulates the next, also catching him by the collar and arm.

'Mr. Arden, can you explain this?' says Mr. Longcluse coolly.

'You may as well give in quiet,' says the third policeman, producing the warrant. 'A warrant for murder. Walter Longcluse, *alias* Yelland Mace, I arrest you in the Queen's name.'

'There's a magistrate here? Oh! yes, I see. How d'ye do, Mr. Harman? My name is Longcluse, as you know. The name Mays, or any other *alias,* you'll not insult me by applying to me, if you please. Of course this is obvious and utter trumpery. Are there informations, or what the devil is it?'

'They have just been sworn before me, Sir,' answered the magistrate, who was a little man, with a wave of his hand, and his head high.

'Well, really! don't you *see* the absurdity? Upon my soul! It *is* really *too* ridiculous! You won't inconvenience me, of course, unnecessarily. My own recognisance, I suppose, will do?'

'Can't entertain your application; quite out of the question,' said his worship, with his hands in his pockets, rising slightly on his toes, and descending on his heels, as he delivered this sentence with a stoical shake of his head.

'You'll send for my attorney, of course? I'm not to be humbugged, you know.'

'I must tell you, Mr. Longcluse, I can't listen to such language,' observes Mr. Harman sublimely.

'If you have informations, they are the dreams of a madman. I don't blame any one here. I say, policeman, you need not hold me quite so hard. I only say, joke or earnest, I can't make head or tail of it; and there's not a man in London who won't be shocked to hear how I've been treated. Once more, Mr. Harman, I tender bail, any amount. It's too ridiculous. You can't really have a difficulty.'

'The informations are very strong, Sir, and the offence, you know as well as I do, Mr. Longcluse, is not bailable.'

Mr. Longcluse shrugged, and laughed gently.

'I may have a cab or something? My trap's at the door. It's not solemn enough, eh, Mr. Harman? Will you tell one of your fellows to pick up a cab? Perhaps, Mr. Arden, you'll allow me a chair to sit down upon?'

'You can sit in the study, if you please,' says David Arden.

And Longcluse enters the room with the police about him, while the servant goes to look for a cab. Sir Richard Arden, you may be sure, was not there. He saw that something was wrong, and he had got away to his own house. On arriving there, he sent to make inquiry, cautiously, at his uncle's, and thus learned the truth.

Standing at the window, he saw his messenger return, let him in himself, and then considered, as well as a man in so critical and terrifying a situation can, the wisest course for him to adopt. The simple one of flight he ultimately resolved on. He knew that Longcluse had still two executions against him, on which, at any moment, he might arrest him. He knew that he might launch at him, at any moment, the thunderbolt which would blast him. He must wait, however, until the morning had confirmed the news; that certain, he dared not act.

With a cold and fearless bearing, Longcluse had by this time entered the dreadful door of a prison. His attorney was with him nearly the entire night.

David Arden, as he promised, had dictated to him in outline the awful case he had massed against his client.

'I don't want any man taken by surprise or at disadvantage; I simply wish for truth,' said he.

A copy of the written statement of Paul Davies, whatever it was worth, duly witnessed, was already in his hands; the sworn depositions of the same person, made in his last illness, were also there. There were also the sworn depositions of Vanboeren, who *had,* after all, recovered speech and recollection; and a deposition, besides, very unexpected, of old Martha Tansey, who swore distinctly to the scar, a very peculiar mark indeed, on the back of his left hand. This the old woman had recognised with horror, at a moment so similar, as the scar, long forgotten, which she had for a terrible moment seen on the hand of Yelland Mace, as he clutched the rail of the gig while engaged in the murder.

The plaster masks, which figured in the affidavits of Vanboeren, and of David Arden, were recast from the moulds, and made an effectual identification, corroborated, in a measure, by Mr. Plumes' silhouette of Yelland Mace.

Other surviving witnesses had also turned up, who had deposed when the murder of Harry Arden was a recent event. The whole case was, in the eyes of the attorney, a very awful one. Mr. Longcluse's counsel was called up, like a physician whose patient is in extremis, at dead of night, and had a talk with the attorney, and kept his notes to ponder over.

As early as prison rules would permit, he was with Mr. Longcluse, where the attorney awaited him.

Mr. Blinkinsop looked very gloomy.

'Do you despair?' asked Mr. Longcluse sharply, after a long

disquisition.

'Let me ask you one question, Mr. Longcluse. You have, before I ask it, I assume, implicit confidence in us; am I right?'

'Certainly—implicit.'

'If you are innocent, we might venture on a line of defence which may possibly break down the case for the Crown. If you are guilty, that line would be fatal.' He hesitated, and looked at Mr. Longcluse.

'I know such a question has been asked in like circumstances, and I have no hesitation in telling you that I am *not* innocent. Assume my guilt.'

The attorney, who had been drumming a little tattoo on the table, watches Longcluse earnestly as he speaks, suspending his tune, now lowers his eyes to the table, and resumed his drumming slowly with a very dismal countenance. He had been talking over the chances with this eminent counsel, Mr. Blinkinsop, Q.C., and he knew what his opinion would now be.

'One effect of a judgement in this case is forfeiture?' inquired Mr. Longcluse.

'Yes,' answered counsel.

'Everything goes to the Crown, eh?'

'Yes; clearly.'

'Well, I have neither wife nor children. I need not care; but suppose I make my will now; that's a good will, ain't it, between this and judgment, if things should go wrong?'

'Certainly,' said Mr. Blinkinsop. 'No judgment no forfeiture.'

'And now, Doctor, don't be afraid; tell me truly, shall I *do?*' said Mr. Longcluse, leaning back, and looking darkly and steadily in his face.

'It is a nasty case.'

'Don't be afraid, I say. I should like to know, are the chances two to one against me?'

'I'm afraid they are.'

'Ten to one? Pray say what you think.'

'Well, I think so.'

Mr. Longcluse grew paler. They were all three silent. After

about a minute, he said, in a very low tone,—

'You don't think I have a chance? Don't mislead me.'

'It is very gloomy.'

Mr. Longcluse pressed his hand to his mouth. There was a silence. Perhaps he wished to hide some nervous movement there. He stood up, walked about a little, and then stood by Mr. Blinkinsop's chair, with his fingers on the back of it.

'We must make a great fight of this,' said Mr. Longcluse suddenly. 'We'll fight it hard; we must win it. We *shall* win it, by——'

And after a short pause, he added gently,—

'That will do. I think I'll rest now; more, perhaps, another time. Goodbye.'

As they left the room, he signed to the attorney to stay.

'I have something for you—a word or two.'

The attorney turned back, and they remained closeted for a time.

Conclusion

Mr Richard Arden had learned how matters were with Mr. Longcluse. He hesitated. Flight might provoke action of the kind for which there seemed no longer a motive.

In an agony of dubitation, as the day wore on, he was interrupted. Mr. Rooke, Mr. Longcluse's attorney, had called. There was no good in shirking a meeting. He was shown in.

'This is for you, Sir Richard,' said Mr. Rooke, presenting a large letter. 'Mr. Longcluse wrote it about three hours ago, and requested me to place it in your own hand, as I now do.'

'It is not any *legal* paper——' began Sir Richard.

'I haven't an idea,' answered he. 'He gave it to me thus. I had some things to do for him afterwards, and a call to make, at his desire, at Mr. David Arden's. When I got home I was sent for again. I suppose you heard the news?'

'No; what is it?'

'Oh, dear, really! They have heard it some time at Mr. Arden's. You didn't hear about Mr. Longcluse?'

'No, nothing, excepting what we all know—his arrest.'

The attorney's countenance darkened, and he said, dropping his voice as low as he would have given a message in church—

'Oh, poor gentleman! he died today. Some kind of fit, I believe; he's gone!'

Then Mr. Rooke went into particulars, so far as he knew them, and mentioned that the coroner's inquest would be held that afternoon; and so he departed.

Unmixed satisfaction accompanied the hearing of this news in Sir Richard's mind. But with reflection came the terrifying question, 'Has Levi got hold of that instrument of torture and ruin—the forged signature?'

In this new horror he saw the envelope which Rooke had landed to him, upon the table. He opened it, and saw the forged deed. Written across it, in Longcluse's hand, were the words—

Paid by W. Longcluse before due.

W. Longcluse.

That day's date was added.

So the evidence of his guilt was no longer in the hands of a stranger, and Sir Richard Arden was saved.

David Arden had already received under like circumstances, and by the same hand, two papers of immense importance. The first written in Rooke's hand and duly witnessed, was a very short will, signed by the testator, Walter Longcluse, and leaving his enormous wealth absolutely to David Arden. The second was a letter which attached a trust to this bequest. The letter said—

> I am the son of Edwin Raikes, your cousin. He had cast me off for my vices, when I committed the crime, not intended to have amounted to murder. It was Harry Arden's determined resistance and my danger that cost him his life. I did kill Lebas. I could not help it. He was a fool, and might have ruined me; and that villain, Vanboeren, has spoken truth for once.
>
> I meant to set up the Arden family in my person. I should have taken the name. My father relented on his deathbed, and left me his money. I went to New York, and received

it. I made a new start in life. On the *Bourse* in Paris, and in Vienna, I made a fortune by speculation; I improved it in London. You may take it all by my will. Do with half the interest as you please, during your lifetime. The other half pay to Miss Alice Arden, and the entire capital you are to secure to her on your death.

I had taken assignments of all the mortgages affecting the Arden estates. They must go to Miss Arden, and be secured unalienably to her.

My life has been arduous and direful. That miserable crime hung over me, and its dangers impeded me at every turn. You have played your game well, but with all the odds of the position in your favour. I am tired, beaten. The match is over, and you may rise now and say Checkmate.

Walter Longcluse.

That Longcluse had committed suicide, of course I can have no doubt. It must have been effected by some unusually subtle poison. The postmortem examination failed to discover its presence. But there was found in his desk a curious paper, in French, published about five months before, upon certain vegetable poisons, whose presence in the system no chemical test detects, and no external trace records. This paper was noted here and there on the margin, and had been obviously carefully read. Any of these tinctures he could without much trouble have procured from Paris. But no distinct light was ever thrown upon this inquiry.

In a small and lonely house, tenanted by Longcluse, in the then less crowded region of Richmond, were found proofs, no longer needed, of Longcluse's identity, both with the horseman who had met Paul Davies on Hampstead Heath, and the person who crossed the Channel from Southampton with David Arden, and afterwards met him in the streets of Paris, as we have seen. There he had been watching his movements, and traced him, with dreadful suspicion, to the house of Vanboeren. The turn of a die had determined the fate of David Arden that night. Longcluse had afterwards watched and seized an opportunity of entering Vanboeren's house. He knew that the baron expected the return of his messenger, rang the bell, and was admitted. The old servant had gone to her bed, and was far away in that vast house.

Longcluse would have stabbed him, but the baron recognised him, and sprang back with a yell. Instantly Longcluse had used his revolver; but before he could make assurance doubly sure, his quick ear detected a step outside. He then made his exit through a window into a deserted lane at the side of the house, and had not lost a moment in commencing his flight for London.

With respect to the murder of Lebas, the letter of Longcluse pretty nearly explains it. That unlucky Frenchman had attended him *through* his recovery under the hands of Vanboeren; and Longcluse feared to trust, as it now might turn out, his life, in his giddy keeping. Of course, Lebas had no idea of the nature of his crime, or that in England was the scene of its perpetration. Longcluse had made up his mind promptly on the night of the billiard-match played in the Saloon Tavern. When every eye was fixed upon the balls, he and Lebas met, as they had ultimately agreed, in the smoking-room.

A momentary meeting it was to have been. The dagger which he placed in his keeping, Longcluse plunged into his heart. In the stream of blood that instantaneously flowed from the wound Longcluse stepped, and made one distinct impression of his boot-sole on the boards. A tracing of this Paul Davies had made, and had got the signatures of two or three respectable Londoners before the room filled, attesting its accuracy, he affecting, while he did so, to be a member of the detective police, from which body, for a piece of *over*-cleverness, he had been only a few weeks before dismissed.

Having made his tracing, he obscured the blood-mark on the floor.

The opportunity of distinguishing himself at his old craft, to the prejudice of the force, whom he would have liked to mortify, while earning, perhaps, his own restoration, was his first object. The delicacy of the shape of the boot struck him next. He then remembered having seen Longcluse—and his was the only eye that observed him—pass swiftly from the passage leading to the smoking-room at the beginning of the game. His mind had now matter to work upon; and hence his visit to Bolton Street to secure possession of the boot, which he did by an audacious *ruse.*

His subsequent interview with Mr. Longcluse, in presence of David Arden, was simply a concerted piece of acting, on which Longcluse, when he had made his terms with Davies, insisted, as a security against the reopening of the extortion.

Nothing will induce Alice to accept one farthing of Longcluse's magnificent legacy. Secretly Uncle David is resolved to make it up to her from his own wealth, which is very great.

Richard Arden's story is not known to any living person but the Jew Levi, and vaguely to his sister, in whose mind it remains as something horrible, but never approached.

Levi keeps the secret for reasons more cogent than charitable. First he kept it to himself as a future instrument of profit. But on his insinuating something that promised such relations to Sir Richard, the young gentleman met it with so bold a front, with fury so unaffected, and with threats so alarming, founded upon a trifling matter of which the Jew had never suspected his knowledge, that Mr. Levi has not ventured either to 'utilise' his knowledge, in a profitable way, or afterwards to circulate the story for the solace of his malice.

They seem, in Mr. Rooke's phrase, to have turned their backs on one another; and as some years have passed, and lapse of time does not improve the case of a person in Mr. Levi's position, we may safely assume that he will never dare to circulate any definite stories to Sir Richard's prejudice. A sufficient motive, indeed, for doing so exists no longer, for Sir Richard, who had lived an unsettled life travelling on the Continent, and still playing at foreign tables when he could afford it, died suddenly at Florence in the autumn of '69.

Vivian Darnley has been in 'the House,' now, nearly four years. Uncle David is very proud of him; and more impartial people think that he will, at last, take an honourable place in that assembly. His last speech has been spoken of everywhere with applause. David Arden's immensely increased wealth enables him to entertain very magnificent plans for this young man. He intends that he shall take the name of Arden, and earn the transmission of the title, or the distinction of a greater one.

A year ago Vivian Darnley married Alice Arden, and no two people can be happier.

Lady May, although her girlish ways have not forsaken her, has no present thoughts of making any man happy. She had a great cry all to herself when Sir Richard died, and she now persuades herself that he never meant one word he said of her, and that if the truth were known, although after that day she never spoke to him more, he had never really cared for more than one woman on earth. It was all spite of that odious Lady Wynderbroke!

Alice has never seen Mortlake since the night of her flight from its walls.

The two old servants, Crozier and Martha Tansey, whose acquaintance we made in that suburban seat of the Ardens, are both, I am glad to say, living still, and extremely comfortable.

Phoebe Chiffinch, I am glad to add, was jilted by her uninteresting lover, who little knew what a fortune he was slighting. His desertion does not seem to have broken her heart, or at all affected her spirits. The gratitude of Alice Arden has established her in the prosperous little Yorkshire town, the steep roof, chimneys, and church tower of which are visible, among the trees, from the windows of Arden Court. She is the energetic and popular proprietress of the 'Cat and Fiddle', to which thriving inn, at a nominal rent, a valuable farm is attached. A fortune of two thousand pounds from the same grateful friend awaits her marriage, which can't be far off, with the handsome son of rich Farmer Shackleton.

The Fortunes of Sir Robert Ardagh

(Later developed into the longer novella *The Haunted Baronet.)*

The earth hath bubbles as the water hath—
And these are of them.

In the south of Ireland, and on the borders of the county of Limerick, there lies a district of two or three miles in length, which is rendered interesting by the fact that it is one of the very few spots throughout this country, in which some vestiges of aboriginal forest still remain. It has little or none of the lordly character of the American forest, for the axe has felled its oldest and its grandest trees; but in the close wood which survives, live all the wild and pleasing peculiarities of nature: its complete irregularity, its vistas, in whose perspective the quiet cattle are peacefully browsing; its refreshing glades, where the grey rocks arise from amid the nodding fern; the silvery shafts of the old birch trees; the knotted trunks of the hoary oak, the grotesque but graceful branches which never shed their honours under the tyrant pruning-hook; the soft green sward; the chequered light and shade; the wild luxuriant weeds; the lichen and the moss—all, all are beautiful alike in the green freshness of spring, or in the sadness and sere of autumn.

Their beauty is of that kind which makes the heart full with joy—appealing to the affections with a power which belongs to nature only. This wood runs up, from below the base, to the ridge of a long line of irregular hills, having perhaps, in primitive times, formed but the skirting of some mighty forest which occupied the level below.

But now, alas! whither have we drifted? whither has the tide of civilisation borne us? It has passed over a land unprepared for it—it has left nakedness behind it; we have lost our forests, but our marauders remain; we have destroyed all that is picturesque, while we have retained everything that is revolting in barbarism. Through the midst of this woodland there runs a deep gully or glen, where the stillness of the scene is broken in upon by the brawling of a mountain-stream, which, however, in the winter season, swells into a rapid and formidable torrent.

There is one point at which the glen becomes extremely deep and narrow; the sides descend to the depth of some hundred feet, and are so steep as to be nearly perpendicular. The wild trees which have taken root in the crannies and chasms of the rock have so intersected and entangled, that one can with difficulty catch a glimpse of the stream, which wheels, flashes, and foams below, as if exulting in the surrounding silence and solitude.

This spot was not unwisely chosen, as a point of no ordinary strength, for the erection of a massive square tower or keep, one side of which rises as if in continuation of the precipitous cliff on which it is based. Originally, the only mode of ingress was by a narrow portal in the very wall which overtopped the precipice, opening upon a ledge of rock which afforded a precarious pathway, cautiously intersected, however, by a deep trench cut with great labour in the living rock; so that, in its original state, and before the introduction of artillery into the art of war, this tower might have been pronounced, and that not presumptuously, almost impregnable.

The progress of improvement and the increasing security of the times had, however, tempted its successive proprietors, if not to adorn, at least to enlarge their premises, and at about the middle of the last century, when the castle was last inhabited, the original square tower formed but a small part of the edifice.

The castle, and a wide tract of the surrounding country, had from time immemorial belonged to a family which, for distinctness, we shall call by the name of Ardagh; and owing to the associations which, in Ireland, almost always attach to scenes which have long witnessed alike the exercise of stern feudal authority, and of that savage hospitality which distinguished the good old times, this building has become the subject and the scene of many wild and extraordinary traditions. One of them I have been enabled, by a personal acquaintance with an eyewitness of the events, to trace to its origin; and yet it is hard to say whether the events which I am about to record appear more strange or improbable as seen through the distorting medium of tradition, or in the appalling dimness of uncertainty which surrounds the reality.

Tradition says that, sometime in the last century, Sir Robert Ardagh, a young man, and the last heir of that family, went abroad and served in foreign armies; and that, having acquired considerable honour and emolument, he settled at Castle Ardagh, the building we have just now attempted to describe. He was what the country people call a DARK man; that is, he was considered morose, reserved, and ill-tempered; and, as it was supposed from the utter solitude of his life, was upon no terms of cordiality with the other members of his family.

The only occasion upon which he broke through the solitary monotony of his life was during the continuance of the racing season, and immediately subsequent to it; at which time he was to be seen among the busiest upon the course, betting deeply and unhesitatingly, and invariably with success. Sir Robert was, however, too well known as a man of honour, and of too high a family, to be suspected of any unfair dealing. He was, moreover, a soldier, and a man of an intrepid as well as of a haughty character; and no one cared to hazard a surmise, the consequences of which would be felt most probably by its originator only.

Gossip, however, was not silent; it was remarked that Sir Robert never appeared at the race-ground, which was the only place of public resort which he frequented, except in company with a certain strange-looking person, who was never seen elsewhere, or under other circumstances. It was remarked, too, that this man, whose relation to Sir Robert was never distinctly ascertained, was the only person to whom he seemed to speak unnecessarily; it was observed that while with the country gentry he exchanged no further communication than what was unavoidable in arranging his sporting transactions, with this person he would converse earnestly and frequently.

Tradition asserts that, to enhance the curiosity which this unaccountable and exclusive preference excited, the stranger possessed some striking and unpleasant peculiarities of person and of garb—she does not say, however, what these were—but they, in conjunction with Sir Robert's secluded habits and extraordinary run of luck—a success which was supposed to result from the suggestions and immediate advice of the unknown-were sufficient to warrant report in pronouncing that there was something QUEER in the wind, and in surmising that Sir Robert was playing a fearful and a hazardous game, and that, in short, his strange companion was little better than the devil himself

Years, however, rolled quietly away, and nothing novel occurred in the arrangements of Castle Ardagh, excepting that Sir Robert parted with his odd companion, but as nobody could tell whence he came, so nobody could say whither he had gone. Sir Robert's habits, however, underwent no consequent change; he continued regularly to frequent the race meetings, without mixing at all in the convivialities of the gentry, and immediately afterwards to relapse into the secluded monotony of his ordinary life.

It was said that he had accumulated vast sums of money-and, as his bets were always successful, and always large, such must have been the case. He did not suffer the acquisition of wealth, however, to influence his hospitality or his housekeeping—he neither purchased land, nor extended his establishment; and his mode of enjoying his money must have been altogether that of the miser—consisting merely in the pleasure of touching and telling his gold, and in the consciousness of wealth.

Sir Robert's temper, so far from improving, became more than ever gloomy and morose. He sometimes carried the indulgence of his evil dispositions to such a height that it bordered upon insanity. During these paroxysms he would neither eat, drink, nor sleep. On such occasions he insisted on perfect privacy, even from the intrusion of his most trusted servants; his voice was frequently heard, sometimes in earnest supplication, sometime as if in loud and angry altercation with some unknown visitant; sometimes he would, for hours together, walk to and fro throughout the long oak wainscoted apartment, which he generally occupied, with wild gesticulations and agitated pace, in the manner of one who has been roused to a state of unnatural excitement by some sudden and appalling intimation.

These paroxysms of apparent lunacy were so frightful, that during their continuance even his oldest and most-faithful domestics dared not approach him; consequently, his hours of agony were never intruded upon, and the mysterious causes of his sufferings appeared likely to remain hidden forever.

On one occasion a fit of this kind continued for an unusual time, the ordinary term of their duration—about two days—had been long past, and the old servant who generally waited upon Sir Robert after these visitations, having in vain listened for the well-known tinkle of his master's hand-bell, began to feel extremely anxious; he feared that his master might have died from sheer exhaustion, or perhaps put an end to his own existence during his miserable depression. These fears at length became so strong, that having in vain urged some of his brother servants to accompany him, he determined to go up alone, and himself see whether any accident had befallen Sir Robert.

He traversed the several passages which conducted from the new to the more ancient parts of the mansion, and having arrived in the old hall of the castle, the utter silence of the hour, for it was very late in the night, the idea of the nature of the enterprise in which he was engaging himself, a sensation of remoteness from anything like human companionship, but, more than all, the vivid but undefined anticipation of something horrible, came upon him with such oppressive weight that he hesitated as to whether he should proceed.

Real uneasiness, however, respecting the fate of his master, for whom he felt that kind of attachment which the force of habitual intercourse not unfrequently engenders respecting objects not in themselves amiable, and also a latent unwillingness to expose his weakness to the ridicule of his fellow-servants, combined to overcome his reluctance; and he had just placed his foot upon the first step of the staircase which conducted to his master's chamber, when his attention was arrested by a low but distinct knocking at the hall-door. Not, perhaps, very sorry at finding thus an excuse even for deferring his intended expedition, he placed the candle upon a stone block which lay in the hall, and approached the door, uncertain whether his ears had not deceived him.

This doubt was justified by the circumstance that the hall entrance had been for nearly fifty years disused as a mode of ingress to the castle. The situation of this gate also, which we have endeavoured to describe, opening upon a narrow ledge of rock which overhangs a perilous cliff, rendered it at all times, but particularly at night, a dangerous entrance. This shelving platform of rock, which formed the only avenue to the door, was divided, as I have already stated, by a broad chasm, the planks across which had long disappeared by decay or otherwise, so that it seemed at least highly improbable that any man could have found his way across the passage in safety to the door, more particularly on a night like that, of singular darkness.

The old man, therefore, listened attentively, to ascertain whether the first application should be followed by another. He had not long to wait; the same low but singularly distinct knocking was repeated; so low that it seemed as if the applicant had employed no harder or heavier instrument than his hand, and yet, despite the immense thickness of the door, with such strength that the sound was distinctly audible.

The knock was repeated a third time, without any increase of loudness; and the old man, obeying an impulse for which to his dying hour he could never account, proceeded to remove, one by one, the three great oaken bars which secured the door.

Time and damp had effectually corroded the iron chambers of the lock, so that it afforded little resistance. With some effort, as he believed, assisted from without, the old servant succeeded in opening the door; and a low, square-built figure, apparently that of a man wrapped in a large black cloak, entered the hall. The servant could not see much of this visitant with any distinctness; his dress appeared foreign, the skirt of his ample cloak was thrown over one shoulder; he wore a large felt hat, with a very heavy leaf, from under which escaped what appeared to be a mass of long sooty-black hair; his feet were cased in heavy riding-boots.

Such were the few particulars which the servant had time and light to observe. The stranger desired him to let his master know instantly that a friend had come, by appointment, to settle some business with him. The servant hesitated, but a slight motion on the part of his visitor, as if to possess himself of the candle, determined him; so, taking it in his hand, he ascended the castle stairs, leaving his guest in the hall.

On reaching the apartment which opened upon the oak-chamber he was surprised to observe the door of that room partly open, and the room itself lit up. He paused, but there was no sound; he looked in, and saw Sir Robert, his head and the upper part of his body reclining on a table, upon which burned a lamp; his arms were stretched forward on either side, and perfectly motionless; it appeared that, having been sitting at the table, he had thus sunk forward, either dead or in a swoon. There was no sound of breathing; all was silent, except the sharp ticking of a watch, which lay beside the lamp. The servant coughed twice or thrice, but with no effect; his fears now almost amounted to certainty, and he was approaching the table on which his master partly lay, to satisfy himself of his death, when Sir Robert slowly raised his head, and throwing himself back in his chair, fixed his eyes in a ghastly and uncertain gaze upon his attendant. At length he said, slowly and painfully, as if he dreaded the answer:

'In God's name, what are you?'

'Sir,' said the servant, 'a strange gentleman wants to see you below.'

At this intimation Sir Robert, starting on his feet and tossing his arms wildly upwards, uttered a shriek of such appalling and despairing terror that it was almost too fearful for human endurance; and long after the sound had ceased it seemed to the terrified imagination of the old servant to roll through the deserted passages in bursts of unnatural laughter. After a few moments Sir Robert said:

'Can't you send him away? Why does he come so soon? O God! O God! let him leave me for an hour; a little time. I can't see him now; try to get him away. You see I can't go down now; I have not strength. O God! O God! let him come back in an hour; it is not long to wait. He cannot lose anything by it; nothing, nothing, nothing. Tell him that; say anything to him.'

The servant went down. In his own words, he did not feel the stairs under him till he got to the hall. The figure stood exactly as he had left it. He delivered his master's message as coherently as he could. The stranger replied in a careless tone:

'If Sir Robert will not come down to me, I must go up to him.'

The man returned, and to his surprise he found his master much more composed in manner. He listened to the message, and though the cold perspiration rose in drops upon his forehead faster than he could wipe it away, his manner had lost the dreadful agitation which had marked it before. He rose feebly, and casting a last look of agony behind him, passed from the room to the lobby, where he signed to his attendant not to follow him. The man moved as far as the head of the staircase, from whence he had a tolerably distinct view of the hall, which was imperfectly lighted by the candle he had left there.

He saw his master reel, rather than walk down the stairs, clinging all the way to the banisters. He walked on, as if about to sink every moment from weakness. The figure advanced as if to meet him, and in passing struck down the light. The servant could see no more; but there was a sound of struggling, renewed at intervals with silent but fearful energy. It was evident, however, that the parties were approaching the door, for he heard the solid oak sound twice or thrice, as the feet of the combatants, in shuffling hither and thither over the floor, struck upon it. After a slight pause he heard the door thrown open with such violence that the leaf seemed to strike the side-wall of the hall, for it was so dark without that this could only be surmised by the sound. The struggle was renewed with an agony and intenseness of energy that betrayed itself in deep-drawn gasps.

One desperate effort, which terminated in the breaking of some part of the door, producing a sound as if the door-post was wrenched from its position, was followed by another wrestle, evidently upon the narrow ledge which ran outside the door, overtopping the precipice. This proved to be the final struggle, for it was followed by a crashing sound as if some heavy body had fallen over, and was rushing down the precipice, through the light boughs that crossed near the top. All then became still as the grave, except when the moan of the night wind sighed up the wooded glen.

The old servant had not nerve to return through the hall, and to him the darkness seemed all but endless; but morning at length came, and with it the disclosure of the events of the night. Near the door, upon the ground, lay Sir Robert's sword-belt, which had given way in the scuffle. A huge splinter from the massive doorpost had been wrenched off by an almost superhuman effort—one which nothing but the gripe of a despairing man could have severed—and on the rock outside were left the marks of the slipping and sliding of feet.

At the foot of the precipice, not immediately under the castle, but dragged some way up the glen, were found the remains of Sir Robert, with hardly a vestige of a limb or feature left distinguishable. The right hand, however, was uninjured, and in its fingers were clutched, with the fixedness of death, a long lock of coarse sooty hair—the only direct circumstantial evidence of the presence of a second person. So says tradition.

This story, as I have mentioned, was current among the dealers in such lore; but the original facts are so dissimilar in all but the name of the principal person mentioned and his mode of life, and the fact that his death was accompanied with circumstances of extraordinary mystery, that the two narratives are totally irreconcilable (even allowing the utmost for the exaggerating influence of tradition), except by supposing report to have combined and blended together the fabulous histories of several distinct bearers of the family name. However this may be, I shall lay before the reader a distinct recital of the events from which the foregoing tradition arose.

With respect to these there can be no mistake; they are authenticated as fully as anything can be by human testimony; and I state them principally upon the evidence of a lady who herself bore a prominent part in the strange events which she related, and which I now record as being among the few well-attested tales of the marvellous which it has been my fate to hear. I shall, as far as I am able, arrange in one combined narrative the evidence of several distinct persons who were eye-witnesses of what they related, and with the truth of whose testimony I am solemnly and deeply impressed.

Sir Robert Ardagh, as we choose to call him, was the heir and representative of the family whose name he bore; but owing to the prodigality of his father, the estates descended to him in a very impaired condition. Urged by the restless spirit of youth, or more probably by a feeling of pride which could not submit to witness, in the paternal mansion, what he considered a humiliating alteration in the style and hospitality which up to that time had distinguished his family, Sir Robert left Ireland and went abroad. How he occupied himself, or what countries he visited during his absence, was never known, nor did he afterwards make any allusion or encourage any inquiries touching his foreign sojourn. He left Ireland in the year 1742, being then just of age, and was not heard of until the year 1760—about eighteen years afterwards—at which time he returned.

His personal appearance was, as might have been expected, very greatly altered, more altered, indeed, than the time of his absence might have warranted one in supposing likely. But to counterbalance the unfavourable change which time had wrought in his form and features, he had acquired all the advantages of polish of manner and refinement of taste which foreign travel is supposed to bestow. But what was truly surprising was that it soon became evident that Sir Robert was very wealthy-wealthy to an extraordinary and unaccountable degree; and this fact was made manifest, not only by his expensive style of living, but by his proceeding to disembarrass his property, and to purchase extensive estates in addition. Moreover, there could be nothing deceptive in these appearances, for he paid ready money for everything, from the most important purchase to the most trifling.

Sir Robert was a remarkably agreeable man, and possessing the combined advantages of birth and property, he was, as a matter of course, gladly received into the highest society which the metropolis then commanded. It was thus that he became acquainted with the two beautiful Miss F——ds, then among the brightest ornaments of the highest circle of Dublin fashion. Their family was in more than one direction allied to nobility; and Lady D——, their elder sister by many years, and sometime married to a once well-known nobleman, was now their protectress. These considerations, beside the fact that the young ladies were what is usually termed heiresses, though not to a very great amount, secured to them a high position in the best society which Ireland then produced.

The two young ladies differed strongly, alike in appearance and in character. The elder of the two, Emily, was generally considered the handsomer—for her beauty was of that impressive kind which never failed to strike even at the first glance, possessing as it did all the advantages of a fine person and a commanding carriage. The beauty of her features strikingly assorted in character with that of her figure and deportment. Her hair was raven-black and richly luxuriant, beautifully contrasting with the perfect whiteness of her forehead—her finely pencilled brows were black as the ringlets that clustered near them—and her blue eyes, full, lustrous, and animated, possessed all the power and brilliancy of brown ones, with more than their softness and variety of expression.

She was not, however, merely the tragedy queen. When she smiled, and that was not seldom, the dimpling of cheek and chin, the laughing display of the small and beautiful teeth—but, more than all, the roguish archness of her deep, bright eye, showed that nature had not neglected in her the lighter and the softer characteristics of woman.

Her younger sister Mary was, as I believe not unfrequently occurs in the case of sisters, quite in the opposite style of beauty. She was light-haired, had more colour, had nearly equal grace, with much more liveliness of manner. Her eyes were of that dark grey which poets so much admire—full of expression and vivacity. She was altogether a very beautiful and animated girl-though as unlike her sister as the presence of those two qualities would permit her to be. Their dissimilarity did not stop here—it was deeper than mere appearance—the character of their minds differed almost as strikingly as did their complexion. The fair-haired beauty had a large proportion of that softness and pliability of temper which physiognomists assign as the characteristics of such complexions.

She was much more the creature of impulse than of feeling, and consequently more the victim of extrinsic circumstances than was her sister. Emily, on the contrary, possessed considerable firmness and decision. She was less excitable, but when excited her feelings were more intense and enduring. She wanted much of the gaiety, but with it the volatility of her younger sister. Her opinions were adopted, and her friendships formed more reflectively, and her affections seemed to move, as it were, more slowly, but more determinedly. This firmness of character did not amount to anything masculine, and did not at all impair the feminine grace of her manners.

Sir Robert Ardagh was for a long time apparently equally attentive to the two sisters, and many were the conjectures and the surmises as to which would be the lady of his choice. At length, however, these doubts were determined; he proposed for and was accepted by the dark beauty, Emily F——d.

The bridals were celebrated in a manner becoming the wealth and connections of the parties; and Sir Robert and Lady Ardagh left Dublin to pass the honeymoon at the family mansion, Castle Ardagh, which had lately been fitted up in a style bordering upon magnificent. Whether in compliance with the wishes of his lady, or owing to some whim of his own, his habits were henceforward strikingly altered; and from having moved among the gayest if not the most profligate of the votaries of fashion, he suddenly settled down into a quiet, domestic, country gentleman, and seldom, if ever, visited the capital, and then his sojourns were as brief as the nature of his business would permit.

Lady Ardagh, however, did not suffer from this change further than in being secluded from general society; for Sir Robert's wealth, and the hospitality which he had established in the family mansion, commanded that of such of his lady's friends and relatives as had leisure or inclination to visit the castle; and as their style of living was very handsome, and its internal resources of amusement considerable, few invitations from Sir Robert or his lady were neglected.

Many years passed quietly away, during which Sir Robert's and Lady Ardagh's hopes of issue were several times disappointed. In the lapse of all this time there occurred but one event worth recording. Sir Robert had brought with him from abroad a valet, who sometimes professed himself to be French, at others Italian, and at others again German. He spoke all these languages with equal fluency, and seemed to take a kind of pleasure in puzzling the sagacity and balking the curiosity of such of the visitors at the castle as at any time happened to enter into conversation with him, or who, struck by his singularities, became inquisitive respecting his country and origin.

Sir Robert called him by the French name, JACQUE, and among the lower orders he was familiarly known by the title of 'Jack, the devil,' an appellation which originated in a supposed malignity of disposition and a real reluctance to mix in the society of those who were believed to be his equals. This morose reserve, coupled with the mystery which enveloped all about him, rendered him an object of suspicion and inquiry to his fellow-servants, amongst whom it was whispered that this man in secret governed the actions of Sir Robert with a despotic dictation, and that, as if to indemnify himself for his public and apparent servitude and self-denial, he in private exacted a degree of respectful homage from his so-called master, totally inconsistent with the relation generally supposed to exist between them.

This man's personal appearance was, to say the least of it, extremely odd; he was low in stature; and this defect was enhanced by a distortion of the spine, so considerable as almost to amount to a hunch; his features, too, had all that sharpness and sickliness of hue which generally accompany deformity; he wore his hair, which was black as soot, in heavy neglected ringlets about his shoulders, and always without powder—a peculiarity in those days. There was something unpleasant, too, in the circumstance that he never raised his eyes to meet those of another; this fact was often cited as a proof of his being something not quite right, and said to result not from the timidity which is supposed in most cases to induce this habit, but from a consciousness that his eye possessed a power which, if exhibited, would betray a supernatural origin.

Once, and once only, had he violated this sinister observance: it was on the occasion of Sir Robert's hopes having been most bitterly disappointed; his lady, after a severe and dangerous confinement, gave birth to a dead child. Immediately after the intelligence had been made known, a servant, having upon some business passed outside the gate of the castle-yard, was met by Jacque, who, contrary to his wont, accosted him, observing, 'So, after all the pother, the son and heir is stillborn.'

This remark was accompanied by a chuckling laugh, the only approach to merriment which he was ever known to exhibit. The servant, who was really disappointed, having hoped for holiday times, feasting and debauchery with impunity during the rejoicings which would have accompanied a christening, turned tartly upon the little valet, telling him that he should let Sir Robert know how he had received the tidings which should have filled any faithful servant with sorrow; and having once broken the ice, he was proceeding with increasing fluency, when his harangue was cut short and his temerity punished, by the little man raising his head and treating him to a scowl so fearful, half-demoniac, half-insane, that it haunted his imagination in nightmares and nervous tremors for months after.

To this man Lady Ardagh had, at first sight, conceived an antipathy amounting to horror, a mixture of loathing and dread so very powerful that she had made it a particular and urgent request to Sir Robert, that he would dismiss him, offering herself, from that property which Sir Robert had by the marriage settlements left at her own disposal, to provide handsomely for him, provided only she might be relieved from the continual anxiety and discomfort which the fear of encountering him induced.

Sir Robert, however, would not hear of it; the request seemed at first to agitate and distress him; but when still urged in defiance of his peremptory refusal, he burst into a violent fit of fury; he spoke darkly of great sacrifices which he had made, and threatened that if the request were at any time renewed he would leave both her and the country for ever. This was, however, a solitary instance of violence; his general conduct towards Lady Ardagh, though at no time uxorious, was certainly kind and respectful, and he was more than repaid in the fervent attachment which she bore him in return.

Some short time after this strange interview between Sir Robert and Lady Ardagh; one night after the family had retired to bed, and when everything had been quiet for some time, the bell of Sir Robert's dressing-room rang suddenly and violently; the ringing was repeated again and again at still shorter intervals, and with increasing violence, as if the person who pulled the bell was agitated by the presence of some terrifying and imminent danger. A servant named Donovan was the first to answer it; he threw on his clothes, and hurried to the room.

Sir Robert had selected for his private room an apartment

remote from the bedchambers of the castle, most of which lay in the more modern parts of the mansion, and secured at its entrance by a double door. As the servant opened the first of these, Sir Robert's bell again sounded with a longer and louder peal; the inner door resisted his efforts to open it; but after a few violent struggles, not having been perfectly secured, or owing to the inadequacy of the bolt itself, it gave way, and the servant rushed into the apartment, advancing several paces before he could recover himself.

As he entered, he heard Sir Robert's voice exclaiming loudly—'Wait without, do not come in yet;' but the prohibition came too late. Near a low truckle-bed, upon which Sir Robert sometimes slept, for he was a whimsical man, in a large armchair, sat, or rather lounged, the form of the valet Jacque, his arms folded, and his heels stretched forward on the floor, so as fully to exhibit his misshapen legs, his head thrown back, and his eyes fixed upon his master with a look of indescribable defiance and derision, while, as if to add to the strange insolence of his attitude and expression, he had placed upon his head the black cloth cap which it was his habit to wear.

Sir Robert was standing before him, at the distance of several yards, in a posture expressive of despair, terror, and what might be called an agony of humility. He waved his hand twice or thrice, as if to dismiss the servant, who, however, remained fixed on the spot where he had first stood; and then, as if forgetting everything but the agony within him, he pressed his clenched hands on his cold damp brow, and dashed away the heavy drops that gathered chill and thickly there.

Jacque broke the silence.

'Donovan,' said he, 'shake up that drone and drunkard, Carlton; tell him that his master directs that the travelling carriage shall be at the door within half-an-hour.'

The servant paused, as if in doubt as to what he should do; but his scruples were resolved by Sir Robert's saying hurriedly, 'Go—go, do whatever he directs; his commands are mine; tell Carlton the same.'

The servant hurried to obey, and in about half-an-hour the carriage was at the door, and Jacque, having directed the coachman to drive to B——n, a small town at about the distance of twelve miles—the nearest point, however, at which post-horses could be obtained—stepped into the vehicle, which accordingly quitted the castle immediately.

Although it was a fine moonlight night, the carriage made its way but very slowly, and after the lapse of two hours the travellers had arrived at a point about eight miles from the castle, at which the road strikes through a desolate and heathy flat, sloping up distantly at either side into bleak undulatory hills, in whose monotonous sweep the imagination beholds the heaving of some dark sluggish sea, arrested in its first commotion by some preternatural power. It is a gloomy and divested spot; there is neither tree nor habitation near it; its monotony is unbroken, except by here and there the grey front of a rock peering above the heath, and the effect is rendered yet more dreary and spectral by the exaggerated and misty shadows which the moon casts along the sloping sides of the hills.

When they had gained about the centre of this tract, Carlton, the coachman, was surprised to see a figure standing at some distance in advance, immediately beside the road, and still more so when, on coming up, he observed that it was no other than Jacque whom he believed to be at that moment quietly seated in the carriage; the coachman drew up, and nodding to him, the little valet exclaimed:

'Carlton, I have got the start of you; the roads are heavy, so I shall even take care of myself the rest of the way. Do you make your way back as best you can, and I shall follow my own nose.'

So saying, he chucked a purse into the lap of the coachman, and turning off at a right angle with the road, he began to move rapidly away in the direction of the dark ridge that lowered in the distance.

The servant watched him until he was lost in the shadowy haze of night; and neither he nor any of the inmates of the castle saw Jacque again. His disappearance, as might have been expected, did not cause any regret among the servants and dependants at the castle; and Lady Ardagh did not attempt to conceal her delight; but with Sir Robert matters were different, for two or three days subsequent to this event he confined himself to his room, and when he did return to his ordinary occupations, it was with a gloomy indifference, which showed that he did so more from habit than from any interest he felt in them. He appeared from that moment unaccountably and strikingly changed, and thenceforward walked through life as a thing from which he could derive neither profit nor pleasure. His temper, however, so far from growing wayward or morose, became, though gloomy, very—almost unnaturally—placid and cold; but his spirits totally failed, and he grew silent and abstracted.

These sombre habits of mind, as might have been anticipated, very materially affected the gay house-keeping of the castle; and the dark and melancholy spirit of its master seemed to have communicated itself to the very domestics, almost to the very walls of the mansion.

Several years rolled on in this way, and the sounds of mirth and wassail had long been strangers to the castle, when Sir Robert requested his lady, to her great astonishment, to invite some twenty or thirty of their friends to spend the Christmas, which was fast approaching, at the castle. Lady Ardagh gladly complied, and her sister Mary, who still continued unmarried, and Lady D—— were of course included in the invitations. Lady Ardagh had requested her sisters to set forward as early as possible, in order that she might enjoy a little of their society before the arrival of the other guests; and in compliance with this request they left Dublin almost immediately upon receiving the invitation, a little more than a week before the arrival of the festival which was to be the period at which the whole party were to muster.

For expedition's sake it was arranged that they should post, while Lady D——'s groom was to follow with her horses, she taking with herself her own maid and one male servant. They left the city when the day was considerably spent, and consequently made but three stages in the first day; upon the second, at about eight in the evening, they had reached the town of K——k, distant about fifteen miles from Castle Ardagh. Here, owing to Miss F——d's great fatigue, she having been for a considerable time in a very delicate state of health, it was determined to put up for the night. They, accordingly, took possession of the best sitting-room which the inn commanded, and Lady D—— remained in it to direct and urge the preparations for some refreshment, which the fatigues of the day had rendered necessary, while her younger sister retired to her bed-chamber to rest there for a little time, as the parlour commanded no such luxury as a sofa.

Miss F——d was, as I have already stated, at this time in very delicate health; and upon this occasion the exhaustion of fatigue, and the dreary badness of the weather, combined to depress her spirits. Lady D—— had not been left long to herself, when the door communicating with the passage was abruptly opened, and her sister Mary entered in a state of great agitation; she sat down pale and trembling upon one of the chairs, and it was not until a copious flood of tears had relieved her, that she became sufficiently calm to relate the cause of her excitement and distress. It was simply this.

Almost immediately upon lying down upon the bed she sank into a feverish and unrefreshing slumber; images of all grotesque shapes and startling colours flitted before her sleeping fancy with all the rapidity and variety of the changes in a kaleidoscope. At length, as she described it, a mist seemed to interpose itself between her sight and the ever-shifting scenery which sported before her imagination, and out of this cloudy shadow gradually emerged a figure whose back seemed turned towards the sleeper; it was that of a lady, who, in perfect silence, was expressing as far as pantomimic gesture could, by wringing her hands, and throwing her head from side to side, in the manner of one who is exhausted by the over indulgence, by the very sickness and impatience of grief; the extremity of misery.

For a long time she sought in vain to catch a glimpse of the face of the apparition, who thus seemed to stir and live before her. But at length the figure seemed to move with an air of authority, as if about to give directions to some inferior, and in doing so, it turned its head so as to display, with a ghastly distinctness, the features of Lady Ardagh, pale as death, with her dark hair all dishevelled, and her eyes dim and sunken with weeping. The revulsion of feeling which Miss F——d experienced at this disclosure—for up to that point she had contemplated the appearance rather with a sense of curiosity and of interest, than of anything deeper—was so horrible, that the shock awoke her perfectly. She sat up in the bed, and looked fearfully around the room, which was imperfectly lighted by a single candle burning dimly, as if she almost expected to see the reality of her dreadful vision lurking in some corner of the chamber.

Her fears were, however, verified, though not in the way she expected; yet in a manner sufficiently horrible—for she had hardly time to breathe and to collect her thoughts, when she heard, or thought she heard, the voice of her sister, Lady Ardagh, sometimes sobbing violently, and sometimes almost shrieking as if in terror, and calling upon her and Lady D——, with the most imploring earnestness of despair, for God's sake to lose no time in coming to her. All this was so horribly distinct, that it seemed as if the mourner was standing within a few yards of the spot where Miss F——d lay. She sprang from the bed, and leaving the candle in the room behind her, she made her way in the dark through the passage, the voice still following her, until as she arrived at the door of the sitting-room it seemed to die away in low sobbing.

As soon as Miss F——d was tolerably recovered, she declared her determination to proceed directly, and without further loss of time, to Castle Ardagh. It was not without much difficulty that Lady D—— at length prevailed upon her to consent to remain where they then were, until morning should arrive, when it was to be expected that the young lady would be much refreshed by at least remaining quiet for the night, even though sleep were out of the question. Lady D—— was convinced, from the nervous and feverish symptoms which her sister exhibited, that she had already done too much, and was more than ever satisfied of the necessity of prosecuting the journey no further upon that day.

After some time she persuaded her sister to return to her room, where she remained with her until she had gone to bed, and appeared comparatively composed. Lady D—— then returned to the parlour, and not finding herself sleepy, she remained sitting by the fire. Her solitude was a second time broken in upon, by the entrance of her sister, who now appeared, if possible, more agitated than before. She said that Lady D—— had not long left the room, when she was roused by a repetition of the same wailing and lamentations, accompanied by the wildest and most agonized supplications that no time should be lost in coming to Castle Ardagh, and all in her sister's voice, and uttered at the same proximity as before. This time the voice had followed her to the very door of the sitting-room, and until she closed it, seemed to pour forth its cries and sobs at the very threshold.

Miss F——d now most positively declared that nothing should prevent her proceeding instantly to the castle, adding that if Lady D—— would not accompany her, she would go on by herself. Superstitious feelings are at all times more or less contagious, and the last century afforded a soil much more congenial to their growth than the present. Lady D—— was so far affected by her sister's terrors, that she became, at least, uneasy; and seeing that her sister was immovably determined upon setting forward immediately, she consented to accompany her forthwith. After a slight delay, fresh horses were procured, and the two ladies and their attendants renewed their journey, with strong injunctions to the driver to quicken their rate of travelling as much as possible, and promises of reward in case of his doing so.

Roads were then in much worse condition throughout the south, even than they now are; and the fifteen miles which modern posting would have passed in little more than an hour and a half, were not completed even with every possible exertion in twice the time. Miss F——d had been nervously restless during the journey. Her head had been constantly out of the carriage window; and as they approached the entrance to the castle demesne, which lay about a mile from the building, her anxiety began to communicate itself to her sister.

The postillion had just dismounted, and was endeavouring to open the gate—at that time a necessary trouble; for in the middle of the last century porter's lodges were not common in the south of Ireland, and locks and keys almost unknown. He had just succeeded in rolling back the heavy oaken gate so as to admit the vehicle, when a mounted servant rode rapidly down the avenue, and drawing up at the carriage, asked of the postillion who the party were; and on hearing, he rode round to the carriage window and handed in a note, which Lady D—— received. By the assistance of one of the coach-lamps they succeeded in deciphering it. It was scrawled in great agitation, and ran thus:

> MY DEAR SISTER—
> MY DEAR SISTERS BOTH,—In God's name lose no time, I am frightened and miserable; I cannot explain all till you come. I am too much terrified to write coherently; but understand me—hasten—do not waste a minute. I am afraid you will come too late.
>
> E. A.

The servant could tell nothing more than that the castle was in great confusion, and that Lady Ardagh had been crying bitterly all the night. Sir Robert was perfectly well. Altogether at a loss as to the cause of Lady Ardagh's great distress, they urged their way up the steep and broken avenue which wound through the crowding trees, whose wild and grotesque branches, now left stripped and naked by the blasts of winter, stretched drearily across the road. As the carriage drew up in the area before the door, the anxiety of the ladies almost amounted to agony; and scarcely waiting for the assistance of their attendant, they sprang to the ground, and in an instant stood at the castle door. From within were distinctly audible the sounds of lamentation and weeping, and the suppressed hum of voices as if of those endeavouring to soothe the mourner.

The door was speedily opened, and when the ladies entered, the first object which met their view was their sister, Lady Ardagh, sitting on a form in the hall, weeping and wringing her hands in deep agony. Beside her stood two old, withered crones, who were each endeavouring in their own way to administer consolation, without even knowing or caring what the subject of her grief might be.

Immediately on Lady Ardagh's seeing her sisters, she started up, fell on their necks, and kissed them again and again without speaking, and then taking them each by a hand, still weeping bitterly, she led them into a small room adjoining the hall, in which burned a light, and, having closed the door, she sat down between them. After thanking them for the haste they had made, she proceeded to tell them, in words incoherent from agitation, that Sir Robert had in private, and in the most solemn manner, told her that he should die upon that night, and that he had occupied himself during the evening in giving minute directions respecting the arrangements of his funeral. Lady D—— here suggested the possibility of his labouring under the hallucinations of a fever; but to this Lady Ardagh quickly replied:

'Oh! no, no! Would to God I could think it. Oh! no, no! Wait till you have seen him. There is a frightful calmness about all he says and does; and his directions are all so clear, and his mind so perfectly collected, it is impossible, quite impossible.' And she wept yet more bitterly.

At that moment Sir Robert's voice was heard in issuing some directions, as he came downstairs; and Lady Ardagh exclaimed, hurriedly:

'Go now and see him yourself. He is in the hall.'

Lady D—— accordingly went out into the hall, where Sir Robert met her; and, saluting her with kind politeness, he said, after a pause:

'You are come upon a melancholy mission—the house is in great confusion, and some of its inmates in considerable grief.' He took her hand, and looking fixedly in her face, continued: 'I shall not live to see tomorrow's sunshine.'

'You are ill, sir, I have no doubt,' replied she; 'but I am very certain we shall see you much better tomorrow, and still better the day following.'

'I am NOT ill, sister,' replied he. 'Feel my temples, they are cool; lay your finger to my pulse, its throb is slow and temperate. I never was more perfectly in health, and yet do I know that ere three hours be past, I shall be no more.'

'Sir, sir,' said she, a good deal startled, but wishing to conceal the impression which the calm solemnity of his manner had, in her own despite, made upon her, 'Sir, you should not jest; you should not even speak lightly upon such subjects. You trifle with what is sacred—you are sporting with the best affections of your wife——'

'Stay, my good lady,' said he; 'if when this clock shall strike the hour of three, I shall be anything but a helpless clod, then upbraid me. Pray return now to your sister. Lady Ardagh is, indeed, much to be pitied; but what is past cannot now be helped. I have now a few papers to arrange, and some to destroy. I shall see you and Lady Ardagh before my death; try to compose her—her sufferings distress me much; but what is past cannot now be mended.'

Thus saying, he went upstairs, and Lady D—— returned to the room where her sisters were sitting.

'Well,' exclaimed Lady Ardagh, as she re-entered, 'is it not so?—do you still doubt?—do you think there is any hope?"

Lady D—— was silent.

'Oh! none, none, none,' continued she; 'I see, I see you are convinced.' And she wrung her hands in bitter agony.

'My dear sister,' said Lady D——, 'there is, no doubt, something strange in all that has appeared in this matter; but still I cannot but hope that there may be something deceptive in all the apparent calmness of Sir Robert. I still must believe that some latent fever has affected his mind, or that, owing to the state of nervous depression into which he has been sinking, some trivial occurrence has been converted, in his disordered imagination, into an augury foreboding his immediate dissolution.'

In such suggestions, unsatisfactory even to those who originated them, and doubly so to her whom they were intended to comfort, more than two hours passed; and Lady D—— was beginning to hope that the fated term might elapse without the occurrence of any tragical event, when Sir Robert entered the room. On coming in, he placed his finger with a warning gesture upon his lips, as if to enjoin silence; and then having successively pressed the hands of his two sisters-in-law, he stooped sadly over the fainting form of his lady, and twice pressed her cold, pale forehead, with his lips, and then passed silently out of the room.

Lady D——, starting up, followed to the door, and saw him take a candle in the hall, and walk deliberately up the stairs. Stimulated by a feeling of horrible curiosity, she continued to follow him at a distance. She saw him enter his own private room, and heard him close and lock the door after him. Continuing to follow him as far as she could, she placed herself at the door of the chamber, as noiselessly as possible, where after a little time she was joined by her two sisters, Lady Ardagh and Miss F——d. In breathless silence they listened to what should pass within. They distinctly heard Sir Robert pacing up and down the room for some time; and then, after a pause, a sound as if someone had thrown himself heavily upon the bed.

At this moment Lady D——, forgetting that the door had been secured within, turned the handle for the purpose of entering; when someone from the inside, close to the door, said, 'Hush! hush!' The same lady, now much alarmed, knocked violently at the door; there was no answer. She knocked again more violently, with no further success. Lady Ardagh, now uttering a piercing shriek, sank in a swoon upon the floor. Three or four servants, alarmed by the noise, now hurried upstairs, and Lady Ardagh was carried apparently lifeless to her own chamber. They then, after having knocked long and loudly in vain, applied themselves to forcing an entrance into Sir Robert's room. After resisting some violent efforts, the door at length gave way, and all entered the room nearly together.

There was a single candle burning upon a table at the far end of the apartment; and stretched upon the bed lay Sir Robert Ardagh. He was a corpse—the eyes were open—no convulsion had passed over the features, or distorted the limbs—it seemed as if the soul had sped from the body without a struggle to remain there. On touching the body it was found to be cold as clay—all lingering of the vital heat had left it. They closed the ghastly eyes of the corpse, and leaving it to the care of those who seem to consider it a privilege of their age and sex to gloat over the revolting spectacle of death in all its stages, they returned to Lady Ardagh, now a widow. The party assembled at the castle, but the atmosphere was tainted with death. Grief there was not much, but awe and panic were expressed in every face. The guests talked in whispers, and the servants walked on tiptoe, as if afraid of the very noise of their own footsteps.

The funeral was conducted almost with splendour. The body, having been conveyed, in compliance with Sir Robert's last directions, to Dublin, was there laid within the ancient walls of St. Audoen's Church—where I have read the epitaph, telling the age and titles of the departed dust. Neither painted *escutcheon*, nor marble slab, have served to rescue from oblivion the story of the dead, whose very name will ere long moulder from their tracery

Et sunt sua fata sepulchris.[1]

The events which I have recorded are not imaginary. They are FACTS; and there lives one whose authority none would venture to question, who could vindicate the accuracy of every statement which I have set down, and that, too, with all the circumstantiality of an eyewitness.[2]

---

1. This prophecy has since been realised; for the aisle in which Sir Robert's remains were laid has been suffered to fall completely to decay; and the tomb which marked his grave, and other monuments more curious, form now one indistinguishable mass of rubbish.

2. This paper, from a memorandum, I find to have been written in 1803. The lady to whom allusion is made, I believe to be Miss Mary F——d. She never married, and survived both her sisters, living to a very advanced age.

The Child That Went With the Fairies

Eastward of the old city of Limerick, about ten Irish miles under the range of mountains known as the Slieveelim hills, famous as having afforded Sarsfield a shelter among their rocks and hollows, when he crossed them in his gallant descent upon the cannon and ammunition of King William, on its way to the beleaguering army, there runs a very old and narrow road. It connects the Limerick road to Tipperary with the old road from Limerick to Dublin, and runs by bog and pasture, hill and hollow, straw-thatched village, and roofless castle, not far from twenty miles.

Skirting the healthy mountains of which I have spoken, at one part it becomes singularly lonely. For more than three Irish miles it traverses a deserted country. A wide, black bog, level as a lake, skirted with copse, spreads at the left, as you journey northward, and the long and irregular line of mountain rises at the right, clothed in heath, broken with lines of grey rock that resemble the bold and irregular outlines of fortifications, and riven with many a gully, expanding here and there into rocky and wooded glens, which open as they approach the road.

A scanty pasturage, on which browsed a few scattered sheep or kine, skirts this solitary road for some miles, and under shelter of a hillock, and of two or three great ash-trees, stood, not many years ago, the little thatched cabin of a widow named Mary Ryan.

Poor was this widow in a land of poverty. The thatch had acquired the grey tint and sunken outlines, that show how the alternations of rain and sun have told upon that perishable shelter.

But whatever other dangers threatened, there was one well provided against by the care of other times. Round the cabin stood half a dozen mountain ashes, as the rowans, inimical to witches, are there called. On the worn planks of the door were nailed two horse-shoes, and over the lintel and spreading along the thatch, grew, luxuriant, patches of that ancient cure for many maladies, and prophylactic against the machinations of the evil one, the house-leek. Descending into the doorway, in the *chiaroscuro* of the interior, when your eye grew sufficiently accustomed to that dim light, you might discover, hanging at the head of the widow's wooden-roofed bed, her beads and a phial of holy water.

Here certainly were defences and bulwarks against the intrusion of that unearthly and evil power, of whose vicinity this solitary family were constantly reminded by the outline of Lisnavoura, that lonely hill-haunt of the "Good people," as the fairies are called euphemistically, whose strangely dome-like summit rose not half a mile away, looking like an outwork of the long line of mountain that sweeps by it.

It was at the fall of the leaf, and an autumnal sunset threw the lengthening shadow of haunted Lisnavoura, close in front of the solitary little cabin, over the undulating slopes and sides of Slieveelim. The birds were singing among the branches in the thinning leaves of the melancholy ash-trees that grew at the roadside in front of the door. The widow's three younger children were playing on the road, and their voices mingled with the evening song of the birds. Their elder sister, Nell, was "within in the house," as their phrase is, seeing after the boiling of the potatoes for supper.

Their mother had gone down to the bog, to carry up a hamper of turf on her back. It is, or was at least, a charitable custom-and if not disused, long may it continue—for the wealthier people when cutting their turf and stacking it in the bog, to make a smaller stack for the behoof of the poor, who were welcome to take from it so long as it lasted, and thus the potato pot was kept boiling, and hearth warm that would have been cold enough but for that good-natured bounty, through wintry months.

Moll Ryan trudged up the steep "*bohereen*" whose banks were overgrown with thorn and brambles, and stooping under her burden, re-entered her door, where her dark-haired daughter Nell met her with a welcome, and relieved her of her hamper.

Moll Ryan looked round with a sigh of relief, and drying her forehead, uttered the Munster ejaculation:

"Eiah, wisha! It's tired I am with it, God bless it. And where's the craythurs, Nell?"

"Playin' out on the road, mother; didn't ye see them and you comin' up?"

"No; there was no one before me on the road," she said, uneasily; "not a soul, Nell; and why didn't ye keep an eye on them?"

"Well, they're in the haggard, playin' there, or round by the back o' the house. Will I call them in?"

"Do so, good girl, in the name o' God. The hens is comin' home, see, and the sun was just down over Knockdoulah, an' I comin' up."

So out ran tall, dark-haired Nell, and standing on the road, looked up and down it; but not a sign of her two little brothers, Con and Bill, or her little sister, Peg, could she see. She called them; but no answer came from the little haggard, fenced with straggling bushes. She listened, but the sound of their voices was missing. Over the stile, and behind the house she ran—but there all was silent and deserted.

She looked down toward the bog, as far as she could see; but they did not appear. Again she listened—but in vain. At first she had felt angry, but now a different feeling overcame her, and she grew pale. With an undefined boding she looked toward the heathy boss of Lisnavoura, now darkening into the deepest purple against the flaming sky of sunset.

Again she listened with a sinking heart, and heard nothing but the farewell twitter and whistle of the birds in the bushes around. How many stories had she listened to by the winter hearth, of children stolen by the fairies, at nightfall, in lonely places! With this fear she knew her mother was haunted.

No one in the country round gathered her little flock about her so early as this frightened widow, and no door "in the seven parishes" was barred so early.

Sufficiently fearful, as all young people in that part of the world are of such dreaded and subtle agents, Nell was even more than usually afraid of them, for her terrors were infected and redoubled by her mother's. She was looking towards Lisnavoura in a trance of fear, and crossed herself again and again, and whispered prayer after prayer. She was interrupted by her mother's voice on the road calling her loudly. She answered, and ran round to the front of the cabin, where she found her standing.

"And where in the world's the craythurs—did ye see sight o' them anywhere?" cried Mrs. Ryan, as the girl came over the stile.

"Arrah! mother, 'tis only what they're run down the road a bit. We'll see them this minute coming back. It's like goats they are, climbin' here and runnin' there; an' if I had them here, in my hand, maybe I wouldn't give them a hiding all round."

"May the Lord forgive you, Nell! the childhers gone. They're took, and not a soul near us, and Father Tom three miles away! And what'll I do, or who's to help us this night? Oh, wirristhru, wirristhru! The craythurs is gone!"

"Whisht, mother, be aisy: don't ye see them comin' up?"

And then she shouted in menacing accents, waving her arm, and beckoning the children, who were seen approaching on the road, which some little way off made a slight dip, which had concealed them. They were approaching from the westward, and from the direction of the dreaded hill of Lisnavoura.

But there were only two of the children, and one of them, the little girl, was crying. Their mother and sister hurried forward to meet them, more alarmed than ever.

"Where is Billy—where is he?" cried the mother, nearly breathless, so soon as she was within hearing.

"He's gone—they took him away; but they said he'll come back again," answered little Con, with the dark brown hair.

"He's gone away with the grand ladies," blubbered the little girl.

"What ladies—where? Oh, Leum, asthora! My darlin', are you gone away at last? Where is he? Who took him? What ladies are you talkin' about? What way did he go?" she cried in distraction.

"I couldn't see where he went, mother; 'twas like as if he was going to Lisnavoura."

With a wild exclamation the distracted woman ran on towards the hill alone, clapping her hands, and crying aloud the name of her lost child.

Scared and horrified, Nell, not daring to follow, gazed after her, and burst into tears; and the other children raised high their lamentations in shrill rivalry.

Twilight was deepening. It was long past the time when they were usually barred securely within their habitation. Nell led the younger children into the cabin, and made them sit down by the turf fire, while she stood in the open door, watching in great fear for the return of her mother.

After a long while they did see their mother return. She came in and sat down by the fire, and cried as if her heart would break.

"Will I bar the doore, mother?" asked Nell.

"Ay, do—didn't I lose enough, this night, without lavin' the doore open, for more o' yez to go; but first take an' sprinkle a dust o' the holy waters over ye, acuishla, and bring it here till I throw a taste iv it over myself and the craythurs; an' I wondher, Nell, you'd forget to do the like yourself, lettin' the craythurs out so near nightfall. Come here and sit on my knees, asthora, come to me, mavourneen, and hould me fast, in the name o' God, and I'll hould you fast that none can take yez from me, and tell me all about it, and what it was—the Lord between us and harm—an' how it happened, and who was in it."

And the door being barred, the two children, sometimes speaking together, often interrupting one another, often interrupted by their mother, managed to tell this strange story, which I had better relate connectedly and in my own language.

The Widow Ryan's three children were playing, as I have said, upon the narrow old road in front of her door. Little Bill or Leum, about five years old, with golden hair and large blue eyes, was a very pretty boy, with all the clear tints of healthy childhood, and that gaze of earnest simplicity which belongs not to town children of the same age. His little sister Peg, about a year older, and his brother Con, a little more than a year elder than she, made up the little group.

Under the great old ash-trees, whose last leaves were falling at their feet, in the light of an October sunset, they were playing with the hilarity and eagerness of rustic children, clamouring together, and their faces were turned toward the west and storied hill of Lisnavoura.

Suddenly a startling voice with a screech called to them from behind, ordering them to get out of the way, and turning, they saw a sight, such as they never beheld before. It was a carriage drawn by four horses that were pawing and snorting, in impatience, as it just pulled up. The children were almost under their feet, and scrambled to the side of the road next their own door.

This carriage and all its appointments were old-fashioned and gorgeous, and presented to the children, who had never seen anything finer than a turf car, and once, an old chaise that passed that way from Killaloe, a spectacle perfectly dazzling.

Here was antique splendour. The harness and trappings were scarlet, and blazing with gold. The horses were huge, and snow white, with great manes, that as they tossed and shook them in the air, seemed to stream and float sometimes longer and sometimes shorter, like so much smoke—their tails were long, and tied up in bows of broad scarlet and gold ribbon. The coach itself was glowing with colours, gilded and emblazoned. There were footmen in gay liveries, and three-cocked hats, like the coachman's; but he had a great wig, like a judge's, and their hair was frizzed out and powdered, and a long thick "pigtail," with a bow to it, hung down the back of each.

All these servants were diminutive, and ludicrously out of proportion with the enormous horses of the equipage, and had sharp, sallow features, and small, restless fiery eyes, and faces of cunning and malice that chilled the children. The little coachman was scowling and showing his white fangs under his cocked hat, and his little blazing beads of eyes were quivering with fury in their sockets as he whirled his whip round and round over their heads, till the lash of it looked like a streak of fire in the evening sun, and sounded like the cry of a legion of "*fillapoueeks*" in the air.

"Stop the princess on the highway!" cried the coachman, in a piercing treble.

"Stop the princess on the highway!" piped each footman in turn, scowling over his shoulder down on the children, and grinding his keen teeth.

The children were so frightened they could only gape and turn white in their panic. But a very sweet voice from the open window of the carriage reassured them, and arrested the attack of the lackeys.

A beautiful and "very grand-looking" lady was smiling from it on them, and they all felt pleased in the strange light of that smile.

"The boy with the golden hair, I think," said the lady, bending her large and wonderfully clear eyes on little Leum.

The upper sides of the carriage were chiefly of glass, so that the children could see another woman inside, whom they did not like so well.

This was a black woman, with a wonderfully long neck, hung round with many strings of large variously-coloured beads, and on her head was a sort of turban of silk striped with all the colours of the rainbow, and fixed in it was a golden star.

This black woman had a face as thin almost as a death's-head, with high cheekbones, and great goggle eyes, the whites of which, as well as her wide range of teeth, showed in brilliant contrast with her skin, as she looked over the beautiful lady's shoulder, and whispered something in her ear.

"Yes; the boy with the golden hair, I think," repeated the lady.

And her voice sounded sweet as a silver bell in the children's ears, and her smile beguiled them like the light of an enchanted lamp, as she leaned from the window with a look of ineffable fondness on the golden-haired boy, with the large blue eyes; insomuch that little Billy, looking up, smiled in return with a wondering fondness, and when she stooped down, and stretched her jewelled arms towards him, he stretched his little hands up, and how they touched the other children did not know; but, saying, "Come and give me a kiss, my darling," she raised him, and he seemed to ascend in her small fingers as lightly as a feather, and she held him in her lap and covered him with kisses.

Nothing daunted, the other children would have been only too happy to change places with their favoured little brother. There was only one thing that was unpleasant, and a little frightened them, and that was the black woman, who stood and stretched forward, in the carriage as before. She gathered a rich silk and gold handkerchief that was in her fingers up to her lips, and seemed to thrust ever so much of it, fold after fold, into her capacious mouth, as they thought to smother her laughter, with which she seemed convulsed, for she was shaking and quivering, as it seemed, with suppressed merriment; but her eyes, which remained uncovered, looked angrier than they had ever seen eyes look before.

But the lady was so beautiful they looked on her instead, and she continued to caress and kiss the little boy on her knee; and smiling at the other children she held up a large russet apple in her fingers, and the carriage began to move slowly on, and with a nod inviting them to take the fruit, she dropped it on the road from the window; it rolled some way beside the wheels, they following, and then she dropped another, and then another, and so on. And the same thing happened to all; for just as either of the children who ran beside had caught the rolling apple, somehow it slipt into a hole or ran into a ditch, and looking up they saw the lady drop another from the window, and so the chase was taken up and continued till they got, hardly knowing how far they had gone, to the old cross-road that leads to Owney.

It seemed that there the horses' hoofs and carriage wheels rolled up a wonderful dust, which being caught in one of those eddies that whirl the dust up into a column, on the calmest day, enveloped the children for a moment, and passed whirling on towards Lisnavoura, the carriage, as they fancied, driving in the centre of it; but suddenly it subsided, the straws and leaves floated to the ground, the dust dissipated itself, but the white horses and the lackeys, the gilded carriage, the lady and their little golden-haired brother were gone.

At the same moment suddenly the upper rim of the clear setting sun disappeared behind the hill of Knockdoula, and it was twilight. Each child felt the transition like a shock—and the sight of the rounded summit of Lisnavoura, now closely overhanging them, struck them with a new fear.

They screamed their brother's name after him, but their cries were lost in the vacant air. At the same time they thought they heard a hollow voice say, close to them, "Go home."

Looking round and seeing no one, they were scared, and hand in hand—the little girl crying wildly, and the boy white as ashes, from fear, they trotted homeward, at their best speed, to tell, as we have seen, their strange story.

Molly Ryan never more saw her darling. But something of the lost little boy was seen by his former playmates.

Sometimes when their mother was away earning a trifle at haymaking, and Nelly washing the potatoes for their dinner, or "beatling" clothes in the little stream that flows in the hollow close by, they saw the pretty face of little Billy peeping in archly at the door, and smiling silently at them, and as they ran to embrace him, with cries of delight, he drew back, still smiling archly, and when they got out into the open day, he was gone, and they could see no trace of him anywhere.

This happened often, with slight variations in the circumstances of the visit. Sometimes he would peep for a longer time, sometimes for a shorter time, sometimes his little hand would come in, and, with bended finger, beckon them to follow; but always he was smiling with the same arch look and wary silence—and always he was gone when they reached the door. Gradually these visits grew less and less frequent, and in about eight months they ceased altogether, and little Billy, irretrievably lost, took rank in their memories with the dead.

One wintry morning, nearly a year and a half after his disappearance, their mother having set out for Limerick soon after cockcrow, to sell some fowls at the market, the little girl, lying by the side of her elder sister, who was fast asleep, just at the grey of the morning heard the latch lifted softly, and saw little Billy enter and close the door gently after him. There was light enough to see that he was barefoot and ragged, and looked pale and famished. He went straight to the fire, and cowered over the turf embers, and rubbed his hands slowly, and seemed to shiver as he gathered the smouldering turf together.

The little girl clutched her sister in terror and whispered, "Waken, Nelly, waken; here's Billy come back!"

Nelly slept soundly on, but the little boy, whose hands were extended close over the coals, turned and looked toward the bed, it seemed to her, in fear, and she saw the glare of the embers reflected on his thin cheek as he turned toward her. He rose and went, on tiptoe, quickly to the door, in silence, and let himself out as softly as he had come in.

After that, the little boy was never seen any more by any one of his kindred.

"Fairy doctors," as the dealers in the preternatural, who in such cases were called in, are termed, did all that in them lay-but in vain. Father Tom came down, and tried what holier rites could do, but equally without result. So little Billy was dead to mother, brother, and sisters; but no grave received him. Others whom affection cherished, lay in holy ground, in the old churchyard of Abington, with headstone to mark the spot over which the survivor might kneel and say a kind prayer for the peace of the departed soul. But there was no landmark to show where little Billy was hidden from their loving eyes, unless it was in the old hill of Lisnavoura, that cast its long shadow at sunset before the cabin-door; or that, white and filmy in the moonlight, in later years, would occupy his brother's gaze as he returned from fair or market, and draw from him a sigh and a prayer for the little brother he had lost so long ago, and was never to see again.

What Was It?

It is, I confess, with considerable diffidence that I approached the strange narrative which I am about to relate. The events which I purpose detailing are of so extraordinary a character that I am quite prepared to meet with an unusual amount of incredulity and scorn. I accept all such beforehand. I have, I trust, the literary courage to face unbelief. I have, after mature consideration, resolved to narrate, in as simple and straightforward a manner as I can compass, some facts that passed under my observation, in the month of July last, and which, in the annals of the mysteries of physical science, are wholly unparalleled.

I live at No. — Twenty-sixth Street, in New York. The house is in some respects a curious one. It has enjoyed for the last two years the reputation of being haunted. The house is very spacious. A hall of noble size leads to a large spiral staircase winding through its centre, while the various apartments are of imposing dimensions. It was built some fifteen or twenty years since by Mr. A——, the well-known New York merchant, who five years ago threw the commercial world into convulsions by a stupendous bank fraud. Mr. A——, as everyone knows, escaped to Europe, and died not long after, of a broken heart. Almost immediately after the news of his decease reached this country and was verified, the report spread in Twenty-sixth Street that No. — was haunted.

Legal measures had dispossessed the widow of its former owner, and it was inhabited merely by a caretaker and his wife, placed there by the house-agent into whose hands it had passed for purposes of renting or sale. These people declared that they were troubled with unnatural noises. Doors were opened without any visible agency. The remnants of furniture scattered through the various rooms were, during the night, piled one upon the other by unknown hands. Invisible feet passed up and down the stairs in broad daylight, accompanied by the rustle of unseen silk dresses, and the gliding of viewless hands along the massive balusters. The caretaker and his wife declared they would live there no longer. The house-agent laughed, dismissed them, and put others in their place. The noises and supernatural manifestations continued. The neighbourhood caught up the story, and the house remained untenanted for three years. Several persons negotiated for it; but, somehow, always before the bargain was closed they heard the unpleasant rumours and declined to treat any further.

It was in this state of things that my landlady, who at that time kept a boarding-house in Bleecker Street, and who wished to move farther up town, conceived the bold idea of renting No. — Twenty-sixth Street. Happening to have in her house rather a plucky and philosophical set of boarders, she laid her scheme before us, stating candidly everything she had heard respecting the ghostly qualities of the establishment to which she wished to remove us. With the exception of two timid persons—a sea-captain and a returned Californian, who immediately gave notice that they would leave—all of Mrs. Moffat's guests declared that they would accompany her in her incursion into the abode of spirits.

Our removal was effected in the month of May, and we were charmed with our new residence.

Of course we had no sooner established ourselves at No. — than we began to expect the ghosts. We absolutely awaited their advent with eagerness. Our dinner conversation was supernatural. I found myself a person of immense importance, it having leaked out that I was tolerably well versed in the history of supernaturalism, and had once written a story the foundation of which was a ghost. If a table or wainscot panel happened to warp when we were assembled in the large drawing-room, there was an instant silence, and everyone was prepared for an immediate clanking of chains and a spectral form.

After a month of psychological excitement, it was with the utmost dissatisfaction that we were forced to acknowledge that nothing in the remotest degree approaching the supernatural had manifested itself.

Things were in this state when an incident took place so awful and inexplicable in its character that my reason fairly reels at the bare memory of the occurrence. It was the tenth of July. After dinner was over I repaired, with my friend Dr. Hammond, to the garden to smoke my evening pipe. Independent of certain mental sympathies which existed between the doctor and myself, we were linked together by a vice. We both smoked opium. We knew each other's secret and respected it. We enjoyed together that wonderful expansion of thought, that marvellous intensifying of the perceptive faculties, that boundless feeling of existence when we seem to have points of contact with the whole universe—in short, that unimaginable spiritual bliss, which I would not surrender for a throne, and which I hope you, reader, will never—never taste.

On the evening in question, the tenth of July, the doctor and myself drifted into an unusually metaphysical mood. We lit our large *meerschaums*, filled with fine Turkish tobacco, in the core of which burned a little black nut of opium, that, like the nut in the fairytale, held within its narrow limits wonders beyond the reach of kings; we paced to and fro, conversing. A strange perversity dominated the currents of our thoughts. They would not flow through the sunlit channels into which we strove to divert them. For some unaccountable reason, they constantly diverged into dark and lonesome beds, where a continual gloom brooded.

It was in vain that, after our old fashion, we flung ourselves on the shores of the East, and talked of its gay *bazaars*, of the splendours of the time of Haroun, of *harems* and golden palaces. Black *afreets* continually arose from the depths of our talk, and expanded, like the one the fisherman released from the copper vessel, until they blotted everything bright from our vision. Insensibly, we yielded to the occult force that swayed us, and indulged in gloomy speculation. We had talked some time upon the proneness of the human mind to mysticism, and the almost universal love of the terrible, when Hammond suddenly said to me, "What do you consider to be the greatest element of terror?"

The question puzzled me. That many things were terrible, I knew. But it now struck me, for the first time, that there must be one great and ruling embodiment of fear—a King of Terrors, to which all others must succumb. What might it be? To what train of circumstances would it owe its existence?

"I confess, Hammond," I replied to my friend, "I never considered the subject before. That there must be one Something more terrible than any other thing, I feel. I cannot attempt, however, even the most vague definition."

"I am somewhat like you, Harry," he answered. "I feel my capacity to experience a terror greater than anything yet conceived by the human mind—something combining in fearful and unnatural amalgamation hitherto supposed incompatible elements. The calling of the voices in Brockden Brown's novel of *Wieland* is awful; so is the picture of the Dweller on the Threshold, in Bulwer's *Zanoni*; but," he added, shaking his head gloomily, "there is something more horrible still than these."

"Look here, Hammond," I rejoined, "let us drop this kind of talk, for Heaven's sake! We shall suffer for it, depend on it."

"I don't know what's the matter with me tonight," he replied, "but my brain is running upon all sorts of weird and awful thoughts. I feel as if I could write a story like Hoffman, tonight, if I were only master of a literary style."

"Well, if we are going to be Hoffmanesque in our talk, I'm off to bed. Opium and nightmares should never be brought together. How sultry it is! Goodnight, Hammond."

"Goodnight, Harry. Pleasant dreams to you."

"To you, gloomy wretch, *afreets*, ghouls, and enchanters."

We parted, and each sought his respective chamber. I undressed quickly and got into bed, taking with me, according to my usual custom, a book over which I generally read myself to sleep. I opened the volume as soon as I had laid my head upon the pillow, and instantly flung it to the other side of the room. It was Goudon's *History of Monsters*,—a curious French work, which I had lately imported from Paris, but which, in the state of mind I had then reached, was anything but an agreeable companion. I resolved to go to sleep at once; so, turning down my gas until nothing but a little blue point of light glimmered on the top of the tube, I composed myself to rest.

The room was in total darkness. The atom of gas that still remained alight did not illuminate a distance of three inches round the burner. I desperately drew my arm across my eyes, as if to shut out even the darkness and tried to think of nothing. It was in vain. The confounded themes touched on by Hammond in the garden kept obtruding themselves on my brain. I battled against them. I erected ramparts of would-be blankness of intellect to keep them out. They still crowded upon me. While I was lying still as a corpse, hoping that by a perfect physical inaction I should hasten mental repose, an awful incident occurred. A Something dropped, as it seemed, from the ceiling, plumb upon my chest, and the next instant I felt two bony hands encircling my throat, endeavouring to choke me.

I am no coward, and am possessed of considerable physical strength. The suddenness of the attack, instead of stunning me, strung every nerve to its highest tension. My body acted from instinct, before my brain had time to realize the terrors of my position. In an instant I wound two muscular arms around the creature, and squeezed it, with all the strength of despair, against my chest. In a few seconds the bony hands that had fastened on my throat loosened their hold, and I was free to breathe once more. Then commenced a struggle of awful intensity.

Immersed in the most profound darkness, totally ignorant of the nature of the Thing by which I was so suddenly attacked, finding my grasp slipping every moment, by reason, it seemed to me, of the entire nakedness of my assailant, bitten with sharp teeth in the shoulder, neck, and chest, having every moment to protect my throat against a pair of sinewy, agile hands, which my utmost efforts could not confine—these were a combination of circumstances to combat which required all the strength, skill, and courage that I possessed.

At last, after a silent, deadly, exhausting struggle, I got my assailant under by a series of incredible efforts of strength. Once pinned, with my knee on what I made out to be its chest, I knew that I was victor. I rested for a moment to breathe. I heard the creature beneath me panting in the darkness, and felt the violent throbbing of a heart. It was apparently as exhausted as I was; that was one comfort. At this moment I remembered that I usually placed under my pillow, before going to bed, a large yellow silk pocket-handkerchief. I felt for it instantly; it was there. In a few seconds more I had, after a fashion, pinioned the creature's arms.

I now felt tolerably secure. There was nothing more to be done but to turn on the gas, and, having first seen what my midnight assailant was like, arouse the household. I will confess to being actuated by a certain pride in not giving the alarm before; I wished to make the capture alone and unaided.

Never losing my hold for an instant, I slipped from the bed to the floor, dragging my captive with me. I had but a few steps to make to reach the gas-burner; these I made with the greatest caution, holding the creature in a grip like a vice. At last I got within arm's length of the tiny speck of blue light which told me where the gas-burner lay. Quick as lightning I released my grasp with one hand and let on the full flood of light. Then I turned to look at my captive.

I cannot even attempt to give any definition of my sensations the instant after I turned on the gas. I suppose I must have shrieked with terror, for in less than a minute afterward my room was crowded with the inmates of the house. I shudder now as I think of that awful moment. *I saw nothing*! Yes; I had one arm firmly clasped round a breathing, panting, corporeal shape, my other hand gripped with all its strength a throat as warm, and apparently fleshly, as my own; and yet, with this living substance in my grasp, with its body pressed against my own, and all in the bright glare of a large jet of gas, I absolutely beheld nothing! Not even an outline—a vapour!

I do not, even at this hour, realize the situation in which I found myself. I cannot recall the astounding incident thoroughly. Imagination in vain tries to compass the awful paradox.

It breathed. I felt its warm breath upon my cheek. It struggled fiercely. It had hands. They clutched me. Its skin was smooth, like my own. There it lay, pressed close up against me, solid as stone—and yet utterly invisible!

I wonder that I did not faint or go mad on the instant. Some wonderful instinct must have sustained me; for absolutely, in place of loosening my hold on the terrible Enigma, I seemed to gain an additional strength in my moment of horror, and tightened my grasp with such wonderful force that I felt the creature shivering with agony.

Just then Hammond entered my room at the head of the household. As soon as he beheld my face—which, I suppose, must have been an awful sight to look at—he hastened forward, crying, "Great Heaven, what has happened?"

"Hammond! Hammond!" I cried, "come here. Oh, this is awful! I have been attacked in bed by something or other, which I have hold of; but I can't see it—I can't see it!"

Hammond, doubtless struck by the unfeigned horror expressed in my countenance, made one or two steps forward with an anxious yet puzzled expression. A very audible titter burst from the remainder of my visitors. This suppressed laughter made me furious. To laugh at a human being in my position! It was the worst species of cruelty. *Now*, I can understand why the appearance of a man struggling violently, as it would seem, with an airy nothing, and calling for assistance against a vision, should have appeared ludicrous. *Then*, so great was my rage against the mocking crowd that had I the power I would have stricken them dead where they stood.

"Hammond! Hammond!" I cried again, despairingly, "for

God's sake come to me. I can hold the—the thing but a short while longer. It is overpowering me. Help me! Help me!"

"Harry," whispered Hammond, approaching me, "you have been smoking too much opium."

"I swear to you, Hammond, that this is no vision," I answered, in the same low tone. "Don't you see how it shakes my whole frame with its struggles? If you don't believe me convince yourself. Feel it—touch it."

Hammond advanced and laid his hand in the spot I indicated. A wild cry of horror burst from him. He had felt it!

In a moment he had discovered somewhere in my room a long piece of cord, and was the next instant winding it and knotting it about the body of the unseen being that I clasped in my arms.

"Harry," he said, in a hoarse, agitated voice, for, though he preserved his presence of mind, he was deeply moved, "Harry, it's all safe now. You may let go, old fellow, if you're tired. The Thing can't move."

I was utterly exhausted, and I gladly loosed my hold.

Hammond stood holding the ends of the cord, that bound the Invisible, twisted round his hand, while before him, self-supporting as it were, he beheld a rope laced and interlaced, and stretching tightly around a vacant space. I never saw a man look so thoroughly stricken with awe. Nevertheless his face expressed all the courage and determination which I knew him to possess. His lips, although white, were set firmly, and one could perceive at a glance that, although stricken with fear, he was not daunted.

The confusion that ensued among the guests of the house who were witnesses of this extraordinary scene between Hammond and myself—who beheld the pantomime of binding this struggling Something—who beheld me almost sinking from physical exhaustion when my task of jailer was over—the confusion and terror that took possession of the bystanders, when they saw all this, was beyond description. The weaker ones fled from the apartment. The few who remained clustered near the door and could not be induced to approach Hammond and his Charge. Still incredulity broke out through their terror.

They had not the courage to satisfy themselves, and yet they doubted. It was in vain that I begged of some of the men to come near and convince themselves by touch of the existence in that room of a living being which was invisible. They were incredulous, but did not dare to undeceive themselves. How could a solid, living, breathing body be invisible, they asked. My reply was this. I gave a sign to Hammond, and both of us—conquering our fearful repugnance to touch the invisible creature—lifted it from the ground, manacled as it was, and took it to my bed. Its weight was about that of a boy of fourteen.

"Now, my friends," I said, as Hammond and myself held the creature suspended over the bed, "I can give you self-evident proof that here is a solid, ponderable body, which, nevertheless, you cannot see. Be good enough to watch the surface of the bed attentively."

I was astonished at my own courage in treating this strange event so calmly; but I had recovered from my first terror, and felt a sort of scientific pride in the affair, which dominated every other feeling.

The eyes of the bystanders were immediately fixed on my bed. At a given signal Hammond and I let the creature fall. There was the dull sound of a heavy body alighting on a soft mass. The timbers of the bed creaked. A deep impression marked itself distinctly on the pillow, and on the bed itself. The crowd who witnessed this gave a low cry, and rushed from the room. Hammond and I were left alone with our Mystery.

We remained silent for some time, listening to the low irregular breathing of the creature on the bed and watching the rustle of the bed-clothes as it impotently struggled to free itself from confinement. Then Hammond spoke.

"Harry, this is awful."

"Ay, awful."

"But not unaccountable."

"Not unaccountable! What do you mean? Such a thing has

never occurred since the birth of the world. I know not what to think, Hammond. God grant that I am not mad and that this is not an insane fantasy!"

"Let us reason a little, Harry. Here is a solid body which we touch but which we cannot see. The fact is so unusual that it strikes us with terror. Is there no parallel, though, for such a phenomenon? Take a piece of pure glass. It is tangible and transparent. A certain chemical coarseness is all that prevents its being so entirely transparent as to be totally invisible. It is not *theoretically impossible*, mind you, to make a glass which shall not reflect a single ray of light—a glass so pure and homogeneous in its atoms that the rays from the sun will pass through it as they do through the air, refracted but not reflected. We do not see the air, and yet we feel it."

"That's all very well, Hammond, but these are inanimate substances. Glass does not breathe, air does not breathe. This thing has a heart that palpitates—a will that moves it—lungs that play, and inspire and respire."

"You forget the phenomena of which we have so often heard of late," answered the doctor gravely. "At the meetings called 'spirit circles,' invisible hands have been thrust into the hands of those persons round the table—warm, fleshly hands that seemed to pulsate with mortal life."

"What? Do you think, then, that this thing is——"

"I don't know what it is," was the solemn reply; "but please the gods I will, with your assistance, thoroughly investigate it."

We watched together, smoking many pipes, all night long, by the bedside of the unearthly being that tossed and panted until it was apparently wearied out. Then we learned by the low, regular breathing that it slept.

The next morning the house was all astir. The boarders congregated on the landing outside my room, and Hammond and myself were lions. We had to answer a thousand questions as to the state of our extraordinary prisoner, for as yet not one person in the house except ourselves could be induced to set foot in the apartment.

The creature was awake. This was evidenced by the convulsive manner in which the bedclothes were moved in its efforts to escape. There was something truly terrible in beholding, as it were, those second-hand indications of the terrible writhings and agonized struggles for liberty which themselves were invisible.

Hammond and myself had racked our brains during the long night to discover some means by which we might realize the shape and general appearance of the Enigma. As well as we could make out by passing our hands over the creature's form, its outlines and lineaments were human. There was a mouth; a round, smooth head without hair; a nose, which, however, was little elevated above the cheeks; and its hands and feet felt like those of a boy. At first we thought of placing the being on a smooth surface and tracing its outlines with chalk, as shoemakers trace the outline of the foot. This plan was given up as being of no value. Such an outline would give not the slightest idea of its conformation.

A happy thought struck me. We would take a cast of it in plaster-of-Paris. This would give us the solid figure, and satisfy all our wishes. But how to do it. The movements of the creature would disturb the setting of the plastic covering, and distort the mould. Another thought. Why not give it chloroform? It had respiratory organs—that was evident by its breathing. Once reduced to a state of insensibility, we could do with it what we would. Doctor X—— was sent for; and after the worthy physician had recovered from the first shock of amazement, he proceeded to administer the chloroform.

In three minutes afterward we were enabled to remove the fetters from the creature's body, and a modeller was busily engaged in covering the invisible form with the moist clay. In five minutes more we had a mould, and before evening a rough facsimile of the Mystery. It was shaped like a man—distorted, uncouth, and horrible, but still a man. It was small, not over four feet and some inches in height, and its limbs revealed a muscular development that was unparalleled. Its face surpassed in hideousness anything I had ever seen. Gustave Dore, or Callot, or Tony Johannot, never conceived anything so horrible. There is a face in one of the latter's illustrations to *Un Voyage ou il vous plaira*, which somewhat approaches the countenance of this creature, but does not equal it. It was the physiognomy of what I should fancy a ghoul might be. It looked as if it was capable of feeding on human flesh.

Having satisfied our curiosity, and bound everyone in the house to secrecy, it became a question what was to be done with our Enigma? It was impossible that we should keep such a horror in our house; it was equally impossible that such an awful being should be let loose upon the world. I confess that I would have gladly voted for the creature's destruction. But who would shoulder the responsibility? Who would undertake the execution of this horrible semblance to a human being? Day after day this question was deliberated gravely. The boarders all left the house.

Mrs. Moffat was in despair, and threatened Hammond and myself with all sorts of legal penalties if we did not remove the Horror. Our answer was, "We will go if you like, but we decline taking this creature with us. Remove it yourself if you please. It appeared in your house. On you the responsibility rests." To this there was, of course, no answer. Mrs. Moffat could not obtain for love or money a person who would even approach the Mystery.

At last it died. Hammond and I found it cold and stiff one morning in the bed. The heart had ceased to beat, the lungs to inspire. We hastened to bury it in the garden. It was a strange funeral, the dropping of that viewless corpse into the damp hole. The cast of its form I gave to Doctor X——, who keeps it in his museum in Tenth Street.

As I am on the eve of a long journey from which I may not return, I have drawn up this narrative of an event the most singular that has ever come to my knowledge.

Ultor De Lacy: a Legend of Cappercullen

Chapter 1
The Jacobite's Legacy

In my youth I heard a great many Irish family traditions, more or less of a supernatural character, some of them very peculiar, and all, to a child at least, highly interesting. One of these I will now relate, though the translation to cold type from oral narrative, with all the aids of animated human voice and countenance, and the appropriate *mise-en-scène* of the old-fashioned parlour fireside and its listening circle of excited faces, and, outside, the wintry blast and the moan of leafless boughs, with the occasional rattle of the clumsy old window-frame behind shutter and curtain, as the blast swept by, is at best a trying one.

About midway up the romantic glen of Cappercullen, near the point where the counties of Limerick, Clare, and Tipperary converge, upon the then sequestered and forest-bound range of the Slieve-Felim hills, there stood, in the reigns of the two earliest Georges, the picturesque and massive remains of one of the finest of the Anglo-Irish castles of Munster—perhaps of Ireland.

It crowned the precipitous edge of the wooded glen, itself half-buried among the wild forest that covered that long and solitary range. There was no human habitation within a circle of many miles, except the half-dozen hovels and the small thatched chapel composing the little village of Murroa, which lay at the foot of the glen among the straggling skirts of the noble forest.

Its remoteness and difficulty of access saved it from demolition. It was worth nobody's while to pull down and remove the ponderous and clumsy oak, much less the masonry or flagged roofing of the pile. Whatever would pay the cost of removal had been long since carried away. The rest was abandoned to time-the destroyer.

The hereditary owners of this noble building and of a wide territory in the contiguous counties I have named, were English—the De Lacys—long naturalized in Ireland. They had acquired at least this portion of their estate in the reign of Henry VIII, and held it, with some vicissitudes, down to the establishment of the revolution in Ireland, when they suffered attainder, and, like other great families of that period, underwent a final eclipse.

The De Lacy of that day retired to France, and held a brief command in the Irish Brigade, interrupted by sickness. He retired, became a poor hanger-on of the Court of St. Germains, and died early in the eighteenth century—as well as I remember, 1705—leaving an only son, hardly twelve years old, called by the strange but significant name of Ultor.

At this point commences the marvellous ingredient of my tale.

When his father was dying, he had him to his bedside, with no one by except his confessor; and having told him, first, that on reaching the age of twenty-one, he was to lay claim to a certain small estate in the county of Clare, in Ireland, in right of his mother—the title-deeds of which he gave him—and next, having enjoined him not to marry before the age of thirty, on the ground that earlier marriages destroyed the spirit and the power of enterprise, and would incapacitate him from the accomplishment of his destiny—the restoration of his family—he then went on to open to the child a matter which so terrified him that he cried lamentably, trembling all over, clinging to the priest's gown with one hand and to his father's cold wrist with the other, and imploring him, with screams of horror, to desist from his communication.

But the priest, impressed, no doubt, himself, with its necessity, compelled him to listen. And then his father showed him a small picture, from which also the child turned with shrieks, until similarly constrained to look. They did not let him go until he had carefully conned the features, and was able to tell them, from memory, the colour of the eyes and hair, and the fashion and hues of the dress. Then his father gave him a black box containing this portrait, which was a full-length miniature, about nine inches long, painted very finely in oils, as smooth as enamel, and folded above it a sheet of paper, written over in a careful and very legible hand.

The deeds and this black box constituted the most important legacy bequeathed to his only child by the ruined Jacobite, and he deposited them in the hands of the priest, in trust, till his boy, Ultor, should have attained to an age to understand their value, and to keep them securely.

When this scene was ended, the dying exile's mind, I suppose, was relieved, for he spoke cheerily, and said he believed he would recover; and they soothed the crying child, and his father kissed him, and gave him a little silver coin to buy fruit with; and so they sent him off with another boy for a walk, and when he came back his father was dead.

He remained in France under the care of this ecclesiastic until he had attained the age of twenty-one, when he repaired to Ireland, and his title being unaffected by his father's attainder, he easily made good his claim to the small estate in the county of Clare.

There he settled, making a dismal and solitary tour now and then of the vast territories which had once been his father's, and nursing those gloomy and impatient thoughts which befitted the enterprises to which he was devoted.

Occasionally he visited Paris, that common centre of English, Irish, and Scottish disaffection; and there, when a little past thirty, he married the daughter of another ruined Irish house. His bride returned with him to the melancholy seclusion of their Munster residence, where she bore him in succession two daughters—Alice, the elder, dark-eyed and dark-haired, grave and sensible—Una, four years younger, with large blue eyes and long and beautiful golden hair.

Their poor mother was, I believe, naturally a lighthearted, sociable, high-spirited little creature; and her gay and childish nature pined in the isolation and gloom of her lot. At all events she died young, and the children were left to the sole care of their melancholy and embittered father. In process of time the girls grew up, tradition says, beautiful. The elder was designed for a convent, the younger her father hoped to mate as nobly as her high blood and splendid beauty seemed to promise, if only the great game on which he had resolved to stake all succeeded.

Chapter 2

The Fairies in the Castle

The Rebellion of '45 came, and Ultor de Lacy was one of the few Irishmen implicated treasonably in that daring and romantic insurrection. Of course there were warrants out against him, but he was not to be found. The young ladies, indeed, remained as heretofore in their father's lonely house in Clare; but whether he had crossed the water or was still in Ireland was for some time unknown, even to them. In due course he was attainted, and his little estate forfeited. It was a miserable catastrophe—a tremendous and beggarly waking up from a life-long dream of returning principality.

In due course the officers of the crown came down to take possession, and it behoved the young ladies to flit. Happily for them the ecclesiastic I have mentioned was not quite so confident as their father, of his winning back the magnificent patrimony of his ancestors; and by his advice the daughters had been secured twenty pounds a year each, under the marriage settlement of their parents, which was all that stood between this proud house and literal destitution.

Late one evening, as some little boys from the village were returning from a ramble through the dark and devious glen of

Cappercullen, with their pockets laden with nuts and "*frahans*," to their amazement and even terror they saw a light streaming redly from the narrow window of one of the towers overhanging the precipice among the ivy and the lofty branches, across the glen, already dim in the shadows of the deepening night.

"Look—look—look—'tis the Phooka's tower!" was the general cry, in the vernacular Irish, and a universal scamper commenced.

The bed of the glen, strewn with great fragments of rock, among which rose the tall stems of ancient trees, and overgrown with a tangled copse, was at the best no favourable ground for a run. Now it was dark; and, terrible work breaking through brambles and hazels and tumbling over rocks. Little Shaeen Mull Ryan, the last of the panic rout, screaming to his mates to wait for him—saw a whitish figure emerge from the thicket at the base of the stone flight of steps that descended the side of the glen, close by the castle-wall, intercepting his flight, and a discordant male voice shrieked——

"I have you!"

At the same time the boy, with a cry of terror, tripped and tumbled; and felt himself roughly caught by the arm, and hauled to his feet with a shake.

A wild yell from the child, and a volley of terror and entreaty followed.

"Who is it, Larry; what's the matter?" cried a voice, high in air, from the turret window, The words floated down through the trees, clear and sweet as the low notes of a flute.

"Only a child, my lady; a boy."

"Is he hurt?"

"Are you hurted?" demanded the whitish man, who held him fast, and repeated the question in Irish; but the child only kept blubbering and crying for mercy, with his hands clasped, and trying to drop on his knees.

Larry's strong old hand held him up. He *was* hurt, and bleeding from over his eye.

"Just a trifle hurted, my lady!"

"Bring him up here."

Shaeen Mull Ryan gave himself over. He was among "the good people," who he knew would keep him prisoner forever and a day. There was no good in resisting. He grew bewildered, and yielded himself passively to his fate, and emerged from the glen on the platform above; his captor's knotted old hand still on his arm, and looked round on the tall mysterious trees, and the gray front of the castle, revealed in the imperfect moonlight, as upon the scenery of a dream.

The old man who, with thin wiry legs, walked by his side, in a dingy white coat, and blue facings, and great pewter buttons, with his silver gray hair escaping from under his battered three-cocked hat; and his shrewd puckered resolute face, in which the boy could read no promise of sympathy, showing so white and phantom-like in the moonlight, was, as he thought, the incarnate ideal of a fairy.

This figure led him in silence under the great arched gateway, and across the grass-grown court, to the door in the far angle of the building; and so, in the dark, round and round, up a stone screw stair, and with a short turn into a large room, with a fire of turf and wood, burning on its long unused hearth, over which hung a pot, and about it an old woman with a great wooden spoon was busy. An iron candlestick supported their solitary candle; and about the floor of the room, as well as on the table and chairs, lay a litter of all sorts of things; piles of old faded hangings, boxes, trunks, clothes, pewter-plates, and cups; and I know not what more.

But what instantly engaged the fearful gaze of the boy were the figures of two ladies; red drugget cloaks they had on, like the peasant girls of Munster and Connaught, and the rest of their dress was pretty much in keeping. But they had the grand air, the refined expression and beauty, and above all, the serene air of command that belong to people of a higher rank.

The elder, with black hair and full brown eyes, sat writing at the deal table on which the candle stood, and raised her dark gaze to the boy as he came in. The other, with her hood thrown back, beautiful and *riant*, with a flood of wavy golden hair, and great blue eyes, and with something kind, and arch, and strange in her countenance, struck him as the most wonderful beauty he could have imagined.

They questioned the man in a language strange to the child. It was not English, for he had a smattering of that, and the man's story seemed to amuse them. The two young ladies exchanged a glance, and smiled mysteriously. He was more convinced than ever that he was among the good people. The younger stepped gaily forward and said——

"Do you know who *I* am, my little man? Well, I'm the fairy Una, and this is my palace; and that fairy you see there (pointing to the dark lady, who was looking out something in a box), is my sister and family physician, the Lady Graveairs; and these (glancing at the old man and woman), are some of my courtiers; and I'm considering now what I shall do with *you*, whether I shall send you tonight to Lough Guir, riding on a rush, to make my compliments to the Earl of Desmond in his enchanted castle; or, straight to your bed, two thousand miles under ground, among the gnomes; or to prison in that little corner of the moon you see through the window—with the man-in-the-moon for your gaoler, for thrice three hundred years and a day! There, don't cry. You only see how serious a thing it is for you, little boys, to come so near my castle. Now, for this once, I'll let you go. But, henceforward, any boys I, or my people, may find within half a mile round my castle, shall belong to me for life, and never behold their home or their people more."

And she sang a little air and chased mystically half a dozen steps before him, holding out her cloak with her pretty fingers, and courtesying very low, to his indescribable alarm.

Then, with a little laugh, she said——

"My little man, we must mend your head."

And so they washed his scratch, and the elder one applied a plaister to it. And she of the great blue eyes took out of her pocket a little French box of *bon-bons* and emptied it into his hand, and she said——

"You need not be afraid to eat these—they are very good-and I'll send my fairy, Blanc-et-bleu, to set you free. Take him (she addressed Larry), and let him go, with a solemn charge."

The elder, with a grave and affectionate smile, said, looking on the fairy——

"Brave, dear, wild Una! nothing can ever quell your gaiety of heart."

And Una kissed her merrily on the cheek.

So the oak door of the room again opened, and Shaeen, with his conductor, descended the stair. He walked with the scared boy in grim silence near half way down the wild hill-side toward Murroa, and then he stopped, and said in Irish——

"You never saw the fairies before, my fine fellow, and 'tisn't often those who once set eyes on us return to tell it. Whoever comes nearer, night or day, than this stone," and he tapped it with the end of his cane, "will never see his home again, for we'll keep him till the day of judgement; goodnight, little gossoon-and away with you."

So these young ladies, Alice and Una, with two old servants, by their father's direction, had taken up their abode in a portion of that side of the old castle which overhung the glen; and with the furniture and hangings they had removed from their late residence, and with the aid of glass in the casements and some other indispensable repairs, and a thorough airing, they made the rooms they had selected just habitable, as a rude and temporary shelter.

Chapter 3

The Priest's Adventures in the Glen

At first, of course, they saw or heard little of their father. In general, however, they knew that his plan was to procure some employment in France, and to remove them there. Their present strange abode was only an adventure and an episode, and they believed that any day they might receive instructions to commence their journey.

After a little while the pursuit relaxed. The government, I

believe, did not care, provided he did not obtrude himself, what became of him, or where he concealed himself. At all events, the local authorities showed no disposition to hunt him down. The young ladies' charges on the little forfeited property were paid without any dispute, and no vexatious inquiries were raised as to what had become of the furniture and other personal property which had been carried away from the forfeited house.

The haunted reputation of the castle—for in those days, in matters of the marvellous, the oldest were children—secured the little family in the seclusion they coveted. Once, or sometimes twice a week, old Laurence, with a shaggy little pony, made a secret expedition to the city of Limerick, starting before dawn, and returning under the cover of the night, with his purchases. There was beside an occasional sly moonlit visit from the old parish priest, and a midnight mass in the old castle for the little outlawed congregation.

As the alarm and inquiry subsided, their father made them, now and then, a brief and stealthy visit. At first these were but of a night's duration, and with great precaution; but gradually they were extended and less guarded. Still he was, as the phrase is in Munster, "on his keeping." He had firearms always by his bed, and had arranged places of concealment in the castle in the event of a surprise. But no attempt nor any disposition to molest him appearing, he grew more at ease, if not more cheerful.

It came, at last, that he would sometimes stay so long as two whole months at a time, and then depart as suddenly and mysteriously as he came. I suppose he had always some promising plot on hand, and his head full of ingenious treason, and lived on the sickly and exciting dietary of hope deferred.

Was there a poetical justice in this, that the little *ménage* thus secretly established, in the solitary and timeworn pile, should have themselves experienced, but from causes not so easily explicable, those very supernatural perturbations which they had themselves essayed to inspire?

The interruption of the old priest's secret visits was the earliest consequence of the mysterious interference which now began to display itself. One night, having left his cob in care of his old sacristan in the little village, he trudged on foot along the winding pathway, among the gray rocks and ferns that threaded the glen, intending a ghostly visit to the fair recluses of the castle, and he lost his way in this strange fashion.

There was moonlight, indeed, but it was little more than quarter-moon, and a long train of funereal clouds were sailing slowly across the sky—so that, faint and wan as it was, the light seldom shone full out, and was often hidden for a minute or two altogether. When he reached the point in the glen where the castle-stairs were wont to be, he could see nothing of them, and above, no trace of the castle-towers. So, puzzled somewhat, he pursued his way up the ravine, wondering how his walk had become so unusually protracted and fatiguing.

At last, sure enough, he saw the castle as plain as could be, and a lonely streak of candle-light issuing from the tower, just as usual, when his visit was expected. But he could not find the stair; and had to clamber among the rocks and copse-wood the best way he could. But when he emerged at top, there was nothing but the bare heath. Then the clouds stole over the moon again, and he moved along with hesitation and difficulty, and once more he saw the outline of the castle against the sky, quite sharp and clear. But this time it proved to be a great battlemented mass of cloud on the horizon.

In a few minutes more he was quite close, all of a sudden, to the great front, rising gray and dim in the feeble light, and not till he could have struck it with his good oak "wattle" did he discover it to be only one of those wild, gray frontages of living rock that rise here and there in picturesque tiers along the slopes of those solitary mountains. And so, till dawn, pursuing this mirage of the castle, through pools and among ravines, he wore out a night of miserable misadventure and fatigue.

Another night, riding up the glen, so far as the level way at bottom would allow, and intending to make his nag fast at his customary tree, he heard on a sudden a horrid shriek at top of the steep rocks above his head, and something—a gigantic human form, it seemed—came tumbling and bounding headlong down through the rocks, and fell with a fearful impetus just before his horse's hoofs and there lay like a huge palpitating carcass. The horse was scared, as, indeed, was his rider, too, and more so when this apparently lifeless thing sprang up to his legs, and throwing his arms apart to bar their further progress, advanced his white and gigantic face towards them. Then the horse started about, with a snort of terror, nearly unseating the priest, and broke away into a furious and uncontrollable gallop.

I need not recount all the strange and various misadventures which the honest priest sustained in his endeavours to visit the castle, and its isolated tenants. They were enough to wear out his resolution, and frighten him into submission. And so at last these spiritual visits quite ceased; and fearing to awaken inquiry and suspicion, he thought it only prudent to abstain from attempting them in the daytime.

So the young ladies of the castle were more alone than ever. Their father, whose visits were frequently of long duration, had of late ceased altogether to speak of their contemplated departure for France, grew angry at any allusion to it, and they feared, had abandoned the plan altogether.

Chapter 4

The Light in the Bell Tower

Shortly after the discontinuance of the priest's visits, old Laurence, one night, to his surprise, saw light issuing from a window in the Bell Tower. It was at first only a tremulous red ray, visible only for a few minutes, which seemed to pass from the room, through whose window it escaped upon the courtyard of the castle, and so to lose itself. This tower and casement were in the angle of the building, exactly confronting that in which the little outlawed family had taken up their quarters.

The whole family were troubled at the appearance of this dull red ray from the chamber in the Bell Tower. Nobody knew what to make of it. But Laurence, who had campaigned in Italy with his old master, the young ladies' grandfather—"the heavens be his bed this night!"—was resolved to see it out, and took his great horse-pistols with him, and ascended to the corridor leading to the tower. But his search was vain.

This light left a sense of great uneasiness among the inmates, and most certainly it was not pleasant to suspect the establishment of an independent and possibly dangerous lodger or even colony, within the walls of the same old building.

The light very soon appeared again, steadier and somewhat brighter, in the same chamber. Again old Laurence buckled on his armour, swearing ominously to himself, and this time bent in earnest upon conflict. The young ladies watched in thrilling suspense from the great window in *their* stronghold, looking diagonally across the court. But as Laurence, who had entered the massive range of buildings opposite, might be supposed to be approaching the chamber from which this ill-omened glare proceeded, it steadily waned, finally disappearing altogether, just a few seconds before his voice was heard shouting from the arched window to know which way the light had gone.

This lighting up of the great chamber of the Bell Tower grew at last to be of frequent and almost continual recurrence. It was, there, long ago, in times of trouble and danger, that the De Lacys of those evil days used to sit in feudal judgment upon captive adversaries, and, as tradition alleged, often gave them no more time for shrift and prayer, than it needed to mount to the battlement of the turret over-head, from which they were forthwith hung by the necks, for a caveat and admonition to all evil disposed persons viewing the same from the country beneath.

Old Laurence observed these mysterious glimmerings with an evil and an anxious eye, and many and various were the stratagems he tried, but in vain, to surprise the audacious intruders. It is, however, I believe, a fact that no phenomenon, no matter how startling at first, if prosecuted with tolerable regularity, and unattended with any new circumstances of terror, will very long continue to excite alarm or even wonder.

So the family came to acquiesce in this mysterious light. No harm accompanied it. Old Laurence, as he smoked his lonely pipe in the grass-grown courtyard, would cast a disturbed glance at it, as it softly glowed out through the darking aperture, and mutter a prayer or an oath. But he had given over the chase as a hopeless business. And Peggy Sullivan, the old dame of all work, when, by chance, for she never willingly looked toward the haunted quarter, she caught the faint reflection of its dull effulgence with the corner of her eye, would sign herself with the cross or fumble at her beads, and deeper furrows would gather in her forehead, and her face grow ashen and perturbed. And this was not mended by the levity with which the young ladies, with whom the spectre had lost his influence, familiarity, as usual, breeding contempt, had come to talk, and even to jest, about it.

Chapter 5

The Man with the Claret Mark

But as the former excitement flagged, old Peggy Sullivan produced a new one; for she solemnly avowed that she had seen a thin-faced man, with an ugly red mark all over the side of his cheek, looking out of the same window, just at sunset, before the young ladies returned from their evening walk.

This sounded in their ears like an old woman's dream, but still it was an excitement, jocular in the morning, and just, perhaps, a little fearful as night overspread the vast and desolate building, but still, not wholly unpleasant. This little flicker of credulity suddenly, however, blazed up into the full light of conviction.

Old Laurence, who was not given to dreaming, and had a cool, hard head, and an eye like a hawk, saw the same figure, just about the same hour, when the last level gleam of sunset was tinting the summits of the towers and the tops of the tall trees that surrounded them.

He had just entered the court from the great gate, when he heard all at once the hard peculiar twitter of alarm which sparrows make when a cat or a hawk invades their safety, rising all round from the thick ivy that overclimbed the wall on his left, and raising his eyes listlessly, he saw, with a sort of shock, a thin, ungainly man, standing with his legs crossed, in the recess of the window from which the light was wont to issue, leaning with his elbows on the stone mullion, and looking down with a sort of sickly sneer, his hollow yellow cheeks being deeply stained on one side with what is called a "claret-mark."

"I have you at last, you villain!" cried Larry, in a strange rage and panic: "drop down out of that on the grass here, and give yourself up, or I'll shoot you."

The threat was backed with an oath, and he drew from his coat pocket the long holster pistol he was wont to carry, and covered his man cleverly.

"I give you while I count ten—one-two-three-four. If you draw back, I'll fire, mind; five-six—you'd better be lively—seven-eight-nine—one chance more; will you come down? Then take it—ten!"

Bang went the pistol. The sinister stranger was hardly fifteen feet removed from him, and Larry was a dead shot. But this time he made a scandalous miss, for the shot knocked a little white dust from the stone wall a full yard at one side; and the fellow never shifted his negligent posture or qualified his sardonic smile during the procedure.

Larry was mortified and angry.

"You'll not get off this time, my tulip!" he said with a grin, exchanging the smoking weapon for the loaded pistol in reserve.

"What are you pistolling, Larry?" said a familiar voice close by his elbow, and he saw his master, accompanied by a handsome young man in a cloak.

"That villain, your honour, in the window, there."

"Why there's nobody there, Larry," said De Lacy, with a laugh, though that was no common indulgence with him.

As Larry gazed, the figure somehow dissolved and broke up without receding. A hanging tuft of yellow and red ivy nodded queerly in place of the face, some broken and discoloured masonry in perspective took up the outline and colouring of the arms and figure, and two imperfect red and yellow lichen streaks carried on the curved tracing of the long spindle shanks. Larry blessed himself, and drew his hand across his damp forehead, over his bewildered eyes, and could not speak for a minute. It was all some devilish trick; he could take his oath he saw every feature in the fellow's face, the lace and buttons of his cloak and doublet, and even his long finger nails and thin yellow fingers that overhung the cross-shaft of the window, where there was now nothing but a rusty stain left.

The young gentleman who had arrived with De Lacy, stayed that night and shared with great apparent relish the homely fare of the family. He was a gay and gallant Frenchman, and the beauty of the younger lady, and her pleasantry and spirit, seemed to make his hours pass but too swiftly, and the moment of parting sad.

When he had departed early in the morning, Ultor De Lacy had a long talk with his elder daughter, while the younger was busy with her early dairy task, for among their retainers this *proles generosa* reckoned a "kind" little Kerry cow.

He told her that he had visited France since he had been last at Cappercullen, and how good and gracious their sovereign had been, and how he had arranged a noble alliance for her sister Una. The young gentleman was of high blood, and though not rich, had, nevertheless, his acres and his *nom de terre*, besides a captain's rank in the army. He was, in short, the very gentleman with whom they had parted only that morning. On what special business he was now in Ireland there was no necessity that he should speak; but being here he had brought him hither to present him to his daughter, and found that the impression she had made was quite what was desirable.

"You, you know, dear Alice, are promised to a conventual life. Had it been otherwise——"

He hesitated for a moment.

"You are right, dear father," she said, kissing his hand, "I *am* so promised, and no earthly tie or allurement has power to draw me from that holy engagement."

"Well," he said, returning her caress, "I do not mean to urge you upon that point. It must not, however, be until Una's marriage has taken place. That cannot be, for many good reasons, sooner than this time twelve months; we shall then exchange this strange and barbarous abode for Paris, where are many eligible convents, in which are entertained as sisters some of the noblest ladies of France; and there, too, in Una's marriage will be continued, though not the name, at all events the blood, the lineage, and the title which, so sure as justice ultimately governs the course of human events, will be again established, powerful and honoured in this country, the scene of their ancient glory and transitory misfortunes. Meanwhile, we must not mention this engagement to Una. Here she runs no risk of being sought or won; but the mere knowledge that her hand was absolutely pledged, might excite a capricious opposition and repining such as neither I nor you would like to see; therefore be secret."

The same evening he took Alice with him for a ramble round the castle wall, while they talked of grave matters, and he as usual allowed her a dim and doubtful view of some of those cloud-built castles in which he habitually dwelt, and among which his jaded hopes revived.

They were walking upon a pleasant short sward of darkest green, on one side overhung by the gray castle walls, and on the other by the forest trees that here and there closely approached it, when precisely as they turned the angle of the Bell Tower, they were encountered by a person walking directly towards them. The sight of a stranger, with the exception of the one visitor introduced by her father, was in this place so absolutely unprecedented, that Alice was amazed and affrighted to such a degree that for a moment she stood stock-still.

But there was more in this apparition to excite unpleasant emotions, than the mere circumstance of its unexpectedness. The figure was very strange, being that of a tall, lean, ungainly man, dressed in a dingy suit, somewhat of a Spanish fashion, with a brown laced cloak, and faded red stockings. He had long lank legs, long arms, hands, and fingers, and a very long sickly face, with a drooping nose, and a sly, sarcastic leer, and a great purplish stain over-spreading more than half of one cheek.

As he strode past, he touched his cap with his thin, discoloured fingers, and an ugly side glance, and disappeared round the corner. The eyes of father and daughter followed him in silence.

Ultor De Lacy seemed first absolutely terror-stricken, and then suddenly inflamed with ungovernable fury. He dropped his cane on the ground, drew his rapier, and, without wasting a thought on his daughter, pursued.

He just had a glimpse of the retreating figure as it disappeared round the far angle. The plume, and the lank hair, the point of the rapier-scabbard, the flutter of the skirt of the cloak, and one red stocking and heel; and this was the last he saw of him.

When Alice reached his side, his drawn sword still in his hand, he was in a state of abject agitation.

"Thank Heaven, he's gone!" she exclaimed.

"He's gone," echoed Ultor, with a strange glare.

"And you are safe," she added, clasping his hand.

He sighed a great sigh.

"And you don't think he's coming back?"

"He!—who?"

"The stranger who passed us but now. Do you know him, father?"

"Yes—and—no, child—I know him not—and yet I know him too well. Would to heaven we could leave this accursed haunt tonight. Cursed be the stupid malice that first provoked this horrible feud, which no sacrifice and misery can appease, and no exorcism can quell or even suspend. The wretch has come from afar with a sure instinct to devour my last hope—to dog us into our last retreat—and to blast with his triumph the very dust and ruins of our house. What ails that stupid priest that he has given over his visits? Are *my* children to be left without mass or confession—the sacraments which *guard* as well as save—because he once loses his way in a mist, or mistakes a streak of foam in the brook for a dead man's face? D—n him!"

"See, Alice, if he won't come," he resumed, "you must only *write* your confession to him in full—you and Una. Laurence is trusty, and will carry it—and we'll get the bishop's—or, if need be, the Pope's leave for him to give you absolution. I'll move heaven and earth, but you *shall* have the sacraments, poor children!—and see him. I've been a wild fellow in my youth, and never pretended to sanctity; but I know there's but one safe way—and—and—keep you each a bit of this—(he opened a small silver box)—about you while you stay here—fold and sew it up reverently in a bit of the old psaltery parchment and wear it next your hearts—'tis a fragment of the consecrated wafer-and will help, with the saints' protection, to guard you from harm—and be strict in fasts, and constant in prayer—*I* can do nothing—nor devise any help. The curse has fallen, indeed, on me and mine."

And Alice, saw, in silence, the tears of despair roll down his pale and agitated face.

This adventure was also a secret, and Una was to hear nothing of it.

Chapter 6
Voices

Now Una, nobody knew why, began to lose spirit, and to grow pale. Her fun and frolic were quite gone! Even her songs ceased. She was silent with her sister, and loved solitude better. She said she was well, and quite happy, and could in no wise be got to account for the lamentable change that had stolen over her. She had grown odd too, and obstinate in trifles; and strangely reserved and cold.

Alice was very unhappy in consequence. What was the cause of this estrangement—had she offended her, and how? But Una had never before borne resentment for an hour. What could have altered her entire nature so? Could it be the shadow and chill of coming insanity?

Once or twice, when her sister urged her with tears and entreaties to disclose the secret of her changed spirits and demeanour, she seemed to listen with a sort of silent wonder and suspicion, and then she looked for a moment full upon her, and seemed on the very point of revealing all. But the earnest dilated gaze stole downward to the floor, and subsided into an odd wily smile, and she began to whisper to herself, and the smile and the whisper were both a mystery to Alice.

She and Alice slept in the same bedroom—a chamber in a projecting tower—which on their arrival, when poor Una was so merry, they had hung round with old tapestry, and decorated fantastically according to their skill and frolic. One night, as they went to bed, Una said, as if speaking to herself——

"'Tis my last night in this room—I shall sleep no more with Alice."

"And what has poor Alice done, Una, to deserve your strange unkindness?"

Una looked on her curiously, and half frightened, and then the odd smile stole over her face like a gleam of moonlight.

"My poor Alice, what have you to do with it?" she whispered.

"And why do you talk of sleeping no more with me?" said Alice.

"Why? Alice dear—no why—no reason—only a knowledge that it must be so, or Una will die."

"Die, Una darling!—what can you mean?"

"Yes, sweet Alice, die, indeed. We must all die some time, you know, or—or undergo a change; and my time is near—*very* near—unless I sleep apart from you."

"Indeed, Una, sweetheart, I think you *are* ill, but not near death."

"Una knows what you think, wise Alice—but she's not mad—on the contrary, she's wiser than other folks."

"She's sadder and stranger too," said Alice, tenderly.

"Knowledge is sorrow," answered Una, and she looked across the room through her golden hair which she was combing-and through the window, beyond which lay the tops of the great trees, and the still foliage of the glen in the misty moonlight.

"'Tis enough, Alice dear; it must be so. The bed must move hence, or Una's bed will be low enough ere long. See, it shan't be far though, only into that small room."

She pointed to an inner room or closet opening from that in which they lay. The walls of the building were hugely thick, and there were double doors of oak between the chambers, and Alice thought, with a sigh, how completely separated they were going to be.

However she offered no opposition. The change was made, and the girls for the first time since childhood lay in separate chambers. A few nights afterwards Alice awoke late in the night from a dreadful dream, in which the sinister figure which she and her father had encountered in their ramble round the castle walls, bore a principal part.

When she awoke there were still in her ears the sounds which had mingled in her dream. They were the notes of a deep, ringing, bass voice rising from the glen beneath the castle walls-something between humming and singing—listlessly unequal and intermittent, like the melody of a man whiling away the hours over his work. While she was wondering at this unwonted minstrelsy, there came a silence, and—could she believe her ears?—it certainly was Una's clear low *contralto*—softly singing a bar or two from the window. Then once more silence—and then again the strange manly voice, faintly chaunting from the leafy abyss.

With a strange wild feeling of suspicion and terror, Alice glided to the window. The moon who sees so many things, and keeps all secrets, with her cold impenetrable smile, was high in the sky. But Alice saw the red flicker of a candle from Una's window, and, she thought, the shadow of her head against the deep side wall of its recess. Then this was gone, and there were no more sights or sounds that night.

As they sate at breakfast, the small birds were singing merrily from among the sun-tipped foliage.

"I love this music," said Alice, unusually pale and sad; "it comes with the pleasant light of morning. I remember, Una, when you used to sing, like those gay birds, in the fresh beams of the morning; that was in the old time, when Una kept no secret from poor Alice."

"And Una knows what her sage Alice means; but there are other birds, silent all day long, and, they say, the sweetest too, that love to sing by *night* alone."

So things went on—the elder girl pained and melancholy-the younger silent, changed, and unaccountable.

A little while after this, very late one night, on awaking, Alice heard a conversation being carried on in her sister's room. There seemed to be no disguise about it. She could not distinguish the words, indeed, the walls being some six feet thick, and two great oak doors intercepting. But Una's clear voice, and the deep bell-like tones of the unknown, made up the dialogue.

Alice sprung from her bed, threw her clothes about her, and tried to enter her sister's room; but the inner door was bolted. The voices ceased to speak as she knocked, and Una opened it, and stood before her in her nightdress, candle in hand.

"Una—Una, darling, as you hope for peace, tell me who is here?" cried frightened Alice, with her trembling arms about her neck.

Una drew back, with her large innocent blue eyes fixed full upon her.

"Come in, Alice," she said, coldly.

And in came Alice, with a fearful glance around. There was no hiding place there; a chair, a table, a little bedstead, and two or three pegs in the wall to hang clothes on; a narrow window, with two iron bars across; no hearth or chimney—nothing but bare walls.

Alice looked round in amazement, and her eyes glanced with painful inquiry into those of her sister. Una smiled one of her peculiar sidelong smiles, and said——

"Strange dreams! I've been dreaming—so has Alice. She hears and sees Una's dreams, and wonders—and well she may."

And she kissed her sister's cheek with a cold kiss, and lay down in her little bed, her slender hand under her head, and spoke no more.

Alice, not knowing what to think, went back to hers.

About this time Ultor De Lacy returned. He heard his elder daughter's strange narrative with marked uneasiness, and his agitation seemed to grow rather than subside. He enjoined her, however, not to mention it to the old servant, nor in presence of anybody she might chance to see, but only to him and to the priest, if he could be persuaded to resume his duty and return. The trial, however, such as it was, could not endure very long; matters had turned out favourably. The union of his younger daughter might be accomplished within a few months, and in eight or nine weeks they should be on their way to Paris.

A night or two after her father's arrival, Alice, in the dead of the night, heard the well-known strange deep voice speaking softly, as it seemed, close to her own window on the outside; and Una's voice, clear and tender, spoke in answer. She hurried to her own casement, and pushed it open, kneeling in the deep embrasure, and looking with a stealthy and affrighted gaze towards her sister's window.

As she crossed the floor the voices subsided, and she saw a light withdrawn from within. The moonbeams slanted bright and clear on the whole side of the castle overlooking the glen, and she plainly beheld the shadow of a man projected on the wall as on a screen.

This black shadow recalled with a horrid thrill the outline and fashion of the figure in the Spanish dress. There were the cap and mantle, the rapier, the long thin limbs and sinister angularity. It was so thrown obliquely that the hands reached to the window-sill, and the feet stretched and stretched, longer and longer as she looked, toward the ground, and disappeared in the general darkness; and the rest, with a sudden flicker, shot downwards, as shadows will on the sudden movement of a light, and was lost in one gigantic leap down the castle wall.

"I do not know whether I dream or wake when I hear and see these sights; but I will ask my father to sit up with me, and we *two* surely cannot be mistaken. May the holy saints keep and guard us!" And in her terror she buried her head under the bedclothes, and whispered her prayers for an hour.

Chapter 7

Una's Love

"I have been with Father Denis," said De Lacy, next day, "and he will come tomorrow; and, thank Heaven! you may both make your confession and hear mass, and my mind will be at rest; and you'll find poor Una happier and more like herself."

But 'tween cup and lip there's many a slip. The priest was not destined to hear poor Una's shrift. When she bid her sister goodnight she looked on her with her large, cold, wild eyes, till something of her old human affections seemed to gather there, and they slowly filled with tears, which dropped one after the other on her homely dress as she gazed in her sister's face.

Alice, delighted, sprang up, and clasped her arms about her neck. "My own darling treasure, 'tis all over; you love your poor Alice again, and will be happier than ever."

But while she held her in her embrace Una's eyes were turned towards the window, and her lips apart, and Alice felt instinctively that her thoughts were already far away.

"Hark!—listen!—hush!" and Una, with her delighted gaze fixed, as if she saw far away beyond the castle wall, the trees, the glen, and the night's dark curtain, held her hand raised near her ear, and waved her head slightly in time, as it seemed, to music that reached not Alice's ear, and smiled her strange pleased smile, and then the smile slowly faded away, leaving that sly suspicious light behind it which somehow scared her sister with an uncertain sense of danger; and she sang in tones so sweet and low that it seemed but a reverie of a song, recalling, as Alice fancied, the strain to which she had just listened in that strange ecstasy, the plaintive and beautiful Irish ballad, "Shule, shule, shule, aroon," the midnight summons of the outlawed Irish soldier to his darling to follow him.

Alice had slept little the night before. She was now overpowered with fatigue; and leaving her candle burning by her bedside, she fell into a deep sleep. From this she awoke suddenly, and completely, as will sometimes happen without any apparent cause, and she saw Una come into the room. She had a little purse of embroidery—her own work—in her hand; and she stole lightly to the bedside, with her peculiar oblique smile, and evidently thinking that her sister was asleep.

Alice was thrilled with a strange terror, and did not speak or move; and her sister slipped her hand softly under her bolster, and withdrew it. Then Una stood for while by the hearth, and stretched her hand up to the mantelpiece, from which she took a little bit of chalk, and Alice thought she saw her place it in the fingers of a long yellow hand that was stealthily introduced from her own chamber-door to receive it; and Una paused in the dark recess of the door, and smiled over her shoulder toward her sister, and then glided into her room, closing the doors.

Almost freezing with terror, Alice rose and glided after her, and stood in her chamber, screaming——

"Una, Una, in heaven's name what troubles you?"

But Una seemed to have been sound asleep in her bed, and raised herself with a start, and looking upon her with a peevish surprise, said——

"What does Alice seek here?"

"You were in my room, Una, dear; you seem disturbed and troubled."

"Dreams, Alice. My dreams crossing your brain; only dreams-dreams. Get you to bed, and sleep."

And to bed she went, but *not* to sleep. She lay awake more than an hour; and then Una emerged once more from her room. This time she was fully dressed, and had her cloak and thick shoes on, as their rattle on the floor plainly discovered. She had a little bundle tied up in a handkerchief in her hand, and her hood was drawn about her head; and thus equipped, as it seemed, for a journey, she came and stood at the foot of Alice's bed, and stared on her with a look so soulless and terrible that her senses almost forsook her. Then she turned and went back into her own chamber.

She may have returned; but Alice thought not—at least she did not see her. But she lay in great excitement and perturbation; and was terrified, about an hour later, by a knock at her chamber door—not that opening into Una's room, but upon the little passage from the stone screw staircase. She sprang from her bed; but the door was secured on the inside, and she felt relieved. The knock was repeated, and she heard someone laughing softly on the outside.

The morning came at last; that dreadful night was over. But Una! Where was Una?

Alice never saw her more. On the head of her empty bed were traced in chalk the words—Ultor De Lacy, Ultor O'Donnell. And Alice found beneath her own pillow the little purse of embroidery she had seen in Una's hand. It was her little parting token, and bore the simple legend—"Una's love!"

De Lacy's rage and horror were boundless. He charged the priest, in frantic language, with having exposed his child, by his cowardice and neglect, to the machinations of the Fiend, and raved and blasphemed like a man demented.

It is said that he procured a solemn exorcism to be performed, in the hope of disenthralling and recovering his daughter. Several times, it is alleged, she was seen by the old servants. Once on a sweet summer morning, in the window of the tower, she was perceived combing her beautiful golden tresses, and holding a little mirror in her hand; and first, when she saw herself discovered, she looked affrighted, and then smiled, her slanting, cunning smile. Sometimes, too, in the glen, by moonlight, it was said belated villagers had met her, always startled first, and then smiling, generally singing snatches of old Irish ballads, that seemed to bear a sort of dim resemblance to her melancholy fate. The apparition has long ceased. But it is said that now and again, perhaps once in two or three years, late on a summer night, you may hear—but faint and far away in the recesses of the glen-the sweet, sad notes of Una's voice, singing those plaintive melodies. This, too, of course, in time will cease, and all be forgotten.

Chapter 8

Sister Agnes and the Portrait

When Ultor De Lacy died, his daughter Alice found among

his effects a small box, containing a portrait such as I have described. When she looked on it, she recoiled in horror. There, in the plenitude of its sinister peculiarities, was faithfully portrayed the phantom which lived with a vivid and horrible accuracy in her remembrance. Folded in the same box was a brief narrative, stating that,

> *A.D.* 1601, in the month of December, Walter De Lacy, of Cappercullen, made many prisoners at the ford of Ownhey, or Abington, of Irish and Spanish soldiers, flying from the great overthrow of the rebel powers at Kinsale, and among the number one Roderic O'Donnell, an arch traitor, and near kinsman to that other O'Donnell who led the rebels; who, claiming kindred through his mother to De Lacy, sued for his life with instant and miserable entreaty, and offered great ransom, but was by De Lacy, through great zeal for the queen, as some thought, cruelly put to death. When he went to the tower-top, where was the gallows, finding himself in extremity, and no hope of mercy, he swore that though he could work them no evil before his death, yet that he would devote himself thereafter to blast the greatness of the De Lacys, and never leave them till his work was done. He hath been seen often since, and always for that family perniciously, insomuch that it hath been the custom to show to young children of that lineage the picture of the said O'Donnell, in little, taken among his few valuables, to prevent their being misled by him unawares, so that he should not have his will, who by devilish wiles and hell-born cunning, hath steadfastly sought the ruin of that ancient house, and especially to leave that *stemma generosum* destitute of issue for the transmission of their pure blood and worshipful name.

Old Miss Croker, of Ross House, who was near seventy in the year 1821, when she related this story to me, had seen and conversed with Alice De Lacy, a professed nun, under the name of Sister Agnes, in a religious house in King-street, in Dublin, founded by the famous Duchess of Tyrconnell, and had the narrative from her own lips. I thought the tale worth preserving, and have no more to say.

Fireside Horrors For Christmas

(*Article written for the Dublin University Magazine.*)

There are two things in particular for which we feel thankful, when we see the year verging to its close, and the dusk falling earlier and earlier every day. The first is, that we never saw a ghost ourselves, and the second is, that other people did. The world does not always consider the debt of gratitude it is under to those who have vision for the invisible. Winter would not limp more tediously away without the long evenings, than the long evenings without ghost-stories. We do not envy the feelings of the man who can get through his December without any deeper shudderings than those produced by physical cold. We have little sympathy with people whose talk, when they hitch their chairs closer together about a well-heaped hearth, does not instinctively turn on haunted houses, nightmares, and warnings before death.

To us, the bars of a grate infallibly suggest the ribs of a skeleton; and as we watch the thin smoke, flitting silently up the chimney, our thoughts are of things in winding-sheets, that glide by moonlight along the aisles of ancient churches. In what manner our own shadow, dancing behind us on the wall or ceiling, might affect our imagination at such a time, we have no means of saying, as we have always felt disinclined to the indulgence of any rash curiosity on the subject. Who knows what other shadow we might see, if we turned round to look at our own: And if we saw none *but* our own, the spell would be broken, the hearth would be disenchanted, the mysterious "behind us" would be spoiled of its mystery, and *that* evening's tale of wonder would be told to listless and incredulous ears. We pity the man who, from his place at the Christmas fireside, has looked behind him; for that man, life has lost its illusions; he has lifted the veil of Isis, and "seen the truth" in the shape of his grandmother; he has leaped into the abyss, and found it just knee-deep.

The law of the winter evening is—look straight into the embers, and think of your favourite horror. When you feel horrorized through and through, begin to talk, still looking straight into the embers. Horrors belong as naturally to the fireside, as the fireside belongs to Christmas. The cold of the season does not more cravingly demand the genial blaze, than the heat of the blaze demands that agreeable chill which a churchyard reminiscence will send with electric swiftness through the blood. The passing shiver that runs over you as you listen to some chimney-corner legend, of wan women with their throats out, that sit down opposite to solitary students at midnight, or of hands thrust out of unhallowed graves, to point to the murderer as he goes by, is as gratefully refrigerant and bracing to the nerves as a raspberry ice in the dog days.

Then, there is nothing that so much heightens the enjoyableness of a ghostly gossip about the Yule fire, in an old rambling country-house, as the thought of the wide staircases you will by-and-by have to ascend, the long corridors you will have to traverse, the dark rooms, with their doors standing open, you will have to pass, with no company but your candle and the echo of your footsteps, on your way from that warm parlour, that lies bathed in the glow of the wood fire, as in the "light of setting sun," to the woebegone, vast chamber, with a bed like a hearse, that awaits you at the furthest end of the scarce half-inhabited mansion. The anticipation of this pilgrimage makes the circle round the hearth a true magic circle, out of the bounds of which no one cares to tread.

The living world has shrunk to the dimensions of that charmed ring, and all beyond its confines is a dark and spectre-peopled void—a world of spirits that have heard you talking

about them. No wonder you have little mind to go out into the goblin domain, with no better amulet against its terrors than a bed-room candlestick. And why should you do so? Why not rather pile on more fagots, and commend yourself to the safe keeping of Vesta, till the "witching time of night" be past? Why not outwatch the ghosts, and betake yourself to your own bed when the first cock-crow summons them to theirs?

If anyone doubts that telling ghost-stories is the proper employment for a winter's night, let him open his window, and look out. Can anything be more spectral? There is not a hill or a hollow in sight, but has put on a shroud, and stares at him with a still, white face, the phantom of itself. The trees stand like giant skeletons, lifting their bleached arms towards the trooping clouds that hurry across the sky, like witches flocking to their Sabbath. What is all that but a ghost-story in dumb-show, told by the earth to the stars? If the doubter can go on doubting in the face of an example like this, nothing that, we could urge in the way of precept would be likely to decide him; we give him up, and can only hope it may not be our fate to have him for a reader. What has he to do with our fireside horrors? He is a horror himself, more horrible than any that we can conjure up, for whatever fireside he sits at.

Thee, actual reader, we well discern to be of a different spirit; come, then, and shudder with us, in the first place, over some ghastlinesses gleaned from a delightful little book, published this year by Mr. Burns, and bearing the title, most germane to our subject, of "Communications between the Seen and the Unseen Worlds."[1]

You are to suppose, then, that a party of friends are assembled, perhaps for the Christmas holidays, at a house, which, from some accidental indications, we judge to be in the country. A starry sky, the sight of which it is pronounced "almost a pity to shut out," leads the conversation of the friends to the compara-

---

1. *The Unseen World; communications with it, real or imaginary, including Apparitions, Warnings, Haunted Places, Prophecies, Aërial Visions, Astrology, &c.* London: James Burns. 1847.

tive beauty of the winter and the summer night; and the gentler season most naturally finds an advocate in a gentle lady of the company, who is introduced to you by the name of Eusebia. Eloquently does Eusebia plead for I he season of her preference. The rare power of "painting with words" is hers in a high degree, and you feel, as you listen, that the influence of the hour she describes is upon you—

> When the west has lost its more gaudy hues, and the only trace of the departed sun is the calm, still belt of green, that reposes above the distant hills, as if they were the barriers of this world, and that quiet ocean of light the gulf which Darts us from the realm of spirits.

Then, she insists further—

> There is the soft scent of the sleeping flowers, the dewiness of the air, the few bright stars that peep through the still faintly-illuminated sky; the joyous song, it may be, of the nightingale; the merry chirp, that seems, wherever you go, to be equally close to you, of the grasshopper. It is repose in its truest sense—life enough to banish the idea that nature, as people talk, can ever sleep—rest enough to lead on the mind to a more perfect, even an eternal repose.

Eusebia's friends will not deny that the summer night is beautiful; but there is one of them, at least—his name is Pistus—who holds that the winter night is more beautiful still, or, in any case, that its beauty is of a more solemn and spiritual character. Too much of this world, Pistus thinks, is mixed up in our ideas of the night of summer. With its flowers, its birds, its dew, and that green brightness over the western hills, it is of the earth, earthy; it does not carry us away to other worlds, but throws a colouring of poetry and illusion over our enthralment to this. It is not so, he exclaims, with the winter night!—

> The sky, and the sky alone, so glorious, yet so awful, so spangled with brightness, so mysterious in its depth, that is all. There is nothing that can remind any sense of earth; nay, the very cold seems to enhance the solitude, to tear

away all connection between yourself and external nature, to make you feel more utterly lonely. And you stand and gaze on those bright worlds, till you seem as if you were banished into the desolate regions of space; and there, without any orb near you, looked forth into the perfect blackness around, and watched the motions of the worlds that above, beneath, and on every side, were moving along in their mysterious path. It is the time when you feel, if ever, that there must be a world of spirits; when the mind seems almost brought into contact with that invisible universe; and when, more than at any other period, it longs to know something of its future home, and to hear some of those 'unspeakable things which it is not lawful for a man to utter.'

The conversation now turns on the strange and dangerous charm which we find in every glimpse, real or imaginary, into things connected with the world of the invisible. How, it is asked, can we but be interested in knowing somewhat of a region of being, to the influences of which we are, perhaps, hourly exposed—and which, hereafter, is to receive us as its denizens forever? And yet, what peril there must be in attempting to raise a curtain which God has drawn, and which may conceal what it would scare the soul from her earthly tabernacle to see disclosed! Has that curtain ever been raised? A thousand traditionary voices say it has. Raised in prophetic dreams and omens; raised in apparitions of the dead; raised in pranks and gambollings of elves, demons and goblins; raised in pacts of the evil one with human kind.

Raised, also, in visits of angels; in miraculous warnings and interferences of heavenly powers in the affairs of men; in visions and glimpses of revelation, from the sphere of essential light, vouchsafed to contemplative souls. That the invisible world has access by many avenues to the visible, the experience of all ages attests, and the friends believe. And now that they have, as it seems, nine December evenings to spend together, what employment more congenial to the time can they find, than ascertaining, if they can, the positions of these avenues, and marking them down, as it were, in a kind of spiritual chart! In other words, what task can engage them, better suited to those long winter nights, than that suggested by Pistus—to inquire into all the methods by which the intercommunion of the seen with the unseen is carried on? They will set about it forthwith. And, hear the wise resolution with which they enter upon the inquiry:—

> In listening to any details which the wisdom of the world would reject as improbable or impossible, we shall, I hope, be guided by a wiser feeling. We will weigh them on their evidence only: if that is sufficient to convince a man in his everyday conduct, it shall be sufficient for us; if not, while we stigmatize nothing as impossible, because it is unusual, we shall return a verdict of 'not proven.'

The plan to be pursued in the investigation is now settled. The mystic symbolism by which material nature, in such a variety of ways, seems to point to spiritual truth, is first to come under consideration; then *aërial* phenomena, fiery crosses, comets, and meteors, whirlwinds, and sudden tempests—viewed as prognostics of momentous events on earth; then the various luminous appearances to which popular belief has ascribed a supernatural character, "stationary lights, corpse-lights, St. Elmo's lights, firedrakes, and Will of the Wisp;" then haunted places, and the tribes that haunt them, whether classic, as "Naiads, Fauns, Satyrs, Dryads, Hamadryads," &c., or romantic, as "The Brown Man of the Moors, Fairies, the Good People, Trolls, Telchens, Pixies and Pixycolts," not forgetting the more peculiar housegoblins, "the old Lar, and our own Robin Good-fellow."

Then the "grand question" is to be debated, "if the spirits of the departed have ever been permitted to visit the living in a visible form;" this will give occasion to speak of the motives of ghostly visitations, of death-warnings, of disclosures of secret crimes, of apparitions in fulfilment of a promise, and so on. After this will come dreams, and the second-sight; and to wind up the whole inquiry, a glance will be thrown at the grounds of the once so general belief in astrology and witchcraft. Truly, as one of the friends remarks, "a comprehensive subject, and, if discussed with an unprejudiced mind, almost fresh ground."

As we are not going, however, to review the book, but merely to cull from it anything that seems to us particularly available for our present purpose, of tempering with a light breath of fear the heat of the Christmas fire, we will not follow the inquirers through the several stages of their task. This it will be well worth the reader's while to do for himself; and, although the friends took nine nights to get over the ground, he will find it easily accomplished in one. If he has a pleasanter night than that one, this December, he will have no reason to complain of his winter. In the meantime, we will hear Pistus, who is the travelled man of the party, tell what once befell him on a mountain excursion in the island of Madeira.

> I believe that people with the strongest nerves have the most dreadful fits of panic when they have them at all. I have wandered far and wide in the most precipitous places of mountains, and never felt it but once. I had a mind to try if the Pico do Cidrao, one of the loftiest, and, at the same time, steepest mountains of Madeira, could not be scaled from the Pico dos Arrieiros. It was a fine day in spring—we tethered our horses on the Arrieiros, and then, with our mountain-poles, and a shepherd for guide, we committed ourselves to the narrow isthmus that joins the two mountains. Narrow it is—for, on either side, it slopes down almost perpendicularly into an abyss of some two thousand feet; while, at the top, it is in many places not more than eight feet broad, and its material of crumbling scoria.
>
> Indeed, so thin is it, that it vibrates, or seems to vibrate, in a heavy gale. When we had accomplished half the distance, we sat down to rest, and gaze at the wonderful chasms which opened below us. Seeing a small crack in the earth, I looked down into that, and lo! the opposite chasm was distinctly visible through it. At last, however, up ladders of rock, assisted by the shepherd's banisters of roughly-spun

rope, round corners where you trusted yourself to the young oak, or the sapling *til,* and hung for a moment over a depth that it makes my blood run cold to recollect—now creeping along this side of the isthmus, now working like worms along that, we stood under the shadow of the great Cidrao itself. Here, on a little platform of turf, my friend sat down, weary and sick at heart, while I resolved, with a good courage, still to follow my guide.

On we went: the path was a ledge of about eighteen inches, a steep precipice above, a steep precipice below, all bare rock—no twining root, or friendly twig, to give the hand a firm, nor even an imaginary hold. Just then the northern gale swept a mass of clouds into the abyss, and it seemed as if we were walking along the edge of the world. I began to feel a little uncomfortable, when my guide, by way of consoling me, wrenched a large rock from its place, and hurled it downwards into the clouds. I lost it in that soft bed, but half a minute afterwards its crash came up from beneath, echoed from crag to crag, and seeming as if it came from another world.

Oh! I shall never forget that moment! My brain seemed to turn round, my limbs to have no power of support, and I felt that horrible desire of leaping after the rock, the descent of which I had just witnessed. That was my only panic, and I thought it would have been my first and last.

There is nothing *obviously* preternatural in the above; but, the question being raised, to what immediate cause we are to attribute the terrible, and apparently malign influences which, in cases of the kind, nature exercises over us, a solution is offered, which gives to these "toys of desperation" a ghastly character indeed. The speaker who undertakes to answer the question is named Sophron, and here is what he says:—

If you ask my opinion, I have long believed it to be the immediate effect of temptation. The name, *panic,* proves that the spirits who were supposed to haunt wild and lonely scenery, were also supposed to be gifted with an extraordinary influence over the mind; just as, in Gothic lore, fairies were gifted with the same power of depriving their unwelcome visitants of reason. Now, that the evil spirits by which we are surrounded, should delight in making God's works, which in themselves are very good, occasions of the misery of man, is extremely likely in itself, and consistent with all analogy. We do not remember, or we will not believe, that the presence of Christians must make an inroad on the powers of darkness; that they cannot exercise the same influence over mankind in such regions, as in wild and lonely mountains, which Holy Church can scarcely be said to have vindicated—almost inaccessible to man—intended, to the end of the world, to be none of his, to whomever else they may be given.

★ ★ ★ ★ ★ ★

True, there is a brighter side to the picture. Angels may delight in solitudes unstained by sin: and peaks, like those of Chimborazo and Himalaya, may be, could we only hear it, vocal with the songs of the just made perfect. But still it is a solemn thought that the doom has been once spoken, which, till the regeneration of the heavens and earth by fire, must remain in some sense in force, 'Cursed is the ground for thy sake.' The church, we know, has a power of reversing this curse; but, till she has blest, it remains, and must remain. The sorest temptations which the history of the church can recount, have taken place in the desert; also, I grant you, some of the most glorious victories. We must expect the one, we may hope for the other.

We should like to know how Sophron would account for the fact, that the same giddy impulse which seizes the wanderer in the solitudes of the Alps or the Andes, is also not unfrequently felt by those who look down from consecrated minster-towers, in which christened bells, the terror of all imps of darkness, are hung. We have felt the solicitations of the dreadful magnetism ourselves, when looking through the open-work of the spire of Strasburg; and more than one dizzy brain has yielded to the fatal fascination, from the same holy height. It is not many years since a laughing young girl, into whose pure, glad soul, the thought of suicide had never thrown its shadow, sprang from that spire, in such a sudden passion of mad terror, to the pavement, five hundred feet beneath. Now we are very much mistaken in Sophron, or he will confess that cathedral steeples, built in the ages of faith, are the very antipodes, spiritually, of those wild and unchristianized solitudes which "Holy Church can scarcely be said to have vindicated." Exeter Hall may sneer at the sacredness of a Strasburg minster, but Sophron does not believe that Luther was the founder of the Christian religion; or that the day of Pentecost was that on which the confession of Augsburg was drawn up. How, then, will he account for panics occurring on the tops of Catholic and devil-dreaded belfries?

Leaving that question, we turn to those enigmatical appearances which, be they natural or supernatural in their origin, are oftenest observed to present themselves in situations unreclaimed, or unreclaimable by the hand of man, from the desolation of the primal curse. Of this kind are the lights that lure unwary travellers into marshes, or that gleam from lonely headlands on stormy nights, and draw the inexperienced seaman upon sandbanks, or the ledges of a rocky shore. Such lights, Pistus tells us, are seen in nights of tempest, along the wild capes and crags of Madeira; glancing up and down precipitous cliffs; leaping over mountain-chasms and ragged beds of torrents; now almost dipping in the surf that beats the bottom of the rocks; now burning on the very brow of the beetling sea-wall.

"The fishermen," says Pistus, "believe them to be tormented souls, thus working out part of their punishment, and testify great horror at the apparition."

All this our philosophy knows how to explain; but Sophron has something to tell, which no theory, that we are aware of, will account for. What does the reader think of this?—

> There is a bedroom in Lulworth Castle, in Dorsetshire, where, on a particular spot on the wall, a pale phosphoric light is always to be seen when the windows are darkened.

> I have heard, that to wake in the stillness of the night, and to see this pale light glaring quietly on you, is a most unpleasant thing. And so the proprietors thought, for they had the wall pulled down and rebuilt, but to no effect; the light appeared again, and is to be seen there to this day.

We confess we do not exactly envy the guest at Lulworth Castle, who has to sleep in this particular bedroom, after an evening of ghost-stories about the Christmas fire.

Under the chapter of death-warnings, the following is related, and has a pleasant touch of horror about it:—

> When a man, whose whole course of life had been marked by the most flagitious atrocities, was lying on his deathbed, near St. Ives (in Cornwall,) a black ship, with black sails, was observed to stand in to the bay, into shallows where seamen felt convinced that no ship of that apparent burden could float. At the moment the soul passed from the body, the vessel stood out again, nor was it ever seen more.

We do not know whether the reader will be affected as we were, by the following account of a dream; but we own that few things of the kind have impressed us more disagreeably. Sophron *loquitur:*—

> A married lady of my acquaintance dreamed that she was compelled one Sunday to stay at home, while the rest of her family went to church; that the house was one which she had never seen before; that she heard a knock at the door, and went to open it; that a man of most ill-favoured appearance entered, and began to insult her, on which she awoke in terror. Sometime after, she removed temporarily to another house, and it so fell out, that one Sunday she stayed at home herself, in order that the rest of her family might be able to go to church.
>
> While there alone, she heard a knock at the front door, and there being no one else in the house, went down to open it. When she had reached the hall, the remembrance of her dream flashed in an instant across her mind, yet she

had not sufficient faith in it to hesitate about opening the door. She did so; and behold! there stood a man, the exact counterpart of him whom she had seen in her dream. She shut the door in his face, locked and bolted it, and awaited the return of her family in great agitation. The man (whoever he was) could not be found. Now that this was a providential warning of danger, it is hardly possible to deny.

The mention of dreams leads to that of second-sight, and this to predictions of death in general. Relating to this topic, a curious circumstance is mentioned, recorded in the account of the plague that depopulated Rome during the pontificate of St. Agatha. In the dead of the night, a knock, sometimes single, sometimes repeated, was heard at the door of doomed houses, whether at the time infected or not; and as many knocks as were heard in the night, so many deaths followed on the succeeding day. There is something horrible in the thought of these knocks, falling at intervals along the silent streets, in the darkness of night. It gives you the feeling as if the plague were going from door to door, making up the list of her next batch of victims. A different kind of death-warning, and one perhaps still more frightful in its character, accompanied, as we have read somewhere, the plague with which Basle was visited at the end of the sixteenth century; the dying themselves, in the unconscious fantastic babblings and delirium of the last moments, announced the names of those who were to die next after them.

Apparitions of the dead affect us with a profounder sense of terror than, perhaps, any other form in which the powers of the unseen realm can approach us. It is not mere terror; it is terror combined with shuddering antipathy—with a loathing which the idea of no *naturally* bodiless being, however evil, awakes. The blood does not curdle so at the thought of a purely diabolical visitation, as at that of finding yourself face to face with one who has been what you are—with a man who has died, and been buried. You cannot, in imagining such a visitant, escape the association of the corpse, and the grave-clothes, and the atmosphere of death, and all the characteristics of mortality which our mortal nature, just because it *is* mortal, recoils from with the most invincible abhorrence. In presenting to the reader, therefore, some account of such apparitions, we feel that we are got to the right horrors, the horrors *par excellence*; and so, without further preface, we transcribe the following story, related by our friend Sophron, in the words of Lady Fanshawe:—

> And here (she says) I cannot omit relating the following story, confirmed by Sir Thomas Baber, Sir Arnold Breamer, the Dean of Canterbuiy, with many more gentleman and persons of that town. There lived, not far from Canterbury, a gentleman called Colonel Colepepper, whose mother was wedded unto Lord Strangford. This gentleman had a sister, who lived with him, as the world said, in too much love. She married Mr. Porter. This brother and sister being both atheists, and living a life according to their profession, went in a frolic unto the vault of their ancestors, where, before they returned, they pulled some of their father's and of their mother's hairs.
>
> Within a few days after, Mrs. Porter fell sick and died. Her brother kept her body in a coffin in his buttery, saying it would not be long before he died, and then they would both be buried together; but from the night of her death, till the time that we were told the story, (which was three months,) they say that a head, as cold as death, with curled hair like his sister's, did ever lie by him when he slept, notwithstanding he removed to several places and countries to avoid it; and several persons told us they have felt this apparition.

Lady Fanshawe's high character, Sophron justly remarks, leaves no room for the least hesitation in receiving this story, one of the most singular that he knows. Pistus agrees that the story *is* singular, and, we think, so will the reader. Nor is it more singular than frightful; we cannot conceive a truer hell on earth than that the being who had been your partner in sin while alive, should refuse to quit you when dead.

Here is a story less horrible, though scarcely less strange. The names of the parties concerned, it is mentioned, are altered, some of them being still alive:—

Lord F. was on his travels on the Continent, when he met a young man engaged in a similar way, with whom he grew very familiar. Mr. G. (for so I will call his friend) gave him, in the course of conversation, to know that the end of his life had been predicted to him, and that he had some grounds for believing that this prediction was not without its weight and credibility. 'As how?' asked Lord F. 'I was travelling with two friends,' replied the other, 'in Italy, and at Florence we agreed to have our nativities cast by a woman there, who had a great reputation for astrological skill. She foretold that none of us would live long, and named the days on which we should each die. My two friends are dead, and that at the time she named: it remains to see whether her prediction will be verified in me.'

'Pooh, pooh!' cried Lord F., 'a mere coincidence; impossible that it should happen a third time. But what is the day she named?' Mr. G. named one about six months distant.

'And where shall you he then?' pursued Lord F.

'At Paris.'

'Why, I shall be there too. Let it be an engagement. Come yon and dine with me on that very day at seven o'clock, and keep up your spirits till then. I shall be found at No.—, Rue de—. Do you agree to the bargain?'

'Willingly,' replied the other, and in a short space of time the friends separated. The six months passed, and a little before the appointed day, Lord F. found himself in Paris.

He sent a note to Mr. G., to remind him of his engagement, and received for answer that he would come. However, a day or two after, another note was brought him, in which Mr. G. said that he was not very well, and must postpone the pleasure of dining with Lord F. till another time; that the indisposition was very trifling, and ere long he hoped to have the pleasure of waiting upon him. Lord F. thought no more of the matter, ordered dinner on the day that had been named at seven, for himself, and about six o'clock sent his servant to Mr. G.'s with a merely formal inquiry how he was.

Seven o'clock came; Lord F. sat down to dinner, when, just as he was beginning his meal, the door opened, and in walked Mr. G. He walked in, it is true, but he said not a word, went up to the table, and went out again. Lord F. was alarmed, and rang the bell, and it was answered by the servant whom he had sent with the message of inquiry. 'How is Mr. G.?' he demanded. 'Dead, my lord,' was the reply: 'he died just as I reached his house.'"

Apparitions of beasts form a puzzling chapter in phantomology, and have something very demonish about them. Everyone remembers

Him of whom the story ran,
Who spoke the spectre-hound in man.

But it is when they come as warnings of the approach of death, that phantom brute-shapes suggest the most disquieting apprehensions. Here is an instance of the kind, which, Sophron says, comes to him so attested, that he really knows not how to disbelieve it:—

A family in the east of England has a tradition, that the appearance of a black dog portends the death of one of its members. It was not, I believe, said that no death took place without such warning, but only that when the apparition occurred, its meaning was certain. The eldest son of this family married. He knew not whether to believe or to disbelieve the legend. On the one hand, he thought it superstitious to receive it; and on the other, he could not, in the face of so much testimony, altogether reject it. In this state of doubt, the thing being in itself unpleasant, he resolved to say nothing on the subject to his young wife. It could only, he thought, worry and harass her, and could

> not, by any possibility, do any good. He kept his resolution.
>
> In due course of time he had a family, but of the apparition he saw nothing. At length one of his children was taken ill, I think with the smallpox; but the attack was slight, and not the least danger was apprehended. He was sitting down to dinner with his wife, when she said, 'I will just step up stairs and see how the child is going on, and will be back again in a moment.' She went, and returning rather hastily, said, 'the child is asleep; but pray go upstairs, for there is a large black dog lying on his bed; go and drive it out of the house.' The father had no doubt of the result. He went upstairs; there was no black dog to be seen, but the child was dead.

Pistus immediately "caps" this story with one of a family in Sussex, in which a white rabbit appears, a few hours before death, to the sick man himself. After all, a white rabbit is not so suspicious a messenger to come for you, from the other world, as a black dog; though they are both of them unclean beasts, too.

Dwarfs, gnomes, and other spirits of a gross nature and sullen mood, have always, and in all countries, been believed to haunt mines, and, as caprice sways them, sometimes to obstruct, sometimes to help, the miners in their work. Many northern tales of the "wild and wonderful" are founded on this belief, which, in some mountainous regions, is not yet extinct. These spirits of the mine were not regarded with unmixed dread; only care was taken not to offend them, for they were easily moved to anger, and their revenge was terrible.

Retzel, a German writer of the last century, who, being a *Bergrath,* or director of mines, must have been well acquainted with the subject, tells us a good deal about them. He says they rarely let themselves be seen in a defined shape, but rather make themselves heard underground, in the pits where the miners work, and particularly when either a great piece of good fortune or a great calamity is near. At night, when few, or on holidays, when none of the miners are in the pits, they have their sport, and make a noise as if the work were going on in the briskest manner, especially in such pits as promise something good. Hence, judges the good Bergrath, it appears that they intend, by such noises, to give a hint to the miners to work in these places, and to win the blessing which God has therein laid, and to bring it to light.

When these spirits are not provoked, they do no hurt to any one; but he who mocks or speaks scornfully of them is sure not to escape their resentment, but, in ascending and descending, is squeezed or otherwise hurt by them. And it is a belief of the miners that he who is so hurt, if he relate before the ninth day what has befallen him, must on the ninth day die, of which there are many examples.

Of these *berg-mannikins* there would seem to be two sorts, for some, when they appear, or make themselves heard, bring good fortune, some evil. They seldom take a visible form; but such as do, show themselves in the appearance of a diminutive miner, with a burning lamp; these portend good luck, and indicate rich veins of ore to be in the places where they are seen. Oftener the light only is seen, gliding swiftly, as if carried by one that ran, but the bearer appears not. These lights burn blue, and the brighter they are, the better the omen. On the other hand, when visions of beasts or of monsters appear underground, it is an evil prognostic, and commonly there follows thereupon great ill-fortune.

These spirits, Retzel says, are no devils or infernal angels, fallen from a better state, but they, as well as the spirits of fire, air, and water, are creatures sprung from the elements, have no higher nature than that of the elements, and will be destroyed with the elements when the present system of things ceases to be. Vice or virtue cannot be attributed to them, any more than to the winds, the floods, or the lightnings; they have their fits of good and ill-humour, their spells of fair weather and foul; they are friendly to man or unfriendly, just as the elements are, with just as little merit and as little blame. But mines are sometimes haunted by a different kind of spirits, as Sophron shows in the following story:—

You know that the Whitehaven mines run out far underneath the sea, and are some of the most terrible in England. A man who had worked all his life in them, and had always borne a high character, was laid on his deathbed, and sent for the clergyman of his parish, to whom he had been previously known. I know not of what kind the disease was; it was one, I am assured, at all events, that did not affect his mind in the least, and that, during the whole of the account which I am going to give you, he was perfectly and most manifestly himself. He related it on the word of a dying man. He assured the priest that it was no uncommon thing in the mines, for the voices of persons, who had long been dead, to be heard as in conversation or debate.

I do not think he said that apparitions were seen, but he affirmed that they were heard to pass along the passages with a loud kind of rushing noise; that the miners, as far as possible, got out of the way on these occasions; that the horses employed in the mines would stand still and tremble, and fall into a cold sweat; and that this was universally known to be a thing that might occur any time. One remarkable instance he gave. The overseer of the mine he used to work was, for many years, a Cumberland man, but being found guilty of some unfair proceedings, he was dismissed by the proprietors from his post, though employed in an inferior situation. The new overseer was a Northumberland man, who had the burr that distinguishes that county very strongly.

To this person the degraded overseer bore the strongest hatred, and was heard to say that some day he would be his ruin. He lived, however, in apparent friendship with him; but one day they were both destroyed together by the firedamp. It was believed in the mine that, preferring revenge to life, the ex-overseer had taken his successor, less acquainted than he with the localities of the mine,

> into a place where he knew the fire-damp to exist, and that without a safety lamp, and had thus contrived his destruction. But ever after that time, in the place w here the two men perished, their voices might he heard high in dispute—the Northumbrian burr being distinctly audible, and so also the well-known pronunciation of the treacherous murderer.

We will give but one more story out of this volume: the scene of it is laid on board a Brazil packet:—

> A lady was lying on the sofa in the ladies' saloon, when, to her surprise, a gentleman entered it from the grand saloon, and passing through it, went out by the door that led towards the hold. She was much astonished, both that anyone should enter the room at all, at least without knocking, and at not recognizing the gentleman who did so, as she had associated with the passengers for some days. She mentioned the matter to her husband, who said that he must have been confined to his berth till then, but that it would perhaps appear, when the passengers sat down to dinner, who he was.
>
> At dinner-time the lady carefully examined her companions, and was positive that no such person was among them. She asked the captain if there were any passenger not then at table. He answered her, that there was not. She never forgot the circumstances, though her husband treated it as a mere fancy, and thought no more of it. Some time afterwards she was walking with him in London, when she pointed out a gentleman in the street, and said, with some agitation, 'There! there! that is the person whom I saw on board the packet. Do go and speak to him—pray do go and ask him if he was not there.'
>
> 'Impossible, my dear,' replied her husband; 'he would think that I meant to insult him.' However, his wife's importunity and agitation prevailed. Stepping up to the gentleman she had pointed out, and apologizing for the liberty he was about to take, 'Pray, sir,' said he, 'may I ask whether you

were on board the— Brazil packet at such a time?'

'No, sir,' replied the person addressed, 'I certainly was not; but may I inquire why you thought that I was?'

The interrogator related the circumstances. 'What day was it?' asked the other. That having been settled, 'Well, sir,' said the stranger, 'it is a very remarkable circumstance that I had a twin brother, so like myself that no one could tell us apart. He died, poor fellow, in America, on that very day.'

"The most remarkable point (observes Pistus) in that story, is its localism, so to speak. A man dies in America, and his spirit is seen, on that very day, on board a ship between America and England, as if crossing from one country to the other."

Here we take leave of this very pleasant Christmas party, not without renewing our recommendation to the reader, to cultivate their further acquaintance. We have put before him some of the stories they tell, but we have said nothing to him of the delightful way in which they talk about these stories. We have passed over all their practical reflections on the subject of their discourse, all their reasonings as to the credibility of the things related, or of preternatural relations in general; all, in short, in the little volume, that is calculated to make the reader a better man. The reason is, we don't want to make the reader a better man, but merely a more uneasy one. We appeal to his nerves, not to his conscience. Our aim is not to improve, but to frighten him. Besides, if he thinks reflections upon the stories ho has been reading would do him good, what is to hinder him from making as many as he pleases?

There they are; let him reflect upon them for himself.

We now turn to another treasury of horrors, to wit, Mr. Joseph Glanvil's *Collection of Relations, in proof of the real existence of Apparitions, Spirits, and Witches*, published in the year 1688, the never-to-be-forgotten epoch of Britain's deliverance from brass money and wooden shoes, and of Ireland's from money and shoes of any material whatever.

The following narrative is contained in a letter of Dr. Ezekias Burton to Dr. Henry More:—

About ten years ago, one Mr. Bower, an antient man, living at Guildford in Surrey, was, upon the highway, not far from that place, found newly murdered, very barbarously, having one great cut cross his throat, and another down his breast. Two men were seized upon suspicion, and put into gaol at Guildford, to another, who had before been committed for robbing, as I suppose. That night this third man was awakened about one of the clock, and greatly terrified with an old man, who had a great gash cross his throat, almost from ear to ear, and a wound down his breast. He also came in stooping, and holding his hand to his back; thus he appeared, but said nothing. The thief called to his two new companions; they grumbled at him, but made no answer.

In the morning he had retained so lively an impression of what he had seen, that he spoke to them to the same purpose again, and they told him it was nothing but his phantasie. But he was so fully persuaded of the reality of the apparition, that he told two others of it, and it came to the ears of Mr. Reading, justice of peace in Surrey, and cousin to the gentleman that was murdered.

He immediately sent for the prisoner, and asked him in the first place, whether he was born or had lived about Guildford? To which he answered, No. Secondly, he inquired if he knew any of the inhabitants of that town, or of the neighbourhood? He replied that he was a stranger to all thereabout. Then he inquired, if he had ever heard of one Mr. Bower? He said, No. After this he examined him for what cause those two other men were imprisoned? To which he answered, he knew not, but supposed for some robbery.

After these preliminary interrogatories, he desired him to tell him what he had seen in the night? Which he immediately did, exactly according to the relation he (Mr. Reading) had heard, and I gave before. And withal described the old gentleman so by his picked beard, and that he was, as he called it, rough on his cheeks, and that the hairs of his face were black and white, that Mr. Reading saith, he himself could not have given a more exact description of Mr. Bower than this was. He told the highwayman that he must give him his oath, (though that would signify little from such a rogue,) to which the man readily consented, and took oath before the justice of all this.

Mr. Reading being a very discreet man, concealed the story from the jury at the assizes, as knowing that this would be no evidence according to law. However, the friends of the murdered gentleman had been very inquisitive, and discovered several suspicious circumstances. One of which was, that those two men had washed their clothes, and that some stains of blood remained. Another, that one of them had denied he ever heard that Mr. Bower was dead, where as he had in another place confessed it two hours before. Upon these and suchlike evidences, these two were condemned and executed, but denied it to the last. But one of them said, the other could clear him if he would, which the bystanders understood not.

After some time a tinker was hanged, (where, the gentleman has forgot,) who at his death said, that the murder of Mr. Bower of Guildford was his greatest trouble. For he had a hand in it; he confesseth he struck him a blow on the back which fetcht him from his horse, and when he was down, those other men that were arraigned and executed for it, cut his throat and rifled him. This is the first story which I had from Mr. Reading himself, who is a very honest, prudent person, and not credulous.

In the same repertory is contained an account of the apparition of Edward Avon, of Marlborough, which was seen by his son-in-law, Thomas Goddard, of the same place, about nine o'clock in the morning, leaning over a stile on the highway between Marlborough and Ogborn. Goddard had a good deal of conversation with the ghost on family matters. It appeared to him several times, and in different places; looked in upon him at seven o'clock of a November evening, through his shop-window, and met him as he rode down the hill on the way from Chilton, "between the manor-house and Axford farm-field," in the shape of "somewhat like a hare," at which his horse started, and threw him in the dirt; on getting on his feet again, after this fall, he saw the ghost in its proper shape, standing about eight feet directly before him in the way, and it said to him, "Thomas, bid Willian Avon (that was the ghost's son) take the sword that he hath of me, which is now in his house, and carry it to the wood as ye go to Alton, to the upper end of the wood by the wayside; for with that sword I did wrong above thirty years ago, and he never prospered since he had that sword." Then, after various other directions about family affairs, the spirit vanished.

Goddard went to the mayor of Malborough, and made a formal deposition of the above circumstances. The mayor ordered him to do as the apparition had directed; and the next morning, at nine o'clock, he and his brother-in-law, William Avon, went with the sword, and laid it down in the copse, near the place the ghost had appointed Goddard to carry it. As they left the spot, Goddard again saw the apparition of Edward Avon, standing by the place where the sword was laid, and called out to his brother-in-law, "There is the apparition of our father!"

William Avon said he saw nothing; upon which, Goddard fell on his knees, and prayed, "Lord! open his eyes that he may see it;" to which the other, instead of "Amen," responded, "Lord! grant I may not see it, if it be thy blessed will."

The apparition then beckoned to Goddard, and said, "Thomas, take up the sword, and follow me." Goddard took up the sword, and followed the apparition about ten perches further into the copse, where he laid down the sword again. At this time he saw something stand by the apparition, like a mastiff dog, of a brown colour.

On Goddard's laying down the sword, the apparition took it up, and going a few paces further, pointed with it to the ground, and said, "In this place lies buried the body of him whom I murdered in the year 1635, (thirty-nine years before,) which is now rotten, and turned to dust."

Goddard asked him why he had committed this murder, and the ghost said, "I took money from the man, and he contended with me, and so I murdered him."

Then Goddard said, "What would you have me do in this thing?" and the ghost said, "This is that the world may know that I murdered a man, and buried him in this place in the year 1635."

The place to which the ghost pointed was a dry and bare spot, on which nothing grew, and which, as Goddard described it, was "like a grave sunk-in." As the two brothers-in-law went away together, Avon confessed to Goddard that he had heard the voice of the ghost, but had neither been able to distinguish the words, nor to see the speaker.

Against the credit of this story, Mr. Glanvil mentions two things that were alleged by people in Marlborough, who knew Thomas Goddard; that first, about a year before he saw, or affirmed he had seen, his father-in-law's apparition, he left off going to church, (of which he had been a diligent frequenter,) and "fell off wholly to the nonconformists;" and the other, that he was sometimes troubled with epileptic fits. But to these reasons Mr. Glanvil does not allow much weight; observing, that a man's falling off to the nonconformists, though it may argue a vacillancy of his judgement, yet affords not any presumption of a defect in his external senses, as if a dissenter were less able to discern when he saw or heard anything than a sound churchman.

In this we agree with Mr. Glanvil: it is not sight that a dissenter wants, but faith. As to the epileptic fits, our own opinion is, that Goddard's liability to these was the very thing that made him also capable of seeing ghosts. However, our author will not say positively but what the apparition may have been "some ludicrous goblin," personating the ghost of old Avon, merely to mystify, or "take a rise out of" the son-in-law. For Porphyrius has noted, that demons do sometimes personate the souls of the deceased; and the learned Von Meyer of Frankfurt confirms this by many instances within his own experience. It ought to be observed that there were no bones found in the place pointed out by the spectre, but this, after forty years or nigh, is not surprising.

Here follows a story "Of a Dutchman that could see ghosts, and of the ghost he saw in the town of Woodbridge, in Suffolk:"—

> Mr. Broom, the minister of Woodbridge in Suffolk, meeting one day, in a barbers shop, in that town, a Dutch lieutenant, (who was blown up with Opdam, and taken alive out of the water, and carried to that town, where he was prisoner at large,) upon the occasion of some discourse, was told by him that he could see ghosts, and that he had seen divers. Mr. Broom rebuking him for talking so idly, he persisted in it very stiffly. Some days after, lighting upon him again, he askt him whether he had seen any ghost since his coming to that town? To which he replied, 'No.' But not long after this, as they were walking together up the town, he said to Mr. Broom, 'Yonder comes a ghost.' He seeing nothing, askt him where about it was?
>
> The other said, 'It is over against such a house, and it walks looking upwards towards such a side, swinging one arm, with a I glove in its hand.' He said, moreover, that when it came near them, they must give way to it; that he ever did so, and some that have not done so have suffered for it. Anon he said,' 'T is just upon us; let's out of the way.' Mr. Broom, believing all to be a fiction, as soon as he said these words, took hold of his arm, and kept him by force in the way. But as he held him, there came such a force against them, that he was flung into the middle of the street, and one of the palms of his hands, and one knee, bruised and broken by the fall, which put him for a while to excessive pain.
>
> But spying the lieutenant lye like a dead man, he got up as soon as he could, and applied himself to his relief. With the help of others he got him into the next shop, where they poured strong water down his throat, but for some

time could discern no life in him. At length, what with the strong water, and what with well chafing him, he began to stir, and when he was come to himself, his first words were, 'I will show you no more ghosts.' Then he desired a pipe of tobacco, but Mr. Broom told him he should take it at his house; for he feared, should he take it so soon there, it would mike him sick.

Thereupon they went together to Mr. Broom's house, where they were no sooner entering in, but the bell rang out. Mr. Broom presently sent his maid to learn who was dead. She brought word that it was such a one, a taylor, who dyed suddenly, though he had been in a consumption a long time. And inquiring after the time of his death, they found it was as punctually as it could be guessed at the very time when the ghost appeared. The ghost had exactly this taylor's known gate, who ordinarily went with one arm swinging, and a glove in that hand, and looking on one side upwards.

In a story of a butler in Ireland, who was like to have been carried away by spirits, because he went out to buy cards for his master on a Sunday afternoon, the most remarkable point is, that he "was perceived to rise from the ground, whereupon Mr. Greatrix (Valentine Greatrix, or Great-rakes, of Cappoquin, the famous magnetizer of the seventeenth century) and another lusty man clapt their arms over his shoulders, one of them before him and the other behind, and weighed him down with all their strength. But he was forcibly taken up from them, and they were too weak to keep their hold; and for a considerable time he was carried in the air to and fro over their heads, several of the company still running under him to prevent his being hurt if he should fall, and was caught before he came to the ground, and had by that means no hurt." This took place at the house and in the presence of the Earl of Orrery.

Another curious point in this case is, that a spectre came to this butler at night, bringing with it a grey liquor in a wooden dish, which it bid him drink off, (as a cure for fits that he had,) but he would not. At this the spectre was angry, and upbraided him with his suspicious temper; but told him if he would drink plantain-juice, it would cure him of one sort of his fits, (for he had two,) but he should carry the other to his grave. He asked whether he should take the juice of the roots or the leaves, and received answer, the roots.

Sophron, in that book about the *Unseen World,* refers to this story, and condemns it as tending to "corporealize our notions of spirits." But this seems to be said without due reflection; for, first, we ought to ask, whence are our "notions of spirits" derived, that we should make agreement with them the test of facts? And then, it is not a very reasonable doctrine that a spirit, which can move a body, cannot move anything that the body can move.

The floating of persons, who are under spiritual influence, in the air, is no uncommon phenomenon. We have been informed by an eyewitness, that one of the ladies at Port-Glasgow, who "spoke with tongues" in the year 1830, flew about the room in which the prophesyings were held, for some time, without touching the floor. A similar phenomenon is the riding of witches through the air to their sabbath. On which subject, Doctor Antony Horneck, a weighty divine of the seventeenth century, speaks as follows:—

> That a spirit can lift up men and women, and grosser substances, and convey them through the air, I question no more than I doubt that the wind can overthrow houses, or drive stones and other heavy bodies upward from their centre. And were I to make a person of a dull understanding apprehend the nature of a spirit, I would represent it to him under the notion of an intelligent wind, or a strong wind, informed by a highly rational soul—as a man may be called an intelligent piece of earth. And this notion David seemed to favour, when speaking of these creatures, Psalm civ. 4, he tells us that God makes his angels wind, for in the original it is רוח; and most certainly if they be so, they must be reasonable windy substances; nor doth

the expression which immediately follows in that verse cross this exposition—*viz.*, that he makes his ministers a flaming fire; for it's no new opinion that some of those invisible substances are of a fiery, and others of an aiery nature: and as we, God gives rational creatures here on earth, bodies composed of grosser matter, why should it seem incongruous for him to give rational creatures above us bodies of a subtiler and thinner matter, or such matter as those higher regions do afford? And if wind, breaking forth from the caverns of hills and mountains, have such force as makes us very often stand amazed at the effects, what energy might we suppose to be in wind, were it informed by reason, or a reasonable being?

A curious thing happened in the year 1659, at Crossen in Silesia, of an apothecary's servant. The chief magistrate of that town at that time was the Princess Elizabeth Charlotte, a person famous in her generation. In the spring of the year, one Christopher Monigk, a native of Serbest, a town belonging to the princes of Anhalt, servant to an apothecary, died and was buried with the usual ceremonies of the Lutheran church. A few days after his decease, a shape exactly like his in face, clothes, stature, mien, &c., appeared in the apothecary's shop, where he would set himself down, and walk sometimes, and take the boxes, pots, glasses off of the shelves, and set them again in their places, and sometimes try and examine the goodness of the medicines, weigh them in a pair of scales, pound the drugs with a mighty noise in a mortar, nay serve the people that came with their bills to the shop, take their money, and lay it up safe in the counter; in a word, do all things that a journeyman in such cases used to do. He looked very ghastly upon those that had been his fellow-servants, who were afraid to say anything to him, and his master being sick at that time of the gout, he was often very troublesome to him, would take the bills that were brought him out of his hand, snatch away the candle sometimes, and put it behind the stove.

At last, he took a cloak that hung in the shop, put it on and walked abroad; but minding nobody in the streets, went along, entered into some of the citizen's houses, and thrust himself into company, especially of such as he had formerly known, yet saluted nobody, nor spoke to anyone but to a maid-servant, whom he met hard by the churchyard, and desired to go home to his master's house, and dig in a ground-chamber, where she would find an inestimable treasure; but the maid, amazed at the sight of him, swooned; whereupon he lift her up, but left such a mark on her flesh with lifting her, that it was to be seen for some time after.

The maid having recovered herself, went home, but fell desperately sick upon it, and in her illness discovered what Monigk had said to her, and accordingly digged in the place she had named, but found nothing but an old decayed pot, with a *hæmatites* or bloodstone in it. The princess hereupon caused the young man's body to be digged up, which they found putrified, with purulent matter flowing from it, and the master being advised to remove the young man's goods, linen, clothes, and things, he left behind him when he died, out of the house, the spirit thereupon left the house, and was heard of no more.

Another curious thing happened in 1673, at Reichenbach in Silesia, in which also an apothecary was concerned, who after his death appeared to divers of his acquaintance, and cried out that in his lifetime he had poisoned several men with his drugs. Thereupon the magistrates of the town, after consultation, took up his body and burnt it; which being done, the spirit disappeared, and was seen no more. This was stated to Doctor Anthony Horneck by a very credible witness.

Webster, a writer against the existence of witches and apparitions, has recorded a story which makes strongly against his own views, and which he nevertheless seems to believe. It is quoted out of his *Display of Supposed Witchcraft*, in Doctor H. More's letter to Mr. Glanvil, prefixed to *Saducismus Triumphatus,* and is as follows:—

> About the year of our Lord 1632, near unto Chester-in-the-Street, there lived one Walker, a yeoman-man of good

estate and a widower, who had a young woman to his kinswoman that kept his house, who was by the neighbours suspected to be with child, and was towards the dark of the evening one night sent away with one Mark Sharp, who was a collier, or one that digged coals underground, and one that had been born in Blackburn Hundred, in Lancashire, and so she was not heard of a long time, and no noise or little was made about it.

In the winter time after, one James Graham, or Grime, (for so in that country they call them.) being a miller, and living about two miles from the place where Walker lived, was one night alone very late in the mill, grinding corn; and as about twelve or one o'clock at night, he came down the stairs from having been putting corn in the hopper, the mill doors being shut, there stood a woman upon the midst of the floor, with her hair about her head hanging down and all bloody, with five large wounds in her head. He being much affrighted and amazed, began to bless him, and at last asked her who she was, and what she wanted? To which she said, 'I am the spirit of such a woman, who lived with Walker; and being got with child by him, he promised to send me to a private place, where I should be well looked to till I was brought to bed and well again, and then I should come again and keep his house.

'And accordingly,' said the apparition, 'I was one night late sent away with one Mark Sharp, who upon a moor (naming a place that the miller knew) slew me with a pick, (such as men dig coals withal,) and gave me those five wounds, and after threw my body into a coal-pit hard by, and hid the pick under a bank, and his shoes and stockings being bloudy, he endeavoured to wash, but seeing the bloud would not wash forth, he hid them there.' And the apparition further told the miller that he must be the man to reveal it, or else that she must still appear and haunt him. The miller returned home very sad and heavy, but spoke not one word of what he had seen, but eschewed as much as he could to stay in the mill within night without company, thinking thereby to escape the seeing again of that frightful apparition.

But notwithstanding, one night when it began to be dark, the apparition met him again, and seemed very fierce and cruel, and threatened him, that if he did not reveal the murder, she would certainly pursue and haunt him. Yet for all this, he still concealed it until St. Thomas' Eve before Christmas, when being, soon after sunset, walking in his garden, she appeared again, and then so threatened and affrighted him, that he faithfully promised to reveal it next morning.

In the morning he wrote to a magistrate, and made the whole matter known, with all the circumstances; and diligent search being made, the body was found in a coal-pit, with five wounds in the head, and the pick, and shoes, and stockings yet bloudy, in every circumstance as the apparition had related unto the miller. Whereupon Walker and Mark Sharp were both apprehended, but would confess nothing. At the assizes following (I think it was Durham) they were arraigned, found guilty, condemned, and executed, but I could never hear that they confessed the fact. There were some that reported that the apparition did appear to the judge, or the foreman of the jury, (who was alive in Chester-in-the-Street about ten years ago, as I have been credibly informed,) but of that I know no certainty.

There are many persons yet alive that can remember this strange murder, and the discovery of it; for it was, and sometimes is, as much discoursed of in the north country as anything that almost hath ever been heard of, and the relation printed, though now not to be gotten. I relate this with the greater confidence, (though I may fail in some of the circumstances,) because I saw and read the letter that was sent to Serjeant Hutton, who then lived at Goldsbrugh, in Yorkshire, from the judge before whom

Walker and Mark Sharp were tried, and by whom they were condemned, and had a copy of it until about the year 1658, when I had it and many other books and papers taken from me.

And this I confess to be one of the most convincing stories (being of undoubted verity) that ever I read, heard, or knew of, and carried) with it the most evident force to make the most incredulous spirit to be satisfied that there are really sometimes such things as apparitions.

Doctor Henry More thought this story so "considerable," that he mentioned it to a friend of his a prudent intelligent person, Dr. J. D., who, of his own accord, offered him, it being a thing of such consequence, to send to a friend of his in the north for greater assurance of the truth of the narration, which motion, he (Dr. H. M.) willingly embracing, he (Dr. J. D.) accordingly sent. The answer to his letter, from his friend, Mr. Shepherdson, was this:—

I have done what I can to inform myself of the passage of Sharp and Walker. There are very few men that I could meet, that were then men, or at the tryal, saving these two in the enclosed paper, both men at that time, and both at the tryal. And for Mr. Lumley, he lived next door to Walker; and what he hath given under his hand, can depose, if there were occasion. The other gentleman writ his attestation with his own hand, but I being not there, got not his name to it. I could have sent you twenty hands that could have said thus much, and more, by hear-say, but I thought these most proper, that could speak from their own eyes and ears.

Thus far, Mr. Shepherdson, the doctor's discreet and faithful intelligencer. Now for Mr. Lumley's testimony, it is this:—

Mr. William Lumley, of Lumley, being an ancient gentleman, and at the tryal of Walker and Sharp, upon the murder of Anne Walker, saith—That he doth very well remember that the said Anne was servant to Walker, and that she was supposed to be with child, but would not disclose by whom. But, being removed to her aunt's in the same town, called Dame Carie, told her aunt that he that had got her with child would take care both of her and it, and bid her not trouble herself. After some time she had been at her aunt's, it was observed that Sharp came to Lumley one night, being a sworn brother of the said Walker's, and they two, that night, called her forth from her aunt's house, which night she was murdered.

About fourteen days after the murder, there appeared to one Graime, a fuller, at his mill, six miles from Lumley, the likeness of a woman, with her hair about her head, and the appearance of five wounds in her head, as the said Graime gave it in evidence. That that appearance bid him go to a justice of peace, and relate to him how that Walker and Sharp had murdered her, in such a place as she was murdered; but he, fearing to disclose a thing of that nature against a person of credit, as Walker was, would not have done it; but she continually appearing night by night to him, and pulling the cloathes off his bed, told him he should never rest till he had disclosed it.

Upon which, the said Graime did go to a justice of peace, and related the whole matter. Whereupon the justice of peace granted warrants against Walker and Sharp, and committed them to prison. But they found bail to appear at the next assizes. At which time they came to their tryal, and upon the evidence of the circumstances with that of Graime of the apparition, they were both found guilty, and executed.

WILLIAM LUMLEY.

The other testimony is of Mr. James Smart, of the city of Durham, who saith—

That the tryal of Sharp and Walker was in the month of August, 1631, before Judge Davenport. One Mr. Fairhair gave it in evidence upon oath, that he see the likeness of a child stand upon Walker's shoulders during the time of the tryal. At which time the judge was very much troubled, and gave sentence that night the tryal was; which was a thing never used in Durham before, nor after.

There is a difference of opinion between Mr. Webster and Dr. Henry More, as to the nature of this apparition—the former holding it to have been the "astral spirit of Anne Walker; the other deriding this as a fantastic conceit of the Paracelsists, and insisting that it was her soul. Perhaps the two opinions are not irreconcilable. However, we will not stop to reconcile them here, but relate one more story, and let the reader go to bed.

Some years ago, when travelling in Germany, it was our fortune to make the acquaintance of a Roman Catholic clergyman, who was the subject of a most strange and frightful spiritual visitation. In the year 1838, he had been appointed to a village parish, and entered upon his work with an ardour that distinguished him in all his pursuits. The first night that he spent in his own residence, he could not sleep; hour after hour, he lay tossing on his restless bed, and rose in the morning without having closed an eye. He attributed this, however, to the excitement of his spirits, the strange bed, the fatigue of his journey—in short, to any cause but what proved to be the true one.

The second night came, and he rested no better; the third and the fourth equally failed to bring him repose. He changed his hour of going to bed, worked hard during the day, did everything possible to win sleep to his pillow, but in vain. It might be on the seventh or the eighth night that he felt, as he lay feverishly turning from side to side, something sitting, as he thought, on the side of his bed. He sat up, groped with his hand over the bed-coverings, to the place where the pressure seemed to be, and was sensible of something that yielded to a push, but immediately after returned to its former place.

He got up, and lighted a candle; there was nothing to be seen on the bed, nothing to be found in the room, that could have been the cause of his sensations. He lay down again, leaving the light burning, and now first did a superstitious awe steal over him, when he felt the weight on the bedside as before, while his eyes assured him that nothing visible occupied the place. Of sleep there was now no hope, and not only for that night, but for many following, till the health of the man, thus at once deprived of his natural rest, and pursued by the terrors of an invisible world, began perceptibly to give way.

This had gone on about a fortnight, when he began to see something. It was the shape of a woman veiled from head to foot, as it seemed, in a gray mist, sitting on the bed. The haunted man began to fear for his reason; he wrote to Schubert, to Dr. Kemer, to Professor Eschenmayer, to everyone he could hear of, as versed in the secrets of psychology; he detailed his sufferings; he supplicated help. As might be expected, the correspondence had no result but that of rendering the case more hopeless. The sufferer travelled from one master of the mystic science to another; and it was while on a visit to Schubert that we became acquainted with him. Of course all that could be done for him was done, and amounted to just—nothing.

He returned in despair to his parish; and, to put the reality of the apparition to a new test, he spoke to it. It answered. He related this to his friends; they smiled, and said his poetical temperament was carrying him too far. More than one said, "Send your spectre to me; if there be anything in her, I'll find it out." He promised to do so, and kept his promise. Sleep, so long a stranger, revisited his bed; but the next morning, the rash inviter was sure to come, and say, one visit was enough for him, a second such night would drive him frantic.

The niece of the clergyman, who was his house-keeper, a good-hearted and religious girl, heard of this, and begged her uncle to send her the apparition; he did it from time to time, to have a night's sleep. The phantom-lady, in all her visits to others, kept silence; no one but the clergyman ever heard her speak; perhaps, because no one else had the courage to speak to her. But *what* she said to him, he could never be induced to tell. So stood the matter when we were brought into contact with him; as, for aught we know, it stands to this hour.

From other sources we have learned that he often passes his

night in the open air, to evade the dreaded visitation, unwilling to lay too heavy a tax on the self-sacrificing affections of his niece. At such times, his village-parishioners often lie awake till the dawn, listening with a heart-clutching fear to the unearthly tones which his voice and his guitar conspire to send forth into the shuddering night.

The Questioning of Paddy Mullowney's Ghost

The following is a literal narrative, the names of some of the actors being modified; every incident in which occurred precisely as we relate.

In a certain flat county of Ireland, between a hill renowned in the Ossianic lays, and the pretty village of Rathangan, stands the hill of Dunganstown, an oblong ridge of limestone about a mile and a half long, and three hundred feet in height. From the top a charming view is obtained over a vast extent of arable land, once occupied by forest, marsh, and meadow, and hunted over by Fionn MacCuumhaill and his warriors, or at least by chiefs of the era in which they are supposed to have lived. From the Grand Canal, distant about a mile, extends a "togher," or causeway, to within a short distance of the hill, and proves of great service to cow-herds and carriers of turf and other country produce. On one side of this togher extends a reclaimed bog, intersected in sundry places by drains never deficient of water in rainy weather, and this causeway and bog form the scene on which our bizarre drama was enacted.

Our authority, now, a business-loving Dublin merchant, assisted at the exhibition which was well calculated to make a lively impression on an intelligent and inquisitive youth of eleven years of age, still in blessed ignorance of bulls, bears, stags, and other monsters, which infest the forest where men of stock take their forenoon exercise.

Mike Donegan was a boy in the service of a farmer in the

neighbourhood, and every evening was in the habit of driving his charge, when milking was ended, to the reclaimed flat we have mentioned. It was enclosed by the "togher" on one side, and a field of rape on the other. Mike was a smooth, easy-going youth, of few words, and as little likely to "set the Liffey, or any greater river on fire" as any boy in Leinster.

One evening, while on returning home after having driven his cattle to their pasture, he met with an acquaintance, the servant-boy of a neighbouring farmer, and addressed him in words to this effect:—"Faith, a strange thing happened to me just now. Just as I was driving the cows into the pasture a big white cat jumped out of the rape field and ran towards me. It was mighty playful at first, and miawed at me, and rubbed the head again my legs, and purred, the way they do when they do be pleased. After a while he stopped this, and began to walk round me, and growl, and the eyes of him sometimes were like two coals of fire, and other times like the green spots in a paycock's feather. Faith myself got frightened, and at last I let a screech out of me, for he looked as big as a dog, and if he flew at my throat with them claws and teeth of his, I had no way to save my life. Well, what would you have of it? the next minute there wasn't a sign of him to be seen; but I made no *flays* in the place you may depend. You must bring the mastiff dog with you tomorrow evening when I'm dhrivin' out the cattle; that's the boy for to match any eat in Ireland."

Next evening the neighbour came, bringing the dog, and accompanied by a few curious village folk, who had heard the story in the course of the day. When they reached the spot indicated, Mike, pointing in an agitated manner to the fence of the rape-field, cried out, "There he is, there he is! Why don't you set the dog at him? Ow, ow, here he comes!"

"Hie, cat! hie, cat!" cried the assistants, getting rather terrified by the boy's apparent fright, and his cries. The dog barked and jumped about in great excitement, but it was evident that he neither saw cat nor rat in any direction. "Oh, don't yous all see him sittin' there on the edge of the gripe? He turned back when

Thigeen began to bark, but he's now lookin' at me, and growlin' like vengeance."The standers-by began to be more frightened at the cat they did *not* see than Mike at the cat he did see; and off they drew without more delay. That evening and the next day the story had travelled a mile or two in every direction, and the following evening, at the same hour, a hundred people, at least, including our authority, were on the spot.

Mike's attention was again painfully arrested by the cat, to the terror of some and the derision of a few. It changed its position several times, and Mike's features were expressive of great trouble, blended with awe. After this state of things had continued for a while someone proposed to send for the schoolmaster, whose house stood by the side of a neighbouring by-road. A deputation waited on him, but on learning their business he scoffed at the thing altogether, said that ghosts or spirits were out of place in the nineteenth century, that he was tired, and that it was too late, and that he would be on the spot next evening, and make a hare of Mike or the ghost, whichever deserved it.

At the usual hour of the cows' visit to the pasture on next evening, our informant was one among a thousand spectators at least. While waiting for the young ghost-seer they formed knots and indulged in various surmises. Some were of opinion that it was what has since been poetically termed a sell, while a young man, who had made the Pantheon his study, and had got a glimpse of the Metempsychosis, conjectured that some evil liver of past days was now obliged to do penance in the shape of the cat, and hinted at the expediency of giving the animal a wide berth. The schoolmaster arriving, and finding a good deal of desultory chat going on, mixed with some laughter (for a little factitious courage is always generated in a crowd), raised his voice, and requested decorum to be observed. "If there is any truth in the boy's story," said he, "the spirit must be either a good or evil one, and in either case levity should not prevail. Oh, here is the spirit-seer!"

The cows were seen approaching, and the young herd, feeling himself the observed of the multitude, slowly advanced, assuming whatever gravity he could in face and movement. When he came opposite the locality of the former apparition, he cried out, in real or assumed fright, "The cat, the cat!" All became hushed and attentive; then, following with his eyes the supposed movements of the apparition towards a little hillock occupied by some women and children, he cried, "Take care! he is going that way!" There was a general scamper among the little group, mixed with some cries and ejaculations, and the operation was repeated a couple of times more with other groups. This caused some general annoyance, and one discontented individual called out, "Now is your time, master, if you have anything to say to Mike or the ghost. You know you boasted last night there was no such thing as ghosts. Let us see what you're good for."

"Well," said he, "one thing or the other must be taking place—a spirit is present in the shape of a cat, or the child is making fun of us all. I do not believe in these apparitions; but if any one of you that has more faith or more folly than myself directs the boy to order the thing, in the name of the Holy Trinity, to appear in its own shape, and reveal what is troubling it, you'll see or hear something out of the common if the boy is not humbugging you all. Mind, I don't believe a word of his story."

A voice was now heard from the fore ranks. "Well, then, I believe in ghosts, but am not a bit afraid of any mother's son of 'em. Mike, my boy, do as the masther says, and I'll be your bail for any harm that can happen you."

Here the mother of the boy rushed at him out of the crowd. "Mick, my darling," said she, "take care what you do! Maybe when you spake them words it's tare you limb from limb he'll do."

"I'm not a bit afeard, mother. I said my prayers comin' along, and do you think the wickedst spirit in the world could have any power over a Christian that wasn't in mortal sin, and was after blessin' himself?"[1]

"That's my brave little boy," said the gratified mother, hug-

1. Making the sign of the cross and invoking the Three Persons of the Holy Trinity, is in our country parlance "blessing one's self."

ging and kissing him. "May the holy angels be about you this night."

"Well," said the schoolmaster, "if you must go through with the ceremony, form a semicircle; let the child go to the front, and then everyone kneel down and pray for God's protection". It was done, and then the stout fellow began. "I command you, in the name, &c.—to, to, to—co,co,co."—

"Master, something is sticking in my throat; will you say the rest, if you please?"

"Well, this is too bad," said the schoolmaster; "but not to disappoint us all, begin again, child." "I command you, &c., &c., to leave that form, to take your own that you had when alive, and answer me such questions as I shall solemnly ask you." A pause.

"Well, Mike, is the cat there still?"

"No; don't you see the smoke?" Here there was a getting up off knees, and a few charges over the togher.

"Keep still," said the schoolmaster. "While you stay on your knees, and arm yourself with the sign of the cross, the devil himself and all his imps won't have power to touch a hair of your head. What now, boy? A face coming like the moon out of the smoke, a three-cocked hat on his head, a long waistcoat, a square grey coat, knee breeches, blue stockings, brogues."[2]

All these came from Mike one after another, his eyes wide open and his teeth chattering. There was no small consternation among the people. The boy now began to move forward beyond the more advanced line of the congregation, and all eyes were anxiously following his movements. One of the nearest to him said. "Where are you going, Mike?"

"Ach! he's beckonin' me farther."

"Have a care. Maybe he wants to get you into his power."

"Oh, never fear! I'm a little in dread, but God won't let him harm me. What had I better ask him first?"

To repeat the babel of directions given to Mike would be neither agreeable nor interesting. Mike proposed the first ques-

2. If Mike was only a clever young pupil of some knave, his tutor had given him a hint of the dress in use just before the Rebellion of 1798.

tion with the adjuration, alluded to before it, and then seemed to listen attentively; and all bent forward, silent as the dead, to catch the answer. But if an answer came, no one heard it but the boy. After he had waited for a while he turned round, and requested to be told what he should ask next. "Let him answer the first question before you go to a second."

"Didn't yous all hear what he said?"

"We heard nothing but your voice asking him."

"Oh, I see, no one can hear him but myself. Well, the answer ho gave was that his name was Paddy Mullowney, and that when he was alive he lived in these parts."

Then issued a volley of observations and ejaculations. "Tshu, tshu! Well to be sure! See, there now! That flogs! I wish we could hear himself! It's all a piece of gosther. Whisht, whisht! no use to be too hard of believing." This portion of the narrative would occupy too much space if given in detail with all the interjections, cross questions, interruptions, &c. So we confine ourselves to the statements made by Mike the interpreter.

"He says that his name was Pat Mullowney; that he lived in these parts; that he was twenty-two years old when he died; that it is twenty-two years since; that he is all that time wandering about Lord Drogheda's demesne, along the banks of the canal, and in the demesne of Oldcourt; that he feels the cold as if he was alive; that what he suffers is what is called a 'cold purgatory;' that it's all because he owed Mr. Jonathan Payne of Oldcourt eight pounds when he was dying; that ghosts cannot reveal their grievances but to those fitted by grace to receive them," &c.

What with adjurations, the proposing of frivolous questions, and other interruptions, the night was far advanced by the time this information was completed, and an adjournment was resolved on.

A deputation waited on Jonathan Payne, Esq., next day, and the awful disclosures made, but they only added to a peck of ill humour he was nursing at the moment of the visit. "How, in the name of Pluto!" (he worded the expression differently) "could he tell whether any thief of the name of Mullowney worked for him or robbed him twenty-two years ago? He was probably a rascally boatman that cheated him, maybe, more than that. His books were in Dublin, and he'd see Mullowney farther off than purgatory, hot or cold, before he'd take the trouble of going so far, or investigating such a cock-and-bull story." He looked at the poor men as he said this with an expression that said as plainly as possible, "I'd see yourselves along with Mullowney in farther region before I'd take any trouble." Just as they were taking leave he condescended to add, "If Mullowney or any of his friends sends me the money I'll take it. I'm pretty sure he or some other knave made me the worse by that sum and a great deal more."

They returned, and acquainted the schoolmaster with the unsatisfactory result. "I am sure," said a man who had taken most offence at Mr. Payne's manner, "that we are imposed on. Would any soul be kept in punishment for owing such a trifle to a cursing ould thief that does not know what to do with the tithe of the money he has?"

"Ah," said the schoolmaster, "but maybe he stole it."

"And sure it's not to purgatory he'd be sent for that."

"But do you recollect what happened to the penitent thief?" said the master. "Well, well! the more I think on this thing the more I'm puzzled. That boy can't be deceiving us, I'm sure. No one of his age could be so deep as to invent all that he has put out of him. We were great ganders for not asking the ghost the most important things to be known. Like Jack in the story, we'll be wiser next time."

The fatal hour coming round again and the crowd—considerably augmented since last night—having taken their station on and near the togher, Mike stood at some distance in front, and announced that the spirit was again visible, being forever freed by the adjuration of the previous evening from the appearance of the cat. In the various answers he redelivered he could not have received any assistance owing to his isolated position, yet he showed wonderful discretion. When he was obliged to ask frivolous or hazardous questions, the ghost, according to him, frowned or remained silent. This evening the following information was elicited. He was a native of Monasterevan; his father and mother and brothers and sisters were dead; one relative, M'Ardle by name, lived at 22, High-street, Dublin, but was unable to assist him; he had been a boatman, and had met his death in his boat at Salins (while sleeping) from the effect of choke-damp; his corpse lay in the churchyard of Clane; the number of his boat was 22.

The frequent recurrence of this number set the thinkers to work, but they could not agree whether it betokened deception or the reverse, and the perquisition continued. "Where were you waked?"

"I was not waked at all."

This reply seemed strange, and the question was repeated. Same answer.

"Why were you not waked?"

"They were troubled times."

This answer electrified the assembly. Twenty-two years before, the rebellion of 1798 was raging. How could the child be up to that piece of chronological information? Very few doubted of his sincerity after this point in the scrutiny.

"What day in the week were you smothered?"

"Sunday. It was a just punishment for working on the Lord's day; but the owner of the boat was more in fault than *me*. He is not far from his end, let him look to it."

This stroke went home also. There was a secret agitation at the time to put an end to Sunday business on the canal. Very many in the crowd would have applauded the ghost if they only knew how to set about it.

Next arose the question of raising the supplies. Some proposed that Mr. Payne should be appealed to for forgiveness; but one of the deputation so feelingly described the reception of the embassy that the proposition fell unseconded, and the demand was formally made of the ghost "how was the money to be raised?"

The answer came, "Mr. Phil Gilchrist, of Glounthann, must

advance it." Here there arose shouts of merriment, for everyone in the crowd was well aware of Mr. Gilchrist's wealth points.

Query. "Why is Mr., G. to advance this money?"

Answer. "He is a very close man. He deals too hard with the poor people that have *conacre*[3] with him. He makes his turf-cutters work from sunrise to sunset in summer. He grinds the faces of the poor that owe him money. His end is not far off, and he must strive to make some reparation before death calls on him."

"I'm sure," cried Phil, "the ghost never said that. Anyhow, I must get time to consider."

"An', faith," uttered a voice in the crowd, "that's the very thing yourself never gave anybody."

There was a general explosion of laughter at this home touch, still without any misgiving in regard to the supernatural presence. Most of the crowd had firm faith in its being there; but, as in other concerns of life, two nights' familiarity had much diminished the awe felt at first. Phil's voice was heard as soon as opportunity was given, announcing, in a very sulky tone, that he, Phil Gilchrist, was ready to advance the money if the ghost of Mullowney would make itself visible to him. Mike having consulted the spirit, beckoned the speaker to come forward to the little hillock on which he himself was standing and have his desire gratified.

The poor victim advanced very leisurely. His terror was not small, but it was mastered by his desire to save his darling guineas. Just as he reached the spot, and was being led a little onward by the young adept, and becoming conscious of the frightful disorder of his ideas and sensations, a loud squib was let off among the people (whether by design or not our authority could never ascertain), and completed the unsettling of the poor man's nerves. He shouted out, "Oh, anything but that! I'll give the money." And without waiting for an interview with the

3. A fanner sets a large field to several poor people, each of whom gets his portion ploughed, and manured, and sown with potatoes, and pays the patron so much for his half or quarter acre, or whatever it may be, before he is allowed to remove his crop. This is *conacre.*

ghost he darted back, preferring the jeering and noisy reception of the crowd to the unknown terrors on the other side.

Here Paul Downey, the schoolmaster, was obliged to exert his authority to restore order. He particularly addressed himself to a man whose name was Darby Duncan, a bruiser, a sheebeen-house keeper, and the owner of a boat or two. He had felt himself aggrieved by the ghost's denouncing of Sunday work on the canal, and seemed zealous to promote a riot among the spectators. Darby, however, was a man of moral as well as physical courage, and boldly turned on the village oracle.

"Mr. Downey," said he, "you are a cunning fellow, but you won't put your finger in my eye. This is a plan contrived to stir up ill-feelings against persons of any property or standing in the place, and I'll uphold you as the head contriver if the ghost does not make his appearance to myself face to face."

"Oh, Mr. Duncan, you need not turn on me. I'm neither art nor part in the matter. I am only striving to ascertain whether the little boy is an impostor or not, and I am very glad of your offer. It will make a cat or a dog of the affair, and speaks well for your resolution. There are very few who would voluntarily seek communication with spirits, for who knows what power they may get over a person to harm him here and hereafter?"

If Mr. Downey was striving by false praise to work on Darby's fears, he did not succeed. "Come, Mike, my boy," said he, "if you are not circumventing us to please the master let us see the spirit."

"Well, Mr. Duncan, come forward a bit, You must put back the people. He says he does not like their breaths. He is moving off into the water, and we must follow him, he is beckoning." Here the urchin paused for a little. "He bids you come a little farther, and he will show himself to you in case you pay the eight pounds."

"Oh, indeed I will, and I am sure to get some help from the neighbours. Mr. Gilchrist, won't you stand to me, and you, Mr. Downey?"

"Oh, we will, we will."

On the side of the hillock farthest from the togher a portion of the flat meadow was at this time flooded by water as deep as three feet in some parts. Into this pool was poor Darby obliged to wade till the water reached his knees. Worse still, at the direction of the ghost conveyed through Mike, he was obliged to kneel down, and there wait, with the water up to his arm pits, till it was the ghost's convenience to reveal himself.

"Speak to him, Mike," said the poor man, feeling his condition verging on the intolerable. Thus exhorted, the youth began his adjuration. "In the name, &c., I command you, ghost of Paddy Mullowney, to show yourself as I see you, to Mr. Darby Duncan, of the Lock public-house."

A pause.

"Do you see him, Mr. Duncan?"

"Indeed and I don't, not a shine of him."

At this point of the drama, there was not a sound from voice or movement in the crowd. All hung on the countenances and voices of Mike and Darby.

After a painful pause the interpreter proceeded. "In the. name, &c., I command you, ghost of, &c., to reveal why you don't appear to," &c.

Another pause.

"He says he can't appear to you."

Confusion. Order being restored, and the ingenious youth requested to demand the reason, the reply came in proper time. "He says that when he strove to appear the weight of sin on your conscience put it out of his power."

Disturbance, cries, shouts, and laughter. "Faith," said the stout bruiser, getting up, and coming forward with the water pouring down from his clothes, "I believe Paddy Mullowney's ghost is not far wrong. Let anyone else take my place that likes."

Incredulity and discontent were fast stealing on the crowd, and schools of discussion were forming, when one of the practical division of the mass cried out, "Be the laws, I'll call on Father Stokes, and bring him here tomorrow night, and we'll see how the ghost behaves to him."

"I'd be glad," said a sage, who had come a distance of four or five miles, "to hear from the spirit whether he'll think well to appear to the priest or not."

"Put that question to the ghost," said one of the people in front.

"He says he won't answer it till the priest is kneeling in the water before him like Darby. He can't bear the smell of any one that's in sin, and Father Stokes is too apt to be meddling with things that don't consarn him."[4]

Here an unlucky Protestant, the only one in the crowd, indeed, jocularly remarked that the ghost must be of the Established Church, he showed so little respect to the clergy. However, he made more haste than good speed, for it was immediately objected to him that the poor spirit's grievance arose from the existence of a purgatory. The controversy, ending in the utter discomfiture of the man without a friend, now assumed such an irreverent shape that we are obliged to omit the particulars.

The mention of the priest's visit introduced much uncertainty into the after proceedings, and the crowd separated without any distinct understanding about meeting or not meeting next evening. There was a gathering, indeed, but it was a poor affair compared with the late ones. Father Stokes made his appearance, and Mike was seen uneasily moving from point to point, unsuccessfully (as it seemed) looking out for the ghost. The priest called Mike and his father before him, but not being satisfied with their answers, he directed both to come to his house next morning. Among the absentees were the schoolmaster and divers worthies known or suspected to belong to the *illuminati* of the neighbourhood.

Father Stokes did not say much on that occasion. He requested the few that were present to go about their business and be more on their guard for the future against hoaxing reports. He had an interview with Mike and his father next day, but as

4. This, translated from ghostly to human speech, meant that the good priest interfered with the movements of the secret society of the neighbourhood more than was agreeable to its ruling members.

neither he nor they could ever after be induced to allude to it, the conference was probably confined to the confessional. Mike assumed a peddler's pack when strength permitted, but found the occupation below a youth of his genius. Mr. Downey emigrated in time to Canada, and his ghostly pupil was obliged to emigrate to Australia, both departures being probably for the good of their country.

We have before us the circumstantial account of this transaction, written in choice English by our friend the Dublin Citizen. We would have much preferred to give the narrative in his own racy and energetic sentences, but needful economy of space interfered. He acknowledges his inability to account for the young rascal's self-possession, and judgment, and discretion, unless by allowing him a remarkable degree of precocious talent, and supposing a strict tutoring on the schoolmaster's part. The question still remains—how was he provided so well for contingencies, when he was out of earshot of promptings by the secret members scattered through the crowd?

The objects of the original contrivers seem to have been to obtain the money which certainly would not have found its way into the strong box of Jonathan Payne, Esq., to expose the priest, and Gilchrist, and Duncan, to contempt, and—what were really desirable things—to confine turf-cutting operations to twelve hours in the day, and to put a stop absolutely to Sunday labour on the canal. The public excitement caused by the imposture aided in a considerable degree to effect both reforms.

LEONAUR

ALSO FROM LEONAUR

AVAILABLE IN SOFTCOVER OR HARDCOVER WITH DUST JACKET

THE COMPLETE FOUR JUST MEN: VOLUME 2 *by Edgar Wallace—The Law of the Four Just Men & The Three Just Men*—disillusioned with a world where the wicked and the abusers of power perpetually go unpunished, the Just Men set about to rectify matters according to their own standards, and retribution is dispensed on swift and deadly wings.

THE COMPLETE RAFFLES: 1 *by E. W. Hornung—The Amateur Cracksman & The Black Mask*—By turns urbane gentleman about town and accomplished cricketer, life is just too ordinary for Raffles and that sets him on a series of adventures that have long been treasured as a real antidote to the 'white knights' who are the usual heroes of the crime fiction of this period.

THE COMPLETE RAFFLES: 2 *by E. W. Hornung—A Thief in the Night & Mr Justice Raffles*—By turns urbane gentleman about town and accomplished cricketer, life is just too ordinary for Raffles and that sets him on a series of adventures that have long been treasured as a real antidote to the 'white knights' who are the usual heroes of the crime fiction of this period.

THE COLLECTED SUPERNATURAL AND WEIRD FICTION OF WILKIE COLLINS: VOLUME 1 *by Wilkie Collins*—Contains one novel 'The Haunted Hotel', one novella 'Mad Monkton', three novelettes 'Mr Percy and the Prophet', 'The Biter Bit' and 'The Dead Alive' and eight short stories to chill the blood.

THE COLLECTED SUPERNATURAL AND WEIRD FICTION OF WILKIE COLLINS: VOLUME 2 *by Wilkie Collins*—Contains one novel 'The Two Destinies', three novellas 'The Frozen deep', 'Sister Rose' and 'The Yellow Mask' and two short stories to chill the blood.

THE COLLECTED SUPERNATURAL AND WEIRD FICTION OF WILKIE COLLINS: VOLUME 3 *by Wilkie Collins*—Contains one novel 'Dead Secret,' two novelettes 'Mrs Zant and the Ghost' and 'The Nun's Story of Gabriel's Marriage' and five short stories to chill the blood.

FUNNY BONES *selected by Dorothy Scarborough*—An Anthology of Humorous Ghost Stories.

MONTEZUMA'S CASTLE AND OTHER WEIRD TALES *by Charles B. Cory*—Cory has written a superb collection of eighteen ghostly and weird stories to chill and thrill the avid enthusiast of supernatural fiction.

SUPERNATURAL BUCHAN *by John Buchan*—Stories of Ancient Spirits, Uncanny Places & Strange Creatures.

AVAILABLE ONLINE AT **www.leonaur.com**
AND FROM ALL GOOD BOOK STORES

07/09

ALSO FROM LEONAUR

www.ingramcontent.com/pod-product-compliance
Lightning Source LLC
LaVergne TN
LVHW050909080826
845145LV00001B/27

* 9 7 8 0 8 5 7 0 6 1 5 6 0 *